Fate and Consequences

Linda Wells

To

Catherine and Tania
Bill and Rick

And to all who supported me while creating this story.

Chapter 1

"What do you mean, they are gone?" Fitzwilliam Darcy's eyes bore into the frightened servant girl's, demanding her immediate answer.

"They left just a few hours ago, sir, Miss Darcy, Mrs. Younge, and Mr. Wickham." She squeaked.

"Wickham!" He roared. "Where did they go?"

"I heard them speaking of Gretna Green, sir. I think they were to stop in Hertfordshire for the night."

"My God!" Darcy ran out to his carriage, where his valet was just seeing his luggage removed. "Roberts!"

"Sir?" Roberts instantly snapped to attention seeing his master's distress, and followed him into the cottage where he watched him scratching out a note.

"Take the coach and go directly to Rosings. My cousin Fitzwilliam should be there visiting Lady Catherine with his parents. Give him this, and tell him he may use this coach if he does not wish to ride."

Stunned by his uncharacteristic behaviour he stared. "But sir, what about you?"

Darcy grew impatient with the delay. "I will hire a horse and leave in a few moments. Now go man! There is not a second to lose!"

"Sir, you must take a change of clothing . . ." The ever efficient valet quickly pulled out a valise suitable for attaching to a saddle, and stuffed in some items. Handing it to his furious and agitated master, he leapt into the carriage. Darcy gave terse orders to the coachman and watched them disappear down the street and out of Ramsgate. Spotting the man who cared for the rented cottage, he demanded the location of the nearest stables and any information of Wickham. He was told that Wickham had been a regular visitor for weeks and seemed quite a favourite of Miss Darcy's. A vision of his innocent little sister in the hands of that cad played before Darcy's eyes. Without a word, he ran to the stables, chose the best horse, asked for the directions given to the coach Wickham had hired there, and was on his way.

He pushed his mount hard, matching his fury and fear, and slowed from the gallop only when he felt the animal labouring. He hoped that travelling on horseback would help him make up the time lost by his delay in following the slower coach. At every inn and post stop he scanned the carriages, riding in long enough to inquire of the servants if they had come from Ramsgate, and then pressing on. During the furious ride, his head filled with thoughts. *I should have paid off the servants for their silence, what will happen if their gossip reaches town? What will Wickham do? Will he marry then abandon her? It must be all for her dowry, he can not possibly love her. And if I find him in time, will he blackmail me to remain quiet? Will this hang over Georgiana's head until she marries?*

It was nearly seven o'clock and his second horse of the day was struggling when he reached another inn at the village of Meryton. He knew he must stop for the night. He was not armed, and travelling alone in twilight or worse, dark, was dangerous as he was unfamiliar with the area. Reluctantly he turned the horse to the stables where he saw one coach parked; its horses in the process of being unhitched. Dismounting, he handed his reins to the groom who ran up. "This horse has had a hard ride. Give him extra care."

"Yes sir!" The eager lad tugged his forelock and caught the coin that Darcy threw to him. For seemingly the hundredth time that day, Darcy wearily asked him, "Can you tell me where this coach is from?"

"Yes sir, Ramsgate, sir. Heading for Scotland, I hear."

Darcy straightened. "Two women and a man?"

"Yes sir!"

Darcy tossed him another coin and nodded. He turned and scanned the building in front of him. He was not too late to save Georgiana from marrying Wickham. Her reputation may very well already be ruined, but at least she would not be married at the age of fifteen to a profligate cur.

He decided to enter through the back door so that he could see the public rooms without drawing notice. The inn's workers cast him odd looks as the well-dressed gentleman made his way through the kitchen to the dining room. The murderous look in his eye was enough to convince them to give him a wide berth, but as soon as he passed, the curious among them crept forward to see what was brewing. The room was nearly empty save for a table at a corner where he saw his sister's golden hair. She sat stiffly. When he saw her head turn, his chest grew tight. Whatever excitement she may have had for her adventure that morning was clearly dissipating. In her face he read discomfort and fear. He tore his eyes away to look at Wickham, and saw his old enemy's false sincerity as he bent towards her and kissed her hand. Darcy's fingers twitched. All he saw of his sister's companion, Mrs. Younge, was the back of her head. That was good. With Wickham's attention on Georgiana, he could step unnoticed into the room.

A voice at his shoulder startled him. "What is your plan, Cousin?"

He spun to see the very welcome sight of Colonel Richard Fitzwilliam. "Richard!" He said in a low voice. "How on earth did you get here so quickly?"

"Your coach made Rosings in two hours, and I was just approaching the stables to take a ride. I knew to head towards Hertfordshire from your note, and this village seemed a logical place for them to break their journey. I made a point of checking the inns as I approached the area, and this was my fourth try. Mother and Father think that I have been called to duty. I was likely not very far behind you the whole way; you could have stopped at Rosings yourself to collect me." He kept his eyes fixed on their quarry. "Have you a plan or do you wish to just confront them?"

Darcy glanced at his cousin and returned his gaze to the table. "I do not wish for a scene, perhaps we can still save Georgiana's reputation if her name is not spoken." He knew in his heart that was unlikely. The servants at Ramsgate were doubtless already talking about it to their friends, and it was only a matter of time before the fresh gossip was spoken to some gentleman or lady on holiday.

Richard watched his face. "Then we shall move quietly. I would like to have my chance at him, as I imagine you would as well, Darcy."

"I have not your sword, but at this moment I feel my hands would serve the purpose well." His glare fixed on Wickham's face.

Richard looked at him closely. "You will call him out?"

"Would I win?" Darcy glanced at him.

Richard considered the question. "Perhaps, you are an excellent shot, and outstanding with your foil, but I would not put it past him to cheat."

"Your faith is heartening, Richard." Darcy said with no little sarcasm. He had relaxed slightly; knowing his cousin and Georgiana's other guardian was there to help. He also knew that violence was not the way to handle his boyhood enemy.

"I will gladly kill him." Richard said quietly. There was no emotion in his voice. He had killed for King and country during his army service, this was no different. He would be ridding the country of some vermin. Darcy saw the cold light in his eyes and knew he was serious. Richard gripped his blade. "Say the word and I will do it now."

"No, not if we are to redeem Georgiana." He put his hand on his cousin's taut arm.

"Darcy, you know it may be too late . . ."

"She is young, perhaps it can be passed as a foolish mistake of youth . . ." He said weakly.

The two men's eyes met. They knew how unlikely that was. "Come on Darcy." They entered the dining room and Georgiana spotted them first. The look of relief on her face was heartbreaking. It was obvious she had not thought through what she had agreed to do, and the reality of her situation was becoming very clear.

Wickham saw her change of expression and looked up. He immediately stood. "Darcy, Fitzwilliam, what a surprise!" Mrs. Younge spun around in her chair, her face reflected her fear.

Darcy's eyes burned into Wickham's but he addressed his sister. "Go to your room Georgiana. I will speak to you shortly."

She sat frozen. His voice grew harsher. "GO! NOW!"

She jumped up and stammered, "Yes, Brother!" and ran from the room.

Darcy's eyes turned to Mrs. Younge. "Be on the next post coach and never darken my door or approach my family again." Feeling the tightly controlled anger in his voice she arose and without a backward glance ran to collect her things and quickly boarded a coach that was just leaving the inn to continue its journey. That left Darcy and Richard alone with Wickham. "Step outside, Wickham." Darcy said harshly.

Wickham shook his head. "I am not a fool; I will remain inside, thank you."

Darcy's eyes blazed and he stepped closer. "Explain yourself!"

Wickham smirked. Not because he was brave, but because he knew it infuriated Darcy. "I am engaged to your sister."

"Not without my consent. She is a child."

"Not according to the law."

"She is not of age."

"That does not matter in Gretna Green, and she wants to be my wife." Wickham smiled widely.

Darcy balled his hands into fists and spoke through clenched teeth. "I do not even want to know what lies you whispered to her. Be gone Wickham, my sister is not marrying you."

He laughed, enjoying seeing Darcy suffer. "Fine, then give me the living at Kympton your father promised me."

"I already paid you its value, we are even and you know it." He spat.

"Hardly. You have now cheated me of the thirty thousand pounds in your sister's dowry. I will extract it from you, in exchange for my silence." His eyes were cold and serious.

Darcy stepped forward, "And you were going to cheat my sister of a settlement before marriage and leave her penniless when you disappeared!"

Wickham laughed, "Would I truly leave my dear, pretty wife? You think so poorly of me Darcy? I would want to have many children with her." His eyes gleamed, watching Darcy's face contort with his anger and disgust.

"I suggest you leave now before I silence you permanently, Wickham!" Richard hissed.

Wickham saw Richard's hand on his sabre and knew to stop. Darcy never frightened him, but he knew enough not to taunt the colonel. He picked up his hat and moved to the doorway. He looked up at Darcy. "I will be in touch for my first payment." He turned and left the room.

"You should have let me kill him. He will bleed you forever."

"I can not have his blood on your hands, Richard. We can not risk being tried for his murder, no matter how justified it may be." He sighed. "Once Georgiana is married Wickham's threats will be meaningless. She will be out in two years . . ." He looked down, knowing already it was hopeless. What respectable man will want her once this news was out? "I have failed her." He said softly.

"No, we both were taken in by Mrs. Younge's credentials. She must be a friend of Wickham's. You saved Georgiana from a marriage of hell to that cur. I doubt he would have remained with her once he had her dowry. You know as well as I do that you would have given it to him, despite your objections. You could not have seen her left with nothing. As soon as he had the funds, she would have been abandoned and back with you."

"But what would have been left of her?" He asked quietly and sighed. "Let us go to her."

"You go. I will just make sure that Wickham is on his way." Richard's posture changed to that of a soldier.

Darcy regarded him warily. "What are you going to do?"

He smiled. "Never mind. Go to Georgiana. She needs you."

Darcy stared at him, trying to read his face, and gave up. He asked the innkeeper to prepare two rooms, taking care to give a false name in an attempt to protect his sister, and was directed to Georgiana's. He found his sister sitting on the bed, clutching a pillow and sobbing quietly.

"Georgiana." He said softly and closing the door, crossed the room. She made no notice of him as he sat beside her and patted her shoulder. "How are you, dear?"

"Oh how can you touch me? How can you speak to me?" She cried. "What have I done?"

Darcy closed his eyes and tried to sound reassuring. "It will be well, we found you in time. You will not be tied for life to him." He kissed her hair. "Can you tell me how this happened?"

Taking a breath, she allowed the story to pour out. "He saw me one day as we walked. He was so kind and charming, I remembered how fond I was of him growing up at Pemberley, and Mrs. Younge encouraged me to spend time with him, and . . . he proposed. I wanted to talk to you, but he convinced me we should elope and surprise you with the news. It seemed so romantic when he spoke of it, but as we travelled further away, I . . . I knew it was wrong, but could not think of a way to stop it." She buried her face in her hands. "I have disappointed you. Oh what have I done?"

Darcy tried to control his emotions. He felt guilty for leaving her vulnerable to such a man, and for choosing Mrs. Younge as her companion. He tried to keep the edge of anger and pain from his voice as he asked, "Did he . . . touch you in any way?"

"He kissed me and held me." She whispered.

He closed his eyes and clenched his jaw as he took her hand. "Nothing more?"

"What else is there?" Her innocence was painful to see. Suddenly she gasped. "Do you mean what . . ." She thought of the teachings of her governess and Aunt Ellen. "Oh no, no, not that!"

Breathing again, he whispered, "Thank God." He rubbed her hand as her sobs renewed.

A knock at the door startled them. Darcy stood and opened it to Richard, then began pacing. Richard sat next to Georgiana, and held her hand. "How are you, dear?" Her sobs continued until she opened her eyes and saw bruises forming on his hand.

She looked up. "What happened to you?"

Darcy stopped his pacing and turned to examine him. "What have you done!?"

"I gave our friend a taste of our displeasure." He said with satisfaction.

"Good Lord, Richard! You beat him?" He clenched his fists in agitation. "You can not fight Wickham with violence, there are other ways to work on him, he is clever, and he will use this to his advantage!"

Richard stared at Darcy. "He ran away from me with his tail between his legs, it was most effective, I assure you!"

"Yes, and as soon as he is out of our sight, he will plot ways to take his revenge." Darcy fumed. "Why can you not keep your hot head under control?! Who knows what he will do now! I have a feeling it will be more than money!"

"What do you mean?" Richard began to realize his error.

"He will attempt to ruin us." Darcy said simply.

Richard brushed that off. "He has no influence in society."

"He only needs to send a letter to the gossip columns. It will grow from there without any help from him. Add to that whatever word comes from Ramsgate . . ." Darcy spun away and stood staring out of the window into the darkening sky.

"But how can he blackmail you if the story is out? I think he will remain silent, Darcy." Richard tried to remain confident.

"Can you not understand, Richard? Facts do not matter to him. He can embellish it as much as he wishes. He can say that Georgiana was compromised." Georgiana gasped. Darcy remembered that she was in the room and hung his head. "I am sorry dear, but you may as well realize now, this could be very ugly for some time." He turned to Richard. "We must secure a carriage and return to London. We need to speak to your parents about how to proceed."

Numb, Richard nodded. "Wickham left without the carriage he hired. We could take that. I will speak to the coachman now." He stood. "It seems this is a mess. I can not imagine what Father will say."

They looked at Georgiana who had curled up in a ball on the bed. Their eyes met. "Georgiana, will you be well? Would you like me to stay with you while you sleep?" Darcy said softly.

She whispered. "Please leave me, Brother. Let me contemplate my transgressions alone." Darcy looked helplessly at Richard, who shrugged. Comforting was not something that Darcy knew how to do. They each kissed her cheek. "My room is just across the hall, if you need me during the night, come to me. Please?"

She nodded and said nothing. The men took their leave and retired to Darcy's room, where brandy and food was ordered. It would be a long night of talking for them.

Darcy stared into the mirror, took another swipe at his cheek with the razor, and cursed, feeling the sharp pain from the nick of the blade along his jaw. He quickly pressed a towel to the cut and looked miserably at the exhausted face that gazed back at him. He swore when he returned home he would give Roberts a pay raise just for sparing him this chore. Searching through the shaving kit he found some alum powder and applied it to the cut. Lifting his chin, he surveyed the damage; *hopefully my cravat will cover the mark.* He finished his task and continued with his rudimentary wash in the basin of the small room at the inn in, *where am I again? Oh yes, Meryton the servant had said.* Drying off, he went to pull on the clean shirt and undergarments his valet had thankfully forced upon him. At least he felt something comfortable next to his skin. His coat and trousers had been brushed by the inn's staff late that night. He could not complain, at least he had something to wear. Richard had only his uniform, although he was used to not changing clothes for days or even weeks at a time.

He walked over to the window and looked out on the main street of the village. It was fairly late in the morning, and the town was bustling with activity. He sipped his tea and took in the scene. It was typical of any other village; there was a butcher, a ribbon shop, a small book shop. If things were different he might stroll over to see if any treasures had found their way there. But things were different, likely drastically different for him and his sister for the rest of their lives. He hated feeling so pessimistic, but it had become a habit to think the worst. Orphaned at the age of two and twenty, suddenly becoming the father figure to a little sister and master of an enormous estate with hundreds of lives left to his care . . . he sighed.

It had been a long five years since his father joined his mother in Pemberley's small cemetery.

He tried to distract himself from his thoughts and concentrated on the people passing by. He noticed a group of four young women entering the street. Their dress was simple but fine, probably daughters of a local gentleman. He watched as two of them, rather too enthusiastic for his taste, ran with undignified speed to accost two local dandies outside of the apothecary's shop. He noticed the other two, obviously older and possessing proper manners, continued their walk and how the smaller one of them seemed to admonish the young girls. He nodded in approval. He watched as they were stopped almost below his window by an older woman, and joined her in conversation. The smaller of the two stood; the blue ribbons of her bonnet blowing backwards and across her back, then further to lay across the nose of a donkey tethered nearby. Darcy watched in fascination as the donkey began nibbling on the ribbon, and with one pull the bonnet was ripped from her. She spun around, grabbing at the hat. Her hair was dislodged and suddenly a great cascade of chestnut curls fell from her head and bounced around her shoulders, almost down to her waist. Darcy drew in a sharp breath. The young lady did not cry out, but instead was laughing. He could clearly see her joyous smile, her dancing eyes, and could faintly hear the musical sound of her voice. It was the most alluring sight he had ever taken in. He felt a warm smile come to his lips as the lady shook a chastising finger at the offending beast, and took back possession of her bonnet from the girl at her side. The older woman appeared to be highly upset and quickly ushered them into a nearby home, most likely to repair the damage.

Darcy found himself twisting, watching the door, hoping to catch another glimpse of the lady, but to no avail. It was only after he gave up that he realized his heart was racing and that his body had responded to the event in a way best kept private. He remained at the window until he heard a knock on the door, and forced himself away.

Richard entered with his call. "Well, the coach will be ready to depart in about ten minutes. They will bring it around to the front door. Have you seen Georgiana this morning?"

Darcy nodded. "Yes, I went to speak to her. She did not say a word. I doubt that she could, her face is swollen from crying. I cannot bear to think what this will do to her if word gets out."

"We should assign someone to read the gossip columns of all the papers, looking for any mention of it."

"I will do that myself." Darcy said darkly. "I do not think that Wickham would go that route right away. I think he would wait to see how I respond to his demands first. But if word has spread from Ramsgate . . . it may be too late already." A knock on the door alerted them to the carriage being in position. Darcy went to pay the innkeeper and Richard collected Georgiana. They made their way down the stairs and outside to the sunshine. Darcy was waiting by the coach; the two horses tied to the back, and saw that the seats were dusty. He asked that they be cleaned off before they boarded, and while they waited, Georgiana started a fresh round of tears, seeing the coach she had sat in the day before. Her handkerchief was hopelessly soaked, and Darcy had no replacement. He looked at

Richard who shook his head, she already had his. He looked about for a shop to purchase one when a voice at his shoulder caught his attention.

"Excuse me, Miss. I think perhaps you could use this." Darcy looked down to see the concerned and kind face of the young woman he had watched from his window. She was holding out a square of linen, embroidered with some pretty small flowers.

Georgiana looked at her through reddened eyes. "Oh, I could not, it is too nice." She spoke for the first time that day.

The woman smiled gently. "Of course you can. We accomplished young ladies are always looking for something new to sew. This will give me a reason to finish all of the other handkerchiefs I have in my workbox. Come, please take it." She pressed the cloth in her hand. "I hope you will soon be well." She smiled at her and glanced up at Darcy.

He was staring at her, mesmerized with her face. "Thank you." He said. She nodded to him with a warm smile and turned away. Richard helped Georgiana up into the coach and entered after her. Darcy remained outside. An unprecedented impulse spurred him to act. "Miss!" He called, and walked up to her and bowed. "My name is Fitzwilliam Darcy. I would like to return your handkerchief when it has been laundered. May I ask your name and where it should be sent?"

"I assure you sir, it is not necessary." She smiled up into his eyes.

"I appreciate that, all the same . . ." He looked at her with his brows raised.

She took in his handsome exhausted face, and noted with pleasure his hopeful expression. She thought that if this brought him some little relief in what was obviously a time of great stress, she would grant him the favour. "My name is Elizabeth Bennet, and I live at Longbourn. This is my sister Miss Jane Bennet." The tall blonde girl beside her curtseyed and smiled kindly at him.

"It is my pleasure, ladies." He bowed again and a slight lift to the corners of his mouth indicated a smile to them. He heard his cousin's call from the coach and looked steadily into Elizabeth's eyes. She felt inexplicably drawn to the intensity of his gaze. "On behalf of my sister, I thank you again." He turned and boarded, and in a moment they were underway. Darcy nodded at the two women as they drove by; trying to memorize the face of one he knew he would never see again.

Chapter 2

The Earl of Matlock sat drumming his fingers on his desk and stared at his son and nephew. "How could you let his happen?"

Darcy looked up at him sharply. "I certainly did not anticipate the son of my father's former steward seducing my sister. Obviously I am at fault for not thinking of such a thing."

"Your sarcasm is not appreciated Darcy."

"Then do not presume to berate me for something I have already accepted as my responsibility. *I* removed Georgiana from school. *I* formed an establishment for her. *I* hired Mrs. Younge. *I* allowed her to go to Ramsgate. *I* stayed in London. It is entirely my fault. Now do you have anything of use to tell me or should I take my leave now?" He stood and went to lean on the mantelpiece of the unlit fireplace, staring intently at the grate, and attempting to control his anger. Between Georgiana's unending tears and his regret and anticipation of disaster, the past week in London had been nothing short of torture.

His uncle relented. "It is not all your fault Darcy. Georgiana must face her own culpability."

"Do not dare blame her!" He snarled.

"She already blames herself." Richard spoke, diffusing the tension between the two men. "You heard her. If she had only insisted on speaking to you before leaving, everything would have been different. She allowed herself to be swept up in the romance she perceived."

"The act of a sheltered, innocent child." Darcy stated with bitterness.

Richard shook his head. "You can not take on all of this. It will do you and Georgiana no good. The ones at fault are Wickham and Mrs. Younge." He looked to his father. "Now, so we can get away from this blaming session, I suggest that we assess our options. Do you have any ideas, Father?"

Lord Matlock's eyes moved from one man to the other, and nodded his head. "Of course you are correct. We must deal with the situation. I assume you will not be calling Wickham out?"

Darcy's gaze remained on the grate. "No. I will not risk Georgiana losing me to a duel or prison."

"How can he be worked on?" Richard asked.

His father laughed. "I am sure he has debts, he always did in the past. If we could find them out and settle them . . ."

Richard's brow rose and he turned to Darcy. "Debtor's prison? Hmm. That is a possibility."

Darcy closed his eyes and said with frustration, "You both fail to realize, Wickham is no longer my greatest concern. I have no doubt that he will try to use this to his advantage and try to harm us in some way, but I would pay his ransom forever if it kept Georgiana's name safe." He finally looked up at them. "Once the rumours start, nothing Wickham does will matter any more. The scandal will spread and will take on a life of its own."

"Are you so sure there are rumours? It has been a week. You may have dodged a bullet." Richard said hopefully.

Lord Matlock agreed. "If by some miracle that was true, then Wickham *is* our concern."

A knock on the door stopped the conversation, and the men stood as Lady Matlock entered the room. She grimly set down a newspaper clipping before her husband. He took it up and read aloud.

The very young sister of a certain FD from Derbyshire was seen departing her holiday love nest for a quick journey to Scotland. The Gentleman is said to be furious and has given chase.

Silence fell over the room. Finally Lord Matlock spoke. "Well, there it is." They all jumped with the sound of Darcy's fist striking the wall.

"Darcy!" Lady Matlock cried.

He stood rubbing his bruised hand. "Forgive me, Aunt." He moved to stare out of a nearby window, his mind such a blur of thoughts, he could not fix on one to address first. Feeling the three pairs of eyes staring at him he sighed and turned. "We will remove to Pemberley immediately."

"No Darcy that is what you will not do. You can not hide. You must go about your business as usual." Lord Matlock rose and began pacing as he thought.

Darcy stared at his moving uncle. "How exactly do I accomplish that? Even if I do go about my normal activities, society's busybodies will not allow me to forget. There are far too many of them hoping for a good scandal to fill the conversation of their dinner tables." He shook his head. "If only it was not the height of the Season, it might die a faster death."

"You are hardly noted as a man who attends dinners and balls. All I ask is that you continue to visit your club, go to a play or concert, attend church. Do not hide. That will show shame. You are a very proud man, remain that way."

He sighed and nodded. "We will leave for Pemberley at our usual time next month."

Lady Matlock spoke. "Would you allow Georgiana to come and stay with us? I think she needs a woman with her."

He stiffened at the suggestion. "I do not think we should be separated . . ."

"I agree with Darcy, Mother. If for no other reason, it would appear that he was ashamed of her and was sending her from their home."

Darcy's eyes flashed. "That is not why I do not wish to be separated!"

"No, but that is how it will be seen." Lord Matlock turned to his wife. "You may go and visit her daily. In the meantime, a new companion must be found."

"I have already begun the search. I hope to interview candidates by the end of the week."

"And what of Wickham?" Richard asked.

"He can do no worse than the speculation of the *ton*. He will get nothing from me." Darcy's glare passed over each of their faces, and they all returned to their seats to prepare for the questions of society.

―――ᴨᴧ―――

"William?" Her voice was almost a whisper, but at least she was speaking. Darcy looked up from the letter he was writing and saw his sister standing nervously before him. She looked drawn and very small.

"What can I do for you?" He said softly.

She held out a neatly folded and pressed square of linen. "This was the handkerchief the young woman lent me . . . did you learn her address? I would like to return it to her. She was so kind to me." Darcy took the proffered fabric and looked down at the delicate flowers so carefully stitched in a corner. Suddenly his mind was flooded with the vision of her laughing eyes. It felt good to forget for a few moments. "Brother?"

He started. "Yes, she told me her name and address. I will take care of it for you, dear." He set the cloth down, and meeting her furrowed brow realized it was somewhat improper for him to communicate with an unmarried stranger. "Perhaps you might like to include a note?" Her face cleared. He breathed. "Her name is Elizabeth Bennet." Georgiana nodded, happy to have a pleasant task to occupy her mind. She turned to go when her brother's voice called her back. "Georgiana, do you happen to know what sort of flowers these are?"

Georgiana's brow creased again. Embroidery was not something that her brother paid much attention. "I believe they are Sweet Williams. Aunt Ellen taught me that stitch a few years ago." She might have imagined it, but a slight curve appeared on her brother's lips, then it was gone in a flash. Seeing he would say nothing else, she left the room.

The silence fell down around him, only the ticking of the clock on the mantle filling the void. Darcy continued to stare at the cloth, remembering the young lady who so caught his attention. He had no idea why Elizabeth Bennet had remained so deeply imbedded in his thoughts. He reasoned that perhaps it was simply because she was a ray of brightness on such a horrible day, and it felt good to think on someone so lovely and obviously full of life; something that he truly had not felt in years.

He leaned back in his chair, gently tracing the flowers and thinking again about the same subject that had troubled him since he jumped on the horse to locate Georgiana. She would not marry now. At least if she ever did, it would not be to the gentleman he would hope for, a peer, or a wealthy landowner. No with this news, her prospects were considerably lowered, especially if the rumours, undoubtedly to be fuelled by Wickham in his attempt to extract money from them, told of her being compromised before he could find her.

Darcy's plans to never marry and leave Georgiana to handle the task of bearing the heir of Pemberley were dashed. He would have to marry and produce the heir himself. After watching the cold union his parents had, and admittedly rejoiced in seeing end after the demise of his mother at Georgiana's birth, he determined he would not subject himself to the union he was raised to expect. A cold marriage of professed but unfelt affection, made solely to bring more funds to Pemberley and to provide a body to occasionally warm his bed and create an heir. He did not want it. Sometimes he allowed himself to feel the twinge of loneliness that marriage might relieve, but he would then think of his unhappily married friends, and that loneliness would be banished to the back of his mind where it belonged. He very rarely allowed himself to feel any emotion; these past weeks were exceptional in that respect. The thought of love in marriage never crossed his mind. He was content. He did not have to put on any pretence of tolerating the company of a woman to decorate his arm, or be interested in conversation that did not challenge. He found society and its ways growing steadily more intolerable. On those increasingly rare occasions when he felt the need for physical release, he would visit a house for gentlemen, but would always leave dissatisfied with the mechanical experience.

He looked again at the cloth in his hand. He did not know this woman, but he found himself wondering about her. In such a brief time he learned several fascinating facts. She was happy. She had a sense of humour and tolerance for the absurd. She had no tolerance for poor behaviour, and she was undoubtedly sympathetic and kind. And she was lovely. He sighed and wondered what it would be like to talk to her, and if that experience would burst the little world he imagined around her. She was obviously below him in consequence but with Georgiana's downfall, what did that matter anymore? The sound of his butler quietly entering and delivering his sister's note startled him. He looked around the room, remembering where he was. He shook his head. There was no point in dwelling on such thoughts. He would never see Elizabeth Bennet again.

Darcy read the note Georgiana had prepared. It was simply a thank you for her kindness. On impulse, Darcy picked up his pen and added a few lines, then sealed it. He set it aside on the top of his desk and taking up the handkerchief, tucked it into the breast pocket of his coat.

A fortnight after the incident, a sennight after the publication of the gossip, Darcy steeled himself and walked to his club. He had put it off as long as he could. It was hard enough attending the theatre with his aunt and uncle, knowing that the opera glasses were all trained on his box and that he was the subject of the barely muffled whispers that he heard as they passed by. Church was its own brand of torture since it added the element of pious disapproval that the hypocrites who attended bestowed upon him and Georgiana as they took their pew, but this place would be a different experience entirely. Here there were no ladies present, and the men, friends and foes alike, would not hesitate to approach him. He entered the main room and paused at the door, searching out his friend Charles Bingley who had agreed to meet him there. He cursed to himself, realizing he had arrived on time, and Bingley had, as usual, been delayed. Placing a look of indifference on his face, he drew breath and entered the noisy confines of the men's lair. Conversations ceased as he strolled deliberately across the room, nodding at a few men as he set a course for an empty corner table. Nobody stopped him on his way, but he knew it was just a matter of time before they began arriving.

A servant silently appeared at his elbow, and taking his order for brandy he disappeared. Darcy picked up a discarded paper and began pretending to peruse it, all the while feeling the eyes upon him. It was a situation that always had made him uncomfortable. Arguably he should be used to being the object of attention in a crowded room. His family was not titled, but its age and extraordinary wealth made it just as important as the peerage. He had been the subject of matchmaking mothers and friends with younger sisters since he came of age, and had resisted them steadfastly through the years. Perhaps that was the one silver lining in this nightmare, perhaps he was not as desirable as he once was and they would leave him alone. He heard voices approaching and noticed several grinning men bearing down on him. Steeling himself, he looked up at them.

"Darcy! We certainly did not expect to see you here!"

He raised a brow and regarded them. "And why would that be, Forrest? I am a member, and I am in town. Why should I not visit my club?"

A man dressed in the finest and tightest of topcoats slid into the booth next to him and said in an eager whisper, "Is it true? Did your little sister elope?"

Darcy looked at him with distaste. "No she did not. You can not tell me that you put stock in the rantings of the gossip rags."

"Come now, Darcy, it is all over town, we heard it from the Dithridges who were staying in the cottage next to hers. She was seen boarding a coach with a man and her companion, and then you were seen arriving and leaving again almost instantly no more than two hours later!" The corpulent man placed both hands on the table and leered at him. "If she is not married, she was certainly plucked before you got to her. What are you going to do with her now? Send her to a convent?" He laughed. Harold Winslow was delighted to see the great Fitzwilliam Darcy knocked down a peg or two.

Darcy rose to his feet. "I will not tolerate such language used in reference to my sister, sir. If you do not wish to face the consequences, I suggest you retract them now!" His voice was low but carrying and the room became silent again. His eyes burned into the rotund, weaker man, who for all of his bravado instantly backed down.

"Just having a little fun, Darcy. You have no sense of humour." He stepped back.

"No man should speak of such things of any respectable woman, let alone of a child." Darcy hissed through clenched teeth.

"Ah but that is the point is it not, Darcy? She is no longer respectable. What man would want her now? I mean any decent man will look away, no matter the dowry. She is good for the desperate ones now, I should think. I certainly would not want anything to do with her."

Darcy rounded on the third man. "Nobody invited you to come calling Pendergast!" He scanned the assembled men. "If you have nothing better to speak of than the filthy gossip of the bored members of society, then I would appreciate you leaving me to my paper."

"Ha, if you did not expect anyone to approach you in this club Darcy, you were blind and have lost what brilliance you once displayed at University." Pendergast said. "You should know there are several betting books already set up. One to determine how soon rid yourself of her by marriage, one as to when the child will be born, oh, and one to determine your wedding date, although that has been in existence for years." The three men, finding courage in their combined solidarity, laughed at him and moved away before Darcy's clenched fists could land on any. The surrounding men who were listening in laughed and went back to their conversations. Darcy glanced around the room, noting the faces, and knowing who amongst them were his real friends. He glanced at the clock in the corner. He would give Bingley five more minutes and he would leave.

Settling back down at the table he picked up the paper and lifted it to his eyes, hiding the red and furious countenance he could not mask. "Darcy!" He slammed the paper down, about to lash out at the intruder and stopped in time to realize the ebullient face before him was that of his friend. He stood and offered his hand. "Bingley! Thank God, I had just about given you up and left. You must invest in a watch."

Bingley laughed and took a seat across from him, and placed a drink order. He regarded his friend. "How are you bearing up? From the expression on your face I would say they have been at you already."

Darcy snorted. "There are betting books open on this, did you know?"

"Yes, I thought it best not to tell you."

Darcy shook his head. "I should not have been surprised." He waved a hand at the crowded room. "Not one of them rose to defend me."

"Do not judge the room too harshly, Darcy. You have friends here, just that some of them are not brave enough to stand up in a crowded room. They will come to you in subtler ways. I have seen Coolidge and Peters there defending you and Miss Darcy in small groups. And Franklin and Wallace, they have had similar experiences with the gossip rags. You are just too far embroiled in this to see them clearly. You have helped too many people over the years with your advice and investments to be left in the cold when you are finally in need."

Relaxing, Darcy met his friend's eyes. "Thank you for that." He sighed. "They may support me, but will it do Georgiana any good?"

Bingley grimaced. "That is another question entirely. If she was compromised . . ." Darcy shook his head. "Well, even if she was not, the rumour is out. Delaying her presentation will be your best hope, I think." Darcy nodded. "It was not to happen for at least another two years, perhaps three would be best. By then a new scandal will surely be at the forefront of the *ton*."

Bingley nodded. "Oh, by that time there will have been dozens of families disgraced by one thing or another. I am sure that at the rate my sister is going, she will undoubtedly be one to create a scandal herself!" He laughed.

"Can I but hope that my ruination by association has dissuaded Miss Bingley from her obsession with me?" Darcy asked, not entirely in jest.

"Ah, well, probably not. She may be put off for the rest of the Season, but you know Caroline, she is quite determined to be Mistress of Pemberley."

"That will never happen, Bingley." Darcy assured him.

"Of that I am well aware, Darcy. Perhaps though, she will stop pushing me to pay attention to Miss Darcy." He smiled.

"She wanted you to marry her? She is not out!" Darcy was incredulous.

"It is all a ploy to get closer to you." He said with a smirk. "Besides, I have a new love, so I am quite occupied, I assure you."

Darcy rolled his eyes. "Not again, Bingley, what is this, the fourth since Christmas?"

"The third and I will thank you not to laugh at me. At least I am enjoying my youth while you waste the best years of your life breeding sheep and collecting rents. There are so many willing young ladies just itching to know you!"

"Knowing me is not what they wish for, Bingley." He said dryly. "And you had better be careful or you will find yourself a father-to-be and a bachelor that was."

"Thank you for the advice, but I assure you, I am under good regulation. I only dance and flirt with the ladies of the *ton*. There are other places, as you well know, for taking care of more pressing needs." He grinned and touched his hand to his heart. "I am saving myself for my one true love."

Darcy almost spat out the brandy he was sipping. "I can not wait to meet the woman who manages to hold your attention long enough to get you to the altar. She will be quite formidable, I am sure."

"No, no, I do not want a challenging, intriguing wife. That is for you. I want one as complacent as myself, a lamb, a beauty, a . . ."

Darcy grew uncomfortable discussing his possible marriage. Bingley struck too close to home for his taste. "Enough of this Bingley. What are your plans?"

"I have decided to buy an estate."

"You have said that for the past five years." He said shaking his head.

"Yes, but I am ready. I have decided to follow your advice and lease something, not commit to anything yet, just get my feet wet. And I have asked my secretary to look for something within easy distance of London, for Caroline's sake. She can not be too far away from her shopping and society, at least not until she marries a certain gentleman who will spirit her away to his spectacular estate in Derbyshire."

"Bite your tongue!"

Bingley laughed. "So, once we find something, will you ride out with me and look it over before I sign a lease?"

"We plan to remove to Pemberley in a fortnight, but if you identify an estate in the meantime, I would be grateful for the day out."

"Good!" Bingley looked up and noticed groups of men speaking and staring in their direction. "Do you think you have put on enough of a show? Are you ready to take your leave?"

Darcy's mouth twitched. "I have been ready since I stepped through the door. Would you like to come and see Georgiana? She would not mind you."

"I would be delighted. I told my driver to return home, so we can take your carriage."

He shook his head. "No my friend, I walked. Come, it will be good for you."

"I am not a walker Darcy." He whined.

"If you plan to own an estate, Bingley, you must leave your study."

The men rose and made their way out of the club. Neither one missed the increased conversation as they left. Strolling down the street they continued their friendly banter. Darcy was grateful for this friend. Bingley always made him feel good. He was just a naturally ebullient man, the complete opposite of himself. They were a good match. Where Bingley provided good cheer, Darcy gave him sound advice. They were walking down a street with many storefronts when Darcy spotted one selling ladies' accessories and told Bingley he needed to stop in. His friend looked at him quizzically and decided he was buying a bauble for his sister. They entered the shop, dripping with feminine items, and felt distinctly out of place. The proprietor spotted gentlemen of quality immediately and bustled up to them.

"Sirs, what can I do for you?" She smiled warmly at them.

"I am interested in some handkerchiefs for a lady." Darcy said quietly.

"Yes sir, plain or decorated?"

"Both."

The woman led him over to a table where a fine assortment of embroidered handkerchiefs was on display. He picked one up with delicate purple flowers and asked, "What stitch is this?" Bingley stared. Darcy ignored him. "Lavender sir, quite unusual. Most handkerchiefs have the fancier blooms. It takes a particular lady to appreciate such a tiny flower." Darcy's eyes brightened. *Lavender.* That was the scent that enveloped him when he stood next to Miss Bennet. He chose two of the cloths embroidered with the pattern, and then picked up one with red roses. He also selected a very fine plain cloth edged with Irish lace. He paid for his purchase and with the slightest of smiles, exited the shop with Bingley in his wake.

"Who are those for?" He demanded.

"A lady."

"Of that I had no doubt. What lady?" He stared into his eyes.

"Nobody either of us will ever know." He said enigmatically, and strode on. Bingley knew enough not to press the point, but filed the information away for future interrogation.

Chapter 3

"*M*iss Elizabeth, there is a special messenger here with a parcel for you. He was told to hand it to you directly." Mrs. Hill, Longbourn's housekeeper, could barely contain her excitement. No such delivery had ever been made to the estate before and she could have been knocked over with a feather when she reached for the pouch of coins she kept in her apron to pay for the post, and the young man assured her that there was no charge.

Elizabeth stared at her eldest sister Jane in bewildered anticipation, and silently thanked heaven that her mother and three other sisters had walked into Meryton that morning. "I can not imagine what this could be!" She grabbed Jane's hand to drag her to the door.

"Miss Elizabeth Bennet?" The dusty young man asked.

"Yes?" She smiled.

"This package was to be delivered directly to you. I was told to wait for any response. If it is convenient, I will go and care for my horse by your stables."

"Oh certainly, would you like something to eat? It must have been a long ride from . . ."

"London, Miss." He smiled. "If it is not too much trouble, Miss."

"It is no trouble at all. Hill, could you see to him, please?" She looked at her housekeeper who was clearly disappointed that she would not see what was in the package. "Yes, Miss Elizabeth."

Elizabeth and Jane returned to the sitting room and examined the parcel. It was addressed in a firm, and she noted, masculine hand. There was no return address, but that would not have been necessary with a special messenger. She carefully opened the wrapping and gasped in surprise as four beautiful handkerchiefs fell into her lap, along with two sealed notes. On the outside of one she saw the words, "open first". Jane picked up the cloths and was admiring the needlework as Elizabeth, a growing suspicion forming in her mind, opened the first letter.

12 June 1811
Darcy House
Park Lane
London

Dear Miss Bennet,
Please forgive me for my tardiness in the return of your handkerchief. I can not begin to tell you how much I appreciated your kindness to me, a complete stranger. You can not possibly understand how deeply needed your generous act

was at that moment, and how looking back, it continues to give me hope that there are good people in this world. I thank you so very much.
Sincerely yours,
Georgiana Darcy

Dear Miss Bennet,
I would like to echo my sister's sentiments. Your kindness touched more than one person that morning. It was a great pleasure to meet you. I thank you.
Sincerely,
Fitzwilliam Darcy

Elizabeth smiled, and then frowned. The letter indicated that her handkerchief was being returned, yet instead she seemed to have received four new cloths. Then she reread the words of the young girl. Something terrible must have happened. That was obvious when she saw her, but this seemed to go beyond just a tragic event, she seemed most grateful that anyone could extend a hand of kindness to her. It was almost as if the girl had done something that she felt deserved her suffering the ill-will of others. Her brow furrowed. Perhaps she was reading too much into the note, but then she looked down at Mr. Darcy's words. She remembered the sombre man who stared so deeply into her eyes, as if he were trying to memorize her face for all eternity. It sent chills down her spine then, and just thinking about it, and seeing his name written in his hand, sent her heart racing once again. She did not even know him but she felt connected somehow.

Jane broke into her musings. "What did the note say, Lizzy?" Elizabeth started and handed it to her, then broke open the seal of the second note.

Miss B,
Surely by now you have realized that your own handkerchief was not returned to you. I could tell a story that it had been ruined in the laundry, but that would be a lie. The truth of the matter is that I simply do not wish to part with it. I observed you in the street that morning, including your conversation with a certain beast of burden, and I was struck. After actually speaking to you, and seeing your kindness to my sister, I can not put into words how I felt. When she came to me asking if I knew your name and address, I took her note and stole your handkerchief. I hope that my choices please you. The stitches are nothing to your Sweet Williams, but the lavender and roses seemed appropriate for you. The plain cloth I leave for you to fill with a bouquet of your imagination. I realize this is entirely improper, and you should instantly burn this note, but I could not let this opportunity pass without expressing my most sincere thanks.
FD

Elizabeth read the note over and over; her hand rose to her mouth and stayed there. Her eyes were opened wide, and rapid breathing joined her racing heartbeat. Who was this man? Would she ever see him again? She looked over at the letter Jane held on her lap. The address was there. Perhaps she could write back to his sister . . . "Lizzy?" She startled again from her thoughts. "What does the second note say?"

She hesitated a moment. "Jane you must promise not to say a word of this note to anyone." Jane's eyes widened and she nodded. Elizabeth handed it over and watched her sister's face as her astonishment grew. Finally she looked up. "Lizzy! This is practically a love letter!" She whispered. Elizabeth nodded. "That is what I thought, too."

Jane squeezed her hand. "Their address is Park Lane. Is that near Grosvenor Square?"

"I believe it is." The sisters stared at each other, realizing the wealth of this family. "Why, Jane? Do you think he is simply toying with me?"

She shook her head. "No, both letters are far too sincere for that. Miss Darcy is clearly in great pain over some terrible event, and Mr. Darcy is obviously grateful for your kindness." She read the second note again. "He seemed quite taken with you and the donkey." She smiled and looked up to see Elizabeth rolling her eyes. "It only proves that I am at my most attractive when I am dishevelled."

"That must be true if you caught Mr. Darcy's eye." Jane said coyly.

"I may have caught his eye, but there is no mention of ever seeing him again. What do I do now?" The sound of approaching footsteps inspired a hurried folding of the notes and quickly secreting them down the bodice of Elizabeth's gown. Mrs. Hill knocked and entered, her eyes scanning for the package. Seeing nothing but the wrapping paper she sighed. "Miss Elizabeth, the messenger has eaten and asks if there is a reply."

"Oh, I forgot about him. Yes, I will write it immediately. Thank you, Hill." Elizabeth ran over to the writing desk and sharpening a pen, pulled out two sheets of paper and quickly wrote her responses. She read them over and nodded with satisfaction, waved the paper in the air to dry the ink, and sealed the sheets together. She wrote on the outside with a definite flourish and smiling at Jane, stood up. "I will be back in a moment." Before Jane could reply she dashed out of the door and found the messenger waiting just outside on the porch. She gave him the note with a smile; he touched his cap, mounted and was gone.

Elizabeth returned to the sitting room where Jane was contemplating the handkerchiefs. "Who did you write to, Lizzy? Mister or Miss Darcy?" She grinned. "Both of them."

———⁓⁓⁓———

A knock on the study door interrupted the daydream Darcy was having. He was in the midst of thinking about Miss Bennet, and her reaction to his small offering. He knew that he had breached the rules of propriety, and for the first time in his life he did not let that bother him. If nothing else, his treatment by society over the past few weeks had shown him that his value, despite all that he had been for his entire life, had been quite significantly lowered. He only hoped that Miss Bennet would not be offended by his behaviour, which was all that mattered. He glanced at the clock; surely Danny should be back soon. It was only a few hours ride to Hertfordshire . . . A second knock brought him fully to attention. "Come in."

Mr. Hendricks, his butler, entered and announced. "Mrs. Annesley, sir."

Darcy stood and walked around to the front of his desk. A woman, likely in her late forties, entered the room and curtseyed. She seemed to be assessing the tall, dark man as closely as he was examining her. Darcy took in the features of the slightly plump woman with a friendly face. He bowed. "Mrs. Annesley, it is a pleasure to meet you. Please take a seat." He indicated the deep leather chair before his desk, and as she made herself comfortable, he moved around to his own chair. "I have had a great many glowing recommendations of you. If half of them are true, I will have been very fortunate to have found you before another family did." She raised her brow at him. "I would hope that all of the recommendations are verifiable, sir."

A slight smile appeared on his lips and disappeared. She was intelligent. That was good. "Forgive me, Mrs. Annesley. I have recently been forced to dismiss my sister's last companion, and her references were seemingly impeccable. You might understand my wariness."

She inclined her head. "I have taken no offence sir. It is fortunate that my last employer's daughter married just last week and you found yourself in need of a new companion for your sister at the same time."

Darcy nodded. "Mrs. Annesley, as my employee, I will expect loyalty and discretion. No discussion of anything that happens in my homes or to any of my family will be tolerated with outsiders, and preferably with no one inside of those homes, although I am aware that the staff does enjoy discussing us over tea in the kitchen." Another slight smile appeared and was gone. Mrs. Annesley noted it with interest. It seemed Mr. Darcy had a kind heart hidden deep under his sombre appearance. "Yes sir, I understand."

"My sister, as you are aware, is fifteen years old, and has no mother. I have done the best that I can since our parent's deaths, but . . . a recent event has made it abundantly clear that she is in great need of someone besides a much older brother to guide her."

"Yes, the elopement." Mrs. Annesley said.

Darcy's eyes flashed. "*You* know about it?"

Very gently she said, "Sir, you are not the only one investigating references. When your name was brought to my attention as a possible employer, I asked my former families if your home would be one that I would feel . . . comfortable entering. I was assured that you were always looked upon in the past as displaying the epitome of honour, however, since your sister's . . . behaviour, your good name has been hurt by association with her transgression."

His jaw clenched. "My sister did nothing wrong. She was led astray by those who wished to take advantage of her naiveté and her good heart."

"I have no doubt of that, sir, but forgive me, if you expect her to heal, she will have to face her part in it, as will you."

"I have already accepted my blame for what happened, madam." He said tersely.

"You misunderstand me. You must accept that your sister played a role." She looked at him with all sincerity.

Darcy said nothing for several moments. "We will be leaving for our estate in Derbyshire in a fortnight. It is my intention to stay there until at least next February. We may be invited to stay at a friend's estate this autumn, but as he has yet to sign a lease, I can not say for sure when or where it will be. In the meantime, if you have never experienced a winter in Derbyshire, I suggest that you acquire some suitable warm clothing prior to our departure." He stood and she did as well. "I assume that the pay I have offered in my letter was sufficient?"

"Yes sir, it was." He nodded. "Fine, let me introduce you to Miss Darcy. When can you begin?"

"I can start tomorrow afternoon, sir. That should give me sufficient time to order the new things." She wondered if she had enough funds to cover this unexpected expense.

He nodded again. "Good. Have the bills for the new items sent to me. I do not expect you to shoulder this burden." He turned and walked from the room. Mrs. Annesley stood for a moment staring at him in surprise, and finding herself alone, hurried to catch up with him.

She followed him into a beautiful room full of sunlight and dominated by a large pianoforte and harp, with comfortable sofas and chairs scattered about, waiting to be filled by an audience. A young girl stood nervously by the instrument, staring at the floor. She watched as he tenderly took his sister's hand and whispered something to her. She nodded and raised her eyes to see her new companion. "Mrs. Annesley, may I present my sister, Miss Georgiana Darcy?" In a soft tone he turned to his sister. "Georgiana, this is Mrs. Annesley, your new companion."

"I am pleased to meet you." Georgiana whispered and looked back down.

Mrs. Annesley was taken aback by the fragile girl before her. She was not at all what she expected after hearing the stories of her attempted elopement. She began to understand more about Mr. Darcy's vehement defence of his sister. She smiled. "I am delighted to meet you too, Miss Darcy."

Darcy let go of her hand. "Well, I will leave you to become acquainted, if you will excuse me?" He smiled reassuringly into Georgiana's panicked eyes and nodded to Mrs. Annesley, then left the room, leaving the two alone. Walking down the hallway he breathed a sigh of relief. He hoped that this woman could help his sister survive the next few years before, well hopefully, she will be successfully presented and she might start over.

He returned to his study and began concentrating on a report from his steward when he was again interrupted by his butler. A little annoyed he looked up to see his personal messenger Danny entering the room. Suddenly all annoyance was forgotten as he watched, with what he thought of as cruel deliberation, Danny removing a sealed letter from his pouch and handing it to him. He saw the swirls and curls of a distinctly feminine hand forming his name on the outside, and instantly his heart started beating faster. He tore his eyes away from his treasure for a moment to address his servant. "Did you have any trouble locating Longbourn?"

"No sir, it seems to be one of the larger estates in the area, and with five daughters, the Bennets seem to be quite well-known." He grinned.

"Five daughters?" Darcy thought back, he only saw four. "So, tell me, what did you learn of the family?"

Danny was surprised, Mr. Darcy was not one for gossip, but he was happy to oblige. "Well sir, the estate, Longbourn, brings in about two thousand a year, there is no son, it is entailed but nobody has seen the heir as yet. The two eldest girls are the picture of propriety, Miss Bennet is said to be the one with beauty, the second eldest, Miss Elizabeth is said to have a sharp wit and kind heart. The younger girls, well, one likes sermonizing while the last two like men in red coats." He grinned again, thinking he would have liked to have met those two. "I hear the Missus is determined to find husbands for them and is rather, uh, loud. The master keeps his sanity by keeping to his study with his port."

Darcy stared at him. "How on earth did you learn all of this?"

He laughed. "Oh, well, Miss Elizabeth took the parcel and asked the housekeeper to find me something to eat while I waited for her response. The maids were just itching to find out what I was about; I guess no such package had ever been delivered like that before. I know not to ever speak of you to anyone sir, so it was easy enough to get them talking about their employers." He shrugged.

"I am happy for your loyalty, Danny." He opened his desk drawer and took out some coins. "Here, for your discretion." Danny smiled widely and touched his cap. "Thank you sir, I will put this to good use!" Darcy shook his head. "I do not care to know." The boy left the room and Darcy looked down at the letter in his hand. He was almost afraid to open it. "Fool!" He muttered, and with a quick movement, broke the seal. To his surprise he found two sheets of paper. One addressed to Georgiana, and one to himself. He bit his lip and unfolded the page for his sister first.

13 June 1811
Longbourn
Meryton
Hertfordshire

Dear Miss Darcy,
I hope with all sincerity that you are recovering from your distress. If I was in any way responsible for bringing you a moment of relief, then I am well-pleased. It was unnecessary, truly, but I thank you for your desire to return my handkerchief. I was thinking, I so enjoy meeting new people and learning about different parts of the country. Would you consider writing me? I have four sisters, one older and obviously three younger, so I am not lacking in female companionship, but I would so enjoy talking with someone who does not occupy another room in my house. Please consider it, and I anticipate your letter. You see! I already expect you to say yes!
Yours sincerely,
Elizabeth Bennet

Darcy smiled. Miss Bennet was offering friendship to his sister, and he could sense that it was offered simply out of kindness, and not in an effort to know an obviously wealthier girl. He doubted that Miss Bennet, no, *Miss Elizabeth*, his smile grew, was anything other than sincere. He saw that she was clever, mentioning the handkerchief but not telling Georgiana what he had done. And she displayed her humour. He sighed. Drawing a breath he bit his lip again and with trepidation picked up the sheet embellished with his name.

Dear Mr. D,

Sir, how can I possibly express my surprise when I opened your parcel and out tumbled not one but four handkerchiefs; and not one of them recognizable as my own? How will I ever explain such finery to my mother? You sir, have no idea the interrogation that awaits me. It is fortunate that I do not know you well or will likely see you again, because if I were to meet you, I would be forced to remain silent in a self-important snit of grand proportions.

In all seriousness, please accept my very sincere thanks for such beautiful replacements for my poor example of sewing. I am afraid I am much better suited to walking and reading than I am to needlework. I can not begin to imagine how you knew the stitch I used, or how you could know that lavender is my favourite flower. I am very fond of roses as well. I think that I shall combine the three to create the bouquet you suggested on the last cloth, and I will remember your generosity whenever I reach for one of these exquisite handkerchiefs. I feel honoured that you were moved to resort to theft to acquire a keepsake of my conversation with a four-legged friend.

With gratitude,
EB

Darcy blew out the breath he was holding and a warm, happy smile spread over his face. It felt so *good*. She had not been offended by his note, by his gift, or by his flaunting of propriety. His heart was thumping. He could not recognize what he was feeling; it was just so oddly exhilarating. She had not rejected him. He sighed, and lifted his chin and stared with relief and accomplishment at his very first note from a lady. There was no doubt in his mind that Georgiana would begin a correspondence with Miss Elizabeth, if he had to write the letters himself.

─────

"Where is he?! Where is my nephew?!" The imperious tones filled the entranceway of Darcy House, and soon the floorboards were creaking with the angry steps and tapping cane of Lady Catherine de Bourgh. Mr. Hendricks tried to stop her advance. "My Lady, please wait, Mr. Darcy is not available at the moment, and he has a guest."

"A guest! Who would want to visit with him?" She glared at the man as if he were an insect.

"Your Ladyship, please, come into the drawing room, and I shall inform Mr. Darcy that you have arrived." Mr. Hendricks had years of experience dealing with this relative of the Darcys'. It was never easy, particularly when she was feeling self-righteous and in control.

Lady Catherine brushed him off. "He is in the study, is he not?" Without waiting for an answer she went to the door and opened it without a knock. She strode into the room where Darcy and Bingley hurriedly rose to their feet.

"Aunt Catherine! What brings you here?" Darcy was offended and embarrassed by his aunt's behaviour, and knowing what was likely to come from her visit, was gathering his thoughts so that he could take her on as tactfully as possible. He glanced at Bingley who had met the formidable woman in the past. "I hope that you remember my friend Mr. Bingley."

Lady Catherine nodded to him. "I am surprised you still have friends." She looked to Bingley. "I have important business with my nephew. I hope that you understand."

Bingley stared at her for being so dismissed, and caught the ire rising in Darcy's expression. "Of course, your Ladyship." He turned to his friend. "We will continue our conversation tonight over dinner Darcy, if that suits you?" Seeing his friend's barely perceptible nod, he walked towards the door.

"Please be seated, Aunt. I will just go and see my guest out." Before waiting for her reply he moved across the room to take Bingley to the front door. As they waited for his hat and gloves to be fetched he said in a low voice. "I apologize for her Bingley. She is obviously ready for a fight, and although I object to her assuming that she is mistress of my home, I do not wish you to be subjected to her display."

"What will she do?" Bingley asked with concern.

"I do not know. Whatever it is, I am sure I will not be smiling when you arrive for dinner." He said darkly.

Bingley patted his shoulder. "Well, then I know all will be normal, for when are you ever smiling?"

Darcy raised his brow. "You have a point there." He sighed and watched as his friend escaped. He turned and straightened his suit, then went in to face his infuriated relative.

"Darcy!" Lady Catherine cried as he entered his study and closed the door. "Your father would be ashamed of you! How could you let this happen?"

He settled himself behind his desk and considered his aunt. "I assure you Aunt, it was not planned."

"Georgiana is utterly ruined, and you are being taken down with her. You must save the family name!" She slammed her cane down for emphasis.

"We are hoping that by the time Georgiana is presented, the memories of the incident will have faded."

She snorted. "As if the board at Almack's would allow you to forget!"

"I am sure some richer scandal will occupy their thoughts in three years time." He said quietly.

"Three years!! You will wallow in this for three years!"

Darcy's anger flared. "Wallow, Aunt? Do you mean to imply that I am enjoying hearing my name disparaged everywhere I go? Do you think that I wish for my sister to feel that she has destroyed hundreds of years of our families' history with one impulsive foolish act? Do you think that I relish hearing whispers behind me when I walk into our church? No, Aunt, I am not wallowing in anything. Georgiana is but fifteen, it is perfectly reasonable to wait until she is eighteen for her presentation."

She gave him a calculating stare. "And what of you? Are you to wait three years to regain your standing in society?"

Darcy watched her and said carefully, "My standing in regards to my fortune remains the same. My desirability as a marriage partner is perhaps reduced, but that does not concern me. As far as participating in society, their rejection is not entirely regretted."

"Well, there is a solution to this entire situation, and I am here today to make all of your troubles disappear instantly!" She sat forward and stared at him with triumphant eyes. "You will marry Anne immediately!"

"Excuse me?" He stared at her. "And how would that save my and Georgiana's reputations?"

"You would be a husband, in possession of two great estates, nobody would dare disparage you. And Georgiana would have a stable home. Her transgressions would be instantly forgotten and soon I will identify a proper husband for her, one who will check this wildness she has displayed and obviously learned by living without proper supervision by you." She sat back, and waited for his praise for her plan, oblivious to the insult she delivered.

Darcy stared at her. "You can not be serious? I have never had a desire to marry my cousin, and doing so now would do nothing to help Georgiana. I take great offence at your implication that she has not been raised properly. While it is true that my marrying may do something to relieve my present difficulties, it is unlikely at the moment that any woman of society would have me. Why, if that is so, are you so willing to sacrifice Anne to me?"

She waved off his objections. "Anne was formed for you Darcy, you know it. Your union was destined since your birth. My sister, your mother, agreed with this."

"My mother barely held me as a baby and only came near me when it was convenient to show off the heir to her friends! I will not satisfy some scheme of hers to marry me off to any woman." He fumed. "IF I marry, it will be to someone of my own choosing, and in my own time!"

Lady Catherine stood and Darcy rose as well. Her voice became placating. "I understand you are upset at present, Darcy, otherwise you would not be speaking so foolishly. I will go and speak to my brother, and he will agree with my plans. Anne will save your name, and you should be grateful that she is willing to make the sacrifice to be your wife. You must remember, Pemberley requires an heir, and Anne will be willing to submit to you."

Darcy recoiled with her last statement. His disgust was evident in his voice. "When I last spoke to Anne, she indicated no desire to marry me."

"Anne will do what she is told." She said icily.

"I, however, will not." He walked and opened the door. "Shall I walk you to your carriage, Aunt?"

Lady Catherine stared up at him. "I have not finished with you, Darcy. You will marry Anne. I will return with your uncle."

"And he will hear the same response, madam."

They entered the hallway just as Georgiana was descending the stairs with Mrs. Annesley. Lady Catherine pointed an accusatory finger at her niece. "This is your fault Georgiana! It is because of your foolish, selfish actions that your brother is no longer welcome in the great homes of this country and no decent man will ever have you!" Georgiana burst into tears. Lady Catherine ignored her and turned to Darcy. "I suggest that you accept your destiny and marry Anne. She is good enough for you, and will save your family. You should realize how low you have fallen because of your sister and be grateful that Anne will accept you."

She turned back to regard her sobbing niece. "This never would have happened if Georgiana had been sent to me after your father died. Perhaps it is not too late. I will speak to my brother about giving custody to me." Georgiana gasped and looked with fear at Darcy.

He attempted to rein in his fury, and with a tightly controlled voice addressed his aunt. "I believe it is time that you took your leave, Aunt Catherine. I have listened to your opinions but I will make this clear now. I will not marry Anne, and no one will ever take Georgiana from me." He opened the door. "Good day, madam." Lady Catherine opened her mouth to argue, and then thought better of it. She would speak to her brother. He was the head of the family, and would make Darcy fall in line. She swept outside without a word and Darcy closed the door after her with a resounding snap.

Taking a moment to collect himself; he breathed deeply then returned to the entranceway where Georgiana stood staring at him. "She can not take me, can she?" The girl ran up and clutched his arm.

Darcy patted her hand. "No, dear. Nobody can ever take you away. Father left you in my and Cousin Richard's care. She has no claim on you. She is just spouting off as usual." He kissed her head.

"Is it true what she said? Have you been hurt so very badly? Will you not be able to marry well?" She said in a very small voice. Darcy lightly touched her shoulder and closed his eyes. "I will not lie to you, Georgiana. The marriage prospects for both of us have changed, and likely permanently. I have hope that by the time you are presented, everything will be as it was. As for me, I do not regret the situation as much as you might expect. Perhaps it will give me a freedom to choose in a way that I previously thought impossible." She looked up at him. "How brother?" He smiled slightly and shrugged. "Who knows?"

"Thank you, Darcy." Bingley said as his friend poured him another finger of brandy. He took a seat and watched him finish pouring his own drink and sit opposite him in the grand library of Darcy House. "That tale is enough to frighten small children from sleeping at night! I can not believe your aunt thought she could bully you into marrying your cousin!"

He took a sip and laid his head back against the corner of the wingback chair. "Well she has tried every other method. You have to admit, she is tenacious."

"I almost regret leaving and missing the fireworks!" He laughed, then seeing his friend's face, stopped. "How is Georgiana? I was sorry that she did not join us for dinner."

Darcy's eyes brightened then he blinked rapidly. Bingley looked away until he spoke. "She now fears that she will be forced to go live with our aunt, and does not believe me when I tell her it will never happen." He blinked again. "She heard all that Aunt Catherine said about our marriage prospects and my standing, and is devastated on how all of this has affected me." He looked up at Bingley's sympathetic face. "Enough. You were about to tell me some news when we were interrupted this afternoon."

Bingley read his desire to drop the subject for now and pasted a happy smile on his face. "Indeed, good news! I have found an estate to lease, and I hope to persuade you to come and look it over with me tomorrow."

"Really! Excellent Bingley, where is this place? Tell me about it!" Darcy was relieved to have such an easy topic to discuss.

"It is called Netherfield. The owner tells me it brings in about five thousand, so it matches my income now. The tenants are good, the house sound. It will come furnished. All he asks is that I keep an eye on things, and work with the steward to identify problems. Any major decisions or repairs will fall to him, but he welcomes me supervising to get some experience. He is willing to sell at the end of the lease. It apparently is a family estate that nobody needed, so he has been leasing it out to a fairly frequent number of people for years."

"Why has nobody ever purchased it?" Darcy asked suspiciously.

"Oh, well he said that the family has just recently decided to sell. They liked the regular income it provided, but now they think they would be just as happy with dividing the proceeds and being done with it." He smiled. "I know what you are thinking, Darcy, it is too good to be true. It is a decent estate with no entail, and available in my price range, but I think it is just pure luck that pointed me to it."

"How did you learn of it?"

"My secretary made some inquiries and this is one of the places he found. I like it because it is fairly near London, in Hertfordshire."

Darcy started. "Hertfordshire?" He started thinking rapidly. *How large could that county be? Perhaps it is not too far away from . . .*

"Yes, near a village called Meryton. Have you ever heard of it?" Bingley was so happy to talk, that he did not notice that his friend looked as if his heart had stopped. "It is only about twenty or so miles from here. We could leave early and ride out, take a look around, speak to the steward and have something to eat in the village. There is bound to be an inn of some sort there, and then be home in time for dinner." He grinned and looked at Darcy. "How does that sound?" Darcy just sat staring at him. His hand had drifted unconsciously to touch the handkerchief in his breast pocket. "I say, Darcy, are you well? Are you clutching your heart?" Bingley sat up with a concerned expression on his face.

Darcy awoke from his stupor and quickly moved his hand. "What, oh, yes, I am fine, Bingley. I . . . I think that sounds like an excellent plan. I look forward to seeing this place. I am sure it will be ideal." He felt himself breathing rapidly. *Yes, it will be perfectly ideal.*

Chapter 4

*T*he Bennet family gathered around the worn dining table for breakfast before scattering to their various activities of the day. An early morning shower had prevented Elizabeth's usual constitutional, but the sun was now brightly shining, and she was anxious to leave the house and walk, and think about her letter and the man who wrote it. Her father's voice somehow managed to break into her pleasant thoughts in a most disconcerting way. "Well Lizzy, I understand that you received a parcel by special messenger. You have not shared with us its contents, as far as I know, so please tell us about it." Her father smiled to see his favourite daughter shoot a suspicious glance at Mrs. Hill, who was standing in the doorway. The table grew suddenly quiet. "A parcel did you say Mr. Bennet? By special messenger? What is this about Lizzy?" Mrs. Bennet demanded.

Elizabeth's sharp look was transferred to her father who did not bother to hide his amusement. "It simply contained a handkerchief, Mama. I lent one of mine to a distressed young lady Jane and I met in Meryton several weeks ago. I told her that she was welcome to keep it, but she insisted on returning it to me. I hope to start a correspondence with her." Mrs. Bennet was distinctly disappointed that the parcel was not more fascinating. Then the thought occurred to her. "The package came by a special messenger. This girl must be of some wealth to have letters delivered in such a way. Is she rich, Lizzy?"

Elizabeth glanced at Jane. "I do not know anything of her circumstances, Mama. I hope to learn more of her if she agrees to our correspondence. She is quite young, so I am sure that she will not be talking of matters of fortune."

"Well, see what you can make of it. If she is rich, perhaps you may go and visit her, and put you in the way of some rich men."

Elizabeth sighed. Her mother's thoughts were fixed on finding husbands for her daughters, and ruled nearly every action and word. It was not an unreasonable goal, but it was very tiresome. "Yes, Mama. That was my hope in writing her." Mrs. Bennet nodded with satisfaction and returned to admonishing her middle girl, Mary for reading at the table. Elizabeth looked up at her father's chuckle. "You handled that with skill, Lizzy."

"I have had years of practice, Papa." He disappeared behind his paper and she could hear his continued amusement as he rattled the pages.

The family separated to their own activities and Elizabeth was tying her bonnet ribbons when Jane whispered in her ear. "I was so afraid that you were going to tell them of Mr. Darcy's gift."

Elizabeth stared and touched her sister's forehead. "Are you well, Jane? You must be fevered to be thinking so foolishly."

Jane giggled. "Forgive me, Lizzy, I should know better."

Mrs. Bennet came around the corner and spotting Elizabeth preparing to walk out exclaimed, "Where are you going, Miss Lizzy? You know we are invited to your Aunt Phillip's this evening, and John Lucas will be there. I will not have you wandering about the countryside all day and appearing dishevelled for him!" Her voice became calculating. "You know he has had his eye on you, and now that he has returned from his tour, he is ready to settle down. You must secure him!"

Elizabeth tried not to roll her eyes. "I will not go far, Mama, I promise, but I am sure that John Lucas will not care if I am dishevelled or not."

"He will if you make an effort!" She huffed. Lydia arguing with Kitty caught her attention and she bustled away to speak to her youngest daughters.

"Not fifteen minutes ago she asked me to have Miss Darcy put me in the way of some rich men!" Elizabeth sighed with frustration. "What do I care if John Lucas looks at me?" She pulled on her gloves. "He is a nice man, but I have never thought of him as anything other than a friend."

"He is well-travelled, and he is the heir to Lucas Lodge . . ." Jane smiled, imitating their mother. "It would be a good match."

"Do not join Mama, Jane, please. Besides, his tour was to Ireland! Hardly the continent!"

She laughed. "Perhaps you have another man in mind who would appreciate you looking dishevelled." She teased.

Elizabeth's movement slowed and she blushed. "I would certainly like the opportunity to know more of him." She said softly. The girls' eyes met and Jane squeezed her arm. "Go walk, Lizzy." She smiled and set off.

———✺———

Darcy and Bingley left London very early that morning on their way to inspect Netherfield. It was the first time since that frenzied ride to find Georgiana that Darcy had been on horseback, and the freedom he felt was exhilarating. The men had been riding for some time in a comfortable and companionable silence, but now Bingley regarded his friend and smiled. "This is the most relaxed I have seen you for some time, Darcy."

He looked over to Bingley, rising and falling easily with his mount beside him. "Nobody knows or cares who I am here."

"I understand." They continued on when a thought occurred to Darcy. "Bingley, have you suffered at all by your open support of us? Has anyone disparaged you?"

Bingley smiled. "Well, let us say, some have made it known that they feel I am hurting myself by associating with such a family."

Darcy was appalled. "Bingley! I am so sorry; I had not once considered how you would be harmed. You can not risk your position by our friendship. I . . ." He was at a loss as to what to do. Bingley stopped him. "Darcy, I am not concerned. Anyone who does not support you, of all people, is not worth my efforts to begin with. I am new to society, that is true, but I am also quite a babe in the woods at identifying who is worthy and who should be avoided. This experience is opening my eyes in ways that I likely would not have known without making some unfortunate choices. I thank you." He smiled wider.

"I find it hard to believe that it is so easy for you to bear criticism for something you did not do." Darcy said in admiration.

He laughed. "Come Darcy, how many years worth of criticism have you borne by being my friend? I am but a lowly man whose money came from trade. I have no property, my sisters are questionable in their airs, and I am, well, some would say painfully naïve, which is not entirely false. But you took me under your wing and ignored the advice of your friends to laugh at me and drop me like a bad habit. No Darcy, my so-called sufferings by associating with you are a pittance, and the least I can do. I am proud to be your friend."

Darcy was overwhelmed. "I thank you, Bingley, I do not know how to respond . . ." He reached his hand over and the men awkwardly shook. "I value your friendship more than I can say."

Bingley smiled and looked ahead. He knew very well that expressing emotions was something that Darcy did very rarely. He was an intensely private man. With him, few words were spoken, but they dripped with meaning. They again rode in silence until Darcy broke their reverie. "We are almost in Meryton."

"How do you know?" Bingley asked with surprise.

He sighed. "It is where I found Georgiana."

"What?!" He stared. "I never thought to ask, it was in Meryton? How ironic! And how painful, Darcy. Perhaps this is a mistake. You should have said something; I could have done this alone."

"Calm yourself Bingley. I bear no animosity for the village or the inn, it is simply a place, and if you think about it, I am happy to be here. This is where my prayers were answered, and I found Georgiana before it was too late." He gave him a small smile and thought to himself, *and this is where I found someone else.* He straightened in the saddle, seeing the familiar outskirts of the town coming into view. He had spoken to Danny that morning when he gave him some things to deliver to Pemberley. He asked him exactly where he had found Longbourn. Now Darcy was picking out the landmarks Danny had mentioned to him. The inn came into view, and he knew that if he were to follow the road from Meryton, cross a stone bridge and ride for about a mile, he would see the red brick house, set at the end of a drive with two enormous and ancient trees in front. He strained his eyes to look into the distance, not knowing what he saw, but hoping for a sign. He looked at the faces of the people in the village as they examined him. It was an odd relief to be studied simply for being a well-dressed stranger on a fine horse as opposed to the disgraced brother to a compromised girl.

Bingley had directions to follow to Netherfield, and to Darcy's disappointment, they seemed to take them in the opposite direction of where he knew Longbourn lay. They travelled up the winding drive and upon rounding a stand of trees viewed the house. They looked at each other and Darcy raised his brows at Bingley's obvious excitement. "Come on, the steward must be here somewhere." They rode to the stables and a groom appeared, directing them to a small house nearby. The steward, Mr. Morris, spotted them from his office window and came out to greet them. He took them on a tour of the house, and found himself speaking more often to Darcy than Bingley, who was bright-eyed and completely unaware of what to ask. After a short break, the men returned to their mounts, and Mr. Morris took them on an extensive tour of the land, showing the fields in full production, the tenant homes, the fences, and the drainage, things that Darcy understood intimately and Bingley listened to with growing trepidation. When Darcy began asking about the number of servants and the taxes paid for them, the windows, the horses, it all began to run together as a frightening blur. He was growing nervous. Perhaps becoming a landed gentleman was not everything he had imagined. Darcy saw that he was worried and tried to reassure him that Mr. Morris would undoubtedly walk him through everything, and since he was leasing, these problems were not yet his concern.

They had come to the eastern edge of the estate's property, and were riding slowly along the fence line near a stile when the figure of a small woman dressed in a yellow gown and walking purposefully appeared nearby. "Ah, there sir is one of your neighbours. This is the border where Netherfield touches Longbourn. That girl is Miss Elizabeth Bennet, the second of the five girls there." Darcy thought he had recognized her but was too afraid to hope. They drew closer. Mr. Morris spoke again. "She's a fine, clever girl, always quick with a laugh, and not too proud to speak to gentleman or servant, she treats everyone the same. She's well-liked, and she's always out walking." Darcy felt his breathing increase to match his pounding heart. Rivulets of perspiration began to trail down his back. He had no idea what was happening to him, but he knew he must speak to her. When the horses drew close enough, Mr. Morris called out. "Miss Elizabeth! How are you this fine day?"

To the other men's surprise, Darcy leapt off of his horse, and holding the reins, stood in front of it and faced her. His expression gave nothing away, but his eyes were watching her with anxiety. Elizabeth reached them and smiled warmly at Mr. Morris, who had joined Bingley in dismounting. "I am very well, sir. I see that you have some company for a change?"

Mr. Morris laughed. "Indeed I do. Miss Elizabeth Bennet, may I introduce you to Mr. Bingley, who is considering taking the lease of Netherfield, and Mr. Darcy, his friend." He indicated the two men. Elizabeth had curtseyed to Bingley, but upon hearing Darcy's name while rising, started and turned to him, her eyes wide. Her smiling face changed to reflect her astonishment and obvious pleasure at seeing him. Her eyes sparkled, her cheeks, already flushed from her exercise, grew pinker, and her entire countenance expressed her unguarded happiness. Darcy was overwhelmed, and drank in the sight.

"Mr. Darcy!" She said with warmth. "I am so pleased to meet you."

Darcy's eyes, normally a pale blue, almost grey, were dark and intense. "Miss Elizabeth, the pleasure is all mine, I assure you." His face to anyone who did not know him well was impassive, but Bingley saw the curl of his lip and the emotion in his eyes. He could not help but stare between Darcy and Elizabeth, wondering what exactly was occurring.

Elizabeth waited a moment, to see if he would say more, but noticed that he had begun shifting from one foot to the other, and was now twisting the reins in a sign of anxiety. He opened his mouth several times to speak, but no words followed. She saw him swallow hard and looked into his eyes, and saw them almost begging her for help. Her brow furrowed. "Will you be long in the area, sir?" She asked cautiously.

He swallowed hard again, internally cursing his awkward behaviour. "Just for the day."

Elizabeth's disappointment was great, and it showed. "Oh." Darcy read her face easily and was both happy and sad to know her reaction.

Bingley jumped in. "I believe that I have made my decision to take the lease here, Miss Elizabeth, so Mr. Morris is correct, we shall be neighbours!" His wide smile and enthusiasm brought Elizabeth's gaze back to him. "That is wonderful news, sir. My mother will be delighted to spread it about the neighbourhood! When should we expect you to come?"

He looked at Mr. Morris. "I believe the lease begins at Michaelmas, am I correct, sir?"

"Yes, you are." He smiled.

Bingley turned to Darcy. "And you will be joining us at some point, will you not Darcy?" He nudged his friend who was standing watching Elizabeth. "Yes . . . yes, Bingley, if your offer still stands, Georgiana and I will come whenever you and your sister are ready for guests."

"Excellent!" Bingley smiled. He looked back at Elizabeth. "I hope that there are events to anticipate in the area about that time, Miss Elizabeth."

Elizabeth was studying Darcy as much as he was staring at her, but looked to him. "Oh sir, I assure you, the families in the area will welcome yours into their homes. Your wife and sister and any other friends will find themselves the subjects of a great many invitations."

"Well done, Miss Elizabeth, but no, I am not married." He grinned. He looked over to Darcy, "And my friend here is not either." They both blushed. "I was not fishing for information, sir, but thank you for telling me because my mother would not rest until she knew." She smiled at him, her embarrassment recovered. "I must warn you, however, both of you, that you should be prepared to be dazzled by the machinations of the country ladies and their mothers." Darcy shook his head while Bingley and Mr. Morris laughed. "That is nothing new, I assure you, Miss Elizabeth." Darcy murmured as his eyes went to his shoes, and Elizabeth's head tilted, trying to catch his expression. He was very confusing.

Mr. Morris stepped in. "Well sir, I imagine that you will be wishing to begin your journey back to London before the hour becomes any later, shall I show you the way back to the house?" Darcy's eyes came up, distress evident, but without any other reason to delay their departure, he could say nothing. Bingley watched him, but not knowing the relationship, could do nothing to help. "Yes, Mr. Morris, I suppose we should be on our way. Miss Elizabeth, it has been a great pleasure to meet you, and I look forward to seeing you and your family in September." He bowed and joined Mr. Morris in mounting his horse. Darcy remained where he was and finally found his voice. "I will be right behind you, Bingley." His brows rose but he nodded and the men rode off, leaving Darcy and Elizabeth alone.

"Miss Elizabeth." He said softly, "I . . . I hope that you were not upset with me for . . . the handkerchiefs." He drew hers from his breast pocket, and she blushed, seeing where he kept it. "I will return yours now, if you wish." He held it out to her, and looked back down at the ground.

"No sir, I think that I have been very fairly compensated for your thievery, and if you were to return my handkerchief, I would be forced to do the same with yours, and I am sorry, I am quite a selfish girl and I do not like returning gifts." She smiled, her eyes danced with humour.

Darcy looked up and seeing her smile relaxed. "I am happy to learn this, Miss Elizabeth, because I rather think you might have had to fight me for it."

She laughed. "A duel sir? Are they not illegal?"

"The law has been known to overlook them between gentlemen." He smiled, enough to crinkle his eyes.

"Ah, but that is the problem, sir, in case you had not noticed, I am not a gentleman." She pursed her lips and raised her brow.

Carried away by her banter he became bold. "I had noticed, Miss Elizabeth, I assure you." Elizabeth blushed. His heart began beating hard. More than anything in the world he wished to reach out and touch her burning cheek, first with his fingers, then with his lips. "Forgive me, I have embarrassed you." He said softly. "I seem to lose all sense of propriety in your presence. I should take my leave. We have been too long alone. I should know better." He began to turn away.

Elizabeth's voice stopped him. "Please do not leave on my account. I am happy to have the opportunity to speak to you." She smiled reassuringly, and met his now shy gaze. The little smile returned to his lips. He watched the sparkle in her eyes. "I seem to remember in your letter that you said if we should ever meet, you would never speak to me. I am happy that you changed your mind."

She laughed. He was so painfully shy, but so terribly eager. She could feel him battling himself on how to speak to her. "Well, it is a woman's prerogative, is it not? My opinions are not set in stone, sir." He smiled. "May I ask Mr. Darcy, how is your sister? I hope that she will wish to begin corresponding with me, I rather have the impression that she would like a friend."

Darcy's face darkened. "She is still recovering; I am very worried for her. I hope that she will write you, and I do hope that when I come to visit Bingley, she will accompany me. With your letters, she may enjoy spending time with you."

"I will be happy to help her." She tilted her head. "Can you tell me of her troubles?"

He looked deeply into her eyes. "Perhaps when we come to visit, and we have time, I could tell you." He thought to himself, *But then, will you still wish to know me?*

"I do take long walks every day." She smiled. "And would be glad of your company." She blushed with her boldness.

He smiled his greatest smile yet, and for a moment, she saw the flash of his teeth. "I would enjoy that, very much, Miss Elizabeth. We will be returning to our estate, Pemberley, in Derbyshire soon, but I will be looking forward to coming here again even more."

A shout from across the field gained their attention and they realized how long they had been talking. "I believe that my friend is growing impatient. I must go." He gathered his courage and took Elizabeth's gloved hand in his and bowed over it. "It was my hope that I would somehow catch sight of you today, this has been more than I could have dreamed. Thank you." He brushed his lips over her hand and quickly turned to mount his horse. At that moment he did not trust himself to stop.

Elizabeth still felt the warmth of his lips on her hand, and unconsciously held it to her rosy cheek. He did not miss the gesture, and again his heart began pounding. "I will look forward to this autumn as I never have before, sir. I hope to receive a letter from Pemberley soon."

He nodded. "I assure you, Miss Elizabeth. You will." He turned the horse and looking back at her one more time, raised his hand and galloped off. Elizabeth stood staring at him until she could see no more.

"Oh Louisa! What shall I do?" Caroline Bingley paced her sister's drawing room in her husband's townhouse in London and lamented her dashed plans. "Mr. Darcy's name is ruined utterly by that horrid little sister! It is not fair! Why should he be blamed for her behaviour? He did nothing wrong! He is just as rich today as he was three weeks ago! Oh what am I to do?" She wrung her hands and wailed, but somehow still managed to observe her appearance in the mirror over the fireplace, and adjusted her turban to a more appropriate angle.

Louisa Hurst sipped her tea and watched her sister. "You waited too long, Caroline; you should have secured him years ago. It is your own fault you know. How many chances have you had?" She hid her lips with her cup and smirked.

Caroline rounded on her. "Do not blame this on me! It is not my fault that Mr. Darcy is so obstinate!" She sat down and picked up her cup and took a gulp, then gasped as it scalded her throat. "It does not matter now."

"Why not? I would think he would be ripe for the picking now, Caroline. He can no longer be so choosy in his selection of wife. If you still want him, I think that he would be grateful for your continued interest and attention, why, look at Charles, he has stayed by his side, so why not you, as well?"

"Charles." She laughed disparagingly. "He will follow whoever leads him, you know that." She sniffed with disgust. "Do you hear what is being said about him supporting Mr. Darcy? That any chances he had of doing well in society are being destroyed by his association? I have spoken to him about this, and yet he refuses to listen. He will drag us all down with him."

"Not us, Caroline, just you. I am married already." She raised her brow.

She sniped back. "Yes, and to a drunken lay about. Whatever do you have to feel proud?"

Louisa shrugged, she knew that her husband was less than desirable, but that happened after they married. "I have this house; someday we will have his parent's estate. I am a married woman where you, dear sister, are rapidly approaching spinsterhood." Caroline gasped at the appellation. "Now, the Season still has some time left in it. I suggest that you either apply yourself to Mr. Darcy when he is weakened, or set your cap for some other gentleman before the *ton* determines that you are on the shelf."

"But I have received so few invitations since Miss Darcy ruined everything! How am I to meet anyone new if I cannot attend the balls and dinners?"

"You have relied too long on using Mr. Darcy's name as your entree into society, Caroline. You seem to have made your own bed." She tilted her head. "Now what was that about Charles dragging down the Bingley name by his continued association with Mr. Darcy? If that is what you feel, why do you still wish to pursue him at all?"

"I want Pemberley. I want his name. I want everything that he represents. I want to be rich and the toast of society." Her eyes lit up with her thoughts. "And Mr. Darcy himself, he is quite the handsome man." She giggled. Then catching sight of her sister's nodding head she narrowed her eyes. "Given time I am sure society will be more concerned with his wealth than his sister's behaviour and will gladly welcome him back. We might have to spend some time at Pemberley, but that will give me ample opportunity to redecorate." She smiled in anticipation of changing everything.

"What of Miss Darcy?"

Caroline's smile disappeared. "She is a problem."

"She is too young to marry off, at least her brother would think so." Louisa speculated.

"Marry off? Who will ever have her?" Caroline sneered.

"Where there is a dowry, there is a man who will take her." Louisa smiled, "Of course, that philosophy has not been successful for you . . ."

Caroline's eyes shot daggers at her sister. "Are you finished?"

Louisa shrugged. "Well, perhaps sending her away would be the solution. Out of sight, out of the *ton's* minds."

"Mr. Darcy would never stand for that." Caroline lamented. "If it were me, I would have had her bundled off to some distant estate in Scotland by now. He has a home there, after all." Her eyes lit up. "Louisa, that is it!"

"What?" She said, sitting up.

"Charles was going to look over an estate to lease in Hertfordshire. He already told me that Mr. Darcy would be coming to stay and help him get started there. If we can convince him that it would be a kindness to his sister to send her away to Scotland for a few years . . ."

"Then she would be gone, and you could press the advantage of convincing him that marrying would further secure her when she returned to society." She smiled. "And of course, who better to marry than you?"

"Yes! What do you think?"

"It has possibilities, but you know, Charles said that Mr. Darcy may bring her with him when he visits, what will you do then?"

Caroline considered the problem. "Perhaps she will have to find herself in another compromising position and have to marry right away." She grinned. "That would take care of everything. She would be gone, his reputation would be restored because of it, and . . ."

"He would no longer need to marry you. You would be back where you were three weeks ago. You need to think of something else, Caroline."

She sighed. "What?"

"You are clever. I have no doubt you will devise a plan to win your man." Caroline narrowed her eyes and nodded.

By the time that Darcy rejoined Bingley and Mr. Morris, his breathing had returned to normal and the flush had left his face, but his eyes were bright, reflecting an emotion that he did not understand but knew without a doubt he wished to experience again. He felt confused and exhilarated. Bingley looked at him closely. He had observed as Darcy spent perhaps ten minutes speaking with Miss Elizabeth, if that, but in that time, his friend had become a different man. Mr. Morris was curious, but as he knew Miss Elizabeth to be a friendly, outgoing girl, with never a word of poor behaviour spoken of her, he thought nothing of the brief conversation alone with Mr. Darcy in full view of anyone, and promptly forgot about it.

The cook at Netherfield, alerted to a potential lease holder, quickly pulled together a simple but satisfying meal for the men upon their return to the house. It was after this that Darcy and Bingley took their leave of Mr. Morris, with assurances that come Michaelmas, the estate would again be occupied. The return ride began in thoughtful silence for both men, with Bingley watching Darcy covertly, and wondering what exactly was passing through his mind as a myriad of expressions passed over his face. He surmised that it most definitely had to do with Miss Elizabeth, and he was dying to know if his theory that they had met before was true. He could not help but be amused with his friend who had never, in all the years he had known him, been reduced to such an obvious state of bewitchment. He was just working out the wording for his question when Darcy broke the silence.

"Bingley, do you think . . . I am . . . that a young lady . . ." He sighed. Seeing his struggle he stopped grinning, and spoke reassuringly. "What is it, Darcy?"

Darcy turned his head to meet Bingley's open expression. "Would it be wrong for me to . . . pay attentions to a lady? Would it be a degradation to her?" He took a breath and returned his gaze to the road ahead.

Charles watched him with interest. Darcy looked back over to him. "What are you thinking?"

"I can only assume that the young lady in question is Miss Elizabeth?" He saw Darcy's flush. "Do you realize that three weeks ago, your question would have been if she would be a degradation to you?"

Darcy furrowed his brow and shot him a look. "Do you think me so shallow?"

"Shallow? No. But proud, or rather, raised to fulfil your duty, and that means marrying from your own circle. Miss Elizabeth is decidedly below you, even with your present distress by association with Georgiana."

"So you believe that in the past I might have felt that I was lowering myself to accept her, and that she should have been grateful for my offer." He said, thinking carefully over the revelation.

"I believe it to be possible. I can not say for sure what would have occurred. I have never seen you in such a state before."

He looked at him sharply. "What state is that, Bingley?"

He could not help but laugh. "You are besotted, Darcy!" He laughed louder seeing his friend's astonishment. "Now, I have been watching you carefully. Tell me, did you meet Miss Elizabeth before? And may I go further; did you perhaps purchase her some finery of late?" He attempted to suppress his grin, but Darcy's completely embarrassed red face was simply too much for him, and he clapped his hands with glee. "Excellent Darcy!! Finally a woman has found a way into your heart. I had practically abandoned hope!! Tell me all, I insist!"

Still deeply mortified that he was easily read, Darcy sighed, then relaxing a little, a small smile appeared. "I hope very sincerely that you are the only one who can read me so well, Bingley. I do not wish to walk around as a besotted fool."

"I have no fear of that happening Darcy, as that is a position where I regularly find myself. I am sure that you will be able to hide this from the world. I was just fortunate to actually see the transformation take place before my eyes." He smiled, happy that his friend's heart could be touched, especially at a time when he undoubtedly needed the distraction. "I might point out that the lady in question was not indifferent to you."

Darcy quickly looked over to him, staring into his eyes. "Are you sure?"

"I am." He said seriously, knowing not to toy with such an important question.

He let out a breath, then met his gaze and looked away. "All right, yes, I did meet Miss Elizabeth the day that Richard and I returned Georgiana home. I observed her with, what I assume was three of her sisters in the street outside of the inn. She . . . I can hardly explain what I saw and felt. Later, when we were about to board the coach, Georgiana was in tears, and was in great need of a dry handkerchief. As Richard and I had no luggage, we had no replacement for hers, and Miss Elizabeth, seeing her distress, offered hers to Georgiana. On impulse I asked her name and direction so that it could be returned to her. She demurred, and I insisted. That is when she gave me her name." He glanced quickly over to him. "I have felt . . . I do not know, something so very . . . very . . . warm, comforting, and more . . . much more ever since." He looked away from Bingley.

Bingley nodded. He knew that speaking of feelings was not something that men did, and this man in particular never opened up. Darcy was struck if he was even attempting to say these things, and it told Bingley how much he was valued as his friend. He would not tease him about it again. "So those handkerchiefs were for Miss Elizabeth?" Darcy nodded. "Have you given them to her?" He nodded again. "And did she feel you were overstepping the lines of propriety?" He shook his head. Bingley smiled. "So what is your next move? You will not see her again for over three months. That will certainly give time for the consequences of Georgiana's behaviour to settle into whatever state it will remain until her presentation. And it will give you time to decide if you will be harming Miss Elizabeth by your interest."

"Yes, that is true." He smiled slightly. "She has agreed to begin a friendly correspondence with Georgiana. They have already exchanged one letter, and Georgiana was thrilled to have befriended someone at this painful time."

"Well done!" Bingley smiled. "And through their letters you can at least know how she is, and perhaps Miss Darcy could tell her of you." Darcy nodded, knowing he could not tell anyone of his writing her himself. "Good, then it seems this time apart will not be as difficult. And Darcy, I think it will give you something pleasant to think about." He nodded to the approaching bustle of London. "You are escaping the censure of town for the peace of Pemberley, but I doubt the situation will be far from your mind."

"No, it seems to have taken up a leaden residence in my heart." He looked over to Bingley again. "You have given me much to consider. I must decide my behaviour towards Miss Elizabeth, and think over how I might have felt about her before. You have opened my eyes to consider my treatment of others, in a way that I never felt necessary before." He looked at him thoughtfully. "Do you think that I behave with disdain towards those lower than me?"

Bingley considered it. "You treat your staff well, which is why they are so loyal, but as to individuals of a lower status? I do not know. You must think on this yourself."

Darcy nodded, and the men separated near Hyde Park to approach their separate homes. Bingley thanked him profusely for his assistance that day, and they agreed to meet again before the Darcys took their leave for Pemberley.

When Darcy arrived home he found a note waiting for him, asking that he come to Matlock House on a matter of some urgency. He thought with a sinking feeling that Lady Catherine was somehow involved.

Chapter 5

*E*lizabeth slowly wandered back to Longbourn after watching Darcy's handsome figure, so straight and tall on his fine horse, disappear from view. He *was* handsome; she thought and smiled, spinning with a little squeal. Imagine such a man paying her any attention at all! She began to wonder about him. He was certainly older than she, surely he was a "man of the world" as her Aunt Gardiner had put it, but Elizabeth thought, he was behaving as if he was unsure of just how to court a woman. He seemed as inexperienced in what to do as she was, and it absolutely delighted her. He completely confused her. His face was inexpressive; it was all in his eyes. The stare that he bore upon her might have disconcerted her, made her feel as if she was failing, if it were not for the undeniable fact that he had written that wonderful, playful, barely concealed love note. How could a man who wrote such a note not be able to speak when in the presence of his object? He must be terribly shy and insecure. But he had his own estate! Or at least his father does? "Oh you are a puzzle, Fitzwilliam Darcy!" She cried out loud. Then she smiled to herself. "A puzzle that I very much wish to understand."

She thought of that little smile that grew as he relaxed and they talked more. Coaxing out that smile would be something she would enjoy very much. *And to make him laugh! Oh, that would be a joy!* She sensed his intelligence, and already knew he was kind. And reserved and worried about propriety, and . . . *Oh so challenging!* Whatever had happened with his sister obviously worried him, and after witnessing the girl's distress, she hoped that her friendship would cheer her. She could not wait to tell Jane that they had met, and hoped so much that the letter from his sister would include one from him. She did not understand this sudden and overwhelming feeling for a virtual stranger, but she felt something, a connection, and a need to know more. It was going to be a very long wait for autumn to arrive.

Upon entering Longbourn she was greeted by the unwelcome sight of her mother bearing down upon her. "Lizzy! Where have you been? Out walking all of this time! What am I going to do with you? I am sure your wildness will be the death of me! As sure as your father will leave us starving in the hedgerows when he soon dies, you will fail to secure a husband when a perfectly good suitor is awaiting you. Now get upstairs and make yourself presentable for Mr. Lucas!"

"Mama, there is plenty of time; we will not leave for hours!" She protested as her mother began pushing her to the landing.

"Never you mind, you know there is one maid to dress all of you, and for whatever reason, Mr. Lucas favours you over your sisters. You must be ready first. Now go!" She pushed her again.

Elizabeth held her ground. "But Mama, I have news!"

That stopped her. "News? What sort of news?"

"Netherfield is let. I met the young man and his friend when Mr. Morris was showing them the line between the estates." She purposely implied Mr. Bingley's marital status to stop her mother's frenzy.

"Netherfield let?? Well tell me all, Lizzy! Who is this young man, and his friend?"

Mrs. Bennet's squeals drew forward the other four daughters who gathered to listen in rapt attention. Elizabeth sent a significant look to Jane, who wrinkled her brow. "The young man is named Bingley. He is not married," Mrs. Bennet screeched and clapped her hand to her mouth, "and he is to sign a lease to begin at Michaelmas."

"Is he handsome, Lizzy?" Lydia asked, giggling to Kitty.

She smiled. "Yes, he is. He is about Papa's height, with blonde hair and green eyes. He was very friendly and was looking forward to meeting everyone in the neighbourhood."

"How old is he?" Mrs. Bennet asked.

"I would say he is no more than five and twenty. He will be coming along with his sister."

Mrs. Bennet nodded. "Yes, his sister will act as his hostess, so he can hold parties and dinners." She nodded again, already scanning her daughters to decide which she would choose for him, and her eyes settled on Jane. "Yes, Jane, you shall marry him."

"Mama!" Jane cried.

"Of course he will want you, dear Jane, for you are by far the beauty of Hertfordshire. Even a blind man would know that!" She patted her cheek. "Yes, you are far more beautiful than Lizzy, I have always said so." Elizabeth, used to this particular insult, just closed her eyes. Her mother was forever telling her how inadequate she was, whether it was her beauty, or her behaviour. It did not matter. Of all of her daughters, Mrs. Bennet made it quite clear that Elizabeth was her least favourite. Mrs. Bennet returned her attention to Elizabeth. "Did you say he had a friend there, as well? What do you know of him?"

Elizabeth looked up at her with a smile. "His friend's name is Mr. Darcy." Jane barely hid her gasp behind her hand. Elizabeth gave her a tiny nod. "He plans to come and stay at Netherfield along with his sister for a visit. As it turns out, his sister is the girl I lent my handkerchief to, so if our correspondence is successful, I will be well on my way to being good friends with her before they even arrive." She looked straight into her mother's eyes, and could see her mind working the information.

"Does Mr. Darcy have a wife, or an estate?" She said steadily.

"He is not married, but yes, he has an estate. I had the impression that he was coming to help Mr. Bingley with purchasing one of his own."

"And . . . did you get on well with Mr. Darcy?" Elizabeth maintained her gaze. "I did."

"Well then, that changes everything! You must write very good letters to Miss Darcy, Lizzy. You must make her fond of you and wish for your company. If you win her good opinion, she will encourage her brother your way." She nodded, her scheme was perfect. "Mark my words; I will have both of you engaged by Christmas!"

Elizabeth shot a look at Jane, who shook her head in exasperation. Elizabeth started up the stairs, but her mother stopped her. "There is no hurry Lizzy, let the other girls dress first. Tonight's company is not important to you!" She took hold of Kitty and Lydia and shooed them up the stairs. "Just like that girl, trying to get in the way of my plans!" She continued talking to herself and Elizabeth watched as Mary melted into the shadows, away to read her book. Jane grabbed her hand and the girls rushed out to the garden.

When they achieved a fair distance from the house, Jane pulled Elizabeth down on a bench. "Lizzy, was it really Mr. Darcy? The man who . . . him?"

Elizabeth grasped her hands and beamed at her. "Yes!! Oh yes Jane. He and Mr. Bingley and Mr. Morris were riding, and Mr. Morris called to me as I walked. I did not look at the other men, as they were strangers, but Mr. Darcy immediately jumped down from his horse, so the other men did as well. Mr. Morris introduced Mr. Bingley, and then Mr. Darcy. That was when I first realized who he was. Oh Jane! He was so shy!"

"Shy? After that note?" She stared at her.

"Yes! He was all nerves and stuttering, but then Mr. Morris said it was time to go and Mr. Darcy said he wished to speak to me for a moment, and then he apologized for taking my handkerchief and offered it back. Jane, he keeps it in his breast pocket!"

"Next to his heart?" Jane was melting.

Elizabeth beamed. "Yes!" She sighed. "Of course I refused to take it back and he admitted he would not give it up without a fight." She laughed. "He finally relaxed a little and smiled." She smiled thinking of it. "He will come with Mr. Bingley, but he said that he and his sister were leaving London for his estate in Derbyshire soon. I suppose they will stay there until coming here."

"How is his sister?"

Elizabeth shook her head. "He did not say much, but from his face, I would say she is not at all recovered. He seemed so pained. I asked if he could speak of the trouble, but he said it would wait until we had more time when he returns." She blushed. "I told him that I like to take long walks everyday."

"Lizzy! You did not!" Jane's eyes were wide.

Elizabeth nodded. "I do not know what came over me, Jane. I was so bold. He was afraid that he had been alone too long with me, and was very concerned over the propriety of us being seen." She laughed. "But then he assured me I would soon receive a letter from his sister when they return to Pemberley, his estate. I just know by the way he looked at me, there is bound to be a note from him inside, too."

"He seems to be quite enamoured of you." Jane winked. Elizabeth blushed. "He kissed my hand." Jane gasped. "After he was worried about propriety?" Elizabeth giggled. "I do not think he could stop himself!"

Jane laughed. "Well, I am very happy that you had the opportunity to see him again, especially so soon after his letter. And I am very impressed with your handling of Mama. Now she has you paired with Mr. Darcy and will leave the matchmaking of John Lucas to another sister!"

"You forget; she has you married off to Mr. Bingley." She grinned.

Jane blushed. "What is he like, Lizzy?"

"He is handsome, very fair, like you. He is friendly; I would think he enjoys everyone and everything. He seemed quite enthusiastic to be coming."

"Would I like him?" She said softly. Elizabeth squeezed her hand. "Yes Jane, I believe you would."

George Wickham sat at the gaming table contemplating his cards. He had won enough, well cheated enough, to have funds to replace the belongings he lost when he fled the inn at Meryton. His face was nearly healed from the beating Colonel Fitzwilliam delivered, but his ribs still ached. His disappointment in failing with Georgiana was great. He knew that Darcy would have given over the dowry, even without his consent, simply to assure the care of his sister. Wickham had no intention of keeping her. Oh, certainly he would take his rights as her husband, but in time, he knew he would tire of the girl and likely put her on a post coach and send her back to her brother, and then take his money and disappear, perhaps to America. But that plan was dashed. What were the odds that Darcy would come to Ramsgate? At least he arrived late enough to prevent the news of Georgiana being compromised from spreading, but what good did that do him? His idea of blackmailing him to remain silent was ruined once the news hit the gossip columns. He took some small satisfaction in seeing Darcy's name ruined along with his sister's, but a name was meaningless to Wickham. As far as he was concerned, Darcy was still triumphant because he was still rich, and all the gossip in the world would not take that away.

He sat and fumed. He had harmed Darcy by ruining his sister, but he had not profited from it. That made him angry. The beating made him vengeful. There must be a way to hurt Darcy, hurt him so badly that everyday for the rest of his life he would wake to misery, and beg for the torture to end. But what could he do? And in the meantime, how would he live? The money he had extracted from Darcy before was rapidly running out. He must find a way to earn a living, and soon.

"What did he mean?" Darcy wondered. He lay in his bed, his hands tucked beneath the pillow, staring up at the canopy in the dark. "Would I have rejected Elizabeth before?" He could not possibly imagine not being just as attracted to her then as he was the day that they met. Ah, but Bingley was not speaking of attraction. He was speaking of pursuit. It was a very difficult question. Other than his servants, or perhaps those persons he used for business purposes, he had very little contact with ordinary people who simply inhabited circles below his own. Well, there was Bingley of course, but he was a special case, and was on the rise through his help. That thought sobered him. Perhaps Bingley should seek out a new friend, he could help him no more. But Bingley had already stated his loyalty, although his sisters would likely say something about that!

He considered Caroline Bingley. Her parents were ambitious enough to put her and her sister Louisa in finishing school, but money does not buy breeding or good sense. They were crass, self-important, far too obvious, and unappealing. Caroline did have her moments of wit, but he found her scathing comments on people, who despite her airs were above her in rank, to be rude. There it was; Bingley's observation. He had thought of Miss Bingley as below him and assigned a tag of dislike to her because of it. He easily rejected all thought of marriage to her for that simple reason even before he knew her enough to dislike her on her own merits. *But not Bingley. And decidedly not Elizabeth. What was different about them? Did he really treat people with disdain?* He hardly knew.

His thoughts drifted back to Elizabeth and he smiled. It felt so wonderful to smile in the midst of all of this torment. How could his feelings for her appear so quickly? He barely knew her, had spoken to her only briefly, but there she was smiling at him in his mind. No other woman had ever occupied his thoughts in such a way, and to even think of her as *Elizabeth*, not even Miss Elizabeth, as if she were his. . . he did not know what to make of it, or even if he had any business pursuing any sort of relationship with her.

Bingley's words wended their way into his musings again. Only a few weeks ago he would have thought himself far above her, but now, she was the one with the untainted background, and he was not worthy of her. But she knew nothing of that, in truth, she knew very little of him. She knew he had a house in town and now knew of his estate, but his income, his property, his reputation, as it was and now is, no, she was ignorant. That gave him comfort somehow, to know that she was smiling at him because she, well, *liked* him. It was a completely foreign concept for him, to be liked because . . . well who knows why she liked him, but it was not because of his worth. Surely she realized he was wealthy, but she did not behave as other young ladies did around him, did she? No. Not at all. She was entirely different. But . . . *I should leave her alone. I should not saddle her with my troubles. She is too special.* He barely knew her and could sense that. But . . . Georgiana desperately needed a friend . . . and so did he . . . and Georgiana writing her would not hurt anything, would it? They would go home, perhaps being away from London would help the rumours die for both of them, life would return to normal at Pemberley, and there would be letters, more wonderful letters full of her teasing words. *For both of them.* She said that she looked forward to his letters, did she not? He could attach a note to Georgiana's. He just would not sign it, just initials, yes. He continued his hopeful thoughts, and wondered once again if he was being the greatest fool that ever lived.

Regardless of Mrs. Bennet's change of plans for marrying Elizabeth off to John Lucas, the news had not been spread to him. He stood in beaming anticipation of seeing his pretty neighbour in the parlour of the Philips' home in Meryton.

"Eliza!" The young man, not homely, not quite handsome, but certainly friendly and good humoured, greeted her near the doorway of the parlour.

Elizabeth smiled at him; she certainly had no reason to treat him any differently than she had before, after all, she barely knew Mr. Darcy, and was hardly betrothed to the mysterious stranger. "Mr. Lucas, it is good to see you again. I understand you have just completed your adventure to Ireland?"

His smile widened and he bounced on his feet, clapping his hands in a mirror of his father's behaviour. She suppressed a laugh. "Indeed! It was beautiful. I can not possibly describe the colour and landscape. It must be experienced!" He delighted in her sparkling eyes.

"Well sir, if I am ever so fortunate as to travel there, I hopefully will return with a greater ability to articulate the sights. All you have accomplished is making me jealous!" She teased.

His face fell, and then he brightened. "Perhaps you will journey there someday, Eliza. I should be glad to hear of your trip." He would like to accompany her on that trip.

"I should be pleased to relate it to you. Tell me your plans now that you are finished with University. Will you be staying at Lucas Lodge?" It was a perfectly reasonable question, truly asked in innocence. But to John Lucas, it sounded delightfully like she was asking if he is ready to take a wife.

He grinned again. "I have not decided as yet, Eliza. I know that I must eventually settle down to learn the ways of running my father's estate, but I am quite young yet. I would like to perhaps study the law, as your Uncle Philips has done, or maybe travel some more. It will be some time before I will find myself in need of learning the ins and outs of estate management. Father is a young man, yet!"

Elizabeth cast a glance at Sir William Lucas and saw a middle-aged man, quite thick around the middle, a beaming face like his son's but hardly the picture of robust health. She raised a brow. "Do you think it wise to simply leave your education of your estate to the future, sir? Would it not be best to be prepared, should something, heaven forbid, happen unexpectedly to your father?"

He looked somewhat taken aback. "Do you think so? I can not imagine there is much to it, after all."

Elizabeth attempted to hide her astonishment. Her father was hardly the example of a fine estate manager, but even watching, and sometimes aiding him in his duties, she saw all that was involved. She was disappointed in John, and thought he had more sense. "Sir, when your family's well-being and the care of your tenants are at stake, it should be of great interest to you." She said gently.

"Perhaps you are correct." He considered her. Yes, she would make a very fine and sensible wife. He was about to ask her to join him in some refreshment when Mrs. Bennet bustled up. She saw the conversation between the two of them, and wished to redirect the young Lucas to one of her other daughters.

"Mr. Lucas! Why how well you look! Do you not think so, Mary?" She pushed the mousy girl forward. John startled. "Yes, Mama." She said then looked away, clutching the sheet music she had brought with her. Mrs. Bennet sighed. The girl was not cooperating. Seeing that John was returning his attention to Elizabeth she spoke up again. "Mr. Lucas, have you heard the news? Netherfield Hall is let at last; Lizzy met the man who will take up residence only this morning!" She turned a pointed eye on her daughter. "Did you not, Lizzy?"

She smiled at John. "I did. And I met his friend, who I understand will be visiting with him this autumn. They seem to be fine gentlemen and will undoubtedly add to the neighbourhood."

John looked at Mrs. Bennet's beaming face with a suspicious mind. "Will the men be bringing their wives and children?"

"Ah, they are unmarried, Mr. Lucas! What fine news for the young ladies!" She looked to Elizabeth and then found Jane. John did not miss her movement and returned his gaze to Elizabeth who was looking at the ground in her embarrassment. John grew up listening to Mrs. Bennet's effusions, and he also grew up seeing Elizabeth's reactions to them. This embarrassment was different from what he had seen in the past. She was interested in these men.

"You say they come in the autumn?" He said quietly.

"Yes, at Michaelmas." Elizabeth looked back up and smiled. "I believe they both will come with their sisters."

"And they will certainly be entertaining!" Mrs. Bennet crowed. She looked at John's disappointed face and nodded. Her work was done there; her wishes were made quite clear.

"I suppose they were very fine gentlemen, Eliza, but such gentlemen would certainly not be looking for more than amusement in the country, nothing more interesting than a good hunt and perhaps a little flirtation. Their futures would be from the ladies of the *ton*. Your mother should not get her hopes up." He watched her face and actually was pleased to see her frown. His words had struck the mark.

"I am sure that Mama is simply pleased to have the empty estate let, Mr. Lucas." She looked up at him, but the crease in her brow remained.

He bowed. "Of course, I am sure that is true." He walked away and started thinking. He had until Michaelmas to win her hand, and it seems, to become serious about learning to run his father's estate.

Elizabeth wandered off to listen to her neighbours' conversation of two young, likely rich, men coming to the neighbourhood. She wondered if Mr. Darcy's attentions were just what Mr. Lucas implied, and that he was merely setting up a pleasant diversion to keep him occupied during his visit. She tried to believe that it was not so.

———~~~———

"Come in, Darcy, come in." Lord Matlock waved in his nephew who was looking at him from the study door. He automatically began to close the door behind him, anticipating a conversation about Georgiana. To his surprise, it stopped moving halfway when his aunt caught it.

"Trying to shut me out, are you?" She smiled and slipped past, giving him a little pat on the arm.

"Forgive me Aunt Ellen, I did not notice you." He finished his task and took the chair his uncle indicated. He sat looking between his relatives expectantly.

"I thought we would see you yesterday. What kept you?"

"I accompanied my friend Charles Bingley to Hertfordshire. He found an estate to lease and wished my opinion."

"Ah, good, good, you continue to keep your friends." Lord Matlock nodded, then templed his hands, looking down at his fingers.

"I have many friends Uncle, although I have certainly learned in recent days the identity of my true friends, and which were merely paying me lip service. It has, I think, been a valuable lesson, despite the reasons behind it."

"What has the reaction been to you?"

Darcy shrugged. "You saw the interest at the theatre, and church was much the same, although with Georgiana by my side, I would say that the barely moderated voices were far more, shall we say, accusatory? I think that the people were rather enjoying pointing their fingers and shaking their heads in false sorrow for her downfall, and of course how it had taken me with her." He said this with disgust in his voice. "She will not be attending again; she did not speak for nearly the entire week after that experience."

"I heard that you stopped at your club." His uncle probed.

"Ah, yes, that is where I learned of the bets laid against my plans and Georgiana's lost virtue." He spat the news.

Lord Matlock met his wife's eyes and sighed. "Yes, it is as I have heard then." He cleared his throat. "Catherine paid us a call."

Darcy laughed hollowly. "Yes, she was kind enough to personally come and tell me of our ruination, and offered me Anne as wife to supposedly save the Darcy name." He shook his head. "And then she had the gall to suggest that Georgiana should be taken from me and go to live with her! As if I would ever allow that! Poor Georgiana was there, was subject to her tirade, and on top of everything else and despite my reassurance, she is convinced that you will somehow order that I send her to Rosings! Or worse, that my shame for her behaviour will cause *me* to send her there; or into exile somewhere." He closed his eyes. "I realize I should respect my aunt, but . . . the damage she inflicted that day . . . it is unpardonable."

Lord Matlock directed his gaze straight at Darcy's eyes. "Your aunt is not entirely wrong. An excellent marriage would instantly retrieve your reputation, as would Georgiana's if she were to marry well."

Darcy stared at him. "You are not actually promoting her ridiculous notion that I marry Anne?"

"It would be a brilliant match Darcy." He said emotionlessly. "You would have Rosings, and Anne's dowry is fifty thousand pounds."

"I could care less what it is. I will not marry Anne. Or anyone without affection." He stated this with great conviction and actually startled himself with his words.

"Affection?" Lord Matlock asked. "What do you mean? Liking your wife? A fondness?" He looked to his own wife, for whom he did have a great deal of affection and met her raised brows. "Yes, I can see how you would wish for that, but marriages in our circle do not occur because of affection, that is simply a fortunate offspring of some matches, like my own." He nodded to Lady Matlock. "It certainly was not the greatest consideration. Why, your own parents. . . "

"Do NOT speak to me of my parents! I was quite well aware of the disparity of their feelings for one another." He glared off into a corner, memories of his childhood flashing through his mind. Again without even realizing he was speaking out loud he said, "It is for that reason that I wish to marry for love or not at all."

"LOVE?" Lord Matlock cried. "What on earth does love have to do with marriage?"

Darcy's brow creased, and he looked at his uncle in a state of blank confusion. *Did I actually say that?* He heard the question over and over again in his head, and then his own voice spoke. "What does love have to do with marriage?" He repeated. *Everything,* Darcy's mind urged, and with growing confidence he stared at him straight on, and declared it aloud. "Everything."

His uncle sat in stunned silence. Lady Matlock touched Darcy's arm and he jumped. "You do realize Darcy how unlikely it is that you would ever make such a match?"

"I am determined not to marry at all without it, Aunt. I was decided before this all happened with Georgiana not to marry, and to leave the task of producing the heir of Pemberley to her. Now, I realize that her prospects are seriously damaged, and I may be forced to take on this role that I so dislike. I also realize that I am not as desirable as I once was, or so society has made clear to me."

Lord Matlock came alive again. "Which is why Catherine's offer of Anne is so perfect! You will have everything with her!"

Darcy's brow rose. "Except love." He said.

Lord Matlock turned to his wife. "Talk some sense into the boy, Ellen!"

"If you are going to further promote a union with my cousin, I do suggest that you save your breath, Aunt." Darcy quietly said. "In fact, I will save you the trouble. I will take my leave now." He began to rise.

"Darcy, stop. Please sit down." She held his arm, and he wearily took his seat. "I do not believe that your prospects are nearly as terrible as Catherine and Henry say. You know as well as I do that the rules for men in society are vastly different than for women. If you were Georgiana's sister, yes, you might be ruined, but you, a man, a very rich man with an estate and old family name? No Darcy, I suspect that the censure you are receiving now is simply the result of society enjoying a good scandal at the expense of one of its most elusive and upright members. I am sure that those who are persecuting you are the same ones who are intensely jealous of you, and that after your return from Pemberley for the next Season, the matrons will welcome you with open arms, and happily direct their daughters your way. No Darcy, you may feel ruined now, you may feel unworthy of any woman, but I have no doubt that should you choose, you may still have any woman in England that you wish for. So, if it is not your desire to marry Anne, do not. And do not force yourself to settle for someone less than yourself because you feel it is all you can have now. Time will take care of your censure."

"Ellen!"

She turned to her husband. "Enough of this Henry! You know that the rules of society are different for men! Do not try to force this ridiculous idea of Darcy marrying Anne down his throat just to satisfy your sister! Tell her you tried and failed. She sees him as weak right now and is pouncing, that is all. I am ashamed of you helping her. You know that Anne is hardly fit for any man!"

He sighed and looked to his nephew. "Forgive me Darcy, your aunt is correct. Marrying Anne is not necessary, although a wedding sooner would be better than later. If you drop this ridiculous notion of love, you could have any woman, just as she says, just wait for it all to blow over for a few months."

"Although I appreciate your withdrawal of this demand from Aunt Catherine, and both of your reassurance that all will be well again for me in a few months time, I am in no hurry to marry, and I was serious about my convictions. I witnessed a loveless marriage. Pemberley was not . . . a happy home." He paused, realizing he was speaking of his uncle's sister. "But in any case, despite your optimism, I do not feel that I deserve any woman's affection after failing my sister so terribly. It is unfair that she will have no future where mine is guaranteed to be whatever I wish. She is ruined when she did nothing wrong."

Lady Matlock said gently. "You must marry Darcy, and Georgiana did do wrong."

"I will not listen to this!" He stood and this time moved out of his aunt's reach. "We leave for Pemberley in three days. If you care to visit, we will be at home. Otherwise, I hope to invite you to join us for Christmas." He bowed and left the room.

The couple looked at each other. "Henry, why on earth did you push him to marry Anne? We needed to talk of Georgiana, not him."

"Catherine was relentless, you heard her." He sighed. "I know; we were going to talk of Georgiana's future. We will visit tomorrow, when he has had time to calm." He closed his eyes then looked at her. "You know the ladies on the Almack's board, what are Georgiana's prospects?"

She considered the question. "If she were coming out next year, I would say very poor. But in two or preferably three years, I believe her dowry will buy her entry there and into the homes of any man's family who needs her. If Darcy could add to it, that would help, I should think."

"You heard him, Ellen; he has the fool notion of marrying for love. If that is what he feels for himself, he will want the same for her. He will not marry her off to rid himself of her, no matter what such a burden may prove to be for his own prospects. I can see him gaining whatever woman he wants based on his own merits, but how many would wish to marry him with Georgiana and her troubles still living at home?"

"So you suggest she go to Rosings?" She asked incredulously. "That would kill the poor thing!"

"I know, I know, and the thought of sending her away to that estate he owns in Scotland is wrong. No, he must not appear ashamed of her, I was just thinking of my friends in the House, and what they have been saying to me."

"Which is?"

He looked sadly at her. "Pack her off to a distant estate and never see her again."

"Lovely friends you have there, Henry." She said dryly. "I would enjoy hearing what they would say if it was their relative."

"I imagine they are simply repeating the gentle gossip they have heard from the ladies gathered in their wives' parlours." He said with a raised brow.

She nodded. "That is more likely. Those cats are savouring this, which is why a wait for her come out is necessary. I imagine the men support banishment to just shut up the yowling they are subject to at home."

He laughed. "You are implying that women are catty, my dear?"

"If it were not for them, no man would care what Georgiana did or did not do, and you know it." She met his smiling eyes with a pointed glare. "It is all about power, money, revenge, and spite. Women are just as ruthless in society as men are on the battleground."

"Just better dressed?" He suggested.

She finally smiled. "Well, of course!"

Chapter 6

"*C*aroline!" Bingley cried upon seeing his sister. "Excellent news! I have signed the lease, and Netherfield is ours for the next year!" He beamed. "Our father's dreams are being fulfilled!" He gave her a peck on the cheek and turned to hug Louisa.

Caroline's eyes lit up. Becoming one of the landed gentry was not only her father's dream, but hers as well. Having a country house was essential to her aspirations to climb to a higher social circle; of course, marrying well would not hurt, either. "That *is* good news, Charles. Now tell us about the house. Is it very fine?"

He laughed. "I am not the one to decide that Caroline. I am afraid that my opinion and yours will differ, but I think it is a good sound home, well furnished; the staff seems to take its care to heart. Darcy approved, so what more can I ask for?"

"Mr. Darcy approved?" She sent a quick glance to Louisa who smirked. "I did not know that he accompanied you yesterday. Why did you not mention it?"

"Did I not?" Charles evaded her. In truth, Darcy wanted no one to know of his company, in case some well-meaning ladies of the *ton* decided to call upon Georgiana in his absence. Of course Charles knew precisely which ladies. He looked upon them. "Oh, well it must have slipped my mind. Yes, he toured the house and grounds with me and supported my decision to take the lease. It is only twenty miles from town, so well within visiting distance should you have a need to go shopping for some finery to impress the locals."

That drew both ladies' attention. "Ah yes, I am sure that they are simply starved for news on the latest fashion!" Caroline snorted. "Forgive me. I am so looking forward to meeting them all!"

Bingley's eyes narrowed. "You do not plan to be rude, do you Caroline? These are to be our neighbours and I wish for us all to get along well. When the lease is up, the owner will be willing to discuss selling. It is too good of an opportunity to let pass. Estates such as this do not come available very often."

"Oh Charles, relax. Caroline will behave." Louisa reassured him. "She has just been looking forward to this for some time and her tongue got a bit carried away with her mirth." She shot a look at her sister. "Is that not so, dear?"

Caroline's eyes were wide and innocent. "Oh yes, of course. I meant no harm, Charles. I am sure the neighbourhood is just lovely."

Placated, Charles' grin returned. "Well, it seems a pleasant village, and I did meet one of our neighbours, a pretty girl whose estate borders Netherfield."

Caroline sighed. "You are not planning to fall in love again, are you Charles? I have no desire to gain a sister from the country. You are doing quite well with the ladies you are attracting here in town . . ." She glanced at Louisa, and began her campaign. "Charles, you were with Mr. Darcy, how is he with all that has happened?" She looked concerned.

For a moment Bingley was drawn in. "He is naturally unhappy. He worries for Miss Darcy; she is distraught, poor girl."

"Does he fear for her future?" Caroline asked prettily.

"Naturally. He worries for both of them. He is convinced that he is not worthy to . . ." He stopped, realizing that the last people Darcy would wish him to speak to about his feelings and worries were his sisters.

"Yes, Charles?" Louisa said a little too eagerly.

He looked between the two. "I am sorry; I am not at liberty to discuss this with you." They sighed.

Caroline tried a different path. "Have you invited the Darcys to come stay with us at Netherfield?"

"Yes, they plan to arrive soon after we do. I hope that they will enjoy their stay." He thought of Darcy and Miss Elizabeth, and hoped very much his friend would find whatever he was seeking with her.

"Well then, that will be wonderful. I will certainly enjoy being in the same household with Mr. Darcy, and you can advance your suit with Miss Darcy."

Bingley startled. "My suit? What are you talking about?"

"Why, this is your opportunity! You could gain Georgiana as your wife so easily now! Even you should realize that this may be your best chance to win a bride with such a fortune, and with her marriage, her name would be restored. We would all be connected to the Darcys!"

"Caroline, I insist that you stop this scheming now. I am not inviting the Darcys to Netherfield to win Miss Darcy's hand or find you a husband. They are coming for peace and companionship. That is all. I hope that you remember that." He looked from one sister to the other. "And Louisa, I will thank you for not encouraging her." They both started to protest and he held up his hand. "I have work to do. Excuse me." He left the room.

Louisa rolled her eyes, while Caroline steamed. "Never mind him, Louisa. Once we are all alone together, we will be in charge of what happens in that house." Caroline smiled slightly. "Perhaps some *compromises* may be made."

———∽∽———

Darcy returned to his home from his uncle's to find that Mrs. Annesley urgently requested his presence in his sister's chambers. Deeply concerned, he hurried up the two flights of stairs and knocked tentatively at the door. It opened and instead of admitting him, she slipped out.

"Mrs. Annesley, what is the meaning of this?"

"Sir, forgive me for alarming you, I thought it best to apprise you of the situation before entering Miss Darcy's chambers."

"What has happened?" He searched her face. She indicated a sitting room; he entered and then turned to face her.

"Sir, Miss Darcy and I were walking in the park, when it seemed one woman after another came upon us, and each saw fit to say or perform some sort of cutting behaviour. They each, in their own way, made it quite clear to Miss Darcy that she was utterly ruined in the eyes of society, and further, that she would be shunned and never accepted amongst them. Sir, it was horrible to witness. Unfortunately we were on the other side of the park when it began, so we were forced to walk through a gauntlet before reaching here. I am afraid that Miss Darcy was completely distraught by the time we arrived. I asked for tea and a mild dose of laudanum to calm her. I am sorry, sir. I did not expect such rudeness, or I would not have suggested the walk."

Darcy listened to all and he closed his eyes. "This is not your fault, Mrs. Annesley. I am afraid that none of us are accustomed to being so treated. Receiving the disdain of others is unfortunately becoming quite familiar. It will be good to leave for Pemberley in a few days. I have hopes that things will have improved by the time we return to town in the spring." He looked back at her and sighed. "Does she sleep now?" She nodded. "Please inform me when she wakes." He walked from the room and slowly descended the steps to his study, the weight of the world on his shoulders, and sat at his desk with his face resting in his hands. He had no idea how long he remained so.

"How are you Cousin?"

Darcy looked up and blinked, his vision blurred. He drew a deep breath and swallowed hard. Richard had the grace to turn and busy himself with the brandy decanter while he put himself to rights. "I am well, Richard." He said, and cleared the hoarseness from his throat. The men's eyes met and he accepted the glass that was pushed into his hand.

Richard settled in the chair across from his desk. "Are you ready to talk now?"

Darcy took too large of a sip and coughed, then nodded. "What is there to say? Georgie took a walk in the park, and experienced the welcome of society." The bitterness was clear in his voice.

Richard sat up. "They cut her?"

"Apparently. Mrs. Annesley did not say specifics, she did not need to. You know what she heard." He closed his eyes. "She is sedated now." He looked back at his cousin. "What can we do?"

"Take her home to Pemberley. She will be safe there."

"Yes." He paused. "I saw your parents today. Your father was pushing me to marry Anne."

Richard rolled his eyes. "Yes, I happened to be in the house when Aunt Catherine arrived. You realize she sees you as weak now and ripe for bullying into accepting her wishes. She claimed that your mother wished for it as well." He laughed at that.

"She did." He said quietly. "I was twelve when she died, and she was already telling me that I was to marry Anne." He shook his head. "I really had no true understanding of it, but when I grew older, my father told me of some agreement she made with Aunt Catherine to join the estates and that the two of them practically cackled with glee over the wealth that would be in the family."

Richard stared. "I thought it was always just a fancy of Aunt Catherine's. I had no idea Aunt Anne was involved."

"Oh yes, Mother wished to use me as a pawn to continue to fulfil her dreams of making her progeny more powerful than her own father. She was angry that her father betrothed her to George Darcy. She, an Earl's daughter, married to a farmer. She was angry from the beginning."

"My father is now the Earl, with all that comes with that title, but the Darcys are so much older, richer, and more influential than the Fitzwilliams, he has always told me this. Your mother did not understand that?"

"She wanted a title. She did not listen to her father's explanations. She entered the marriage with anger, but was pleased with Pemberley and the riches my father gave her, so she played the part well."

"Why did your father choose her?" Richard asked, hearing all of this for the first time.

He laughed harshly. "She was stunning, and she had a pedigree with a healthy dowry. She performed well in society, and would ornament his arm. They had nothing in common. I remember meals spent in silence and the sounds of argument from her bedchambers each night when she refused him. Sometimes he would not accept her response." Darcy took a long sip of his brandy, and went on without emotion. "Of course, at the time I did not know of what they argued, but I would sit in the hallway outside the door, listening. She would say he had his heir and he should be satisfied with that. She told him to go buy a mistress. So he did." He looked up at his cousin's shocked face. "I would come to London with him, and I would see him leaving for an evening out. Sometimes I would be rising when he came back in, and he would give me a wide smile. I understand now." He took another sip, and continued his purge. "They would host guests who would stay for weeks. I think they did so to keep from speaking to each other. Oh, they put up a perfect front in company, but I heard the doors opening, the footsteps and laughter in the hallways. Pemberley was a den of fornication, by both of them." He said the last with disgust.

"I am surprised your father did not remarry after your mother died, if his marriage was so bleak."

"By that time he realized he did not require a wife to keep him company." He glanced at his father's portrait on the wall. "He actually discovered he had a son and lavished his attention on me. He swore I would not marry Anne, he would sooner see me married to a scullery maid than see any wish of Mother's fulfilled."

"Darcy, forgive me, but you seem to intimate that he gave you his attention to spite your mother's neglect, and not out of any affection for you."

He gave him a grim smile. "I do not intimate it at all, Richard. I accepted the attention for what it was. I benefited from his words, and he actually seemed pleased to train me to understand my duty." He sighed. "No, that is not quite correct, he always was proud to have an heir. He was extremely proud of Pemberley, and our heritage. It was instilled in me from an early age the importance of my duty. That was truly the only time I saw the man he was, who he could have been." He said the last softly.

Richard was watching him carefully. "You never said a word." Darcy shrugged. "It would change nothing, so why bother?"

"Good Lord, Darcy. I had no idea." He began to understand his deeply private, intensely protective cousin. He rarely expressed emotion; he grew up knowing it meant nothing. How empty he must feel. Richard's own upbringing was in a household with affectionate, kind parents, who did care for each other. He did not know if it could be labelled love, but it certainly was vastly superior to what Darcy experienced. One thing was for certain, he loved Georgiana.

Darcy was lost in another memory of his childhood when he was startled back to the present by his cousin. "What of Wickham? How do you explain your father's attraction to him?"

He frowned. "He was the son of a loyal servant, was gifted with charm, and cunning enough to see how to achieve his wishes. Father also knew that it enraged Mother to see him lavishing her son's funds on a servant's child. I think it was the only motherly instinct she ever displayed for me, and he delighted in throwing it in her face. He had no idea what he created by giving Wickham a taste of what he would never attain." He sat back and said thoughtfully. "It was rather cruel if you think about it."

Richard found the thought of Wickham receiving a gentleman's education by his uncle Darcy anything but cruel. "And Georgiana? What of her?"

"I do not know that he was entirely convinced she was his, but he never treated her poorly. Actually, I think that he rather delighted in her, how could he not? She was raised by her governess, and your mother has influenced her. I was in school most of the time after she was born until father died. She was the only reason I came home."

"Do you know why my father would support Aunt Catherine's bid to marry you off to Anne? Mother did not seem to."

"No, she did not. I think that Uncle Henry knew that his sister's wish was that I marry Anne, he knew that mother was unhappy in her marriage, and that for him, seeing that her wishes were fulfilled, would be a way of honouring her memory."

"That is ridiculous! It is your decision who you marry, not his!" He shook his head. "One great benefit to being orphaned Darcy, you are without question head of your house. You decide what you will do. My father can give advice but can not do anything to you."

"And neither can our aunt. Her desire to take Georgiana from me is impossible. We have custody. She has no rights to her at all."

"No woman does. The children always go to the father or male relative. She is just trying to scare you."

He muttered darkly. "I do not scare easily with empty threats."

"And what of real ones? What of Georgiana?" Richard brought up the most pressing concern. Darcy sighed. "I will take her home and hope the world forgets about us."

"Well there is an advantage to living so far north; nobody will wish to visit once the weather closes in." He screwed up his eyes in thought. "And Wickham, have you heard anything from him?"

Darcy's countenance stiffened. "Not a word. I am undecided how I feel about that. He obviously realizes he is too late to benefit from blackmail. Georgiana's experience in the park proves that." He laughed with satisfaction. "So much for his wish of profit from me. But in truth, I do not believe he will hesitate to extract revenge if he can. There is just too much between us."

"So you must remain prepared." Richard said, patting his scabbard.

Darcy saw the gesture and said dryly, "And retreat to my fortress in Derbyshire?"

"Have you ever thought of digging a moat, Cousin?" Richard grinned.

Darcy raised a brow. "I have enough problems with the cesspits, do not add to them." He did manage a small smile, then sighed. "What will I do when I get her home?"

"You will concentrate on the estate, and Mrs. Annesley will do her job."

Darcy nodded and thought, *and maybe, she will receive some letters.*

Elizabeth walked swiftly out of the door, tying her bonnet ribbons as she put distance between herself and the bed where she had attempted to find sleep the night before. It was hopeless. After John Lucas put the idea in her mind that Mr. Darcy was only coming to Netherfield to find some pleasant diversion in a country girl before returning to the ladies of London, she had felt her ire rise to a level of indignant unreasonableness such as she had never felt before. "How dare he trifle with me?!" She stormed. "Giving me handkerchiefs and writing his pretty words, when all along he knew he would be coming back to the area. Of course he would wish to have some young lady with whom to flirt!" She stormed on, not paying any attention to her direction or destination. "John was quite right, how clever of him to see right through them! I always thought of him as clever!"

Elizabeth stopped to catch her breath and she saw that she had arrived at the very spot where only yesterday Mr. Darcy had stood nervously before her, unable to find his voice, but caressed her with his gaze and his lips on her hand. She trembled and whispered, "Oh my," and leaned back against a tree, feeling the rush of shivers travel from her shoulders to her toes.

"Stop being a fool Lizzy Bennet! How could a man who completely lost the ability to speak, who had no idea he would encounter you ever again, who wrote such honest, sweet things, be trifling with you?" She sank down to the ground and drew her knees up to her chest, hugging them. *What is wrong with me? Why do I care if Mr. Darcy comes to Hertfordshire in September? He is . . . I do not know!* She picked up a stone and threw it in frustration. *It is all John Lucas' fault! I was quite happy with the thought of writing his sister and him, and anticipating his return. Why would I let John's comments bother me so? He is not clever! He has not even bothered to think about his future! I can not possibly respect a man who has such responsibility and such potential before him and does nothing to prepare for it! Surely his father has tried to teach him? I must speak to Charlotte about her brother. But why should I care? I am not going to marry him, am I?* She shook her head. Her future as one of five daughters with very little dowry and little else but her charms to recommend her was quite questionable, and despite her romantic conviction that she wished to marry a man she could respect and love, and who felt the same for her, the intelligent mind that was both her gift and curse knew the reality of her situation all too well. John Lucas' attentions might just have to be accepted.

Her thoughts turned back to the man who stared at her so intently the day before. *What troubled him so, and how could I help him?* She stood and brushed off her skirts, and began the long walk home, composing a letter to Miss Darcy in her mind.

Darcy sat back in his chair, watching Georgiana. She was picking at the keys of the pianoforte. She had not spoken a word since the assault in the park by the well-bred ladies of London. *I can not wait to leave here!* He could not imagine what the three-day journey to Derbyshire would be like, but thankfully, the people at the inns where they would stop would have no idea of Georgiana's fall from grace, and the further they were from London, the more at peace she should be.

"Will you play for me, dear?" He asked. She looked up, startled. His quiet request had the effect of a whip lash she looked so pained. He immediately went to her side and awkwardly patted her shoulder. "Georgiana, please, I do not mean to upset you." He had no idea how to comfort her, never having been comforted himself. "What can I do for you?"

She looked up at him. "I am so sorry, William." Her eyes filled with tears and she got up to run upstairs just as Lord and Lady Matlock were announced. She dropped a curtsey and ran from the room.

They turned to face Darcy who had risen to his feet. "I am sorry, she . . . she met some ladies in the park yesterday and they were quite clear to her how ruined she was. It has affected her deeply." His face was a mixture of fury and pain.

Lady Matlock turned to her husband. "I will go to her." She whispered in his ear. "Remember, we are here for Georgiana." He rolled his eyes and nodded.

Darcy gratefully watched her go, and then looking to his uncle he said. "Uncle Henry, perhaps we would be more comfortable in my study?" He led the way out into the hallway and down to the door. Opening it, he stood aside and waited for his uncle to precede him, and then shut it soundly. After providing him a glass of wine, they sat in silence for a few moments.

Lord Matlock began. "Darcy, we ended our conversation yesterday before we had an opportunity to discuss Georgiana."

Wearily Darcy sat back in his chair. "Do you have some cousin you wish her to marry? Richard perhaps?"

"That was unnecessary, Darcy." Lord Matlock said sharply.

"Forgive me, Uncle. It has been a very long day, and it is only two o'clock." He sighed.

His face softened. "Has anything else happened, aside from the confrontation in the park yesterday?"

Darcy shrugged and waved his hand over his desk. "It seems all of my long-lost Darcy relatives have decided to suddenly lend their voices to the fray. My Uncle Harold, you may remember him; my father's brother, has decided that I am unfit to be the heir of Pemberley, and has told me so." He shook his head. "He invents ideas to unseat me quite regularly. It is fortunate for James that Richard is not a disgruntled second son, as he knows how to kill with a sabre as opposed to angry words in an apoplectic letter."

Lord Matlock looked at his nephew sympathetically. "I take it he was unhappy that one so young would come into such a huge inheritance."

"Yes, my father was five and thirty when his father died, a decent age to become master of an estate, by my uncle's estimation. He did not take to the life in law with happiness, although it was entirely his own choice." He sighed. "And there are other letters, calling me an unfit brother, telling me I have sullied the Darcy name forever, and even worse things of Georgiana. It is fortunate we meet them all so rarely, because after their sweet letters of support, I doubt I could abide any of their faces again." He closed his eyes momentarily and then looked up to his uncle. "So tell me, what words of wisdom do you have to impart?"

"Your aunt and I were going to suggest that you take Georgiana on an extended holiday to the continent, or perhaps simply have her come and stay at Matlock for the winter, to give you a respite. We could see how hard this has been for you."

"I seem to recall you telling me that sending her away would make it appear as if I were ashamed of her? Would that not be the effect of sending her to Matlock with you?"

"No, because we will have all removed from Town, nobody knows what you do at Pemberley, do they?"

He bowed his head. "That is true; however, I believe Pemberley is where she should be. I . . . think she will do well there."

"And travel; what of that idea?" He asked. "We could go as a family party, to Italy perhaps?"

Darcy shook his head. "No, I do not think a sea voyage is what she needs right now, despite the delights of the destination. She is . . . she is ill. I wish her to be in peace at home. Nobody will bother her there. She will not be forced to wear a happy countenance to please her companions."

"I suppose you understand her best, Darcy. These were simply some suggestions your aunt and I devised." He paused. "I want to apologize for pushing Anne on you yesterday. Richard spoke to me of your conversation."

Darcy's head snapped up. "What did he say?"

Lord Matlock's brows furrowed, wondering all that had passed in their meeting. "He said that your mother had already declared that she wanted you to marry Anne, and that your father said it was devised in some combined retribution by my sisters towards my father, to make you greater than he."

Darcy relaxed and nodded; sinking back down in his chair. "Yes, that is what I understood. Do you disagree?"

"No. Your mother, my sister, never did accept that a titled family could be lesser than a non-titled one. But there was more to it than that. You see, she was caught in a compromising position with the son of a peer, whose father refused to allow the wedding because she was considered to be ruined, despite the fact that his son is the one who perpetrated the act. Your father had expressed interest in her, and so she was attached to the wealthiest man who would have her at the time, to hush up the scandal immediately."

Darcy stared. "Am I not George Darcy's son?"

"Oh no, no, you are his son. No child resulted from her foolishness. No Darcy, you were born about a year after your parents wed. Anne had been bitter about her suitor's abandonment, never accepting her culpability in the affair, and further never accepted her forced marriage to a man who essentially was the best bidder at the time. But she did give the marriage her best attention for that first year, as she realized how miserable her life would be if the news of her being compromised had been spread about society. She was grudgingly grateful to your father for essentially rescuing her from a life of shame. However, once she bore him his heir, she felt that she had fulfilled her duties to him, and she allowed her anger to take over." He sighed. "Your father was devoted to her for the first few years, but he grew frustrated and just as embittered as she. I suppose that is the marriage that you remember, and is the reason behind your attitude towards marriages of convenience now."

Darcy absorbed this news in silence. It was all so overwhelming, and the dull throbbing headache he felt when he awakened that morning was growing to a pain of mammoth proportions. "You are telling me that my mother was compromised and rather than face scorn, she was married off to my father?"

"Yes." He said simply. "Which is why I hold out hope that Georgiana will someday marry. However, your aunt and I both feel that she must accept that she was in some way responsible for what happened before she can contemplate marriage to anyone at all, if she hopes to be happy in her situation. Now, you may need to increase her dowry . . ."

He shook his head, and chose not to think of Georgiana's own guilt. "I will not sell her to the highest bidder."

"I am not suggesting that. It is reasonable that a man truly will care for her. I just wish to hold out your mother as an example of a woman who was compromised and found respectability again in marriage."

"To a man she did not respect, she considered him below herself, and did all she could to make his offer of redemption in marriage a farce, driving him to a life with mistresses and affairs, just as she did the same with men who came to our home. Forgive me uncle if the hope you present to me does not send me to dancing a jig."

"Your parent's example is not necessarily how things will be for Georgiana." He said steadily.

Darcy rubbed his temples. "No, no, you are right. It is not, and it should give me hope. This has all been rather . . . overwhelming." He sighed and looked up. "I do wish to simply take her home. Perhaps she will wish to accompany me to Hertfordshire at the end of September. Nobody will know her there either, and we might enjoy the change of scenery by then. Perhaps she might make some friends there. Netherfield is not as remote as Pemberley."

Lord Matlock nodded. "All right, Son. You handle it as you see best. Please know that your aunt and I are ready to assist or welcome her or both of you to Matlock whenever you wish, and we do intend to accept your offer of hospitality at Christmas, the whole family will come."

Darcy nodded and looked to him with gratitude. "Thank you, Uncle Henry. I can not tell you how much I appreciate your support."

―――⁓⁓―――

The next morning, Darcy sat alone at the breakfast table, holding *her* letter in his hand, and dying to open it. For whatever reason, this letter represented hope to him. He lightly traced his fingers over the words on the envelope, and imagined her bent over a writing desk. Would she write deliberately as he does, or quickly, her mind so alive with thoughts that they fairly flowed from her pen? He thought of her pausing to consider her words, perhaps chewing on the pen, its tip caught in her straight white teeth, or perhaps resting on soft pink lips. His eyes closed as his breathing increased. "What is wrong with you?" He whispered. When Georgiana finally appeared he practically shoved the letter in her hands and stared at her until she opened it and began to read.

25 June 1811
Longbourn
Hertfordshire

Dear Miss Darcy,
I hope that this letter finds you well. I have found myself wondering about you since your last letter, and I decided that I must satisfy my curiosity. Ordinarily I would not be so forward, but I find that once I fix an idea in my head, I must act upon it. I assure you, such ideas quite often send me off on adventures that no proper lady should admit, and if my mother ever knew, why I would never hear the end of her fluttering. Oh do not think me too wicked, shall I tell you? All right, it shall be our secret. I climb trees. There, it is said. I also read absolutely everything that I can get my hands on, including those books that my father keeps locked up in his cabinet. I learned where the key is kept long ago, although, as I think about it, I do believe my father made no pretence of hiding its location from me. Oh my, do you think that he actually meant me to read such things? Miss Darcy, forgive my ramblings, but simply writing down my thoughts has helped me to realize something that I did not actually comprehend before. How extraordinary! Well, that settles it. I must write to you often if it brings such moments of clarity!
If we are to be correspondents, I must know of you. I know that you have a brother and a cousin who, I think, is a colonel? I know that you live in Derbyshire at an estate named Pemberley. That is all I know. How old are you? Do your parents live? Do you have other siblings? What do you enjoy doing with your time?
I realize it is hardly fair to ask such things without providing you information about myself so I will tell you. I am just twenty. I walk daily and far. I have never ridden a horse. I have many times been a passenger on one, but was certainly never in charge. As I said, I enjoy reading, and arguing with my father. I dearly love to laugh, so am quite proficient with teasing. I play a little, but rather poorly, and you have seen the evidence of my skill with a needle. I understand that you may come to stay at the estate that neighbours mine in the autumn. If you do, I hope that you would enjoy my company, and that of my sisters. I do hope that your travel to Derbyshire is comfortable. Please send your brother my greetings, and tell him that I await our next duel with anticipation.
Sincerely yours,
Elizabeth Bennet

Darcy watched intently as she read. He was itching to rip the letter from her, and delighted in the appearance of a slow, small smile on her pale face. He breathed a sigh of relief. Elizabeth had touched her.

"What does Miss Elizabeth have to say, Georgiana?" He asked as casually as he could.

She looked up with brimming eyes. "She is so nice, William." She handed him the letter and he turned his eyes to it, eagerly drinking in the simple happy words. Soon the little smile on his own lips grew to the warm one he seemed to have found only for her. *A duel. She asks for satisfaction.* He nodded. *So be it, Miss Elizabeth Bennet. I shall sharpen my pen to take on your wit.*

He looked up to see he was undergoing a close scrutiny by his sister's wide blue eyes. "Georgiana?"

She looked at him in wonder. "You are smiling, William. I . . . I have not seen you smile so in a very long time." She looked down.

He reached out and touched her hand. "I could say the same of you, dear. It seems that Miss Elizabeth's letter has made us both feel happier. I hope that you intend to write to her today."

"Oh yes, I should!" She bit her lip. "What should I say?"

He gave her fingers a squeeze. "Anything you feel comfortable saying, Georgiana. Perhaps you should start by answering her questions, they are simple enough." He gave her an encouraging smile.

She nodded. "Yes, I can do that." She said softly.

He handed the letter back to her. "Be sure to give her the direction for Pemberley so she can send her reply to you. Oh, and Georgie, before you seal it, please allow me to add a few lines."

They finished their meal; Darcy was pleased to see her eat more than a piece of toast. He watched her rise and leave the breakfast room, and let out a sigh of relief. Elizabeth Bennet had given him many new clues to add to his growing catalogue of her. He looked forward to a great many daydreams on the long trip to Pemberley.

Chapter 7

"Come now, Bennet, you know it would be a most welcome match! Your Eliza and my John! They have been friends for years!" Sir William Lucas was comfortably ensconced in an armchair within Thomas Bennet's bookroom, a full glass of port in hand.

"That is true Sir William; however, I have no intention of brokering Lizzy's marriage. If John is to win her, he will have to do it on his own." Mr. Bennet's lips twitched. "I would not want to be the young man Lizzy was coerced to marry."

"Ah, there is something in that." Sir William nodded. "Eliza does have a fiery personality."

"Fiery? I would say obstinate, but regardless, at least while I live, she will be allowed to follow her heart."

"It would be a fine match," he paused, "you know, he was presented at a levee at St. James' this spring . . ."

Mr. Bennet rolled his eyes. "As may be any recent graduate of Cambridge, even I."

Sir William cleared his throat. "Yes, well, we are returning there for a gathering, the last of the Season as a matter of fact, quite soon." Mr. Bennet remained silent and unimpressed.

Seeing his lack of audience, Sir William dropped the subject. "John does care for her."

Mr. Bennet tilted his head. "Do you not wish for a girl with a greater dowry?"

In a rare show of humility Sir William spoke. "Certainly, I wish the best for him, but Lucas Lodge is not even as large as Longbourn, and . . . with my roots in trade . . . well . . . one thousand pounds and a gentleman's daughter is nothing to sneeze at. And I would prefer to see him happy."

"As I would my Lizzy." Mr. Bennet said with an understanding nod.

"Ah-ha! Then we are agreed!" He clapped his hands. "Capital, capital!"

"Not so fast, sir. We are agreed we wish our children happy. That is all." He raised his brow.

Sir William's eyes narrowed. "How does Mrs. Bennet feel about this?"

Mr. Bennet laughed. "Do not attempt to employ my wife against me, sir. I am an expert at resisting her charms."

Sir William snorted. "Enough said!" He swallowed his port and stood, as did Mr. Bennet. "I have done my best. As you say it is up to the children. May I just say it would please me immensely to see the union. She is the brightest jewel in Hertfordshire."

"Well finally we are in agreement, sir!" The men shook hands and Mr. Bennet escorted his guest to the door in time to meet Elizabeth and Jane returning from a trip to Meryton. Sir William greeted them, giving Elizabeth a great wink and continued on his way. She turned to regard her father. She eyed him with suspicion. "What has Sir William so pleased, Papa?"

"Come into my bookroom, my dear." Elizabeth glanced at Jane who lifted her shoulders, and followed her father in. He settled behind his desk and she took her usual chair across from him. "Well, well, Lizzy. It seems you are the subject of interest by a young man of the neighbourhood." He watched her, his lips pursed and his chin resting on his folded hands.

Elizabeth's startled eyes studied him, and then comprehension dawned. "John Lucas."

"Well done, Lizzy." He smiled. "What are your thoughts on the boy?"

She gave a sigh. "Boy is the word, Papa."

"Ah, you see that. Good. He has not earned your respect, I see."

"No, Papa. Nor my admiration. I see him only as a pleasant friend." She began thinking through the situation. "Did Sir William think otherwise?"

"Let us say he hopes for a union?" He suggested.

She was incredulous. "John Lucas sent his father to present his suit?"

Mr. Bennet laughed. "Well, whether Sir William came at his son's behest or not, I can not say, all I do know is he sees the alliance as favourable to all, and desirable to his son."

"How nice for his son." She said dryly. "I hope you have not given me away, Papa."

"No indeed, I told him as long as I live; your choice of spouse is your own." He then looked at her seriously. "Just be sure to make your choice before that day. I have no desire to see you forced to make a decision you do not truly desire." He continued, "It is a very prudent match for you, Lizzy."

Elizabeth nodded, recognizing her father's rare expression of his fears. "Yes, Papa." She rose and stood by his chair to kiss his forehead.

He closed his eyes for a moment then resumed his usual sardonic smile. "Off with you child." He shooed her from the room.

"Mr. Darcy, Miss Darcy, welcome home!" The beaming countenance of their housekeeper Mrs. Reynolds greeted the siblings as they walked into the foyer of the great house. Georgiana fell into the woman's outstretched arms and embraced her so tightly she gasped. "My goodness, Miss Darcy! Well, I certainly missed you as well!" She smiled then looked at the young girl. Her smile disappeared. "Are you ill, dear?" She looked over to Darcy, who looked just as haggard. "Sir, what has happened to the two of you? Surely this must be more than exhaustion from your trip?"

Georgiana looked to her brother and whispered, "I am feeling tired, will you excuse me?" She gave Mrs. Reynolds another quick hug and whispered. "I missed you so much, Mrs. Reynolds!" Then turning, she ran up the stairs.

Darcy and his housekeeper stood watching her disappear then turned to each other. He met her raised brow. "Come to my study please, Mrs. Reynolds. I have some news to tell you. I am rather surprised you were not informed already."

Twenty minutes later Mrs. Reynolds emerged from Darcy's study, a handkerchief clutched in her hand. He remained behind. The peace of Pemberley lasted for almost two minutes before reality intruded. Wearily he rose to his feet and made his way to his chambers. He entered, hearing his valet busily putting away his clothes. Roberts knocked and walked into the sitting room. "Sir, will you want a bath before dinner?"

Darcy nodded. "That would be welcome, Roberts, thank you." He went to the window and leaned on the frame, gazing out at the lake. He would go riding tomorrow with his steward and look over the estate. The harvest was approaching, and there was much to do. He thought of the fine new stallion he had purchased at Tattersall's two months previous and sent to Pemberley. He looked forward to trying his new mount. The thought of riding brought to mind Elizabeth's note. She had never been in charge of a horse that she had ridden. He smiled, wondering if she meant that she had been lead by someone holding the reins or if every horse she had ever ridden had followed its head. What would it be like to teach her to ride? Looking out over the vast expanse of the green lawn he imagined his great black stallion, he seated upon it, sitting tall, one hand clutching the reins, the other firmly wrapped around Elizabeth's waist, her chestnut curls loose and bouncing around her with each step of the animal. Her soft form would be pressed back against his chest, and her face, glowing with the exertion of the ride, would be turned back and looking up at him, her sweet, parted, smiling lips begging to be kissed . . .

"Excuse me sir, your bath is ready." The sound of Robert's low voice jolted him from his daydream. "Ah, yes, thank you. I will be there directly." Roberts disappeared and he looked back out of the window. The vision was gone, but his heart was still pounding. He let out a slow breath and tried to calm his body before going to his bath. He wondered if she had received his letter yet.

———～～～———

Mrs. Bennet was nearly hysterical when Mrs. Hill appeared at the dinner table to announce that Miss Darcy's personal messenger was at the door with a letter for Miss Elizabeth. "Well go, Lizzy, go!" She urged her.

Elizabeth rose and meeting Jane's wide eyes and her father's lifted brow, she quickly went to the front door. Recognizing the same young man as before, she smiled. "We meet again, it seems."

He grinned. "Yes, Miss. I was told by the master to get used to the journey." They smiled and he opened his pouch. "He asked that the letters be delivered right into your hands; no one else was to take them. Oh, and this," He handed her a purse, "is for postage on the letters that I can not deliver. He does not wish to have to burden you with the cost, and he said; he did not wish to limit the length of the correspondence." Danny screwed up his eyes and said his speech very slowly, obviously trying to get Darcy's words just right. He finished and grinned down at her. "I'd appreciate it; Miss, if you could tell him I gave you the message."

Elizabeth, recovering from the surprising statement startled. "Oh, of course. Will you be waiting for a reply?"

He shook his head. "No, Miss. I want to make my other deliveries, but I'll be coming through here fairly regular, I'm sure." He pulled on the brim of his cap and grinned. "Have a good evening, Miss."

"Thank you, oh what is your name?" He grinned again. "Danny, Miss." She smiled. "Thank you, Danny, and thank Mr. Darcy for his kindness." He nodded and leapt up on his horse and galloped off.

Elizabeth looked down at the two envelopes in her hand. One addressed to her in a feminine hand, the other simply addressed to "Miss E" in his clear writing. Her heart skipped. She quickly concealed his letter inside of her bodice and opened the little purse and gasped. There was a small fortune in coins enclosed. *Surely he did not expect to send that many letters!* She did know that the last thing she should do is let her mother see it. She would speak to her father about it privately. Drawing a deep breath she returned to the dining room where every eye, including those of the curious servants', watched her as she resumed her seat.

"Well, Lizzy, what was that all about?" Mr. Bennet asked.

She smiled. "It is a letter from my new friend, Miss Darcy. Her brother's messenger was on his way north and stopped here with her letter to save us the postage."

"Well that is most considerate of the girl! Quite kind!" Mrs. Bennet nodded. "What does she say in her letter?"

"I have not read it yet, Mama; I thought I would wait until after dinner."

"Nonsense! I insist you read it now, so we all can hear!"

Mr. Bennet fixed a stare on his wife. "Mrs. Bennet, I am sure that if there is any news that would be of interest to you, Lizzy will undoubtedly share it with you. In the meantime, leave her correspondence to her."

"Oh Mr. Bennet, you do vex me! Do you not know? Miss Darcy's brother is unmarried, and will be coming to Netherfield with Mr. Bingley. If Lizzy is good friends with his sister, why he will have to meet her, and of course, he will wish to marry her!"

Mr. Bennet saw Elizabeth's blush, but assumed it was out of embarrassment from her mother, and not because that thought had ever crossed her mind. "Well Lizzy, tell us, is that your plan?" He smirked. "A rich man with a fine estate, well no wonder you are not interested in our local young men." He laughed at her flushed face and returned to his plate.

Elizabeth closed her eyes and tried to ignore her mother's effusions, while she could feel *his* letter pressing against her body. She could not wait for the evening to end. In the parlour after dinner, and under the watchful eye of her mother, she had no choice but to open Miss Darcy's letter. She hoped that she would not say anything too revealing because her mother was just poised to pounce upon the sheets.

30 June 1811
Pemberley
Derbyshire

Dear Miss Elizabeth,

I wish to thank you for your very welcome letter. I was so happy to learn more of you. I have never had a correspondent before who did not know me already, so when I asked my brother what I should write, he suggested that I do the same and tell you about myself.

I am fifteen years old. William is my only sibling, and he is twelve years my senior. Our parents are both passed, my mother at my birth and my father five years ago. We live during the late summer until February at Pemberley, which is near the village of Lambton, and the rest of the time in London, except when we are visiting with relatives. I was recently taken from my school, and it is good to be home with William all of the time again. I have missed him so much. Well you have met him, so you know how kind he is. He shares my guardianship with our cousin Colonel Richard Fitzwilliam, you were correct about his rank. He has been to war several times, but is thankfully in London now, training new men for the cavalry.

Unlike you, I do not walk very often, although the park at Pemberley is beautiful, and offers many paths to explore. I mostly keep to the gardens when I am on foot. I do enjoy riding though. William taught me when I was very small, and last year he bought me a new pony. He was so very patient with me. I was terribly afraid, but he sat with me in the saddle and made sure I would not fall. Before I knew it, I was on my own and sometimes we even race! I do hope that you are not afraid of horses, if you are and you ever come to visit, perhaps William could teach you to ride, too!

I think that my greatest accomplishment is music. I enjoy playing very much, although I have not had the desire to play for some weeks now. Perhaps when I reach home I will take it up again. I hope that we stay at Pemberley for a very long time. I have no desire to ever return to London again.

Please tell me all about your family, and the music you like to play. And thank you so much for wanting to write to someone like me. I do look forward to your next letter so very much.

Sincerely,
Georgiana Darcy

Elizabeth read the letter through several times before folding it and thinking over Miss Darcy's words. What had happened to her was in London, and it was enough to make her wish to never return. Was that simply the overstatement of a young girl, or was it truly so horrible that any person would dread returning? She thought back of Mr. Darcy and his cousin, and their grim faces when she met them. No, this girl was not overstating her feelings. Something truly terrible happened. But what could it be? Her parents were already gone; it must be something that personally affected her. She felt her father's eyes upon her as she thought.

"Is all well with your friend, Lizzy?"

She looked up and smiled. "Yes, she tells me she is happy to be home at their estate and hopes they stay for some time. She invites me to visit her someday."

"Well, Lizzy! That is great news! Where is her estate?" Mrs. Bennet demanded.

"It is called Pemberley and is located in Derbyshire, near Lambton."

Mrs. Bennet's brow furrowed. "Lambton? Mr. Bennet, is that not the town where our sister Gardiner lived?"

"I believe it is."

Mrs. Bennet nodded. "I shall write to her directly and ask if she knows anything of the family."

Elizabeth's eyes grew wide. "Oh Mama, I will do that, I am a letter in her debt in any case. I will tell you if she has any news of her."

"Good, that is fine; I do not have time for writing letters." She shook her finger. "You be sure to tell me what you learn!"

Elizabeth rolled her eyes. "Yes, Mama."

Mrs. Bennet nodded again. "Yes, and you will visit her. But you must behave yourself to her parents!"

"Her parents are gone, Mama, it is just she and her brother."

Elizabeth instantly knew she made an error when Mrs. Bennet's eyes widened and she practically purred. "Mr. Darcy is master of his estate, and so young, too? Well, that is excellent news, is it not, Mr. Bennet?"

"Excellent, Fanny. Now I will retire to my bookroom. Goodnight." He left and Elizabeth soon followed. He looked up with surprise when he turned to close the door. "Lizzy, is there a problem?"

"No Papa." She bit her lip and drew out the purse. "Mr. Darcy's messenger gave me this. He said it was to pay the postage on any letters his sister sends. He did not wish for her to have to limit her replies, but did not wish for us to be burdened with the cost either, and his messenger would not always be available to deliver here."

He opened the pouch and could not hide his surprise. "This is quite a gesture, Lizzy." His gaze fixed on her expression.

"I think it was done in kindness." He nodded, and she realized he would think that the young man was trying to impress her with his wealth.

"You know him better than I my dear, if that is what you believe, than I will as well. I will keep this locked in my desk. If the funds are necessary, I will take them from here, but not until we cannot afford to pay the postage ourselves."

Elizabeth smiled. "Thank you, Papa." Instead of returning to the parlour she sped up the stairs to her room where she closed the door, and hurried to the window to open his letter.

Dear Miss E,

I hope most sincerely that this note finds you well. I must before anything thank you very much for writing my sister. Your letter arrived in the midst of a very difficult time and to see Georgiana with a smile on her face because of your words brought me more happiness than I have felt in a very great while. I thank you.

I understand from your letter that you wish for a duel. Please be aware Miss E that I am quite skilled with the foil, and I suspect you are not. What shall our weapons be? The pistol? No, for our duels should be of a long duration; and a pistol's action is rather short-lived. That leaves words, Miss E. Are you up to the challenge? Shall I begin by examining your rather revealing letter to my little sister?

You confessed many things that beg to be addressed. What is this habit of climbing trees? Do you contemplate your life when up in their limbs? Do you dream of the future? Do you imagine what lies beyond the horizon and wish to go there? I will not criticize your action as it is one that I have often enjoyed myself. Yes, I enjoy escaping into the embrace of a magnificent tree, although it has been many years since I last took the opportunity. Would you accept some company in your tree?

I am quite curious of just what books you have discovered behind your father's locked door. That is a wicked confession, Miss E. I wonder if the books you have found are of the type I imagine, and if so, your mind has been broadened in quite fascinating ways! Tell me, what have you been reading? As you have been so forthright in your confession, I will make one of my own. I have escaped into the ridiculous fantasy of one of my sister's novels, and found it, mindless but strangely satisfying. I will never admit to this again, and if you mention it, I will deny ever making the statement. I also ask what is this problem you have with four-legged beasts? A donkey accosts you and it seems that horses are hardly your friends either. I must find this out Miss E. I must know all.

I confess to you now that I am perhaps not quite prepared for a duel. I sat down to write you a charming, witty letter, and reading it over, I fear that what I have given you sounds anything but, in fact I fear that it sounds forced. I wish to assume no disguises with you, Miss E. What I do wish for, what I hope for; is a friend.

I am in the midst of a trouble I can not control. Since my becoming master of Pemberley, I have been able to manage every aspect of my world, but this time I can not, and it affects my dearest sister in a way that will mark the rest of her life. I am powerless to stop it, and desperate for help. I am alone and I do not know what to do. I do not know what fate has brought you to me at this time, I have thought over our introduction countless times over the past weeks and wondered if I would have behaved differently if our meeting had occurred before my sister's troubles began.

In honesty I do not know, I would like to think that were I at my leisure that day I first saw you, I would have hurried down the steps of the inn and introduced myself to you. I do not know if the man then would have had the courage to do such a thing, but the man I am now, more hardened against the rules of society, would perpetrate that heinous act of speaking to a single lady without a proper introduction from a third party. The day before I met you I could not possibly have considered breaking the rules of propriety by writing to you as I have, sending you my token, or speaking so plainly. How such a little amount of time can change a man, how the act of another can change the course of one's life so suddenly. I ask you, Miss E, can you bear to be the friend of two Darcys? I anticipate your reply more than I can possibly say.

Sincerely,

FD

Elizabeth sank slowly down upon her bed, the letter clutched in her hands. She read it through again. "Who is this man?" She whispered in wonder. "Why would he wish a friendship with me?" His sister, she could understand. They had formed a little bond of sorts over an act of kindness. But this man was obviously one of wealth and power, master of his own estate, and surely he would have any number of friends at his disposal to help him through this trouble with his sister. Why choose a stranger? Well, not quite a stranger anymore, but still, he could hardly know her well enough to be sure of her trust. She thought back over their last meeting, and how tongue-tied he was, and how troubled. There was more to him than simply his sister's pain.

She looked back over his words, and saw a man desperately trying to be light hearted and banter with a girl who had, she blushingly admitted, caught his eye, but in the end he gave in to the truth. He needed a friend, and he had no one else to help him. That thought made her feel more sad than honoured. A man of such wealth could also be so alone. She again thought of his difficulty in speech and realized that through the comfort and distance afforded by the pen, he would be able to express himself, and take the time to clearly form his thoughts without them tumbling out in an incoherent jumble. She began to understand the puzzle of Fitzwilliam Darcy. He liked her; he was somehow attracted to her. He wished to know everything of her, and her letters brightened his world. To have such an affect on another person was gratifying in a way she had never before experienced. She read his letter over again and smiled. "Yes, FD, William Darcy, I will be your friend." A knock at the door startled her and she quickly folded his letter and stuffed it under her pillow. "Come in?" She called and was relieved to see Jane.

"Are you well, Lizzy? You never returned to the parlour." Jane looked at Elizabeth's flushed face. "You are ill! Do you have a fever?"

Elizabeth touched her burning cheeks and laughed. "No, Jane, I am well, I assure you. I was just reading my letter from . . . him." She ended in a whisper.

Jane's eyes grew wide. "Another letter?" She whispered. Elizabeth nodded and handed it to her. She watched as Jane read, at first smiling and raising her brow, obviously over Elizabeth's confessions, and then she saw her brows knit in concern. "He is in great pain."

"Yes, that is what I concluded as well. I have decided to honour his request, I will be his friend." She looked at Jane anxiously. "You do think he is sincere, do you not? He is not trifling with me?"

Jane looked back up from the letter to meet her hopeful eyes. "No Lizzy, this letter is very sincere. I believe he has never been so honest before." She reached for and squeezed her hand. "Be careful with your heart, and be careful that Mama and Papa do not learn of this correspondence. You must protect yourself from the impropriety."

"Yes, I will be careful." She took her hand. "Oh Jane, do you think I can help him, cheer him?"

She smiled. "If anyone can make a man laugh, it will be you."

Darcy paced the confines of his study. *Surely the post will have arrived by now?* He looked again out of the window and groaned with frustration. By his calculation a letter from Hertfordshire should arrive this day. Elizabeth received his letter five days earlier. That would have given her a day and a half to compose her reply and post it. *It must arrive today!* He strode about the room, picking up books and casting them aside. *Why did I send that letter?!* He thought. *It was a mistake. IF she writes back, it will surely be to tell me that I was overstepping the lines of propriety and that I should never contact her again. She will likely tell me to discontinue Georgiana's letters as well. I will never forgive myself if Georgiana loses Elizabeth's friendship because I can not control my . . . What do I feel for her?!* He continued his circuit of the room, finally alighting by the mantle of the fireplace, and staring down into the grate. He closed his eyes, the picture of tension, and twisted furiously the ring on his finger. A knock at the study door made him jump. "Come in." He rasped.

"Sir the post has arrived. . ." The servant could say no more as Darcy strode forward and snatched the pile from the salver. He dropped them on his desk and began rifling through. His heart stopped seeing two letters from Longbourn, one for Georgiana, the other for him. Drawing a deep shaking breath, he took his letter to his chair, sat down, broke the seal, and closing his eyes for a moment, readied to learn his sentence.

Dear FD,

I do not know what fate brought us together that day, but I should like to tell you that I would be honoured to be considered your friend. The troubles you and your sister face must be heavy indeed. Her letters indicate that she is undeserving of any kindness and yours shows the signs of a man who is so alone that he reaches out to a stranger for help. If you sense that I can indeed be of aid, if only for the contribution of a willing ear, I will be glad to lend it. I propose that we write honestly to each other. Tell me what has happened, and I will do my best to provide comfort and any ideas for relief. We may drop the pretence of flirtation, and instead move to what a friendship should be, companionship and support. Does that suit you, sir?

Now, to answer some of your questions, I do spend my time in trees to escape my rather noisy home and contemplate the world. I find that nobody looks up when they walk, so I am free to observe life below and dream of what life could be in my little sanctuary. I will not tell you what I have read in my father's cabinet because I blush to think that you have read such things as well, but I assure you, I am far fonder of poetry and histories than of anatomical diagrams. Oh, I just told you what I saw! Oh dear! As for my friendship with beasts of the field, I have been led away by a headstrong horse far too many times for comfort. Your sister suggests riding lessons. Do you know anyone who might be willing to teach a girl who is often as obstinate as her mount?

I must tell you that Danny delivered your letters and money for the post, as well as his well-rehearsed speech. I gave the funds over to my father, who was concerned that you were attempting to impress me with your resources. I corrected him by saying that I believe you were simply being kind. He accepted my assessment, as he knows very well that my motivation in friendship is not based on the wealth of my object, but rather on their character.

Now sir, tell me. Tell me your trouble, and I will endeavour to help you any way that I can. You have my permission. Please talk to me.

Your friend,
EB

Darcy attempted to read the letter again but was stopped by the blurred words. He reached into his pocket, drawing out the only tangible symbol of Elizabeth he owned. He pressed her handkerchief to his eyes and then kissed it before secreting it back in his coat. He took some time to collect himself and settled down to write. This time there was no pretence. As he steadily scratched his pen on the paper, he felt driven to tell everything of Wickham and the events of the past six weeks. When finished, he sat looking over the sheets, wondering if there were any details he left out, or if in fact, what he had written had been too raw for a lady to read. He felt empty. It was painful and soothing at the same time to write out his feelings, his perception, and his reality of what had happened. It was the first time that he truly bore witness to another person the pain that seemingly gripped his heart so hard that he could scarcely feel it beating anymore. He held out so much hope for this truly extraordinary offer of help from such a kind woman. He sighed and sealed his long letter, finally rising to take up Elizabeth's letter for Georgiana, wondering what it contained to cheer his sister, and left the room.

When he knocked on the door to the parlour where Mrs. Annesley was working on a lesson with Georgiana, he was pleased to see her appearing calmer, and at least for the moment, more like herself. It was indeed correct to bring her home to Pemberley. She looked up with a small smile. "William, what brings you here?"

He smiled and held out her letter. "Miss Elizabeth has sent you a reply, my dear." A small gasp of pleasure was released and she rushed forward to take the letter and spun to face her companion. "Oh Mrs. Annesley, may I read my letter now? It should not take long."

Pleased to see any happy emotion from her charge she smiled. "Of course, Miss Darcy. I will go busy myself in the library until you are ready to begin again." She nodded to Darcy, exchanging a look with him, and a glance at Georgiana before leaving the room. Darcy had no intention of leaving, but wished to watch his sister read Elizabeth's words. He settled in a chair and delighted in the growing smile.

Dear Miss Darcy,

So, you wish to know of my family, well, my sister Jane is two years my elder, and is the sweetest, gentlest young lady you could ever wish to know, and my dearest friend. We spend much of our time talking and managing our younger sisters, as alas, they are largely without supervision. We have no governess, and our mother has seen fit to allow all of us to be out, from the eldest to the youngest, who like you, is fifteen. Her name is Lydia, and her partner in all things concerning ribbons, lace, and men in red coats is my sister Kitty, who is sixteen. They are silly young things, Lydia being bold as brass, and Kitty an enthusiastic follower. My last sister is the middle child, Mary, who is eighteen. She is fond of reading and music, though the choices she makes in both are questionable. She prefers sermons to sonnets, and ponderous pieces to jigs. They can be a trial to bear at times, which brings me closer still to my sister Jane. My father is a good man, very fond of reading and teasing, though perhaps negligent in some aspects of his life. My mother's primary concern, other than gossip and a good table, is to marry her daughters off as soon as possible. It is frustrating to say the least, but I realize she does it with good reason, as she worries for our fate should our father die. She is silly and frets, but sometimes, I can look beyond her manners and see the reasons behind it all. But then she will be silly again and make me wish to take up my bonnet and escape for a long walk, far away from her demanding voice.

As for me, I enjoy all types of music, but prefer those musicians who make you feel something through their work. I enjoy the lightness of Mozart and the deep movement of Beethoven. You seem to be withdrawing from your favourite activity due to some sadness you feel. I would think that you might use your music instead to help relieve your burden. Choose pieces that you find soothing or perhaps that lift you to a place far away from whatever presses on your heart. If you are able to find escape in this way, and if indeed the distance you now enjoy from London is helping, you may find that you become restored to the happiness you felt before.

If I had such a great teacher as you did, I imagine I would also employ my riding skills as a means to relieve my stress. I walk, and I feel the exertion helps to tire my body and the solitude encourages me to think of solutions to my trouble. You could just as easily do the same with your riding. When did you last ride, Miss Darcy?

I will close now with the hope that the next letter I receive from you contains news of your latest composition and words assuring me that you beat your brother in a race.

Sincerely,
Elizabeth Bennet

Darcy could sense the restorative that was Elizabeth's letter as a look of peace appeared upon Georgiana's face. "What does Miss Elizabeth have to say, dear?" He asked softly. Georgiana looked to him and stood, handing him the letter. She kissed his cheek. "It is so good to have a friend." She whispered. He nodded and she left the room. As his eyes took in her words, he could hear for the first time since Georgiana left for Ramsgate, the sound of the pianoforte. He closed his eyes and listened. "Yes, it is so good to have a friend."

Chapter 8

*J*ohn Lucas followed his father into St. James' Palace for the last concert of the Season. He was hoping they would be attending something more exciting, a ball perhaps, where all of the debutantes whose first Season was coming to an unsuccessful close might be more willing to look upon the heir to a country squire's small estate with favour. He had made no progress at all with Eliza, in fact, he felt he was actually losing ground with her for some reason. Although he was certain that his father's overtures with Mr. Bennet would eventually be welcomed, and he would in fact win the hand of his pretty, obstinate neighbour, he still would not mind meeting other ladies in the meantime. He was young after all! Unfortunately it was not a ball, but a concert, and the ladies he was overhearing were not pretty or young, but married and vicious.

"Well Margaret, I heard that Mr. Darcy has finally taken his sister from town."

"It is about time! She ruined everything for him this Season. He could not possibly court a woman with her scandal surrounding him."

"Was he really finally seeking a wife?" One excited voice asked.

"I do believe he was, Henrietta, I did see him dance several times!" Gasps were heard.

"And the foolish girl ruined herself and her brother by her shameful behaviour!"

A disappointed whine cried, "Oh is he really ruined?"

"Would *you* accept him now?!" A haughty woman exclaimed.

"Would I not? Why he is rich beyond anything! His must send Miss Darcy far away of course, but he *surely* will be welcomed back next year."

"As long as Pemberley is in need of a mistress . . ."

"What exactly did his sister do? There are so many stories." Asked another.

An authoritative woman spoke. "Well, I heard that she was inviting him into their cottage every night!" Gasps were heard. "To visit?"

Laughter filled the air. "Well *of course* to visit. He would be seen leaving in the morning!" A breathless voice asked, "NO! Really?"

"Oh yes! And when Mr. Darcy arrived and learned what she had done, he beat all of the men servants and dismissed the women. He then drew a pistol and went in search of the man!"

An admiring purr sounded. "Well who knew he could be so physical! He is such a sombre man."

"Still waters run deep, my dear." A voice said sagely.

"Where was she found?"

"Nobody knows for sure, I heard that she was found in a bed with the man, and Mr. Darcy called him out! But you can not be quite sure of that." The voice sounded disappointed, then brightened. "However, there she was, proud and primped, with the gall to walk into church on her brother's arm! Oh my! I was sure the vicar was going to cast them out, if Mr. Darcy had not purchased those new stained glass windows last year."

"They are very nice." Murmurs of agreement were heard. "Oh yes, yes, they are."

"Well *surely* he does not think she will ever be accepted back in town?"

"I suppose he will try to marry her to some man or another. I would send her to his farthest estate forever." The clipped superior tone of an older matron declared.

"I agree, Margaret. He is ruined as well, at least until he rids himself of her."

"Have you heard of his habits?" A voice whispered loudly.

"His? He is never out with the ladies. He always comes alone!"

"Ah, but where does he go afterwards?" The sage voice asked.

An excited woman spoke. "He has a mistress?"

"He must; a man of his age and wealth? He certainly would not spend his nights without companionship."

"Oh no, he would not." Another agreed, "She must have learned it from him."

"Serves them right to suffer for their behaviour. Just like their parents, so I have heard." Silence fell over the hens. "But he is very rich, and handsome . . . and still unmarried. I could overlook a mistress for him. . ." The tittering voices faded away into the general noise of the crowd.

John rolled his eyes. Whatever this scandal, it involved a single rich man and his obviously permanently ruined sister. He felt pity for the man. *Darcy his name was? Something like that.* What a shame to have such a scandal ruin his time with the ladies. But, he knew enough of society to realize the man would recover where the girl is shunned. It was a shame. He thought of his sisters Charlotte and Maria. *No, neither of them would ever disgrace the family.*

He moved away and sipped the drink he held in his hand. He felt the eyes of the surrounding people assessing him, taking in his clothing, his appearance, and knew that he was found wanting. He did not belong there. A university degree and his father's ceremonial knighthood did not go far in these halls. He may have been invited to the party, but he was not allowed to participate. Watching a group of debutantes speaking in a small group, he realized his income would not buy them the jewels they were wearing that night, let alone give them the pin money they would require as a wife. Another group appeared behind him, discussing some other poor man and his scandal, this time the name was Harrison. Moving around the room he heard more tongues wagging with more names speared with derisive comments and cackling laughter, so many that his head fairly spun with the gossip. John looked over to his father who was taking in the atmosphere with eyes as wide as a child's. This trip would give him stories to tell for months. He sighed; thinking of hearing them incessantly, and thought instead of the grouse season to open soon, and looked forward to returning home to hunt the birds and renew his addresses with Elizabeth. She was in his circle, which was where his aspirations should remain. He had no doubt that she was certain to be his.

"What did Aunt Gardiner have to say, Lizzy?" Jane walked out to the garden where Elizabeth was taking lavender cuttings for preparing scented water.

"Oh, she said she never met Mr. Darcy's parents, although she saw his father occasionally in her village. He was said to be very proud of Pemberley and ran it well." She looked away.

"Lizzy?" Jane touched her arm.

Elizabeth turned a distressed face to her sister. "Oh Jane, Aunt Gardiner knew the sister of a maid who worked there. Mr. Darcy's parents did not get on well at all, they fought, and they had guests who . . . behaved poorly." She whispered.

Jane was confused. "What do you mean?"

Elizabeth closed her eyes and leaned in close to her. "There were rumours of infidelity." Jane gasped. "Mr. Darcy must have been just a boy at the time. His mother died when he was but twelve. I wonder how much he understood." She looked at Jane sadly, but her sister's face bore a look of comprehension.

"How old were you when you understood our parents, Lizzy?" Jane said gently.

Elizabeth closed her eyes again and nodded. She was eight when she realized that her parents did not love each other. "How terrible to grow up in such an atmosphere, no wonder he begged for my friendship."

Jane nodded. "You should hear from him soon, I think." She gave her a knowing smile. "I believe you are beginning to like him."

Elizabeth's smile returned, but she could not meet her eyes. "Oh, Jane, you are always looking for romance!"

Jane pursed her lips and prodded her. "Tell me the truth, Lizzy, you like him!"

"Well, he does have the loveliest eyes . . ." The girls giggled and gathered more of the herb. When they finished, the sound of a lone horse brought them through the garden to see their visitor. "Danny!" Elizabeth cried, somewhat forgetting herself in her excitement.

The young boy grinned. "Good day Miss Elizabeth." He jumped off of his horse and reaching in his bag drew out two letters. "Here you go, Miss, only written two days ago."

"Will you wait for a reply?" He smiled and shook his head. "No, Miss. I have to move on to London and back to Pemberley quickly for Mr. Darcy."

Struck by a thought, Elizabeth bit her lip. "Could you wait just for a few moments? Water your horse, he should appreciate it?" His brow crinkled. "All right, Miss."

Elizabeth handed the letters to Jane and taking the basket of cuttings from her, ran into the house. She returned a few minutes later with a bulging envelope. "Please give this to Mr. Darcy."

Jane watched with great interest as he took the missive and placed it in his pouch. "Well, I'll be off then." He touched his cap and jumped on his mount. He grinned. "I'm sure I'll be back soon!"

Elizabeth smiled and he was on his way. She turned to meet Jane's questioning eyes, and blushed. "I did not wish to miss the opportunity to send him a short note. Is there something wrong with that?" She asked a little defensively.

Jane smiled. "No, Lizzy, not at all." She hooked her arm in Elizabeth's and accompanied her to a bench where she drew out the letters. Elizabeth could not help herself. She had to read Mr. Darcy's first.

Jane sat and watched with growing alarm as Elizabeth's eyes scanned with increasing speed the numerous pages of the letter. They filled with tears again and again. Her face expressed pain, fear, anger, and sorrow. Elizabeth's heart was racing. Mr. Darcy did not attempt to spare her any of the experiences of the past six weeks of his life. She realized that the grim faced man she met that day was only hours into this torture. He had completed that desperate search only to feel the disdain of society, and to witness his sister's shunning. This was the reason for his reaching out to her with such honesty; she represented a ray of kindness in the midst of his turmoil. *He must feel so terribly alone.* She wondered how supportive his family was, and if his friends had deserted him. The account he gave of the man responsible for this pain, Mr. Wickham, was numbing. She could feel there was much more in their history than the favour given by his father and his payment in lieu of a bequest. Knowing what she did of his parents from Aunt Gardiner, she suspected a great deal more. She reread again the closing lines of his letter.

Now you know it all Miss E. I will understand if you feel that association with my disgraced sister and her guilty brother is too much for you. I release you from your promise of befriending us, if you choose. All I ask is that you keep the details to yourself, although in truth, they are likely already known.
   Your hopeful friend,
   FD

She felt a fierce sense of protectiveness rising in her breast for him, and his sister, who she now understood. "Lizzy?" Jane's concerned voice interrupted her rapid thoughts. She met her gaze and Jane held out a handkerchief. Elizabeth did not realize she had been crying. She instead drew out the cloth William had given her, and wiped her eyes. *William.* She handed Jane the letter, and sat tracing the pattern of lavender as Jane read and gasped. When she finished, she too was in tears. The sisters embraced. "Oh Jane, first his parents, and now this!"

"Poor Mr. Darcy!" Jane whispered. "And his poor sister! What can be done for her?" Elizabeth stared at the ground. Georgiana's swollen, stricken face in her mind. Then she remembered her letter, and quickly broke it open.

I have taken your advice and returned to my music. You were so correct. I should have been losing myself in the sounds of the composers, instead of the voices that haunt me. I think that it pleased my brother. He smiled a little today. He agreed with me that I am so fortunate that you would wish to be my friend. May I call you Elizabeth? I would like very much for you to call me Georgiana. I hardly deserve your attention but I thank you for it. Perhaps tomorrow William will take me riding.
   Your friend,
   Georgiana

She closed her eyes for a moment, and then turned to Jane. "She is improved but her confidence is destroyed." She took the letter back and folded it, hiding it along with William's inside of her dress. "I need to think about this."

———~~~———

"Come now Henry, you can not possibly support Darcy's obstinacy. You know that his marrying Anne is the best solution to his disgrace." Lady Catherine strode around the sitting room at Matlock House.

Lord Matlock tiredly rubbed his face. "Catherine, I have spoken to the man. He will not bend to your will. He will not be disgraced forever. You know as well as I do that a man as wealthy as Darcy will not suffer the censure of society for long. He is far too valuable to the families in need of his support. Too many wish him for a son."

She snorted and resumed her seat. "He has shown no sign of marrying any woman, so why not Anne if he is so disinterested?"

"His reticence makes him all the more sought." He regarded her warily. "You will drop this Catherine. He has enough trouble without your demands." She rolled her eyes and huffed, but said nothing. "Catherine, I once supported this plan because our sister wished it, but after speaking with Darcy . . . he is very bitter over his mother's treatment of him. He feels no compelling desire to honour anything that she might have wished for him. I doubt that he would plant her favourite roses at Pemberley, so he most certainly will not marry Anne. Give this up."

Lady Catherine glared at him. "I suppose his father was against the union?"

Lord Matlock sighed. "I suppose he was."

"That man!" She spat. "It was all his doing. If Anne had not married him . . ."

"She would have been shunned just as Georgiana is now, and you, dear sister, would have been ruined along with her." Lady Catherine, about to retort, snapped her mouth shut. Lord Matlock quietly spoke. "*She* is our concern now. I have hopes that she will someday be able to marry. She is very young. There is time to recover her reputation."

She shook her head. "She was completely compromised."

"She was not."

"How do you know?"

"Darcy asked her." He said simply. Lady Catherine sniffed with disbelief. "Catherine, is Georgiana George Darcy's daughter?"

Her eyes flashed. "What do you mean?"

"I mean that I am aware of our sister's habits, as well as our brother's. I knew the goings on at Pemberley. They were the subject of much gossip in years past, although, the behaviour at the house parties there were not unlike many other of the great homes." He looked at her carefully. "I ask, is she the daughter of another man?"

She would not meet his eye. "I do not know."

He nodded. "There is nothing to be done if it were true. George Darcy had his doubts, but he accepted her. I always thought it curious that Anne named Georgiana after the husband she disliked, as if the name would curry his favour for the girl when she knew she would die." Lady Catherine looked at him sharply.

"No matter, what is done is done. She is a Fitzwilliam at the very least, so that is good enough for me. I will do all I can to help Darcy through this mess." He stared pointedly at her. "And you will return to Rosings." He held up his hand at her furious protest. "No Catherine, I am the head of this family. You will not follow Darcy to Pemberley; you will go home to your daughter."

Lady Catherine considered him for a moment and realized further discourse was not going to be productive. She decided to write Darcy. "I am not through, Henry!" She stood, and in a swirl of skirts she strode majestically from the room.

Lord Matlock sat silently for some time thinking over the conversation. He knew if Catherine could devise a way to force the wedding she would, but only a total compromise of Anne . . . and even after that, he doubted Darcy would ever give in. He was strong, he would resist. Georgiana however, was she truly a Darcy? He supposed they would never know. He summoned his butler and informed him the family would remove to Matlock in three days. He could not wait to put London and the gossip behind him.

—⁓—

"Mr. Douglass, it is a pleasure to see you again." Darcy met the heavyset man in front of the house where he had been taking in the breeze during a break from his endless paperwork.

Mr. Douglass smiled and shook his hand. "Mr. Darcy, you are looking well, and Pemberley is as magnificent as ever. Your father would be proud of the care you have taken here."

Darcy smiled. Mr. Douglass was a very wealthy man, a brewer, owning at least one hundred alehouses in Derbyshire and the surrounding counties, and a very good customer of Pemberley's crops. He was here for his annual visit, to discuss the harvest, and any ideas for the next year's production. "I see that you have an assistant this year?" Darcy acknowledged the young man beside him, who could not hide the wonder in his eyes, taking in the beautiful home.

"Ah, yes, Fitzwilliam Darcy, may I present my eldest son, Marshall?" Darcy bowed as did Marshall. "It is a pleasure, sir. I understand that you have recently finished at University?"

The young man nodded. "Yes, I did sir, Oxford. Now Father is bringing me along on his calls."

Mr. Douglass grinned as Darcy led the way into the house. "Yes indeed, I am glad to finally have him by my side. It will be a few years before my next son can join us."

Darcy nodded, "Quite a few, as I recall, he was just entering Eton last year."

Mr. Douglass beamed. "Excellent memory, sir. I always like how you and your father remember every detail, whether it be of the granary or my daughter's favourite sweet."

They were about to enter Darcy's study when Marshall stopped dead, and stared down the hallway. Georgiana had emerged from the music room and stood staring in open-mouthed surprise at the young man. She gave a little cry and disappeared back into the room, firmly closing the door. His head tilted, watching her go, and when he turned at the sound of his father's clearing throat he startled and straightened. Darcy's imperious gaze caught his eye and he looked away. The men took their seats around the desk and began to discuss the year's barley, rye and wheat production. Mr. Douglass suggested trying hops and Darcy took notes, as did his steward who was sitting at a desk nearby. "I understand that you have acquired several more alehouses of late, you have expanded greatly in the past year."

He nodded. "Yes, it seems that the proprietors are pleased to have someone supplying the brew, rather than making it themselves. They can concentrate on other aspects, like their food or in some cases, running a good inn. I have men overseeing the houses, of course, making surprise inspections. Nothing with my name on it will be shoddy!" He looked over to his son. "Marshall is coming around with me to see the entire operation, and will decide which part he would like to take over."

Darcy raised his brows. "Perhaps you should spend an extended period in each, so that you will learn it all well. My father had me mucking out stalls and harvesting wheat long before I went to Cambridge. I must say that as much as I disliked it, the experience has been invaluable, and gives me more authority when speaking to my labourers and farmers. I have the scars from my first attempt at shearing sheep, and the respect that earns me is worth every bit of the humiliation I suffered."

Marshall smiled. "I believe that I have poured enough ale to make all of London drunk, sir, and made enough leaky kegs to waste a year's worth of profits."

The men laughed, and Darcy nodded at him. "I do hope that either your skills improved or someone recognized that the position of cooper was not your calling."

He grinned. "Ah yes, I was smartly sent off to work with the brew master." A knock at the door interrupted them.

"Come." Darcy called.

Mrs. Reynolds entered. "Forgive my intrusion sir, Miss Darcy asks if your guests will join you for the meal."

Darcy looked at the men with raised eyebrows, "Well, Mr. Douglass? You are welcome."

He smiled. "We would enjoy it, I know. Pemberley has always set a fine table, but we must move on soon. We want to be on our way home tonight. My wife Sarah's birthday is in a few days, I dare not miss it!"

Darcy turned to Mrs. Reynolds, "It seems it will only be the two of us then, Mrs. Reynolds." She nodded and curtseyed. "Yes sir."

Darcy looked back to his guests and saw Marshall biting his lip. "Was the young lady in the hallway Miss Darcy?" Darcy watched him carefully. "Yes, that was my sister."

"She seemed, looked . . . very sad." He wrinkled his brow. "Is she well?"

Darcy drew a breath and touched his chest briefly. "She has received a shock recently, but is recovering." He looked away, obviously unwilling to say more.

Mr. Douglass saw his discomfort. "Was that Miss Darcy? Well, she has grown up. I remember coming here to see your father, and she was hanging onto his leg for dear life." He laughed. "She must be seventeen now?"

Darcy smiled slightly, remembering her never leaving his father alone. "Fifteen."

Mr. Douglass grinned. "Well, that is a relief; I am not as old as I thought." He glanced over at his son, who looked disappointed at hearing her age. He grinned. "Too young for you, my boy."

He startled and his eyes met the stern gaze of her older brother. "I . . . I thought she was very pretty." Darcy's eyes narrowed. "But yes, too young." His face reflected his regret.

"Well, we have taken enough of your time, sir." They all rose and shook hands. "Let me know the yields when the harvest comes in, and we'll decide on what we would like to purchase for the spring."

Darcy nodded and showed them out the door. "Very good, I certainly enjoy doing business with you, and look forward to contacting you or Douglass in the future."

Marshall could not stop himself from glancing down the hallway again when they left the study, a move observed by both of his companions. Mr. Douglass met Darcy's eyes with raised brows. Darcy watched them board their coach and slowly returned to the house, thinking over the young man's reaction to Georgiana. He wondered if they had known the news of her ruin would she still have earned his interest, or if she was not suitable for a brewer's son either. It was a match he never would have considered before, thinking her a candidate for the son of a peer, but to be courted by the son of a wealthy brewer was very respectable as well, but something for the distant future. He sighed and returned to the silence of his study.

—⁓⁓—

Danny arrived at Pemberley four days after his delivery to Longbourn, and looked forward to delivering Miss Elizabeth's message. He was a simple lad, seventeen, orphaned four years earlier when his parents' home burned taking his two sisters and brother. They had been tenants of Pemberley. He easily could have been sent to a workhouse, but Darcy saw how fond he was of horses and found him a place in the Pemberley stables. Darcy watched him exercising the horses one day, and noticing his skill asked how he felt about working as his personal messenger. Danny, already deeply loyal to his master, jumped at the chance to see the countryside. He had formed a friendly sort of banter with the man that most everyone else saw as so solemn and sedate they were sure his face would crack if he smiled. But since Danny started bringing these letters to and from Longbourn, his master had definitely changed. Being a healthy young man, Danny could well imagine why when he saw Miss Elizabeth's sparkling eyes. He kept his views to himself, but he had a feeling he would soon be wishing his master joy.

Darcy was just entering his study after a day in the fields watching the harvest begin when Danny made his appearance. "Sir, I have your letter from the solicitor." He began to open his pouch.

"I am surprised to see you so soon. I did not expect you until tomorrow."

He grinned. "Ah well, I had a feeling I should move as fast as possible, sir."

Darcy smiled slightly at his enthusiasm. "I appreciate that, but there was no pressing need to make such haste."

"Aye, sir, but that was not the only letter I have, sir." He pulled out Elizabeth's envelope. "Miss Elizabeth asked me to wait a moment after I delivered your letters. She went into the house and came back with this." He handed the bulging envelope to the suddenly speechless Darcy. His heart was in his throat and his hands fairly shook as he received the missive.

"You say that she gave you this before she read the letters?"

"Yes sir, I could not stay for her response."

"Oh." He looked from the envelope, to Danny, to the door.

Danny caught the hint. "I'll just be going, sir. Oh, and sir, I don't think I've ever seen someone so happy to get a letter before." He touched his cap. "Good day, sir!" He grinned at the dumbfounded expression on Darcy's face and left the room, closing the door behind him.

His heart beating hard, Darcy carefully opened the oddly folded envelope. Inside the sheet he found a small bunch of lavender, tied with a yellow ribbon. He lifted it to his face and drank in the scent, feeling surrounded by her. He looked down on the page and gazed in wonder at the simple words.

I miss you, my friend.
Elizabeth

His knees suddenly failed him and he sank down into his chair. "Oh Elizabeth." He gently caressed the ribbon he just knew she wore in her hair. "What have you done to me?" He lifted the bruised leaves to his nose again. "Have you read my letter, Elizabeth? Do you regret sending this token now?" What he was feeling was something he could not name. It was so unfamiliar, but all he knew was that it was so very welcome. He closed his eyes and held the lavender, brushing the wilting leaves to release the scent again. "I hardly know her." He spoke to the empty room. "What am I doing?" He thought of the smile she wore when she spotted him standing by his horse and his heart lurched again. He shook his head. How could she ever entertain a relationship with him, let alone a friendship, now that he had confessed all to her? And he, what was he doing? If there was any hope at all of restoring Georgiana's place in society, the last thing he should be doing is contemplating a . . . friendship with a daughter of a country squire.

Darcy felt the war raging between his heart and head. He feared Elizabeth's rejection and deeply needed her . . . friendship. Her still unknown reaction to his letter forced him to turn to the only solid knowledge he possessed, his duty. Darcy stood, straightened his shoulders, and drew a deep breath. He should very quickly marry, and well. That would help more than anything, Aunt Catherine was correct in that. It did not have to be Anne, Uncle Henry assured him he would be welcome in town the next Season, he could just find some heiress and make that marriage of convenience, sacrifice his happiness for Georgiana's future. *Yes. That was what I should do. Stop this foolishness now!* He took the small token and turned to toss it in the grate, and realized no fire would be lit there for weeks. He went to pick up a tinder box on the mantle to set it alight, but found his hand shaking when he opened it. He then went to his desk and pulled open a drawer and dropped the symbol of Elizabeth's friendship within and closed it soundly shut. He let out a long breath and stared at the closed drawer. His chest grew tight, and he unconsciously reached inside his coat to rub the pain, and found himself drawing out her handkerchief. He looked down at the cloth in his hand and sighed. "Oh Elizabeth, what am I to do?"

Chapter 9

*A*fter another sleepless night, Darcy arose at dawn, eager to join his steward at work on the estate. They were to the grist mill that day, to watch the installation of the new grinding stones, then off to interview tenants about the new type of barley they planted that year, anything, anything to occupy his mind away from the sure knowledge that today a letter would come from Longbourn. During his night of tossing in his bed and then rising to pace the room to stare out at the moonlit lawn, Darcy struggled with the feelings he was carrying for Elizabeth. He refused to label them. If upon receiving her letter, or worse, never hearing from her again, he found himself rejected, he did not want to know that he had offered anything of himself other than his friendship. He had lost friends before, simply by growing apart or by argument, but to lose this friendship, when he knew already it was more than anything he had ever experienced with any woman . . . it would leave him unable to contemplate ever trying again. So he avoided his home, and worked the day through. Finally exhaustion and hunger forced his hand and he did return. Upon entering he eyed his study door, located just at the right of the entrance, and turned for the stairs. He bathed, he dressed, he descended to the music room where Georgiana could be heard playing. He stood in the doorway, quietly watching her concentrate, and tried to relax.

Georgiana finished the piece and spotted him. "William!" She stood and smiled at him. "Oh I am so glad you are home!"

He was stunned. "Georgiana, what has happened to you? Forgive me, but you seem so different, so much happier, what has inspired such a wonderful improvement?"

"I received a letter from Elizabeth today." Her eyes glowed with excitement.

"You did?" Darcy hardly recognized his voice, it was suddenly hoarse. The letters had come. At least one had. "What did Eliz . . . Miss Elizabeth have to say?"

"Oh, William, it was so . . . positive, so . . . she told me that whatever was in my past I could not control, but my future I could. She said that even if my future did not become what I had always envisioned, there was no reason that I could not be just as happy, or happier with whatever it did hold for me. She said that it was up to me to determine what caused me to behave the way that I did, and to accept responsibility for the consequences, but that I also must not spend the rest of my days regretting it."

He stared at her in wonder. He knew that Elizabeth had taken what she had learned from his letter and combined it with the melancholy of Georgiana's and determined a way to reach her. A feeling of hope for Georgiana, and for himself, began to rise in his breast. "Eliz . . . Miss Elizabeth told you that?"

"Yes, she told me to talk about it, too." She looked over to Mrs. Annesley. "We have been talking quite a great deal today, have we not?"

She smiled encouragingly. "Indeed we have, Miss Darcy, and we will for some time, I am sure."

Darcy looked between the two and smiled a little. "Would you like to talk with me? I would be happy to hear you, Georgiana."

She looked down and her smile faded. "No, not yet Brother. I . . . I have much to think about. My behaviour affects you in some ways more than me, and I must . . . I must work through it." She glanced up with trepidation.

He gave her hand a squeeze. "Whenever you are ready."

They moved into the dining room, and enjoyed a conversation about what each had done during the day, both of them speaking more than they had in weeks, and afterwards, she entertained him for some time with her playing. Eventually he decided that he was being a coward and excused himself to work in his study.

He entered the room and closed the door. There on his desk in the centre of the blotter sat a stack of letters. "Go on man, get to it." He said softly. He approached the desk and slowly lifted each letter, glancing at the direction, and set it aside. When he finally reached the bottom of the stack he found a letter covered in ink blotches, a certain giveaway that the author was Bingley, but any pleasure he may have felt at seeing a letter from his best friend was effectively eliminated by the complete absence of a letter from Elizabeth.

He rifled through the envelopes again, thinking that perhaps he had missed it. He rang for Mrs. Reynolds, demanding to know if any other post had arrived and been placed elsewhere. He paced the room, his eyes darting about, searching out corners, thinking the missing letter would magically appear, perhaps dropped on the floor or hidden behind a curtain. His pacing ended with his halt in front of the desk. He ran his hand through his hair. "Calm yourself, Darcy, it will be fine, the letter is simply delayed, is all. It will come tomorrow. It will be well." He dropped heavily down into his chair and sat, his hands tightly gripping the arms of the chair. "What are you so upset about? Only yesterday you decided to have done with her. You decided to marry some heiress for Georgiana's redemption." He felt his chest tightening. "You tried to burn her gift, for God's sake!!"

His chin dropped and his hands came up to wipe the hot tears that were tracking down his cheek. "This is what you wanted, is it not?" He looked up and saw the blurred sight of his desk drawer. Reaching forward he opened it and drew out the slowly drying lavender cuttings, entwined the yellow ribbon through his fingers, and closed his eyes. "Tomorrow. Tomorrow all will be well, tomorrow it will come."

———

"Eliza!" John Lucas called to catch Elizabeth's attention as her family approached the entrance to church. She turned along with Jane and waited for him to reach them. She smiled, but it was not the brilliant smile of the past, now it held some wariness. "Good Morning!" He smiled and bowed, then held out his arm. "You look particularly lovely this morning, Eliza, may I escort you inside and sit with you?"

Elizabeth immediately took a firm hold of Jane's arm and smiled disarmingly. "Oh, Mr. Lucas, I am sure that your own family would miss you if you were to sit with the Bennets."

John looked at her with disappointment, but dropped his arm to his side and covered the move by taking his walking stick in that hand. "Oh, of course. But perhaps I might join you on your return home?"

Elizabeth knew of no reasonable excuse to refuse him. "I am sure that Jane and I will welcome your escort."

John felt even more disappointed to have Jane's company, but smiled. "Yes, I would be honoured." Jane squeezed her arm and they walked into the church.

Elizabeth whispered worriedly to her. "What am I to do? You do not think he is going to try to court me now, do you?"

Jane regarded her seriously. "Are you sure that you do not wish his addresses? After all, Lizzy, there is no guarantee that Mr. Darcy will court you when he comes."

Elizabeth sent her a sharp look, but sighed. She shook her head. "How can I respect a man who sends his father to present his suit to Papa?"

Jane held her hand. "I would just proceed carefully, Lizzy, hear him out."

Elizabeth said nothing. She stared forward at Reverend Mosby, but heard nothing of what he said. She thought instead of William. *Had he received her letter yet?* She hoped that it brought him comfort, he poured out his heart to her, telling her things that she was sure that he had kept locked away, and only the distance of a letter gave him the ability to tell him his pain. *How could he think that I would reject him or his sister?* She wondered, but then the answer was obvious, all of society had very soundly rejected them, it was not too much of a leap for him to expect the same from her. *Oh William.* She thought of his eyes, staring at her, as if he was trying to see into her soul. She wanted to wrap her arms around him and tell him everything would be fine, at least if he gave her a chance. Jane was correct, she did like him, in fact, and she more than liked him. She wondered what he felt for her. *Well, I should hear from him in a few days, and then I will know.* The sound of the benediction roused her from her musings and soon she was walking back home with Jane, following the rest of the noisy Bennets, when John caught up with them.

"Eliza?" He came up to her side. "May I have a word?" He looked pointedly at Jane.

Elizabeth looked at her sister's raised brows and nodded. "I will just walk a bit ahead of you."

Jane stepped up her pace and John fell into step with Elizabeth. He looked over to her. "I have been hoping to speak to you alone for some time, but there always seems to be a family member about." He smiled at her.

Elizabeth looked over to him and clasped her hands behind her back. "What would you wish to speak to me about, Mr. Lucas?"

"Mr. Lucas? What has happened to calling me John?" He smiled again.

"I think that we are too old to call each other by such informal names, sir." She said stiffly.

He laughed at her obstinacy. "Come now, Eliza, we have been friends since we were both babies. If that does not give us the right to address each other by our Christian names, what does?"

She shook her head. "I prefer it this way." He smiled and leaned towards her, "And I prefer to call you Eliza."

She unconsciously moved away from him. "What did you wish to speak to me about, Mr. Lucas? Surely it is more than how to address each other properly?"

He laughed again. "Indeed it was." He drew a breath. "I wish to tell you that I am taking your advice and am beginning to apply myself to learning the workings of our estate."

"That is an admirable occupation. I am happy for you and your father." She remained looking straight ahead.

He tilted his head, watching her face. "I was hoping that it would sufficiently impress you so that you might think me mature, and worthy."

Her natural impertinence could not be held back. "Worthy of what, sir? Managing tenants? Paying your taxes? Planting a field? What are your goals?"

"Worthy of winning your hand." He whispered as he leaned in close to her. Elizabeth's head came up and she looked at him in shock. He laughed. "Surely this does not come as a surprise, does it?"

Disliking his self-assurance she snapped. "Surely it does, for it is the first I have heard of it from you!" She stopped walking. "What makes you think that I would accept the suit of a man who has not the courage to speak to my father himself? A man who sends *his* father to do his bidding? And why was I not consulted beforehand? No sir, this is a surprise!" She turned and began walking quickly.

John regarded her with confusion for a moment and hurried to catch up. "Eliza! Have I insulted you somehow? I am sorry if my father's speaking to yours first was seen as a slight in some way, I only wished for him to open the negotiations."

"Negotiations!" She turned to him. "And what, pray tell were they negotiating? The terms of my surrender?" She strode off again. "No thank you sir, I am not interested in taking part in such a scheme; that is IF I had been asked in the first place!" She stopped and turned again. "And what makes you think that I was interested?" Her face was red and she was furious. John was completely taken aback. "Do you think that I have been eagerly awaiting your addresses?"

He felt as if he had been slapped. "But Eliza, do you not think that this will be the best chance of an offer of marriage you will ever receive?"

Her eyes burned with her rage. "Who are you, John Lucas, to say such a thing? What makes you such a great catch that you would insult me in this manner? You come to me, not ever once indicating your interest in anything other than friendship, send your father to do your bidding, and simply assume that I will fall at your feet at the first mention of an attachment!! I have more self-respect than that!! I will not marry a man I do not love! And do not dare proclaim that you love me, if you did, you would not treat me in this cavalier manner!" She picked up her pace again.

John's own anger at the rejection was growing. "And what are you waiting for Eliza Bennet? Do you pin your hopes on those rich men who are coming to live at

Netherfield as your mother proclaimed? Do you think that if you catch their attention they will want you for anything other than a tryst in the country? I have been to St. James'; I have heard the tales of these men and their flirtations and mistresses. I assure you, they will not be faithful simply because they are rich. Stick with your own, Eliza. Stick with the company in which you were born. Your circle is the same as mine."

"I may be in the same circle as you, but that does not mean I am limited to it, and furthermore, simply because my mother wishes me to marry as well as possible does not mean that I do. My marriage will be one of mutual respect and love. You have shown me today that you wish for neither from me." She moved up to Jane and took her arm.

John caught up. "I will leave you now, Eliza. You are obviously overwrought. I will speak on this again when you are calm." He made a brief bow to the both of them and hurried off down the path to Lucas Lodge.

Jane looked at the tears tracking down her sister's face and offered her handkerchief. Elizabeth drew out William's instead and dried her eyes. "What did he say Lizzy? It was clear that you were arguing, but I could not make out the words. I am grateful we are so far behind the others, nobody noticed your conversation."

"I would not care if they did. It might have made it easier to have them hear his insult." She drew a deep breath and clutched the cloth as if it were a lifeline. "Oh Jane, he wants a marriage of convenience. I believe that he went to London and discovered how low he was in comparison to the other men at court, his father is knighted, but the truth is his fortune is from trade, and he realized that his best chances of winning a wife was here, with me." She wiped her angry tears away. "Is it truly too much to simply want to be loved?" Jane squeezed her arm and they continued on their way. *Three days, surely in three days I should hear from William.* She looked down at the sodden handkerchief and willed him to write her.

Eight more days passed and Darcy had sunk into a depression so deep that nothing could touch him. No letter had come from Longbourn. Georgiana sent a reply two days earlier, giving in to Darcy's demand that she wait for Danny's return so that he could deliver it instead of relying on the post, but he could not bring himself to write her. Not after his last letter had been so obviously rejected.

The letter he finally opened from Bingley spoke of his excitement over moving into Netherfield soon. He wrote of his anticipation to begin the path to purchase an estate and fulfil his father's dreams. He hoped that the time at Pemberley had been healing for both Darcy and Georgiana, and looked forward to finally hosting and welcoming them into his home. He also intimated his interest in renewing his acquaintance with a certain neighbour and was sure that Darcy shared the sentiment.

Darcy read his friend's words and thought darkly that his appearance in Hertfordshire was not to be the joyous reunion with Elizabeth he had desired, but rather a constant reminder of how far he had fallen and what he had lost. He had no doubt that Caroline Bingley would welcome him with enthusiasm, now that the

Season was over and they were far from London, but that was the expected behaviour of a conniving fortune hunter. He clearly was not worthy of a good woman such as Elizabeth Bennet anymore. If he was, she would have written him by now.

Georgiana saw his despair and thought it was over her, so she remained afraid to speak to him of her experience. What she did not know was that her brother was torn with happiness that Elizabeth's continued friendship with his sister had such a positive impact, while he felt increasingly jealous of that same friendship. He coveted and needed it so much, and did not understand how she could accept his sister, who was guilty of the act, and reject him, who was hurt only by association. Did she blame him for it all happening? When he gave Georgiana's reply to Danny for delivery, the young lad paused. "What is it, Danny?" Darcy said with irritation at his hovering.

Danny was confused at his abrupt address. "Sorry sir, I was just waiting for your letter."

"There is no other letter." He said curtly.

"Oh, sorry sir. Is there anything . . . "

Darcy cut in. "You have your assignment; I suggest you be on your way."

"Yes sir." He turned and hurried across the room, but stopped at the door and looked back at his master. He was staring at a yellow ribbon. He watched as Darcy snatched it up and slammed it into a drawer. He looked up at Danny and could not hide the pain in his eyes. Danny turned and left immediately, leaving Darcy to his sorrow.

———～～～———

"Charlotte!" Elizabeth called upon seeing her friend enter the garden of Longbourn. Charlotte smiled and quickly joined her.

"Good morning, Eliza!" She took her hands and gave them a squeeze. "Oh, I am so happy!"

Elizabeth saw her joy and demanded immediately the cause. "What has happened? I do not remember the last time you appeared this excited!"

"Why we are to be sisters!" Charlotte exclaimed. "I will have my best friend as my sister, oh Eliza; I am so happy that you will be Mistress of Lucas Lodge someday!"

Elizabeth's smile left her face. "I am sorry Charlotte, but I have no idea of what you are speaking. I am not engaged to your brother."

Charlotte frowned. "But, he said that you will be his bride, he returned from London determined to propose, and that was weeks ago, surely he has approached you by now? Papa spoke to your father, he said so."

Elizabeth's eyes narrowed. "Indeed, Sir William came and spoke to Papa about John's desire to marry me, but Papa made it clear to him that who I marry is my choice, not his. He was not going to broker my marriage." She frowned. "Has your brother actually been going about proclaiming that we are attached?"

Charlotte's brow furrowed. "Well, not exactly, but he has declared that after seeing the ladies of London, there was no more doubt in his mind that his future lay in the company of a certain lady of Longbourn. And we all know how he has admired you for years."

"Charlotte, if he has admired me for years, he has certainly maintained the information in a very secretive manner. I had no idea that we were more than good friends from childhood. Until recently, I do not believe that he made any special effort to speak to me." She shook her head remembering their argument many days earlier. "Mama perhaps thought it was a possibility, and may have spoken to your mother about it, but I assure you, I am quite out of the negotiations, and I further assure you, it shall remain that way. I will not be pushed into a marriage with any man."

Charlotte knew very well how obstinate Elizabeth could be if her ire was raised and tried to calm her. "Eliza, please, do not allow the well-wishes of your friends and family stop you from considering the great possibilities such a marriage would provide. You would have a home and would be safe when your father dies."

She regarded her with shock. "You know full well that I wish to marry for reasons other than that."

"It is necessary to be practical. You are not getting any younger."

"I am twenty!"

"And I am seven and twenty. I know how foolish I was to pass on a good offer of a secure home for romantic ideals. I do not wish to see you in the position I am in, dependent on my family forever. Although he is obligated to care for me and my mother and sister, it will be by my brother's good will that I shall be allowed to remain at Lucas Lodge after Papa passes. With you there, I should be able to stay, and not have to go out and earn my way as a governess or companion. You would not send me away, would you Eliza?" She took her hands and looked at her imploringly.

Elizabeth pulled away. "Charlotte, I am not marrying your brother. Please do not make this harder. If he had put any effort into courting me, I might consider the possibility, but as yet, he has only made assumptions which I refuse to abide. I have made it clear to you and your brother that I will not marry a man I do not respect and love deeply. John has earned neither of those emotions from me."

"Do not be foolish, Eliza!" Charlotte admonished. "Think of your family, they would have a home when your father leaves you!"

"Yes, all of us, including your mother and sister all wedged into Lucas Lodge to live together. Do not try to convince me that is ideal."

"And if your father died today, all of you would be living with your Aunt Philips or Aunt Gardiner, you have no security until you marry!" Charlotte closed her eyes. "John assured me that you would marry him."

Elizabeth knew full well the reality of her situation, but it would not drive her to accept a man she did not love. "Well, that is his fantasy, and now I must speak to my father so he can set this to rights before the entire neighbourhood hears the gossip." She thought, *And before William arrives, oh why has he not written me?*

The voice of Mrs. Hill calling brought her attention back. "Miss Elizabeth, the messenger is here for you!" She called across the garden.

"Danny!" Elizabeth whispered with relief, a smile lit up her face. Charlotte stared. "Excuse me; I will be just a moment."

She hurried away and Charlotte had to follow. She watched as Elizabeth was met by a dusty young man, and was handed an envelope. As she approached she heard him speak. "I am on my way back to Derbyshire, Miss. If you like, I can wait for your reply this time."

Elizabeth looked at the lone envelope with confusion. "Is this the only letter you have for me?" She searched his eyes.

He watched her closely, seeing the acute distress. He knew there must be some misunderstanding between the master and his lady, and thought he had to do something about it. He lowered his voice. "Yes, Miss. I asked the master specifically if there was another, and he said no, but Miss, when I took another look at him, he looked as if, well, as if his whole world was ending, he looked so broken up. Do you know what is wrong?"

Elizabeth stared at him, trying to understand, and shook her head. "I might have an idea, but . . ."

Danny noticed another girl coming closer and said in a low whisper. "I'll just wait while you write your letters." He looked at her pointedly.

Elizabeth startled. William's messenger was telling her to write him. "Oh yes, here, let me take you to the kitchen for something to eat while you wait." She saw Charlotte approaching. "I have a letter that I must answer right away Charlotte, before the messenger returns to his master. Do you mind?"

She tilted her head and regarded her flushed face with curiosity. "No, I will visit with Jane while you are occupied."

They entered the house, leaving Danny in the care of Mrs. Hill, and found Jane at work in the parlour. Mrs. Bennet was sitting nearby working on a new screen, and Lydia and Kitty giggling over some ribbons they were using to decorate their bonnets. "Lizzy, did Hill find you?" She saw an envelope in her hand. "Oh I see she did. What does Miss Darcy have to say today?"

Elizabeth grimaced. "I do not know yet, Mama, but the messenger said that he was on his way back to Derbyshire if I wished to send my response with him. I must not delay him long."

Mrs. Bennet nodded. "Well do not keep him waiting, you must maintain this friendship, soon her brother will be here, and we want her to encourage him towards you." Elizabeth blushed, wondering if her impetuous gift had hurt any possibilities of that ever happening. Mrs. Bennet finally noticed Charlotte's presence. "Ah Charlotte, what brings you here? I would think that your mother would need you at home, she invited us all for dinner tonight."

Elizabeth looked to her suspiciously, but her friend looked away. "Yes, Mrs. Bennet, I will return soon."

Mrs. Bennet nodded. "You know of course that Netherfield is let at last, and the young man who has taken it is bringing his good friend and his sister along. Elizabeth has already met them both, and is a regular correspondent with the girl, are you not, Lizzy? I have hopes for a match between the two of them." She smiled widely. "He is quite rich, you know."

Elizabeth had taken a seat at the writing desk and was about to open Georgiana's note. "Mama!"

Mrs. Bennet ignored her. "Well he must be if he keeps sending his own servant with letters from his sister!" She turned back to Charlotte. "I have hopes that Mr.

Bingley, the man who will lease Netherfield, will like Jane." She looked at her daughter fondly. Charlotte looked between the women, realizing that this was likely the reason why Elizabeth was so vehemently against her brother. She wondered what the relationship was with this girl, how it had happened, and how well she knew the brother. If nothing else, it was clear that her brother had an uphill battle to fight, and it would take more than wishful thinking to gain her good friend as her sister.

Elizabeth opened the letter, reading it carefully, concern crossing her brow. Georgiana wrote of William's increasing despondency, and how he insisted that she wait to write back to Elizabeth until Danny could return from a delivery to Scarborough. He seemed to be waiting for the post everyday, as if he expected something important, and every day he would search through the letters, and would always ask if there were any more. He even had a man go to the post stop and enquire there if any lost letters were turned in. He seemed almost desperate for news from someone specific, but would not say who. And then when she mentioned Elizabeth's name, he would rub inside of his coat, as if his heart hurt. Georgiana was so worried about him, and just knew that she was the cause of it. She begged Elizabeth for advice.

Elizabeth attempted to concentrate on the clues that Georgiana and Danny had given her. She wondered if perhaps her last letter to him had been lost, and that he was desperately awaiting word from her. Her hand flew to her mouth as she stifled a gasp. After opening himself to her and laying out all of his troubles, he had received nothing from her. He was rejected. Tears welled up in her eyes, realizing the pain he was feeling, not just out of sympathy for him, but also realizing what she meant to him to be acting so oddly. She thought of Georgiana saying he rubbed at his heart when Elizabeth's name was mentioned, and she remembered where he kept her handkerchief. *Oh William!* Whatever feelings she had for him before grew a hundredfold. She wrote a note to Georgiana, trying to calm the distraught girl. She certainly could not tell her what she thought was distressing William, she had no idea of their correspondence, but Elizabeth tried to tell her she thought all would be well soon. Then taking a second sheet she wrote him, praying that her conclusions were correct, and that her words would assuage his fears.

The letters were sealed and she rose. "Excuse me; I will just give this to the messenger." She hurried from the room and found Danny finishing a piece of pie. She walked out to his horse with him and gave him the missives. He smiled seeing there were two. "When should you arrive?"

He looked at her, seeing the same pain he noticed in his master's eyes. "Two days, Miss. I should be there by dinner time."

She nodded, no longer able to hold back the tears. "Have a safe journey." He jumped up on his horse. "I will, Miss."

Elizabeth stood watching him disappear and prayed that her words would arrive safely, and would relieve him. She knew that she had found in him the love she had always declared she wanted, and realized, it was not a romantic feeling at all, but one of caring so deeply for someone that his pain was hers. The realization surprised her. She managed to wipe her eyes and pull herself together, and then returned to the parlour in time to hear Charlotte asking about Miss Darcy. She turned to Elizabeth. "How did you meet her, Eliza?"

She sent a look to Jane who nodded and smiled. No secrets had been revealed. "I saw her in Meryton in need of a handkerchief, she was distressed over something. I offered her mine, and she insisted on learning my name and address so she could return it. Some weeks later she did, and we have struck up a friendship through letters." She smiled. "She is but fifteen, and has no sisters. She is very happy to have another lady to talk with. Her mother is passed, and her brother is hardly suitable for discussing the concerns of a young girl."

"You have met her brother?" Charlotte asked.

"Yes, of course, he was with her when we met, and then I happened upon him with Mr. Bingley and Mr. Morris when they were touring Netherfield."

"Oh." It was all very innocent and reasonable, and Charlotte saw her brother's hopes of winning Elizabeth dwindling. And it was all because of his lax attitude towards the relationship. He thought that she was there for the picking. She knew that she needed to get home and relay this information to the family. "Well, I must be on my way. I will see you all tonight." Elizabeth walked with her to the door. She turned. "Do you follow your mother's wishes to become attached to Mr. Darcy?"

She met Charlotte's eye. "I will only do that which will constitute my own happiness. I have only spoken to Mr. Darcy twice, and I can hardly base my future on such a brief acquaintance." Charlotte searched her face and nodded. "That is wise."

———∼∼∼———

The carriage bringing Lord and Lady Matlock, Richard, and his older brother James arrived exactly on time, which would have pleased everyone immensely if Darcy had opened the letter Lord Matlock sent a week earlier announcing their intention to visit. Darcy had opened nothing since Bingley's letter. There was only one missive that he had any interest in ever reading, and that, it seemed, was becoming less and less likely to ever come. Darcy sat alone in his darkened study, contemplating a bottle of brandy, and wondering if sinking into a drunken stupor would help dull the pain of Elizabeth's rejection. A knock at the door was ignored. The knock came again, louder this time. Again, he ignored it. The knock became a hammering, with what sounded like an army, and Darcy finally jumped up, ran to the door, turned the key in the lock and pulled it open, snarling, "LEAVE ME ALONE!!"

His face, haggard from lack of sleep, and pale from lack of food shocked his family. "My God, Darcy! What has happened to you?" Richard pushed his way in and grabbed onto his cousin, staring into his bloodshot eyes. James went and pulled open the heavy drapes, flooding the room with light. Darcy squinted and attempted to cover his face, the heavy growth of beard making him appear even wilder. Richard dragged him over to a chair and pushed him down. He sat on a table and leaned in, placing his hand on Darcy's arm. Lord Matlock pulled another chair over and sat down, while James closed the door and then walked over to join them. Richard's grip tightened. "We arrived to find that nobody knew of our visit. Georgiana said that you have been locked up in this room for nearly a fortnight.

She said the only thing you ask about is the post. What is it Darcy, what has happened?"

Darcy looked up at the concerned eyes of his family and shook his head. "Leave me, please. Nobody who is here can help me."

"Well then who *can* help you? Darcy, I have never seen you so, what has put you in such a state? Georgiana said that she does not know what happened. She is beside herself with worry."

He laughed hollowly. "She will be fine. She has a friend."

The three men looked at each other in confusion. "What friend does she have?" Lord Matlock asked.

Darcy raised his eyes to his uncle. "Ask Georgiana. I will not speak her name." Suddenly he broke free of them and strode to the doorway, threw it open and left the house.

"Should we follow?" James looked to his father and brother.

Richard watched as Darcy kept going down the drive. "No, let him burn it off. He will return eventually. In the meantime, we should speak to Georgiana, and perhaps Mrs. Reynolds can shed some light on this."

Lord Matlock walked around to the desk; it was littered with unopened letters. Amongst the pile he recognized his own, sent over a week earlier, announcing their plans. He scattered the envelopes about, recognizing some as business-related, some seemed to be from friends he knew, and one from a person he definitely recognized, his sister. He picked up that letter and slipped it in his pocket. Whatever it contained, the information was not something that Darcy needed to read just then.

Darcy continued his rapid stride down the drive of Pemberley. He saw the surrounding beauty and all he could think about was how sure he was that Elizabeth would love it. She who confessed to taking long walks as an escape and rejuvenation, who loved to climb trees and think. Darcy stopped his walking, the lack of food and sleep finally sapping his strength. He leaned against a tree, wishing he had the energy to climb, but instead he stayed where he was, nearly a mile from the house, but still in the middle of the great park that surrounded it. He knew he could not continue this way, but he knew also he could not face Elizabeth. He could not go to Hertfordshire. Georgiana could continue to correspond with her if she wished, but he would ask that her name not be spoken. He could not bear it. He took out the handkerchief he cherished so much and wiped his eyes. This he would keep with him always, as a sign of what his negligence towards his sister had cost him. The sound of a horse coming down the gravelled drive caught his attention and he recognized Danny approaching. The boy spotted Darcy right away, a tall spot of black against the green of the shrubbery.

He reined in his mount and jumped down. "Sir! Are you well?" He looked at his appearance with shock. It was so much worse than it was four days earlier when he left.

Darcy attempted to straighten. "I am perfectly fine. Do you have a letter for Miss Darcy?" His heart ached knowing there would be nothing for himself.

"Yes sir, I have letters for both of you." Danny watched as comprehension dawned on his master's face. Darcy's eyes became sharp for the first time in weeks.

"What was that? You say we both have letters from Elizabeth?" He was standing staring down upon Danny, his hands itching to grab the bag or his lapels.

Danny smiled, realizing that he was right; it was a letter that was needed. "Yes sir, I brought Miss Darcy's letter and Miss Elizabeth was sorely disappointed that you had not sent one. She looked so worried and she started to cry. She had been waiting for some word from you." He watched Darcy as he processed this information.

"She was crying? Over *me*?" He said in disbelief.

Danny reached into the pouch and drew out the letters. "Would you like these now, sir, or should I take them to the house?"

Darcy awoke from his vision of Elizabeth in tears and fairly snatched the letters from him. "I will take them. You go and take care of your horse." He began to turn away then looked back as Danny mounted. "Danny, thank you."

He touched his hat. "It is an honour, sir." He urged his horse on without looking back.

Darcy put Georgiana's letter in his pocket and stared at his. There it was; his name in her hand. He took a shuddering breath, and at last opened her letter, to finally learn his fate.

Chapter 10

On her way back from seeing Charlotte off, Elizabeth knocked on the door of her father's bookroom. He bid her enter and she walked in and closed the door. "Lizzy, what brings you to me? Is your mother busy planning your wedding to Mr. Darcy?" He grinned at seeing her blush. "Ah, I embarrass you. Come child, sit down. I saw the young messenger, if he continues coming, I will have to return the little fortune Mr. Darcy has provided us." He tipped his head, seeing that Elizabeth was not joining in. "What is it?" He asked seriously.

"Papa, Charlotte Lucas was just here, and she was under the impression that I was engaged to her brother."

Mr. Bennet's brows rose. "Is that so? Are you?"

"Certainly not! The man has hardly attempted a courtship; he seems to assume that I would accept him simply because he is available and willing! Why, he even implied that he was my best chance for marriage!" She huffed. "I maintain my position Papa, I am not interested in Mr. Lucas, but what am I to do if his family persists in spreading rumours of our engagement? I am certainly not obligated to him, am I?" The horrific thought crossed her mind that she would be forced to marry him simply to protect her reputation.

Mr. Bennet sat up, concern crossing his brow. "No Lizzy, you will not be obligated, and in fact, I will speak to both Sir William and his son about this privately tonight. We will stop this now. The Lucas' are good friends, but they also like to spread gossip and speculate, much like your mother does. You will not be forced to accept a man you do not want. I promise you that."

Elizabeth came over and embraced him. "Thank you, Papa."

He watched his daughter leave the room with concern. Few things could rouse Thomas Bennet to action. One certain thing, however; was Elizabeth's well-being. She would not be forced to accept a marriage with any man she did not want. *She* would not have to live the miserable marriage that he was forced to accept, through no fault of his own.

Elizabeth entered Lucas Lodge and felt the eyes of the room upon her. She looked from one face to another, seeing emotions from speculation to outright affront. She drew a deep breath and pulled her shoulders back. Her courage began to rise, and she prepared for what promised to be a challenging evening. Lady Lucas was the first to approach her. "Lizzy! Why it is so good of you to come, we were afraid that you would wish to stay away, after all, you do not seem to think much of our home."

Elizabeth was taken aback by the statement. "Lady Lucas, I do not have any idea how you could come to such a conclusion!"

She smiled thinly. "Oh, it was just something that I assumed. I understand that you have set your sights quite high for your future." She glanced over at Charlotte, who was determinedly paying attention to a conversation with Jane.

Elizabeth closed her eyes. She knew that Charlotte had undoubtedly repeated the entire conversation from that afternoon to her mother. "I assure you, I have not set my sights on any man. You should know as well as anyone that my mother's effusions should be taken with a grain of salt."

Lady Lucas' haughty demeanour relaxed. "Well, yes, I suppose I should know better." She smiled and patted her shoulder. "I am pleased to know that you are not being foolish, looking for a connection with a man who is so far above you, and who is not even in the neighbourhood yet. After all, he may find some other girls quite more to his liking." She smiled over at her plain-faced, spinster daughter Charlotte, and the overly eager sixteen-year-old daughter Maria. Elizabeth's eyes widened, imagining William paying attentions to either girl. Lady Lucas' smile came back to her. "Surely you are not so vain as to think you are the only woman of beauty in the county?"

Elizabeth stared. "I am not vain at all, at least I hope not, and I certainly hope that all of the ladies are considered beautiful in their own way." The matron nodded and taking her arm; directed her across the room towards John. Elizabeth saw where she was going and broke away. "Excuse me; I believe that my mother needs me."

She walked across the room towards Mrs. Bennet, all the while wondering what else might happen that night. *Vanity!* She thought. *Am I vain? I suppose a little, growing up with Jane being so beautiful; it can not help but make me more sensitive to comments about my appearance. Mama certainly tells me often enough that I am not at all pretty, but compared to Charlotte . . . stop it now, Lizzy, stop being catty!* She arrived at her mother's side in time to hear her crowing to her sister Mrs. Philips that Elizabeth had received another letter from Miss Darcy.

"And you know, dear sister that will mean that Mr. Darcy is sure to want to come calling, to meet his sister's good friend!" She turned to Elizabeth. "You must treat him very well, Lizzy! None of this running on with your impertinence around Mr. Darcy! I will not have it!! You must secure him! I would think Jane would do for him quite well, but of course, I plan to have her with Mr. Bingley. He is quite handsome, so Lizzy says. But of course, you can not really go by her judgment can you? After all, she rejected John Lucas!"

Mrs. Philips nodded enthusiastically. "Yes, but he will be a wonderful match for your other girls. Who shall you pair him with, Kitty? I do not see Mary with him. She has spinster written all over her, just like Charlotte."

Elizabeth cried. "Aunt!" The sisters ignored her and went on with their conversation. Elizabeth escaped in time to see Mary slinking away to a corner, obviously overhearing what was said. She went to speak to her younger sister but was instead caught unexpectedly by a hand on her elbow. She looked up to see it belonged to John. Flustered she tried to pull away, but he drew her across the room to a quiet corner.

"Ah, at last I have you by my side, Eliza." She stepped from him to gain some distance. John sidled up beside her. "I hope you are well." She stiffened.

"I am quite at ease, Mr. Lucas."

He smiled at her persistence in her address. "At ease is hardly how I would describe you now, Eliza. I was hoping that we might have a chance to talk again, now that some time has passed and you have had the opportunity to think of your future."

She gave him an icy stare. "I assure you sir, I think of my future quite often, and I believe that I made it clear that it does not include you."

He moved to stand in front of her and smiled. It was not a friendly smile, rather it seemed almost feral. "Never say never, Eliza. I understand from Charlotte that you are corresponding with the sister of one of the future residents of Netherfield. Quite a coincidence, do you not think so? You meet his sister and he takes the opportunity to come into the vicinity? He must be assuming a pretence of furthering his sister's friendship, and of course, he would need to be sure that you are a proper friend, and would be required to spend time in your company. Yes, quite convenient, indeed."

"I have no idea what you are implying, Mr. Lucas." She stared into a far corner. He moved in front of her, brushing his arm against hers. "I doubt that you as innocent as you appear, Eliza."

"Sir, you forget yourself!"

He stepped back. "Forgive me if I offended. I assumed that you would be aware of the machinations of men. I see now that I should be concerned that the brother of your friend may take advantage of an inexperienced lady of the countryside, and may simply see you as a welcome diversion while visiting. I have only your best interests in mind."

She looked for some sign of true regard in his eyes, and to her surprise, actually did see it. She closed her eyes and pulled herself together. "Sir, I have no fear that my friend's brother is anything other than an honourable man. If I learn otherwise, I will be very surprised, but I have no expectations of his attentions in any case. As I just told your mother, my mother's crowing is something with which you should be well acquainted by now, and should also be ignored. Now sir, I would like to return to the party."

John opened his mouth to argue but realized it was not the time or place. He nodded. "I will importune you no longer tonight, Eliza, but I want you to know, if you need me, I will be by your side in an instant. You need only ask."

She met his eyes briefly and nodded. "I do not feel that your help will be necessary, however I thank you for the offer." She moved away quickly and went to Jane. The sisters put their heads together. "Jane, I seem to be the subject of a great deal of speculation and interest tonight. If it is not Mama exclaiming about Mr. Darcy, it is Lady Lucas angry over my rejection of her son and assumption that any resident of Netherfield would want me, and just now John Lucas was practically threatening me that I am about to be ruined by Mr. Darcy!" She sighed with frustration. "What am I to do?"

Jane squeezed her arm. "There is nothing you can do, Lizzy. Mr. Darcy will arrive soon and that will either confirm or end the speculation. I am afraid in the meantime you must simply bear it with equanimity."

John approached Charlotte. "Any success?" She asked.

He shook his head. "It is hard to say. She is, I think, far more intelligent than I. Flattery and fears are not the way to win her."

Charlotte agreed. "No brother, the way to Lizzy's heart is to earn her respect, and I am afraid that you have done nothing to earn hers."

He sighed. "I just hope that what she said is true, and that she is not hoping to win this man who comes to Netherfield. Darcy. That name seems familiar somehow, but I just can not put my finger on it." He looked over to Elizabeth. "I do not wish her to be hurt by some man who would not ever lower himself to accept her."

Charlotte observed her brother watching Elizabeth. "Do you truly have feelings for her?"

His gaze became sharp. "Of course I do. I would not be acting like an idiot if I did not. I could have any girl of the neighbourhood, the Long sisters, for instance. I just never thought that I would have to compete for her." He returned his gaze to Elizabeth.

Charlotte nodded. "So this is not just a marriage of convenience? Elizabeth has stated clearly she will not settle for such a thing, but then, she is still young."

John watched the wistful expression on her face, avoided the question and instead asked, "You would settle for such a marriage, would you not?" Charlotte looked up to him. "Yes. If the opportunity ever presents itself, I will take it."

The guests all settled down to dinner. Elizabeth took her seat and was dismayed to see that Lady Lucas had placed her between John and her Uncle Philips, a man of little conversation. Across from her was Mary, silent as ever, and at the head of the table was Lady Lucas herself. She felt trapped. Lady Lucas smiled and nodded. "Since you have assured me that you have no interest in the gentlemen coming to Netherfield, you may now freely accept the attentions offered by John."

Elizabeth closed her eyes. "I am certain that any number of ladies would welcome Mr. Lucas' interest. I am not seeking any man's attentions at the moment."

Lady Lucas' eyes narrowed. "Is there something wrong with my son?"

John's eyes turned to study her face. She felt his leg brush against hers and she pulled away. "No, he is a fine young man . . ."

Lady Lucas interrupted. "Well then, what is the problem?" She turned to her son. "John, is there anything objectionable about Lizzy?"

He looked from his mother to Elizabeth's flushed face. "No, nothing at all." He smiled.

Lady Lucas nodded. "It seems to me that there is nothing to stand in the way of this attachment!" She smiled and looked at her son's satisfied expression and ignored Elizabeth's panicked one. "It seems we are to have a courtship between our homes! Is that not delightful?"

Elizabeth's heart was pounding. "Lady Lucas, I . . ." Her stricken face had finally caught her father's attention.

"Lady Lucas, I would appreciate it if you would discontinue your matchmaking. If your son has something to say, he may speak to me directly. But the dinner table is not the appropriate place."

Lady Lucas snapped her mouth shut, then murmured. "Of course, Mr. Bennet. I was simply excited with the prospect." He nodded and sent Elizabeth a small smile as she closed her eyes in relief.

John leaned over. "You see, I kept my promise not to say anything else tonight."

She opened her eyes to glare at him. "Do not start now." He laughed, and turned back to his meal, and enjoyed the flash of her eyes.

Fortunately the remainder of the evening continued without any further hints or outright declarations of Elizabeth's future attachments. She stationed herself with Jane, and regarded the approach of any Lucas with suspicion. She even began to evaluate her longstanding friendship with Charlotte. When it came to her own future, Charlotte was obviously going to be ruthless in securing it, even if it meant helping her brother to win his reluctant neighbour as his wife. Mr. Bennet did take the opportunity after dinner to speak with Sir William and John. He informed them that no hints, gossip, or unsubstantiated declarations of attachment between the houses would be tolerated. If John Lucas was to win Elizabeth, it would have to be done honourably. John assured him that he had no intention of forcing the issue, and that Elizabeth's resistance only made him more inspired to win her. Mr. Bennet could do nothing else but assure the boy that he would only approve a match to which she agreed. He was on his own.

Darcy stood holding the letter he both anticipated and dreaded. What lay inside, his absolute rejection, an explanation for its delay, or something more? He stared at the now familiar hand and touched his name. "Fool!" He admonished. He sat down against the tree and broke the seal, pulled out the sheets, and steeling himself, began to read.

Dear William,

I have been so worried, I have heard nothing from you since I sent that impulsive gift of lavender and my ribbon, and I was sure that I had offended you in some way. I was afraid that I was appearing to be nothing more than one of those ladies who have undoubtedly put themselves in your path all of your life, but I assure you, the gift was not meant in that way, I simply wished to tell you that I miss you. But then no word came, not from you, not from Georgiana. I read your letter, and William, I wrote you back that very day. From the hints that Danny gave me, I am wondering if only Georgiana's letter was received. Oh, William, I am so sorry. I can not imagine how my letter could have been lost, and if you have been hurt by the absence of my assurances after opening yourself to me so completely, I apologize. I felt confused, but you must have felt deserted. But now I will tell you again exactly what I said in my lost letter.

Stop this silly nonsense, imagining my rejection of your friendship at once! If you think that I will let the admittedly foolish and likely life-altering behaviour of your sister end what I sincerely believe is a very welcome and mutually enjoyed friendship between us, you are very mistaken, and disappoint me greatly.

I have the strong impression that you believe yourself now unworthy of my friendship by her behaviour, and that you have been ruined along with her. I admit that I felt a similar wonder at you wishing to further your acquaintance with me, a girl so far below you in consequence. But sir, you are a gentleman, and I am a gentleman's daughter. As far as I am concerned we are equal. Perhaps that is an oversimplification of the situation. I only wish to assure you that I feel nothing but respect for you. I do not pity you, but I do ache for your pain. I admire you for trying to care for your sister, for taking over your father's estate and your heritage at such a young age, and succeeding.

You have my friendship; you have my admiration and support. I agreed to a friendship without pretence sir, and that means honesty. You naturally needed to wait to tell me such a painful and terrible story, it would not have been appropriate to tell me sooner, and yet, it truly would not have been appropriate to wait longer. I needed to know what troubled both you and Georgiana if you expected anything more from me than impertinent banter. Stop your worry, I accept both of you. Remember, you have yet to meet my family, so I hope that you extend the same charity to me when you come to Hertfordshire. You are still coming are you not? Please come, your letters are everything wonderful, but I need to see you.

Darcy had to stop reading and wipe his eyes. It was well. Everything would be well. He wondered what she would look like if she were saying those words to him. He imagined her standing and shaking her finger as she did with the donkey, and he smiled. "Yes, Darcy, you are an ass." His smile grew at the thought and he felt a chuckle rise in his throat. His eyes travelled to her salutation. "She calls me William." His smile grew even wider. "She misses me!!" He shook his head, realizing she was putting herself through her own torture of doubt, wondering if her token had offended him. "Silly girl, how could your affection ever offend me?" He drew a deep breath and felt the devastation he had been fighting for weeks finally start to lift.

He wiped his eyes again and finally turned to the rest of the letter. He read of her shock and anger at the tale of Georgiana's seduction and disregard of everything she had ever been taught to agree to such a scheme. She lay most of the blame at Wickham's feet, but still reserved some for his sister. That made him pause; he had been entirely unwilling to blame any of this on her. Elizabeth assured him that Georgiana must accept her own culpability for not ever mentioning that Wickham had been calling on her for weeks, let alone the proposal of elopement. She suggested as she did in Georgiana's letter that they talk about it, his feelings as well as hers. She suggested that when they come to Netherfield, Georgiana meet her sisters, and mix with girls her age, and learn how to make friends. Nobody knew of the gossip there, she would be free to gain confidence in herself and be with people who did not look at her with disdain. She said that Georgiana could not hide forever. Elizabeth held out hope. A commodity he had found elusive in recent weeks, and he was grateful for it.

Now then sir, we have addressed your fears, and your pain. We have solved the mystery of the missing letter, and I hope I have reassured you of my constancy towards our friendship. Now it is time for you to start telling me about yourself. What do you do in that great house (I am assuming of course that it is a great house), how do you spend your time? Do you read? Do you ride? Do you embroider cushions? What are your accomplishments? After all, young ladies are measured by their accomplishments, so why not young men? Tell me sir; I want to know everything of you!!

I will wait for your next letter with great anticipation. I sincerely hope that it arrives here intact, and very soon. I hope that you are smiling again, I will when I see your letter in my hands. I look forward to your arrival more than I can possibly say. God Bless you, William.

  Your friend,
  Elizabeth

Darcy could not help but laugh at her close, the tears fell again, but this time it was with relief. He closed his eyes and sighed, thanking her, thanking Danny for whatever he said to her, thanking God for bringing her to him. All was well. She missed him! She was waiting for his letter as desperately as he waited for hers. Somehow, knowing that she was sharing his misery made him feel even closer to her.

With a rare feeling of optimism, Darcy settled back against the tree and read again the words of the woman who had been tying him up in knots since the first moment he saw her. He read her plans, and nodded his head. Her ideas were sound. Elizabeth had earned not only his admiration, but his respect, and now he finally admitted to himself that she was exactly who he needed by his side, in everything. He put a name to the unfamiliar feeling he was experiencing. He was sure that he had fallen in love with her. He was not sure if he knew how to love her, but he did know that he wanted to try. It was terrifying and exhilarating, and he thought; when he and Georgiana arrive in Hertfordshire, he would speak to her. He would ask for her permission for a courtship. He would speak to her father. One thing was certain; the thought of resigning himself to a marriage of convenience was banished forever.

Darcy pulled from his pocket the now dried lavender sprigs, and held them to his nose. He swirled the yellow ribbon through his fingers and closed his eyes. He imagined Elizabeth standing before him, smiling, enticing him, and daring him to take her in his arms. He moaned softly as he thought of holding her face in his hands, tipping her chin up, and then drawing his thumb across her ruby red lips. He wanted to possess those lips; he wanted to caress and taste them with his own. He wanted to pull her tightly to him and feel her soft body melt into his and feel her heartbeat race as his lips pressed against the pounding pulse on her throat. He wanted to wind his fingers through those beautiful chestnut curls. He wanted her to feel how much he desired her. And he wanted, dearly, to be desired by her. His imagination carried him away, and upon opening his eyes, he lifted the lavender once again to his face and knew he would not allow anything to stop him from marrying this woman.

Inside of Pemberley, the Fitzwilliam men joined Lady Matlock in the parlour where she had been interviewing Georgiana. Richard sat by his ward and took her hand, the girl was in tears. "It is all my fault, I am sure of it! I have sent William into this state. He must be so ashamed of me, and he has been trying so hard to make me happy. I suppose he just could not pretend any more. I have ruined both of us!" She sobbed again. Richard looked to his mother for help.

She shrugged. "I can get nothing of sense from her. She says that Darcy has been growing increasingly despondent for weeks now, but he has been shut up in his study exclusively for the last four days, ignoring his duties completely. I understand that he has not eaten, bathed, or slept in that time."

Richard squeezed her hand. "Georgiana, Darcy said something about you having a friend and not needing him anymore, but demanded that her name not be mentioned. Who is he talking about?"

Georgiana sniffed and looked to him with confusion. "Friend? I have only one friend now, Elizabeth."

Everyone's attention focused on her. "Elizabeth? I do not know her do I?" Richard's brows contracted.

"You saw her. I do not think you were introduced. It was at the inn." She said softly.

Richard stared at her, but he was seeing the inn at Meryton, remembering the faces of servants, but nobody stood out until . . . "Do you mean the young woman who lent you her handkerchief?"

Georgiana nodded. "Yes, that was Elizabeth Bennet. William introduced himself to her and took her address so that I could return her handkerchief."

Richard looked at his father who nodded, then back to his cousin. "And did you return it?"

She smiled, "Yes. William was going to do it, but suggested that I write her a note to thank her, and he added a few lines of thanks as well."

Richard's eyes met his mother's raised brow. "And what happened after that?"

Her smile grew. "Oh, we have become regular correspondents! She has encouraged me to learn from my mistakes, but to look to the future instead of wallowing in the past. She told me there is no reason I can not be happy, even if it is not the future I once anticipated." She looked to Mrs. Annesley. "She has encouraged me to talk about what happened so that I know what I did wrong."

Lady Matlock was impressed. "And what has she asked in return?"

Georgiana's face grew confused. "Why, nothing at all. She simply is happy to be a friend. She tells me of her family and stories of her sisters. She is looking forward to seeing us when we go to visit in Hertfordshire at the house Mr. Bingley is leasing."

Lord Matlock stepped in. "Ah, so she is hoping to further her acquaintance with your brother! A fortune hunter!"

Georgiana gasped. "Oh, no, I do not think that at all. I think she is very kind. Ask William, he has read every letter."

"Has your brother written to her again, besides those few lines he added to your first letter?" Lady Matlock asked.

"I do not believe so, it would be improper for him to do so, and William never does anything improper."

The Fitzwilliam family could only agree with that statement. "What can you tell us of this girl?"

Georgiana spoke eagerly. "She is twenty, and has four sisters; her father is a gentleman with a small estate."

Lord Matlock muttered. "At least she is gently-bred." He looked to his concerned wife. "This must be stopped, and soon."

She nodded. "Yes, an attachment to a woman outside of our circle will not help him to return to society."

Georgiana was confused. "But William is not attached to her."

The adults in the room all thought otherwise. Hearing this story and seeing Darcy, it was now very clear that his behaviour was that of a lover, not a brother distraught over his sister's behaviour. "We will talk to him when he returns." At this point Mrs. Reynolds knocked and entered with a message from Darcy. He had returned to his room and was resting, and planned to join them all for dinner. He invited them to enjoy the household as they saw fit until he could assume his hosting duties.

Lady Matlock closed her eyes with relief. "Well at least he is returned and recognizes he needs to pull himself together. I suggest that we do not broach this topic until he has had a full night to sleep, unless he brings it up himself."

Lord Matlock agreed. "Fine, we shall wait until tomorrow. We have a great deal to discuss." He looked over to his niece and searched her face for any sign of Darcy blood. Shaking his head he left the room and went down to Pemberley's great library to settle in a chair and read his sister's letter. After taking in her demands he struck a match and threw it into the grate. Her words were not needed at this time.

———⁓⁓⁓———

George Wickham stepped away from the gaming tables, a large grin on his face. "Good evening, gentlemen, I thank you for your generosity!" He bowed and ignored the growls of the angry men calling good riddance to him and went to a corner booth to count his winnings. He had enough to get by for at least half a year if he was careful. He knew he could not rely on gambling to fund his lifestyle, but until he was better dressed and had more disposable cash, he could not cosy up to some rich widow and exchange his attentions for her funding. It was a game he had played for years. It took him into the society he craved, and with his charm he could almost seem to fit in.

A group of men in red coats entered the tavern and caught his eye. He glanced at them briefly when one man seemed to be standing and staring at him. "Wickham?" He said as he walked over. Wickham flinched, wondering if this was the brother of a girl he might have defiled, but relaxed when he recognized an old acquaintance. "Denny! Why it has been years! You are in the army?" The men shook hands and Denny took a seat at Wickham's table, waving to his friends who had moved across the room. "Militia actually. We are headed out to our winter quarters in a few weeks, so we have some leave in London before we go. What are you doing now? Did you ever use that degree?"

Wickham laughed. "No, but it does impress the ladies." He regarded his old acquaintance thoughtfully. "How is the pay in the militia?"

Denny shrugged, "It is not riches, but as your rank increases, so does the coin. I am comfortable as a lieutenant, and I imagine I'll make captain in a year or so. Why do you ask, are you thinking of joining?" He laughed but stopped when he caught the speculative look in Wickham's eye. "I say, if you are serious, then come and meet Colonel Forster when we return to Brighton tomorrow. We should be leaving for our winter quarters early in the month. Come along and see if you would like to join up."

"The militia." Wickham laughed at how far he had fallen. "Very well then Denny, I think I may just have to take you up on that offer." The men rose and moved over to join the other soldiers at their table, and Wickham began to learn of his new career. If nothing else, he would be fed and housed with no problems for awhile.

———∿∿∿———

The bright sunshine poured through the windows and fell upon Darcy's sleeping face. He lay stretched out on top of the bed, still clothed in the breeches and shirt he had worn for the past five days. All that was missing were the topcoat and boots he had removed in preparation for his bath nearly sixteen hours earlier. He returned from his escape feeling lighter than air. Elizabeth's assurances of her devotion erased the torment of rejection he had carried for weeks. She had never rejected him. Her letter, now lying clutched in his hand, said so much more than simply the affirmation of her friendship. Darcy was very intelligent, and he saw the letter for what it was, a declaration of her love. He knew it. She was as lost as he.

That incredible knowledge sent him to find the peace of sleep, and he dreamed of waking in the security of her arms. The sound of movement in the next room finally permeated his consciousness and he blinked open his eyes, and immediately saw the letter. He settled his head deeper into the pillow and lying on his side, read it through again. He smiled and looked across the vast empty expanse of his bed. "I do not think I will be sleeping alone here much longer." He whispered, and ran his hand over the counterpane, thinking of the woman whose rightful place that was. "No separate beds for us, Elizabeth. None of that nonsense, as you would say." He laughed out loud and smiled. Rubbing the beard that was making his face itch he stood and looked into the mirror over the fireplace, barely recognizing the white teeth of the grinning bearded fool staring back at him. Lifting his chin he examined his new appearance and wondered if Elizabeth would like it. It seemed he would have a full beard within a week if he let it go any longer. Then another smile came to his face. *No, it must go. When Elizabeth's lips finally kiss my face, I want to feel them on my skin.* A thrill of anticipation ran through him at the thought of her affection, and he had to turn his back to the dressing room door to hide his reaction when Roberts poked his head into the room. "Sir, I thought I heard you. Will you want a bath this morning?"

Darcy, trying to calm his body, said to the man's reflection, "Yes, a bath and a shave. Be sure the razor is sharp, you have some work ahead of you."

Roberts saw him rub his jaw and nodded. "Yes sir, I will prepare accordingly. The bath will be ready in half an hour if you would like to begin?" Sufficiently able to walk into the room, he took care of necessities and settled into the barbering chair. He saw four blades ready for the task.

Glancing up at his man Darcy smiled. "You are prepared!"

Roberts' lips twitched. "I added a new blade each day, sir." Darcy lay his head back and let his man get to work. Roberts had the unprecedented need to remind his master several times to stop smiling so that he could finish the job.

Darcy ran his hand over the smooth skin and grinned. "Much better. I hope to never be left in such a state again."

After bathing and thankfully dressing in clean clothes, he went downstairs. It was still fairly early in the day, and upon inquiring, he learned that only his cousin Richard was up, and out riding. He went into the breakfast room and took in the enormous meal his near-starvation required and set off to his study. The room was spotless. Obviously when he finally vacated it the day before, Mrs. Reynolds set the staff to work. He settled behind his desk and began dealing with the correspondence that had been neglected. He took care of the business letters first, and then his steward came in with a report on the harvest. He had been at work over two hours when a knock at the door brought in Richard.

Darcy stood and shook his hand. "It seems that I slept through dinner last night. I hope that your parents were not too offended."

He returned to his seat behind his desk and Richard dropped into the chair opposite, and regarded him appraisingly. "No, actually I would say that Mother was relieved to hear that you stayed in bed. From what we were told, you have been hiding in here or haunting the halls at night. Would you care to enlighten me as to what happened? You seem to have made a miraculous recovery; it can not be simply because you have relatives in the house." He watched Darcy as he wound a ribbon around his finger. "Georgiana seems to think that it was her fault."

Darcy startled. "Her fault?" He shook his head. "That seems to be a Darcy trait, to jump to the worst possible conclusion when a simple explanation will solve it all."

Richard prodded him. "And, that simple explanation is . . .?"

Darcy smiled. "Private, cousin."

"That is not going to be accepted, Darcy, and you know it. If you intend to keep something private after your behaviour, it will be best if you leave Pemberley before my parents come downstairs." Darcy frowned. "Does this have anything to do with Miss Elizabeth Bennet?" The sudden jerk of his cousin's head and wide eyes answered the question. "I see it does. What has the chit done to you?"

A glare of deadly force was fixed upon his cousin. "Richard, if you do not wish to be called out, I suggest that you rephrase that question. Miss Elizabeth is a lady, and deserves your respect. She is not only Georgiana's good friend, but has become mine as well."

Before he could answer, Lord Matlock and James entered the room and closing the door, took seats around the desk. "You look much better, Son." He looked between the two men and saw the challenge in Darcy's eyes and the raised brow of his son. "What is the standoff about?"

Richard's gaze never wavered. "We were just discussing Miss Bennet."

"Miss Elizabeth." Darcy said quietly.

"I stand corrected." Richard nodded. "I was asking Darcy what she had done to him, and he objected to my description of her."

Darcy's eyes narrowed. "As I said to Richard, she is a lady, and my friend. I will not tolerate any insult thrown her way."

Lord Matlock watched him carefully. Darcy showed every sign of being in the throes of infatuation. He settled back. "It seems to me this woman is more than a friend. Did you have a quarrel with her; is that what sent you over the edge? You can not behave in such an irresponsible manner Darcy and expect the family to allow Georgiana to stay under your care."

Darcy's head snapped to his uncle. "Do not even *think* of lecturing me about responsibility, Uncle. You know better."

Lord Matlock backed down. "Forgive me, I merely wished to point out the extent of your fall. We hardly recognized you yesterday, and frankly I am shocked at the transformation today. I demand to know the cause of each. Without anymore dancing, if you please." Although Lord Matlock was unquestionably the head of the Fitzwilliam family, he was not head of the Darcy house. He was really under no obligation to honour his demands, other than by familial respect, and Darcy did possess that for this man.

He bent his head. "I have been corresponding with Miss Elizabeth for nearly three months. We have become very good friends; in fact, I feel affection for her that I have never hoped to feel for any woman. I finally told her all about Georgiana and my history with Wickham. When I did not receive a reply, but Georgiana did, I felt that I had been rejected by her in the same way that society had dismissed us. It . . . it drove me to the state in which you found me yesterday." He looked down, winding and unwinding the yellow ribbon around his finger.

The three men exchanged glances expressing surprise and shock that Darcy would break with propriety in such a way, and that he would actually open himself to anyone at all about his private affairs. Lord Matlock cleared his throat, reserving his opinion for the moment. "And the transformation we see now?"

Darcy looked up. "When I left the house yesterday I met my messenger, arriving with her letter. She had written, and only when he came with a note from Georgiana, but not me did she realize what had happened. She was afraid that I had rejected her, it had been so long since I last wrote . . ." His voice trailed off, a vision of her face in tears entered his mind.

Lord Matlock blew out a breath. "What are your intentions, Darcy?"

Blue eyes met brown. "I will make her my offer. I will marry her."

Richard and James began to voice their protests but the Earl spoke over them. "No Darcy, you will not. The family will not support a match between you and a woman so far below you. You have been lured by a fortune hunter."

Incensed. Darcy stood. "She is NOT a fortune hunter!" He struck the desk, causing the stack of letters to fall over. "I am sorry to hear that we will not have your support, but I believe that we have had this conversation already. I will not marry without affection or love. I have witnessed the effects of a marriage of convenience firsthand. I will not be party to it. I will marry as I choose."

Lord Matlock attempted to remain calm as Richard and James exchanged glances. This was the first time they had heard of their cousin's convictions. "Sit down, Darcy. I wish to speak in a civilized manner." Darcy sent them all a cold glare and resumed his seat.

"Your position in society is, at the moment, tenuous. I expected you to be welcomed back next Season. Perhaps there will be some who continue to cast their poor opinion your way, but that is to be expected, and likely they were people who did not like you to begin with. However, there is every reasonable expectation that the majority of society will forget your part in the scandal and accept you. But that will not be at all likely if you marry below yourself. Your Aunt Ellen and I are in agreement that you must marry, not as Catherine would wish, it does not have to be Anne, but you must marry, and you must produce the heir of Pemberley."

Darcy nodded at him. "And that is what I intend to do. I intend to marry Miss Elizabeth."

The Earl shook his head in frustration. "You are not listening to me, Darcy. You can not risk your position in society by taking on the daughter of a country squire. It will do you no favours. My words will be seen as mild compared to theirs."

The venom in his response struck them all. "Do you truly think that I care of my position in society?" He hissed. "The only reason that I maintained the contacts I did was for promoting Georgiana's future marriage. As it is clear that she is unlikely to ever be accepted in the first circles again, unless it is by some family so desperate for her dowry that they are willing to take on a girl with a damaged reputation, what does it matter who I marry?" His stare would have sent a lesser man running.

Lord Matlock closed his eyes to avoid the glare and stated the bald truth. "Darcy, she would not be accepted, and do not expect any support from us in making her so." He implored, "If you care for her as you say, do you truly wish to subject her to the same disdain you see Georgiana facing now?"

Darcy stopped, considering Elizabeth's strength. He was not sure, but somehow, he simply knew that she would not crumple under society's censure. "Uncle, I do not ask for your support. I would appreciate your civility when in her company, but as to Town, I already know who my friends are. I need nothing else. I will be perfectly content to spend my days here, and Miss Elizabeth is a country girl, I suspect she will feel the same." He fixed his eyes on his uncle. "I will marry no other. It is truly a miracle that I found her. I admit to considering the possibility of choosing a lady of fortune to help Georgiana, but now that I have the possibility of felicity, I will not let it go." He stood up and walked to the window and stared out at the gardens. "I will not marry if it is not to her."

"Darcy . . . Darcy, you *must* be the one to marry. You can not leave it to Georgiana." Lord Matlock's voice was almost pleading. Darcy turned. "I have become increasingly convinced that Georgiana is not your father's daughter. To be sure that a child of Darcy blood is born, he must come from you."

"Have you proof of this?" Darcy had, in fact, suspected this truth for years, which was always the chink in his plan to leave the creation of the Pemberley heir to his sister, but now after all that had happened, he really did not care. She was raised as a Darcy, she WAS a Darcy.

"I have the indications from your Aunt Catherine that it was so." He said quietly. "She will not say more, I do not know who the father may be."

"Well then, if a child with the Darcy blood is to be born, it will come of my union with Miss Elizabeth. Otherwise, the bloodline will end with me." He returned his gaze to the garden, his hands working the ribbon incessantly while the Fitzwilliam men spoke amongst themselves.

Richard looked over to him. "Have you presented your suit yet?"

Darcy turned back. "No. I will be travelling to Hertfordshire in less than a fortnight with Georgiana. I intend to ask Elizabeth's permission for a formal courtship and speak to her father then. If she will have me, I sincerely hope that we will be married before Christmas. I wish to begin my life. I have waited long enough." He looked at them all seriously. "I hope to have your acceptance, but if I do not, it will not change my decision."

His eyes were drawn down to the worn yellow ribbon, now wrapped around the third finger of his left hand, and he smiled at the irony. He thought of the gold band he hoped to place on Elizabeth's hand and said softly, "At last, I will know love."

Chapter 11

*D*arcy finally escaped his unhappy uncle and cousins by simply refusing to speak any further on the subject. He opened the door and left the room after hearing his uncle state once again that if he chose to marry Elizabeth, he would receive no support from the family. Striding down the hallway, he felt a great many emotions, anger, hurt, but oddly it was freedom that overwhelmed his senses. He felt released from society and all that went with it. He found himself in the library built by his ancestors and fell into a chair, thinking.

Elizabeth grew up completely removed from the *ton*, and she was happy. She was dressed, fed, educated, walked, laughed, and *lived*, all without society. What would he, *they*, be missing if he suffered the disdain of society for making Elizabeth his wife? Culture, certainly, but there really was no reason why they could not still go to London and attend the theatre. What they *would* miss would be the balls, parties, and social occasions that he so dreaded attending already. He would perhaps lose friends, maybe not be welcome in his club, but was that really a loss if they did not think well enough of him to accept his choice? Perhaps he would miss out on some business opportunities, or would he? Money would apparently save him from being ruined by Georgiana's mistake; undoubtedly his wealth would be more important to the men of society than who he chose to marry. Perhaps it was not really so bad after all. He saw what society did to his parents, and he swore it would not happen to him. It seemed that his wish could be realized.

He would write to Elizabeth and ask her if she cared for London. He did not even know if she had ever been there. They had so much to learn of each other. He smiled and thought of her letter, she had demanded to know all of him. He rose and settled down at a writing desk set next to a window overlooking the rose garden. The blooms were no longer present, but the foliage remained lovely, just beginning to yellow with the coming autumn. He made a note to speak with his gardener, and have a lavender border planted for Elizabeth. He thought it should be set near the mistress' study, so that the scent would fill her room when she opened the windows and worked there. He closed his eyes and imagined her in the long-abandoned room, wondering how she would adjust to such an enormous task and smiled; they would take it on together. How very good that sounded!

With a new lightness in his heart he settled down to write. He took his time. This letter had to be perfect. It was, he realized, the most important letter of his life. Six pages and two pens later, he scattered fine sand over the ink and read it over, trying to imagine who wrote such an effusive letter. He was about to seal the envelope when he thought that he should include a token of some sort. This was more difficult for a man, ribbons would not do. He considered sending a handkerchief embroidered with his initials, but that would surely cause her trouble if it was found. Drumming his fingers and thinking he finally decided on his gift. Ten minutes later he bit his lip and sealed the letter. He hoped it made her happy.

—⁓⁓—

Georgiana had been standing outside of Darcy's study about to knock on the door, when the raised voices of the men filtered through the wood. What she heard about her paternity; and the demands on her brother's future and his desires overwhelmed her, and she fled, with no idea of her direction. Her eyes flooded with tears, she bounced off a wall and into the arms of a startled footman who inquired after her well-being. She stammered out some excuse and continued on. The footman immediately notified Mrs. Reynolds of the girl's distress, and she in turn found Lady Matlock. Together the women searched out and finally found her sobbing in the Pemberley chapel. Mrs. Reynolds left the small sanctuary to find her master, and Lady Matlock draped her arm around her. "What is wrong, Georgiana?"

"Oh, Aunt Ellen, I just heard the most dreadful thing! It can not be true!" She renewed her sobs.

Lady Matlock brushed away the hair that had fallen from her pins. "What have you heard, what is not true?"

Georgiana watched her aunt's concerned face. "I am not a Darcy." Lady Matlock closed her eyes and Georgiana read her expression and whispered. "It is true?"

Her aunt saw her devastation. "We can not know for sure, Georgiana. At the time that you were conceived, your mother was . . . not always faithful to your father, as he was not faithful to her." She tried to be gentle, but the girl was old enough now to hear the truth. She saw the pain she was causing but ploughed on. "Your father suspected that you were not his daughter, but yet he still accepted and loved you. He raised you as a Darcy."

Georgiana's tears were flowing, but the sobs had stopped. "Uncle said that William must marry. He must be the one to provide an heir so that the Darcy blood would continue to live in Pemberley."

Lady Matlock nodded. "There is no doubt of his heritage. Your parents were still faithful at that time; it was only after his birth that they changed."

Georgiana persisted. "I heard William say that if he did not marry the woman he chose that the bloodline would die with him."

Lady Matlock's face was grim. "I am sorry to hear that, but yes, if your parentage is questionable, and Darcy does not create an heir, that fact is true. I hope that he rethinks his position."

"He loves my friend Elizabeth, does he not?"

A deep voice answered her. Darcy had entered the chapel and silently approached, listening to the conversation. "Georgiana." He sat down next to her and took her hand. "First, you should know that I consider you as much a Darcy as I am."

She stared up at him. "But you said that if you do not marry Elizabeth, the bloodline would die with you."

"That is true, dear, because I will marry no woman but she." He lifted his eyes to meet his aunt's then looked back down at Georgiana. "I do not know if our uncle's claims of your paternity are true, and I do not care. You are my sister regardless, and I love you. As Aunt Ellen said, Father accepted you as his. As far as I am concerned, there is nothing else to discuss."

"But if they do not let you marry as you wish, you could be the last . . ."

Darcy stopped her. "Georgiana, the only one who has any say in who I chose to take as my wife is Elizabeth. While I hoped our family would wish to share my happiness, they have made it very clear that they reject her without ever knowing her. You and I know how wonderful she is." Lady Matlock felt the sting of his anger, even though his voice was very soft.

"Is it true? Have you been writing her?"

"Yes, for as long as you have." He reached into his pocket. "This came for you yesterday. I fell asleep before I remembered to give it to you."

Georgiana took the envelope and saw it was in Elizabeth's hand. "Were you ill over me, William?"

He brushed back the loosened hair and smiled sadly. "No, I was ill because I was heartbroken. I thought that Elizabeth had rejected me." Lady Matlock stared in disbelief as he continued on. "You see, I told her about you and Wickham."

Georgiana gasped. "She knows!"

He nodded. "I trust her, and she cares very much for both of us. But when I did not receive a letter from her after my confession, I thought that she . . . well . . . that does not matter now. Her letter was lost and she was feeling just as worried that I did not . . . we were both very silly."

"How can you love her? You have only seen her once?"

Darcy smiled. "Twice." Georgiana smiled back. "Through our letters I grew to know her in a way that would have never been possible during a traditional courtship. I had the opportunity to know and fall in love with the woman, and not be distracted by her beauty or physical presence. Of course she is very lovely, and I anticipate spending a great deal of time with her when we go to Netherfield. I hope that you would like Elizabeth as your sister."

"Oh William, I would love her as my sister!" She squeezed his hand, and he laughed. Lady Matlock looked on the scene with astonishment. The happiness that she saw between the siblings was highly unusual. Georgiana grew concerned. "But our family disapproves of her?"

"They do, and likely we will not be welcomed by most of society, and I will have to tell Elizabeth of that, but if she will have me despite those facts, I hope very much to make her my wife and bring her to Pemberley." He smiled at the thought. "And if she says no, I am afraid that we will be staying at Netherfield for some time as I court her incessantly until she says yes! Shall we go to Netherfield in two weeks time? Or do you prefer to stay here?"

"Oh no brother, we will go together. I must be sure that you do not ruin my chances of winning a sister!"

Darcy laughed. They stood, and he looked down at his aunt. "I suppose that if the family disapproves of my wife, we will simply live here without them. It is up to them. My course is set." Without another word they departed, and Lady Matlock was left alone in the chapel to contemplate her nephew's words.

After three days of rain and entrapment inside of the house, Elizabeth could take no more. At the first sign of dry skies she grabbed her bonnet, announced to her mother that she was going walking and fled. Her head was spinning. Lydia had been laughing for days about their mother pushing Kitty to make eyes at John Lucas as it was obvious that Mary would not do for him at all. Kitty protested loudly that she did not want to marry some farmer; she wanted a soldier, a tall blonde one. Mrs. Bennet followed her around the house proclaiming that she had better change her attitude. Whenever she had the chance she would turn to follow Elizabeth, chastising her for encouraging John to be attracted to her instead, and then she would launch into a long-winded diatribe against Lady Lucas, practically engaging Elizabeth to him at the dinner table. "Why, how could she even think that her daughters would be looked at once by Mr. Bingley or Mr. Darcy? Trying to steal them away from my girls! You mark my words Lizzy, and you too Jane, there will be hordes of women trying to take them away. You must be on your very best behaviour. The nerve of her!! Why Charlotte is an old maid! What would a young gentleman want with that? And Maria, she is a silly thing, far too young."

Elizabeth heard her mother's voice ringing in her ears as she put distance between her and the house. "Maria is too young? She is the same age as Kitty and you want her to marry John!" She left the garden and entered the lanes, slowing her rapid pace. Although she certainly was encouraged by her mother's assurance that she would marry William, she still had no guarantee of that from him. He should have her letter by now. She hoped so much that it helped. Danny seemed so concerned for him, and that made her feel worse. And now, with all this mess concerning John Lucas, should she tell him about it? After all, she was not encouraging him at all. She had twice made that clear, but although university-educated, it did not seem to be sinking in. She supposed he resembled his father in that way.

Unconsciously she made her way towards Netherfield, and before long found herself at the spot where she had last seen William. She climbed up on the stile and sat, watching the breeze blow the long grass, and looked off to the distance where she had last seen him as his horse disappeared over the hillside towards the house. Soon he would come. And what would come with him? *A proposal?* She smiled and chastised herself. "Do not get your hopes up Elizabeth Bennet." She closed her eyes and thought about it. They had been courting for nearly three months. Was it possible to court someone in such a way? Do you need to physically be with someone to know them?

"Eliza." The sound of her name jolted her out of her reverie and she opened her eyes to see John standing before her. She hurriedly climbed down from the stile. "I did not hear your horse, Mr. Lucas."

"I was walking him; I thought you might be asleep." He was looking at her without the calculation she had seen of late.

"And yet you decide to wake me anyway." She said with her brows raised. John smiled. She was teasing, not fighting. He relaxed. "Yes, forgive me. I could not miss the chance to speak to you. I wish to apologize for my behaviour at dinner."

Elizabeth looked at him carefully. "Mr. Lucas . . ."

He shook his head. "John, please."

She sighed. "Mr. Lucas, I was very offended at dinner. Not just by you, but by the presumption of your mother. I felt that if my father had not stepped in when he did, she would have declared our engagement to the village at church on Sunday. I do not appreciate being forced to do anything, whether it be sewing or marrying. The harder I am pushed, the harder I will resist."

"Yes, I realize that now. Eliza, I have liked you since we were children, and I know that we have seen little of each other over the past few years with me away at school, but you have changed, have grown up so beautifully, and I was just overwhelmed when I returned after graduation to see that you were not a girl anymore. I found myself very drawn to you." He stepped a little closer. "All I ask Eliza is that you give me a chance. I will stop pushing. I will tell my mother to stop. I know that you are angry with Charlotte for telling us what she heard about your mother's wishes for you with Mr. Darcy when he comes, but she hopes for you to be her sister."

Elizabeth waved away his statement. "She is looking out for her future. That is all. She worries that you will throw her from the house when your father dies. Would you truly do such a thing? Why would she worry so about that?"

He kept his eyes on hers. "I would let my wife decide."

Elizabeth closed hers to break the contact then looked away. "You can not divorce yourself from your family when you marry. I expect whoever marries me to accept that my parents and sisters do exist, and may someday need our help, even if they do not live with us."

"I would do that, Eliza." He assured her.

She shook her head and studied him. "How can I believe that when your own sister is unsure of her fate? Why do you pursue me, Mr. Lucas?"

He smiled. "There is something about you that I can not name." He lifted his hand as if to touch the long curls resting on her shoulder, but stopped when he saw her flinch. He sighed. "Tell me I have a chance. Give me the opportunity to redeem myself."

More than anything in the world she wished to tell him that she was attached to William, but could not. He had made no offer, and she certainly could not expose him to censure by speaking of their letters. She was helpless. "Mr. Lucas, I can offer no hope."

His temper rose. "You are hoping for Mr. Darcy. You truly think that he will want you?"

Elizabeth's eyes flashed. "I expect nothing from him!"

"Then what is it? Why will you wait for him, a stranger, and not me, a man you have known all of your life??" He began to pace, then stopped. "Do you wish to have men fighting over you? Is that the game you are playing?"

"Mr. Lucas!"

"Eliza, I will do as you wish. I will take on this Mr. Darcy. I will win. You will be mine." He walked up and stood inches from her and breathed raggedly. His eyes travelled to her mouth. She shivered, not knowing what to do. With a groan he took possession of the gloved hand that was resting protectively over her chest and kissed it. He stared into her eyes again and turned to mount his horse. "I promise Eliza, I will make you want me." He kicked the horse and was soon gone.

Elizabeth finally let the breath go she was holding and moved from her frozen state, reaching out for support from the fence. She attempted to calm herself and whispered. "Oh William, please come soon."

———❦———

"May I speak to you?" Richard asked quietly. It was the morning after the family confrontation. Darcy chose to eat a quiet dinner alone the night before, and had not spoken to anyone since leaving the chapel. He stood and regarded his cousin in silence. Richard shifted uncomfortably. "You are as much my brother as James. I have no desire to be estranged from you. I just . . . Darcy you can not understand how shocking it was to see you in that wild state. Never have I thought you could fall so low, and when I realized it was caused by a woman . . . you and a woman . . . forgive me Darcy . . . I found it difficult to feel charitable towards her."

Darcy stared into his eyes. "And now?"

"And now I would like to hear . . . anything you have to tell me." He met his stare. "Please."

Darcy relaxed slightly and indicated the study door. Richard breathed out his tension and stepped past his glowering cousin. They sat down and Richard noticed that Darcy once again wrapped the yellow ribbon around his fingers. "Richard, never let me hear you speak against Miss Elizabeth again. I *will* marry her."

"You have never been drawn to any woman, Darcy. You have been pursued since you came of age. I should have known that you would know the difference between true regard and a fortune hunter. Can you understand our reaction, though? This girl is . . . from a different circle . . ."

He watched him struggle and finally relented. "All right Richard, enough. I know very well that Miss Elizabeth is not from our circle. I know that she likely has no significant dowry or connections. But since I have watched Georgiana's treatment by these so-called models of society, I no longer measure a person's value by their status, but rather by their character." *Something Elizabeth taught me.*

Richard nodded. "I can accept that." He considered the situation. "You know that Mother and Father feel that if you were to marry a . . . favoured woman of society it would be beneficial to Georgiana's future."

"I do, and as recently as a fortnight ago, I may have agreed or rather, forced myself to settle for such an arrangement. In fact, that conflict between Georgiana and my own wishes caused a great deal of pain for me. I debated the problem and realized that the best way that I may serve her is to be happy. I believe sincerely that Elizabeth Bennet will bring me the happiness I have missed all of my life."

With an expression akin to wonder, Richard studied Darcy. "I have never heard you speak of happiness before."

"That Cousin is because I did not understand what it was until I was blessed with Miss Elizabeth's friendship."

He sat forward on his chair, his elbows on his knees, as if he were trying to see into his cousin's head. "How did this come about? You saw her for moments before we left. How can you be so sure of your feelings when you have spent no time with her?"

"I observed her for some time in front of the inn with her sisters." He smiled with the memory.

"What did she do?" Richard asked urgently.

Darcy's smile grew. "She had a conversation with a donkey."

"She what?!" Richard stared at him.

Darcy grinned. "You heard me, and no I will not elaborate."   He relaxed. "Richard, I know that I broke every rule of propriety by engaging in a correspondence with her. At the time, I think that, well, I was feeling so raw, that her simple gesture of kindness touched me deeply and I wished for more. The fact that she was willing to engage in the surreptitious exchange told me that she was missing something in her life as well. Our letters began as light, teasing notes, but as time went on, we opened up to each other. I believe we conducted a far more productive courtship in this manner than we ever would if I had been calling on her every afternoon with a nosegay and conversation about the weather. We know more of each other now than I daresay a couple married for convenience would learn in years of proper behaviour. Knowing the little I do just makes me thirst for more. She is intelligent, well-read, and happy. I feel myself going through my day wishing I could tell her what I am doing and asking for her advice. I need her." He ended simply.

"I find it difficult to believe that any woman could be so extraordinary." Darcy internally smiled at his obstinacy while Richard thought about his next statement. "Are you certain, beyond doubt, that she is not playing at some game, pretending friendship to Georgiana simply to become closer to winning you?" He saw the ire appear in Darcy's eyes. "It is a perfectly reasonable question, Darcy. I am Georgiana's guardian as well. If you are blinded by this woman, I must be sure that she is not using both of you for her own plans. I realize that you are experienced in fending them off, but she is so unusual that she might have found a way through your guard. If she is so willing to break with propriety, is there something more in her background that you do not know about? Could an attachment with her make things worse?"

He watched as Darcy reached into his coat and rubbed at his chest while closing his eyes, then removed his hand to again twist the ribbon entwined in his fingers. "I am sure." He opened his eyes. "Georgiana and I will be going to Netherfield to stay with Charles Bingley and his family. There I intend to enter into a formal courtship and make my proposal. I hope to return to Pemberley a married man. If society rejects us, so be it. If you or your parents choose not to support us, we will miss you. Some young man will marry Georgiana, and as long as they love each other and he can support her, I will not question his status. Society has already declared her ruined, so why should we dance to their tune? We have more than enough here without them, and I know how to make Pemberley grow. Miss Elizabeth will not miss what she never has experienced or expected. My decision is made. What is yours?"

"I would like to reserve my decision until after I have met her."

Darcy nodded. "That is reasonable and fair. If I am successfully married by Christmas, you and the rest of the family will be invited here."

"I would like to repeat this conversation to my parents and James." Darcy waved his hand to the door. Richard stood and walked from the room. Darcy felt oddly complacent. His decision was irrevocably made. He resumed the work he started the day before and it was over an hour later that a footman brought a note requesting his company. He shook his head at it and sighed, preparing for the attack.

"Darcy." Lord Matlock came forward and held out his hand. Darcy looked down at the offered hand then back up to his uncle and saw sincerity. He briefly clasped his hand and remained standing as his uncle resumed his seat. "We have been discussing your . . . choice. We understand your anger with society. You have endured more than enough to justify your position. We still feel that a marriage with a woman from our circle would be greatly beneficial to you and that marrying so far below yourself will likely cause more unwanted talk, possibly describing you as unmarriageable to anyone better by those disappointed in losing you."

"I am sure that would have been the case regardless of who I married. There was bound to be someone disappointed. Too many have chased me for too long."

"I will concede that point." He sighed. "Darcy, we all wish you to be happy. We know, well we can not truly know, but we have a fair idea of your childhood . . ."

"Uncle, I do not expect you to hold a ball in our honour. I do not expect any social obligations at all. What I would like is that you give Miss Elizabeth a chance, and when in company, treat her with civility. I expect nothing from Aunt Catherine, but I hope at least that from you. Miss Elizabeth knows of everything that has happened with Georgiana, and I intend to speak to her father about it. It is hardly a secret in London, and he deserves to know. I would hope that the news not be spread in Meryton while we are there, simply to give Georgiana an opportunity to make friends. She has come such a long way since June, and no little reason for that is due to Miss Elizabeth's care and encouragement. What better sister could I have found for her?" He sighed. "Richard said that he would reserve his opinion until he meets her. Perhaps you could do the same. In truth, I do not need your approval."

Lady Matlock stood and walked to stand before him. "I understand that you have invited us for Christmas."

He nodded. "I have, I hope to have Miss Elizabeth by my side."

"And your wedding?"

"You would come?" He looked at her with surprise.

Richard spoke. "I must return to London soon, but it is near enough to Hertfordshire that I could easily come for a few days and meet her. Mother and Father have agreed to accept my judgment. If I find that Miss Elizabeth is all that you believe, and that you have not been taken in by a . . . woman unworthy of your regard, I will communicate the fact to them."

Lady Matlock agreed. "You are correct Darcy, you do not require our approval in anything, but, if this woman truly is all that you say, and I admit, I have already seen the difference she has made in both you and Georgiana, perhaps our presence at the wedding would be of some aid in both of your futures. This all depends on Richard's decision. Regardless, we will treat your wife with civility if she shows the same to us and especially, you."

Darcy nodded. "Very well. I will write to you Richard when I feel that the time is right for your presence. I am sure that Bingley will not object at all to your visit. Perhaps it will distract his sister from me." He smiled at Richard's grimace. He looked to his aunt. "I would love to have my family around me at my wedding, no matter the reason."

"Well then. I believe we will depart for Matlock, and leave you to your courtship." Lord Matlock and James stood. Darcy could see that both were very unhappy with the decision, but the fact that they had agreed to it spoke volumes to him of their affection and hopes for him. Georgiana was summoned to say her farewells and soon the two siblings were left alone again.

Charles Bingley watched with great excitement and pride as the servants bustled about, unloading the luggage cart and settling him, his sisters, and his brother Gilbert Hurst into Netherfield. It was finally happening. The first tentative steps to owning an estate had been taken, and so far, all had gone well. Almost as soon as their wagons came to a stop at the front door, he received a call from one of his neighbours, Sir William Lucas and his son John, welcoming him to the neighbourhood, and inviting his party to attend an assembly dance the following Tuesday. Bingley happily accepted the invitation, knowing that Darcy would be arriving the day before with Georgiana. Sir William informed him of his being the parent of two lovely daughters, and of course Bingley exclaimed with delight that he looked forward to meeting them. His task completed, Sir William departed leaving John looking about for the missing man who he considered his competition, and was disappointed upon learning that Darcy had not yet arrived. Bingley returned to the drawing room to the varying degrees of amusement of his family.

"You had better watch yourself, Bingley. I think that the mamas of the neighbourhood have you in their sights!" Hurst laughed.

Bingley smiled. "I think that I will rather enjoy the experience Hurst. In London I am but one of many, and really quite unimportant. But here, ah I will enjoy the display that is meant just for me!"

Caroline rolled her eyes. "Charles, you will not fall in love with a country miss. I forbid it! You were doing quite well in Town."

Bingley shook his head. "Yes, Caroline, anything you say, Caroline." Hurst laughed and the two men set out to find the billiards room while Caroline and Louisa supervised the unpacking. Within the hour the heads of house for six more families paid their respects. Amongst them was Mr. Bennet.

Upon his introduction, Mr. Bennet took a long look at Mr. Bingley. He was handsome, Lizzy was correct. That would please Mrs. Bennet. He had an urge of compassion to warn the man of what his wife had planned, but decided he would prefer to watch it all unfold instead. He looked over the other man. Surely this was not Mr. Darcy? Bingley finished his bow and gestured to his companion. "Mr. Bennet, may I introduce my brother, Mr. Hurst?"

Mr. Bennet bowed. "I am pleased to meet you sir! I was under the impression that you were to host another family, the Darcys."

Bingley grinned. "Ah yes, I understand that your daughter Miss Elizabeth has begun a correspondence with Miss Darcy? They are to arrive Monday afternoon." Mr. Bennet nodded. "Lizzy will be pleased to hear that, the letters that pass between the two are undoubtedly wearing out her brother's messenger, to say nothing of his horse!" The men laughed, and Mr. Bennet departed, looking forward to telling Lizzy of his news.

"I paid a call on Mr. Bingley today." He said casually at dinner.

All conversation ceased and six pairs of female eyes fixed upon him. He said nothing, enjoying the tension. Mrs. Bennet could stand no more. "Well? What did he say? What did he look like? Is he amiable?"

He laughed. "He was gracious and excitable. I suppose he is handsome. Lizzy's description, I think was quite accurate. I met his other guest as well." He watched Elizabeth's face as her breath caught. "A Mr. Hurst." He saw the disappointment and wondered at it. Perhaps there was something in this Mr. Darcy theory of his wife's. "He and his wife, as well as Mr. Bingley's other sister, are in residence." Elizabeth looked sadly at Jane, who squeezed her hand. "Some more guests are expected soon. Mr. Darcy and his sister will arrive Monday." Elizabeth could not hide the delight in her eyes and she smiled with relief. "I thought that would please you, Lizzy. You will see your friend at last."

Elizabeth met his eyes. "Yes, Papa, I look forward very much to finally seeing my friend in person." Mr. Bennet raised his brow and nodded. He knew there was much more meaning in her statement than she let on.

The meal was interrupted by Mrs. Hill. "Miss Elizabeth, the messenger is here." Elizabeth shot up out of her chair and left the room before anyone could draw breath.

Mrs. Bennet watched her disappear. "Well, finally the young men will be here, and my plans will be fulfilled. Now Jane, I am sure Mr. Bingley will attend the assembly on Tuesday. You and Lizzy must come with me into Meryton and we will buy you both new gowns. You must look your best that night." Mrs. Bennet prattled on about dresses and lace while Kitty and Lydia petitioned for their own new things. Mary began to sermonize about the need for female modesty in their dress, and Mr. Bennet watched the door for Elizabeth's return. She missed the rest of the meal.

"Danny!" She came to the door to greet the young man. She stepped out onto the porch, and away from curious ears. "How was your trip?"

He grinned. "Very nice, Miss. I'm learning a few quicker paths here, now!"

She laughed then asked carefully. "And how are the Darcys?"

He bowed his head as he opened his bag. "Mr. Darcy was a sight when I brought your last letter, Miss, but when he gave me this one, I doubt a week of scrubbing could wipe the smile off his face." Elizabeth blushed with pleasure as he retrieved the two envelopes. "He told me to wait as long as necessary for your reply. I'll just head over to the stable and take a rest if you don't mind, Miss."

Elizabeth was weighing the thick envelope and looking at it with curiosity. "Oh yes, please do."

She returned to the house, and avoiding the noisy dining room went upstairs to sit on her bed. She determinedly placed William's letter aside and first opened Georgiana's. The girl's emotion was heartbreaking. She was overwhelmed and grateful that Elizabeth would still wish to be her friend despite her horrible fall. Elizabeth could feel her isolation. Somehow though, Georgiana's sadness struck her, something else was haunting the girl. She wondered what it could be. She amazed Elizabeth by telling her knowledge of William's correspondence. Why would he confess such a secret?

I can not wait to see you Elizabeth. I hope so much that we will have the opportunity to talk. My aunt and my companion have helped, but I have not had the courage to speak with William. I love him so much and he was so unhappy over the past weeks when he thought that you no longer wished him to be your friend. Elizabeth, you must know that William thinks the world of you.
Your friend,
Georgiana

Elizabeth studied the last sentence and wondered what he had told her. She set Georgiana's letter down and nervously retrieved his. Running her fingers over the fine paper, she carefully broke his seal and upon pulling open the sheets, something fell out onto her lap. Looking, her breath caught. It was a lock of his hair, tied in a piece of worn yellow ribbon. It was some minutes before she could control her emotional tears, but when she finally did, she clutched the gift in her hand and read. He was serious at first, describing his fears and torture over her seeming rejection, then he was emotional telling her of his elation when Danny found him and delivered her assurances. Then he was passionate, telling her about his home. He described Pemberley with pride. He asked how she felt about living in the country and if she preferred it to town. He asked if she had an urge to be a part of society, or if she wished to live a quiet life. He told her of his relatives' hopes for his future, and then stated plainly his disagreement. In short, he was asking her if she would like to live at his beloved estate, without the support of society or his family.

In closing, my dearest Elizabeth, my friend, I must tell you that I look forward to seeing you and finally hearing your musical laughter, and gazing upon your incomparable beauty once again. I count the days, and I dearly hope that the friendship that we have begun will only grow when we are at last together. I have great hopes for us.
Yours,
William

Elizabeth read his letter through again, it was difficult to see the paper through her constantly streaming tears. She opened her hand to behold his gift, and stroked the soft black hair, lifting it to brush against her cheek and lips. He had given her a piece of himself to hold and treasure when he was away. Closing her eyes she brushed the feathery token on her face again and imagined that same hair grazing against her as he took her in his arms and bestowed her first kiss. A shiver ran through her at the thought. She practiced kissing him deep in the dark of night, when nobody could hear her whispering to her pillow. Maybe, maybe she would feel his tender touch soon.

She settled at her writing desk, absurdly small for a grown woman in a little girl's room, and wrote him everything that she was feeling at that moment. The paper she sprinkled with the lavender water kept in a bottle on her dressing table, and kissed the envelope before sealing it. She penned a letter to Georgiana assuring her of her willing ear and her fondness for her brother then escaped the house to find Danny, who was sleeping against some hay in the barn. Nudging him awake he blinked sleepily. "Aye Miss, that took a while, but I will be on my way back now." Elizabeth insisted that he stay the night, and he laughingly refused. "Once the master is here, Miss, I imagine I'll be getting caught up on my sleeping." Soon enough he was on his way, with Elizabeth wishing him Godspeed.

Two days later, Darcy finished reading Elizabeth's reply. He drew a deep breath and slowly exhaled. The smile he wore would light up a darkened room.

I believe, my William; that I have addressed your concerns and hope with all of my heart that my responses bring you the happiness you seek. I too count the days until I can see you before me and no longer in my imagination. The day after you arrive there shall be an assembly in Meryton. Shall I be so fortunate to find myself dancing a set or two or more with you? I wait for the feel of your hand holding mine.

    Yours,
    Elizabeth

Darcy looked at the shortened ribbon he clutched in his hand as he read her letter, and hoped she would wear yellow the night he first danced with her. "Oh yes my love, there is no other partner for me but you."

"Mr. Darcy!" Caroline Bingley purred. Darcy nodded and murmured his greeting then quickly sidestepped her, and grasping Georgiana's arm, walked up the stairs to greet Bingley. After the two long days of travel, the last thing he needed to do was bear her attentions.

"Darcy! Welcome! How was your journey? Miss Darcy! You look lovely! Welcome! Come in, come in!" Darcy smiled and looked at his sister whose eyes were wide at Bingley's effusions.

"Thank you, Bingley. Our journey was comfortable." Darcy took Georgiana's arm and escorted her inside.

Caroline and Louisa had made their plans, but they would not put them in motion for a week or so. Until then, they would simply be very kind and sweet to the young girl. "Oh Miss Darcy, come, you must want some tea after that long trip!" Caroline gushed. "How are things at Pemberley; is it still beautiful? I always enjoyed visiting there in August, and was disappointed to not come this year."

Georgiana, always intimidated by the woman who so clearly was chasing her brother could not find her voice. Darcy stepped in. "Miss Bingley, as I knew that Bingley was preparing to take up residence at Netherfield soon, I was sure that the travel to Pemberley would be inconvenient for him." He turned to look at his friend.

"Indeed, I am afraid that I would have had to refuse the invitation Darcy. I was quite overwhelmed by the details." He smiled and gave Darcy a little wink. "Miss Darcy, perhaps you would like to see your chambers and rest a bit before dinner? I put you in a room next to your brother. Caroline could you escort Miss Darcy and her companion upstairs? I would like a word with Darcy." He looked at her pointedly and she smiled.

"Of course, Charles." She began to leave and turned. "Oh, Mr. Darcy, there is an assembly to be held in the village tomorrow evening. I hope that you do not mind, but Charles has already accepted the invitation. I know how you detest such gatherings, so I will be quite pleased to stay behind and keep you company should you choose not to attend." She smiled at Georgiana. "I am sure that you will be remaining behind, as you are not out."

Georgiana looked to Darcy nervously. "Indeed, I would prefer that Georgiana stay here with Mrs. Annesley. I, however; would hardly be a good guest if I did not accompany my host to whatever entertainment he has planned during my stay." Smiling slightly to Bingley he added. "I am sure there are many in the neighbourhood I should meet."

"Oh yes, of course, I was only thinking of your comfort, Mr. Darcy." Caroline's disappointment was fierce. She was positive Darcy would beg off any social engagement, and it would give her a chance to work her wiles on him. She moved to her secondary plan. "I hope to see you dancing then." She batted her eyes.

Darcy kept the slight smile. "I can guarantee that you will see me dance." Sure that he was complementing her she giggled and taking Georgiana's elbow, led her upstairs.

Bingley watched them go and said softly. "I apologize for Caroline, Darcy."

They entered the study and took seats before the fireplace. "For which offence, her barely civil fawning over my sister or her barely concealed pursuit of me?"

Bingley had the grace to appear repentant. "I will speak to her."

"I maintain my stance, Bingley. I will not ever pay Miss Bingley any attentions." He glowered at him.

Bingley nodded. "I believe that she expects that you will be dancing with her."

Darcy's expression changed. "I am afraid that my dance card is full. I shall have a partner." He met Bingley's eye. "I have already been promised any set of my choosing, even if it is every one."

Bingley laughed. "You know that is not possible, Darcy, no matter how much you wish it. How did you know of the dance?"

Darcy smiled enigmatically. "Miss Elizabeth told Georgiana about it. I told her of my interest in securing her as my partner." Bingley studied him and gave up. When Darcy wished to keep a secret, it was impossible to cajole it out of him.

He nodded and said carefully. "I met Mr. Bennet." Bingley laughed at Darcy's instant attention. "Your head will snap off of you move it that quickly again!" Taking pity on him he relented. "He asked after you."

Darcy's eyes grew wide. "What did he say?" Bingley smiled at his friend's sudden anxiety. "He was at first concerned that Hurst was you and seemed relieved to find that he was mistaken." Darcy feigned horror, and Bingley laughed again. "Relax man, he only mentioned Miss Darcy's correspondence with Miss Elizabeth and that she looked forward to seeing her friend."

Darcy nodded. "I hope to know Miss Elizabeth better now that I am here."

"I imagine you have read every letter she sent to Pemberley." Bingley grinned.

"Indeed I have." Darcy smiled. He became serious. "Have you met John Lucas?"

"Sir William's son? Yes, he came here calling when we moved in, paying the respects of the community. I believe that Sir William is actually the host of the assembly tomorrow. Odd man, very friendly, seems particularly thrilled at his knighting, talks incessantly of St. James'. But you asked after the son. He is fresh out of Cambridge I hear, affable, not like his father, actually someone I could enjoy knowing. The father was promoting his two daughters to me and to you as well. They asked after you." He caught the dark look on Darcy's face. "What is it?"

"Miss Elizabeth mentioned something of bearing Mr. Lucas' attentions." Darcy would not be able to say more without exposing their correspondence, something he wished to keep quiet here in Elizabeth's neighbourhood.

Bingley saw his friend's concern. "Darcy, you can hardly be surprised if Miss Elizabeth attracts the attentions of local gentlemen. She is a very lovely young woman." Darcy's sharp stare landed on his friend who quickly held up his hands. "Do not spear me with that gaze, Darcy. I have no designs on Miss Elizabeth. Her sister, however, is a different story." Darcy relaxed. "Miss Bennet?"

"You do know about the family!" He smiled. "I caught sight of her when I returned Mr. Bennet's call. Lovely, simply lovely." Darcy rolled his eyes. *Here he goes again.* "How many this year so far, Bingley?" He attempted to look offended, but failed under Darcy's raised brow. "Oh all right, six. Are you happy now?"

"No, actually I am not. Quite honestly Bingley, if you are to dally here in the countryside, I wish that you would do it with someone other than Miss Bennet. I do not wish her to be hurt by your bad habits."

"You wound me Darcy! What if she is the love of my life?" He smiled that winning smile.

Darcy did not play along, this was his future sister. "I am serious, Bingley. Do not trifle with Miss Bennet. Your sisters would not stand for it, and you know it. They have high hopes for you."

Bingley's smile disappeared. "As I have been frequently reminded." He stood and went to a side table and picked up a heavy cut glass decanter and poured them both some brandy. He handed Darcy his glass and resumed his seat. "I will not ask of your concerns for Miss Bennet, as I am sure they are tied to Miss Elizabeth, and I am sure also that some element of your sister's situation makes you concerned for the well-being of any innocent woman." He paused. "I do, however; feel an uncommon attraction to Miss Bennet and given the opportunity, I would like to pursue it. I promise to not behave as I usually do. I know the difference between a lady and a debutante."

"And what is that difference, Bingley?" He sipped his brandy and looked at him with amusement.

"One, my friend, you dance with, and the other, you marry." He nodded significantly and raised his glass.

Darcy shook his head. "Very well then. By the way, I have it on good authority that Mrs. Bennet has already engaged Miss Bennet to you, so it seems you only need the lady . . ."

Bingley spit out the swallow of brandy he had been taking. "WHAT?" Darcy brushed some droplets from his trousers. "Oh, yes. And I am to marry Miss Elizabeth. Shall we plan on a double ceremony?"

Bingley shook his head and took out his handkerchief to wipe off his topcoat. "That was bad form, Darcy." He smiled. "But it is good to see you feeling better. This time away has been beneficial to you."

"Yes, in some ways it has been, but I am anxious to begin again." He stood. "I think I will change and relax before dinner." He looked over the spotted cravat his friend wore. "Perhaps you should do the same?" He laughed as he dodged the chair cushion thrown his way.

Darcy found his assigned chambers and Roberts laying out his dinner clothes. He sat down near the window and closed his eyes, thinking over the little bit of information Bingley had given him. He was almost positive that Elizabeth was his; she had practically said yes with her response, all he needed to do was ask. He looked out over the fields towards Longbourn and his future. "Until tomorrow, my love."

Chapter 12

*D*arcy awoke at dawn. He was alive with anticipation, and nothing would stop him from rising, dressing, and saddling his horse to ride off through the lightly frosted grass in a certain direction, the one that he knew drew him closer to Elizabeth. After the dinner and entertainment by Bingley's sisters the night before, he pled fatigue from the journey and escorted Georgiana upstairs early. When the sun showed its first hint of light across the sky, he was already anticipating its setting that evening, and in whose company he would be. He needed to somehow be near her. Taking the one trail he remembered from his last visit, he soon found himself approaching the fence line where he last beheld her and there, to his utter surprise and delight, he found her again. It could be no other. No young lady he had ever known would walk unescorted in the early morning light. Only Elizabeth; and he was grateful for it.

Hearing a horse approaching, Elizabeth turned and her breath caught. There was no mistaking the tall man. His carriage was assured, his gaze penetrating. She could not have moved even if she wished it. She felt captured. Darcy halted the animal and leapt down, rapidly throwing his reins over the fence rail. He stepped up before her, and they stood staring at each other. There was so much to say.

Darcy moved first. He removed his gloves and looking deeply into her eyes, he reached up to brush an errant curl from her cheek, shuddering with his first touch of her warm skin. "Elizabeth."

She felt her eyes filling with tears, and whispered. "William."

His eyes had become equally moist. His hand dropped to take hers, and slowly he tugged the fingers of her gloves, finally pulling them free. Tucking them into the pocket of his greatcoat, he took her small hands in his, pressing and enveloping them between his own, stroking gently, conveying the emotion he felt so deeply.

Looking up he saw her flushed cheeks and how her eyes never stirred from observing his unceasing movement. Her lips parted and he could feel the increase in her breathing as he watched. Her eyes lifted again to his and they became lost in the gaze. Darcy gently released her hands and lifted his to cup her face, just the way he had imagined. Elizabeth pressed her palms to his chest and he stepped forward to close the gap between them. They were almost touching. Darcy ran his thumb along her lower lip, felt her tremble, slowly bent his head while lifting her face and brushed his mouth to hers. He paused, looking into her eyes and seeing them close, he caressed her mouth again, and again, then tenderly traced his tongue across the soft, full lips as she responded by parting them in welcome. Without hesitation he deepened the kiss, and moved one hand to remove the bonnet and bury in her hair, the other dropping down to encircle her waist and draw her firmly to his heated body.

His kisses grew in intensity, abandoning the gentle caress and now exposing the raw edge of his passion. He felt her mouth begin to move with his, learning how to respond. Her acceptance only made his demand stronger, and his tongue entered her mouth to touch and stroke, and was met with the same fervent response from her. He felt her arms wrap tightly around his waist as she moulded her body to his. They kissed, moving their lips to taste each other's faces. His mouth trailed down her neck to feel the pounding pulse, and he forced himself not to suckle her, not wishing to leave a mark, no matter how deeply he longed to brand his body onto hers. Instead his lips returned to hers and his hands possessively stroked her back as he felt her hands run over his. He had never felt so desired.

Without letting go, he moved to kiss her ear. His warm breath filled it and his whisper sent a shiver straight to her toes. "Be mine, Elizabeth. Always."

Her heart pounding, she tried to focus on his meaning. "Yours?" She managed to breathe out.

"Yes, Elizabeth. Please, there will never be anyone but you. I love you. I need you. Be my wife."

"Oh William." She whispered.

"Does that mean yes?" He asked as his lips scattered kisses over her face.

"Yes, my love, yes."

His happiness was displayed by his mouth recapturing hers and kissing her so deeply she nearly succumbed, and wished it would never end. He finally pulled away and breathing hard, he again took her face in his hands. Elizabeth stared into his passionate, searching blue eyes. "You did say yes, you will be my wife?"

She smiled and his heart soared. "Yes, William. I love you. I will be yours."

Darcy lifted her and spun her around, making her squeal with delight. She heard for the first time his deep chuckle which became a laugh of unquestioned elation. She saw a huge, delighted smile, and she sensed that this was an exceptionally rare sight. Knowing that she was the one who drew such emotion from him only made her love him more. She laughed and his soul flew, for the first time knowing joy. He set her down and hugged her. Kissing her lips, he could not hold back the grin. "Perhaps I should have begun by wishing you a good morning."

Elizabeth smiled brilliantly and lovingly ran her fingers through his hair, laughing at his contented sigh. "I believe sir, that you did most impressively."

"Elizabeth." His smile disappeared and his voice shook with emotion. Her happy tears began to flow and possessively he gathered her to him and again their lips met, already their kisses felt like home. He drew away to rest his cheek on her head, and felt her sigh as she nestled against his chest. "I love you." Darcy whispered into her fragrant hair.

"I love you, William."

His embrace tightened. "Why is it that I feel as if we have been together forever instead of mere minutes?" He closed his eyes, realizing that this was the first time anyone had ever held him.

"I think that you know more of me than anyone." Elizabeth confessed.

"I think that we were able to be honest in our letters in a way that we could never have been in your mother's drawing room." He kissed her hair and heard her soft laugh. Looking down he smiled slightly. "What is it?"

Her eyes danced. "Oh William, I dread you meeting Mama."

"From what I understand, she will welcome me with open arms. Is that to be dreaded?" He became lost in her beautiful gaze, and then grew concerned when her expression changed to worry.

"She will embarrass me, and likely mortify you. Please do not hold my family against me."

Darcy relaxed and kissed her nose. "I can hardly do that when I have already told you of my family's concerns, although, they did improve after I wrote you."

She rose up on her toes and kissed his chin. "How did it improve?"

His mouth brushed her warm cheek. "My cousin Richard wishes to come here and meet you . . ."

He felt her smile grow under his lips. "Ah, and send his extensive report back home."

Darcy drew back and saw a delicately arched eyebrow. "Yes, to gain their support and have them present at our wedding . . . well, it may help us down the line." He watched carefully for her reaction.

Elizabeth regarded him seriously. "William, I wrote you that I do not care if we ever participate in the activities of London. I have only been there to visit my Aunt and Uncle Gardiner, and they hardly move in the same circles as your family. In all honesty, it will worry me to face the society of London regardless of the circumstances. I would do my best for your sake, but I would be so concerned of embarrassing you."

He kissed her wrinkled brow. "What worries you so? I have the impression that you would be quite the formidable woman in the presence of the cats of the *ton.*"

Elizabeth had to smile at that. "Thank you for your confidence. I think that I would be not so much intimidated by the women; I can hold my own particularly if someone were to be blatantly rude, but truly I have very little experience with . . ." She sighed. "Well, all that you likely learned in your cradle." She looked up at him, seeing him trying to understand.

"You lack confidence because you have never been in those situations and do not know how you would perform. Is that it?"

She nodded and traced her fingers over his cheek. "I also have the unfortunate knowledge of what those people have done to Georgiana."

Darcy pulled her close and gave her a reassuring squeeze. "Well, when that time comes, I assure you that I will be by your side. In all likelihood, as with my supposed downfall after Georgiana's ruination, my status will eventually bring me back into the good graces of society no matter what I do or whom I marry. Hopefully my family, despite their current concerns, will help to guide you."

She gave him a small smile. "I would like to be accepted by your family."

Darcy saw worry cross her brow, and knew she was thinking of their objections. "I have told them that I will only marry for affection and love. They have had a difficult time understanding that. You see, most marriages in my circle are based on less emotional issues."

"Connection and wealth."

He nodded. "My own parents did not marry for affection, rather it was . . ." He put his head down.

Elizabeth stroked the fringe of hair that fell across his face. "You can tell me anything, my love."

Darcy turned to kiss the hand that caressed him. "My parents were very unhappy; it was a very difficult situation." He shook his head. "No, I will not mar this moment with terrible memories." She reached up again to touch his hair and he felt her hand wander to the back of his head. Darcy closed his eyes and sank into her gentle touch. "What are you doing?"

"Seeing where you cut your hair, ah, there it is!" She smiled. "Did you do that yourself?" He nodded, smiling shyly at her. "And did your valet notice?"

He chuckled. "I heard nothing but I did notice a pause when he rinsed my hair the first time."

She laughed then became very serious. "I can not begin to tell you how much I treasure your gift."

He swallowed hard and whispered. "Thank you." They kissed and leaned their foreheads together.

"What on earth did you do to my ribbon?"

He laughed softly, amazed with her movement from serious subjects to light hearted in barely a breath. "I hold it when I need you." He watched as her eyes instantly expressed her feelings.

"Oh my."

They kissed again and the wind blew, sending a shiver through her. The air was growing cooler even as the sun rose. Without a word, Darcy unbuttoned his greatcoat and pulled her inside, wrapping the heavy wool around her. Lowering his head, he lovingly kissed her again.

"It occurs to me that a short engagement is in order." Darcy whispered. Her soft laugh roused him and he lifted his head to seek her eyes. "You do not agree?"

"Oh William, how can we have a short engagement when as far as anyone, particularly my father, knows, we have only met twice briefly? I am afraid we must suffer a courtship for a little while."

He closed his eyes and groaned. "Oh no, Elizabeth! Now that I have held you, I am to go back to praying for a chance to touch your hand? How am I to survive?" He looked miserable.

"I do not look forward to it any more than you do, sir." She stared at him pointedly.

"Well, I am very pleased to know I will not suffer alone." He stole a kiss. "Extraordinarily pleased."

Before he could return to his preferred activity Elizabeth spoke. "Could you bear a month? Perhaps tomorrow you could come and speak to Papa, and then after a month we could officially be engaged. I admit we probably should try courting in the same room for a change. Just to be sure that we truly are compatible." She lifted her brow as she teased.

"There is no doubt in my mind of that." Darcy growled and recaptured her mouth for several intense moments. Sighing he pulled away and again rested his cheek on her head. "Very well, I actually had not planned on proposing the instant that I saw you, and I did expect that we would court formally." Then looking down at her, the only expression on his face was the twinkle in his eyes. "I will present my suit to your father after a magical night of dancing, where I was enchanted by you . . ."

"And I was swept off of my feet by you . . ."

"And we will be officially engaged in one month . . ."

"And marry . . ."

"No more than one month later." He regarded her with great seriousness. "I will wait no longer, and I wish you at Pemberley for Christmas. Agreed?" His blue eyes searched her warm hazel gaze and she smiled with her first glimpse of the commanding master of Pemberley.

"Agreed." He nodded and sealed the bargain with many more kisses.

"I should probably be returning home. My family will rise soon." The regret was clear in her voice.

Darcy obstinately refused. "No, Elizabeth. I have waited far too long to see you, and we have too much to discuss. Once our courtship is official, who knows when we will be allowed this privilege again?" Darcy purposefully tightened his embrace. He whispered seductively in her ear. "Come, there must be some comfortable place nearby where we can rest and talk. I have many things I wish to say to you."

Elizabeth was very pleased with his resistance but needed to ask. "Will Georgiana miss you?"

"I hope so!" He smiled at her laugh. "Mrs. Annesley will look after her and keep Miss Bingley and Mrs. Hurst from bothering her." Seeing her confusion he continued. "Miss Bingley has been quite determined to be mistress of Pemberley for several years now. It is obvious to all but apparently her, that it will never happen. If ever there was a determined fortune hunter, it was she."

Elizabeth laughed. "Should I be worried about you living under the same roof with such a single-minded woman?"

Darcy kissed her then rubbed his nose with hers. "I lock my door whenever she is about." She nestled her face on his chest and giggled. Darcy drank in her dancing eyes and rosy cheeks. It felt so good to have such joy in his arms. They finally drew apart and Elizabeth leaned over to retrieve her bonnet and his fallen hat while Darcy untethered his horse. Holding hands she led him to a secluded patch of trees, and disappearing into the growth, she indicated a path for them to follow. He led the horse in far enough so no passer-by would notice him, tied the reins off and following the impatient tug of her hand, he laughed and obeyed her command to move. The path wound about for a short way then turned around an ancient oak tree where they came upon a stream. Protected from the breeze, it was warmer amongst the trees. Darcy removed his coat and spread it on the ground to make a blanket for them.

"Oh William, it will be ruined!"

He laughed. "It will require a good brushing perhaps, but will hardly be ruined. The ground is not wet here." He sat down and held out his arms. "Come, my love." Laughing she accepted his aid and sat beside him, cuddled to his chest. He wrapped her up in his arms again, kissing her forehead. "Elizabeth, I have never experienced . . . never expressed . . . never knew that I could feel . . ." He sighed with frustration. He had been doing so well speaking to her without tripping over his tongue. Shaking his head he met her fine eyes. "I am very poor with conversation. I do not know what to say, I have a difficult time . . . blast!" He saw her surprise. "Forgive me. I just become so angry with myself. I want to tell you so many things but I have never. . ." He cast his eyes back down and took her hand, caressing it.

"You have never had anyone to talk to about your feelings before?" She asked softly. He nodded. "Well, perhaps when you are a little more comfortable with me it will become easier."

His head snapped up. "But I am comfortable with you! It is not you, it is . . ." He closed his eyes.

"You are shy." She squeezed his hand.

"I suppose I am. A trait you will see in my sister as well."

Elizabeth decided a change in subject was necessary. "William, in Georgiana's last letter, she seemed somehow sad. Was it because of your family's objections to our union?"

Relieved to talk about something that did not require opening his soul he answered. "I am sure their words likely have contributed to her worry. But I have assured her that whatever our relatives, or for that matter, society says, I will marry no other but you." Elizabeth blushed and looked down. Darcy appreciated her obvious pleasure in his declaration. "Georgiana has also said that she is delighted you will be her sister. What I think bothers her is learning that she may not be my father's daughter."

Elizabeth gasped. "You mean that your mother conducted . . ."

Darcy nodded. "As did my father. It was not a happy marriage." He closed his eyes as a memory intruded. He felt Elizabeth's arms holding him and her simple gesture was something that he realized immediately he had craved for a very long time. "Thank you." She did not press him about it further, remembering the letter from her aunt. After some moments in silence he continued. "I assured her that she is as much a Darcy as I am, but my relatives said that it was up to me to produce an heir. You see, I had previously planned to never marry and leave the heir to Georgiana. Now that her future is in doubt, and there is apparently a good chance that she is not of Darcy blood, they were pushing me to marry a woman of the first circles as soon as possible. They argued quite strongly against you. They felt that marrying a woman of society would aid both of us in retrieving our reputations, and that marrying you would make everything worse." He saw the hurt in her eyes. "I am so sorry Elizabeth, I told you of this in my letter, perhaps I was not as explicit . . . but you deserve to know exactly what their objections are based upon." He hugged her to him. "They have always expected a different fate for me."

Elizabeth pulled away, leaving him confused. "I wonder if you would have spared me a second glance if you had not already been rejected by the *ton*. Will you find me, a simple country girl, enough to satisfy you forever? As well as I think of myself, I am aware of my deficiencies. I do not wish to wake up one morning to find that my husband regrets his choice."

"I do not know what I can say to reassure you of my confidence. I have lived in society for ten years. I know what it has to offer . . . and then I met you. I forced myself to consider my behaviour of the past towards those in other circles. I hope most sincerely that I would have approached you regardless of my state of acceptance in society."

She studied him, still feeling hurt. "I would not have been worthy of your attentions, at least not the attentions of a suitor. Perhaps I would have been good enough for a tryst." Her eyes burned into his.

Alarmed by her obvious anger he quickly tried to explain. "Elizabeth, I admit, I have experienced a great change in my way of thinking of others since witnessing Georgiana's shunning. I have never been a great participant in society. I hate large social gatherings, I am terrible with conversations with no substance, and I can not pretend interest in society's activities. I grew up witnessing the devastating effects of an arranged marriage based on need rather than affection and determined never to subject myself to such a circumstance. I now base my opinion of others on their character rather than their status, as I know you do . . . I have never in my life conducted a . . . tryst . . . as you call it, with any gentlewoman simply because I could. I never would have come here and attempted such an experience with you. I truly wish to believe that had I come here without this event ever happening to Georgiana, I would have met you and been swept off my feet." He wrapped a finger around a curl and studied her face as her gaze softened. "Why do you say such things?"

She looked down and felt terrible for the pain she heard in his voice. "Forgive me William, I am feeling unnecessarily insecure, and lashing out at you for your family's understandable objections. You see . . . it was recently suggested to me that you and Mr. Bingley would only wish to engage a country girls' attentions for momentary pleasure, and then leave the neighbourhood to return to the ladies of society."

Darcy closed his eyes, already knowing the answer to the question. "Who suggested this to you?"

"John Lucas." She said softly.

Darcy's anger and jealousy rose. "And on what occasion did he have the opportunity to bestow such wisdom?"

"On several occasions." She saw his blue eyes turn black with anger and quickly continued. "He heard of Mama's desire to pair me off with you, and Jane with Mr. Bingley. He has told me many times that you would only wish me for your pleasure. When he asked if I would give him hope and I refused, he became angry and said that I was trying to win the attentions of two men and swore that he would win me in the end."

Darcy swore under his breath, and pulled Elizabeth back to him, his intense gaze searched her face. "And do you wish for men to fight over you?"

She placed her hands on his cheeks, reassuring him. "No, I told him to find his future elsewhere. I so wanted to tell him that I loved you, but I could not then, there was no agreement between us."

Darcy kissed her, lifting her onto his lap and possessively to his chest. His hands held her firmly and his voice filled her ear with a terse promise. "I protect what is mine." His tight clutch communicated more to her than anything he could say. Elizabeth turned to softly kiss his cheek, and gently ran her fingers through his hair. Without opening his eyes, his lips sought hers and they joined in a slow exchange, relieving the tension of the conversation and returning them to the indisputable joy of their promise to marry. Darcy's hands gently stroked her back and he hugged her. "I need you, Elizabeth. I wish I knew how to tell you, show you . . ."

"You have dearest, with every touch, and every word. We just need to be together now." She very softly suckled his lower lip and he groaned. "I think that talking in person will be much more productive than letters." Her dancing eyes met his passion-drugged gaze.

"You, my love, are a temptress." He growled as he bent to reclaim her mouth.

The sound of a gun startled them. "We should return." She whispered. This was dangerous, and he knew it. Hunters were near, and they could be so easily discovered. He nodded reluctantly and she stood, touching her hair, readjusting the pins, and carefully fixing her bonnet over the dislodged curls. He brushed off his coat, put it back on and replaced his hat.

He placed his hands on her shoulders. "I love you, Elizabeth. I will take care of you, whether it be relatives, unwanted suitors, or errant hunters."

She smiled. "I love you, William, and I trust you." He smiled with the honour. Her eyes sparkled as she reached into his greatcoat pocket.

"What are you doing?"

"Retrieving my gloves." His hand instantly dropped and trapped hers in the pocket.

"No."

Elizabeth looked at him with disbelief. "William, I can not walk into Longbourn without my gloves!" He smiled slightly, but his eyes were twinkling, and he shook his head slowly. "Fitzwilliam Darcy!"

"No. I want a keepsake of this moment. I will buy you a dozen more, but I want this pair. They are the last things that touched your hand before you gave it to me." His voice was deep and hoarse, and it sent a shiver down Elizabeth's back. She withdrew her hand from his pocket, and he took both of her hands in his, stroking them and lifting first one, then the other to his lips. "Thank you." Elizabeth removed her hands from his grasp and slipped her arms around his waist. Darcy's arms surrounded her and they stood embraced in silent communion for a few more precious moments.

They made their way back to his horse, and before leaving the cover of the trees indulged in a last sweet kiss then stepped back out into the meadow. Darcy walked with her to Longbourn as far as he could before they might be seen. He extracted a promise from her to include riding lessons and morning walks as part of their courtship. He demanded all of her dances that night and Elizabeth laughed, promising three, the first, supper and last. She knew what it would signal to the neighbourhood, and was thrilled about it. Reluctantly they finally parted; both instantly feeling the loss.

～∿～

By the time that Elizabeth returned to Longbourn, it was nearly ten o'clock. She had been gone for almost four hours. She crept into the house, hearing the family at breakfast. Removing her bonnet and pelisse, she looked into a mirror, fixing her hair and seeking any sign of Darcy's attentions. She saw nothing amiss, so taking a breath, smiled and entered the dining room. "LIZZY BENNET! WHERE HAVE YOU BEEN?!" Mrs. Bennet's screech filled the air and brought all activity to a sudden stop. "Out wandering the fields? Today?! You know the assembly is today. Oh my poor nerves! What will I do with such an ungrateful child! You will meet Mr. Darcy tonight! You must look your best, and where are you, at breakfast with your family? No, out trying to climb a tree or a mountain. If you had twisted your ankle I would never have forgiven you!!"

"I am sorry Mama, I did not think I would be gone so long, it was such a lovely morning that I am afraid I forgot the time." She slipped into her seat next to her father who was regarding her carefully. Jane sat across from her and stared with wide eyes. Elizabeth worriedly wondered if she had missed something when she looked in the mirror.

"I expect you to stay in this house for the rest of the day. You must bathe and wash your hair. Your new gown will be here by noon, and I want you and Jane to be ready first." She turned to Jane. "Of course dear Jane you will be lovely in no time, you require very little help to prepare, but you know that Lizzy needs every extra moment of Susie's time."

Jane looked away from Elizabeth and murmured. "Yes, Mama." Elizabeth closed her eyes in frustration. She wondered if she would ever do anything that would earn her mother's praise. She opened them to see her father.

"You will be lovely I am sure, Lizzy. Pay her no mind."

She gave him a small smile. "It is difficult sometimes." He nodded. "Come and visit with me before you dress this evening." She nodded, and glancing at Jane she hurriedly ate while the rest of the family finished their meal and departed. Elizabeth escaped her mother's fluttering and ran upstairs where she found Jane in her room, sorting through her hair combs. "Jane!" She whispered excitedly.

"Lizzy, what is it?" Jane took her hands and laughed as she pulled her down onto the bed. Elizabeth started to speak, then jumped up to close and lock the door. She ran back to the bed and threw her arms around Jane. She whispered excitedly in her ear. "Oh Jane, he proposed!"

"What??!!" She pulled back. "Who?"

"Shhh!" Elizabeth pressed her hand against her mouth. "William . . . Mr. Darcy. I was walking and he was riding and we kissed and he asked me to marry him and he will ask father to court me tomorrow and . . ."

"Lizzy!" Jane whispered urgently. "Calm down!!"

Elizabeth caught her breath then lay back on the bed, clutching a pillow and remembering William's body pressed to hers. Jane lay beside her. "Now slowly, please. You saw Mr. Darcy this morning when you were walking . . . and he asked for your hand?"

"Yes!" She beamed.

"Oh my!" She smiled in surprise and delight. "He kissed you?" She whispered.

"Oh, yes." Her smile became dreamy.

"Lizzy!" Elizabeth turned to her. "Oh and you would not kiss the man you love when he wraps you in his arms and begs you to marry him."

Jane's eyes widened. "Is that what he did?"

Elizabeth cried joyously. "Oh yes, Jane, yes!"

"Oh Lizzy." She sighed. "But . . ."

Elizabeth interrupted. "We agreed to keep it secret and conduct a courtship for a month. He will speak to Papa tomorrow."

Jane smiled. "You have thought of everything, it seems. Mama's worry is for nothing."

Elizabeth closed her eyes and sighed. "Jane, did I look different when I came in?"

Jane nodded. "Yes, you did. I could not put my finger on it then, but now Lizzy, I would say that you are glowing."

She laughed. "I am." The sisters spent the rest of the morning talking of most of what happened between Elizabeth and Darcy. Some secrets Elizabeth reserved for herself.

Darcy returned to Netherfield in a state of happiness he could not remember ever experiencing before. He swung down from his horse and caught a glimpse at his reflection in the water trough and was taken aback to see a grinning fool staring back at him. He rubbed his face, feeling muscles he never knew he possessed beginning to ache. He laughed softly and taking a breath, made a concerted effort to school his features back to their normal state of solemn seriousness. He thought he was successful until entering the house and meeting Bingley.

"Darcy, there you are! I was going to propose a hunting party this morning and learned that you took an early ride. Where have you . . ." He stopped and studied his friend.

Darcy's brow creased. "What is it?"

Bingley turned to a passing servant. "Have a breakfast tray sent up to Mr. Darcy's room." He gave his friend a grin and taking his arm hustled him towards the stairs.

"Bingley!" They ascended the stairs, fortunately avoiding the ladies of the house and Bingley opened the chamber door, pulling Darcy in.

Roberts appeared. "Sir, will you like your bath now?"

Darcy removed his gloves and hat and looked to Bingley. "Well Bingley, tell me, shall I bathe?"

He smirked and nodded to Roberts. "He will be ready to bathe in a half hour, and I have already requested a tray." Roberts looked between the men and retreated to the dressing room, closing the door. Bingley shut the chamber door and stood with his arms crossed, a huge grin on his face. "You saw Miss Elizabeth?"

Darcy was stunned and sat down. "You can tell?"

Bingley laughed and took another chair. "It is all in your eyes, man. I would daresay you could hide it from my sisters, but not yours and I have made a study of your face for years now. I can see an expression I have noticed only rarely on you, the last time was the day that we came to look over Netherfield." Darcy stood to look at his face. Bingley was correct. His expression was normal, but his eyes were alive. He turned back and broke out a smile. Bingley jumped up and shook his hand. "Tell me about it, my friend!"

Darcy sat down and sighed. "Yes, I saw her. I went riding towards Longbourn and there she was, walking in the light of dawn. I stopped, we talked." He did not elaborate.

"And?" Bingley prodded.

Darcy smiled. "I will be speaking to her father tomorrow about our courtship."

"Well done, Darcy!!" He shook his head. "You move quickly, man. Why you barely know the girl!" Darcy flushed. "I always thought you would jump on the opportunity when the right girl came along, damned if you did not!" He laughed as Darcy pulled out the ribbon and began twisting it. "A token?"

He startled and began to hide it and sighed. "Yes. And Bingley, I will not elaborate, but Miss Elizabeth and I do know each other very well. This is not the work of a moment."

Bingley's brows rose with his curiosity, but he knew not to push. He nodded. "Very well, I am sure that whatever is between you two was done with just this result in mind. If there was ever a man I would trust with my sister . . ." Darcy looked at him in alarm. Bingley laughed. "Well, you know what I mean." Darcy shook his head with a small smile. "So, what can you tell me?"

He settled back in the chair. "She is beautiful."

Bingley suppressed a laugh. "You sound like me."

Darcy smiled. "No, then I would be calling her an angel."

This time Bingley did laugh. "Touché!"

"We talked; we spoke of my family's objections to her." Bingley's brows rose to hear that this truly was not a spur of the moment decision. "We spoke of her other suitor." Darcy's countenance clouded and he looked up to his friend's concerned face. "John Lucas. He has been quite persistent, and from what I could tell, has both angered and worried Miss Elizabeth."

Bingley was surprised. "He seems very affable. What has he done?"

"He outright told her that he would win her from me." Darcy's eyes turned black. "That is impossible."

"Well, as his father is more or less hosting the assembly tonight, he will undoubtedly be there."

Darcy nodded. "I hope that we will arrive on time. I do not wish to leave Miss Elizabeth alone with him." Bingley thought to remind him that there would likely be scores of people there, but knew not to argue with a jealous man.

"There is no other reason you would wish to be on time?" He smiled.

Darcy met his smile with one of his own. "Well, I do have a partner for the first set."

Bingley laughed. "Ah, you do have it bad. Imagine; Fitzwilliam Darcy concerned about arriving on time to a dance!" He stood and offered his hand. Darcy stood and they shook. "Congratulations, Darcy. I only met her briefly, but I knew even then that she was a lovely woman. I hope you will be very happy."

"I will, and I thank you." He looked down and sighed. "Please do not say anything to your family. I would prefer to leave our courtship a secret until I have spoken with her father."

Bingley opened the chamber door and waved on his way out. "Have no fear, but you had better decide what you will say to your sister. That, or hide your face from her for the rest of the day!" He grinned and closed the door behind him.

Darcy watched the door close and sat back down in the chair. He was not sure why he did not tell Bingley that he was, in fact, engaged to be married, but somehow he just did not want his friend to know yet. He did not wish to tell Georgiana either. She knew full well his ultimate intentions, but they still had not spoken of what happened with Wickham. He had already broken the rules of propriety with their letters, and he somehow felt that he needed to set some sort of an example for her. The seemingly sudden courtship would be hard enough to explain to the neighbourhood, let alone if the news was of an engagement. If Georgiana did notice his unusual happiness, he was sure that she would just decide it was due to his being near Elizabeth again. He did dearly need to tell someone though.

Roberts knocked and re-entered the room. "Sir, your bath is ready and the tray has just arrived." Darcy looked up and saw the man who knew him more intimately than any other, and knew he could trust him.

"Thank you Roberts." He watched as the man bent to remove his boots. "Roberts, I have some news, but it is not to be discussed with anyone."

He stood and set the boots down. "Yes sir?"

Darcy drew a breath. "I am engaged to be married."

The servant's eyes widened. "Truly sir? I had no idea that you were courting . . . pardon me sir!" He cast his eyes down. Then biting his lip he asked. "May I ask the lady's name, sir?"

Darcy smiled. "Miss Elizabeth Bennet."

Robert's eyes came up. "Not Miss Bingley?" Then seeing the horror in his master's face he immediately looked down. "Forgive me sir, it was the talk below stairs that she would stop at nothing . . ."

He was surprised by a deep chuckle and looked up again. "It is all right Roberts. I should not be surprised that was a topic of conversation. But I assure you that never would have happened. I hope that the staff will be pleased with their new mistress. Nonetheless, it is to be kept between the two of us, and for your information, we will be courting for the next month. I will let you know when the engagement begins and the staff may be notified."

If the valet was confused he hid it well. "Of course, sir." Darcy looked at him and grinned. Telling someone made it all real. He watched Roberts leave the room and removed Elizabeth's gloves from inside of his coat. He marvelled over how small her hands were, and felt his heartbeat increase as he stroked them lovingly. He stood and quickly crossed the room, locking them away in a large ebony box, then went to prepare for the day.

The rest of the morning Darcy spent working with Bingley and his steward, helping him to understand the workings of an estate. They met the ladies and Hurst for an afternoon meal. Georgiana stared with curiosity at her brother and he met Bingley's amused eye. Apparently his happiness was still evident to those who knew him well. He shrugged at him and smiled at Georgiana. "Would you like to take a walk in the garden after we eat, dear? I have not seen you all day."

Before she could reply Caroline jumped in. "Oh what a lovely idea Mr. Darcy, we can all go walking. Do you agree, Louisa?"

She nodded her head. "Yes, it is a fine day, and we have had little opportunity to spend time with you, Mr. Darcy. Why, Caroline has been looking forward to your visit so much!"

Darcy hid the grimace he felt and turned to Caroline. "I am sure that we will miss your company, however, I need to speak with my sister on some private family matters. I hope that you understand." He saw the displeasure flash briefly in her eyes and raised his brow.

"Oh, of course, sir."

He smiled slightly. "Besides, I imagine that you will wish to prepare quite carefully for the assembly. I am sure that you wish to impress the neighbourhood with your particular style."

Caroline flushed with pleasure at his supposed compliment. "Oh Mr. Darcy! Yes, I do have something particular planned tonight. I do hope that you will like it!" Darcy glanced at Bingley's twitching lips and back at Caroline. "I have no doubt that the gentlemen of the assembly will be impressed."

He stood and offered his arm to Georgiana. "Excuse us, please." They made their escape.

"William, what has happened? Miss Bingley was so upset when she came down to breakfast and found that you had disappeared. It was as if she felt you should have asked her permission!"

Darcy stared at her. "Really?" He shook his head. "Well I will tell you, I went riding and came upon Miss Elizabeth this morning. We talked for a long time, and she accepted my offer of courtship. I will speak to her father tomorrow, so please do not mention this to anyone until it is official."

Georgiana listened to him with a growing smile. "Oh William!" She threw her arms around his neck and kissed him.

He laughed. "I take it that you are pleased?"

"You know that I am!" She reclaimed his arm and they began walking again. "How is she? Was she surprised?"

"She is beautiful, and I do not know if I can truly describe her emotion when I asked, but she is happy, just as I am."

Georgiana smiled. "Yes, brother, it is all in your eyes."

He laughed. "To those who care to see, yes it is."

—⁓—

"Papa, you wished to see me?" Elizabeth entered her father's bookroom and took her usual seat before his desk. Mr. Bennet studied her for a moment.

"You have a new glow about you, Lizzy. Can you tell me what it is?"

She startled. "Oh, I could not say."

Mr. Bennet raised his brows, and pressed the tips of his folded hands to his lips. "I wished to speak to you because tonight you will likely meet your friend's brother. I know that your mother has determined that you will marry this man, despite either of your opinions. Just as I have told you with John Lucas, I want you to know that I take the same stance with Mr. Darcy. You will not be forced to suffer the attentions of any man that you do not favour, and if you wish, I will speak to your mother about her machinations with this young man. I imagine that he is of some status and wealth, and is used to mothers pushing their daughters on him, and would appreciate one less being forced his way."

Elizabeth was unsure of how to respond. She could not tell him of her courtship, much less of her engagement to William. She bit her lip. "I assure you, Papa, that despite Mama's unwelcome interference, I was impressed with Mr. Darcy when I twice met him, and I would not object to his attentions were he to bestow them upon me."

Mr. Bennet tilted his head a bit and regarded her carefully. Her face was flushed, her hands were twisting, and her eyes, everything was always in his daughter's eyes. He saw it now. She was lost to this man. He sighed and hoped he would not break her heart when he returned to London without her, and wondered if he would be intelligent enough to see the treasure his Lizzy was. "Very well, child. I will say nothing for now. I do think that I will come to this dance tonight. I look forward to seeing your battle to ignore one suitor and win another!"

"Papa!" He laughed and shooed her away. He wondered at all of those letters that came to Longbourn, why there always seemed to be two either arriving or leaving. His suspicions were aroused. "Yes, this dance will be interesting indeed."

Chapter 13

*C*aroline stood poised at the top of the stairs, ready to make her entrance. Down below she watched as Hurst and Bingley stood with arms folded, sending amused comments to Darcy who was wearing a path in the carpet with his incessant pacing. "What are you waiting for?" Louisa asked. "We will be late enough as is, and Mr. Darcy is clearly impatient to go."

"I just want him to look up." She hissed. Louisa rolled her eyes and called out. "Mr. Hurst, are you ready?" The question produced the intended result and all three men looked up to see Caroline descending majestically. Darcy blew out a frustrated breath and taking in the overly dressed, overly bejewelled women, inwardly shuddered and stepped to the servant who held his coat and hat.

Caroline arrived and instead of pleasure, she saw ire in the man's eyes. "Please excuse the delay, Mr. Darcy. You did say that I should look my best this evening."

"You look tolerably well, Miss Bingley. Now, we should be on our way."

She started at his comment, but then shook it off and smiled knowingly. "Oh, Mr. Darcy, you know that it is fashionable to be late to these affairs."

He detached the hand that had claimed his arm. "Miss Bingley. It is difficult to repair a bad first impression. I would prefer not to lose the good opinion of the neighbourhood by our tardy appearance." He stepped back and watched as Bingley offered his arm to her and walked outside to the carriage. Darcy hoped that she would be sufficiently silenced by his reply to stay away from him that evening.

At the assembly Elizabeth stood looking out of the window, nervously worrying the chain to the locket where William's token was kept. Jane joined her. "Oh where are they? The dance will begin at any moment!"

"I am sure they are on their way, Lizzy." Jane was almost as nervous as Elizabeth. She had seen Bingley when he visited Longbourn and caught him staring at her. She was taken by the handsome young man, and despite her protests to her mother, hoped he would ask her for a dance. "Look there is a carriage, perhaps it is theirs." The door opened and both girls deflated, seeing another family exit. The sound of music starting signalled the beginning of the dance.

"Eliza."

Elizabeth stiffened and turned to face John. "You look beautiful tonight." He took in the yellow fabric of her well-cut gown, the three long curls draped over her shoulder, the ribbons of yellow and white woven through her hair and smiled. "I have never seen you so lovely."

She felt Jane squeeze her hand. "Please call me Miss Elizabeth, sir." He continued smiling, and she sighed. "Thank you, Mr. Lucas for your compliment. You look well yourself." She felt trapped.

"You seem to be waiting for someone." He glanced out at the empty street. "Punctuality is admirable, is it not?" He held out his hand. "May I have this first set, Eliza? I will be much honoured." He gave her a genuine and warm smile.

Elizabeth fumed at his refusal to honour her request to be addressed formally, but did not wish to create a scene. She looked once more out of the window, willing a coach to appear, then to Jane. Both girls knew that if she refused, she would have to sit out the next two dances, and she did not wish to risk that if William did arrive soon. "Thank you, Mr. Lucas." She reluctantly accepted his hand and he led her to the floor.

Mrs. Bennet's eyes narrowed and Lady Lucas smiled. "Oh look, Eliza is dancing with John."

Mrs. Bennet sniffed. "The Netherfield party is following the fashion of entering late. All people of society do."

Lady Lucas nodded and her smile grew. "Ah yes, but it seems that those who are late miss the desirable partners."

John stood opposite Elizabeth and enjoyed taking in her entire form. The music began and they waited for their turn to move. Elizabeth's eyes kept travelling to the doorway. When their turn arrived she sighed and giving John a weak smile, took his offered hand. Her mind travelled through many emotions, worry that William was ill, hurt for leaving her waiting, and concern that he regretted his proposal. John took her hand and smiled. "Come Eliza, we must have some conversation."

"Must we?" She arched her brow.

He laughed. "Why of course!" John moved around her. "What shall we discuss?"

"You are eager, Mr. Lucas. I will allow you to choose the subject."

He considered her carefully. She was clearly unhappy with him. "I wish to apologize." Elizabeth was not expecting that. "Apologize?"

He nodded and holding her hand, moved beside her. "Indeed. I am afraid that my attentions have made you uncomfortable. I have little experience with courting, and I hope that you will bear with my awkward attempts." Again he smiled with sincerity and contrition.

"Mr. Lucas, I agree that I find your methods . . . disconcerting; however, I also do not seek your attentions. I would prefer that we simply remain the friends we have always been." She looked around the room, seeing the groupings of local matrons whispering together and nodding. By dancing the first set with him, expectations in the neighbourhood were being raised.

John noticed the same reactions and smiled, all was going well. "I will always wish to be your friend. . . Eliza." She glared. "Oh come, give me this little privilege."

With the eyes of the room upon them she held her tongue. She could not deliver a set down and remain at the dance, and she would not leave and miss William. She smiled slightly. "Tell me of your trip to Ireland, Mr. Lucas." Clearly she was deflecting his advances, but at least she was paying attention only to him. He happily began regaling her with the details of his trip.

The Netherfield party finally arrived. Darcy could hear the music from the street and his heart sank. The dance had begun. He glared at Bingley who looked at him with sympathy, and offered his arm to Caroline before she had a chance to attach herself to Darcy. He looked up at the windows, blazing with light. It was precisely the kind of place he hated visiting, but Elizabeth was somewhere inside. After leaving their outerwear at the door, he followed the couples upstairs and tugged at his coat, resisting the urge to pull out his ribbon. He needed to face the real woman now. Searching the hall, he barely heard Sir William's welcome. He managed to politely endure the introductions, noticing the curiosity with which he was examined by their host and his family. Charles, of course, asked Charlotte for the next set, and Darcy noticed Caroline moved towards him. He murmured something and advanced into the room. Elizabeth was nowhere in the crowd. *Where is she?* Every woman was examined, then his eyes turned to the dancers, and there she was, a vision in yellow, just as he had hoped. She had not seen him, and he stood at the edge of the dance and fixed his unwavering gaze upon her, watching her move gracefully through the pattern. The smiling man who was her partner took her hand in his and Darcy's heart twisted. *That should have been me! Why did she not wait for me?* He thought angrily, but knew the rules as well as she did. She had no choice. Watching to see if there was pleasure in her face, all he could see was a fixed smile, and that she was engaged in a conversation that apparently pleased her partner. Darcy wondered who the usurper was.

Bingley's voice at his ear answered the question. "It seems Miss Elizabeth was claimed by Lucas in you absence, Darcy."

He spun around. "What!?"

Bingley nodded. "That is John Lucas."

Elizabeth sensed his presence and began searching the room. She looked up and directly across from her was William. He turned back and witnessed the moment she spotted him. His distress was evident, and it was only her obvious happiness at seeing him that stopped his immediate advance to tear her away from her partner. John noticed her changed expression and saw Bingley standing with the tall stranger. His frustration appeared and he remarked bitterly. "It seems that the men of London deigned to appear tonight; how very gracious of them."

Elizabeth looked sharply at him. "I am sure that there was a good reason for their delay, Mr. Lucas."

John met her glare. "You need not make excuses for them, Eliza."

When the music ended, John purposely led her in the opposite direction from Darcy. His eyes narrowing, he quickly advanced to meet them. He bowed. "Good evening, Miss Elizabeth. May I apologize for our unfortunate delay? I hope that you will forgive me and allow your company for your next available set." His eyes stared into hers, trying hard to display his regret. Elizabeth saw it.

"I admit to being disappointed in missing our set, sir. Unfortunately I am not available until the third."

Darcy's eyes expressed his hurt. "Thank you." He said softly. He glanced at John, who was grinning at his supposed set down.

Elizabeth looked between the men. "Mr. Darcy, may I present Mr. Lucas? He is the son of Sir William, who you met at the door. Mr. Lucas, this is Mr. Darcy, a guest at Netherfield Hall." The two men nodded slightly and stood sizing each other up.

"Miss Elizabeth?" She turned to see a youth standing nervously, and looking worriedly between the two angry men.

"Mr. Harris." Elizabeth smiled warmly. "Are you ready for our dance?" Darcy and John both swung to take in the boy.

His eyes grew wide. "Y-y-yes." Relieved to escape the standoff, Elizabeth hooked her hand onto his arm and led him to the floor. Darcy watched her go, appreciating already that she purposely accepted the young boy as a consideration for him. He looked back at John.

"So you are Darcy." He leaned against a wall. "Your name is oddly familiar."

"Is it? I am familiar with yours as well."

John's brow rose. "Eliza seems to be under the impression that you are interested in her."

Darcy's eyes narrowed, hearing him speak of Elizabeth in such a familiar way. *Eliza, I never liked that name. She is Elizabeth.* "Miss Elizabeth is a very astute woman."

"I agree; I have had the pleasure of knowing her all my life, quite intimately. How long have you known her, Darcy?" John baited him, watching to see his reaction.

Darcy growled. "Long enough to know that she deserves the best."

John laughed. "A rich man's argument." He took in Darcy's handsome features and fine clothes. "What is your game, Darcy? What do you want with my Eliza?"

His eyes flashed dangerously. "I think that Miss Elizabeth would object to your claim of possession, it shows a lack of respect."

John stood up straight and glared at him, his smirk gone. "And I think that you could have any woman in England. This one is spoken for."

Darcy stepped closer. "Do not presume Lucas." His eyes were black with his warning.

Before John could respond a low voice interrupted. "Gentlemen, I believe that this is not the place for a cockfight. We are here to dance." Mr. Bennet stood between the men. "Lucas, could you introduce me to your friend?"

John continued glaring at Darcy. "This is the fabled Mr. Darcy." He said with clear derision.

Mr. Bennet nodded. "Ah, I thought as much. Forgive me for interrupting, sir. I am Thomas Bennet."

Startled, Darcy ripped his gaze away from John. "Mr. Bennet." He bowed and met the man's inquiring eyes. "I had hoped to meet you under . . ." he glanced at John, "calmer circumstances."

A small smile appeared on Mr. Bennet's face. "Well sir, I am sure that the opportunity will arise soon. You will bring your sister to visit Longbourn?"

Darcy relaxed. "Yes, Georgiana is looking forward to putting faces to the names in Miss Elizabeth's letters."

"Ah yes, the letters. Your sister was most prolific in her writing; sometimes I noticed two letters in Lizzy's hand." Mr. Bennet's brows rose watching Darcy's startled reaction. His eyes widened, and he shifted uncomfortably.

"Yes, Georgiana often thinks of more to say after she finishes a letter." He wondered what Mr. Bennet suspected.

"How kind of you to save us the cost of delivery by employing your own messenger."

John stepped in. "A worthy woman would not be impressed with such extravagance."

Darcy's glare returned. "It was hardly an extravagance when my servant was travelling between Derbyshire and London. It is also faster and more reliable than the post."

Shifting his gaze away from Darcy, John turned. "I am sure, Mr. Bennet, that you are curious what would inspire such a wealthy gentleman to bestow his attentions on your daughter. I hope that you will warn the lady that he could not possibly be serious."

"My daughter will determine if the attentions from ANY man are welcome. I believe that you are familiar with my opinions." Mr. Bennet's eyes took on an unusually serious cast as he stared at John.

Knowing he had stepped over the line with the man whose opinion mattered, John nodded. "Yes, sir." He glanced at Darcy's raised brow and walked away.

Darcy eyed Elizabeth's father. "Sir, I do hope to pay a call to Longbourn tomorrow. I would appreciate a few moments of your time."

"Would you? Well as you barely know my Lizzy, I can be assured that the conversation will not be about how you have fallen madly in love with her by reading your sister's letters, correct?"

Mr. Bennet's amused smile disconcerted him, but he raised his chin and answered truthfully. "Correct, sir."

Mr. Bennet laughed. "Very well then, until tomorrow, sir." He looked across the room to where John stood watching them. "I must say, it is quite fascinating to watch this play out." Darcy's gaze was again fixed on Elizabeth as she danced and was not listening. Mr. Bennet saw the intensity of his concentration. "Yes, quite fascinating." He stepped away and taking a cup of punch, moved to the periphery of the dance floor to watch and see what might transpire next.

The dance ended, and Darcy saw Elizabeth directing the boy to escort her off of the floor and to him. He acknowledged the lad, who would not look at him, but nervously bowed and thanked Elizabeth for the dance, then with a look of utter relief departed. Elizabeth laughed watching him go, and smiling widely looked up to Darcy's unrelenting and very warm gaze. "You are beautiful."

Elizabeth blushed and looked down. "Thank you." She whispered.

He stepped closer. "I can not begin to express how deeply sorry I am that I missed the opening set. To find you dancing with another man when it should have been me . . . I can hardly put my feelings into words, particularly when I learned his identity. Can you forgive me, my love?"

Elizabeth glanced up at him. He was so sincere, and she could tell it was only with a great effort that he did not take her into his embrace. She drew a deep breath and looked him head on. "Sir, I was very unhappy to find myself in such a difficult position." She lifted a brow and tilted her head. "I shall consider your excuse then render my punishment."

Darcy's eyes widened and a slight smile appeared. He whispered so only she could hear. "I daresay any punishment of yours will be a pleasure to suffer, my dearest Elizabeth."

She laughed. "Well, sir, I am waiting."

Darcy drank in the sight of her beautiful laughing eyes. *Punish me dearest, let me take you away from here and do your worst, I will gladly win my place back in your good graces.* He pulled himself together and nodded over to a corner where Caroline and Louisa were holding court. "Do you see those two women over by the refreshment table?" Elizabeth stood near his shoulder and he inhaled her light scent, and longed to caress her hair with his lips. She nodded. "The one in blue is Louisa Hurst, Bingley's eldest sibling. Beside her is Caroline Bingley, his elder sister. She is the reason for our delay tonight."

Elizabeth turned to look up to him, finding his person close enough to feel the warmth of his body. She felt enveloped in his clean manly scent, and wished they were back in the seclusion of the forest. She regained command of her feelings and looked into his eyes. "Oh, and I assume that they were trying to repair the damage to their appearance and were unsuccessful?"

Darcy held in his amusement, and returned from his fantasy. "I do not see why you fear taking on the *ton*, Elizabeth, you have just proven that the spirit of cattiness lives in every woman." She giggled. "In all seriousness, the sisters, I imagine; wish to show the poor residents of this village what it is to be a woman of society. They planned to come late to draw attention. I imagine Miss Bingley is wishing for my attention as well. This is the longest I have gone for some time without her attaching herself to my arm." He shook his head.

"So you have a Mr. Lucas, too." His expression darkened. "The man is not easily dissuaded from you." He watched her carefully. "Does he have your permission to call you Eliza?"

"I have asked him to stop." She said quietly. "He persists nonetheless, and continues to insist that I call him John."

"Do you like the name Eliza?" He asked softly, and watched as her face changed expression.

"I used to, when I came out our neighbours stopped calling me by my family name of Lizzy, and switched to the more adult name, but now, it just makes me hear his voice whenever it is spoken." She caught his serious eye. "Please never call me that."

He shook his head. "I will not."

The music began again and they smiled at each other. "Finally it seems we shall have our dance." Darcy held out his arm and Elizabeth gladly took it. It just felt so right to feel the strength lying beneath the coat. They took their places and looked across at each other. Nobody else was in the room. There was no need to speak, they were lost in the movement, their steps seemingly choreographed perfectly, as if the music, the night, the atmosphere was all designed for just they two. Gloved hands touched and parted, warmth was sensed and drawn away as they moved around and near. It was as if they were making love without ever touching.

Those in the room who observed the striking couple saw that there was certainly a connection. Mr. Bennet stood up and moved closer, carefully watching their faces. Mrs. Bennet saw nothing of the emotion, but crowed in triumph to the ladies around her. On opposite sides of the room two others looked upon the scene with great displeasure. Caroline began whispering furiously to Louisa, trying to determine who this country nobody was who not only had won a dance from Mr. Darcy, but his attention. John watched seeing only the desire in the eyes of the woman he wanted. His jealousy grew.

When the dance ended, the spell was broken and both of the lovers felt weak with the intensity of their exchange. Flushed, Darcy offered to bring Elizabeth some refreshment and led her over to where he saw Bingley standing with Jane. A familiar look in his eye awakened Darcy from his bewitched mood and back to reality. "Bingley." He said, startling his friend.

"Darcy!" He smiled and looked at Elizabeth. "Miss Elizabeth, what a pleasure to see you again. I do apologize for our delay this evening. My sisters were determined to make a grand entrance." He nodded to the corner where Caroline and Louisa were staring at them, now trying to see who their brother had latched onto.

"Mr. Darcy explained it all to me, and I have decided to forgive him." She smiled.

"You have?" He looked at her with surprise. "I think that I am disappointed. I was rather looking forward to hearing my penance."

Elizabeth laughed. "I have no doubt that you will raise my ire again in the future, sir."

He smiled, and leaned down to whisper. "I look forward to it." She blushed.

Looking up she saw her sister's amused smile. "Mr. Darcy, do you remember my sister, Jane?"

Darcy bowed to her. "Yes, Miss Bennet, I am delighted to meet you again. I see that you have been suffering the attentions of my friend. I hope that his charming manner has not been too overwhelming."

"Mr. Bingley has been everything a gentleman should be, sir."

Darcy looked at Bingley and cleared his throat. "I was just going to fetch some punch for Miss Elizabeth. Would you care to join me?"

They moved to the refreshment table and Bingley nudged him. "You and Miss Elizabeth seemed to get on well. She accepted your apology so easily?"

"Yes, although she suggests that we take two carriages from now on." Bingley laughed. "She was not impressed with your sister's fashion efforts."

Bingley glanced at Caroline and grimaced. "Neither am I, but she was out to draw your attention, I think." Darcy shuddered. "You will have to dance with her Darcy."

Sighing he nodded. "Perhaps the next, then I will be free for Miss Elizabeth." He tilted his head. "What do you think of Miss Bennet?"

"Oh Darcy, she is an angel!"

Darcy sighed. "Bingley, do not trifle with her, please."

Bingley looked offended. "I never trifle with ladies!"

"A lady of the *ton* is likely more aware that you are only wishing to enjoy her company for a brief time. I fear that a sheltered country girl might have a more fragile heart."

Bingley's brow rose. "And she is Miss Elizabeth's sister."

He looked at him pointedly. "Please behave carefully."

"Did it ever occur to you, Darcy; that I already am?" Bingley picked up his two cups of punch and led the way back to the ladies. Darcy studied the back of his head, wondering if he was serious.

Across the hall, Caroline had enough. "Come along, Louisa, we must stop Mr. Darcy and Charles before they are drawn in by these country upstarts."

"I seriously doubt that Mr. Darcy is susceptible to the charms of these girls, Caroline. He has never paid attention to anybody. Miss Elizabeth is simply a friend of Georgiana's." Louisa said as they slowly walked across the room.

Caroline glanced at her. "You saw how he looked at her when they danced. He never dances outside of his party! Something is very wrong! I will not have these Bennet girls upset my plans for Mr. Darcy or Charles!"

Bingley and Darcy made their way back towards the ladies and very nearly lost their cups of punch when two wildly giggling girls ran in front of them. They arrived to find Jane blushing and Elizabeth's mouth set in a grim line. "Will you please excuse me, Mr. Darcy? I need to speak to my sisters."

"Those girls are your sisters?"

Elizabeth met his incredulous eyes. "Yes sir, please excuse me." He realized her embarrassment, but she was striding away before he could apologize for his clumsy reaction and was left looking after her, still holding the punch.

Elizabeth reached Lydia and Kitty. She whispered in a furious tone, "What are you doing? You are making fools of yourselves in front of the entire neighbourhood!"

Lydia looked around her sister to peer at Darcy. "Oh pooh, Lizzy! You do not know how to have fun! Is that the Mr. Darcy Mama has been going on about? He looks far too stiff, and he never smiles. John Lucas is far more entertaining. I think you should accept him."

Kitty eagerly chimed in. "Yes Lizzy! Mr. Darcy is handsome, I suppose, but I hope you do not marry him.

Although, he is rich . . ." Kitty giggled. "That would make up for his dour face." Lydia grabbed her arm and the two began whispering together.

Elizabeth took hold of both of their arms. "Neither of you have any sense nor can you judge another person by the expression on their face. Now, settle down!"

She began to return to Darcy when again she heard the soft voice near her ear. "Eliza."

She closed her eyes in frustration. *Will he not take a hint?* She turned. "Mr. Lucas, I am not in the mood . . ." He caught up her hand and kissed it. "Mr. Lucas!" Her eyes flashed.

"Forgive me, but I could not resist. You look even lovelier when your eyes burn so passionately."

She closed her eyes, her hands balled into fists. "Mr. Lucas, you wish to be friends. Why do you insist on . . . approaching me like this?" She attempted to control her anger and the volume of her voice. "Surely there is another suitable candidate for your attentions somewhere in this room!"

He drank in the fire he had never seen in any other woman. Beauty and strength, and he wanted it for his own. "Dance with me, Eliza." He urged, reaching for her hand again.

"Mr. Lucas, I can not." She started back to where she left William.

"Mr. Darcy is engaged for the set, he is not your excuse." He nodded to the floor where she saw William dancing with Caroline. Elizabeth turned back and saw the satisfied smile on John's face.

Charlotte appeared at her side. "Eliza." She jumped.

Lady Lucas approached from behind, she was surrounded. "Ah, Eliza, I knew you would not be fooled for long. These men from London are not here to find wives, no matter what your mother says. Why, they have barely acknowledged Charlotte and Maria."

"Mr. Bingley did dance with me, Mama." Charlotte said quietly.

Elizabeth felt for Charlotte's discomfort, and tried to change the subject. "Lady Lucas, please . . ."

"Why are you not dancing?" She smiled and gave her a firm nudge towards John. Charlotte pasted a smile on her face and began to speak but was interrupted by Mrs. Bennet's screech. For possibly the first time in her life, Elizabeth was grateful to see her mother.

"Lizzy! What are you doing? Mr. Darcy is dancing with Miss Bingley. Now get back over there, he must see you. You can not let him be distracted. The girl is better dressed but you were charming him so well. He is living under her roof; you must give him something to remember when he leaves!"

Seemingly by magic Mrs. Bennet grabbed Kitty from the crowd. "Kitty I have not seen you dance with John Lucas tonight." She pushed her forward. "Surely that was an oversight, sir!" John looked at Elizabeth, then Kitty.

He smiled tightly. "Of course, Kitty, shall we dance?"

"All right, but we must hurry!" She moved quickly away.

John looked back at Elizabeth. "I will claim another set with you, Eliza." She felt as if the room was spinning.

Lady Lucas nodded. "You danced the first with John, it is only right that you dance the last as well."

"Lady Lucas, that set is already taken." She gratefully announced.

"By Mr. Darcy?" Mrs. Bennet demanded.

"Yes, Mama."

"Oh my clever girl!" She crowed. Lady Lucas stared at them. She wanted her son married, and he wanted only Elizabeth. She would find a way to make this happen.

"Eliza, may I speak to you?" Charlotte asked quietly.

Elizabeth looked again to the dance floor where she spotted William watching her as he moved. His face was expressionless, ignoring Caroline's chatter, but his eyes burned into hers. "I will speak on any subject other than gentlemen, Charlotte."

Clearly this was not the time to push her brother's suit. "Oh I was just thinking that Jane looked pleased with Mr. Bingley."

Elizabeth saw the two were talking with Mrs. Hurst. "Yes, she does seem to get on well with him." The mothers departed and the girls spoke of their friends and neighbours, Elizabeth gradually relaxed. The set ended and Darcy took Caroline back to her family, and immediately approached Elizabeth and Charlotte. He wished to speak to her alone, but Charlotte would not give up her post, and ignored the subtle hints they both dropped. In frustration Darcy asked Elizabeth to introduce him to her mother.

"Sir, are you sure?" She asked as they moved away, both surprised and alarmed.

"I could see that she rescued you from Lucas, Elizabeth. That act alone wins her my undying admiration."

She laughed and smiled up at his warm gaze. "Remember those last words, sir."

"William." He whispered.

"William."

Their eyes met. "I apologize for dancing with Miss Bingley when you clearly needed . . ."

Elizabeth touched his arm. "Shh. I know that you were obligated to do so sometime tonight."

Darcy looked back at her hand, now at her side. "I wish that we could leave here, if only for a few moments." Darcy was standing as close as possible to Elizabeth without touching her. He searched the crowded room, wondering if there happened to be a convenient balcony or curtain where he could lead her for a few stolen kisses. He wished she would take his arm. "Elizabeth . . ." He leaned and whispered. She looked up and smiled. He bit his lip and gently nudged her arm with his elbow and raised his brow. She blushed and biting her own lip instead dropped her hand to briefly caress his. As she began to return her hand to her side he captured the retreating fingertips and entwined his own with hers, hiding their hands by moving to block the view. Elizabeth's blush deepened and she chanced a peek up at his face. Once again they were alone in the room.

Jane was watching them and smiled. She glanced up to see Bingley was watching them as well with a delighted expression. Bingley leaned over to her. "I have a feeling that you are as pleased for your sister as I am for my friend, Miss Bennet."

"I have never seen her so happy."

Bingley nodded. "I can swear this is a first for my friend. He is a very good man. You have nothing to fear."

Jane looked at him with surprise. "I never thought to worry. Was that naïve of me?"

"No actually it is refreshing." He smiled.

Darcy and Elizabeth awoke from their solitude by Mrs. Bennet's appearance. "Mama, may I introduce Mr. Darcy?"

"Oh, Mr. Darcy, I am delighted to meet you at last! Lizzy has so enjoyed your sister's letters! It is always so exciting when your messenger arrives. I do hope that we will meet her soon? She is not here tonight?"

"Mrs. Bennet." He bowed. "My sister remains at Netherfield, she is not yet out. However, I have spoken with Mr. Bennet and we plan to visit Longbourn tomorrow afternoon."

Mrs. Bennet beamed. "Lizzy! Did you hear that? You will have to show Miss Darcy a very good time. We do not wish you to hurt this friendship with your impertinent ways, so you must be on your best behaviour."

"Yes, Mama." She closed her eyes, and mortified, moved away from William.

Mrs. Bennet nodded knowingly. "Mr. Darcy, my Lizzy will be an excellent friend for your sister.

"She already is."

Elizabeth looked up to his warm eyes and relaxed. "Thank you, Mr. Darcy."

He smiled and seeing Mrs. Bennet's head turned, mouthed "William." Elizabeth blushed and nodded.

The remainder of the assembly Elizabeth found she was oddly more popular and was asked for every dance. To her surprise, John's last approach was refreshingly formal. He addressed her as Miss Elizabeth and the conversation was neutral. She had no idea what inspired the change, but was glad for it. Darcy danced once with Mrs. Hurst after supper, and once with Jane. The rest of the evening he stood on the periphery watching Elizabeth's partners and paying great attention to John's location and his attention to her. He wondered at his varied behaviour. He could not question the man's attraction to Elizabeth, that was unquestionably obvious, but he admittedly wondered why he would not seek a gentleman's daughter with a larger dowry. Was this love or a physical attraction? Was this man's heart engaged in the same way his own was?

After Elizabeth was relinquished by John, the last dance arrived. When Darcy took her hand they both felt the relief of finding home. "This has been quite a day." Elizabeth smiled while taking his arm in a turn.

"I loved the way it began." He whispered as she passed by again. "I would dearly love for it to end the same way."

Elizabeth blushed. "So would I, William."

When the dance ended Darcy bowed deeply to her, and lifted her hand to his lips, brushing the fabric of her glove with a lingering warm kiss. Her blush matched his, and he wanted so much more. He tucked her arm around his, and escorted her to collect their coats, then out to await the family carriage. Mr. Bennet watched from the street. His suspicions of a deeper connection between the two grew. The Bennet carriage arrived and meeting Mr. Bennet's eye, Darcy handed Elizabeth in, bowing over her hand and upon rising whispered, "I love you." Their eyes met, and he smiled at her loving gaze, and then closed the door after her father. He stood for a moment watching her carriage roll in the wrong direction, then entered Bingley's coach, no longer so alone.

Chapter 14

"Welcome to the militia Wickham!" Denny shook his friend's hand. "You look quite well in that uniform; you should know that it is a very useful accessory when attracting the ladies." He grinned and laughed at Wickham's raised brow.

"Ah, I thought as much, I have yet to see any soldier without a lady on his arm." Wickham glanced around. "Well, now that I am here, do you have any idea where we will be spending our time? I suppose we will not be so lucky as to spend the winter in London."

Denny shook his head. "Not the militia, my friend. You caught me there because we were on leave. No, our lot is to reside in the countryside. Rumour has it that we are heading for Hertfordshire, but nothing is set in stone until the Colonel says the word."

Wickham nodded. "Hertfordshire, well at least we will not be spending the winter in the north, I experienced enough of Derbyshire to appreciate the warmer climate."

"You grew up there didn't you? I seem to recall you saying your father was a steward of a large estate?"

"Yes, Pemberley, may the Darcys rot in their graves." He spat.

Denny's brows rose. "Come on man, there is a story in that!"

Wickham shook his head. "Another time. It is too raw now. Just let us say that their beneficence is what leads me to this handsome uniform today." Denny laughed and taking the lead, escorted Wickham into their headquarters to meet the rest of his new comrades.

"Anne, do not slouch. You are a lady!" Lady Catherine barked at her daughter. "I wrote to Darcy weeks ago and have had no answer." She eyed Anne. "Have you heard from him?"

"No Mama. Cousin Darcy has not written to me for months." Anne looked down at her teacup. The absence of letters from her cousin was unusual. He had always taken the time to write her. She was aware that her mother was pushing him harder than ever to marry her, now that Georgiana had been ruined in the eyes of society. Perhaps that was the reason. Any show of family affection would be taken as proof that he was going to propose. Her mother would have an announcement in the paper before he could blink an eye.

"Have you heard from your other cousin?"

Anne knew she referred to Georgiana, but that she had taken to not speaking her name. "No Mama. I have only heard from Cousin Fitzwilliam."

Lady Catherine's eyes widened. "Ah, and does he have news from Pemberley?"

"He and his parents and Viscount Matlock visited some weeks ago. He said that Georgiana and Darcy were well." She was not about to elaborate. Richard reported that both of their cousins were carrying heavy burdens. She often thought of Darcy. In many ways they were alike. Both shared mothers whose senses of worth were entirely tied to their title. Her Aunt Anne had rejected what could have been a comfortable and happy life at Pemberley to instead be bitter. Her mother had married her father because he was titled and wealthy; there was never any affection in the relationship. Somehow Anne thought that the combined experiences of the cousins might make for a tolerable marriage. She would not have objected to her mother's demand that she marry Darcy. She did not love him, but they were both such unhappy people, it would not matter. It was abundantly clear that he never would marry her, but nonetheless . . . she sighed inwardly. She had her chance. Darcy asked her directly what her feelings were on the subject, and rather than suffer watching the repulsion appear on his face, she told him she did not wish for it. Her decision was clearly correct because he could not hide the relief that his eyes expressed. She accepted it. She knew that a man such as he would want a beautiful, vivacious woman, not a sickly domineered shadow of a girl. There would be no rescue from Rosings from a knight wearing the Darcy crest.

"I will have to write to him again. Or perhaps I should simply go to Pemberley . . ." She eyed her daughter. "Would you care for a trip?"

Anne's eyes lit up. "To Pemberley?"

Lady Catherine nodded slowly. "Perhaps. But . . . no, your uncle would find out." She glared as her brother's face appeared in her mind. "Nothing will come of this until your cousin is dealt with, there must be someone suitable I can find to marry her . . ."

"But she is not yet out, Mama." Anne bravely spoke.

Lady Catherine looked at her sharply. "Do you think that I am not aware of that!?" Her fingernails tapped on the fine polished wood of the table by her side. "Who would accept a ruined girl? Especially one such as her?" She thought, remembering the name of the man she knew was Georgiana's father. She would have to avoid that family, of course. But surely there were plenty of other titled or at least wealthy families willing to accept her in exchange for that tidy dowry . . . she decided that she must begin writing letters.

"Darcy will not marry until his sister is removed from Pemberley. She is the albatross around his neck. It is her presence that keeps him from taking you as his wife." She nodded with new resolve. "Yes. I will find a suitable husband for her and get that girl out of our home."

Anne thought to protest that Darcy would likely be unhappy with this decision, but instead thought she would write her Cousin Fitzwilliam about it instead.

"Lady Catherine, Mr. Collins is here." The footman announced. She nodded. "Send him up." The man bowed and several minutes later a small, greasy-haired man, made even smaller by his stooped entrance, appeared.

"Lady Catherine, how can I thank you for your kind acceptance of my poor company? Your most-esteemed attentions are gratefully received and I beg your forgiveness at my delay in appearing. I only received your message within the hour. I was called away from the parsonage to tend a dying parishioner."

"I hope that you did not bring his disease in with you?" She eyed him.

"No, My Lady, I stopped and changed my attire and washed my hands most thoroughly to remove the . . . fluids." He cast his eyes down. Anne stared at him, wondering just what "fluids" had been removed. Mr. Collins noticed her and turned, bowing. "Oh, and Miss de Bourgh, please forgive me, I . . ." His effusions were interrupted by his noble patroness.

"Sit down, Mr. Collins." He found a low chair and sat, staring up to her. "I understand that you are to inherit an estate."

He smiled. "Yes indeed. Now that my father has passed, I am the benefactor of the entailment which lies upon Longbourn, a property located in Hertfordshire."

"Have you seen the property?"

"No, My Lady, my cousin Bennet, whose family has held the property for generations was estranged from my father. He has only five daughters, so the entailment was not broken with his issue. With my father's death . . ."

"You will write to him. You will heal the breach in your family." She ordered.

"Yes, My Lady!"

She looked at him coolly. "I do not like my rector not having a wife. You must marry, and you must provide an example to the parish of felicity."

"Yes, My Lady!"

"Choose a wife from these five cousins of yours. They will lose their home upon their father's death. If you marry one, they will not be cast out. This should assure you of winning one of them." He nodded eagerly. "Yes, a gentleman's daughter; not born too high, but of good sturdy stock. Pick her well, Mr. Collins, and I shall visit her."

"Oh, and she will be honoured for the condescension, My Lady, I will make sure of it!"

"Now be off with you. When you receive your cousin's reply, I will arrange for a replacement so that you may settle your marriage. I will give you a fortnight away to complete the transaction."

"Yes, yes, My Lady, certainly that will be more than enough time to select my bride!" He stood and bowed as he backed out of the room, then scurried back to Hunsford parsonage to write Mr. Bennet.

Lady Catherine watched him go and smiled. "I enjoy seeing him grovel." She looked speculatively at Anne. A husband for her like that would be amusing, but she needed Pemberley. No, a grovelling fool for Georgiana would be excellent. She stood. "I have some letters to write. Go take your nap Anne."

Anne sat still after she left, listening to the tapping of her cane fade. Her shoulders slouched. After thinking about it she too stood, and went to her room to write Fitzwilliam.

Darcy awoke, and in his half-conscious state reached to draw Elizabeth against his aroused body, and felt a sudden and deep disappointment when he realized that she was not there, and not his wife. Fully awake he fell back against the pillow and stared up at the canopy, fighting both the physical ache and the one he recognized as loneliness. One he could relieve, the other would have to wait two long months. At least after this day he would have the right to protect her from John Lucas and any other interloper who tried to claim her attention. Last night he could only watch and fume. His glare was all he could offer her. He would be sure that his changed status was made very clear to all.

He arrived in the breakfast room to find that Georgiana was the sole occupant. She jumped up at his entrance. "William!" She kissed his cheek. "How was the dance? Did you see Elizabeth? How is she?"

He smiled and patted her shoulder. "Please let me take some coffee dear, before the inquisition begins." Georgiana resumed her seat and watched him pour a cup, then fill a plate from the covered dishes on the sideboard. He settled into his chair and looked up to her expectant face and chuckled. "Yes, I saw Elizabeth. We danced three times. I met her parents and family, and you and I will be visiting there this afternoon."

Georgiana clapped. "Oh, I can not wait to see her! Were her parents nice?"

Darcy leaned back with his cup and took a sip. "They were . . . unique." He saw her confusion. "I believe you will have to experience them to understand. I have asked for a private conference with Mr. Bennet."

Her eyes grew wide. "You will ask for permission to court her?" He nodded. He also had a feeling that an explanation about the letters would be requested.

Georgiana reached out and took his hand. "I truly have never seen you so happy, Brother."

He smiled. "Thank you, dear. I truly am. I want to bring her home." Georgiana looked at him with surprise. He rarely referred to Pemberley as home.

Before more could be said, the sound of boots in the hallway was heard and Bingley made a sleepy appearance. "Good Morning." He looked around, bleary-eyed. "You would think that I would be used to late nights, but I just could not fall asleep after we returned."

Darcy raised his brows. "Something on your mind?"

A slow, wide grin spread across his face. "Something like that." Darcy rolled his eyes. Miss Bennet was obviously going to receive his attentions.

"Bingley, please, remember what I said last night." He looked at him pointedly.

Bingley's gaze sharpened. "Darcy. I believe that we have addressed this subject."

The men's eyes met, and Darcy nodded. "Very well. Georgiana and I will be calling at Longbourn this afternoon."

Bingley smiled. "Ah, do you mind if I tag along?"

Darcy shook his head and smiled slightly. "I am sure you would be welcome." A companionable silence fell over the room as the three ate, and was subsequently disrupted by the arrival of the Hursts and Caroline.

"Well Charles, are you happy with the neighbourhood? There was very little of fashion or style evident at that assembly last night. I imagine the people of importance stayed away from such a public event. Hopefully we will meet neighbours of quality soon."

Bingley looked up as Caroline selected her breakfast then met Darcy's cold eyes. "This is not London, Caroline. I do not know why you are placing the standards of the *ton* upon the neighbourhood. Everyone I met was welcoming and kind. I am pleased with our reception."

She sat and huffed. "I am merely pointing out a few deficiencies. Some of the families did seem tolerable, but others . . ." She looked at Darcy pointedly, ". . . were quite unsatisfactory, the Bennets for instance."

"I found Miss Jane Bennet to be quite lovely." Bingley said, meeting her eyes.

She bowed her head. "Yes, she was the exception. She is a sweet girl. But her sisters. . ." She shuddered. "I can not imagine what society would think of them. That Miss Eliza Bennet was without any grace at all. She would be laughed out of the drawing rooms. She quite belongs in the country." She stared at Darcy who did not hide his ire. "Surely that is obvious. However, I understand that Mr. Lucas is very interested in her. His mother told me that he has been pursuing her quite vigorously but she is resisting. She apparently has set her sights on someone with a fortune. Lady Lucas agrees with me that she should keep to her own. She will be happier there."

Georgiana and Bingley both looked to Darcy whose mouth was set in a thin line. "I imagine that Miss *Elizabeth* will be interested to hear of your counsel. I will be sure to relay your opinion when I call on her this afternoon."

Caroline was silenced. Louisa looked at her sister's stunned expression. "You are to call on Longbourn, Mr. Darcy?"

His cold gaze fixed on her. "Indeed. I will accompany Georgiana to visit her friend. I look forward to spending time with all of the Bennets, Miss Elizabeth in particular."

Louisa's mouth opened and closed. "I will be joining them." Bingley added. His sisters stared and Hurst watched the tableau and snorted with his amusement.

Darcy stood. "I have some work to finish. I will be in the library should you need me, Georgiana." He bowed and left the room. Georgiana whispered her excuses and left to join Mrs. Annesley.

Bingley was left with his family. "Caroline, what are you about?"

She looked affronted. "I was merely pointing out the deficiencies of the Bennets. Mr. Darcy seemed uncommonly blind to them last night. I wish only to protect him from an obvious fortune hunter."

"I have said this once and I will say it only one more time. The Darcys are here to relax after a difficult summer. I do not wish any desires of yours to interfere with their visit. Darcy is welcome to spend his time as he sees fit, without your unwanted advice." He stood and put down his napkin. "And Caroline, Louisa, I do not want to hear another word disparaging the Bennets." He nodded to Hurst and left the room.

"Well!" Caroline huffed.

"I do not think this will be as easy as you supposed, Caroline." Louisa whispered. Hurst shovelled more food in his mouth and listened.

Caroline glanced his way and dismissed him. "It is perhaps more difficult. I did not expect Mr. Darcy to be suddenly infatuated with another woman. But having another suitor nearby is useful."

Hurst swallowed his tea and stood. "Ladies." He strolled from the room and down towards the library. Knocking, he entered and closed the door behind him.

Darcy looked up from the desk which was spread with papers. "Hurst."

He dropped down in a chair and considered Darcy in silence for several moments. "I thought you should be made aware that my wife and sister have plans for you."

"What do you mean?" He put down his pen.

Hurst shrugged. "Nothing specific, but the addition of Miss Elizabeth has upset them. I would be prepared for a possible compromise if I were you. Keep your door locked, if you know what I mean." He nodded, then seeing the disgust crossing Darcy's face stood. "Just be on guard. You have had enough this summer." He turned and left the room.

Darcy sat back. The length of his courtship was just going to have to be shortened. It was convenient to be at Netherfield, but until he was engaged officially, it would be like living in a nest of vipers.

———～ル～———

Elizabeth wandered the garden, reliving the past day. It seemed as if it was only a dream, but the memory of William's kisses was very real. She crossed her arms around her chest, hugging herself. If she closed her eyes she could almost feel his strong embrace, and imagine the scent of his cologne enveloping her when he expressed so warmly the emotion he felt. She drew a deep breath and slowly blinked her eyes open again. It was extraordinary, at nearly this exact time a day before she was a naïve girl, pretending to kiss her lover in her pillow at night, and suddenly she was different, her mind rapidly pulling together the new feelings, smells, sensations and reactions that she had now experienced, and imagining what it would be like to become William's wife. She pressed her hand to the locket and attempted to still her rapidly beating heart.

The proposal, well, the meeting itself, had been such a surprise, but to see him there before her, saying all that was in his heart, when she knew how hard it was for him to express himself, was overwhelming to her. To know that she, Elizabeth Bennet, could arouse such passionate emotion from such an extraordinary man nearly took her breath away. She thought back over the assembly and smiled. He was practically grief-stricken, staring at her dancing with John. She felt his pain just as deeply, but she had been without recourse at the time, and he thankfully understood that she was not slighting him. Even for the second dance with John, William knew that she could not refuse and still dance the last with him. Elizabeth thought there might be some gossip today amongst the neighbourhood. His attentions to her were very marked. *Three dances! And only one other with a lady outside of his party.* She shook her head. Tongues *would* be wagging today. She wondered if they would be pleased that he, a wealthy man, had shown the sense to single out one of their own, or if they would be disparaging him because he did not choose one of the other girls. Elizabeth sighed; she supposed he could not win, no matter what he did. Mr. Bingley had clearly made a good impression on them all. For him, that was more important, since he was to be living there, and William was merely a visitor. She would have to speak to him about at least attempting to be a little more approachable in company. She laughed. *Listen to you, Lizzy! You are already acting like a wife!*

A wife. She closed her eyes again, thinking of all that the word entailed and shuddered, realizing now that the strange aching she experienced was obviously shared by him. All she could think about was how she wanted to feel it again. It was as if a darkened room had been filled with blazing light, and the words that she had read in secret without comprehension suddenly made sense. A month of courtship and a month of engagement seemed entirely too long now. He wanted to marry right away . . . perhaps they should talk before he meets with her father.

She was startled out of her reverie on William's passionate kisses with Jane's voice. "Lizzy, are you well? You looked so deep in thought. Has something happened?"

She smiled at her concerned sister, and did not even consider explaining the feelings she was reliving. Jane would not understand. "I am fine, Jane. I was just thinking of William. What do you think if we shortened the courtship?"

"Shortened? Oh Lizzy, you are only asking for a month now, it would surely cause talk if you made it less."

Elizabeth bit her lip. "I know, but, Jane I wish . . . oh, it is so hard to explain!"

Jane touched her hand. "You love him, Lizzy. You simply wish to begin your life."

Elizabeth smiled. "I suppose that is it." She sighed. "It would be so much easier if John would just give me up." She shook her head. "He was so odd last night. Sometimes he was kind, sometimes jealous or angry, and then at the end, he was so formal. I do not know what to make of him. He frightens me at times."

"Has he threatened you?" Jane asked with concern.

"Well, if telling me that he will win my hand is a threat, then yes, he has. I tried to convince him to look elsewhere, but it is as if he is obsessed with me. I do not recall ever doing anything to inspire it. Do you?" She searched her sister's eyes.

Jane shook her head. "No, not at all. It was as if he returned from Cambridge this way." The girls hooked their arms and walked along.

"Mr. Bingley seemed most taken with you, Jane."

She blushed and looked at the ground. "I like him, Lizzy."

Elizabeth smiled and squeezed her arm. "I am so glad to hear that. Perhaps he will come calling with the Darcys today."

She looked up hopefully. "Do you think so?"

Elizabeth laughed. "Well, if he does not, he is a silly fool!"

———∽∾∾———

"The post, sir." Hill entered the bookroom and handed the letters to Mr. Bennet. He closed the atlas he was studying and picked up the envelopes. The first was from an unfamiliar address in Kent. He frowned at it, and then studying the return remembered why he knew the name, Collins, the heir to Longbourn. He put that letter aside. He lifted the second and recognized the handwriting immediately, but still looked at the address. There was no name, there never was. Ever since his sister had been banished to Scotland she was too ashamed to ever speak her family name again. Her letters were always a bittersweet gift for Mr. Bennet. He loved her, but her mistake was what led him to the marriage he had now. The sound of Mrs. Bennet's screech carried through the doorway, and he looked down at the letter again. He loved his daughters, was miserable with the marriage he had to accept, and only he remembered Sarah Bennet. His daughters had no idea that they had another aunt. He had no desire to read her words just then.

He picked up the last letter and his brow wrinkled. It was filthy. Covered in mud, the direction was obliterated. *How did they know to bring it here?* He wondered, and then examining it closely, he saw that only a portion of the return was legible. Longbourn, Meryton, Hertfordshire, he made out. He thought it was Lizzy's writing, but it was difficult to tell. The seal was intact so he decided to open it. If it was Lizzy's he would just return it to her so she could write her friend anew. Breaking the seal he found one muddy and one nearly pristine sheet. He opened them and his eyes grew wide.

Dear William,
I can not imagine why you would think that our friendship would end now. Your sister's behaviour, while foolish was not your fault.

Mr. Bennet could not stop himself. He read the entire letter through. He learned through Elizabeth's reassurances to Mr. Darcy everything. They were correspondents, obviously of some time. He had entrusted her with the secret of his sister's ruin. Mr. Bennet's heart suddenly ached with the memory of his own sister's shame. He read of Elizabeth's support for both of them, her ideas for helping Miss Darcy regain her life, if not her place in society, and he read what was in every sentence of the letter but as yet unwritten. She loved him. He looked at the end of the letter and saw her signature: *Yours, Elizabeth.*

Mr. Bennet sighed and wiped the tears that were falling silently down his face. He suspected that perhaps Elizabeth had exchanged a few friendly notes with him. After the dance he even suspected that they were forming a romance, but this? He shook his head and again read the letter. *This was what it looked like to read of love.* He thought of his own lost love, the one who rejected him after . . . He set the letter down. The rules of propriety had been broken. *What should I do?* The sound of a carriage arriving took him to the window and he saw Mr. Darcy descend, his sombre face remained but his eyes were bright with anticipation and joy. Mr. Bennet clasped his hands behind his back and began to pace.

———∽∿∼———

Mrs. Bennet was beside herself at the sight of the Darcy carriage through the drawing room window. She called out to each of the daughters to arrange themselves in as natural a manner as possible, while posing them in various attitudes of work. She especially directed Elizabeth, even jumping up to pinch her cheeks one last time to give her already healthy blush an extra glow. The visitors were announced and they all stood to receive them. Darcy's eyes flew to Elizabeth's and they exchanged a smile that barely hinted at their rapidly beating hearts. "Mr. Darcy, Mr. Bingley how very good to see you again!" Mrs. Bennet cried, stepping forward. "And sir, may I presume that this is your sister?" She looked over the very elegantly dressed girl. Georgiana was excited to come, but the moment she stepped into the house, she retreated so far into her shyness that she could not lift her eyes from the floor.

Darcy looked down at her then back to Elizabeth with concern. "Yes, Mrs. Bennet, may I present my sister, Miss Georgiana Darcy?" She curtseyed but still would not speak.

Elizabeth came forward and said softly. "It is so wonderful to see you again, Georgiana."

She looked up to Elizabeth and swallowed. "Yes, it is."

Smiling, Elizabeth took her arm and led her into the room. All of the sisters examined her. Obviously she was shy, but Kitty and Lydia were only concerned with her clothes. Mary wondered why a girl with all the advantages of life could possibly be so afraid to enter a room, and thought they might be alike in some ways.

Jane sat beside her on the sofa and patted her knee. "I doubt that you remember me, Miss Darcy. I am Elizabeth's sister Jane." Elizabeth took the opportunity to introduce the rest of the family, and slowly Georgiana relaxed. There was nothing to fear here. Nobody in this place knew of her ruin, she was simply accepted for who she was.

Darcy sat in a chair next to Elizabeth's sofa and watched her work magic on his sister. Their eyes met and her warm smile helped to relieve some of his tension. "I wonder if I might have a moment to speak to you before I see your father." He looked at her anxiously.

She looked out of the window, it was a fine day. "Mama, I would like to show our guests the garden."

Mrs. Bennet, watching Bingley staring at Jane, and Darcy staring at Elizabeth, wholeheartedly approved the plan. "Of course! The flowers are yet in bloom, by all means go outside, and when you return we will have tea."

Darcy stood and smiled at her. He bent down and whispered. "You are clever, Miss Elizabeth."

She laughed. "Do you really think that my mother would stand in the way of matchmaking?" He laughed and offered one arm to her, and his other to Georgiana. He had already told her that he needed to speak to Elizabeth alone for a few moments when they arrived.

In the garden, Georgiana stayed with Jane and Bingley, and Elizabeth led Darcy to an area that afforded them some privacy. He looked around very carefully and when he was satisfied that they could not be seen, pulled her against him so quickly that she gasped. "William!"

His arms wrapped around her waist and his eyes travelled over her face. "Elizabeth, I have thought little of anything but holding you in my arms again." His face lowered and her lips were tenderly brushed with his, then feeling her response, Darcy groaned and kissed her deeply. His hands moved, one supporting her back, the other drawing her hips against him. Elizabeth's arms moved from his waist to around his neck and she drew his head down, entwining her fingers in his hair and pressing the length of her body to his. He drew away from her mouth only far enough to kiss his way to her throat. "Darling, please, I can not bear to wait two months for you. Let me tell your father of our letters. At least let him know that we are long beyond courtship." His hair brushed against her face as his head bent to claim the sensitive skin beneath her ear.

Elizabeth moaned and he reacted by holding her tighter against his aroused body and suckling ever so delicately her throat. She trembled. "Oh William."

Her moan drove him to run his hands over her, feeling the curves, and again firmly held her to his chest. He lifted his face to look into her eyes. Passion burned there. "What is your answer Elizabeth?" Her eyes closed and her mouth hungrily claimed his. The provocative move drew out his moan, and they stood exchanging their kiss for several more moments before she began to draw away. "No, no, please . . ." He tried to bring her back to him.

"We must . . ." She panted, ". . . we must . . . stop . . . William." She looked up and saw his blue eyes had disappeared and been replaced by the blackness of his desire. She swallowed, trying to calm her breathing.

He panted raggedly. "What shall we do?"

Elizabeth stroked back the hair that fell against his eyes and he took her hand, kissing the palm, and then held it to his pounding heart. "Tell him everything, my love. I will come in and reassure him. He will be unhappy."

He nodded. "Any father would be unhappy to lose his daughter to another man. I can understand after I almost lost Georgiana."

She nodded. "Will you tell him of her actions?"

Calming, he stepped back and held both of her hands in his. "Yes, I think that he must know it all. Everyone in London knows of it, or some version of it. I would prefer he know the truth. It is only a matter of time before the news is learned here."

"Lizzy!" They startled. Jane had given them as much time alone as she dared. "Mama said that tea is ready."

Elizabeth straightened Darcy's neck cloth and he gently rubbed a thumb over her lips. "I am afraid that you will need an explanation for this." Then his fingertips brushed her neck. "I am sorry."

She drew in a breath. "Is it very bad?"

He smiled. "It depends on who you ask. I think it is beautiful." She raised her brow, and he laughed. "Call Miss Bennet over and see her reaction."

"Jane, could you come here for a moment?" Elizabeth looked up at him with her arms folded. Jane appeared around the corner and took one look at Elizabeth and gasped. She glanced at Darcy and her eyes focused on his swollen mouth. "Well, that answers that question." Elizabeth sighed. "Now what do we do?"

Jane looked from one to the other. "Lizzy!"

She patted her arm as she walked past. Darcy quickly caught up to her, and took her hand to place on his arm. "Oh Jane, we are engaged!"

He smiled and leaned down. "Well, not officially."

Elizabeth glanced up. "So you were toying with me?"

Darcy kissed her hand. "Not at all, my love. We just need your father's sanction, remember?"

"Well, after he sees our faces, I have a feeling he will have no choice but to grant it."

His eyes widened. "You mean I have compromised you?"

She laughed. "I believe, Mr. Darcy that you have!"

He joined her laughter. "So I have."

They had by then joined Bingley and Georgiana. The two men eyed each other, one with raised brows and a smile, the other with a challenge. Georgiana looked at her brother with confusion, then to Elizabeth and gasped. "William!" Elizabeth took a firm hold of Georgiana's arm and they entered the house. When they reached the door to Mr. Bennet's bookroom Darcy and Elizabeth paused while the others continued on.

She fussed with his coat and tie, arranged his hair and he stood, taking in her activity and smiling warmly down at her, his eyes twinkling. "Am I presentable, Miss Elizabeth?"

She brushed off some imaginary lint and looked up. "You will do, sir." He laughed.

The sound of the door opening startled them both. "Mr. Darcy, are you ever going to knock or shall I sit here listening to your courting all day?" Mr. Bennet stood looking at the suddenly silent and guilty pair. He took in the appearance of the two, noting the blushed cheeks and more significantly, the blushed lips.

He stared at Elizabeth with a look of surprise and she met his gaze unashamedly. "I will just go in and see to Georgiana. If you have any need of me, please call." She nodded to her father, smiled warmly at Darcy and turned to disappear down the hall.

The two men stared after her and Mr. Bennet cleared his throat. "Will you come in, sir?" Darcy nodded and drawing a breath, entered the room.

Chapter 15

"**M**r. Darcy?" Indicating the chair placed in front of his desk, Mr. Bennet settled into his own, and resting his elbows on the arms, laced his fingers and regarded the young man before him. Darcy's face was unreadable. Mr. Bennet did not know him well enough, but to one who did, seeing the slow flexing of his fingers, the lifting and twist of his chin and the periodic bite of his lower lip, the evidence of his discomfort would have been clear. Mr. Bennet had the upper hand in this interview, and he meant to keep it as long as possible. The men sat in silence until Mr. Bennet made the first move.

"Well, Mr. Darcy, you requested this meeting. To what do I owe this honour? Last night you assured me you were not coming to announce that you have fallen in love with my daughter by reading her letters to your sister."

Darcy nodded. "That is quite correct, sir, although, I have had the distinct privilege to have read each letter that Georgiana received from Miss Elizabeth, and I am grateful that she has found such a caring friend." Mr. Bennet bent his head, knowing the meaning behind the man's sincere words. Darcy began searching for the way to tell Elizabeth's father that he had broken the rules of propriety by writing her when Mr. Bennet spoke.

"Mr. Darcy. It was an amusing conjecture of mine that perhaps you had in fact exchanged some sort of friendly correspondence with Lizzy, perhaps added a line or two to your sister's letters, and perhaps she would do the same to her own for your benefit. I came to this conclusion after observing the surprising behaviour you displayed last night. You were acting as a man with a firm interest in my daughter. Your dancing with her almost to the exclusion of all other ladies, your obviously protective reaction to the approach of Mr. Lucas, and your vigil on the edge of the dance floor whenever she was engaged with another man made you a fascinating study." Darcy's eyes never wavered from Mr. Bennet; he waited for the coup de grâce. "However entertaining my surmises were, the unquestionable evidence of a far deeper relationship is clearly displayed on your, and I am shocked to say, my daughter's face. Sir, I am well within my rights to demand an explanation from you, and much more. My Lizzy is a good girl, and I am at a loss to understand what is clearly a willing, and I assume long-term, breach in propriety by her, with you. I do hope that this is the subject you wished to address with me today, sir, as I will entertain no other."

Darcy steeled himself. It would be uncomfortable, but the opening to tell the truth had been given. "Mr. Bennet, indeed, this is precisely the subject I wished to speak about." He gathered his thoughts, and while doing so, unconsciously reached into his coat pocket and drew out the worn ribbon. He entwined it in his fingers and felt better. "Sir, when my sister and I met Miss Elizabeth, it was at a moment of great pain in our lives. She brought my sister a little comfort and agreed to a correspondence with her. I did indeed add a line to the first letter, thanking her for her care." He wrapped the ribbon around his index finger and unwrapped it again, all the while staring at Mr. Bennet, who glanced at the man's occupation with interest. "I would now like to acknowledge that I too derived comfort from Miss Elizabeth's letters and began to write her myself. What began as a light banter became a friendship, and has grown, sir, into a very deep regard."

He took a deep breath and met Mr. Bennet's eye. "I have fallen in love with Miss Elizabeth, sir. I regard the past three months of letters that we have shared as a courtship I could not have dreamed of ever having. I honestly never hoped to find a wife, let alone love, but sir, the opportunity to know your daughter through letters has been the greatest gift of my life. A courtship performed within the recognized bounds of propriety would have left me trying to make small conversation in a crowded drawing room. I am of no use in such a situation, and would have failed miserably. In our letters we were able to . . . express ourselves without fear. I believe that I know Miss Elizabeth better now than I would in a year of tea and polite conversation." He swallowed. "It is for this reason that yesterday morning, when I went riding and came upon Miss Elizabeth on her walk, I could not hold back. I had intended to ask her for a formal courtship upon my arrival at Netherfield, but finally seeing her, and witnessing that she shared my feelings, I offered her my hand, and she accepted. We are engaged to be married." He blew out a breath and released the ribbon that was so tightly wound on his finger he could no longer feel sensation. He watched Mr. Bennet digest the declaration. "Sir, I realize that some sort of courtship would be desirable for appearance's sake, but I also wish to tell you that Miss Elizabeth and I are agreed that we would like to marry as soon as possible."

"Are you?" Mr. Bennet said sardonically. He was both appalled and relieved with Darcy's confession. A forced marriage, not that he would have demanded one, was not required. He thought that he knew Lizzy, but the plain truth was that she hid this secret so well, that he had no idea she was losing her heart gradually to a man he knew next to nothing about. "Mr. Darcy. For the moment, I will set aside the breach of propriety that led you and Lizzy to this juncture and address the most pertinent matter. You have asked my daughter to be your wife?"

Darcy sat up straight. "Yes sir and she *has* accepted me."

"I know little of you, sir."

Darcy relaxed. This was a subject that would only make him worthy. "My father passed five years ago, and at that time I became the master of Pemberley, our estate in Derbyshire. My income from the estate is ten thousand a year, but I have a great many more investments and properties, and my total income is nearly twice that sum. I also own a house in town. Miss Elizabeth will have an excellent settlement sir; I am not miserly or mean; she and our children will want for nothing. She will never fear for her future." Mr. Bennet surmised Darcy was rich, but he did not anticipate this.

"That is quite impressive and welcome news, Mr. Darcy. And although my daughter's financial situation is naturally of great importance, I value far more her happiness. She has told you that she loves you?"

Darcy nodded; a small smile and look of pride crossed his face. "She has."

Mr. Bennet noted how it changed the man. He regretted what he was about to say. "Love sir, is an extraordinary gift. Are you sure that this is not some passing fancy?"

Darcy's expression changed to one of concern. "Mr. Bennet, I assure you, this is not the work of a moment. Already we have endured a time of doubt and pain between us, and it has only made our mutual conviction stronger."

Mr. Bennet had an inkling of what he referred to and let that pass for the moment. "And sir, what do you think my daughter's reception would be in society?"

Darcy sighed. "I have no interest in participating in society, sir. They have proven their worth lacking."

"Your sister has been shunned."

It took a moment for that statement to sink in, but when it did, Darcy's eyes widened and he sat up. "What do you know of my sister?"

Mr. Bennet opened a drawer, drawing out the muddy envelope. "This letter arrived today in the morning post. The direction was unclear and I opened and read it. It was meant for you." He held it out and Darcy took it, already knowing what it was. He stared at the letter. "Will you not read it?" Mr. Bennet asked, watching Darcy caress the paper.

He shook his head. "I waited so long to receive this." He swallowed, his eyes suddenly filled with emotion, and he stood to walk to the window and look out at the drive.

If Mr. Bennet had any doubt of the man's affection for Elizabeth, it was now erased. "Mr. Darcy." There was no response. He stood and laid a hand on Darcy's shoulder. "Son, I understand more than you can know the pain and consequences of a sister's compromise." Darcy turned to him.

"My own sister, just a girl of fourteen at the time, allowed herself to be seduced by a boy who worked in the stables. He was nineteen, and knew what he was about. The tryst was discovered when my sister presented with a pregnancy. She was sent away to Scotland, never to return. To this day, her name is not spoken and my own daughters know nothing of her existence." He returned to his chair. Darcy remained standing. "Our family was deeply affected by the scandal. My mother was never the same, my father gave himself to drink and I am sure it hastened their deaths. The young lady I loved could not tolerate the shame and did not support me. I lost her to another. Then, one night at an assembly; I danced with Fanny Gardiner. She was very pretty, but silly, entertaining enough for a dance." He closed his eyes. "I have never been an accomplished dancer. I turned wrong and stepped on her gown, tearing it. Her father saw an opportunity to attach his daughter to a gentleman and demanded that I marry her. Fanny had no objections; she wished to be the mistress of an estate, instead of the wife of a tradesman, as she expected to be. My parents said that the family could not bear another scandal and I found myself married to a woman I can barely abide within a month."

Darcy walked over and resumed his seat, sitting forward and listening intently. "I regret my marriage daily, Mr. Darcy. The only saving grace is my daughters, particularly my Lizzy." His eyes were now teary. "I swore that she would never suffer my fate. She would choose her future. If she has chosen you, then so be it, but I will not have her life begin with the taint of scandal lingering over her. You will not marry her right away, no matter the reasons. You will have to endure a courtship and engagement period. I will have no whispers follow her. Do you understand me, sir? Given your sister's experience, I imagine you should."

They sat staring at each other. Darcy realized anew how fortunate he was to have Elizabeth love him, and not abandon him when she learned of the scandal. "I will not lie and say that I like this news, but I do understand completely, sir." He swallowed. "How long must we wait? I had hoped to bring my wife home in time for Christmas."

"That is under three months away." Mr. Bennet said unhappily.

Darcy nodded, feeling his heart sink. "Yes, I know, but the roads to Derbyshire very quickly become difficult to navigate, and I wanted us safely home before . . ."

Mr. Bennet waved him off impatiently. "Mr. Darcy, you are not concerned of the roads. You wish to have your wife. The evidence was clear on your faces when I opened my study door." He calmed. "Before you made your unexpected proposal, what was your original plan?"

"We were to court openly for a month then announce the engagement, and marry at the end of November." He said it quickly, hoping for approval.

Mr. Bennet closed his eyes and remained silent, feeling Darcy's eyes bore into him he looked up. "I will approve this on certain conditions." Darcy leaned forward. "Your displays of affection must be restrained."

Darcy closed his eyes and nodded. "Yes sir." He opened them again. "Is that all?"

Mr. Bennet nodded. "I think that will be challenging enough for you."

Darcy let out a long breath. "That is true." The men's eyes met and they both smiled, sharing the common knowledge. "Sir, I would like to teach Miss Elizabeth to ride. Mr. Bingley has a pony in his stable which I believe would be suitable for her. With your permission . . ."

Mr. Bennet regarded the hopeful expression in the man's eyes. "You are aware of my daughter's poor success with the activity?"

He smiled. "She has alluded to it."

Mr. Bennet laughed. "Well, if you are willing to try, I give you leave."

Darcy smiled. "Thank you, sir!"

Mr. Bennet smiled and stood, Darcy rising with him. They walked to the door and Mr. Bennet extended his hand. "I will speak to Lizzy about this later, but I believe that it is safe to say, welcome to the family, Son. You have my blessing and consent."

Darcy shook his hand gratefully. "Thank you sir, I will treasure her always."

Mr. Bennet nodded. "See that you do." The men walked out of the bookroom together towards the drawing room where the ladies and Bingley were gathered. Arriving in the doorway, Darcy's smile was erased upon seeing Elizabeth sitting on a small sofa with John Lucas beside her.

Elizabeth saw the crease in his brow and smiled at him. His eyes asked if she was well, and the almost imperceptible nod reassured him enough to relax. His body had been poised to rescue her if necessary. Mr. Bennet did not wish to announce their courtship until he had spoken to Elizabeth, but Darcy was no longer comfortable with the delay. "Mr. Bennet, could we tell our news?" He said softly.

A small smile played on Mr. Bennet's lips. "Anxious to assert your territory, Mr. Darcy?" The light of amusement returned to his eyes.

Darcy met his gaze, feeling anything but amused. "Sir, I am very much aware of Mr. Lucas' desires."

"Relax sir; she is in no danger of being wooed from you here in her home. I suggest that you take a seat, and meet your future family." Darcy entered the room and took an empty chair next to Elizabeth's end of the sofa.

"Is everything settled?" She whispered, leaning towards him.

He smiled slightly and leaned closer to her. "Your father will speak to you. He has given his consent, but we must wait." The disappointment that crossed her face went a long way to relieving his own distress, and it was all he could do not to take her hand in his. His fingers began to move when he caught the raised brows on Mr. Bennet's face and sighed.

"Mr. Darcy, I do believe that you need a new ribbon." Elizabeth smiled looking at the sad bit of satin in his hand.

He looked down and smiled at her. "I did not even realize I was holding it." He tucked it back in his pocket. "I needed you with me." She blushed. John watched but could not hear the quiet exchange, and felt the need to interrupt.

"Mr. Darcy, I was just asking Mr. Bingley if you might like to join a party for a day of sport."

Darcy looked at him appraisingly. "Shooting? Yes, that is something I looked forward to doing while staying at Netherfield. I am afraid that the ladies will not always wish for our company."

He glanced at Elizabeth who raised a brow. "What ladies do you refer to, Mr. Darcy? Surely Miss Bingley would welcome your company at any time."

A loud cough was heard from Bingley as he choked on a biscuit.

Darcy turned towards him. "Are you quite well, Bingley?"

He took a long sip of tea and regained his composure. "Yes, quite." Georgiana watched the bantering exchange with fascination.

"Of course, perhaps you could take her along; she would be quite useful carrying the birds." Elizabeth suggested.

Darcy pursed his lips. "No, thank you Miss Elizabeth, although I am sure that Miss Bingley is very accomplished, I doubt that her education included the skills of a good hound."

"I beg to differ, Darcy, she is very accomplished at rooting out the eligible men in any parlour." Bingley smiled at him then turned to Elizabeth. "Miss Elizabeth, my sister will be delighted to know that we have spoken of her in her absence."

She laughed. "As you are not leaping to her defence, I have a feeling that she was kind enough to speak of me in mine?"

Bingley's smile widened. "Ah, you are a very clever woman! I thought that of you when we first met, and now it is proven true. You are as clever as you are lovely."

Elizabeth laughed. "And you are a golden-tongued charmer, Mr. Bingley!"

Darcy watched the exchange with increasing unease. He did not at all like how easily Bingley brought out Elizabeth's teasing nature. "Bingley . . ." He glowered at him, and all he received in return was a raised brow.

John watched Darcy's obvious jealousy increase, and wondered if he had another man to fight for Elizabeth's affections. Unfortunately for him, his half hour of visiting had neared its end, as he had not been invited to stay longer, he must depart. He was determined to show himself to be just as polite and gracious as Darcy. He rose. "Mrs. Bennet, I believe that I should be taking my leave. I will be sure to tell my mother of your acceptance of her invitation, and yours as well, Mr. Bingley. We look forward to seeing you all at Lucas Lodge next Wednesday." He turned and bowed formally to Elizabeth. "Good afternoon, Miss Elizabeth. It has been a very great pleasure to again enjoy your company."

She stood and curtseyed to him. "Thank you Mr. Lucas." John's eyes looked into hers and searched for some sign of emotion, happiness in his attentions, regret that he was leaving, but all he saw was a cautious smile. He had truly botched his courtship royally. He took his leave of the rest of the room and Mrs. Bennet directed Kitty to show him the door.

Darcy immediately claimed the seat next to Elizabeth. "Are you well? What did he want?"

She could not help but laugh at his demanding tone. "He came to extend his mother's invitation. He was the model of politeness. I have no idea what he is about, but I can complain of nothing."

Darcy stared at the doorway darkly. "I do not trust him."

Elizabeth touched his hand. "Perhaps he knows that his suit is futile and wishes to make amends."

Darcy continued his glower. "I am not so easily swayed." Elizabeth's retort was interrupted by her father.

"Lizzy, I would like a word with you." He turned and left for his bookroom, and she followed.

Behind the closed door Mr. Bennet took her hands. "Lizzy, Mr. Darcy has told me of your engagement. I know of your letters, and of his sister's situation. I am also aware of your expressions of affection." He looked at her seriously. "I have given my consent and blessing, however, I will not allow a hurried wedding simply to satisfy your desires, I am aware that you feel you have already been courting for three months, but as it has occurred well outside of public view, to say nothing of propriety, I am forced to demand a courtship period of at least a month. Mr. Darcy has prevailed upon me to allow your wedding at the end of November. Now Lizzy, do you truly love this man? Is this really what you want? I know that he is rich, but his and his sister's reputations are in tatters, and I might add, his circle of society will not look kindly on you capturing one of their own, despite his temporary fall. Do you know of his family's feelings about you? Are you prepared to face what his circle will do to you?"

Elizabeth was overwhelmed. Never had her father spoken to her so seriously before. "I . . . Yes, Papa. Mr. Darcy and I have discussed all of the concerns you raise and yes, I am prepared to accept whatever society or his family deals to me. I enter this marriage with eyes wide open."

Mr. Bennet squeezed her hands. "Do you understand why I insist on the courtship and engagement? I do not wish you to be angry with me."

"I do understand." She looked down, hiding her disappointment.

"And Lizzy, you must curtail your displays of affection, at the very least until you are engaged officially." She looked up, her eyes now expressing her hurt. "Papa, I can not . . ."

Mr. Bennet kissed her forehead. "Yes, Lizzy, you can."

They returned to the drawing room and Darcy looked up anxiously. Mr. Bennet indicated that he should join them and addressed the room. "I am delighted to announce that Mr. Darcy has requested Lizzy's and my permission to court her. He has assured me that his intentions are honourable, and I hope for a greater announcement in the future."

Darcy took Elizabeth's hand and kissed it gently before Mrs. Bennet's screeching filled the room. Bingley stood and wrung his hand and excited conversation started amongst the family. Georgiana took it all in, trying to understand where she fit into the general upheaval when Mary sat down beside her.

"Miss Darcy, are you happy for your brother?"

She looked at the previously silent girl. "Yes, very happy. Elizabeth has been a wonderful friend to me, and I hope to call her sister one day."

Mary nodded. "She is so full of life. I wonder sometimes how we can be related. I am just not able to summon the joy she feels without effort, but I do love watching her." Georgiana listened with interest. Her impression of Mary was that of a girl who preaches morality and not one who would covet her sister's liveliness. She wondered if it was all a mask that she wore, like the one that William wore with everyone but his very closest friends. "I understand that you play, Miss Darcy, perhaps we could practice together while you are visiting the area. I have a feeling that your brother will be rather occupied now." She smiled over at Darcy who was already testing Mr. Bennet's proclamation by keeping a firm grip of Elizabeth's hand which rested on his arm.

Georgiana caught Elizabeth's eye that looked between her and Mary and gave her an encouraging smile and nod. She smiled at Mary. "Yes, I would like that Miss Mary. Thank you."

With Darcy and Elizabeth completely occupied in a soft conversation, Bingley was finally free to give his full attention to Jane. "Miss Bennet, I can not begin to express how delighted I am with this announcement. I do hope that you are pleased."

She smiled softly and nodded towards the engrossed couple. "Mr. Bingley, my sister has astonished me of late with her anticipation to see Mr. Darcy, and now with her finally having his company, I have felt nothing but joy for her happiness."

Bingley followed her gaze and smiled, seeing Darcy surreptitiously brushing his hand on Elizabeth's arm. "I must admit, I feel a certain amount of jealousy for my friend."

"Jealousy, Mr. Bingley?" She asked with surprise, and then cast her eyes down.

He looked back at her and tilted his head, trying to see her face. "Yes, he saw your sister and realized at that moment that she was someone he wished to know. He then referred to her as someone he would likely never see again, and I was struck by the disparity in the pain of his statement and the way his face lit up when he was thinking of her. I had until then not understood how a few moments in a woman's company could change a man so suddenly."

"Until then?" Jane continued to look at her folded hands. "Has something changed, sir?"

He did not reply. He waited for her to lift her head and look at him. When their eyes finally met he smiled. "Yes, Miss Bennet. Something has changed." He paused. "I would like your permission to come calling. I would like to know you better."

Jane smiled and Bingley wanted to shout. "Yes, Mr. Bingley, I would like that very much."

"Excellent!" He grinned. "Perhaps I could accompany my friend when he visits; you and I could volunteer to be chaperones." He looked over to Darcy who resembled so much a lost puppy he almost snorted. "I believe that your sister might appreciate it."

Jane observed Elizabeth and started laughing at the expression on her face. "I believe they both would, but I do suggest that we do not give them too much time alone." She raised her brows and smiled.

Bingley laughed. "Well, perhaps we could give them their time, but also allow a good long chance to repair the damage before returning to company."

Jane covered her mouth and giggled. "Mr. Bingley, you are wicked." She whispered.

He shrugged. "I am only doing for him what I wish he would do for me."

Their eyes met and she blushed. "How very kind of you."

"Yes, it is, actually." Bingley laughed at her surprised expression. "Miss. Bennet, if you understood Darcy's past, you would be just as happy to waive the rules as I am. He has had a very lonely life. Your sister is a godsend for him. I have never seen him so happy. I will do anything I can for them. He has done so much for me." He looked at her soberly. "I hope that you do not think me. . ."

Jane interrupted. "I think you a good friend, Mr. Bingley."

He smiled. "Thank you." He saw Mr. Bennet leaving the room. "Perhaps I should pay my respects to your father now that he is free. Excuse me." He stood and bowed, then catching Darcy's eye, winked as he left the room.

"What was that about?" Elizabeth asked. Darcy looked at his retreating friend speculatively. "I imagine Bingley is going to speak to your father."

"About what?" She demanded.

He smiled, seeing the protective flash in her eyes. "He wishes to make a good impression; I suspect that he will be calling on Miss Bennet."

Her eyes grew wide. "Courting her?" He shook his head. "Why do ladies always jump right to thoughts of marriage? Calling, my love, simply calling on her."

Elizabeth regarded him with pursed lips. "I take great offence at your presumption, sir. Not all ladies are instantly desirous of a wedding when meeting a young man. Some ladies care to know more of him than his income and skills on the dance floor."

He laughed. "Which ladies?" His eyes travelled to the lips he knew were so soft and sweet, and delighted in how they drew together.

"I believe that you know one."

He feigned confusion and looked about the room. "Who?" He watched a delicate pink slipper tapping out her ire and bit back his smile. "Do you mean,

Miss Elizabeth that you value more of me than my income and obvious skill when wooing a lady?"

She snorted and covered her mouth, her eyes dancing at inspiring his lifted brow. "Excuse me; I have no knowledge of your skills for wooing, as I was not subjected to them."

Darcy shook his head and leaned closer. "That is fortunate. I fear that if you had been, I would not know the taste of your lips now."

Elizabeth's breath caught. "Oh my."

Darcy sat back, satisfied with the dreamy smile that had appeared on her face. "Elizabeth, your father has demanded that we curtail our displays of affection until we are engaged . . . I fear that I will be unable to restrain myself. You will have to keep me in check."

Her expression changed. "But I do not want to!" She cried. Heads in the room turned her way and she blushed, looking down. She peeked up to see Darcy's delighted smile. "I was hoping that you would help me. I am afraid, William, that I am as lost as you."

Now his breath caught and they stared at each other. "We will work this out, my love." He whispered. She nodded. "Your father has granted me permission to give your riding lessons at Netherfield."

Elizabeth smiled. "How very convenient." He nodded, and glancing around the room, ran a finger down her wrist to her palm. "Yes, indeed."

———⁓⁓⁓———

John sat back in the chair in his father's study, thinking over his visit to Longbourn. It had gone surprisingly well, at least until Darcy appeared with Mr. Bennet. Eliza had been cautious, but friendly. She obviously appreciated the change in his addresses. Their conversation began rather stilted, but as time passed he could see that she relaxed.

He threw down the pen he had been twiddling in his fingers and looked over the accounting books spread before him. He was learning the duties required to run the small estate. His father's decision to take the place after his knighting was a reflection of his self-importance. He thought that any man with "Sir" before his name was instantly of greater value than all others, but in reality, he was simply a man with an honorary title granted in recognition of a small service to the crown, nothing more. He was certainly not a peer, though watching him trying to talk up Darcy was both amusing and mortifying. Anything to disrupt Darcy's attention to Eliza was welcome, but why did he have to be so blatant about it? He sighed. It was no use; he supposed everyone had relatives to blush over. Look at Eliza, her mother . . . how on earth did Mrs. Bennet produce Eliza? Or Jane for that matter? And now she was clearly pushing Kitty towards him, when only a few months ago she was welcoming his attentions to Eliza.

He pounded the desk in frustration. He had his opportunity. Clear sailing, and what did he do? He squandered it by behaving as a self-important fool, just like his father. He thought himself so good that she could not possibly resist him, and acted a jealous, possessive idiot, frightening her in the process. And now Darcy was here, and speaking to Mr. Bennet alone. John had a distinctly queasy feeling when he left Longbourn. He caught the smile on Darcy's face just before he was spotted. He had asked Mr. Bennet for permission to . . . what? Court or marry her? He would find out soon enough, gossip of this magnitude would not be secret long. Why not simply admit defeat and walk away? There are many other pretty girls in the neighbourhood, some with fortunes. He shook his head. Not like her. "No, as long as there is no ring on her finger, she is fair game. Wednesday night, I will approach her again." He closed his eyes, and began to plan his strategy. There must be something about Darcy that he could use to his advantage.

--- ∿ ---

Hurst stood outside of the doorway to the sitting room where Louisa and Caroline talked. "What do you think? Will it work?" Caroline asked urgently.

Louisa's voice reflected her doubt. "I do not know, Caroline, I think that it has a great potential to go very wrong. I know that you wished her to be compromised and married to allow Mr. Darcy to re-enter society, but with Charles? Why?"

"Why not?" She laughed. "He would be Mr. Darcy's brother; we would be in company with them all of the time. No titled family will ever take her now, so it would certainly be the only opportunity Charles would have to marry into some family with such a pedigree. Surely he would understand the advantage to us all, why we would be members of the first circles with the family connection to Mr. Darcy."

"Even through his ruined sister?"

"But that is just it, Louisa, once she is married, she is no longer ruined!" Her voice reflected her avarice. "And she has the dowry. Imagine what a grand estate Charles could buy with the addition of her thirty thousand to Father's funds! Why it could rival Pemberley!"

"That is extremely wishful thinking Caroline. Besides, you are wrong, many a titled family would welcome her dowry, they are always in need of funds." Louisa grew silent for a moment. "Do you think Charles would give in?"

"Of course he would, he is always easily manipulated to whatever I wish." She sniffed dismissively.

Louisa disagreed. "Not of late, have you noticed that he is asserting himself more frequently? It seems that watching Mr. Darcy deal with society and all that has happened with his sister has affected Charles. He seems to be learning to emulate Mr. Darcy's strength. He may refuse even if the compromise you plan is witnessed. After all, she is already ruined, it can not get worse. You are determined to win Mr. Darcy at any cost." She studied Caroline. "What about Miss Elizabeth? He was very taken with her at the assembly. He danced three times with her. Three! You know the significance of that! He practically declared himself. It was quite singular. It is very unusual for Mr. Darcy to forget the rules of proper society. He must not have been himself last night."

"You do not need to remind me." Caroline said bitterly. "What is that chit about? She must be discouraged. I have tried to talk to him about it, you know. I told him in the carriage on the way home, well you heard me! I told him that he was putting himself in great danger of falling victim to a fortune hunter! He is blinded by her!" Louisa nodded; this discussion had taken place endlessly since last night. "Mr. Darcy is far too rich and important to show favour to a country nobody. Do you think he is simply seeking a distraction while here? He never behaves so . . . obviously in town, maybe he thinks that he can take advantage of the naïve population, nobody needs to know . . ." She wrinkled her brow, trying to understand her prey's behaviour.

"Caroline, I can not presume to know his motives, but I must say that Mr. Darcy has never displayed any signs of such easy behaviour towards women in the past, and we have kept a very close eye on him for years. There must be something more to it."

"But what?!" Caroline paced around the room. "Even if he does not marry me . . ." She stopped and closed her eyes, clutching her heart at the thought, ". . . he is ruining his chances to marry well when he returns to town, to say nothing of further hurting his sister's opportunities if she ever returns to society." Caroline began to stride from the room.

"Where are you going?" Louisa called.

"I must speak to him. I must tell him he is behaving foolishly. I must make it very clear what a worthless nobody that Elizabeth Bennet is, before the entire neighbourhood has them married. He will thank me for pointing out the truth!"

Louisa stopped her. "I do not believe that he has returned from his visit to Longbourn with Charles yet."

Caroline deflated and sat down. She looked at the invitation that had arrived earlier and lay on the table next to her chair. "I imagine the Bennets will be invited to this dinner at Lucas Lodge. I will have to remind Miss Elizabeth of her place there. And remind Mr. Darcy of his."

Louisa smiled. "You are ruthless."

Caroline lifted her brows. "I am merely doing what is necessary." The conversation turned to other subjects and Hurst nodded his head and thought. *I will apparently have to do what is necessary as well.*

Chapter 16

15 October 1811
Rosings Park
Kent

Dear Fitzwilliam,

I hope that this letter finds you and the rest of the family well. I have not received a letter from Darcy for several months, and am unsure of his location. If you are in contact with him, he must know that Mother has decided to find a husband for Georgiana. Mother feels that if she is safely married, Darcy will come around and finally marry me. As you know, he does not desire such a union.

From what Mother said, I believe that she will be writing to respectable families that are in need of funds. She will propose that a son marry Georgiana to restore her place in society in exchange for her dowry. Mother will not tell Darcy of her actions until she secures a suitor.

I would not wish this for myself, much less my young cousin, and I hope that you or Uncle might bring this to an end somehow. I do not wish to be the one to tell Darcy. I will attempt to secure her letters before they are posted, but I have little hope of success.

Your cousin,
Anne de Bourgh

Richard blew a low whistle. "My Lord." He stood and walked down the hall and knocked on the door to his father's study. Hearing his call, Richard entered and closed the door.

Lord Matlock and James were bent over a table, examining a map of the estate. "What is wrong? You look as if you have received some bad news." He glanced at the letter in his hand.

Richard grimaced and handed him the letter. "Aunt Catherine has reared her head again." He sat down and watched as his father and brother leaned over it.

James spoke first. "I hate to say this of our aunt, but is she deranged? Who gave her the authority to bargain Georgiana's future away?" He looked at Richard. "Surely you do not approve?"

He stared. "Surely you jest! No, as wonderful as it will be someday to find Georgiana married and restored to society, this is not the method that should be followed." He sighed. "Darcy will be furious."

"Darcy furious!? I am furious! She has stepped far over the line this time." Lord Matlock began pacing. "The Season is over, all the families are back in the country, and the talk was dying. This will only dredge it all up again!"

"Darcy's consent would still be necessary; does she really think he would bend to her will?" James asked as he watched his father's rapid stride.

"She certainly would not receive mine." Richard muttered darkly.

Lord Matlock stopped. "There is nothing for it. I must go to Rosings. A letter will not do."

"What authority do you have over her?" James asked.

"I know the terms of Sir Lewis de Bourgh's will." Richard and James glanced at each other.

"And?" Richard prodded.

"Upon Anne's thirtieth birthday, if she is not married, Rosings is hers. She will have the right to send Catherine to the dowager's home. That is less than two years from now. Perhaps I can speak to Anne about her plans; she is becoming quite old to marry, and with Rosings in her possession, she will likely never marry, she will be free to make her own choices."

James nodded then was struck by a thought. "Would Aunt Catherine be displaced if Anne were to marry?"

Lord Matlock laughed without humour. "Not if she married Darcy. He would wish to remain at Pemberley, and Catherine would be able to continue at Rosings for her lifetime. Any other man would have sent her packing; that, along with our sister's wishes to show up our father with the joined estates are her incentives." He glanced at his sons. "I will go speak to your mother. She will be incensed and will likely wish to come along and strangle Catherine personally."

"Well, I must return to London soon, so I will travel with you. Further, as Georgiana's guardian, I should be there in any case." Lord Matlock nodded and strode from the room to find his wife.

The brothers watched him go. "Will you tell Darcy?" James asked.

Richard sat back and closed his eyes. "He is in Hertfordshire now, wooing Miss Elizabeth." James laughed shortly. Richard's eyes opened. "You do not support him?"

James picked up a pen and started fiddling with it. "Darcy and I were raised to follow certain standards when marrying. As first sons and heirs, we are to marry women of the highest circles, bringing their dowries and connections to the estates. He is mocking his position by taking on this fortune hunter in his ridiculous quest for love."

"Do you really think she is a fortune hunter? Mother seems to be softening towards the match, and she is no fool."

"She is a woman."

Richard cocked his head and raised a brow. "Obviously, James."

He waved his hand dismissively. "All women are overly romantic."

"So you are calling Darcy romantic?" He laughed. "You do not know him well. Darcy would have no idea how to express love let alone feel it. He had no ability to comfort Georgiana after we found her. I hardly did better, but at least I have the memory of an affectionate mother. He has nothing."

James listened, thinking of the warmth his mother taught him without even realizing it. "So why this girl? Why not someone from his circle? Surely there must be some lady of society who could fulfil whatever his need is."

Richard shook his head. "Miss Elizabeth found the key to awaken his numb heart. I will meet her sometime next month or sooner if this mess with Aunt Catherine requires my seeing him. I will reserve my judgment until then."

"All right, go, look her over, and render your opinion. Please do not be swept away by a pretty smile. Too much is at stake for him and Georgiana."

"One crisis at a time." They looked up as the door opened. Lord Matlock appeared; his face was bright red. "Richard, I suggest you have your things packed quickly or your mother is liable to leave without us."

Richard and James laughed. "Ah, leave it to Mother. She will set Aunt Catherine straight in no time."

"That is a fine weapon, Mr. Darcy." Sir William looked at the gun Darcy held with admiration.

He nodded. "Thank you, it was a recent purchase, but I have not as yet had the opportunity to try it." Darcy made a special effort to be a little more approachable. Elizabeth's gentle chastisement during one of their walks was still running through his mind. He smiled inwardly. How could this slip of a girl so quickly become a part of his consciousness? Several other men in the shooting party stepped over to inspect the new purchase. Darcy handed it to Mr. Goulding and watched as he held the gun to his shoulder and aimed at a passing bird. The group was gathered at Lucas Lodge, the men of that house, the occupants of Netherfield, and six other neighbours had met in the still foggy morning air to seek out the pheasant that were beaten out of the grass by servants. When Darcy enquired after Mr. Bennet, he was told that he rarely joined them. Darcy retrieved his gun and set out on the walk, separating himself slightly from the group. He enjoyed the activity, but was simply not comfortable with so many he did not know. He listened to the idle conversation of guns, dogs and horses. Bingley was urged to host a fox hunt when the season opened in November and he looked at Darcy with alarm, never having done such a thing.

Darcy gave him a slight smile. "I can tell you what must be done, but I am sure that your steward is well aware. I am only sorry that my best hunter is at Pemberley. I should have had my own horses brought down."

"I am sorry that my poor equestrian choices will limit your enjoyment, Darcy." Bingley jabbed.

Darcy laughed. "As I recall, they are not your horses. Perhaps you can have them included as part of the purchase if you decide to take Netherfield."

"That is an excellent idea!"

He smiled and wandered further away. The beaters cried out with success and a flock of birds suddenly rose up in a great squawk. The men hurried to fire their guns. Darcy made his shot, watching his bird fall, and was preparing to take another when suddenly his hat flew from his head and landed some five feet away on the ground. He spun around to see John Lucas standing alone behind him, gun in hand, and an unreadable expression on his face. "What the devil are you doing?!" Darcy cried. "I could have been killed!" He strode up to the man, his eyes blazing. The other men saw the incident and Bingley bent, picking up the hat, and stuck his finger in one of the holes. The location was just where the top of Darcy's head would reside. They gathered around the two men.

John finally reacted. "I am sorry, Mr. Darcy, I was aiming and the hound bumped against me just as I pulled the trigger, and threw me off balance. It was an accident." He looked over at Bingley holding the hat and saw the hole. He then glanced up at Darcy's head and blanched. A trickle of blood was running down his temple. "Mr. Darcy, you have been wounded."

Darcy's eyes widened and his hand went to his hair as the rest of the party murmured. He drew his fingers away and looked at the smear of blood. Hurst stepped forward with a clean handkerchief and pressed it to his scalp. "Lean down, man, you are far too tall for me to see the damage." Darcy bent and Hurst moved his hair about. "Just grazed, but a bit further south and we would not be enjoying this discussion." Bingley drew out his own handkerchief and wiped the blood from Darcy's face. He stood and accepted their ministrations, and tried to control his feeling that this was no accident.

John could practically read the thought as it crossed his face. "Mr. Darcy, I swear, I was not attempting to harm you. I realize that we have . . ."

Darcy held up his hand. "I believe that I have lost my interest in hunting for today. If you will excuse me gentlemen, I will return to Longbourn and join my sister as she visits with the Bennets."

Sir William bustled up. "Please sir, it is but a scratch, and an accident to boot. Do not let this spoil your sport."

Darcy looked at him, then John. "Thank you, but I believe a walk will do me good." He took his hat from Bingley and placed it back on his head. All eyes travelled to the hole. He picked up his gun from where he threw it down, and nodding, began the long walk.

"Darcy wait, I will come with you." Bingley caught up to him.

"No, it is important for you to establish relationships with the neighbourhood. I will be fine. I would prefer Elizabeth's company in any case."

"Very well, we will come by Longbourn when we are finished. I will lead your horse over."

He nodded and grasped his shoulder. "Thank you." Both realized how close he had come to death.

They all watched Darcy leaving and then the eyes turned upon John. "I swear; it was an accident!"

Bingley stepped up to him and spoke softly. "You do not know how fortunate you are that Darcy let this go so graciously. It takes a far stronger man to walk away from a fight." John gritted his teeth. "I did not aim for him!" Bingley looked him over. He was doubtful.

Sir William called out. "Shall we continue, gentlemen?" The party wandered deeper into the fields as the gamesmen picked up the birds. John lagged behind, wondering if he had unconsciously aimed for Darcy. The news of his courtship with Elizabeth came as a hard blow. He looked behind him and just saw Darcy's tall form as it disappeared from view, and thanked God nothing worse was damaged than his hat.

"Finally I get to spend time with you!" Elizabeth hooked her arm in Georgiana's and they made their way through the garden and to begin their walk. "I was afraid that Mary was going to take all of your time. You certainly have become fast friends." She smiled at her.

"I do like her very much. She is a little older than I, but we seem to share a love of music."

"Indeed you do, I hope that you might convince her that all she plays need not be ponderous, and perhaps hint that playing is far better than singing." She winked at her.

"Elizabeth!" Her eyes were wide. "I can not tell her that she sings poorly!"

Elizabeth sighed. "I wish someone would." Georgiana giggled. "So, tell me, how are you getting on with Miss Bingley and Mrs. Hurst?"

"Oh, they are nice." Elizabeth tilted her head. Georgiana's expression was hardly enthusiastic. "Well, maybe a little too friendly. They keep telling me how wonderful I am, how accomplished, it all seems a bit much, really. The way they go on, you would think that I outshine every girl in society, when I am but fifteen. Even if I were to believe their flattery, I doubt that I could ever approach their description of me."

Elizabeth nodded. "That is very wise, Georgiana. Why do you think they flatter you so?"

"I do not know. Everyone else in town has been very clear in how ruined I am." She cast her eyes down and whispered. "I am not fit for anything now."

Elizabeth stopped and lifted her chin so that Georgiana had no choice but to look at her. "You are fit for a wonderful life. It may not be what you expected, but did you ever think that it may be even better?" She smiled as she watched her eyes widen, and then patting her arm they set off again. "Did it occur to you that they want something? I know them but little, and even with that brief introduction I see them both as rather manipulative. Do they do anything else that strikes you as odd?"

Georgiana worried her lip. She was unaccustomed to thinking ill of anyone. "I . . . well; Miss Bingley has presumed a closeness with William."

Elizabeth's brow rose. "A closeness?"

Georgiana looked up. "Oh, taking his arm, complimenting him excessively, following him around, getting in his way, drawing attention to herself . . ."

Elizabeth laughed. "I have a feeling you could go on forever. I imagine your brother finds the interest annoying."

Georgiana smiled. "Yes, but he is too polite to do much more than make a face when he thinks nobody can see." They laughed. "They seem to push Mr. Bingley towards me." She said softly.

Thinking of Jane, Elizabeth asked. "And how do you feel about that? He has begun visiting frequently and it is clearly to call on my sister Jane."

"Yes, I know. He is not interested in me, and I like him, but certainly not as more than my brother's good friend." She sighed. "Honestly Elizabeth, if it were not for you and your family being here, I would much rather go home."

"Well, with any luck, we will all be home soon." Elizabeth said softly. Georgiana looked at her with confusion. "We?"

"Oh." Elizabeth took her hands. "I see that your brother has not told you. He has proposed and I have accepted. My father insists on a public period of courtship, as nobody but we know of our letters. William and I are bearing with it for appearance's sake, but we do hope to announce our engagement soon and be married in about seven weeks." She smiled. "So, WE will be sisters."

Georgiana stood with her mouth agape. "Really?" She did not know how to react. "May I . . . may I embrace you Elizabeth?"

"Why of course!!" Elizabeth pulled her in for a great hug and Georgiana burst into tears. "Whatever is wrong?" Elizabeth held her close, rubbing her back and rocking her. "Georgiana?"

The tears continued, but she managed to speak. "Is this something that sisters do? Do they comfort each other?"

Elizabeth pulled back. "Has nobody ever held you?"

"Not since Papa died. Sometimes my aunt does, but I see her so seldom. William tries, but he is so awkward. He does not know how to express his feelings. When he was small, whenever he did, Papa would call him weak, and Mother, well from what I have heard, she rarely interacted with him at all. He just learned never to show anyone anything." She looked up. "Until he met you." They walked over to a bench and sat down. Elizabeth held her hands and listened. "He was changing every day, since your letters, but now that he is actually here with you, he is so different. I wish he had met you months ago, then maybe I would not have . . ." She grew quiet.

"You can trust me Georgiana. Why do you wish I had met William sooner?"

"Do you know why I agreed to elope with Mr. Wickham?" Elizabeth shook her head. Georgiana sniffed. "He expressed affection for me. He told me I was beautiful and held me and . . . I just did not want to lose that. Ever since Papa died, I have missed that so much."

Elizabeth closed her eyes and embraced the girl. "I understand now. That is why you did not tell William about Mr. Wickham coming to call. You did not want to lose the affection that he was expressing to you, even if you knew it was wrong." She nodded. "You do not continue to have feelings for him, do you? You realize that he only wished for your dowry and to hurt your brother?"

"I have ruined us all because of it."

Elizabeth kissed her forehead. "You were following a foolish dream. You were lonely and inexperienced, and I gather that Mr. Wickham is quite adept at what he did to you. You are not the only one."

Georgiana looked up. "I am not?"

"No. Your brother and I have talked about it. He still does not understand why you acted as you did, and you should tell him. You do understand what was so wrong about what you did, why you should never have hidden this from William?"

"Yes, I knew all along, it almost seemed as if I was living a story from a romantic book. But then we climbed into the carriage, and at first it was all so exciting. It was not long before I realized how stupid I had been and all I could think about was how to make it all stop, but it was too late then, I thought that there was no hope, and I would never see William again." She began sobbing. "I was so grateful when I saw him standing in the doorway with Richard, I had been praying all day long for him to find me. I deserve everything that has been said of me, and will bear it for the rest of my life as my punishment, as long as I still have my brother. I just feel so terrible for hurting him. He has suffered so much because of me, and I do not even belong in his home." That statement caught Elizabeth's attention.

"Is there anything else that you wish to talk about while we are alone?" Georgiana thought of telling her about her doubtful paternity, but just could not bring herself to speak on it. She shook her head. Elizabeth could sense that she was holding back but followed her lead and smiled. "Are you sure Georgiana? I promise; I will not judge you."

The sympathy in Elizabeth's voice finally helped her to overcome her fear and she blurted it out. "He never would have suffered this humiliation if I had never been born." She sobbed anew. It was several minutes before she could speak. "I am not a Darcy. My mother . . . I do not know who my father is."

Elizabeth hugged her tightly, and remembered William telling her this news, and searched to find the comforting words the young girl needed to hear. Georgiana continued. "The whole family knows, has at least suspected it since my birth, you see, my parents . . . my mother and Mr. Darcy did not get on well, they . . ."

Elizabeth shushed her. "I understand." She began to wonder about William's tormented childhood. "What has William said to you about this?"

Georgiana sniffed and looked up. "That I am as much a Darcy as he is." Elizabeth smiled; proud of the man she would marry.

"So, why are you worried? He accepts you, and that is the most important news of all, and apparently Mr. Darcy accepted you, too. You are William's sister, and soon you will be mine." She took out her lavender embroidered handkerchief and wiped her face. "Do you think of Mr. Darcy as Papa, still? He must have loved you, his loss affected you deeply. If he had been indifferent, you would not have felt the absence of affection that he obviously gave you, and you would not have been so easily influenced by Mr. Wickham's attentions."

She sniffed and kept her face buried in Elizabeth's shoulder. "I do still think of him as Papa. It was just when I learned this terrible news last month; it seemed that I finally knew why this had all happened to me. I am not a Darcy. I do not deserve the name because it is not mine. I deserve to be shunned and driven away. William should never have suffered with my behaviour because Papa should have rejected me at the beginning. He should have sent me away . . ."

Elizabeth kissed her hair and tried to find the words to help the anguished girl. "Do not be ridiculous Georgiana. I know that you are a source of joy for William. He would have been so terribly lonely without you." She searched for the right thing to say. "William told you that you are as much a Darcy as he is, correct?" Georgiana nodded. "And you definitely share the same mother, so you are agreed that you are definitely his sister by blood?" She nodded again. "Well, my dear, if my brother did not protect me when I behaved foolishly, I would be devastated. But your brother is the best of men, and has stood by you and defended you as well as he can. You are not living on some Scottish moor now are you?"

Georgiana lifted her face from Elizabeth's shoulder and looked at her. "No." She whispered.

"Then I suggest that you stop belittling yourself and thinking that you are undeserving. You are only undeserving if you listen to the nonsense that anyone who shuns you says. You are a good and beautiful girl who made a terrible mistake. William and I will do our best to be sure that you have a happy life, whatever it may be, but we can only do so much without your assistance. You have to decide that you are worthy."

Georgiana hugged her and whispered. "Thank you for caring about me."

"I will always care about you." She kissed her forehead and smiled. "There, we had our first sisterly talk. What do you think? Can you bear to have a lifetime more?"

She sat up and smiled, dabbing at her eyes with her own handkerchief. "Yes, I believe I can."

Elizabeth laughed and looking across the garden she spotted a tall solitary figure approaching them. "What brings William here?"

Seeing the look in Elizabeth's eyes, Georgiana stood. "I will just return to the house." They exchanged smiles and Elizabeth patted her arm, and then walked to meet him.

Before he could say a word she spotted the hole in his hat. "William!!"

He sighed. "I was hoping you would not see that." He placed her hand on his arm and led her away from the house, and behind a garden wall. She began to ask a question and he muffled it by pulling her deep into his embrace and kissing her. He carefully removed her bonnet. "Just hold me, my love." He whispered.

Even with their brief time in each other's company, it was clear that something was wrong, and how very much he needed her comfort. She lay her head against his chest and squeezed him tight, as he rested his cheek on her hair. They stood in silence for several minutes until she heard him draw a shaking breath. She squeezed him again. "This would be so much easier without this heavy coat of yours."

A soft chuckle moved his chest. "I can think that it would be far more enjoyable as well." He drew back and smiled down at her with shining eyes. "I missed you."

Elizabeth reached up to brush the hair from his forehead and felt it stick. She pulled and he winced slightly. She looked at her fingers, now stained with his blood. "William, what happened?"

Darcy looked into her eyes and saw love and concern and ire. His heart was nearly bursting with the joy of receiving her affection. He could not possibly hold back and drew her against his body and reclaimed her lips. "Do you know how much I love you?" He whispered.

Not to be distracted Elizabeth drew away. "William, please tell me, why are you bleeding? What happened to you? Are you in pain? Let me see, we must clean your wound."

He smiled at her demands. An inch lower and he would be lying dead in that meadow, instead he was standing safe in her arms. "Shh."

Elizabeth saw the emotion in his eyes. "William?"

Darcy kissed her, and she realized that what he needed was for her to love him. Explanations could wait. Elizabeth pulled his face forward and ran her tongue over his mouth, then began suckling his upper lip. "Oh, Eliz. . ." She covered his mouth and began stroking his tongue with her own. She could feel his body trembling and it only made her want to love him more. He eagerly accepted her kisses, stroking her back and holding her tight, while their mouths hovered and slid and embraced. Darcy felt his control slipping, his hands were moving of their own volition, trying to open her coat and expose her warm flesh. She was not helping at all; the sensuous kisses were driving him wild in a way he had never before experienced. He managed to unbutton the spencer and his lips moved hungrily down her neck and found her shoulder. His hands moved around her body to stroke over her breasts, and he felt the nipples hardening into tight buds, waiting for his tongue to warm and soften them again.

"Will . . ." She moaned. He looked up and into her eyes, dark with the same passion he was feeling, and pulled her roughly back against him, reclaiming her lips as his own.

"Lizzy!!" Jane called her sister's name for the fifth time and looked worriedly at the house. She stood just beyond where the couple was embraced. She was about to close her eyes and try to pry them apart when she heard her sister's weak and panting voice respond.

"Jane?"

She closed her eyes in relief. "Yes. Papa asked Miss Darcy where you were and she told him that Mr. Darcy had arrived and you were talking to him. He was about to come out when I said that I would go and fetch you."

She was met by silence. "Lizzy?" She heard a low rumble of laughter, followed by Elizabeth's giggle. Several minutes later Elizabeth came around the corner, holding Darcy's hand.

Jane looked from one to the other and shook her head. "You look worse than last time!" Darcy's smile lit up his face and both girls gasped.

"You must do that more often, sir! It is quite irresistible!"

He laughed and kissed her hand. "I think that would not be wise, dearest, your father is not at all pleased with my charm." She reached up and lovingly rearranged his hair and he smiled at her warmly.

"Come on you two, before Papa does appear." Jane turned and walked into the house.

Darcy offered his arm and bent down. "Miss Elizabeth, I must ask a question before we face your father." She stopped retying her bonnet ribbons and smiled up at him. "Have you ever kissed a man before me?"

Her expression changed to one of concern. "You are the *only* man I have. . . Why do you ask? Am I doing something wrong? I am sorry . . ."

He pressed a finger to her lips and shook his head. "I only ask because my love, your kiss takes my breath away, I can only imagine what it will be after you have had some more practice."

Elizabeth blushed and looked down. "Really?" She peeked up to see his rapidly bobbing head and laughed. "Well, we all have our accomplishments, I suppose!" Darcy kissed her hand, and they entered the house.

Mr. Bennet stood in the entrance, arms folded, looking most unhappy with them both. "Mr. Darcy, if I may have a word?" Darcy sighed and began to let go of Elizabeth's arm when she interrupted.

"Could you speak to him later, Papa? He has been injured and it should be tended."

"Injured?" He saw Darcy's hat. "Sir, were you shot?!" His eyes went from the hat to the trace of dried blood on his face. Elizabeth gasped and suddenly understood what he had tried to distract her from seeing. She not once considered a bullet as the cause of his injury.

Darcy removed the hat and leaned his gun against the wall, then ran his hand through his hair. "Grazed, sir. Mr. Lucas said his hound nudged him and he misfired."

Their eyes met. "Is that so?" Mr. Bennet's expressed his doubt. "You do not think it was deliberate, do you?"

Darcy said nothing for a moment. "Of course not." His expression was unreadable.

Elizabeth grabbed the hat and looked at it carefully, then up to his forehead. Tears sprang into her eyes and her hand covered her mouth. "I almost lost you today."

"Elizabeth . . ." Darcy took her hand as she began to shake, whether in fear or anger he could not tell.

She searched his face then looked to her father and spoke in a steady, determined voice. "I will see to William's injuries, Papa." She boldly took his hand and led him to the kitchen. Mr. Bennet looked after them and wondered about the incident. He also recognized that Elizabeth had drawn a line in the sand.

"Sit down, Mr. Darcy." He looked around the busy room. He rarely entered his kitchens. The servants normally were gossiping and laughing as they worked, but with Darcy's presence, they were silent. Elizabeth spoke to Mrs. Hill, who returned with a bowl of water, several cloths, and some brandy. Elizabeth dipped the towel in the water and began gently cleaning his forehead.

Darcy's gaze was on her face. "You know, you should not be doing this."

Her eyes flicked down to his and back to her task. "And who do you suggest care for you, sir?"

"My valet would . . ." Elizabeth interrupted. "If you have failed to notice, he is not here."

He smiled at the flashing eyes and pursed lips. "I could wait."

She glared at him. "I can not." His smile grew.

"Thank you." He said softly.

Elizabeth glanced down at him and huffed. "Men." She started working through his hair.

Darcy closed his eyes and attempted to ignore the gentle touch. "What does that mean?"

"Silly fools going about and shooting at each other." She pronounced.

He looked back up at her. "We were not at war. We were hunting." Their eyes met, and Elizabeth's filled with tears. She blinked them away and scrubbed a little harder. Darcy reached up and to take her hand and squeezed. They both drew deep breaths. He let go and she examined the wound.

"You do not appear to need stitches. It should heal nicely." She applied the alcohol and he flinched. Elizabeth bent near his ear. "Big, strong, man." She smirked, then straightened and smiled.

Darcy mouthed, "I love you." She gathered up the supplies and Mrs. Hill bustled over to take them away.

Elizabeth turned back to him, and on the pretence of checking his wound once again bent near his ear. "As I love you." He wished to kiss her then, but out of the corner of his eye noticed Mr. Bennet had been standing and watching the exchange in the doorway. When Darcy turned his head, he saw that he was gone. Elizabeth wiped her hands, and held one out to him. "Shall we join your sister and the rest of my family?"

"Of course." He stood and tucked her hand on his arm.

"Georgiana and I had a talk today." She looked at him steadily.

They walked into the hallway and he studied her. "Wickham?"

She nodded, "and her father."

He drew a sharp breath. "How was she?"

Elizabeth closed her eyes for a moment. "She cried; she worries of losing you. I tried to reassure her, it was hard to know what to say, but I think my holding her helped."

Darcy looked down at the floor, his face was so sad. "I should have told you more. I should have prepared you for this." He looked up and away from her. "It has been quite a day."

Elizabeth touched his cheek and he turned back to her. "Whenever you wish to tell me of your parents . . . I gather from Georgiana that it was not a happy home."

He laughed shortly and kissed her hand. "No, it was many things, but happy was not one of them." He paused. "Thank you."

They had almost reached the parlour and could hear the sound of the pianoforte. "Oh, William, I am sorry but in the midst of our conversation I told Georgiana that we would marry. I did not realize you had not told her . . ."

He shook his head. "No, no, it is fine. I am not sure why I did not tell her, I guess that I enjoyed keeping it as my own precious secret." He looked at her lovingly. "I can not wait to bring you home."

Elizabeth pushed open the door and they were greeted with a blast of noise from the sister's arguing, Mrs. Bennet's screeching, and Mary's music. She raised her voice and grinning declared, "I can not wait either!"

―――――⁓⁓――――

Monday morning Darcy looked out of the window in the Netherfield Library at the sodden view. It was too wet to ride and the roads too muddy for a coach. He would have to remain in the house that day. He looked up at the poorly filled library shelves and thought that his housewarming gift would be more reading material, but then he smiled and realized that he would likely be the only one to ever open the volumes. His mind drifted back over the fields to Longbourn and to its home. He thought of Elizabeth constantly. The months of communication had opened their hearts and minds to each other, and inspired what he thought was love. But now knowing her physical presence, and hearing her voice and thoughts, she had been transformed into someone who was utterly indispensable. After only a few days, a few dances, a few long, precious walks with her, he could no longer conceive his life continuing without her by his side. He only wished that he could express it to her somehow. He wondered if she understood the depth of his feelings.

A knock brought his attention to the door and he was surprised by Danny's entrance. "Here you are, sir, the letters pile up when you are away." Danny drew out a tall stack of letters from his pouch as Darcy seated himself at a table.

"Thank you, Danny." He examined the missives and knew he would be all day answering them, but at least it would keep him away from Miss Bingley. He looked out at the rain. "Why did you keep pushing in this weather? You know it is dangerous."

"Ah it wasn't so bad. I was too close to stop, so I just kept on." He grinned and winked. "Besides, I wanted to stop at Longbourn."

"Longbourn?" Darcy sat back and looked at him quizzically. "What would take you there? Both Miss Darcy and I are only three miles away, there are no letters to deliver or retrieve."

Danny shuffled and coughed then looked up at his master sheepishly. "Ah, you might say I was stopping for personal reasons, sir."

A small smile appeared on Darcy's lips, and he raised his brow. "Really? Who is she?"

Danny lifted his chin. "Miss Susie Prewett, sir, the maid that takes care of the young ladies. I kind of got to know her when waiting on Miss Elizabeth's letters."

"You get on well, do you?"

Danny stood up straight. "Well enough, sir." Darcy laughed.

He glanced through the stack before him, "Well it seems that I will have several letters for London. I will make arrangements for you to stay here overnight and I will have them ready for you in the morning. At least it will keep you out of the rain, unless you go calling somewhere." Looking up at his loyal messenger for a moment, he took a piece of paper and quickly wrote a note, and sealed it. He handed it to Danny. "Now you have an excuse to pay your call."

Danny's grin grew. "Yes, sir!"

Darcy looked at him and was struck by a sudden idea. "While you are in town, you will stop at the house and pick up anything that has arrived there in my absence. I also will give you a note to ask Mr. Hendricks to retrieve something for me. I will tell you now that it is very important and should be guarded carefully."

The young man became very serious. "Yes, sir, that I will, sir."

Darcy nodded, dismissing him, but as the boy reached for the door he called out. "Oh and Danny, the item is Miss Elizabeth's engagement present."

His face broke out in a glowing smile. "I knew it! I knew she would be our mistress!"

Laughing, Darcy said, "I imagine that you knew long before we did. It is not official yet so say nothing to the staff, only Roberts knows."

"Yes sir!" He left the room and after Darcy called the housekeeper about finding him a place in the servant's quarters, he sat back and thought about the jewels that were kept in London. The majority of the Darcy heirlooms were at Pemberley. Most of the items in London were purchased by his mother. His father refused to spend any of his funds on her once their marriage effectively ended with his birth. Darcy was glad of it. He did not want Elizabeth to wear any of his mother's jewels. They would go to Georgiana when she was presented or came of age, depending on what happened in the future. Elizabeth would wear the jewels of his grandmothers. He closed his eyes, going over the inventory in his mind, then nodding, he wrote out a note to his butler and sealed it. He had found a way to express his feelings for her.

Chapter 17

"Danny, what brings you here?" The young man stood on the front step, dripping wet and grinning at Elizabeth.

"I had some post for the master, mistress, and I mentioned that I was going to come over here to visit . . ." His eyes grew wide and he blushed deep red.

Elizabeth stepped outside quickly and pulled the door shut. "Danny, please, you must watch yourself!"

"I'm sorry, mistress, I just wanted to see Susie while I am here." He shuffled his feet and looked up at her.

She stared at him in confusion. "Susie? Our lady's maid?" He nodded. Elizabeth blinked and then shook her head. "Danny, that is not what I meant, twice you called me mistress."

His eyes grew wide. "Oh. . . . Oh I am sorry, the master just told me the news, and . . ." He sighed. "I guess that I have thought of you as the mistress for so long now, it just seemed right."

Elizabeth could not help but smile. "So you knew before we did?"

He grinned. "That's what the master said!"

She laughed. "Very well Danny, just see that you do not do it again, not for a while."

He nodded, then remembering his purpose he drew out the note Darcy had given him. "This is from the master, Miss. Should I wait for a reply?"

Elizabeth took the note and her heart leapt. "Oh yes, why not go around to the kitchen, I think that Susie is there."

He started to walk away and stopped. "Oh, and the master said that if the day is fine tomorrow he will send the carriage for you at eleven for your riding lesson."

"Thank you, I will come to the kitchen with my reply."

She opened the door and returned to the sitting room. Without thinking, she began to open William's note as she walked and was startled by her mother's voice. "What is that, Lizzy? A note from Netherfield?" She stood and quickly crossed the room, her hand out and ready to snatch it away from her.

"Mama, this is from Miss Darcy, and she invites me to come to Netherfield tomorrow for a riding lesson. She will send the coach for me at eleven."

Mrs. Bennet stopped. "Riding?" She huffed. "Well, I suppose it is something you must learn, although you have never shown any talent for it." She returned to her chair and started her sewing. "You should take a change of clothes with you. You will be covered in mud after all of this rain." Elizabeth relaxed and let her held breath go. She did not feel that she had lied since Georgiana would likely join them.

"Yes Mama that is an excellent idea. The messenger is waiting so I will just write a note back now."

Mrs. Bennet nodded. "You must look your best tomorrow and do very well. Mr. Darcy must think that riding is important or he would not have his sister teaching you. You must continue to hold his interest. He has not offered for you yet, and you must not miss this opportunity. Behave properly and do not drive him away!"

Elizabeth rolled her eyes and looked at Jane who hid her smile behind her hand. "Yes, Mama." She took a seat at the writing desk safely across the room from her mother and finally opened the note. Her breath caught.

My love,
I look out of the window at this interminable rain and miss you. I hear the fire crackling, and think how much warmer it would feel if you were sitting before it, safe within my arms. I wait for the day that my home is yours, and your place is with me, until tomorrow, my darling.
William

Elizabeth's hand went to her mouth and she tried to hold back the tears that sprang to her eyes. She looked up to see Jane watching her, and she smiled, then drew out a piece of paper and wrote her reply. She glanced around the room, and seeing everyone else was occupied, she pulled a ribbon from her hair and enclosed it carefully in the paper so the gift would remain safely inside, and sealed it. Standing, she left and went to the kitchen where she saw Danny sitting up very straight, a silly smile on his face as he stared dreamily at Susie, who was sitting opposite him folding linens and talking. She laughed and began to think; maybe she could persuade her father to let Susie come with her to Pemberley as her abigail. She cleared her throat, and Susie looked up. "Yes, Miss?"

Elizabeth looked to Danny. "I have my reply ready, Danny."

He startled and his face fell, then he stood and regained his composure. "Ah, yes Miss. I will take that back to Netherfield right away."

She looked between the two. "There is no rush, take your time." She turned and left the room, and Danny sank back down in his chair, doe-eyed once again.

Upon returning to the drawing room she heard the discussion that had begun. "I think that he tried to shoot Mr. Darcy. He is heartbroken."

"Oh that is just silly, Kitty! Who would be heartbroken over Lizzy?" Lydia grabbed a ribbon Kitty was holding and started to attach it to her bonnet. "I think that he is just a terrible hunter." She giggled. "Did you ever see Sir William shooting targets? I spied on him one time. He is awful!"

"Lydia, Kitty that is enough. I will not have you saying lies about Mr. Lucas. And Kitty, I want you to wear your blue gown Wednesday night. I want you to look your best for him."

Kitty's eyes widened and she looked around the room. "Me? Why me? Why do I have to look good for him? Why not Lizzy? He likes her!"

"Lizzy is being courted by Mr. Darcy!" Mrs. Bennet scolded.

"But Mama, have you heard the news? The militia is coming to quarter here this winter; we will have scores of officers to meet!" She leaned back in her chair dreamily imagining all of the young men in their dashing uniforms and sighed. Then she sat up. "I will not settle for some boring man who wants my sister. I want an officer!"

Lydia chimed in. "Ohhh, yes! I hope there is a ball soon, I want to dance and dance with all of them!"

The girls fell into excited giggling and Mrs. Bennet smiled at them indulgently. "I loved an officer once, but then the chance to be mistress of this estate came about." Elizabeth listened. She rarely heard her parents speak of their reasons for marrying; she always wondered how it came to be.

Seeing the opportunity she asked. "Did you and Papa court for a long time?"

Mrs. Bennet focused on Elizabeth and realized she had slipped. Mr. Bennet had sworn her to secrecy on anything to do with their wedding or his sister. "No, and the rest is not your concern Miss Lizzy. You should be thinking about how to secure Mr. Darcy." She nodded at Jane. "And you are doing very nicely with Mr. Bingley. I am sure he will come speak to your father any day now." Her eyes swept the room. "Where is Mary?"

"I am right here, Mama." Mrs. Bennet twisted and saw her middle daughter sitting on the same sofa. "Oh well, what are you doing to find a husband?" Mary's mouth opened and closed and Mrs. Bennet stared at her then shook her head, and began talking about what they should wear to the Lucas' Wednesday night. Elizabeth sent Mary a look of sympathy and she smiled back weakly.

Jane patted the sofa and Elizabeth joined her. "Was that a note from Mr. Darcy, Lizzy?" She whispered.

Elizabeth nodded, but would not share this note with her sister. "He is wonderful." Elizabeth sighed, touching the note, and tucked it inside of her gown. "Georgiana told me that he has never been able to express his feelings, but he certainly knows how to write them."

———～～～———

Darcy sealed the envelope of his final letter and set it aside in the stack for Danny, then flicked through the envelopes to be placed in the post. That finished; he looked out at the wet garden and then at the clock on the mantle. "Surely he should be back by now." He stood and paced, then settled against the mantle and stared at the dancing flames. A knock startled him. "At last!" He called out, "Enter."

"Mr. Darcy, there you are! You have been hidden away all day in here." Caroline glanced at the piles of letters and the neatly arranged desk. "It seems that your work is finished. Will you not join us for some tea?" She glided up to him and slipped her hand on his arm then smiled up to his expressionless face. "Georgiana quite misses you." His eyes flickered. Caroline triumphed, mentioning his sister was bound to make him react.

"I suppose that I should eat something." He started to move and glanced down at the hand tightly gripping his arm and sighed. Silently they proceeded to the drawing room where tea was laid out.

"There, you see, I knew I could persuade Mr. Darcy to join us." Caroline declared as they entered the room.

Bingley caught his attention and rolled his eyes. "I hope that we did not tear you away from anything pressing."

Removing Caroline's hand he took a chair near Bingley. "No, I had just finished when Miss Bingley arrived." He looked about the room. "Where is Georgiana?"

"Here I am." She said softly. Caroline leapt to her feet and hurried over to the doorway. "I think you will be most comfortable here by Charles." She practically pushed her down next to him on the small sofa.

Bingley stared at his sister then smiled at Georgiana. "I suppose you can bear my company, Miss Darcy." She nodded and looked to Darcy, whose eyes moved between Caroline and Louisa, and narrowed with suspicion. His reaction was not missed by Hurst.

"It is quite nice to have our whole party together for once. We have seen so little of you, Mr. Darcy. You seem to never be about."

He met her gaze then turned to Bingley. "Forgive me if I have been a poor houseguest."

Bingley smiled. "No, you are certainly under no obligation to spend your time with us. I wanted you and Miss Darcy to enjoy your time here. Obviously you have found suitable distractions in the neighbourhood." He winked.

"Indeed I have." Darcy smiled at him then back at Georgiana. "We have made many new friends here."

"Yes, Elizabeth already was my friend, but we are so much closer now. And I think that Miss Mary and I are getting on well, too."

Darcy nodded. "Perhaps you will meet some other young ladies at the Lucas dinner."

"You intend to go?" Bingley asked carefully.

Darcy turned back to look at him. "I choose to believe that it was an accident, Bingley. I have spoken at length with Mr. Bennet and Miss Elizabeth on the subject."

Caroline was not at all pleased with the time Darcy spent with the Bennets. "I have accepted several invitations from other families in the area; of course you will be joining us, Mr. Darcy. You can not spend all of your time with the Bennets, delightful as they are."

He turned a blank face to her. "I will consult with Miss Elizabeth before committing to any other engagements."

"Come now Mr. Darcy, you are not obligated to follow their schedule! You are far too important to be spending your time with such insignificant people."

He addressed her coldly. "I am courting Miss Elizabeth, Miss Bingley. I hardly would term her or her family as insignificant."

Caroline pressed on. "I can not help but wonder what exactly has drawn you to her. She is hardly the type of woman I would have expected to entrap you. What allurements has she used?"

"I am not entrapped, Miss Bingley, and just what type of woman would you expect me to choose? Certainly not one who overestimates her own value?" It was a jab that flew above her head.

She nodded. "But obviously Miss Elizabeth does if she has targeted you. I am sorry that you may be unaware sir, but she shows all the signs of being a fortune hunter." Darcy stared at her. "And I must sadly inform you sir, that she was quite attached to Mr. John Lucas mere days before you entered the neighbourhood. I am sure that when she saw you at the assembly she jumped at the chance to attract you. I do not wish you to be blinded to the machinations of an accomplished temptress." She nodded knowingly at him then smiled over at Louisa. Darcy looked to Bingley, who had closed his eyes in mortification. Hurst snorted. Georgiana was bright red with her embarrassment.

Darcy stood and towered over Caroline. "I am quite aware of everything there is to know about Miss Elizabeth, and I will thank you to keep your opinions to yourself, they are not welcome." He turned and strode over to the window, cursing the rain that kept him from Longbourn. Bingley cleared his throat and Caroline sat staring at Darcy, feeling the sting of his rebuke. Gradually conversation filled the room and Darcy ignored the buzz, instead drifting into the memory of the walk he took with Elizabeth the day before.

They met at the stile where he had proposed. After a long embrace and passionate kisses, she suggested they walk to Oakham Mount, where they settled on a rock, holding hands and talking. He opened up a little to her about his childhood, and she listened without interrupting. When he finished he felt drained, but knew he had only scratched the surface. He had told her of fights he overheard and witnessed, as well as the complete withdrawal of affection by his mother, and his attempts to win his father's rare praise. He admitted that he had felt no emotion other than relief when his mother died. When his father passed, he felt regret, because although they never were close, he did respect him. He sensed that his father did feel pride for the man he had become, and somehow knew that if he had married differently, his father could have been a very loving man. His mother had effectively killed that emotion for both of them. He felt nothing while speaking of his parents. His heart had long ago become numb to them.

Elizabeth described her parents' unhappy marriage, and how growing up witnessing such a poor union was what led her to the determination to only marry someone she could both respect and love with her entire being. Darcy considered telling her the story Mr. Bennet had confessed about his sister and how he came to marry Mrs. Bennet, but thought he should share that news himself. Instead, Darcy told her that growing up with his parents had set him so against marriages of convenience that he determined he would never marry at all. It was Georgiana's ruin and the recent, seemingly true revelation that she was not a Darcy by birth that made him reconsider . . . and he said, meeting Elizabeth.

They talked over Georgiana's confession about Wickham, and Darcy was filled with guilt. He felt that it was his own inability to express love that drove her to this life-changing decision to accept Wickham's advances. Elizabeth disagreed and told him what he already knew, that Wickham was a master at playing on girls' hearts, and that Georgiana freely admitted she knew she was doing wrong at the time. Perhaps a more affectionate brother might have helped, but the love of a brother is not the same as the kiss of a lover. She punctuated her statement by taking his teary face in her hands and kissed him so tenderly his heart nearly burst with emotion. He admitted that at first he felt guilty for having fallen in love, he actually felt grateful that Georgiana had run away, because through her ruin he had found his Elizabeth. She waved that away. They would have met anyway, the timing would have been different, but he would have come to Netherfield to be with his friend, and they would have begun then.

It was a conversation that reassured him, and gave him such a bright look into the future. He imagined sharing so many concerns with her, not only of the heart, but of the estate. He hoped that she would be interested in his affairs. It was an unusual view for a man, but he had been alone for so long, he wanted to share his life with her, at least so that they could talk out the problems and decisions he must face so that she could understand and contribute. He anticipated bringing her home so very much. During the conversation he found that he had wrapped Elizabeth tightly in his embrace, and was afraid to let her go. He felt almost desperate for her expressions of love, and clung to every squeeze, smile, laugh, and touch. Her kisses made him feel alive, and he realized that only she could have coaxed him to show his feelings.

Darcy's musings were interrupted by the arrival of a note on a salver. "Sir, your messenger brought you this, but did not wish to dirty the carpets with his attire." Darcy nodded and picked up the awaited envelope. He looked up and noticed the eyes of the room were upon him. He turned back to the window and broke the seal of the carefully folded sheet, feeling a small lump inside. He held it out of everyone's view and slowly opened it, finding the new yellow ribbon. He could not hold back the brilliant smile that lit his face. He slipped the ribbon in his pocket then read the note.

Dearest,
I received with surprise and delight your words of love, and I return them to you with this fresh token to hold until I may take my proper place with my hand in yours, where I hope to always reside. I eagerly await my lesson tomorrow, not simply because I will be with you, but because it is something that you love, and I wish to share everything with you. Now, if you could simply speak to the horse about cooperating with its inept rider, I would dearly appreciate it.
Yours always,
Elizabeth

Darcy laughed out loud and grinned. Then realizing where he was, quickly folded the note and placed it inside of his coat next to her precious handkerchief, and relaxed. He turned back, not seeing the stunned expressions on the faces of the room's occupants to hearing him laugh, and took his seat, ready to bear Caroline's attentions again.

———— ∼∼∼ ————

Lord Matlock's carriage rolled into Rosings early on Tuesday morning. They stayed at their London home overnight, so everyone was refreshed and ready for the short trip to Kent to take on Lady Catherine. On the long journey from Derbyshire, they discussed their options, including stopping at Netherfield to consult with Darcy. Together the family decided to spare him this trial, and Richard spent the time as they approached London describing his search for

Georgiana in detail. His parents listened in fascination, as mile by mile marked the ever growing ruin of their niece.

The party was announced and Lady Catherine stood to welcome them. "Henry, Elaine, Fitzwilliam! This is a great surprise; I thought you were in Matlock!" Her sharp gaze moved between each of them. The last thing she wanted was for her brother to be present, not when suitors for Georgiana's hand were arriving. "I would have expected a letter announcing your plans; I have several guests coming this afternoon to stay. I am afraid that I am ill-prepared to host any others."

Lord Matlock sat down as did his wife and son. Lady Catherine paused, and then resumed her chair. "Rosings has, I believe, twenty bedchambers. I sincerely doubt that we would be forced to sleep in the dining room."

Lady Catherine cleared her throat. "Yes, well, I will ask my housekeeper to prepare your rooms . . ."

"Catherine, it has come to our attention that you have been casting about for a husband, not for your daughter as we would expect, but for Georgiana. What have you to say about this? I sincerely hope that it is not true, as I specifically told you not to interfere." He met her glare with one just as imperious.

"You told me not to approach Darcy, and I have not." She lifted her chin and sniffed.

Lady Matlock had held her tongue long enough. "Catherine, stop this ridiculous dancing! How dare you impose yourself on the Darcys in this way? Even if Georgiana was of age or at least presented, Darcy would never go about searching for a husband in such a cold manner. He knows better than anyone the mistake of marrying devoid of feeling, and he is seeking to correct that in his own life. He will not take kindly to your behaviour!"

Her head snapped around to her sister. "Does he know?"

She regarded Lady Catherine with disgust. "No, we have sought to spare him this trial. He has enough. But, I assure you, he will know." She laughed derisively. "So you admit to your scheme? Are you so afraid of losing Rosings? Do you truly believe that marrying off Georgiana would change Darcy's attitude to marrying Anne?"

She looked surprised. "Of course, he would do his duty!"

Clenching her fists tightly, Lady Matlock declared, "His duty is to his sister, and to Pemberley. Not to you." She glared at her. "Who have you contacted, who is coming here?"

Lady Catherine looked away and became evasive. "Some interested young men and their families."

"You will send them on their way, telling them that you made an error."

"I will do no such thing! The girl must be married quickly to restore her reputation and restore the family name."

Lady Matlock narrowed her eyes. "If that is the case, we will then be here to greet them and assure them that you were obviously displaying the signs of dementia that have worried the family so much recently when you sent off your nonsensical letters."

She stood. "You would not dare tell such a lie!"

Standing eye to eye with her, she glared. "Would we not? Henry is prepared to have his lawyers draw up the papers to declare you incompetent and unfit to care for Rosings, giving it immediately to Anne's control. She could then decide if she wishes you to remain or to go to the dower house, unless of course you prefer Bedlam? I can just imagine you being prodded by the sticks of the voyeurs who come to visit the insane." She raised an imperious brow to her.

"Henry!" Lady Catherine turned to him. He nodded without expression. "I will Catherine. I have put up with your behaviour for years. Perhaps you truly are touched. Our sister must have been to have behaved as she did. And this auction you have proposed for our niece only gives me proof of your questionable sanity, to say nothing of your absence of compassion."

Richard sat back and watched the entire show, smiling and thinking of the letter he would write to Darcy that evening. But he did feel as Georgiana's other guardian he should speak. "Oh and Aunt Catherine, I assure you, no scheme of yours would ever be approved by me or Darcy, you would require our consent, and you hold nothing over either of us. I would say that your plans are rather poorly conceived. I think that I agree with you Father, perhaps she should be declared incompetent."

Lord Matlock nodded to his son. "Thank you. Tomorrow we will return to London and begin the procedures."

Lady Catherine looked from one serious face to another and crumpled. "I will withdraw my invitations. I will be a laughing stock in society."

Richard grinned. "Tell them that consumption is in the house, that will send them away quite efficiently, I should think."

Lord Matlock's eyes twinkled, feeling the tide turning in their direction. "And I imagine the families you chose were hardly of the best financial status, anything they say will be laughed at in any case."

They all looked to the very disappointed woman before them. "Very well."

"Fine. We will remain for the night. If I hear of any more schemes of yours to disrupt or control Darcy's life, I assure you, I will follow through on my threats." Lord Matlock stood and began to leave the room.

"Who told you . . .?"

Anne interrupted. "I did."

Lady Catherine looked in shock at her daughter. "YOU!"

"Yes Mama, and if you do not stop trying to control my life as well, you will find yourself put out of Rosings as soon as I become mistress."

Lady Matlock beamed. "Good for you, Anne!"

"Lizzy, please join me for a moment before you go." Mr. Bennet was standing in the doorway to his bookroom.

She glanced out at William's carriage through the front window and sighed at the delay. "Yes, Papa."

Mrs. Bennet bustled over. "Mr. Bennet, do not delay Lizzy! Mr. Darcy is probably waiting alongside his sister!"

He looked at his wife sternly then transferred the gaze to his daughter. "Mr. Darcy will have to wait a few more minutes." He looked up to see the approach of yet another set of curious neighbours, hoping to catch sight of Mr. Darcy and

Elizabeth, and to gossip about the good fortune that had found the Bennets with such a wealthy suitor for their daughter. "Lizzy?" He indicated the door and stepped aside. She passed before him into the room and waited while he closed the door. He did not beat about the bush. "Lizzy I wish to remind you to refrain from displays of affection with Mr. Darcy." She began to protest and he held up his hand. "I overlooked your behaviour earlier this week when both you and Mr. Darcy were understandably emotional following his injury, however, Netherfield is not Longbourn, and witnesses there will be quite happy to spread rumours of your unsuitability as Mr. Darcy's wife far and wide. You do not wish him to have to give you up to save his reputation."

"Papa, if you would allow our engagement to be made public, our small displays of affection would not be noticed, and even expected."

He ignored the suggestion. "Your displays have hardly been small, and Lizzy, a gentleman would not press you in such a way."

She bristled. "Are you accusing Mr. Darcy of not being a gentleman?"

Mr. Bennet sighed. Elizabeth was an equal, if not superior combatant, and he knew well enough she would not meekly accept his pronouncements as Jane would. "Lizzy, I am sure that Mr. Darcy is a fine man. I simply wish you to . . . be careful."

Elizabeth relented; she knew that he was only trying to protect her, though why after a lifetime of indifferent parenting he chose this moment to assert himself was a mystery. "Papa, I will not disgrace our family. Mr. Darcy's sister's predicament is in my mind."

"I should realize that you are not Lydia or Kitty."

"Thank you for the compliment, Papa. May I go now?" He kissed her forehead, and turned to the window to watch her board the carriage. It pulled away and already he could feel her loss, she was steadily leaving him behind.

———〜〜〜———

At Netherfield, Darcy was pacing in front of the house. The carriage was late. It should have arrived at least a quarter hour earlier. He had the route memorized; the timing fixed, and had hardly slept the night before in anticipation of this day. His great disappointment was that Georgiana determined she should participate. That was decidedly not in his plans, but he could neither deny her superior knowledge of riding side saddle, nor her desire to further her relationship with Elizabeth. Or for that matter, avoid Miss Bingley and Mrs. Hurst. Georgiana stood watching him pace in absolute fascination. The sound of the carriage approaching garnered their attention and Darcy strode forward to open the door. His eyes expressed everything that he physically could not. "Miss Elizabeth, at last." He took her hand and kissed it. A footman removed a small trunk. Darcy looked at it and whispered. "Are you making my dreams come true and staying here?"

Elizabeth laughed. "Mama felt it would be muddy riding and insisted I bring a change of clothes.

"I admire your mother's reasoning."

She rolled her eyes. "Oh, Mr. Darcy, please reconsider that statement or I will fear for your competency."

He smiled and leaned close. "I missed you so much yesterday. Thank you for my new ribbon." He drew it out of his pocket. She touched it, and briefly hooked her index finger with his.

Their eyes met and she swallowed under his burning gaze. "You are welcome. What have you done with the old one?" He leaned close again.

"I have placed it in my treasure box." The expression on his face changed. He blushed and was biting his lip, looking for her reaction.

She looked up with surprise. "You have a treasure box?" He nodded and smiled shyly. "What else is in it?"

"I will show you someday." Elizabeth smiled; delighted that such a reticent man could possess such a boyish secret.

Georgiana walked forward. "I am so glad you have come today." Elizabeth immediately embraced the girl and kissed her cheek. Darcy instantly felt jealous.

"I am glad to see you, too. Will you be observing my lesson?"

Georgiana flushed from the hug and smiled. "Yes, I remember when William taught me and thought I might be able to tell you things he can not."

Both of them looked at Darcy who smiled slightly. "I believe that I could do fine on my own, however, I am happy for the additional advice."

Elizabeth saw his barely hidden disappointment and hooked her hand on his arm. "Well then, sir. Take me to my doom!"

He bowed his head solemnly. "Right this way, my Lady." He paused and held his other elbow out. "Georgiana?" She bit her lip and hurried to take his arm. Elizabeth smiled at him and he began walking proudly, his two greatest loves on his arms.

From a parlour window, Caroline and Louisa watched the scene. "I was not aware that Miss Elizabeth was coming today." Caroline seethed. "I am the mistress of this house; surely I should have been informed."

Hurst's voice was heard. "I believe that Darcy spoke to Bingley about it yesterday, and as he is master of the house, I daresay he acted properly."

Bingley stuck his head in the door. "Oh, Caroline, I forgot to tell you, Miss Elizabeth is coming today and I think you should plan on her remaining for tea."

Caroline gritted her teeth. "Thank you, Charles." He smiled brilliantly and left, as Hurst stifled a laugh and strolled from the room. He remained outside of the door to listen to the sisters' reaction.

"What does he see in that chit?!" Caroline fumed. "There must be some way to stop this!"

"They are not engaged, Caroline. He may change his mind yet." Louisa soothed.

"But their courtship is public knowledge. You know that is practically a declaration of his intentions. She would be a fool to refuse him. They sat together in church! They may as well have published the banns!" She watched them disappear from view. "I was not prepared for competition here. I was sure that I would have him all to myself, with no other fashionable women nearby; it should have been so simple! I must find a way to be alone with him." She turned away from the window and began walking around the room.

Louisa sat and watched her progress. "You still wish to try for a compromising situation?"

"I think that is my only chance. My ideas for winning his regard are useless with this courtship. The neighbourhood clearly expects an engagement, and Mrs. Bennet was ridiculous in her effusions, and yet none of the behaviour seems to have put him off. It is as if he is actually willing to tolerate the attention. I have never seen him so uncaring of the society he keeps! No, if I can not find a way to be alone with him and resurrect his sense of duty . . . unless . . . Louisa, perhaps I could find a way for John Lucas to compromise her or win her back." She looked at her sister with bright eyes. "He is obviously jealous, look at what he tried to do to Mr. Darcy!" Hurst rolled his eyes and moved away from the doorway. It was time to speak to Bingley.

———

The Darcys and Elizabeth approached the stable and he felt her tremble. "You are not afraid are you?"

She grimaced. "No, not afraid, but suitably cautious."

He smiled at her refusing to admit fear. "I will allow no harm to come to you, my love." He whispered. She squeezed his arm and looked at the light brown pony standing by the mounting block. "This is Buttercup, Elizabeth." She smiled and reached out to rub the velvety nose, and laughed when the pony immediately nuzzled into her palm.

"What a sweet name!"

Darcy laughed. "Obviously named by a lady."

She cocked a brow and continued stroking. "You would not choose such a name?"

"Never."

"I suppose you favour names such as Beelzebub or Fury."

"Actually I name my horses after literary figures."

"Ah, so you like Othello or Macbeth?"

His lips twitched and his eyes twinkled. "My horse is named Benedick."

She grinned. "A comedy? Why does that surprise me so?"

Darcy shrugged. "I am not always so serious, at least when alone."

Elizabeth reached up to touch his face and remembered Georgiana. "You have spent too much time alone, Mr. Darcy." He nodded and swallowed. To distract himself from the moment he helped her to mount, and went about adjusting the stirrup to give her a secure foothold. He stood back.

"Your seat is perfect, Elizabeth." Georgiana observed. Darcy was happy that she made the comment because the sight of Elizabeth atop the horse sent his heart racing. Too many times he imagined her riding astride a different mount entirely.

"Oh, my seat was never the problem, Georgiana; it is once the horse moves that I lose control." She gathered the reins and looked nervously at William.

Recovering himself, he spoke, "Well, could you try a walk? Perhaps we could determine the problem that way." Elizabeth bit her lip, sending him into another bout of imagining, this time of his teeth nibbling on that luscious flesh or better yet, her teeth nibbling . . . *Stop it now!* He determinedly concentrated on her riding.

Georgiana nudged him and whispered. "See how she holds the reins? It is too loose, they should be shorter, and her hands are not together. And the horse's head is not looking forward."

Darcy nodded, casting a critical eye at last. "That is it Georgiana. She has no control. No wonder her mounts all take their own head." He gave her a smile and drew her close for a quick hug. "Very good, dear." He let go and strode forward, missing the surprised and delighted smile Georgiana wore.

"Elizabeth, I believe we have determined the problem."

"It is that obvious? I can no longer blame the horses?" She tried to laugh, but was embarrassed to appear so terribly inept in front of two very accomplished riders.

He read the discomfort in her face and smiled. "I am afraid not, it is definitely you." He caught up to the slowly moving animal and pulled sharply on the reins, issuing the command to stop. In a second he slipped his foot in the stirrup and swung himself up and behind her.

"William what are you doing?"

He reached his arms around her and placed his hands over hers where they gripped the reins. "I am teaching, my love."

Georgiana called out. "It is all right, Elizabeth. It is how I learned."

Elizabeth blushed and whispered fervently. "Sir, my father delayed my visit here today to admonish me about our behaviour."

Darcy adjusted his seat, while achieving the great pleasure of feeling her body rest against his chest. "William. And this is a common teaching technique."

She looked up at his disconcertingly close face and into those soulful blue eyes. "Why do I fail to believe you?" The eyes crinkled.

"I would not lie; Elizabeth." He stopped himself from becoming lost in her gaze. "Now, let me teach you how to control your mount." They moved around the paddock slowly. Darcy tried to concentrate on the work at hand, Elizabeth tried to remember his soft directions, and both failed to hear Georgiana's calls of advice. Finally Darcy felt that they needed both more room and privacy. He told the groom to open the gate. "We will attempt the drive. We will not be gone long." Georgiana wished them luck and Darcy showed her how to urge the pony into a canter. They moved away and were soon beyond the sight of the stables and quite alone.

Directing the horse behind a tall hedge, he scanned the area to confirm their privacy. Assured, Darcy could hold back no longer. He brought the horse to a stop, quickly pulled her closer and deftly untied the ribbons of her bonnet, lifting it off and laying it on her lap. He lowered his mouth to hers. "I can not begin to tell you how many times I have imagined this, Elizabeth." Their lips met and the kiss began as gentle caresses, and rapidly became the deep and passionate exchange they both craved. Darcy's mouth stroked over hers and he smiled, chuckling softly.

Elizabeth's eyes opened. "What is it?"

He tenderly kissed her frown. "I love that sound." He smiled and kissed the crease in her brow.

"What sound?" She demanded. He pulled his glove off and ran a finger from her temple down her cheek to lift up her jaw.

"The little moan you make when I kiss you."

"I do not moan!" She tried to pull away, but he held her tight.

"Yes, you do." He whispered and nibbled her earlobe.

"Ohhh."

He chuckled. "No, not like that." She tried to move away again. "Forgive me, Elizabeth." He looked at her with contrition. He was irresistibly handsome, but she would not give in so easily.

"We should return. We have been too long away."

He slowly shook his head. "No, I can not give you up so soon." He cuddled her and nuzzled her neck, whispering warmly, "or ever." Darcy felt her melt into him and spoke softly in her ear. "You do not really wish to return either, I think."

"No, I wish we could urge this pony on to take us far away." She listened as his heartbeat quickened and she heard its pounding, even through his heavy coat.

"Do not encourage me, my love." The rich sound made her heartbeat race.

Elizabeth looked up to his very serious gaze. "You would run away with me?"

"Why must we wait to begin our lives together?"

She pulled his head down and caressed his lips in the sensuous way he loved. "Because you require Papa's consent, at least until my next birthday."

"When?" He asked in a strangled voice.

"Months, my sweet William, June."

He groaned and rested his chin on her shoulder. "We cannot elope." He said with regret. Elizabeth shook her head and kissed his smooth cheek. "No."

They stayed in their silent embrace until the pony began to shift them around. "One more kiss?" He begged. "Please?"

Their mouths joined again and they slowly made love the only way they could. Darcy's hands travelled over her captive form, and as one arm held her securely, he unbuttoned her spencer, slipping his hand inside to caress her breasts. "Oh, my love, how I want you." He murmured, trailing kisses over her face, and down her neck. Elizabeth tilted her head back to give him more room, and her hands wandered to the buttons of his coat, opening it and sliding inside to caress his chest and drifted lower, coming upon his prominent arousal. She touched it and he groaned so loudly that she drew back as if stung. Her eyes were wide.

"I . . .I am so sorry, did I hurt . . ." Her mouth was instantly engulfed with his kiss and she felt his hand taking hers and resting it back on top of the bulge. He kissed her with demanding strokes, as he showed her not to be afraid to touch him. Panting raggedly, he drew away long enough to stare into her eyes and allowed her to see the deep desire he felt. They closed again, and reclaiming her mouth, his hand moved back to her breasts, a thumb making endless circles over the tightened bud. Her muffled moan drew out his groan and his lips moved to below her ear, where he licked and kissed and breathed. The sensations that were spreading over her body were overwhelming Elizabeth, and she was rapidly approaching the point where she would succumb and beg for him to take her wherever he wished to go. The movement of the pony suddenly reminded her of their location, and the memory of her father's voice sounded in her ear.

"William, we must stop." She panted and felt him draw her possessively to him. Darcy could not bear to let her go. "William . . ."

With a tremendous effort he stopped his ministrations and attempted to calm his breathing. He placed his hands over hers, and kissed her gently, meeting her eyes. "I love you Elizabeth. I did not mean to become so carried away. . . I meant no disrespect . . . I just needed to show you . . ."

She placed her fingers on his lips and he kissed them. "I love you William." She swallowed, calming her own desires.

He buried his face on her shoulder. "I have dreams of us loving each other. I imagine waking up with you in my arms, and I am so disappointed when you are not there. I know this seems a short courtship and engagement but it is interminable to me." He looked up. "Do I shock you?"

"No, I feel the same, I dream of you also, and now I do not have to worry of you thinking me improper, hoping that you would want me by your side at night."

He breathed a sigh of relief. "Night, day, all times." He kissed her and they rested their foreheads together. "Do not move." Darcy whispered. Her position pressed against him was an exquisite torture. It was no use; he would have to suffer the discomfort of his desire. A frustrated sigh drew his attention and he opened his eyes to see Elizabeth appeared just as miserable. "Darling are you well?" She blushed and shook her head. He smiled "Neither am I."

She met his gaze. "You feel this . . . ache too?"

His smile grew. "Oh yes, constantly."

Her eyes widened and she bit her lip. This time he leaned forward and took a nip. "William!" He laughed and squeezed her. Somehow it was easier to bear knowing she wanted him just as deeply, even in innocence.

Darcy kicked the pony and they turned. "We should return." He declared. She nodded, they were in a secluded area, but they were risking too much the chance of being seen, and she knew how tempted they both were to yielding to desire. She replaced her bonnet while he watched her curls disappear with regret. Darcy gave her instructions and soon the pony was galloping, his hands not on the reins, but around her waist. She was smiling with her success and he was fulfilling his fantasy as they rode, their bodies rising and falling against each other in perfect rhythm.

They arrived at the stables to find Bingley and Hurst talking with Georgiana. Darcy told Elizabeth how to slow the pony and they came to a stop before them, his hands had moved to rest on his thighs as soon as they came in sight of the others. Elizabeth beamed with her accomplishment. "Well done, Miss Elizabeth!" Bingley cried. Darcy quickly dismounted, not willing to linger with so many witnesses about, and held up his arms to help guide her down.

Elizabeth slid down the pony's side and he stepped back immediately. She smiled. "Thank you." She turned. "And thank you, Mr. Bingley, although I suspect you should be congratulating Mr. Darcy more than I. Without his guidance, I am afraid this pony would never have stopped!"

The group laughed. "Well, it was an admirable display. Perhaps for your next lesson, Darcy may ride his own mount." Bingley winked at him and Darcy glared.

Hurst chuckled. "Leave him alone, Bingley."

"No, I have waited years for this opportunity." He took Elizabeth's hand and placed it on his arm, and began walking. "Miss Elizabeth, have I ever told you the story of how my good friend Darcy and I met?"

"Bingley!" Darcy bellowed.

She turned back to Bingley. "No sir, but I would enjoy the tale." He grinned and they set off. Elizabeth looked back at William and smiled apologetically. Besides his ire, he was obviously feeling possessive. Darcy's eyes never left them.

"Come Georgiana." She took his arm and he nearly dragged her, trying to catch up.

Hurst followed. "Slow down, man. He will do no harm." Darcy's gaze smote him and he shrugged. By the time they reached the house, Elizabeth and Bingley were laughing heartily and Darcy recognized a familiar light in his friend's eyes. He knew what it meant. Bingley had discovered the joy of his Elizabeth.

"Not this time." He muttered.

Georgiana looked up at his dark countenance. "William?" He did not answer. They entered the house and Elizabeth immediately let go of Bingley's arm. Darcy watched and saw the disappointment register on his face.

"Miss Elizabeth, do you wish to change your dress?" Darcy blurted out. She stared at him with surprise. "I . . . I only ask because your mother did insist. . ." He just needed her to go away from Bingley.

"Your dress is in my bedchamber." Georgiana offered. "Come, and I will help you to change."

Elizabeth smiled. "Thank you, I suppose I should change if I am to stay for tea."

"You are?!"

She laughed at William's wide eyes. "Mr. Bingley was kind enough to invite me."

"It is my pleasure." Bingley bowed.

Darcy's eyes met hers and he saw the warmth he knew was just for him and relaxed. He held out his arm and offered his escort upstairs.

The trio left and Bingley watched them go. "You are playing with fire, Bingley." Hurst said when they were alone.

They entered his study and sat by the hearth. "Why do you say that?"

Hurst snorted. "Come on, I saw the same thing that Darcy did. You are attracted to Miss Elizabeth."

Bingley looked confused. "Well, who would not be? She is beautiful, vivacious, intelligent, kind . . ."

"And spoken for."

He stared. "I am not attempting to take her from Darcy. I would never do that!"

Hurst rolled his eyes. "Bingley you go through women almost as quickly as my wife goes through abigails. It is a compulsion with you. I think you can not help yourself." Bingley's brow creased. "I thought you were interested in Miss Bennet."

"I am!" He said defensively.

"Are you?" He shook his head. "Well, I need to speak to you on another subject. Are you aware that Caroline and Louisa are plotting to somehow compromise Darcy or ruin Miss Elizabeth in his eyes?"

Bingley was still wrestling with the thought of him merely toying with Jane, and startled. "What? Darcy has known of Caroline's ridiculous wishes for years.

Even if he were somehow trapped alone with her, he would never marry her. We have discussed this many times."

"I am not as concerned for him as I am for Miss Elizabeth. They spoke of Lucas, and trying to convince Darcy she was unworthy. Who knows to what lengths Caroline may go?"

Bingley's brow creased in confusion. "Surely his courtship should have ended this fantasy of hers."

"I believe it is making her desperate. She has presumed very openly that he would eventually offer for her."

"Good Lord, can not the man fall in love in peace?" Hurst raised his brows. "I swear I did not know I was doing anything!" Bingley insisted.

"Perhaps it is time that you do, before Darcy murders you." Bingley stared. Hurst sighed. "You wish to be a respected member of society one day, start with your own house."

With no little resentment, he asked, "What makes you suddenly so wise, Hurst? As I recall, you spend your days drunk or asleep."

"That is to avoid your sisters." He closed his eyes. "I am not always drunk or asleep, and in that position I hear things. Are you aware that your sisters plan a compromising position between you and Miss Darcy?"

Bingley startled. "What?"

Hurst nodded. "You are not prepared as Darcy is to avoid any chance of being caught alone with Caroline. You should take precautions to avoid the same with Miss Darcy."

"Good Lord. Should we speak to Darcy?"

"Leave the man alone. He has enough. We can handle this ourselves."

"How?"

"I was thinking, I could speak to Louisa or . . ." He grinned. "We could let them try to trap you and turn the tables on them."

Bingley sat forward. "And do what?"

"I do not know, but I would love to teach them a lesson." He laughed. "What say you?"

Bingley nodded eagerly. "Yes, it is time that I finally take charge."

Chapter 18

*A*fter the transportation debacle to the assembly, Darcy was determined that his arrival at Lucas Lodge would not be dictated by Miss Bingley. He ordered his carriage readied, and when it pulled up to the front of Netherfield, he, Georgiana, and Bingley boarded and went on to the dinner. Hurst volunteered to stay behind and escort his wife and sisters, and looked forward to listening to the complaints and plotting that were sure to ensue. Darcy wanted to arrive to not only see Elizabeth, but to observe John Lucas. The decision to overlook the shooting incident was not an easy one; the man's behaviour that evening would determine if it had been correct.

"Welcome, welcome!" Sir William cried. "Mr. Bingley, so good to see you, but your sisters and Mr. Hurst, are they not coming?" He looked worriedly at the empty carriage as it pulled away from the door. The addition of the Netherfield party was the highlight of his evening, such rich and socially connected people were just the sort of guests Sir William craved.

"Ah sir, my sisters are preparing quite carefully tonight. They wish to grace your home with the latest of fashion. We simply decided to come ahead." Bingley's beaming smile matched Sir William's in every aspect.

The older man relaxed. "Well, capital, capital, then please come in!" He ushered Bingley past and turned to greet Darcy. He hesitated. It was clear that he was somewhat conflicted in how to address him. "Mr. Darcy." He bowed solemnly and checked his effusions. "My house is honoured with your presence. I do hope that you are quite recovered from . . ." He glanced up at Darcy's scalp and cleared his throat at the sight of his raised eyebrow and set jaw. "Uh, yes, well, and who is this lovely young lady on your arm?" He smiled at Georgiana, who was studying her toes.

"Sir William Lucas, this is my sister, Miss Georgiana Darcy." Sir William bowed low. "We are delighted to have you join us this evening, Miss Darcy." She managed to peek up at him and saw a kindly face and smiled a little. "Thank you, Sir William, I am happy to be here." Sir William looked up to Darcy who was watching Georgiana with concern. "You remind me of my youngest daughter, Maria. I hope that you will have an opportunity to meet her tonight, I believe that she is helping her mother at the moment."

Darcy nodded. "Perhaps she will." He bowed and they proceeded into the room.

The whispers swirling around them were hardly unexpected, but still annoying. There were the usual discussions of his income, speculation over the identity of the girl on his arm, men's words over the shooting incident, and most predominantly, he heard his and Elizabeth's names, as well as John Lucas mentioned. Realizing that he would be watched carefully that night, he sighed and began looking about the room for Elizabeth. He could hear the unmistakable bubbling laughter of his beloved, and his height gave him the advantage he needed to help him locate her in the crowded room. Darcy bent to Georgiana. "I have spotted Elizabeth, shall we join her?"

She finally looked up and nodded. "Yes, please." She whispered. He gave her hand a squeeze and moved them steadily to the corner where he found Elizabeth talking to Jane and Bingley.

"There you are, Darcy, I was wondering what was delaying you." Bingley smiled and turned to Elizabeth. "Obviously he found something of interest in the crowd."

Elizabeth smiled up at William, "Is that it, Mr. Darcy? Here I was; all anticipation for your company and I find that you are so easily distracted by others. Perhaps I should not have wasted my time waiting for you when there are so many other interested parties about." She waved her hand eloquently to encompass the eager faces and leaning heads of the rather indiscreet eavesdroppers who surrounded them. Elizabeth obviously saw everything that he had, and displayed no intention of allowing it to bother her.

Darcy felt his tension easing. "I assure you Miss Elizabeth, had I known that you were so eager for my presence, I would have entered through this conveniently placed door behind your sister, and avoided the crowd all together."

They laughed and Bingley clapped his shoulder. "I have no doubt of that at all!" Bingley moved Jane off in another direction, leaving the three others behind.

Elizabeth hugged Georgiana. "I do hope that your brother behaves himself tonight, once he starts talking it is difficult to make him stop."

Georgiana relaxed and stopped clutching his arm. "Oh Elizabeth, do stop teasing him! He is so happy to be seeing you tonight, he was like a caged animal all day waiting to come, and was dressed at least an hour early." Elizabeth's expression changed and her eyes shone as she smiled radiantly at him.

Darcy was flushed with embarrassment. "Georgiana, nobody needed to hear that!" He admonished quietly.

Elizabeth touched his arm and his eyes lifted from the floor and met hers. "I did. Thank you, William." He swallowed hard and resisted the impulse to take her up in his arms, crowd be damned.

The moment was broken by Charlotte's arrival. "Eliza, I have not seen you in so long, what have you been doing?" She insinuated herself between Darcy and Elizabeth. Darcy tilted his head in question, and Elizabeth shrugged slightly.

"Charlotte, you remember Mr. Darcy and his sister from church; do you not?" Charlotte turned and curtseyed. "I have been spending a great deal of time with both of the Darcys."

"I am sure that has been most entertaining, but you must not neglect your old friends. Look, here comes John!" She waved him over and he walked warily forward and regarded the scene. Darcy was staring at him coldly, as was Elizabeth. Georgiana felt the tension, and spotting Mary, murmured an excuse and slipped away to join her.

"Miss Elizabeth, Mr. Darcy, how good to see you both." John met Darcy's piercing eyes. "I do hope that you are quite recovered, sir.

Darcy nodded curtly. "No permanent harm was done. Accidents do occur, even amongst the most experienced hunters."

The relief on John's face was evident and he relaxed. "Yes, I am grateful that we are able to agree on that. I will certainly never again position myself behind another man when I shoot."

"That is wise." Darcy did not appear as if he was going to further the conversation, so John turned to Elizabeth.

"Miss Elizabeth, you and your sisters are all turned out very prettily tonight. You honour my father's home." She recognized a truce had been agreed to between the men, and as much as she wished to berate him, she could not ignore his obvious efforts at civility.

"Thank you Mr. Lucas, you are very kind."

John shifted uncomfortably, it was clear that his presence was unwanted, but he had no desire to leave her alone with Darcy, so he stayed. "How long do you intend to remain in the area, sir? Perhaps we can try another hunt before the fox season begins."

"My plans are not yet determined, but I do expect to remain at least through the end of November." He looked to Elizabeth and smiled slightly.

John saw her blush and wondered at it. "I imagine you will be anxious to return to your estate for the winter, it is in Derbyshire, I believe?"

"Yes it is. The Peaks are beautiful any time of year, but I especially enjoy them in winter."

John nodded. "I imagine it becomes quite cold there, with the higher elevation. Are you snowed-in frequently? Are you trapped in your home with no contact with the outside world for weeks? I have heard that often the roads are impassable for much of the season, not even affording such a luxury as going to church. You must be quite adept at entertaining yourself, sir."

Darcy's eyes narrowed. "I must admit that indeed, the winter can be rather harsh, however, I have an exceptionally well-stocked library, filled with the selections of my ancestors. I doubt that a lifetime will afford enough time to peruse them all. Then there are winter activities such as sleigh rides and skating. And of course, the winter is when an estate as large and complex as mine prepares for the coming year, the land may sleep, but the planning never ends. But I am sure that you are aware of the work involved in estate affairs. Although only a fraction of the size of Pemberley, I am sure that Lucas Lodge experiences similar issues."

John saw that Darcy was no fool and realized what he was doing. He turned to Elizabeth. "Is it not fortunate for us to live in such a temperate climate, so we never feel stranded in a cold, white, lonely desert for bleak months? We suffer from rain and mud, but that never lasts for long. You are free to enjoy your walks through every season here, Miss Elizabeth. I hope that upon your next foray into the vicinity, you might take note of the new fencing I have been installing between our estates. I noticed the need when I began the oversight of the daily operations last month. It is good to know that on that unhappy day when my father leaves this earth, I will be fully prepared to take on the responsibilities that I was born to accept."

"You are fortunate that your father is still here to teach you. Mr. Darcy lost his father at about the same age that you are now, and he was left to manage Pemberley, his home in London, and do you not own other properties, sir?" She smiled at him.

Darcy's lips curved up as he appreciated her subtlety. "Yes, I own an estate in Scotland, and many other properties which I lease out for farming or livestock, as well as tending to my other investments."

Elizabeth tilted her head, "And of course you have had the responsibility of your staff and sister to take all of the rest of your time. No wonder winter seemingly speeds by for you."

His smile grew. "Indeed Miss Elizabeth, it seems that this brief period after the harvest is when I have my most leisure."

"How very fortunate we are to have won your company this year." She smiled warmly at him.

Darcy's eyes burned into hers. "Indeed, how fortunate for me and my sister."

Charlotte saw that her brother was not doing well. "Eliza, I am going to open the instrument and I insist that you play."

"Oh no Charlotte, I have no desire to offend the ears of your guests with my poor singing and fingering. You are much better off persuading one of the more accomplished ladies. I am sure that Miss Bingley would be very pleased to exhibit."

Charlotte firmly took her arm. "Please, I must insist."

She pulled her away, and Elizabeth shook her head and smiled first at William, then at John. "It seems that I must acquiesce to my friend. Gentlemen, I suggest that you find a suitable activity to distract yourselves from the poor sounds which will soon fill this room." She looked back at William and followed Charlotte to the pianoforte.

"Have you heard Miss Elizabeth, sir? I have had the pleasure countless times. Do not let her fool you, she is quite accomplished. Perhaps not in a technical way, but her emotion is evident in her presentation." Darcy looked at John sharply, and saw that he was staring after Elizabeth with admiration and longing. Darcy felt compelled to walk away before he drew him outside to thrash him soundly for staring at his wife in such a way. He strode across the room and stood at the side of the instrument. Elizabeth was looking through the sheets of music and noticed him immediately.

"Sir, I would be grateful if you could turn the pages for me." She said softly.

Darcy smiled and happily took his place at her side. "It is an honour, Miss Elizabeth." Elizabeth leaned against him for a moment and heard the sharp intake of his breath. She could not look at him but saw from the corner of her eye his warm gaze. Other guests saw the couple sitting together on the bench, and gathered around to hear the song. Elizabeth began to play, and Darcy was lost in the sound of her soprano voice, as fine as any soloist he had ever paid to hear. Her playing was, as Lucas had said, not technically perfect, but emotive of the essence of the song. He felt carried away, and nearly missed his cues to turn the pages until he realized that Elizabeth would gently lean into him a few bars ahead to gain his attention. He smiled to himself, seeing her save him from the embarrassment of appearing a lovesick fool before a roomful of people. The song ended and the crowd clapped, demanding another.

She looked up to see him staring at her with open admiration. "Well sir, may I employ you for one more performance?"

He leaned in and whispered, "No, for a lifetime of them. I believe we have found another way to pass the lonely winter at Pemberley." She blushed and pulled out a lively Scottish air to relieve the heady mood. Darcy drew back and was able to pay better attention to the music without the bewitching sound of her voice in his ear.

Beyond the instrument, conversations continued. Mrs. Bennet was very pleased to see the couple seated next to each other, and did not hesitate to voice her expectations of a forthcoming offer by Mr. Darcy. Mr. Bennet stood in an alcove and watched their behaviour. It had been obviously warm, but no objections could be said. He was relieved to see that they could behave properly when in public. Lady Lucas took in the scene and saw that her son's cause was lost, and resolved to identify a new candidate for her daughter, and determine ways to convince her son of the truth. Caroline and Louisa; finally arrived and quite unhappy with the transportation arrangements, set about learning everything they could about her. To their unhappy discovery, Elizabeth was found to be universally liked. Caroline then spotted John Lucas standing nearby, staring longingly at her. "Mr. Lucas?" Caroline sidled up to him.

He startled, and as the song ended and Elizabeth refused to play again, he shifted his focus to the extravagantly-dressed woman by his side. "Yes, Miss Bingley? What may I do for you?"

"Mr. Lucas, I have heard that you are most interested in Miss Eliza Bennet, is this true?"

He straightened, and observed her carefully. "I would like to think that we are good friends."

"Good friends, indeed! You grew up almost side-by-side! How wonderful it would be to see such childhood friends marry! What a wonderful gift for both of your families! When may I wish you and dear Miss Eliza joy?" She smiled and batted her eyes at him.

He grew suspicious. "Miss Bingley, as you are aware, Mr. Darcy has entered a courtship with Miss Elizabeth. I am afraid that my hopes may be dashed."

"Nonsense sir, she is still free until her wedding day. You must not give her up!" Caroline nodded at him encouragingly, but her strained voice indicated her desperation.

"Why would my choice for a bride interest you, Miss Bingley?"

Caroline flushed prettily. "Well, if you must know, Mr. Lucas, I have a long-standing admiration for Mr. Darcy, and until he was distracted by Miss Eliza, I believe that he would have made his offer to me during his visit to Netherfield."

John crossed his arms and leaned back against a wall, nodding. "So, it seems that you lost the suitor you wished for and I lost the lady I chose by their unfortunate meeting. What exactly do you propose, Miss Bingley?"

Caroline smiled her most cat-like grin. "Have you thought of taking the matter into your own hands, sir?" He tilted his head and looked confused. Caroline was frustrated that he did not follow. "I understand that Miss Eliza enjoys long walks about the countryside alone." She nodded at him significantly and raised her brow. She saw the light of comprehension come into his eyes.

"You are suggesting that I . . ."

She smiled, "Oh, nothing overt, but enough to be noticed by a witness or two?" She nodded again. "I see that you understand me, Mr. Lucas." She tapped his arm and moved away, leaving John staring after her. He shuddered at the thought of being married to her, and pitied Darcy for a moment for being her object. Then he looked back across the room to where Darcy and Elizabeth stood comfortably by the pianoforte, watching Mary play as Georgiana turned the pages. He wondered, perhaps this was the only way.

Elizabeth caught Georgiana's eye and glanced at Mary, who was shuffling through the sheets of music, looking for a new song. Georgiana picked up a lively piece and gave it to her. "Mary, perhaps the guests would like to dance."

Mary looked at her. "But everyone seemed to enjoy the song I just played, and besides, they are all talking."

Lydia came running up. "Play a jig, Mary! It is far too quiet in here!"

Sighing, Mary took the music and put it up. "I will do this only because you asked first, Georgiana." The girl smiled and looked up at Elizabeth who was nodding her head.

Mary struck the first notes and Darcy turned to her. "I believe, Miss Elizabeth that we should honour your sister's playing by dancing to her song. Will you join me?" He smiled and offered his hand.

"I would be delighted." She took his hand and they moved to an area where other couples were lining up. Lydia dragged a laughing young man to the floor and Kitty was looking about, hoping to catch some man's eye when she felt her mother's hand on her arm.

"Mr. Lucas, surely you will not miss a chance to dance! Here is Kitty! You made such a delightful couple at the assembly!" She pushed Kitty forward and John looked at her, and then at her mother with some distress.

"Madam, I . . ."

Mrs. Bennet would brook no opposition. "Go on, get out there, you still have time to join."

John sighed and took Kitty's reluctant hand. "Come, Miss Kitty." John stood opposite her, waiting for their turn to move, and watched Darcy smiling and holding Elizabeth's hand as she swung around him. He noticed Miss Bingley glaring at the couple from the other side of the room, and then looked up to take note of Charlotte glaring at them as well. He wondered how many people in that room were unhappy with this particular pairing, and noticed that Kitty was certainly unhappy with him. It seemed that the only female member of the Bennet family who favoured him that evening was Mrs. Bennet

The remainder of the evening passed without incident. Elizabeth was unsurprised to find herself seated beside John and across from Charlotte, and to see that William was far down the table on the same side, so there was no possibility of them even looking at each other during the courses. Lady Lucas clearly had intended to promote her son and dissuade William, but was not actively encouraging any conversation during the meal. Elizabeth was able to converse in a friendly manner with her dinner partners, and John was exceedingly polite, although he seemed to have something on his mind. He persisted in extolling the virtues of Hertfordshire, as well as its proximity to London. He made note of Mr. Bingley's attentions to Jane, and suggested that if a happy event occurred in that quarter, would it not be wonderful to know that her sister would not be taken far away upon her marriage, as he knew how close she was to Jane. He knew that he had struck a significant mark with that statement and was pleased to see her startle and look carefully at Jane's flushed face, she clearly was enjoying Mr. Bingley's attentions, and he was earnest in his delivery. Elizabeth had been so caught up in her own romance that she really had not paid much attention to the progression of Jane's.

Georgiana fortunately was seated across from her brother and Mary, so she was able to enjoy the meal in some peace, but she was also able to observe Elizabeth from her position, and the alarm she displayed while watching her receive John's attentions was noted by Darcy. He was desperate to know what was happening, but could not call across the table for a description. Finally he leaned across, "Georgiana." She looked away from the couple. "Is she well?" The anxiety was evident in his eyes.

"I am not sure, she appears worried." Darcy sighed with frustration and leaned back, trying to see her face down the row of diners, but only managed to catch the briefest glimpse of her hair. Even that sight sent his heart racing. Mr. Bennet sat on the opposite side of the table, almost exactly between the couple, and was watching them. They were both clearly unhappy with the table arrangements, and he noticed John saying things to Lizzy that gave her pause. He wondered if another talk might be necessary with the young man.

Upon the separation after dinner, Bingley could not stop his delighted rambling about Miss Bennet, and Hurst shook his head and smiled at Darcy. "It seems my brother is in love again. You had nothing to fear about him and your Miss Elizabeth."

Darcy looked at his friend's faraway and dreamy smile. "Do you think it will stick this time? I do not wish to see Miss Bennet disappointed."

Hurst regarded one man, then the other. "I do believe this might be the one, Darcy. It seems Bingley will be your brother after all." Darcy looked at him sharply. "Oh come on man, it is clear as day what your intentions are. My wife and sister are quite convinced of it." Darcy smiled slightly and shook his head. Hurst looked at him seriously. "Do be careful of Caroline, Darcy. I listened to her complain of Miss Elizabeth the entire way here."

"Thank you, I am well aware of not being caught alone with her, not that I would capitulate if I were."

Hurst grinned. "I have always admired that about you, Darcy, duty and honour are your bywords, but you show uncommon sense as well." He raised his glass and walked away. Darcy laughed slightly and looked at the clock, soon this ritual would be over and he could return to his Elizabeth.

Sir William approached with an officer. "Mr. Darcy, may I introduce you to Colonel Forster? His militia will be quartering in the area for the winter."

Darcy bowed. "It is an honour to meet a man who has dedicated his life to protecting our country, sir."

The Colonel smiled with pleasure. "Thank you, Mr. Darcy. I wish that we received such a warm welcome from all residents, I am afraid we are often regarded as a menace, particularly by the fathers of young daughters." He smiled sadly. "I try to instil proper behaviour in the men, but . . ."

"Vice of some form or another abounds, yes, I know, sir. If not ladies, it is drink or gaming. My cousin is a colonel with the regulars, and often bemoans his troops, although he has had great success in reforming or perhaps the word is, restraining them." He smiled slightly.

Colonel Forster looked interested. "Really? What is his name? Perhaps we have met."

"Fitzwilliam, Richard, with the cavalry stationed in London. He fought on the peninsula. He will visit the area in a few weeks; perhaps he can pay you a call."

Colonel Forster nodded his head. "Yes, I am always interested in meeting another man in regimentals." He laughed. "Well, good evening, sir." They bowed and Sir William took him off to meet more members of the neighbourhood. Darcy was watching them go when Mr. Bennet strolled to his side and nodded after the colonel.

"My daughters are beside themselves in anticipation of the militia's arrival." Darcy exchanged glances with him.

"You should watch them carefully sir, while the colonel has made this his career, most of these men are there by lottery, not choice."

"Yes five years, unless the regulars do something about Napoleon . . . ah well, that is another subject entirely." He took a sip of his port and gestured his glass across the room. "Mr. Darcy. I was pleased to see you getting on so well with Lucas."

Darcy smiled grimly. "You mean you were pleased I did not beat him for shooting me or strangle him for approaching Miss Elizabeth?"

Mr. Bennet laughed. "Well, something along those lines." He stood looking around the room. "I think that one more week should be sufficient, sir."

Darcy's head snapped up. "Sir?"

Mr. Bennet nodded. "I have listened to the murmurings of the neighbourhood. Expectations are high. One more week, and I will be satisfied." He patted Darcy's shoulder and walked away. Darcy drew a deep breath and reached into his pocket to wind Elizabeth's ribbon around his fingers. *One more week and we may announce our engagement. Thank you, Lord.*

When the men reunited with the ladies, Darcy had no further opportunity to spend time alone with Elizabeth. He was always near, but so were his sister, her sisters, Bingley, the Bennets, Miss Lucas, seemingly everybody who ever had any interest in either of them was there to get in their way. Caroline seemed to attempt a permanent attachment to his arm and he was continually shaking her off like an overly affectionate dog. He was desperate for a moment alone with Elizabeth, and finally had the opportunity as they walked outside to the carriages. "Elizabeth," he whispered, "will you walk in the morning?"

She looked around and seeing everyone occupied she stepped near. "Yes, if there is no rain, I hope to be out by eight. You will ride?"

He nodded. "I will meet you at the stile. I have good news." He smiled, unable to hide his joy.

"Tell me now!" She whispered.

"No, I want to tell you when we might celebrate properly." His gaze sent a warm fire down to her belly.

Elizabeth pursed her lips, but her eyes were dancing. "Very well then, make me suffer."

Darcy laughed with delight, then Jane called Elizabeth and they looked at each other with regret. He kissed her hand with a lingering caress. "Dream of me, my love." One more look then he watched her board the carriage, and lifted his hand as it rolled by. He turned to help Georgiana into his carriage and Bingley climbed in after him. They had not gone far before his ribbon was again wound around his fingers, and his thoughts were with a pair of fine eyes.

Roberts was moving about the dressing room when Darcy entered. "What are you doing, Roberts? I thought I told you not to wait for me."

"Yes sir, but Danny arrived and I am afraid I was late with my preparations for the night." He took the coat and waistcoat Darcy handed to him.

"Gossiping, Roberts?" He raised his brow.

His valet cleared his throat. "Just gathering the news from London, sir." Darcy smiled to himself, knowing full well what news the two loyal servants would be discussing, and handed him his cravat. He sat down so his boots could be removed.

"I see."

"I left your letters on the writing desk and your package from Mr. Hendricks there by the bed, sir."

Darcy looked over to the old velvet box and nodded. "Thank you." He removed the rest of his clothing and poured some water from the ewer into the basin and began washing off the grime of the evening. His man stood with his eyes averted and handed him a towel. "Thank you, Roberts; that will be all. I wish to be riding by seven-thirty." The valet bowed and wished him a good night, and Darcy slipped the long nightshirt over his head. He stood and looked at himself in the mirror, and wondered if he would please Elizabeth. The mere thought of her seeing him dressed in such a way . . . or better yet undressed, brought him to instant arousal. He glanced down at the tent pole he created and moaned with no little frustration. "What are you doing to me, Elizabeth? This has become a permanent affliction!" He climbed into the bed with a handkerchief and again lay back to find relief alone. His back arched as his hips thrust, and he fell into that heart-stopping abyss that his body craved. It grew more intense each time. He relaxed in the warm lassitude that always followed then opened his eyes to look over at the box. He reached for it, and rolling onto his side, rested his head on the pillow and opened it carefully. The jewels captured the light from the fire and came alive, dancing like her eyes. He settled deeper into his pillow and set the box next to him, watching the sparkle, and fell asleep, imagining that she was there.

Mr. Bennet rarely slept through the night, and never with his wife. He was in his bookroom early the next morning, finally opening and reading the letter from his cousin William Collins. The letter was so ridiculous that he found himself laughing at the man's curious style. Instead of resenting the fact that because of the entailment set down by his grandfather he was forced to relinquish his family's estate to a distant cousin, he looked forward to the character study the obviously foolish parson would present. He also wondered at the thinly-veiled motives for the visit, as the presence of five unmarried daughters in the house was mentioned several times. "Well, Lizzy will be safe from him, and she and Mr. Darcy can easily afford to care for the rest of the girls if it becomes necessary. Perhaps Jane will soon be safe as well." It was sobering to think of his girls leaving home, but knowing that they would go to good men and not be left to accept the attentions of someone like Collins was a relief. He sharpened a pen and wrote to the man, inviting him to mend the fences. When he finished he set about answering his sister's letter, and heard the front door open and close again. He looked out of the window to see Elizabeth adjusting her gloves and setting off at a brisk pace. He wondered if she was meeting Mr. Darcy, then decided he really did not want to know.

———✑✑✑———

Elizabeth reached the stile, and looked in the direction of Netherfield. There was no impressive figure on a horse approaching, so she drew out her watch and saw that she was a quarter hour early. She sighed and sat down to wait. Her fingers went to her neck and followed the chain down to her locket, caressing it while imagining William's face. He seemed so excited when they parted, what could his good news be? So many ideas crossed her mind, each more fanciful than the next, and she finally stopped herself. "Silly girl, you will know soon enough." Instead she thought of the kisses they shared during her riding lesson, and the look of pride and admiration on his face as she responded to Miss Bingley's thinly veiled criticism during tea. She laughed, remembering how she took a seat beside William on the sofa, only to look up to see that Miss Bingley had not noticed her and was about to sit on her lap. Even Georgiana managed to laugh at that. Elizabeth was pleased with the improvement she slowly saw coming from her, but she was so withdrawn at the party last night. She resembled William very much in their mutual unhappiness in crowded rooms. The sound of a horse brought her from her reverie and she looked around eagerly only to see with disappointment John Lucas dismounting and approaching with a smile.

"Miss Elizabeth! Good morning, this is a welcome surprise!" He beamed at her.

The smile of expectation was instantly wiped from her lips, and the heart that had been beating so quickly in anticipation now clenched. She tried to regain her composure and glanced towards the empty path to Netherfield. "Mr. Lucas, good morning, I would think that you would not have arisen so early this day." He stopped and held out his hand to aid her down from her seat on the stile, squeezing her fingers.

"I could easily say the same of you." She smiled slightly, but felt uncomfortable being alone with him, particularly after receiving his barely concealed attentions the night before.

"No, I did not have a house full of guests."

He laughed. "Well that is certainly true. I simply found that sleep did not come. I had too much on my mind." John's eyes met hers and she instantly knew that she was the subject of his musings and flushed. He drew a deep breath. "Miss Elizabeth, I realize that I made a very poor beginning with my attempts at a courtship, but I have taken your admonishments to heart. I have begun to learn and accept the responsibilities of my position, and I hope that you have noticed my attempts to change and treat you with the respect you deserve. I hope with all of my heart that it is enough to allow me to ask for a second chance."

Elizabeth bit her lip and closed her eyes, holding back the retort that came to mind. He was behaving civilly and she did not wish to cause him pain. "Sir, yes, I have noticed your efforts, and I do appreciate them, but you are aware that I have accepted Mr. Darcy's offer of courtship. I can not entertain any others."

John fully knew this but pressed on. "And if this courtship should end?"

"Why should it?" She demanded. "Mr. Darcy has been a gentleman at every turn, and I have no reason to end our friendship."

John looked at her earnestly. "What do you truly know of him? He sweeps in with his tales of wealth and property, a stranger to us all . . . Look at me, Miss Elizabeth. You know everything of me. I will never be able to give you endless supplies of funds or an enormous home, but I know you. Those are things that matter little to you. Your love is family, nature, simple things. Those I can give you in abundance. You do not belong in the world where he lives any more than I do. You belong right here in Hertfordshire. You belong with me." He stepped forward. "You know it is true, Miss Elizabeth." He looked longingly into her eyes.

"Mr. Lucas, do not speak of such things. Do not presume to know me or where my place should be. Not once have you ever considered my opinion in your plans, that presumption is the furthest thing from respect." She drew herself up and stared straight into his eyes. "I am courting Mr. Darcy. You have no business telling me your feelings."

He shook his head in frustration. "Then what should I speak of? Shall I tell you of my suspicions that Mr. Darcy is not all that he seems?"

She looked at him sharply. "What do you mean?"

John took her hand. "There is something wrong with him. I feel it! He is so dark, brooding, and I just know that he is hiding something. His sister, I watched her last night. She barely spoke a word and behaved like a frightened doe whenever he looked at her. If his own sister is afraid to open her mouth in his presence, what will he do to you, Miss Elizabeth? I can not bear to see you hurt. Something is terribly wrong in that family."

Elizabeth pulled her hand away from his and stepped back. "Sir, I assure you, Mr. Darcy is simply a man who is uncomfortable in large gatherings and his sister is a mere girl of fifteen and very sheltered and shy. The only person who is seeking to hurt me is you, with your unwanted attentions and interference in my affairs."

Seeing that he was rapidly losing any improvement in her opinion that he may have gained, he spoke urgently, stepping close to her again. "You are not Charlotte, you are only twenty. Please do not rush to accept this man. Please do not regret the choice you make merely to secure your future. You could be secure with me. I swear, I will take care of you, and any in your family who needs our help. Truly Miss Elizabeth, I feel that Mr. Darcy is not the man he appears to be. I know that I have heard something of him when I was in London, it nags at me constantly, but I can not put my finger on it. I can not watch you go to your destruction when I know that I could have stopped it." He took her chin and lifted it. "If you do choose to go with him, and find that he has . . . been ungentlemanly, come to me, I will care for you. I am in no hurry to marry; I will wait until I am sure you are safe. But dear Elizabeth, I do so hope that I will not have to suffer that torture, and you will come to me now." He spoke softly and his eyes dropped to her lips.

Elizabeth wrenched away from him and slapped him full across the face. "How dare you touch me!!" Her hand stung with the slap and John stared at her in shock. "How dare you address me in such a familiar manner, and how dare you speak to me of such things after my father came and told you that I was not interested in your attentions!" She turned and looked towards Netherfield, and spotted a horseman galloping at great speed across the field. It was William. "Do you think that behaving in this manner is going to win you my favour? Look to a true gentleman, sir." She pointed to William's rapidly approaching horse.

Disregarding Darcy, John reached out to grab her arm as she began to climb up over the stile to get away from him. Desperately he spoke. "Elizabeth, please, do not be afraid of me, I have never wished you harm. I was a fool who thought that I could have everything I wanted because of who I was. My father instilled an overblown sense of pride in me, and I have learned very quickly it was worthless outside of my home county. It was a difficult realization, and it happened at the same time that I discovered the fascinating woman that you had become. No woman I have ever known has your life, Elizabeth. I could marry any number of the ladies of Hertfordshire, but I have fallen for you. But I learned of this all too late; and insulted when I should have listened. My feelings, I admit at the beginning were not nearly so strong, not as they are now. I am so afraid that I am too late, but I want you to know, I will wait and hope, and dream of you, my dear Elizabeth."

"You insult me now, Mr. Lucas! You insult me with your every touch and look and thought. I have asked repeatedly for you to leave me alone, and you persist, even when I am publicly and formally courting another man who DOES have my father's consent. I have never wanted your attentions, sir!"

Darcy came over the rise from Netherfield and instantly spotted Elizabeth speaking to a man. He was halfway across the field when he saw him take her hand, and was nearly there when he saw her slap his face and try to get away. That she was fighting him with words was obvious, but he knew full well that she would be no match for him if he chose to become physically violent. His heart pounding, he recognized John, and urging his horse to gallop faster, they leapt over the fence and landed, startling them with the sound. In a flash, Darcy was dismounted and striding forward. He looked at Elizabeth's flushed and furious features and grabbed a firm hold of John's shoulder, pulling him roughly away from her. He raised his fist and struck him in his stomach. John doubled over in pain, gasping. Darcy pulled him upright and struck him again, this time across his jaw. He fell back into the tall grass. Darcy leaned down to pull him up to his feet, and pinned him against a tree, his hand at John's throat. He glared and said in a low dangerous voice through clenched teeth. "What did you say that drove her need to slap your face? Why would a woman need to defend herself against a gentleman who claims to admire her? I know of your fascination with Miss Elizabeth, Lucas. If you value your future, I strongly suggest that you direct your attentions elsewhere. I chose to overlook the shooting as an accident, now I know that your intentions were to kill me. You are fortunate that I am not armed sir, because *I am* an excellent shot." Darcy again raised his fist and struck him in the stomach. John began to retch, and Darcy stepped back in disgust. He stood staring at the man, ready to hit him again if necessary.

John spat and stood up, gasping. "Go ahead, strike me again. Show her the brute you truly are. You have managed to hide it long enough, or perhaps we should ask your sister?"

Darcy's eyes were black with fury. "What are you saying of my sister? What has she to do with this?"

"She stands in your shadow, cowed by your presence. I will not have you do the same with Miss Elizabeth!"

Darcy's eyes darted to her. "What is he saying?"

She stepped forward, feeling shocked at the display but proud of William. "He thinks that I require protection from you. He questions your worthiness as my suitor."

Darcy's face reflected his shock. "What??" He spun to face John, who regained some of his breath. "You know nothing of me."

John nodded and raised his hand to point at Elizabeth. "That is exactly what I was telling Miss Elizabeth. She knows nothing of you. I have offered her my protection, should she ever need it, whether now, or after she comes to regret accepting you." He breathed deeply.

"Your protection?! To anyone who happened upon this scene, Miss Elizabeth would have been considered compromised. Is that what your plan was? To grab onto her and force a marriage that you otherwise never would have had?" Darcy stood between them. "You have been told by Miss Elizabeth, and her father, and now by me, to leave us alone. Your attentions are not desired, your protection is a front, and your friendship is now over. I will not permit you to come near her ever again. Do not try, or I will deliver the message in the same manner as I have today, and as often as is necessary. Am I clear?"

John addressed Elizabeth. "My offer remains Miss Elizabeth. It will only be a matter of time before I am proven correct."

"If you continue to persist, sir, I will be forced to call you out." Darcy took a step forward.

"Mr. Lucas, you have allowed your disappointment to overwhelm your reason. I assure you that Mr. Darcy is the very best of men." She walked up to William and stood by his side.

John stood and stared at her, trying hard to understand why he had failed so utterly with her, and how she could have been taken in by the man who stood glowering beside her. He also was feeling ashamed with his inability to defend himself. He glanced at Darcy's burning eyes and flinched when his hand flexed back into a fist. "Very well, I will refrain from expressing my beliefs until they are confirmed elsewhere, but in the meantime, remember my words." Casting a wary eye at Darcy, he went to mount his horse. He took one last look and galloped away. Elizabeth instantly embraced Darcy and could no longer hold back her tears. He took her in his arms, and held her tight, confused and angry.

"Elizabeth, darling, please, tell me, are you well?" He felt her nod, and thanked heaven that he had come in time. He had no idea how to comfort her, but removed her bonnet and rested his cheek in her hair, his head moving as she cried out the emotion of the last half hour. When she quieted, he continued to hold her, rubbing her back and kissing her hair. She moved away and took a long breath, and he drew out her handkerchief to wipe the tears. "Are you better?" He asked tentatively.

She nodded and reached up to caress his face, wiping away the tears he did not know he shed. "I was so excited to come here today, and then this had to occur."

He walked her to the stile and sat on the step, drawing her onto his lap. "What exactly did occur? I came over the rise to see a man holding your hand, and touching your face. I saw you slap him and your attempt to escape. I did not know what was happening, only that I needed to come to you immediately. Did he hurt you?" He searched her face.

Elizabeth shook her head. "If I had not been so angry, I would have been more frightened. No, that is wrong, I was frightened, but my courage rose when I saw you coming." She caressed his cheek. "Mr. Lucas was confessing his feelings for me and offering me marriage."

Darcy sat up straight and his eyes grew black with anger again. "He did what?!" He looked around. "HERE? I should have killed him!" Elizabeth could not help but laugh and embraced him. He searched her face. "Why do you laugh?"

She drew his head down and kissed him. The crease in his brow remained. "Oh William, if I do not laugh, I will cry again, and you do not know what to do with me then." She sighed. "It seems that he must have heard some of the gossip of Georgiana when in London, but does not yet connect your name with what he heard. I know that he visited St. James' one evening at the end of the Season."

Darcy closed his eyes, and nodded. "I am sure that you are correct." Darcy met her eyes and shook his head. "My love, I do not know what to say, the position he put you in . . . what did you say?"

"I hardly know, mostly I told him to leave us alone."

He caressed her face. "I am so sorry, Elizabeth."

"For what? None of this is your doing. Mr. Lucas was never someone I wished to marry. I have never felt anything more than friendship for him. He has taken any emotion he has ever felt for me and added this new protectiveness to it. I just hope that he keeps his word and does not spread his mistaken beliefs throughout the neighbourhood."

"I am sorry that this man imposed himself upon you. I am sorry that you were forced to bear his attentions, and I could not do anything to stop him because our engagement is not public. And I am sorry that you had to witness me behaving in such an ungentlemanly way."

Elizabeth took his right hand and held it gently. "Does this hurt?" She kissed the bruised knuckles.

He flexed his hand and smiled ruefully. "It is not too bad."

"I liked seeing you defend me." She looked up and Darcy's eyes darkened again, but this time with passion.

"Elizabeth." He searched her face and in a sudden movement seized and crushed her against him. Elizabeth gasped and he claimed her lips in a ravenous kiss, devouring her mouth and stroking his hands possessively up and down her body. She clung to his neck and pressed as tightly to him as she could. Their lips and tongues fought in a desperate competition to consume the other. Darcy dragged his mouth across her face, and breathing heavily whispered hoarsely. "You are mine, Elizabeth. No man touches you but me." He reclaimed her lips hungrily then pulled away to take her face in his hands. "I have waited my entire life to feel love." Her hands took his face and she could feel his jaw working to control the emotion.

Elizabeth caressed him. "My love is yours alone, William." Darcy closed his eyes and held her to him, resting his cheek on her hair as Elizabeth's arms encircled his waist. She rested her head over his pounding heart.

"I saw you trying to escape him. My God, what might have happened if I had not come when I did?" He squeezed when she gasped in understanding.

"You do not think he would have harmed me?"

Darcy said nothing, and only clutched her tighter. "I need to make you mine."

His words reverberated throughout Elizabeth; they contained a multitude of meanings. "I want to be yours." She whispered, and then looked up to him.

He swallowed hard and touched her cheek. "And I want to belong to you." He said softly before kissing her gently. They both knew that their desire could not be fulfilled at that moment, so instead they remained in their embrace, calming, and Elizabeth felt the arousal that had been pressing against her slowly die away. Only then was Darcy able to relax his grip.

Elizabeth looked up and kissed his chin, and he smiled with a small upturn of his mouth. "Now, what was your wonderful news? I could not sleep last night trying to imagine it."

His smile grew. "Well, perhaps it is even better news than I thought at the time, following this morning's activities." He laughed at her raised brow. "Your father told me one more week of courtship and we may announce our engagement. Apparently the neighbourhood is convinced we will marry." He cried out as Elizabeth threw her arms around his neck and kissed him with enthusiasm. He laughed and drew away, smiling into her sparkling eyes. "Your excitement is very gratifying my love. I look forward to your reaction after you open this." He drew the velvet box from his pocket and handed it to her, watching her eyes widen with wonder.

"What is it?" She whispered.

He turned her around so that her back was to his chest and rested his chin on her shoulder. He reached his arms under hers and opened the lid. Her gasp swelled his chest. "This was my grandmother's favourite necklace." He lifted it from the box and carefully placed it around her neck.

Elizabeth touched the simple diamond choker with shaking fingers. "It is so beautiful." She turned and kissed him. "I do not know what to say. Thank you for trusting me with your family's treasures."

Darcy smiled warmly into her eyes. "You, my love, are my greatest treasure; this necklace is merely an adornment."

Elizabeth turned and wrapped her arms around his neck, "I love you, and not because of this magnificent gift, but because you are the man I always dreamed would love me. I can not imagine marrying anyone but you."

Darcy swallowed the lump in his throat and held her face in his hands, tracing her lips with his thumbs. "I am . . ." He moaned and his lips fell upon hers. As she began to lose herself in his kiss, the sound of William's horse awakened her to their location.

She gently put her hands on his chest and pushed away. He only clung tighter. "William, we must stop, we may already have been seen."

He held her and murmured. "I do not care." Elizabeth managed to loosen his grip and slipped off of his lap.

"Yes, you do." She held out her hand. "Come, we should tell Papa what has happened."

He stayed seated, staring at her, then closed his eyes and nodded. "Very well, I agree that we need to inform him of this morning's events, but I also believe that it would be wise to announce our engagement before Lucas makes any of his claims public." He took her hand and stood.

To her surprise, he lifted her up and placed her on the horse. Seeing her settled, he took a hold of the bridle and began walking beside her. "Do I seem incapable of walking, Mr. Darcy?"

He smiled. "I do not think you incapable of anything, Miss Elizabeth; however you may recall that you did not receive much of a lesson the last time we kept company with a horse."

She raised a brow and held onto the unnecessary reins. "Whose fault was that?"

He laughed. "Well, mine perhaps, but I do believe I had a willing partner." He met her gaze and she stopped pursing her lips and smiled.

Across the field John watched the couple depart. Their obviously tender behaviour confused him. It was not the image of Darcy he had built in his mind. He shook his head, no of course he was correct, something was wrong with Darcy and Elizabeth in her innocence was fooled. John was determined to learn the truth and rescue her. He rubbed his swollen jaw and debated how he would explain his bruises to his parents.

The couple arrived at Longbourn just after nine o'clock. The rest of the family was just beginning to rise after their late evening and the servants were busy with their duties. Only Mr. Bennet witnessed Elizabeth sliding down the horse's flank and into Darcy's waiting arms. And only he saw those arms wrap around his daughter as the man bent to bestow a lingering kiss. Mr. Bennet was standing in the hallway when they entered the house, hand in hand.

"Mr. Darcy. I would like a word with you immediately." Mr. Bennet's face reflected his anger.

"Mr. Bennet that is exactly what I would like with you. Events have transpired this morning of which you need to be informed."

Mr. Bennet recognized the deadly serious expression on Darcy's face then looked to see the equal emotion on Elizabeth's. Their unexpected reaction startled him from his anger over their displays of affection. "Well then, come in. Lizzy, please leave us." She began to protest when Darcy spoke.

"Sir, I ask that Miss Elizabeth remain."

Taking in their solidarity, he nodded. "Very well, then. Come in."

They entered the bookroom and closed the door. Between the two of them, the story of John's behaviour and their reactions was told. To say that he was shocked was an understatement. "He tried to compromise you while proposing? Are you well, Lizzy?" Mr. Bennet looked at his daughter with great concern.

Elizabeth smiled. "Yes, Papa. Mr. Darcy was my rescuer."

Darcy reached over and took her hand, kissing it. "You were defending yourself most effectively, I am only happy that I arrived when I did."

Mr. Bennet watched the tender regard between the two and realized he could no longer delay the inevitable. "Thank you sir, for defending my daughter." He noticed the swollen hand. "It seems you will be in need of her nursing once again." Darcy flexed his fingers and smiled at her.

"I will gladly accept it."

Elizabeth raised her brow. "Are you sure? I could always send for your valet."

"I was trying to follow the rules of propriety."

Her eyes danced. "Well we seem to fail that quite regularly, sir."

He kissed her hand again. "William."

Mr. Bennet cleared his throat, interrupting the exchange. "I believe that I should call on Lucas Lodge."

Darcy immediately focused on him. "I will accompany you, sir."

He shook his head. "No. I am, although it seems merely ceremonial at this point, still Lizzy's guardian and you sir, despite your displays, are not her husband . . . yet. It is my duty to warn off Lucas and threaten to call him out if he persists." He sighed. "It is evident, however, that the announcement of your engagement should occur sooner than I anticipated." He spotted the necklace sparkling around Elizabeth's throat. "Your mother's raptures will be deafening, Lizzy. If you wish to spare my hearing, perhaps you could reveal that rather impressive gift after I have left the house."

Elizabeth touched the jewels and blushed. "Yes, Papa." Darcy drew out the old velvet box and gently removed the necklace from her throat. A knock at the door alerted them that breakfast was ready and they made their way to the dining room.

Mrs. Bennet stared in surprise to see Darcy joining them. "Mr. Darcy, this is an unexpected pleasure, what brings you here so early in the day?" She looked from her daughter to her husband and back to Darcy, suspecting what had happened. Jane looked at Elizabeth with wide eyes and she smiled back, nodding her head.

Mr. Bennet cleared his throat. "Well, I am pleased to announce that Mr. Darcy has asked for Lizzy's hand and I have granted my consent and blessing."

As predicted the effusions were deafening, "Oh my Lizzy!! My dear, dear girl! You have done it! I knew that this correspondence with Miss Darcy would help you to capture her brother's eye, and it did! Oh and what a fine husband you will make for my Lizzy, Mr. Darcy! What pin money, what jewels you shall give her! And she will be a good and obedient wife for you, will you not Lizzy!" She barely drew breath.

Elizabeth grasped Darcy's hand under the table and he squeezed hard. She leaned over to him. "I am so sorry that you have to witness this, William." The table was awash with excited feminine voices, all voicing their opinions of the match, Elizabeth's future, wedding plans, and general excitement. Lydia and Kitty were demanding new clothes along with Elizabeth's trousseau. Mary made suggestions from her sermons about the proper conduct of a betrothed woman. Jane sat and watched them with obvious longing, and Mr. Bennet felt a growing sadness in his heart.

Darcy looked over the general melee and smiled. "This may come as a complete surprise to you Elizabeth, but although perhaps your younger sister's behaviour should be refined, I welcome this excitement. I look forward so much to being part of a family, and I hope that they will come to visit us at Pemberley. I can not wait to fill our home with the sounds of our children, even if it means I will never have a moment's peace again."

Their fingers entwined and she leaned in close to him. "It is my dearest hope to fulfil your wish, but when you do find those moments of peace, I want them to be spent in my embrace."

Darcy stopped before he kissed her, but whispered in return. "That is where I belong."

Chapter 19

"**W**hat do you think Darcy's reaction will be to our interference with Catherine?" Lord Matlock asked Richard. They were comfortably ensconced in two armchairs before a roaring fire in his study at Matlock House in London.

Richard took a sip of wine and looked thoughtfully at the portrait of his grandfather hanging in a corner of the room. "If I know Darcy, and I like to think that I do, well at least as much as anyone can, I believe that "interference" is exactly the word he would use and he is feeling very unhappy with his relations at the moment."

"I was afraid of that. Well there is nothing to be done for it now. I hope that he will see reason once he cools down." Lord Matlock glanced at the portrait as well. "My father would be appalled with Catherine's behaviour."

"I do not really remember him. I must have been . . . six at the time that he died." He looked at his father, who nodded.

"He lived to see most of his grandchildren born."

Richard sat up. "I imagine that he lived to see both Aunt Catherine and Aunt Anne reject their marriages."

"And their children." Lord Matlock sighed. "It broke his heart. Mother was gone fairly soon after Anne married, so she thankfully did not witness it. Darcy's grandmother on his father's side doted on him, but I doubt that he remembers it, since she died when he was about four or so. Well, I do hope that he understands that we acted out of concern for both him and Georgiana."

"What was it like for him? I mean, I have heard tales of the parties and the rumours of infidelity at Pemberley, but nothing of what he actually experienced day after day. He never speaks of it. I know that he did not even seem to acknowledge his mother's death."

Lord Matlock was silent for a few moments. "I remember paying a visit, unannounced, to Pemberley one time. I was admitted to the house, of course. The servants were silent, unusually so. Not even gossiping as the maids worked, you know how they are." He closed his eyes, as if seeing it in his mind. "I asked if anyone was about, and was told that Mr. and Mrs. Darcy were in her boudoir. I started walking that way and heard a woman's voice pleading with someone. I followed the sound and found Mrs. Reynolds, the current housekeeper, and Darcy's governess bent in front of an armoire in a room next to the study. Darcy was hiding inside of it. They saw me and looked quite frightened and relieved at the same time. I did not understand why until I opened the door and pulled him out. He must have been no more than five. He was curled, hugging his legs, but not crying. He just stared at me. I tried to hold him and ask what had happened, but he said nothing. From the next room I heard raised voices, it was my sister and brother arguing. Darcy cringed at the sound then put a finger to his lips and pressed his ear to the door, listening, and when they finally emerged, he smiled and tried to win their attention, and was told to be quiet and leave them. He flinched at the reprimand, and I suggested bringing him to Matlock to visit for awhile. My sister was indifferent, but my brother said that his son would not leave home. I never knew exactly what they did, but that is a small example of his early life."

Richard was aghast. "I knew that he was essentially told never to express weakness, but I had no idea that it was beaten into him."

"I do not know that it was. There was undeniably an absolute absence of affection from his parents, and at some point he just stopped trying to express it or win it for himself. It may all have been verbal abuse, or simply the exposure to his parent's unending fights, I can not say, I was not there. It is rather extraordinary that he became the good man he is, it could so easily have gone the other way. I suppose that his governess is responsible for that." He paused. "I have been thinking long and hard about his declaration of affection for this Miss Bennet. For Darcy to feel so strongly, well to allow himself to express emotion as he has about this woman is truly an exceptional event. I wonder just what this woman has done to break through the walls he put up around himself. It actually makes me ashamed that I would try to dissuade him from his choice."

"Then why have you, knowing all of this?" Richard asked, sitting forward and studying his father carefully.

Lord Matlock met his eye. "I suppose that I can not forget that little boy, trying desperately to win some affection from his unhappy parents, and I am afraid that this woman has taken advantage of him. I pray that it is not the case, but I could not protect him when he was a lad. I had no right to take him from Pemberley, and now that he is an adult, I can not protect him either. All I can do is talk." He looked down. "I am counting on you Richard, to go and find out if he is truly making the right decision."

Richard sat back again. "James thought that he was a fool. I admit to perhaps feeling some of that same sentiment, but was willing to support him and believe that what he has found is real." He nodded. "Well, I am on leave now, and I believe that I will invite myself to Hertfordshire. Will you return to Matlock?"

"Yes, Catherine is under control, and as long as she does not get wind of Darcy's marital hopes, I imagine she will behave. I will not put it past her to try and disrupt his plans if he has proceeded with his courtship."

"But Anne has said she will not marry him."

Lord Matlock laughed. "She is angry now, Son. He has refused her daughter and ruined her long-held plans. Do you truly believe that she will allow Darcy to find peace and happiness? If I know my sister, she will be vindictive and try to stop him somehow."

"You have threatened her to stop interfering!"

He laughed again. "She has nothing left to lose. Surely she realizes that our threat of Bedlam was simply to shock her. She will end in the dower's house with the rest of her settlement, so why not on her terms? She would like that better than simply being banished there by Anne. No, Catherine is not through, I am sure of it."

"She is not quite sane, is she?" Richard asked.

Lord Matlock shrugged. "I honestly do not know. She is a bitter woman."

"Well, I have some things to finish up here in London, and then I will go to Hertfordshire in a day or so. I will let you know what I find." Lord Matlock stood and placed a hand on his son's shoulder. "I hope that you find a happy man."

Despite his protests, Mr. Bennet was very pleased that Darcy insisted he accompany him to Lucas Lodge. Confrontation was not something that he did well, standing on the side and making observations, whether to himself or others; that was something that he could do, but taking on his neighbours over improprieties committed upon his daughter, no, he was glad for the company. Particularly as Darcy, now officially engaged to his daughter, had every right to be there, as he vehemently argued in the bookroom after breakfast. Mr. Bennet examined his future son-in-law. His expression was unreadable as ever, but it was clear that he would not frighten easily. "How is your hand?" Mr. Bennet asked as he watched Darcy wince when he pulled on his glove before mounting.

"It is a bit larger than it was this morning."

Mr. Bennet laughed. "Well, it was done in a good cause. Have you ever struck a man before?"

Darcy glanced at him. "No, I have actually never expressed much emotion over any subject. It has earned me a reputation of being rather cold from the whisperings I have heard."

Mr. Bennet tilted his head. "Did you feel that to express emotion was ungentlemanly? I do not mean emotion of the heart so much as emotion such as anger or even fear?"

Darcy's face became like stone. "I was encouraged to express nothing at all to anyone at anytime." He stared straight ahead. Mr. Bennet wondered what sort of upbringing this man experienced. Darcy wished to redirect the conversation. "Sir, how do you wish to approach the Lucas'? They are your friends and neighbours; I will speak only if you wish it. I am here to demonstrate my devotion to Elizabeth and support of her family." Darcy relished the new right to use Elizabeth's Christian name publicly.

"In all honesty, Mr. Darcy, I do not know what I will say. I think that we should see what our reception is first."

Nodding, he looked out into the distance, losing himself in thoughts of the morning. He did not lie. He had never in his life hit a man, or even defended himself. All of those years of admonishment by his father not to ever express emotion, and the neglect by his mother, had taken their toll on him. When he was older, stronger, wiser, he used his wits to extricate himself from difficult situations, or more likely to avoid them all together. The only man who ever challenged him enough to drive him to desire violence was always Wickham, and for him, he always walked away. His father's seemingly blind devotion to him made Darcy hesitant to ever put him in his place. He knew now, after thinking it over for years, that he was afraid that if he knocked down Wickham, he would lose whatever affection his father did hold for him. Perhaps that is why Wickham felt that he could take Georgiana away, he felt that Darcy would never fight back.

They arrived at Lucas Lodge and dismounting, approached the door. Mr. Bennet glanced up at Darcy. "Thank you for coming with me."

Darcy looked at him with appreciation. "It is my honour, sir."

The housekeeper took them to Sir William's study where he stood in surprise. "Gentleman! What brings you here this fine morning?" He waved them to seats, offered them drinks and settled in behind his desk, smiling expectantly.

Mr. Bennet looked at him quizzically. "Has Lucas been here to see you this morning, Sir William?"

"John? No, he was off early on an errand, and I believe he was going to inspect the drainage. He has really been throwing himself into his estate duties of late." He chuckled. "I believe that was at Eliza's encouragement." He grinned at Mr. Bennet then catching Darcy's piercing gaze stopped and cleared his throat. "Well, so, ahem, John is out, so may I be of service?" He looked between them.

Sighing, Mr. Bennet began. "It seems we are to be the bearers of bad news. Lizzy went for a walk this morning and Lucas came upon her. He took the opportunity to present his suit in a most unwanted and insistent manner, to the point where she had to slap his face to convince him to let go of her." Sir William's smile fell away and he stared at Mr. Bennet. "Mr. Darcy was riding and came upon the scene in time to witness the slap and Lizzy attempting to escape your son by climbing over a stile. He rapidly rode to her aid and in the course of the confrontation struck Lucas three times." He looked at Darcy who nodded.

Sir William transferred his gaze to Darcy. "You struck him, sir?"

"I did, twice in the abdomen, and once on his jaw. I regret resorting to violence, but he clearly was not listening to Miss Elizabeth's demands to let her go and leave her alone. Perhaps I could have negotiated with him more rationally if it were not for the fact that I am engaged to be married to her, and my feelings may have understandably obscured my reason."

"Engaged?" Sir William sat back, dumbfounded by what he heard. "Is there any chance that his actions could have been misconstrued?"

Darcy leaned forward and drove his finger onto the desktop. "Sir William, he was holding Miss Elizabeth's face in his hand. If it had been anyone but me witnessing the event, the rumours of compromise would be running wildly through the countryside."

He nodded silently and turned to Mr. Bennet. "I am sorry, Bennet. You warned him, well all of us, away from making a match that Eliza did not want. I believe that I have honoured that request, and Lady Lucas has. . ."

Mr. Bennet snorted. "Except for the seating at last night's dinner."

Sir William cleared his throat, "Ahem, well, yes, there was that, but no harm was done, I suppose . . ." He glanced up at Darcy's cold blue eyes and looked away. "Well nobody knew of your engagement then!" He defended himself.

"Now you do." Darcy said quietly. "I have informed your son to stay away from my betrothed, and not to attempt any communication with her. I have told him that if he persists, I will call him out. He apparently is labouring under the impression that I am somehow misrepresenting myself to Miss Elizabeth. She and Mr. Bennet know everything of me, and if they are satisfied, then that is all that matters. I do not need to prove myself to someone so wholly unrelated to our situation. Your son was aware that we were courting; not knowing of our engagement is no excuse for his behaviour. Do I make myself clear, sir?"

"Yes, yes, of course, capital, yes; indeed. Well sir, I am sure that my son will think long before approaching another lady again, and I will be sure to speak to him about his behaviour. Sir, I apologize most sincerely on behalf of my son and my family. Bennet, I do hope that this incident does not sour the relationship that we have between our houses. Mr. Darcy, may I wish you and Eliza great joy? When is the happy event to take place?" He stood and was ushering them out the door as he spoke. Mr. Bennet glanced at Darcy and smirked.

Darcy saw an opportunity and took it. "No later than the end of November. As your son said, the roads in the north become quite treacherous in the winter, and I wish to bring my bride home safely."

Sir William coughed and nodded. "Yes, very good, I can certainly see that, you have no wish to bring her to London for a time? You will have to have her presented; of course, so that you may attend events at St. James', perhaps we could meet there when you are in town? Yes?" He continued shooing them along. Lady Lucas appeared and looked at them with a quizzical eye. "Ah, Lady Lucas, so sorry my dear but our guests were just leaving. I must tell you the happy news; Mr. Darcy is engaged to marry Eliza, is that not wonderful?"

She gaped at them. "Engaged? Oh, well, how very nice for you all."

Sir William gestured to the servant who held their hats and gloves. "Yes, yes, very nice, indeed. Well, do not hesitate to call again, and bring dear Eliza with you, Mr. Darcy." He smiled and bobbed. The door was firmly shut behind them and Darcy and Mr. Bennet stared at each other in bemused silence.

They walked to their horses, mounted and were back in the lanes before either spoke. "He could not send us away fast enough, could he?" Mr. Bennet laughed.

"I imagine he is very embarrassed."

"Yes, indeed." He looked sideways at Darcy. "You did very well. You kept your temper and stated the facts plainly. I am quite proud of you. A man in your position could very easily have done a great deal of damage to the Lucas'. Your choice to handle this quietly is impressive."

Darcy startled. "Thank you, sir." He looked down. "Elizabeth and I will be gone from the neighbourhood soon; you must address your future relationship with the family, not I. In any event, I am quite accustomed to conducting difficult negotiations, this situation was no different."

"I beg to disagree." Mr. Bennet only had the vaguest idea of Darcy's wealth, but it was enough to know that he was at least equal to a peer of the realm, and he possessed the power to harm if he chose. "I wish that I had your strength, and then perhaps I would have been able to reject my father's demand that I marry Mrs. Bennet."

Darcy looked at him. "But sir, then neither of us would have Elizabeth." They rode in silence, contemplating that salient fact. Darcy did not return to Longbourn, but instead continued on to Netherfield. Elizabeth would learn the details of the meeting from her father, and her mother had already demanded that she spend the day with her, to begin the wedding plans. She would see him the next morning for a riding lesson.

"Ah, back again." Wickham looked about the village as the militia rode into Meryton. Denny lifted his chin and looked over at him. "You have been here before?" Wickham laughed. "I passed through."

"There is a tale in that, I'd wager." Denny grinned.

"Quite a tale." Wickham muttered, and saw the inn coming into view. "Good inn, though."

Seeing that he was not going to be hearing more at the moment, Denny changed the subject. "And the ladies? Did you have an opportunity to meet any?"

Wickham smiled, "I was not here long enough, but I do believe that our primary goal is to explore the ladies and the drink of our new home, is it not?"

Denny smiled, "And do not forget to add to our winnings by meeting the local gentlemen." The two laughed and looked at the villagers watching them enter. Some appeared excited to see them, particularly the young ladies who were staring at their uniforms. Wickham was sorry to leave their last camp at Brighton, a town ripe with his favourite activities, but winter meant moving inland, and for whatever reason, his militia had been assigned here. Money must have exchanged hands somewhere along the line.

The officers were to stay in a rooming house in the village, while the rest of the men set up tents in a field rented for the purpose. They would erect more substantial structures for the winter, but nonetheless, Wickham was grateful for his simple accommodations in an actual building. Colonel Forster sent word around that an evening had been planned two days hence to introduce the officers to the local gentlemen, a sort of welcoming party. Wickham leaned into Denny as they left the room where they had gathered. "We will have the chance to see which of our new hosts will make the best companions. Too bad the ladies will not be invited."

"Come on, let's walk around and see what is to be seen." They left the house and went into the street, and were soon aware of two young girls standing and giggling behind their hands at them. Wickham smirked. They approached and bowed low. "Good afternoon, ladies. I am Lieutenant Wickham, and this is my friend, Lieutenant Denny, we are very happy to be spending our winter protecting the good citizens of Meryton."

Lydia giggled and affected a superior air. "Good afternoon sirs, I am Lydia Bennet, and this is my sister Kitty. We are delighted to meet you." They curtseyed and fell into more giggles. Wickham sent Denny a look with a raised brow, and he grinned, nodding. Yes, these girls were perfect.

Wickham presented his arm to Lydia. "Might I ask you to give us a tour?" Still giggling she took his arm, as Kitty accepted Denny's and together, the couples strolled around the village.

Elizabeth arrived at Netherfield in Darcy's coach, and was disappointed to only see Georgiana waiting outside for her. She stepped down with the aid of a footman and walked up, noting her troubled expression. "Georgiana is something wrong?"

She wrung her hands. "I do not know. William was fine this morning, and until he read a letter at the breakfast table, he was happy, but he stood up and stormed from the room, nearly knocking over a servant on his way. I heard a door shut, and Mr. Bingley said that he had sealed himself in the library and begged not to be disturbed." She took Elizabeth's hand. "What could it be?"

Elizabeth shook her head. "Well, obviously it was something in the letter. Do you think he would speak to me?"

"I confess I hoped you would offer. I was afraid to knock. Miss Bingley has been hovering outside of the door, but thankfully has not gone in." They entered the house and after giving up her outerwear to a servant, Elizabeth followed Georgiana to the library door.

Caroline stood outside. "Miss Eliza, what brings you here?" She looked over the riding attire. "Oh yes, you were to receive a lesson today. Well, I am sorry to tell you that Mr. Darcy is far too occupied to spend time with you. I will call for the carriage to return you to Longbourn right away."

Smiling sweetly, she met Caroline's eye. "Although I am sure that Mr. Darcy appreciates your concern, I am also sure that he would not wish you to speak for him. I will just confirm this with him, then I will either return home, or perhaps Georgiana would like me to visit with her if he needs to alter our plans."

She looked at Georgiana who nodded her head gratefully. "Oh yes, I would like that very much. I already told William that I would rather not accompany you today, it is too windy." Elizabeth smiled and patted her hand, then raising her brows to Caroline to step away from the door; she lifted her hand and knocked.

"Please leave me alone!" The angry voice called.

Elizabeth was taken aback by the very uncharacteristic tone, but glancing at the smirk on Caroline's face she drew herself up. "Mr. Darcy, it is Miss Elizabeth, may I speak to you for a moment?"

The rapid sound of boots on hardwood was heard and the door was unlocked and pulled open. Darcy's eyes were dark and searching. He stepped back and she entered. He glared at Caroline, then looked with pain at Georgiana, and closed the door, locking it again. "What is he doing? He can not be alone in that room with her!" Caroline fretted. Georgiana stared at her, and did not hear Hurst walking up.

He spoke softly so that Georgiana would not hear. "What are you afraid of Caroline, that she will be considered compromised and would have to marry Darcy?" He laughed softly and winked at Georgiana as he passed by.

Caroline turned to him and whispered furiously. "He is most certainly not compromising her! Do you hear me?" She looked at Georgiana and raised her voice. "She is perfectly able to speak to him alone. And I do not want to hear another word about it!" She spun on her heel and stormed away.

Georgiana looked after her in confusion and Bingley stepped up. "Come Miss Darcy, obviously Miss Elizabeth is who he needs right now. I believe that Mrs. Annesley is in the drawing room if you would care to join her." She nodded her head and walked away, wondering at the distress in William's eyes, and suspecting it had to do with her somehow.

Inside the library, Elizabeth had just turned as William closed and locked the door when she suddenly found his arms encasing her and his face buried in her hair. They stood for several minutes in silence while she held him tight, feeling his body shaking with emotion. As his breathing calmed he whispered. "Thank God you are here."

"What is wrong, William? I understand that you were fine until you read a letter?" She rubbed his back and pressed herself to him. He nodded and drew back a little. His eyes had returned to their customary blue, but remained full of anger and pain.

"I received a letter from my cousin Richard, the colonel?" She nodded. "Apparently my aunt, Lady Catherine de Bourgh, decided that I was mishandling the reformation of my sister and that she would step in to find her a husband." Elizabeth gasped. He nodded and let go of her, stepping back and running his hand through his hair. He took her hand and kissed it, then held it tightly in his. "She sent out letters to various families in need of Georgiana's dowry, offering her money in exchange for a saved reputation." He took her to a sofa and they sat. His face displayed his disgust. "Apparently she thought that if she approached me with the suitor in tow, I would give my consent."

"Why on earth would she do this? She is but fifteen! Will your aunt not allow time a chance?"

Darcy laughed bitterly and squeezed her hand. "Saving Georgiana was not her goal. She felt that I would not marry as long as Georgiana was ruined. She thought that I was ruined unless I made a good match, and of course the only good match in her mind is to her daughter."

"What?" Elizabeth stared. "Do you mean this is some elaborate scheme for you to marry . . . your cousin?" Darcy nodded and looked away. Elizabeth closed her eyes. "Do you wish for such a marriage, William?"

His head snapped back. "No!" He gathered her into his arms and held her to his chest. "No, Elizabeth, no, I never wished for Anne. My mother and aunt wanted it, and that made me more determined than ever to never consider it, besides the very real fact that I do not care for my cousin in any way other than as a family member." He gazed into her eyes. "Only you, Elizabeth; I will marry no woman, but you." His lips gently caressed hers, and then he searched her face.

She smiled. "I had to ask."

He gave her a little smile. "I know." He kissed her softly. "I have told nobody here as yet, but as your father has announced the news to your family and the Lucas' I am honour bound to marry you."

Gently she stroked back the fringe from his brow. "I do not care for the reasons, as long as you do." Resting their foreheads together, they closed their eyes. "I assume by this letter that your family has somehow learned of the scheme and stopped it?"

She felt his head nod. "Yes, Anne wrote Richard, who told his parents, and they travelled to Rosings in time."

"I imagine that you feel grateful for their swift response."

He sighed. "I am."

Elizabeth pulled back and caressed his face. "What makes you so angry, your aunt's actions?"

Leaning into her touch he studied her while thinking. "No, I mean, yes, her actions, but I suppose it is simply not being in control."

"Do you feel that your family should have consulted with you first?"

He kissed her palm and settled back on the sofa, drawing her to rest her head on his chest. "I would have wished that, yes. It makes me feel that they think me incapable of protecting my sister."

She squeezed him. "I sincerely doubt that they thought that at all, William. It seems to me that they wished to act expeditiously, and they wished to spare you additional pain. Is not your cousin also Georgiana's guardian? Would not his actions be in accordance with your father's wishes that he care for her as well?"

"You are being far too sensible." He murmured against her hair.

Elizabeth laughed. "Forgive me. Perhaps when you write your family to thank them, you could say that in the future, you would appreciate them including you in their plans."

"You mean make my displeasure known subtly." He smiled into her eyes.

She caressed his cheek. "Yes. It is obvious to me how hurt you are. Does it make you feel inadequate? Weak? I imagine with all of the things that you must care for, you feel hurt that you could not be trusted to handle yet another item. Perhaps though, they feel that you have enough on your plate, and merely wished to spare you more stress. Perhaps they wished to show you support after treating you so poorly upon your last meeting."

"Do you know how much I love you?" He kissed her lips.

"Are you saying that I am correct?" She twinkled up at him.

"You can put into words the frustration I feel. I am so used to caring for everyone, even before my father died, as he became weaker, I was running Pemberley. By the time he passed, the transition was hardly noticed. I am simply unwilling to accept help sometimes."

Elizabeth held his face in her hands. "There is no shame in asking for or needing help. You are no longer alone, and I hope very much that you will never be afraid to ask me for anything, even if it is just to hold your hand."

He drew a deep breath and blinked rapidly. "Nobody has ever . . ." He buried his face in her shoulder. "Thank you for loving me."

Blinking back her tears she whispered, "I do, and always will." They stayed embraced for several minutes. She felt him swallow hard. "Do you wish to write back to your family, or would you like to give me my lesson? I think it may rain later, so we must go soon if we wish to accomplish anything at all. Georgiana said that she would welcome a visit if you have work to do." She laughed. "Of course, we could stay in here all day and drive Miss Bingley mad!"

She felt his shoulders move then heard a deep chuckle. His head came up and he kissed her with a smile. "I think that we should ride."

"One horse or two?"

He laughed. "As much as I enjoy one, I believe that two would be best, that is if you expect to learn anything."

They stood and he held her close. "Thank you, my love."

Elizabeth squeezed him. "I did not do or say anything that you would not have accomplished on your own. I have great faith in your reasonable mind."

He smiled and shook his head, and they walked to the door. He unlocked and pulled it open quickly, and Caroline nearly fell in. Darcy raised his brow and watched her attempt to regain her dignity. "Why Miss Bingley, you really should be careful about leaning on doors, you never know when they might open." Elizabeth bit her lips to suppress her laughter and they walked down the hallway to don their coats and begin their ride.

"My dear Miss Eliza, you do appear rather pale, perhaps we should call the carriage for you to return home right away?" Caroline's sincerity, although questionable, did not belie the fact that indeed, Elizabeth was very pale.

The ladies were gathered in a parlour, taking tea. Darcy was upstairs, trapped in his chambers by Bingley demanding to know what had upset him that morning. He and Elizabeth had been out riding for an hour when the heavens opened and a cold rain fell upon them in torrents, aided by a bitter wind. Darcy was protected with his heavy greatcoat, but Elizabeth's spencer was no match for the storm, and very soon she was sodden and shivering. They took shelter in an abandoned barn on the property, and brought their horses inside to wait out the weather. Darcy searched around and found some old blankets, likely used beneath a saddle, and while dirty and musty, they were dry. He wrapped them around Elizabeth, and then held her tightly to his body as they sat together on a bench, looking out the open door. There was nothing to do but wait. Elizabeth's shivering never ceased though, and Darcy became increasingly worried. She laughed it off through her chattering teeth, and instead insisted that he tell her stories of his childhood when he would be caught in snowdrifts or was lost in the Pemberley woods. She countered with tales of catching toads and bringing them home to show her horrified mother. Despite his worry, Darcy had to admit that those hours spent in such a miserable situation were amongst the happiest moments of his life. He was holding the woman he loved, laughing, feeling nothing but the joy of her filling up the empty places in his heart. It felt wonderful, and selfishly, if she had not been so obviously cold, he would have wished it never to end. But as soon as the rain abated to a steady drizzle, they were upon their horses and returned to Netherfield.

Bingley and Georgiana fussed over both of them. Caroline attempted to take Darcy's arm and lead him away to his chambers herself, exclaiming over the horror of having been trapped with Elizabeth for so long. Elizabeth rolled her eyes and followed him upstairs where she went with Georgiana to take a warm bath and dress in the clothes her mother had insisted she bring with her. Georgiana's abigail dried her hair and within an hour she was comfortably resting near the fire with her tea. It was not until she came to rest there that she realized that she did not feel herself.

"Elizabeth, are you well?" Georgiana asked quietly.

She shivered and smiled a little. "I can not seem to warm, but I am sure this tea and fire will take care of me quickly and I will be out of your way." Georgiana looked at Mrs. Annesley worriedly. It was obvious that Caroline and Louisa were not going to make any suggestions to help her.

Mrs. Annesley was watching Elizabeth carefully and walked over to her. "Miss Elizabeth, may I?" She held her hand near her head. Elizabeth nodded and the woman gently touched her forehead. "No fever as yet, Miss, but I suspect it will not be long."

Elizabeth sighed. "I hope not. I am sure that as soon as I warm, I will be fine. The wind simply made the rain colder."

The gentlemen entered the room, Darcy looked tired, but that was more due to his interrogation than the drenching. He spotted Elizabeth by the fire and took a seat nearby. "Are you feeling better? Your mother's insistence that you bring a clean dress worked to your advantage today." She smiled, but he saw a difference. "You are not well." His eyes reflected his concern.

"I am fine, sir. I assure you. I have simply not warmed yet." As the words left her mouth, her pale face suddenly flushed pink then red. She closed her eyes, and it was only Darcy's quick movement that saved the tea from pouring all over her dress. He took the cup and placed it on a table and kneeling before her chair, wrapped his arms around her. "Elizabeth!" She leaned heavily on his shoulder.

"Get her off of him!" Caroline screeched. She ran forward to pull Elizabeth out of his arms and was met with a glare that could have set her hair on fire.

"Miss Bingley, she is ill. I will carry her upstairs, and you will do everything necessary to make her comfortable."

Without waiting for an answer, Darcy lifted Elizabeth up in his arms. He rested his cheek on her face. "She is burning up with fever."

Mrs. Annesley touched her forehead. "I knew it would come." Darcy nodded to her and she and Georgiana followed him up the stairs. Automatically he went down the corridor where his chambers were located and stood in the hallway, not sure where to take her. He wished to lay her on his bed, and had half-turned there when Georgiana opened the door to a room directly across from his.

"This is empty, William." He carried her in and Mrs. Annesley pulled back the counterpane so he could lay her carefully down.

Georgiana pulled the bell and a servant arrived at the same time as Caroline. "No, Mr. Darcy, this room is too cold; you should put her in the other wing."

Darcy had no intention of moving Elizabeth any farther away from him. "Every room that is not occupied is cold, Miss Bingley." He looked at the waiting servant. "Please build a fire in here quickly." The girl bobbed and set to work.

"Really, Mr. Darcy, she would be far more comfortable away from . . ."

Before she could finish the thought, he glared at her again. "Miss Bingley, perhaps you could send a note to Longbourn and inform them that Miss Elizabeth is ill and will be staying here tonight. Perhaps Miss Bennet will wish to be with her. You may send my carriage for her."

Caroline began to retort when Bingley appeared. "Go ahead and write the note, Caroline. I will take care of the carriage, and then have the next room prepared for Miss Bennet."

Turning on her heel, she left, furious that not only was Eliza staying the night, but now Charles' latest love interest would be there as well. There must be some way she could use this to her advantage. She would talk to Louisa.

Darcy remained kneeled on the floor by the bed, caressing Elizabeth's burning face. Bingley cleared his throat. "Um, Darcy, perhaps we should move out of the ladies' way?" Darcy looked at him without comprehension.

"Brother, we should change Elizabeth's dress if she is to be in bed." Georgiana whispered. He closed his eyes and nodded. He caressed Elizabeth's cheek again, and lifted her hand to bestow a kiss. Georgiana and Mrs. Annesley averted their eyes and Bingley smiled widely at him.

"Tell me of any change." Darcy instructed before he left the room, and giving her one last concerned look, walked out, hearing the door close behind him.

"Come on man, there is nothing we can do for now. We will go round up Hurst for some billiards, what do you say?" Darcy shook his head and finally agreed.

Jane arrived along with a trunk of clothes for both sisters, and was ushered upstairs immediately to Elizabeth's side. Georgiana was sitting with her, and Darcy was hovering in the hallway. As Jane entered he stepped in as well. "William!" Georgiana cried. "You should not be here!" He did not move, but looked at Elizabeth, her hair was unbound and her face was red. Georgiana was sponging her forehead with a damp cloth and Mrs. Annesley sat on the other side of the bed.

"Is there anything I can do?" He asked anxiously.

Turning, Jane placed her hand on his arm and firmly pulled him towards the door. "No sir, you can do nothing, she needs to rest, and I know that she will not wish you to worry. I will let you know if there is any change." She pushed him out into the hallway and shut the door. Darcy stood staring at the dark wood, feeling powerless and alone, then drew himself up and went downstairs to the library where he buried himself in work, and tried not to dwell on his heart lying in a bed upstairs.

A knock at the door an hour later made him start. "Come in!" He called, hoping for news, and was deeply disappointed to see Caroline enter. "Miss Bingley." He bowed and resumed his seat.

She smiled sweetly. "Mr. Darcy, you have been hidden in here far too long; I came to ask you to join us in the parlour until dinner."

"I have too much work to do." He said abruptly, and then added. "Thank you."

She walked around and stood by the desk, brushing his arm with her gown, and touching the letters. "Oh so many letters you write sir, letters of business, how tiresome. Surely there must be something else that you would find more worthwhile of your time?" She bent down, so that her décolletage was directly in his eye line.

He drew back. "Miss Bingley, what is your purpose?"

"I do not know what you mean?" She batted her eyes, and leaned closer, her breasts practically under his nose; and prepared to fall into his lap.

Darcy saw her leaning and instantly stood and moved away from her. She lost her balance and grabbed for the arms of the chair to stop her forward motion, missed, and sprawled with a thud onto the floor. Darcy's eyes narrowed as she awkwardly straightened, and offered no assistance to help the humiliated woman rise. "You entered this room anticipating my solitude, and clearly attempted to execute a compromising circumstance. It will not happen, will never happen, and if by some quirk of fate your brother came in and found the two of us engaged in some act of your design, he would not demand, and I would not agree to, a marriage with you. Ever. So I do suggest Miss Bingley that you employ your assets towards a gentleman who cares, because madam, I assure you, I do not."

A chuckle rose from a sofa in the back of the room and they looked over to see Hurst sitting up and grinning. "I say Darcy that was well done! I have been wondering when Caroline would make her move, and to think she chooses the moment when the woman you are courting lies nearly above your heads in the grip of a fever was a truly callous touch. Ah, Caroline, you have met your match in this man. I daresay you could trip into his bed with a hundred witnesses and he would still never give in. Face it; Mr. Darcy will never marry you."

Caroline's face was red with her embarrassment. "I do not know what you mean! I was not orchestrating anything!"

Darcy exchanged a look with Hurst. "Then what exactly were you doing, Miss Bingley?"

Another knock was heard and Bingley entered, looking upon at the scene. "What happened?"

Hurst settled back in a chair near the desk and gestured. "Caroline was trying to compromise Darcy."

She spun around. "I was not!"

Bingley was disappointed. "You mean I missed it?" Darcy stared. "Sorry old man, but we were expecting her to do something of the sort. That is why Hurst took his nap in here; we were sure you would hide away in the library after you left Miss Elizabeth and expected Caroline to try to take advantage while you were distressed." He nodded over at his gaping sister. "I was convinced that something was afoot when Louisa said to go see her in the library. When was the last time you looked at a book, Caroline?"

Darcy turned to Hurst. "So you were here to save me from a fate worse than death?"

The men laughed and Caroline screeched. "I was not trying to . . ."

Bingley interrupted. "Do not lie; Caroline, of course you were." He looked at Darcy then back at his sister, "And dear sister, we know of your plans to throw me and Miss Darcy together. So do not even try. Like Darcy, I will not be forced to accept a marriage I do not want, even though Miss Darcy is a lovely young lady, my interests lie elsewhere." He glanced up at the ceiling.

An incredulous expression appeared on Darcy's face. "Do you mean that you wished to involve my sister in your schemes? I knew that you hoped for a marriage between Georgiana and Bingley, but that you would actually consider orchestrating a compromise of her . . . Miss Bingley, I am appalled!"

"I do not have any idea to what you refer." She turned and began to leave the room.

Bingley placed a hand on her arm. "I hope not, Caroline. You have overspent your allowance, and I am of a mind to cut you off entirely until your interest from the funds replaces your debt, in fact, yes, that is what I will do. You will receive nothing else until then. By my calculations, that means you will live on what money you have until next March."

"Charles!"

He shrugged. "You knew your limits; it was my fault for letting you exceed them. I am merely correcting my error."

Hurst nodded. "I believe that I should have a similar talk with my wife." He stood and grinned. "Excuse me, gentlemen." Caroline was speechless and flew from the room, pushing Hurst out of the way. He turned and laughed. "Well, I had hoped we could teach them a lesson, perhaps we have." He nodded and strolled out. Bingley dropped into the chair that Hurst had vacated, and grinned.

"That felt good." He smiled at Darcy who tilted his head and raised his brow as he resumed his seat at the desk.

"To be the man in charge or to thwart their plans?"

"Both actually." He leaned forward. "I am sorry; Hurst has been overhearing them plotting to compromise you with Caroline, and Miss Darcy with me, for weeks now. We did not wish to bother you with it, but after seeing your reaction to your family's interference with your aunt this morning, we thought that we should expose Caroline as soon as possible, and before you. I hope that you do not mind."

Darcy sighed. "No, I appreciate it, and I suppose I did overreact to my family this morning, Elizabeth set me straight when we talked." He looked down at his hands. "I do appreciate you caring for Georgiana and me so much to bring such unhappiness to your sisters."

Bingley spoke softly. "I needed to take the reins of my family, Darcy; it is time for me to grow up, not only with my sisters, but with my own life. I am considering speaking to Miss Bennet while she is here and asking if I may court her, then go and speak to her father."

"Are you sure Bingley? Dowry is not an issue for me, but it could be significant for you and your ambitions." He bit his lip. "I am happy to hear that you are not interested in Elizabeth, you had me quite concerned with the attentions you paid her, and I am afraid that I did consider some rather violent responses to them."

"Darcy! I swear, I never . . ." He hung his head. "This is not the first time my attentions to Miss Elizabeth have been brought to my attention, I . . . I am sorry. I have some serious thinking to do about my behaviour towards ladies, particularly if I am serious about aligning myself with Miss Bennet, and yes, I have considered the issue of dowry, but I believe that I would like to emulate my best friend and put my happiness first." He peered into his friend's eyes. "You *are* engaged to Miss Elizabeth?"

A rueful smile appeared. "It is that obvious?"

Bingley laughed. "Darcy, I have known you for years, and I have never seen a man so besotted, or one who so frequently has swollen lips after visiting a woman he is courting. What exactly happened during that riding lesson you took the other day?" Darcy flushed with embarrassment. Bingley laughed harder. "Honestly, I suspected as much when you were alone with her in the library this morning, and went riding without a chaperone. Something significant must have occurred. When do you announce?"

"Mr. Bennet actually announced it to the family yesterday, after the incident with Lucas."

Knowing the story, Bingley nodded. "You wasted no time."

He closed his eyes. "I have a confession to make. Elizabeth and I have corresponded with each other since we met here at Netherfield."

Bingley stared. "You mean; you have exchanged letters? You said before that you knew each other well, but I suppose I never really considered how that happened."

"Yes, we grew very close through our correspondence and I proposed the first morning after we arrived here. As I told you that morning, it is not so very sudden at all." He looked up. "Are you shocked?"

"Completely! And Mr. Bennet, does he know?"

Darcy nodded. "He knows all. He forced us to maintain the courtship for appearance's sake, and we will marry at the end of November. I have sent Danny to London to pick up the settlement from my attorney, and although it is not necessary, I wrote the archbishop and applied for a special license. I thought it would please Mrs. Bennet."

Bingley sat back in stunned admiration. "I am proud of you."

Darcy's head turned sharply. "Really? I thought you would be ashamed."

"Why? You have been bereft of love since the day you were born, when you found it, you snapped it up with eagerness. She is a lovely, wonderful woman, and I know you will be very happy." He stood and offered his hand. "Congratulations, Darcy!"

He stood and smiled. "Thank you, Bingley, for everything."

Chapter 20

arcy knocked lightly on the door. Jane opened it and bit her lip to hide her smile when she saw the poor worried man standing before her. Darcy's brow was creased, he was shifting from one foot to another, and a ribbon was wound around the fingers of his left hand. "Mr. Darcy?"

"Miss Bennet, how is . . . is Miss Eliz . . . Elizabeth . . . Is she well?" He tried to see past her, and then stared anxiously into her eyes. Jane smiled kindly. "She is sleeping."

"Is she . . . does she need a physician? A surgeon . . . anything? I will send for our family doctor in London."

Jane touched his arm. "No, it will not be necessary, I am sure she will be fine in the morning. Elizabeth very rarely becomes ill, and it never lasts long."

His eyes widened. "She rarely is ill? It is my fault! I made her ill! I never should have taken her riding; she knew it was going to rain. What have I done?"

"Mr. Darcy, please!" Jane looked up and down the hallway and seeing nobody stepped back into the room.

He instantly followed her and she quickly closed the door. He stood perfectly still, staring at the flushed figure tossing in the bed. "Oh Elizabeth." He whispered, and moved cautiously forward to kneel down beside her. He stroked a damp curl from her brow. "She is so warm, it is worse!" Her movement calmed with his touch.

"No sir, it is better, I think." Jane reassured him.

"She looks so . . ." His voice trailed away and he took her hand in his.

Alarmed, Jane gently touched his shoulder. "Mr. Darcy, I think you should retire." He looked at her as if she was insane.

"I can not leave her."

"She is fine, sir. Do you see how quiet she is now? I will be in the next room should she need anything."

He stared and asked anxiously. "You will leave her alone?"

"She only needs sleep. Now sir, you really should go." He did not move. Jane sighed. "I will step into the dressing room so that you may wish her good night."

He heard the door close and bent to gently kiss her lips. "I love you." He rested his head on her shoulder and felt her chest rise and fall. Far too soon Jane returned and he felt her hand again touch his shoulder. He rose slowly and disregarding Jane; kissed Elizabeth's lips and whispered in her ear. He met Jane's blushing face and reluctantly left the room.

Returning to his chambers he mechanically changed into his nightshirt and robe, and then took a seat in a chair near the door. He listened as the household settled, and finally heard the door across the hall open and close, followed by another door nearby doing the same. Jane had retired. He waited another quarter hour then stood and slowly opened his door to look out. Biting his lip he stepped into the empty hallway and walked quickly to Elizabeth's door. He turned the handle and slipped inside. The light of the fire showed her alone and sleeping restlessly. He turned the key in the door, then went to the dressing room and did the same. Drawing a shaking breath, he removed his robe, lifted the counterpane, and slipped beneath. His heart pounding, he lay on his side and drew Elizabeth against his chest, tenderly kissing her cheek. "Sleep my love, your William is here." He nestled his face into her shoulder. Elizabeth's restless movements ceased and he felt her press her body so it rested perfectly spooned to his. Darcy heard a long sigh. "William." His eyes grew moist as he cuddled her to him, and soon fell gratefully to sleep.

Jane woke just past midnight to go check on Elizabeth and was confused to find that the door was locked. She turned away then stopped and looked across the hall to the room she knew belonged to Darcy, then back to her sister's door. She gasped and quickly returned to her bed, and hoped it was Elizabeth who had turned the key.

Hearing the clock chime four times, Elizabeth woke. She felt so safe and comfortable. A pleasant, heavy weight was resting against her back and she felt surrounded by warmth. The soft sound of deep, steady breathing brought her fully awake, and she realized that the heavy warmth was a body, and the hand resting on her breast and the arm lying across her waist belonged to a very large, very sleepy man. "William." She whispered. She tried to turn but her movements made him pull her closer.

"Lizzzzzy," he murmured and kissed her hair. He sighed and squeezed her. "I love you." He whispered and nestling his face deeper into her neck he fell back to sleep.

Elizabeth smiled; she was Lizzy to him now. She lifted his hand and kissed it. His fingers entwined with hers. "I love you, Will." He must have heard as she felt him cuddle closer to her. He should not be there, and he must leave soon . . . but she did not want him to go. It felt so wonderful. This is what it would be to sleep with the man she loved. Elizabeth laughed softly. She would never be cold on a winter's night again. She relaxed and let her thoughts wander, amazing herself by not once feeling that she was breaking with propriety. It simply felt perfectly right that William should be in her bed. When the clock struck five times he moved, rolling onto his back. She took the opportunity to shift position and had just turned onto her other side when she felt his strong arm scoop her up and cuddle her to his chest. It seemed he would not relinquish her for a moment. Elizabeth nestled against him and listened to his heart. She heard a deep sigh and looking up she saw a pair of blue eyes gazing lovingly at her. "Good morning." He whispered. "How do you feel?"

She smiled and rubbed the beard that had sprouted sometime during the night. Darcy took her hand and kissed it. "I am much better, the fever broke. I must admit though, I have never felt so comfortable. I must thank my bed warmer."

He smiled. "It is very much my pleasure." He ran his fingers through her hair. "I have imagined seeing you like this again ever since I first saw your hair down."

Blushing, she touched the tangled curls. "I can imagine what a terrible sight it is now." Her brow creased. "When . . . oh, the donkey!"

He smiled and nodded. "That was the moment that I fell in love with you."

She sat up. "But you had never spoken to me, how could you possibly feel love?"

Darcy shrugged and drew her back down to him. "I know that I had never seen a woman who had so bewitched me, and when we left I watched you, thinking I would never see you again. My heart knew what my mind did not." He smiled slightly, "And yet, here you are in my arms." He kissed her cool forehead. "The last day has been . . . you will think me odd, but it has been so wonderful."

She laughed, "Oh yes, lying in bed with a fever was a joy!"

He laughed softly, "No, that was not, but our talk in the library made me think of how we will work out problems when we are married, and our time in the barn made me think of the happiness that your friendship and companionship will bring, and I admit, I even enjoyed worrying about you being ill, and finally sleeping with you this night . . . I can not describe the peace. I hope so much that you are too ill to return to Longbourn, because I can not fathom sleeping without you ever again."

"Oh my dear, sweet, love." She laid her cheek on his and suddenly he lifted her up so she was lying on top of him. He wrapped his arms around her waist. "William!" She whispered furiously.

He laughed. "What happened to Will?" She held his bristly face in her hands and smiled down at him.

"That is for very special occasions."

He lifted his brow,

"Such as?" She answered by kissing him with soft, caressing strokes to his lips. He opened his mouth and they kissed deeply, Elizabeth's fingers entwined in his hair. Darcy's hands ran up and down her back, then to her bottom. As their kiss continued to grow in passion, he drove his hips up and Elizabeth's legs naturally parted, and felt his arousal pressing against her. Only the thin muslin separated them and Darcy's hands were bunching up the fabric, pulling it higher and up over her hips. She felt his warm hands on her bare thighs and then one hand slipped beneath to stroke between. He touched the soft curls and moaned, feeling the wetness, and caressed her. Elizabeth's breathing hitched with his touch, and then increased.

"Oh Will . . ." She moaned. He continued his steady caress with one hand, and tangled the other in her hair, holding her mouth captive against his.

Darcy felt her begin to writhe against him, and it took every bit of his willpower not to lift his nightshirt and plunge into her. Instead he opened his eyes and watched with pride as the flush spread over her face when she found her pleasure. He moved his hands back to her waist and held her to him, collapsed against his body. He kissed her forehead. "Are you well, Lizzy?" She nodded, breathing erratically. He smiled, "I think I helped to relieve your ache."

"That felt so . . . indescribable." She lay still, listening to his heart pounding, feeling his hardened flesh still pressing into her, and suddenly understood the feelings he had always evoked in her. "This is what it is to love each other."

He kissed her. "Almost." She looked into his eyes. "When we become one body . . ." He whispered.

"Yes." Elizabeth realized that he was still aching and sensed that he would want to feel her touch. She slid off of his chest.

"No, where are you going?" He tried to pull her back, but a moment later he drew a sharp breath as he felt her small hand slide up his thigh. "Lizzy, you do not have to touch . . ." His eyes closed and his head lay back on the pillow. She nestled her head on his chest and closed her eyes while he wrapped one arm around her waist. Her hand touched the unfamiliar curls and tentatively encircled his arousal, then she instinctively fondled and stroked him, remembering how he wanted her to touch there when they rode. He laid his steady hand over her trembling fingers and demonstrated how to move.

"Oh, Lizzy." He breathed. "Oh yes . . . please . . ." He had dreamed of her touch for so long it did not take much effort for him to find rapture. She gasped to see his body twist and shake so violently, and to feel the warm flood of his essence over her hand. His cry he muffled in her hair when he clutched her tightly. Panting, he slowly recovered, and opening his eyes, saw her watching him. "I love you." He said, and was rewarded with a soft kiss.

"I love you." Elizabeth looked away and bit her lip. "Did . . . did . . . *this* . . . feel good?"

She heard his soft chuckle and looked up to him. "Oh Lord, Lizzy, YES! More, please, yes!" He smiled and caressed her cheek, and she smiled with relief at his obvious elation. "Did it not feel good for you?"

She blushed and nodded. "Oh yes, William . . . I can not describe . . ." She looked up to see his delighted smile and relaxed. Elizabeth's gaze travelled to the thick milky fluid, and he wiped it from her hand with his nightshirt. "This is what creates a child."

He studied her and joining their hands asked softly, "How do you know these things?"

Elizabeth blushed again. "I do live on a farm, and . . . those books of my father's . . . I spoke to my Aunt Gardiner about them. She has been willing to answer some of my questions. I have never spoken to anyone else about this." She looked at him worriedly. "Are you upset that I am not completely naive? I know that girls are not to know anything of . . ."

Darcy interrupted. "No, my love, not at all. I am surprised, but grateful that you had someone who was willing to answer such questions. I know that most girls come to marriage knowing nothing, and come to it with great fear." They held each other in silence for several minutes, slowly recovering from their first intimate experience, and knowing how far their relationship had suddenly advanced.

He rolled onto his side and held her to him. "I know that we have broken with propriety almost from the first moment we met, and I do not want you to feel that I am asking you to . . . I never thought that I would kiss or touch the woman I would marry the way we have before our wedding night . . . let alone come to sleep with her, and experience what he just have . . ." She watched as he struggled to express himself. "I never want to let you go again, Lizzy. I . . . I need you." He kissed her gently. "I have sent for the settlement, and will bring it to your father to sign as soon as it arrives."

"That is not necessary, William, I trust you." She whispered.

"My love, besides the horror of Georgiana being married to Wickham, the terrible tragedy of her eloping would have been for her to marry without the protection of a settlement. I would never subject my own wife to such a thing, and your father would never allow you to marry without it. I have made sure that Pemberley will always be your home, no dower's house for you when I die, and provided for an income for you and our children when I leave you." His last words struck her painfully, knowing just how deeply she had come to love and need him.

"Stop, please stop!" She cried and buried her face in his chest. Darcy held her and kissed her head. "What is it? Lizzy?"

Her voice breaking she whispered. "Please do not speak of dying."

His heart swelled with her affection and he held her to him. "I just wanted you to know that you will always be safe." He felt her shoulders shake and the tears on his neck. "Shh, I will not speak of it again, dearest." He closed his eyes and cuddled her, feeling her gradually quiet and relax again. He blinked back his own tears. Darcy never thought that anyone would ever care if he lived or died, not anyone outside of Georgiana or the Fitzwilliams. Elizabeth's love filled him up in ways he never thought he would experience.

The sound of the dressing room door handle rattling startled them both. They looked at each other; it was likely a maid coming to stoke the dying fire. "You should leave soon." She said softly, and he whispered with regret. "I know."

He rolled over and wrapped her in his arms, then began to slowly caress her lips, gently tracing his tongue over them until she parted her mouth and they kissed over and over, expressing their love. She already knew that she would have to be the one to withdraw, she knew him well enough now to realize that he needed her touch so much that he simply could not let her go. She turned her head and rested her face in his neck, and he closed his eyes, kissing her hair, and worked to regain control. He desperately wanted to love her again. His breathing gradually calmed and Elizabeth let go and moved away.

Caressing her face he murmured with regret, "I must go." She nodded and sat up. Darcy stood to don his robe, and turned to find her standing by his side. He took her hands in his. "Do you think you will be too ill to return to Longbourn?"

She laughed. "I think I have proven already that I am quite well now, and Miss Bingley will doubtless point that out immediately."

He shook his head. "No doubt, but I have a feeling that she will no longer bother us." He lifted her chin and kissed her lovingly. "I will see you downstairs at breakfast, since you are so well." She nodded, and stepped to the door to unlock it, then peeked out.

"It is safe, go." He gave her hand a squeeze and slipped out and into his room, turning to look back at her as she closed the door. Elizabeth unlocked the dressing room door and climbed back in her bed, laying her head on his pillow and drinking in the faint scent that lingered. She thought over the words that he struggled to express. She knew that he was a man who felt deeply the bounds of propriety. He saw daily the effect that his sister's behaviour had wreaked upon her life and his, and yet they had just shared an act that was even more scandalous, with the only difference being that they were engaged. She knew that what they had done was not simply an expression of ardour and love; it was an act to be experienced between a husband and wife. How close they had come to abandoning everything!

And, she realized, how gladly she would welcome his touch again. A thrill ran through her just thinking of touching his . . . and wanting to give him that pleasure again. The burst of energy she felt upon waking and loving William was rapidly disappearing, and the lingering effect of her illness slipped over her. She closed her eyes and as she drifted back to sleep, her last thoughts were of wishing that he would return to her. She no longer wished to sleep alone.

Jane appeared at seven, knocking tentatively and sighing with relief when she heard her sister's call. "How do you feel, Lizzy?" She felt her forehead and stroked back her hair.

"Much better, I felt almost myself until I began walking around, but I confess, I did seem a little dizzy after a few steps."

"You did suffer for many hours with the fever. I suspect it will be another day or two before you are restored." She turned away and picked up a brush from the dressing table and returned to begin brushing out the tangled hair.

Elizabeth saw her worried expression and stilled her hand. "What is it Jane?"

She sighed. "Lizzy, I came to check on you during the night, and found that the door was locked. Did you rise and lock the door?" She searched her face.

Elizabeth blushed. "I did not wish for anyone to enter. It is a strange house, and I did not know you were here."

Jane nodded and closed her eyes. "I was afraid that someone did enter, and spent the night with you." She opened them to see the guilt in her sister's face. "Oh Lizzy, did Mr. Darcy sleep here last night?"

Elizabeth nodded and looked down. "I woke in his arms."

"Lizzy!"

She took Jane's hands in her own. "I am not ashamed, Jane. We did nothing but sleep and hold each other and talk . . . and express our feelings, nothing more!"

"Mr. Darcy should know better! His sister's reputation was ruined for a carriage ride!"

Elizabeth sighed, hearing her sister voice the same thoughts that she had already considered and accepted. "I know, I know, but we are engaged, and he has the settlement and it will not be long . . ."

Jane squeezed her hands and looked at her seriously. "Exactly, it will not be long. You must curb this . . . feeling until you are married!"

Elizabeth's eyes flashed. "What do you know of this feeling, Jane? Have you ever been in love?"

Jane flushed. Elizabeth stared at her and the realization hit her hard. "You are in love with Mr. Bingley! I have been so caught up with William and Georgiana that I did not see it. Not that you display your emotions very readily, but still, I should have known . . . I thought that you liked him, but I saw no tender regard on your part, and he is so kind to everyone, even me, and . . ." She nodded, working out the clues she had not paid any mind. "He has been visiting Longbourn just as frequently as William, and even John Lucas mentioned to me that you seemed to be attached. It is odd that he would notice what I did not. You do love him."

Jane began brushing her hair. "I do not know what you are talking about." She glanced at Elizabeth's face and stopped. "I do not know what I feel. It is so confusing."

"Do you wish to spend every waking moment with him?" Elizabeth asked, tilting her head and smiling.

She blushed. "I do not know if I want to spend every moment . . . but a great many of them, yes." She caught her sister's raised brow and bit her lip, looking down.

A bubbling laugh filled the room and Elizabeth grinned. "Perhaps I should remain ill for a few more days, so that you and Mr. Bingley can spend some time together, without Mama's help."

Jane's eyes grew wide. "Lizzy! You can not pretend to be ill!"

"I was not lying, I felt fine until I started to walk about. I know that whatever this is will be lingering. If Mr. Bingley does not mind the extra houseguests, I would just as soon recover here than at home." She leaned forward and looked up to her sister's lowered face. "What do you think?"

"What of Mr. Darcy?"

Elizabeth looked at her seriously. "If he comes to hold me in the night, I will not shut him out. I do not believe that he would ever . . . demand more than I am ready to give."

Jane warred with herself; she wanted to stay and be near Mr. Bingley but was frightened by Elizabeth's seemingly heedless behaviour with Mr. Darcy. For once she put her own desires first. "Please be careful, and please do not tell me about it until we are home." They embraced and Elizabeth thanked her.

A warm bath helped a great deal to revive her, but by the time her hair was dried and she was dressed, Elizabeth was again feeling fatigued. They slowly made their way down to the breakfast room, where Darcy immediately stood. "Ladies, good morning! How are you feeling Elizabeth?" He smiled warmly at her then noticed her tired eyes. "Lizzy?" Jane looked at him with a startled expression. Darcy was at Elizabeth's side and helped her to a nearby chair. He took the chair beside her. "You are not well, what happened?" Elizabeth glanced at Jane and was grateful that no other members of the household were present, since William obviously would have forgotten them as much as Jane.

"I simply felt the effects of the illness once I arose, that is all." She watched as the conflict of his thoughts played out on his face.

He could not feel regret for the attentions he paid, he treasured the experience, and it would be a lie to pretend otherwise. He had tried to explain to her how he felt about their break with propriety, and thought she understood. What he did feel was guilt for paying those attentions while she was ill; and he had been chastising his selfish behaviour since he left her room. *But she had seemed so recovered at the time!* He was disgusted with his attempts to justify his behaviour, then began blaming his actions for making her ill once again, and took her hand.

"You will remain here." It was not a question.

"Yes, William, I will." Darcy kissed her hand, and remained very concerned. "You need to eat. What shall I bring you?" He stood and walked to the sideboard.

"Some tea and toast would be fine." He was about to argue, but decided against it. He brought her the food and sat down beside her again after moving his plate. Jane felt completely ignored, but was pleased to watch how attentive Darcy was.

Bingley and Hurst wandered into the room and greeted the sisters. Bingley instantly took the place by Jane. "Miss Bennet, it is truly a pleasure to begin my morning with your company at my table. Although I regret Miss Elizabeth's illness, I can not help but be pleased with the unexpected benefits." He smiled at Elizabeth. "And I imagine Darcy does not object either."

Elizabeth smiled and laughed softly at William's unceasing gaze. "I believe that if he would speak he might agree, sir." She leaned back and closed her eyes.

Bingley looked concerned. "I do hope that you are not planning to leave us today, Miss Elizabeth. I insist that you remain here as long as necessary to recover."

"I agree, Bingley. I am certain that your family home is hospitable, but I do not think you should risk the exposure to the elements that a carriage ride would incur." Darcy took her hand under the table and squeezed.

Before she could answer Hurst piped in. "Come now ladies, please put them out of their misery and agree to stay. If for no other reason than to save me from having to cheer them from their hangdog appearance after you depart."

Elizabeth and Jane smiled at each other. "Of course, if it is to save you Mr. Hurst, we will remain." All three men grinned.

Bingley's eyes widened. "Oh, I say, Darcy, Hurst, we have that dinner tonight with the officers." He looked at Jane with distress.

Darcy shrugged. "I have no problem remaining here. They will be in the area until spring, and we can certainly meet them some other time." He smiled at Elizabeth.

She squeezed the hand that rested on her leg. "Sir, I do not wish you to miss an evening that has obviously been planned. You accepted the invitation and should go. Besides, I will likely retire early, so any evening here would be spent without my company in any case."

"William." He mouthed. She smiled. "Are you sure?"

Elizabeth nodded. "I will be safely asleep when you return with tales of war and horses, or whatever men talk about when they are alone. I am certain that you will regret missing the evening. Please do not stay here on my account." She looked at Jane. "Do you agree?"

Jane was not so ready to relinquish her evening as Elizabeth, but nodded. "Yes, Mr. Bingley, since you are an important part of the community now, you must go."

"It seems that everything is settled, then." Bingley said with regret.

Hurst nodded. "I will have them home in good time, ladies."

The remainder of the day Elizabeth spent under a blanket by the fire in the library, alternately dozing or reading while Darcy worked and looked up to smile at her. It was a scene of a home life he had frequently imagined. He would rise when she woke to come talk with her and laugh, sometimes reading to her, and stealing kisses and holding hands whenever they could. He apologized for his disregarding her illness and she shushed him before the words had fully formed on his lips, reassuring him of her welcoming his attentions. Georgiana came and kept them company, but Caroline and Louisa kept to themselves. Both were angry about their punishment for attempting to interfere in Darcy and Charles' lives, and Caroline was too embarrassed to face Darcy again anytime soon. The news that the Bennets remained brought additional unhappiness, and Georgiana's casual mention and guileless joy over her brother's engagement mortified Caroline and provided no end of amusement to Bingley and Hurst.

That evening Darcy and Bingley reluctantly left their ladies, with Darcy bestowing a lingering kiss to Elizabeth's hand and a gentle caress to her cheek in front of the entire party. The three gentlemen left to board the coach to the officer's dinner.

From a window at the assembly hall where the dinner was being held, George Wickham was standing holding a drink and observing the arrivals. He instantly recognized Darcy and started, wondering what could bring him back to this village of all places. He was just casting his eyes about for a place to stand and observe when he noticed another man watching Darcy, and rubbing a bruised jaw. He saw his glare and decided that this was a man he needed to know.

Chapter 21

"*M*iss Bingley, I am Colonel Richard Fitzwilliam, Mr. Darcy's cousin and an acquaintance of Mr. Bingley's. Please forgive my intrusion, but I received a note from my cousin Darcy to come, and I do believe that your brother knew that I was planning to stop and visit here during my leave." Richard bowed over Caroline's hand in the drawing room at Netherfield and smiled his most charming smile. The fact was that Darcy had not summoned him as yet, and he only hoped that his cousin had informed Bingley that he might be visiting.

"Oh, Colonel Fitzwilliam, I am sure that my brother simply forgot to mention it to me. He does seem to remember invitations in a delayed fashion." She glanced at Louisa, who rolled her eyes. "But of course you are welcome here. I will have a room prepared for you immediately. I am only sorry that Mr. Darcy and my brothers are not presently at home. They are attending a dinner with the newly arrived militia, but they did not expect to be away very late." Caroline was no fool, she was not going to deny room to Mr. Darcy's cousin, and she knew that he was the son of an Earl, a second son, but a son nonetheless.

"Thank you, Miss Bingley. You are a gracious hostess to put up with my sudden appearance." He smiled and looked enquiringly at Louisa.

"May I introduce my sister, Mrs. Hurst?"

He bowed. "A delight, madam."

The sound of happy laughter was heard coming through the doorway and suddenly Richard found himself tackled. "Richard!"

He drew back and grinned. "Georgiana! You look wonderful! What has happened to you?"

She blushed over her demonstration. "I am simply happy. William is engaged to be married, did you know?"

He stared at her in surprise. "No, I did not . . ." He looked over at the two young women who were standing nearby. "May I be introduced to your friends?"

"Oh, I am so sorry, I am just so happy to see you . . ." She drew a breath and spoke very formally. "Colonel Richard Fitzwilliam, may I present Miss Jane Bennet, and her sister, Miss Elizabeth."

Richard bowed to Jane, noting her beauty with pleasure then turned to see the real object of his trip. Elizabeth's face still bore signs of her illness, but her eyes were alive and dancing at him, and she smiled widely. That morning in front of the inn was so emotional that he really had not looked at her then, but now, seeing this small, sparkling, enticing woman, a warm feeling began to spread over him under her bewitching gaze. "Miss Elizabeth." He bowed and took her hand. "I understand that congratulations are in order."

Elizabeth raised a brow and tilted her head. "Indeed sir, they are. I am only sorry that you are learning the news without your cousin's presence. I am sure that he will be disappointed to have been absent."

"I confess that I am surprised to find you here."

They all took seats and Elizabeth sighed. "I am as well, sir. I fell ill yesterday after being caught in the rain while William worked to improve my riding skills. I am staying here at his and Mr. Bingley's insistence until I am recovered enough to attempt the harrowing carriage ride back to Longbourn."

He laughed. "And how far is this ride?"

She pursed her lips. "Three miles, sir."

Richard laughed louder. "Ah, yes, clearly you must be spared such an adventure . . . for I would say a period of days, perhaps weeks?"

"Oh, at least until the wedding." Elizabeth laughed.

"Lizzy!" Jane admonished.

Richard held up a hand. "Miss Bennet, please do not stop your sister. I can see that she is of a good humour, and that must indicate that she is feeling much better. In all honesty it does my heart good to see that my cousin has won a lady who might inject some levity into his sombre mien."

Georgiana smiled at her then took her cousin's hand. "She has already Richard; you will not recognize him when he returns."

He gave the hand a squeeze. "I look forward to it. Miss Bingley indicated that the gentlemen would not be gone for long, I believe that I understand why now." He turned to his hostess. "It must be quite gratifying for you to witness a romance blooming right in front of you."

The smile on Caroline's face was frozen in place. "Yes, quite."

The housekeeper arrived to announce that Richard's room was prepared. He excused himself to change and would return to join them for dinner. He left and Georgiana smiled at Elizabeth. "He likes you."

"Well, I certainly hope so, we will soon be related."

Georgiana shook her head. "No, I mean . . ." She glanced at Caroline and Louisa and whispered. "I think that he is here to make sure that you are . . ." She blushed and looked down.

Elizabeth's mouth formed an "O" and she nodded. "I see. I remember William mentioning that he would come. He will report back to the family, is that it?" Georgiana glanced up and nodded. "From what I understand, they are not entirely happy with me?"

"They are protective."

Elizabeth laughed and looked at Jane who was concerned. "Well, all I can do is to be myself. In the end, it is William's decision, so I will simply continue as I have. I seem to please him, and that is all that matters to me."

Colonel Forster welcomed the men from Netherfield into the assembly hall and directed them to his second-in-command, who in turn took them around the room, making introductions. Bingley naturally fell into conversation immediately with a group of neighbours and officers, and Darcy stood nearby, listening, and contributing occasionally when the talk turned to the war. There was much interest in Napoleon's latest moves, as well as the military's efforts with the Luddites in the North, and he was following the news as closely as the rest of them. Hurst wandered away, examining the refreshment table and finding friendly conversation over the season's sport. He saw John Lucas speaking with a lieutenant and noticed them looking towards the group that included Darcy.

"Tell me sir, how did you acquire that jaw, or is it too painful to discuss?" Wickham asked.

Glancing at the soldier and rubbing at it he muttered, "It is of no consequence." John returned to his occupation of glaring at Darcy. Wickham followed his gaze, stepping behind him when he saw Darcy's eyes flick in his direction.

"Very well." He paused. "You seem interested in Mr. Darcy."

John's gaze returned to him. "Do you know him?"

Wickham saw the immediate reaction and smirked. "Indeed I do. We grew up together at his estate, Pemberley in Derbyshire."

John's eyes widened and he turned to face Wickham. "So you know him well, what sort of a man is he?"

Smelling an opportunity, Wickham started asking questions. "Do you not know his character? I imagine he has established himself well in the neighbourhood. Has he been here long?"

"He arrived a month ago with his sister. You could say that he is established quite well. He is engaged to be married." John sent a deadly glare Darcy's way. Wickham raised a brow. "A month, and with Miss Darcy, well, this engagement news comes as a great surprise, I had always thought he would marry his cousin Miss Anne de Bourgh, but from your indication, he has chosen a local girl?"

John nearly spat. "Yes, a local girl, my local girl. He has somehow convinced her that he is better than me."

Wickham cast an amused glance at the obviously inconsequential gentleman. "Well, he is rather rich, I imagine that she is looking at the estate she will win, and he is undoubtedly attracted to her dowry."

He spoke defensively. "She is not mercenary; he has her fooled of his affections. And it is not her dowry he is attracted to, she has nothing to offer."

"Really? I am curious, sir, what can this girl have that would cause two gentlemen such interest?"

John looked at him and then back at Darcy. "She is indescribable."

Wickham grinned. He really wanted to meet this girl. "And what is this vision's name, if I may ask?"

"Miss Elizabeth Bennet."

"Miss Elizabeth? I believe that I have met two of her sisters, Miss Lydia and Miss Kitty." He glanced at John then Darcy; those girls were not even close to what he would imagine any gentleman wanting for more than an afternoon of pleasure. "Is she like them?"

John laughed. "Her younger sisters are silly flirty things, quite enamoured with a uniform." He glanced knowingly at Wickham who nodded with a smile. This man understood him. "No, she is beautiful, intelligent . . . extraordinary." He shook his head.

"And belongs to him now." Wickham said softly. John looked at him sharply. "Yes."

"What a pity, to know that a woman you favour would be tied forever to a man such as him."

John immediately picked up on the insinuation. "What do you mean?"

Wickham indicated that they move to a private corner of the room. "Darcy's father hated him, but as he was his only son, he had no choice but to accept him as his heir. He preferred my company and provided me with the same benefits as Darcy."

His brow furrowed. "Are you a relation?"

"No, I was the son of his father's steward."

"Why would the master of an estate bestow such favours upon you?"

Wickham's eyes flashed. "I told you he hated his son." Something did not sound quite right, but John encouraged him to continue. "He sent me to school with Darcy, and then when my father died he decided to continue his beneficence. He gave me a university education, and provided for me in his will. I would have been set for life, had not Darcy denied the bequest."

"Really?" John glanced at Darcy. Wickham nodded, watching the movement. "I was to receive a valuable living as pastor of the Kympton parsonage."

"And Darcy denied it in revenge for his father's favour towards you?"

Nodding, Wickham smiled to himself. "Exactly."

John turned back to regard him. "But surely you could have taken him to court. The will would have been upheld and he would have no choice but to honour his father's wishes."

"That was not an option." Wickham was not happy with the way the conversation had turned.

Returning his gaze to Darcy, John murmured, "I am sure that I heard rumours of him when I was in London this summer." Wickham's ears perked up. He wished to hurt Darcy, but now was not the time to mention Georgiana. He needed to think.

"I am sure that rumours abound around such a rich man."

John sighed and looked away. "I imagine they do. I just wish there was something I could do to convince Miss Elizabeth she is making a mistake. She is very loyal, and it will be difficult to change her mind."

Wickham watched him carefully. "Has the young lady defended him?" John nodded, but did not elaborate. Wickham looked again at Darcy then saw him glancing in their direction again. It was getting too dangerous; he did not want to be seen. "Well, I must be taking my leave, sir. I wish you luck in your attempts to win Miss Elizabeth back. Perhaps we can meet again sometime?"

He looked at him in surprise. "You are leaving? But what of the dinner?"

Wickham smiled. "I have duties to perform; it is my lot as a soldier."

"Courtesy of Mr. Darcy."

"Well, perhaps." He bowed and left before John realized he had not caught the man's name. He looked back over at Darcy, who was speaking with Mr. Bennet. Clearly Mr. Bennet had welcomed Darcy as his soon-to-be son. His eyes travelled over to his own father, and his face reddened, remembering their conversation where his father had essentially reprimanded him as a schoolboy for approaching

Eliza and pressing her. He told of Mr. Bennet's and Darcy's visit, and their news of his behaviour. It destroyed John's tale of falling off his horse and knocking his jaw on a rock that he had concocted. He could see the disappointment in his father's eyes, but how could he understand what it was like to be so completely rejected, by a woman whose value John was only just beginning to comprehend. Even this soldier recognized her worth by, even without knowing the circumstances, understanding how her defence of Darcy was extraordinary.

Darcy quietly accepted the congratulations of the group of men he had joined when Mr. Bennet introduced him as the man his Lizzy would marry. The surprise of the local gentleman was subdued, obviously Mr. Bennet was correct; the match was expected. Some men offered their hands in congratulations, some eyed him with speculation, wondering at the rapidity of the attachment, but it seemed one and all recognized that winning Elizabeth was winning a treasure. With that, Darcy could not agree more, although they seemed to value only her beauty and wit, where he knew there was so much more to his dearest friend then they could ever imagine. He was extraordinarily uncomfortable being the centre of attention and turned the conversation away from himself, encouraging discussion of the war news, and breathed a sigh of relief when he was able to remove to the background again. Darcy wondered how much longer he must stay to have put in a respectable appearance. All that he wanted to do was return to Netherfield. He was anticipating another night in Elizabeth's bed, although he swore that he would not allow their displays of affection to go beyond what they had already experienced. He felt a tightening of his breeches at the memory and shifted uncomfortably. He glanced across the room to find a distraction and spotted Lucas. In an instant his warm amorous thoughts changed to those of heated anger.

Mr. Bennet spotted the change in his expression, and followed his gaze. "Mr. Darcy, you do not need to begin a free-for-all here tonight. Try to restrain yourself."

He turned to Mr. Bennet in amazement. "Do you think that I would fight him here?"

"No sir, I was merely stating something ridiculous to draw your attention. It worked, did it not?" He raised his brow and tilted his head, a move so like Elizabeth that Darcy actually smiled.

"Indeed." He relaxed. Lucas could not harm him, the engagement was official. "You remind me of Elizabeth."

Mr. Bennet laughed. "Well, I suppose I should!" He sobered. "I will miss her terribly when you take her away."

"Sir, I appreciate that more than you know; please be assured that you and your family will be welcome at Pemberley or in London when we are in residence." Darcy regarded him with sincerity.

"I thank you for that. I hate to let her go, but I know that she does not belong here. She is meant for bigger things. She can learn so much from you."

"It is odd that you say that sir, because I feel that I have learned a great many things from her already." The men smiled.

"Will she be returning home soon?" Mr. Bennet asked quietly.

Darcy looked down and said reluctantly, "She is feeling better, but she spent most of the day sleeping. I believe the decision is hers."

Mr. Bennet laughed. "Well, that is certainly true. She will declare herself well and there will be no stopping her, whether she is or not." He looked over the wistful expression on Darcy's face. "You will be married to her soon enough. I do envy you. I went into marriage without any expectation of happiness, and I see you, all anticipation. It is good to see such love for my daughter." He nodded over at John. "I do not believe that would have been the case with Lucas. I think that he would have been triumphant over the prize, but would not have appreciated the gift."

"I believe you are correct." Darcy looked around the room. "Will you tell Elizabeth the story of your marriage? I think that she would appreciate your trust, as well as knowing her aunt. I will be honest with you sir, I feel uncomfortable not telling her, but feel that it is your story to explain."

Mr. Bennet shook his head. "I am not ready to tell her." Darcy nodded and jumped when he felt Bingley touch his arm.

"Come gentlemen; let us take in this meal so we can return to our homes."

Mr. Bennet laughed. "Mr. Bingley, I rather expect you to be paying me a private call sometime soon." He lifted his brow and Bingley flushed. "Yes, sir."

On their way in to the dinner, John sidled up to Darcy. "I know what you did."

Turning to him, Darcy looked at him. "Pardon me?"

"You denied a man his inheritance from your father's will. You denied him a living. You are not worthy of Miss Elizabeth." Darcy's head tilted, watching him. This story sounded painfully familiar.

"What man do you speak of? Give me his name."

John flushed. "I. . . I do not know his name."

"Then how do you know that what he speaks is true?" Darcy's eyes travelled the room, seeking out a familiar face, but came up empty. He looked back at John. "Be sure of your facts before spreading rumours, sir. It does you and nobody you know any good." He stepped away and approached the dining room, his appetite gone. Finding Bingley he leaned down. "I think that I will return to Netherfield. I will send the carriage back for you."

Bingley stood. "What is wrong?"

Darcy shook his head. "It is nothing."

Bingley looked at his friend carefully. "It is not nothing; Darcy." He signalled Hurst who strolled over. "We are going to return home." Darcy protested but Bingley ignored him.

"Is there a problem?" Hurst asked. Darcy stared at his hands then looked away. "Well, apparently there is. Come we will farewell our host." The brothers left to express their regrets to Colonel Forster and Darcy was approached by Mr. Bennet.

"Leaving so soon?" He asked with an amused smile.

"Uh, yes sir, we . . .'"

Mr. Bennet stopped him by holding up his hand. "Please do not even try to explain, just wish my daughters good night for me." Darcy flushed and nodded, then turned to join Bingley and Hurst.

The men arrived back at Netherfield well ahead of their expected time, and were informed that the rest of the household was at dinner. Bingley spoke to his butler as their outerwear was collected and he bustled off to give orders to lay three more settings at the table. Bingley took Darcy's arm and pulled him into the darkened library; Hurst followed and closed the door. "You have not said a word since we left there, Darcy. What happened?"

Darcy began pacing and ran his hand through his hair. "It will sound foolish but Lucas approached me with a very familiar accusation, it made me uncomfortable."

"What accusation?" They watched Darcy's progress. "It has to do with my father's will; and a bequest . . ." Darcy stopped moving. "I need Elizabeth." It was a simple statement but Darcy saw their confusion, and looked from one man to the other. "You do not understand do you?" He shook his head. "It is not so long ago that I would not have understood either."

Bingley watched him stare distractedly out the window. "They are eating; you must compose yourself before entering the room. I understand that your cousin the colonel has arrived. Did you know of his plans?"

Darcy startled. "Richard is here?" He closed his eyes; the news was welcome but a curse all at once. He nodded. "I was going to ask you for permission to allow a visit. He was to meet Elizabeth and report back to the family."

"Ah, to determine their approval of the match?" Hurst nodded.

Looking over at him, Darcy sighed. "Yes, I was going to ask him to come after the engagement was generally known . . ." He thought of the odd accusation by Lucas and wondered how he could have known. Perhaps this was the rumour he heard in London; and not the story of Georgiana at all. Wickham certainly had not held back in spreading his tale of woe far and wide. "I need Elizabeth."

Bingley exchanged a glance with Hurst. "Well, then it is good that she remains in this house. Come, let us join the party." He opened the door and they proceeded down the hallway.

The three place settings had been prepared and Darcy sought out Elizabeth as he entered, and found her sitting next a newly laid place, with Richard across from her. She smiled warmly at him and he felt better instantly. Bingley was rapidly explaining away their early return as Darcy strode in. "Richard, this is an unexpected pleasure, what brings you here so soon?"

"Ah Darcy, I thought that I had been invited." He stood and raised his brows while tilting his head at Caroline, who was furrowing her brow at him as they clasped hands.

Darcy shook his head. "Well, I had planned to invite you . . . but it seems no harm was done by your early arrival." He was too preoccupied to give his cousin any leeway. He pulled out his chair and sitting down, took Elizabeth's hand, squeezing it tightly. She immediately felt the tension in his grip.

"What is wrong?" She asked softly, leaning towards him.

"I can hide nothing from you." He whispered and raised her hand to his lips. He looked at her carefully. "You are tired."

"And you are angry." She continued holding the hand that now lay in his lap. "What has happened?"

He shook his head. "After dinner." Elizabeth looked at him with concern, but noticing the eyes of the table upon them she nodded reluctantly.

Richard could see that something was upsetting Darcy, but he also saw something new and unexpected. He was seeking and receiving comfort from Elizabeth. They could not hide the small touches and glances, and clearly neither one was able to eat comfortably as their hands appeared to be joined beneath the table. Despite the mysterious reasons for his upset, Richard was happy to see his cousin so obviously attached, and after spending some time with Elizabeth, he could easily see why he was so besotted. The conversation throughout the meal could not help but be lively with Bingley, Richard and Elizabeth at the table. Caroline did her best to dominate Richard's attention since she was not really speaking to her brother and Darcy's display did nothing but infuriate her. Georgiana was just happy to see her brother smile, though he did look at her sadly from time to time. Louisa spoke to Jane and Caroline, while Hurst ate and enjoyed watching the scene.

When the meal ended, the men left for Bingley's study. Darcy paused before leaving. "You should retire; I can see that you are in need of sleep."

Elizabeth refrained from stroking his cheek with difficulty. "I am perfectly fine, and I want to know what has happened. You are unhappy."

"I am very unhappy. I must speak to my cousin, but . . . may I come to you tonight? We can speak privately there."

She searched his eyes, they were the sole clue to his feelings, but she had learned how to read him. "Of course, I will be waiting for you."

He raised her hand to his lips. "Thank you my love. I will be forever grateful that you fell ill at this time."

Darcy watched her ascend the stairs and then entered Bingley's study. Richard accosted him. "Well, I understand that something was said to you of your father's will by a competitor for Miss Elizabeth's hand. What is this all about?" Darcy sank heavily into a chair and accepted a glass of port from Bingley, then repeated the essentials of his conversation with John. When finished, Richard gave out a low whistle. "So, somehow this Lucas has heard of Wickham's claims. Well you are correct; he spread that manure all over England, why would you allow that to bother you now? He very likely could have heard that in London, your name was bandied about quite freely this summer. You won the woman he was pursuing; naturally he will seek anything he can to disparage you. Do you think he will try to use this information to change her mind? Or her father's?"

Darcy shook his head. "I hope not. I just hope that is the extent of his knowledge. I could not bear to see Georgiana shunned here, she is doing so well."

Richard leaned against the mantle and folded his arms. "I think that if he knew of her ruin he would not have hesitated to mention the subject to you. He had the perfect opportunity. I believe that this news is the worst he has, and as he does not even have Wickham's name, he really can not claim good knowledge. It will be regarded as rumour concocted by a rejected suitor, nothing more."

"Then why do I have a bad feeling about this twisting in my gut?" Darcy said softly.

Bingley clasped his shoulder. "Because my friend, you have always looked at the worst of things."

Darcy looked around at the men and saw three knowing smiles and shrugged. "It is not without experience."

They sat sipping their drinks, contemplating the problem. Richard broke the silence. "It seems that you need to speak with Mr. Bennet before this Lucas character does."

Darcy nodded. "Yes, I suppose that as much as I hate to relinquish her company, Elizabeth is undeniably well enough to return home, although she did appear very tired just now." The others smiled.

"I will gladly host her and Miss Bennet for any length of time, Darcy." Bingley volunteered.

"Yes, we all know your opinion." Darcy smiled.

"You mean that she is taken as well?" Richard caught Bingley's sharp glance and laughed. "Two lovely ladies . . . are there more at home like them?"

Hurst laughed then. "Uh, the rest are to be experienced, sir." Richard frowned.

Darcy's sigh ended the amusement. "Well, as I said, Elizabeth will likely return to Longbourn tomorrow, so I will take that opportunity to speak to her father. Hopefully he will know not to believe the rumour that Lucas will undoubtedly repeat to the neighbours. I certainly can prove that I am not the ogre that Wickham claimed, so I will be acquitted easily. There is really nothing that I can do about him disparaging me, I have been part of common conversation in London for months, and hopefully this is the worst of his knowledge. I hope that he thinks twice before saying it publicly, without Wickham's name or a good idea of the facts. I suppose he will resort to anything in his quest to see Elizabeth reject me." His voice trailed away and his eyes dropped to the glass in his hand.

Richard watched him carefully. "I doubt that she would reject you."

Darcy continued staring at his glass. "I do not know what else he has heard, or what he might say. I should not have beaten him."

Bingley stood up and shook his finger at him. "Darcy, he had his hands on her face, he was grabbing her arm, and she was trying to escape. Frankly if you had not beaten him, I would have beaten you for allowing such liberties to the woman you say you love."

Richard grinned. "You beat him up? Excellent Darcy!"

He looked up at his cousin and smiled slightly. "I knew you would like that." He sighed. "I can not say that I regret it, but . . . I know it will come back to haunt me."

"What I do not understand is why you are not telling the world what he has done?" Richard gestured with his glass. "Bring the fool to his knees!"

"And tell the world that he compromised Elizabeth?!" He reigned in his flaring anger and continued in a softer tone. "To broadcast the news would make me no better than the gossips of the *ton* who dragged me down with Georgiana. He has two unmarried sisters, and parents who are somewhat important in the area. I will not harm them." Darcy met Richard's eye.

"You are too generous, Cousin."

"I am hopeful that my talk with him will prove sufficient." He sighed again. "Why can this not be easy?"

"It seems that you are in need of Miss Elizabeth's cheering. She will knock that permanently morose attitude out of you." Darcy's mouth turned up again and he nodded, acknowledging Hurst's words.

Still marvelling over his cousin's decision, Richard began planning for what may come. "Well it seems to me that you need to have a conversation with the lady, about this and any other rumours that flew about you while in London. What did you hear that was specifically about you?"

Darcy shrugged. "You probably heard more than I did. What was the worst?" He looked at the three of them and Bingley shifted uncomfortably.

"Um, there was the rumour of your mistress." They all stared. "What?!" Darcy exclaimed. Bingley looked at the floor. "Um, yes, I heard that you did not keep company with any ladies of the *ton* because you kept . . . a lady that you would visit regularly."

"My God!" Darcy stood and ran his hand through his hair distractedly.

"Darcy, relax!"

He paced and looked up at his cousin. "This will surely make her reject me!"

Bingley grabbed his arm. "Darcy, this is simply a rumour I heard, not Lucas, it is not being spread about Meryton! Nobody has spoken of this outside of this room. She will not reject you over a rumour, Miss Elizabeth is far too sensible for that!" Darcy stopped his pacing and stared down at his shoes.

"She might if she thinks I keep a mistress." Darcy said quietly.

Hurst's short laugh made him lift his head. "I am sorry, but I was just thinking that Caroline or any number of the ladies of society would be quite willing to overlook that habit."

"Elizabeth would not."

"The behaviour is hardly uncommon . . . do not fix me with that glare Darcy, you are no innocent, however I acknowledge that in your case it is most definitely not true. If you feel the need to confess, simply tell her so now and get it out of the way." Richard watched the turmoil that showed only in his eyes. "When are you to marry?"

"The end of November . . . four weeks."

Richard's brows rose. "Well, I should send a note to Mother and Father, so they can arrange their schedule. Oh and Darcy, I sincerely suggest that you keep this from Aunt Catherine until the event is finalized, Father suspects she is not through with you."

Darcy made a frustrated groan. "What else can go wrong?" He drained his glass and stood. "I have had enough. I am going to wish the ladies goodnight and retire. Thank you for your support gentlemen, if any of you think of a better way to approach this problem, I would welcome your ideas." They all stood and entered the sitting room where Darcy kissed Georgiana and bowed to the rest, then departed for his chambers. Jane watched him going with trepidation and noticed Richard observing her. She blushed and turned to the conversation. Richard looked out the door speculatively; his cousin was certainly a changed man.

—·∿∿·—

Elizabeth opened the door at the sound of a gentle knock, and quickly shut it as William slipped inside. She turned the key and had barely drawn breath when she was encased in his arms. "Will . . ." Her voice was silenced by his mouth. His kiss was different, she could feel a sort of desperation in the way he clutched her to his body. His lips were dominating her in a way that made her feel undeniably wanted. Darcy lifted her into his arms, barely breaking the kiss, and reclaimed her mouth instantly. Elizabeth's arms wrapped around his neck and he carried her towards the bed, stopping with a jolt when his knees struck the mattress. He bent and laid her down, and quickly took his place beside her. Their eyes met and locked. His hand caressed her face then stroked downward possessively, coming to rest on her breast. Deliberately he pulled the pink ribbons of her nightdress; opening the fabric just enough to reveal one soft mound, and she moaned as his mouth lowered to suckle her hard dusky nipple. Elizabeth closed her eyes, holding his head and caressing his hair with her lips. "Ohhhh, oh Will . . ." The plea in her moan brought his mouth back to love her lips again, then down to her throat, where he felt her soft moans vibrating as he kissed and licked her tender skin. She clung to him so tightly and he finally gave in to his need, rolling so he lay over her, the sensation was exquisite torture. Elizabeth's legs had instinctively parted under his weight, her welcome was clear, she could not possibly know what her body was telling him, but he did. She wanted him, and it made him nearly insane with desire.

Darcy thrust his potent arousal against her and groaned. "Oh God I want you, I want to make you mine, Lizzy. Nobody can take you away from me once you are mine." He moved his hips rhythmically, imagining loving her, and revelled in the small gasps against his ear as he stimulated her core. Groaning he moved them back onto their sides, kissing her face and again finding her sweet parted lips. His hand drew up her gown, then began to stroke her lovingly. He watched her eyes close and felt her body tremble. "Does this feel good, my love?" Elizabeth nodded, unable to make a coherent sound. Darcy was dying to slip a finger inside of her and experience her warmth, but limited his touch to resting his hand over the chestnut curls. Slowly he began rubbing over her pearl, and enjoyed her writhing as her hips bucked up against his unceasing hand. She bit her lips as the exquisite feeling of pleasure began to build, and Darcy instantly needed to nip that luscious flesh, then soothed their bites with his tongue. The warm evidence of her ecstasy spread over his fingers as her back arched and her body blushed. When she opened her eyes, she saw that he was staring at her longingly.

Elizabeth pulled his hands and urged him to again lie on top of her. "Love me." He shook his head. "I want to be yours Will, please." Darcy moaned softly and closed his eyes, settling over her. Stroking her hair, he held her tightly as they kissed. His erection was there, and he could sense the wetness and the warmth drawing him in. The intoxicating scent of her body surrounded him. Her legs parted further, and he felt warm hands pulling up his robe and nightshirt, caressing over his bottom and up his back, stroking him and urging him forward.

"Oh my Lizzy." He moaned, experiencing the pleasure of her touch, and kissed her deeply. Darcy looked into her eyes and saw the love he dreamed of, and somehow, with a strength he did not know he possessed, he managed to tear his body from hers and roll off onto his back. He covered his face with his arm and panted; the pain of denying his desire was overwhelming. Elizabeth felt instantly bereft of his body, but did not feel rejection. Instead her feelings for him grew stronger. She realized that *he* was the one in control, and that she really had to depend on his ability to stop, as she could not yet understand what was to happen between them.

Laying her head on his chest, she closed her eyes and stroked her fingers over his aching arousal, hearing a low groan. "Let me love you." She whispered, touching him the way he showed her. His eyes were closed, and she felt the tension in his body. Her fingers glided over him, gently rubbing the moist tip. Darcy jumped and his arm flew from his face. "Did I hurt you?" She asked worriedly.

"No." He said in a strangled voice and watched in fascination as she smiled and lowered her head back to lie upon his chest, and began to caress him again. "Ohhhhhhhhhhhhhh." Darcy muffled his moan by pressing his arm across his mouth. Elizabeth continued, slowly increasing the motion, pleasuring her William until she achieved a rhythm that he matched with his driving hips. Suddenly Darcy lifted her shoulders from him and dragged her up to his mouth where he kissed her desperately, and she felt his body buck beneath her as his essence spread over her legs. Darcy clutched her and breathed raggedly. "Do not move, please." Elizabeth settled atop him and felt the tension in his muscles leave as his body sank into lassitude. Eventually his eyes opened and he spotted a handkerchief. He gently lifted her away and carefully wiped the spending from their bodies. He then drew her back into his embrace and covered them with the counterpane. "I love you." He closed his eyes and kissed her. "I did not mean for this to happen, I planned to just kiss you and hold you, but I . . . I guess that I can not let go of you. Please forgive me, Lizzy."

Elizabeth nestled onto his chest and ran her fingers through the black curls that bloomed through the open neck of his nightshirt. "Do not apologize William, I am as much to blame as you." His disgusted laugh made her angry and she sat up. "Excuse me sir, but I am not completely helpless. You have witnessed me slap one man who tried to accost me, do you truly think that I would have remained yielding and compliant if I was not a willing participant in our activity?"

Darcy stared up at her and was about to retort when he was instead overcome by her beautiful flashing eyes. "What am I to do, Elizabeth? When you smile I am lost, and when you glare I am just as deeply entranced. It is hopeless; I am clay in your hands."

Her anger subsided. "That is a very dangerous confession, sir." She smiled and kissed him.

He chuckled, seeing her satisfied with herself, and ran his fingers through her hair. "I am sorry, though. I know that you are still ill, but I come here and disregard your obvious fatigue and wish to satisfy my own needs. It was wrong of me. Are you feeling any better?"

She settled back onto his chest. "I am. I believe the fatigue you saw was merely the result of spending an evening fending off the kind advice of Mr. Bingley's sisters."

"What did they say to you? Did they bother Georgiana, too?" He asked with concern.

"Nothing that I could not address, Miss Bingley is rather disappointed in our engagement, I gather. Did her brother make her angry somehow?"

Darcy smiled. "You might say that . . . he has curtailed her spending until the spring."

"Ah, that would explain her burning the newest issue of *The Lady's Magazine* and crying that she would have no use for it." She laughed. "If you ask me, she desperately needs the advice, but that would be unladylike to make such a remark, so of course, I will not."

Darcy's laugh rumbled in her ear. "Oh, Lizzy, I enjoy being with you so much."

"You enjoy hearing nonsense?"

He hugged her. "I enjoy hearing anything you have to say."

She snuggled into him. "And I enjoy lying beside you." He stiffened and she felt it. "Please tell me what is wrong. You returned from the dinner without eating. What happened?"

He closed his eyes and blew out several deep breaths. "I had a conversation with Lucas; he spoke of my father's will and implied knowledge of Wickham, the man who tried to elope with Georgiana?" His eyes reopened to meet her gaze. "Lucas did not know his name though, so I assume that he heard this story from his time in London. Wickham spread his tale quite widely." He sighed and tightened his embrace. "I fear that he will attempt to speak to your father and perhaps you to warn against me. I am afraid that what he repeated to me was just the smallest hint of the stories that he heard, and I do know that the stories were quite fantastic. I can defend against the claims that I cheated Wickham of his inheritance, but as to these other rumours, if he has heard them, and finally connects my name to them . . . I do not know what they are, so I can not prepare. I would hope that he would not repeat them around the neighbourhood. I think that his goal may be a wish to see you reject me." Elizabeth sat up and regarded him with great concern. "I hope Lizzy, that if you hear these things, you will remember me, the man who has written you, and attempted to court you, and not believe the ugly accusations. I hope that you will still wish to be my wife."

"William! How could you possibly believe that I would reject you? I surely am not enamoured of John Lucas, what could these stories be that would turn me against you?"

"Bingley told me the worst of what he heard about me." He paused and said quietly. "They spoke of my mistress." He watched in horror as all colour drained from her face and he pulled her down to him. "It is not true, I swear, I have never kept a woman."

Elizabeth rested stiffly in his arms, staring up at the canopy. "I would be foolish to think that you are innocent, especially after what we have experienced these last two nights, no matter how much I wish it to be true."

Darcy sighed. "No, Elizabeth. I am not. But neither am I a rake." He felt her tension. "It has been so long since I last . . ."

"Will I ever meet her?"

Darcy started at the thought, cursing the pain he was giving her, and saw that her eyes remained fixed on the canopy. "They were always demimondes." He said softly, and read her confusion. "Une chére-amie." He sighed; pretty words would not change the facts. "They were paid for their favour." He studied the canopy as well. "I am seven and twenty, and I never expected to marry. I went, I never stayed longer than an hour, and I always left disappointed."

They. She attempted to stop thinking about how many women that could mean. "Then why did you return?" Elizabeth fought back the tears that pricked her eyes.

"I wished to feel something, even if for only a moment." He turned and held her face in his hands. "You are the only woman I have ever slept with. You are the only woman I have ever held in my embrace. You are the only woman I have ever wanted to love. You alone are my future. These last two evenings with you have given me . . . oh Lizzy I can not describe the joy I feel with your touch."

Elizabeth searched his sincere and pained expression and knew he spoke the truth. "I believe you." He clutched her to his chest and kissed her forehead fervently. "I am glad that I heard this from you. If I had been confronted with the tales from anyone else, it would have been difficult to . . . stop the hurt."

"I do not mean to hurt you." He whispered.

Elizabeth sighed. "I know, but it does nonetheless, and even though it was before you met me, and it is likely an unreasonable reaction, I do not care. You are mine, and I hate knowing that someone else knows what I someday will. Do you not feel the same way about me?"

Darcy swallowed and again cupped her face in his hands. "Elizabeth, you saw how I felt about Lucas touching you . . . I . . . I would likely kill any man I knew who did anything more, no matter how long ago it was."

"So my reaction is not at all unreasonable?" He shook his head. His soulful eyes stared into hers, and he tenderly kissed the tears from her cheeks.

Elizabeth drew a breath and blinked. "I have never liked sharing." She smiled slightly and stroked back the hair on his forehead.

He watched her carefully. "Neither do I my love, which is why I burst in here and accosted you so . . ."

"Enthusiastically?"

He smiled a little. "I was going to say desperately, but I will accept enthusiasm, it does not sound so . . ."

"Desperate." She gave him a small smile, and they both laughed quietly, feeling the tension ebb.

"Is that the worst of it?" Elizabeth settled back into the safety of his arms, she had not offered forgiveness and he had not sought it.

An enormous feeling of relief flowed through him; she hopefully accepted that it was the past. "I believe so, at least as pertains to me. I did not hear it all, but I can not imagine what else they would say, there was a story that I shot the man Georgiana eloped with, obviously that is not true. I do worry over the many things I heard of her while in London. Nothing kind, and unfortunately she heard them as well. I dearly hope that Lucas keeps his conversation to your father, if he speaks at all, and does not remember anything else of what he may have overheard when in town. I hope that he realizes that this is a child he would be disparaging, not just me. It would likely be useless to visit him and try to make him see reason, or try to convince him of Wickham's guilt. I am hardly someone he would wish to believe." He gave her a tight squeeze and kissed her head. "I will speak to your father tomorrow when you return to Longbourn, and bring him the settlement to sign. Danny brought it while I was away."

She looked up at him. "I am returning?"

Darcy smiled and stroked her cheek. "My love, I stopped tonight only by the skin of my teeth. I am afraid that if you remain here another night, we will need to be married the next morning. I desperately want to make you mine in every way."

Elizabeth sighed. "I do not object."

"Neither do I, but even tonight when your father announced our engagement to the party, I noticed some eyebrows rose at the supposed expedited nature of the news. They were not surprised of the attachment, it did seem to be expected, but as far as they all know, we only met a month ago. Your father's caution was wise."

She kissed his chest and closed her eyes. "I understand." The sounds of the rest of the household moving to their rooms were heard and doors opened and closed. Darcy and Elizabeth listened in silence as the footsteps and conversation died away, and gradually the movement in the other rooms quieted. He finally removed his robe and climbed back into the bed, spooning their bodies together. Darcy rested his face on Elizabeth's shoulder and entwined their fingers.

"Good night my love." He whispered.

"Good night Will, I love you."

Chapter 22

*E*lizabeth awoke feeling cold. For a few moments she thought that she was in her bed at Longbourn until she realized that the fine fabric beneath her cheek would not have been wasted on a pillow, but would have been fashioned into a dress or a shirt for her father, just as her old gowns were remade again and again. She became aware of deep steady breathing nearby, and opened her eyes to see William. The moonlight through the window provided just enough illumination for her to lie still and simply appreciate his handsome relaxed features. She was surprised that he was not holding her in some way, and even, she admitted to herself, disappointed. Trying to roll to her back, she found it was impossible to move. Upon lifting the counterpane to discover the reason, she saw that William had gathered up the fabric of her nightdress and clutched it in his hand, like a child sleeping with a favourite blanket or toy. A bright smile lit Elizabeth's face and her disappointment vanished. He *was* holding her. Seeking to reward him, she scooted to his side and instantly felt warm again.

Darcy's arm wrapped around her waist and he sleepily nuzzled her neck. "Lizzy." He whispered and his lips wandered up her face to find hers. They held each other and kissed deeply. When Darcy finally opened his eyes, he was astonished to discover this was no dream. Elizabeth held his face and laughed, watching his expression of surprise turn to one of absolute delight.

"You are real!" He smiled widely and hugged her tight.

"Did you forget about me?" She laughed.

"Never. I just am not used to having my dreams come to life . . . oh what a wonderful way to awaken!" He proceeded to leave a trail of kisses from her temple to her neck. His muffled voice tickled her ear. "You are not well enough to return to Longbourn."

With difficulty, Elizabeth tried to speak coherently. "I . . . believe that . . . you decreed . . . I should."

"I was overwrought. I have rested and I am thinking clearly now. You will stay until we wed." The wandering lips were joined by his firmly caressing hands.

"But . . ." His hands began lovingly fondling her breasts. "Ohhhhh . . ." Darcy's face lifted. "Please stay." He whispered.

'Will . . . I truly wish to stay, but Papa . . ."

Darcy sighed and pulled her against his very aroused body. "He wants you home. I know." The sound of resignation was clear in his voice. He kissed her forehead and valiantly attempted to control his desire. "Will you leave me a token, Lizzy, so that I can survive the night without you?"

"What would you like? You have my ribbon, my gloves, and my handkerchief, what else of me would satisfy you?" Darcy's intense gaze answered the question without words. Elizabeth blushed, which did nothing to cool his ardour. His hands began stroking her face and he was staring at her parted lips. She smiled, and trying to regain control of the moment, brushed back the fringe of hair that covered his eyes, and raised her brow. "I am waiting for your answer."

Darcy nipped her lip lightly and dragged his eyes up to hers. With a decidedly roguish glint, he made his demand. "Leave me your nightdress."

Her eyes widened. "My nightdress!"

"It carries your scent, my love. Leave it behind or I will not permit you to go." His face took on a stubborn set.

Elizabeth giggled then pursed her lips. "Fine sir, but on one condition."

"Will." He smiled. "What are your terms?"

She caressed his bearded cheek. "You must leave me yours."

His smile was bright enough to light the room without a lamp. "Done, madam!"

They laughed and snuggled together, sealing the bargain with a kiss. "I will speak to your father about the settlement today."

"Will you tell him of Mr. Lucas' claims?"

He sighed. 'Yes, I wish to keep no secrets from him."

"I think that you need to have another conversation."

Darcy lifted his head from the pillow of her hair and smiled. "With whom; and on what subject?"

"Georgiana, about everything. She is so afraid that she has angered you somehow, or that she has behaved improperly, she remains so timid. Even Mr. Lucas remarked on it."

Darcy's face immediately clouded and he spoke tersely. "I look forward to bidding Mr. Lucas farewell. That man has done nothing but disrupt what should be a joyous time in our lives."

Elizabeth gently ran her fingers through his hair, and kissed the frown that had formed. "Yes, but if he has noticed Georgiana, then others surely have as well. She deserves your attention, William."

"Have I neglected her?" He asked worriedly. "I thought that we have been getting on very well."

Elizabeth smiled at him kindly. "I think that I have been a distraction."

Darcy closed his eyes and buried his face back in her hair. "No, you have not. Without you, I would have been drowning in the sorrow of Georgiana's ruin, as would she. I am grateful for you." He breathed in the lavender that lingered faintly. "I know that I have much to learn about how to . . . give attention. I think that I am improving my ability to accept it." He looked down at her. "You must teach me."

Elizabeth caressed his face. "Someday you must tell me more of your youth. We spoke of it once before, but I could tell that you only touched on the subject."

Darcy's face became as stone and he spoke without emotion. "I cannot."

His reaction worried her; he was so quick to retreat back into the fortress of self-preservation he had erected. "Will . . ." His eyes softened and he blinked rapidly as he gazed at her. "I can not understand what you experienced, but I do understand what it is to grow up with parents who do not feel love. I am sure that my youth is nothing to yours, but . . . well, whenever, if ever you are ready, you may talk to me without fear."

Darcy swallowed hard and nodded, then rested his face back in her hair. "I will speak to Georgiana when we return from Longbourn."

He felt her head nod. "That seems like a fine idea."

They dozed in their embrace for one more hour, both desiring so much more. Darcy knew that if he began to caress her as he wished, it would be his undoing. It took a great deal of willpower not to give in to the siren call of her soft, intoxicating form. He instead cuddled her to him and imagined the coming winter, where he would forever be warm. Elizabeth took comfort from his steadily beating heart and the hardness of his body, holding her so possessively. It was a security she had never before experienced. Her parents rarely embraced her, not since she was very small, and a hug from Jane was no comparison at all to being loved and desired by William. It was very hard to let go, but the morning was advancing and they forced themselves to rise.

Elizabeth went into the dressing room and returned wearing a robe. She smiled and handed William her folded nightdress, which he immediately held to his face. Withdrawing from the still-warm fabric, he smiled and handed her the nightshirt he held behind his back, and watched her breathe in his scent as well. Darcy set down his gift then gazing into her eyes, untied the belt of her robe, opening it to expose her nude body. He did not look away from her eyes, but let his hands wander over her, feeling her soft skin, caressing her breasts, and memorizing the shape of every curve. Elizabeth became lost in his warm blue eyes, and drawing a shaking breath untied his robe and ran her hands over the thatch of hair on his chest, allowing her fingertips to caress it, down over his tightly muscled stomach, and followed the hair trailing down to narrow hips and below to his arousal. Her touch made him shudder and he pulled her to him, holding her tightly, skin to skin. "My love, how I want you." He kissed her throat, and pressed his body to hers. "I want to remember how you feel; it will seem an eternity before I can touch you like this again." His lips rose to hers and claimed her mouth for the hungry kisses they needed. Knowing that he must leave or make her his own, Darcy closed his eyes and pulled her robe together, tied the belt and stepped back, immediately tying his own. He caressed her cheek with the back of his hand and kissed her. Without a word, Elizabeth held his hand and opened the door. Darcy picked up his token and with her nod, slipped back out across the hall. He could not look back.

—⁓—

Wickham settled back in his bed, his hands behind his head, and stared out at the gradually rising sun. He had spent a sleepless night in the tavern of the Meryton inn, plotting his long-awaited revenge upon Darcy. He thought of Mr. Darcy, knowing now that he initially won his attention simply because he was a convenient child on whom he could shower gifts and infuriate his wife. But after she died, and his impetus was gone, Mr. Darcy continued to support the young boy who worked so hard to charm him. Wickham never questioned why he was chosen, never wondered why Darcy did not seem to earn his father's praise. He just accepted the attention and enjoyed watching Darcy trying to win a bit of it himself, and ultimately withdrawing completely in failure. Wickham felt that HE was the favoured son, and made a point of making Darcy's life hell. He noticed though that as Darcy grew older and the time passed after Mrs. Darcy died . . . his father gave him a different sort of attention, it was harsh and demanding perhaps, but it was the attention of expectation and pride in his heritage. Darcy was being groomed for his future, and Wickham felt his fantasy of winning Pemberley slipping away. It angered him. He decided that he had been employed as the dancing fool for Mr. Darcy's entertainment, and he subsequently ignored the truth of the enormous gift of education and the bequest that had been left him. After seeing Darcy accept his place as master of Pemberley, Wickham's delusion of entitlement and quest for revenge grew.

He returned to his rooms no further along, but continued his musings. "Darcy engaged to a dowerless country girl . . . I can not imagine it!" He crowed. "Perhaps this is all that is left to him; perhaps his value has fallen so low because of Georgiana's ruin that no woman of society would have him!" The grin fell from his face. "No, that is not the case at all, those rich heiresses will fall all over him forever, damn his luck! If I were he I would spend every night in a different bed!" His face reddened with his jealousy. He shook his head. "This is getting you nowhere . . . Think!"

Closing his eyes, he mulled over what he knew. "Miss Elizabeth Bennet, an extraordinary woman. Fought over by two gentlemen, extraordinary enough to drive Darcy to beat a man, he did not even beat me over his sister. This woman is extraordinary indeed!" A sudden thought struck him. "Darcy is in love!"

Wickham threw his head back and laughed, practically braying at the moon in his incredulous amusement. "That is it!" He grinned. "I will take his love away from him!" He knew that he could never claim the dowry he lost, but to make Darcy miserable for the rest of his life . . . "Ah, yes, that would be almost worth the loss of the money, I wonder if I could turn her against him, but how?"

He stood and walked across the room, and looked into the empty tankard sitting on the window sill with disappointment. He made use of the chamber pot and pushing it beneath the bed, stood at the window. "He can not know I am behind this. That man, the rejected suitor, I will employ him. Yes, I will learn the name of this man, it should not be difficult to discover from a gossip in town. I will spread the news of Georgiana's ruin through the village. So while the rejected suitor welcomes my aid, the village will disparage Darcy and that will ruin him in the eyes of Miss Elizabeth! The suitor claims that she is not mercenary, so it must be a love match for her as well. I could perhaps play up other rumours that I have heard of him." He stared out the window, thinking hard.

His eyes narrowed as another thought intruded. "But would her parents reject such a husband for their daughter? He is richer than they could ever dream . . . there must be more I can suggest about him." He thought of the beating the suitor received. "Perhaps if I imply that Darcy is violent in his home . . . that might frighten the parents away. I must speak to this suitor and learn what I can of the beating."

Wickham heard the movement in the adjacent chambers and swore. Life as an early rising soldier did not agree with him at all. It only made his desire for revenge grow. He was invited with some other officers to tea at the home of Mrs.

Philips that afternoon. As the aunt of the Bennet girls, perhaps Miss Elizabeth would be there, and perhaps he could discover why she attracts Darcy. He began to dress for the day, and looked forward to the afternoon.

———ᴗᴗᴗ———

"So, Lucas has a new story about you, but no proof, and no names." Mr. Bennet sat back in his chair and watched Darcy as he paced the confines of the bookroom. "But the story he tells is recognizable to you?"

"Yes sir, it is. I have heard it repeated to me seemingly everywhere I go. Apparently the money I paid the . . . fool in exchange for the living he refused was spent visiting the places I might go to spread his tale. I can not tell you how many people have told me versions of it." Darcy glared at a painting of a horse hanging near the door; it resembled the hack Wickham rode at Cambridge. He tore his eyes from the animal and looked at Mr. Bennet. "I imagine that this is the tale that Lucas heard when he was in London, but I can not pretend that he did not hear others. The city was replete with them this summer. I asked my cousin and Bingley what they heard . . . sir, they were ugly, but I assure you my conduct has always been that of an honourable man. If Lucas or any other tells tales of me, or God forbid my sister who was disparaged far more grievously than I, please, speak to me of it before taking the rumours as the truth." Darcy had stopped his pacing and had fixed his sincere gaze directly at Mr. Bennet.

"Do you know of any specific rumours?"

His eyes turned away and his face flushed. "They claimed I kept a mistress." He looked back at Mr. Bennet. "I assure you it is not true."

"But you are not without experience." Mr. Bennet said quietly.

"No, sir." Darcy's voice was soft.

Mr. Bennet read the expression on his face. "I do not hold you in contempt, sir. In my youth I was encouraged to find relief frequently, why I remember reading advertisements in the papers from women looking for . . . well, in any case, I do understand. I assume that you will keep your past habits from Lizzy."

Darcy attempted to wrap his mind around the different mores of the older generation and shook his head. "I have already discussed my past with her."

"Have you?" Mr. Bennet regarded him with great surprise, and marvelled at this unique relationship they had formed. "Mr. Darcy, I have known you but a month, and my Lizzy has known you four, but I do believe your statement that you are a trustworthy man. If I do hear of rumours, I will ask you for an explanation. Please realize that I live with a woman who thrives on gossip. I am well aware of how a simple story can grow into a tale of gargantuan proportions in the blink of an eye. Your sister's interrupted elopement is ripe for exaggeration."

Darcy hung his head and nodded. He sank heavily down into the chair opposite Mr. Bennet's desk. "Indeed sir. I hope to God I never meet Wickham again."

"Wickham?" Mr. Bennet started.

"Yes sir, George Wickham, he is the man . . . who claims I offended him, and the man who . . ." He looked down again, "ruined my sister in the eyes of society."

"Mr. Darcy, I do not know if this will please or anger you, but . . . there is a Mr. Wickham in Meryton."

Darcy's head snapped up. "Pardon me?"

Mr. Bennet nodded, sitting up. "In fact, he was here, in my parlour drinking tea with my daughters and wife yesterday afternoon. A tall man, almost your height I would say. Dark hair, from the behaviour of my daughters I would say they found him handsome. Very gentlemanly manners, a bit too solicitous for my taste, and perhaps a bit overly familiar. . ." He watched Darcy's eyes turn black. "Does this sound like the man?"

His fists clenched in anger Darcy hissed. "Yes sir. May I ask how Wickham came to be in your parlour?"

"He is in the militia, my daughters Lydia and Kitty met him and another officer in Meryton and they asked to call." He saw Darcy struggle with the emotion he was feeling.

"Sir. I respectfully suggest that you tell your daughters to keep away from this man. He will do them no good."

"I believe that I had already reached that conclusion, Mr. Darcy. He will not be welcomed here again." He saw a ribbon appear in Darcy's hand. "What will you do?"

Looking up, Darcy shook his head. "I do not know. I will need to speak to my cousin about this. He is visiting Colonel Forster as we speak; a courtesy call upon a fellow officer while in the area." He glanced down at the bit of satin in his hand. "He wished to come and meet Elizabeth's family, but I . . . I wanted to say my farewells . . ."

Mr. Bennet interrupted. "You need not say more." He smiled and then chuckled softly. "It is not as if you are never going to see her again."

Darcy smiled slightly. "It only seems that way."

"Well then, let us rejoin the party, shall we? I assure you, if this Wickham is the man who hurt your family, and speaks ill of you, or your sister, I will not listen." Darcy slipped his token back in his pocket and stood.

"Thank you, sir."

—⁓⁓—

Wickham sat across from John in the tavern and took in the earnest man's face. It was quite a fortuitous circumstance that John had ridden into the village that morning in the hope of spying the soldier he had spoken with the evening before, and Wickham was more than happy to begin spinning his web of lies in the convincing manner he had perfected over the years.

"Sir, I have been thinking over the news you told me last night of Mr. Darcy, I have a memory of hearing his name in London this summer, I attended an event at St. James' and I am sure that I heard Darcy's name spoken . . . and not in a complimentary way. I wonder, as you know him so well, can you confirm these things?"

Wickham smiled, this was going to be even easier than he thought. "Of course, Mr. Lucas, please tell me what you heard."

John looked down into his tankard and spoke softly. "I understand that Miss Darcy was involved in an attempted elopement, and that she is ruined in the eyes of society."

He glanced up to see Wickham nodding his head solemnly. "That is indeed quite true. She was shunned by all."

John's eyes widened. "Then, what I heard is true, she was caught in the bed of her lover at an inn . . . and Darcy found them and shot the man?" Wickham raised his brows and stared at him. John drew his own conclusions; Darcy had told him that he was an excellent shot. He continued in a low voice. "I understand that she was with child, but as I have seen her, it must not be true."

Wickham shrugged. "She may have lost it, or perhaps Darcy learned of the methods used by his prostitutes . . . she is certainly ruined, if she was in the man's bed, it was not to sleep, was it?" He smiled knowingly at John.

"Such a young girl, what could have driven her to go?"

"Well, knowing her brother's reaction, perhaps she wished to get away from him, look at what he did to you, after all. How did that come about?" Wickham's eyes flicked over to John's jaw.

He rubbed the bruise unconsciously and avoided the question. "Do you think that he is violent with her at home?"

"You said yourself that she is unusually timid." He watched as the thoughts turned in John's mind. "What have you heard of Darcy himself?"

John looked up. "I understand that he keeps a mistress, perhaps more than one."

Wickham smiled at that unlikely thought. "Ah, well, I must admit that there was a constant stream of questionable ladies in our rooms at Cambridge. I know that he was forever settling gaming debts as well." He watched with amusement as John's eyes narrowed at Darcy's supposed behaviour, which was really his own. "Can you imagine how much his reputation suffered in Town with his sister's downfall? He could no longer hide behind his mask of respectability. I imagine that he has been quite angry with her for lifting the veil on his habits." Wickham delighted in watching the effect his suggestions had.

John was not innocent, but he kept his liaisons to the gentleman's houses. He never paraded women into his chambers at school. "Yes, perhaps . . . Do you think that he is violent with her? Threatens her? I swear; she barely speaks above a whisper in his presence."

Wickham shrugged, knowing full well Georgiana's shyness, how long had it taken him to coax kisses out of her? "I can not say. The Darcys never expressed themselves openly. Who knows what happens behind closed doors? I can only feel concern for the ruined girl . . . and for the future of Miss Elizabeth."

At this John sat up. "What do you mean? Do you think he will be harsh with her?"

He shook his head sadly. "If as you say the girl is not mercenary, but fancies herself in love with him, she will be blind to his behaviour. I imagine that her parents are delighted that such a rich man would want their dowerless daughter, and would do nothing to stop the match, but . . ."

John stood and exclaimed. "Everyone should know his character! There is time! I must save her!"

Wickham grabbed his arm and pulled him back down, whispering urgently. "Yes, you must save her, but how? She will not listen to you; she will think that you are making up lies to convince her to return to you."

Pounding his fist on the table, John swore. "There must be a way! I will not see her hurt!"

"You will not see her in Darcy's bed, you mean."

John's face grew red. "No, I will not."

Wickham nodded knowingly. "I suggest that you tell everyone you know of the truth. Tell them of Miss Darcy's ruin. Tell them of Darcy's proclivities. Let the combined voices of the neighbourhood accomplish what your single cry could never do. Miss Elizabeth's parents surely will not wish to connect their family with one containing such a ruined girl. It would taint their other daughters, and her father would not wish to connect her with a potentially violent man, no matter how good the settlement would be." He knocked on the table. "Then when the Darcys are driven back to their estate, you will be here to offer her comfort, and she will ask for your forgiveness for ever rejecting you in the first place. She will beg for your favour again."

His eyes grew unfocussed, the vision of Elizabeth begging for his attentions was gratifying indeed, and clouded the reality that Elizabeth begging any man for such a thing was unlikely in the extreme. "I thank you sir, for telling me these truths. I will begin to spread the news of the Darcys' unworthiness. Knowing the thirst for gossip in the neighbourhood, I daresay the news will be spread far and wide by dinnertime tomorrow, especially with church tomorrow, yes, I will be sure to tell it to everyone."

Wickham smiled. "Excellent, sir. I believe you will soon have your Miss Elizabeth in your arms."

John smiled at the thought and he stood along with Wickham, shaking his hand. He took his leave and strode out of the inn with purpose. He felt that he was a knight going to save his lady, and not once considered that he was now the victim of a master of manipulation.

Yes! Wickham chortled to himself as he watched John approach a group of men. *The fool believed it all! He is dying to tell the world, and will soon speak to her parents. Now, I believe that I should go dress for tea.* Wickham stopped by his rooms to check over his uniform, then meeting Denny and some other officers, made his way to the home of Mr. and Mrs. Philips, and hoped he would meet Miss Elizabeth.

Darcy was afforded no private moment with Elizabeth to tell her of his discovery, but did manage to whisper a request to walk with her the next morning before church, if the weather was fine. He relaxed, thinking that she was to stay home and rest, and with Mr. Bennet's assurance that Wickham would not be allowed entry; he would not have to worry about her meeting him before they spoke. A kiss on her hand was all that he was allowed, and with sadness the two parted. He returned to Netherfield with Bingley to hold the long-delayed conversation with Georgiana. Elizabeth found herself thrown back into her mother's frenzied wedding plans.

Almost as soon as the gentlemen left; Mrs. Bennet demanded Elizabeth's attention. "Lizzy! Oh there is much to be done! We have lost precious time while you were lounging around Netherfield!"

Elizabeth's eyes rolled to the ceiling. "Mama, I was hardly lounging, I was ill!"

"Yes, but I could not make calls with you when you were there!" Mrs. Bennet was itching to parade Elizabeth around the neighbourhood.

"But Mama, Mr. Darcy was very pleased to have my company, do you not think it has helped to cement our engagement?"

Mrs. Bennet paused and turned to take in her now favourite daughter. "Oh, what a clever girl you are Lizzy!" She beamed and clutched her hand. "Yes, yes you were so wise to take advantage of your location. Why, I never thought of it!" She turned to Jane. "You should thank your sister for arranging her illness so conveniently Jane! Mr. Bingley was certainly paying close attention to you today; you must have pleased him very much during your time there! Very good indeed, girls!" Elizabeth and Jane exchanged exasperated glances.

It would do no good to argue with her. "Yes Mama, I am sure that Mr. Darcy and Mr. Bingley were pleased."

Mrs. Bennet bustled about. "Now, we are going to my sister Philip's for tea. She has invited a number of people there to announce your engagement, and while we are in the village we will begin selecting fabrics for your trousseau. I know that you must go to London for most of your things, but we can begin ordering your morning dresses here, they are not so important." She was almost talking to herself.

"Mama, please, must we do this today? I am still rather tired . . ."

Mrs. Bennet snapped around. "You looked fine when you were batting your eyes at Mr. Darcy just now. You are quite capable of going to tea." She looked her over and did see signs of fatigue. "Very well, we will postpone the trip to the dressmaker until Monday, but that is all!"

Elizabeth and Jane went upstairs to change and Jane followed Elizabeth into her room. The trunk from Netherfield lay on the bed, untouched as yet. Elizabeth heard Susie coming down the hall and quickly closed the door. Jane watched her with curiosity as she opened the trunk and drew out a folded white cloth, and placed it in her closet.

Before she could ask, Susie knocked. "Miss Elizabeth? I came to collect your things for washing." Elizabeth stood by the open trunk and handed her the soiled items.

"Susie, I was speaking with Mr. Darcy, and he said that his messenger Danny has been calling on you."

Susie blushed deep red. "We don't do anything improper, Miss!"

Elizabeth smiled. "I did not mean to suggest that you did. I only ask because I thought that I might ask my father if you could come with me to Pemberley as my abigail when I marry. Would you like that?"

"Go to Pemberley?" Susie's face lit up. "Do you mean we could . . . oh yes! Yes, Miss Elizabeth!"

"Very well, I will speak to my father. I know that my mother and sisters will be disappointed to lose you, but I do hope to have a familiar face with me there, it will be intimidating enough to face my new position on my own."

Susie lifted her chin. "Well Miss, I will be proud to be your lady's maid." She gathered up her laundry and bobbing, exited the room, barely containing her excitement.

"So, you steal our maid and arrange a romance at the same time." Jane smiled at Elizabeth who grinned.

"I am sorry, but Danny is such a sweet boy, and after William and I marry, he would likely come here but rarely. I could not bear to see them parted."

"You are an incurable romantic, Lizzy." Jane walked over to the closet and opened the door. "Now, what exactly did you hide away in here?"

Elizabeth closed the door and looked her in the eye. "Nothing."

"Lizzy, it looked like a night dress. Why would you hide that?" Jane watched as a blush crept up Elizabeth's face. "It is not a night dress."

Jane crossed her arms in front of her chest and stared. "Well?"

"Oh Jane, please, let me have a little secret!"

It is not a nightdress . . . She gasped. "Lizzy! Is that Mr. Darcy's night shirt?" She whispered urgently, her eyes darting back to the closet.

Elizabeth bit her lip and closed her eyes, then nodded. She opened them slowly and saw Jane's gaping mouth. "I told you not to ask." She took her sister's hands. "William and I slept together, but I promise, you have nothing to fear."

Jane searched her face. "But why . . ."

Elizabeth smiled. "It carries his scent. Someday you will understand . . . with Mr. Bingley, perhaps?" It was Jane's turn to blush.

Mrs. Bennet opened the door. "Girls! You must dress, we leave in an hour!"

She disappeared and Elizabeth grinned. "We will talk all about Mr. Bingley tonight. I think it is time for you to be embarrassed for awhile!"

———~~~———

"You wished to see me, Brother?" Georgiana asked softly.

Darcy stood and smiled. "Yes, come in, dear." He walked from around the desk in Netherfield's library and took her hand. "I thought that we could do with a talk." He settled her on a sofa and went to close the door. Richard was in the hallway and looked at him with raised brows. Darcy signalled him to mind his business and made sure he turned the key. Trying to remember all of the ways that Elizabeth drew him out, he put a smile on his lips and took a seat next to his sister.

"I wished to speak with you today because I am afraid that you are concerned with my rather unhappy behaviour of late, and that it might be because of something you did?" He tilted his head, trying to see her eyes which were cast down at her nervously twisting hands. As it was clear that she would not speak, he made himself continue. "For example, the morning that I received that letter and shut myself away in here, I apologize for acting so poorly. You see, it was news concerning Aunt Catherine, and you can imagine that any word from Rosings would not be received with delight by me."

"Does she demand something of you?" She whispered.

"Actually she demanded something of both of us." Georgiana finally looked up into his concerned eyes. "She wished to acquire a husband for you, in the hopes that I would then marry Anne."

Georgiana stared in shock. "She . . . she wished to send me away with some man I had never met?"

Darcy nodded, and seeing the tears begin to form; he instinctively took her hand. "That is why I was angry dear; it was because of her presumption and, well because Richard and his parents acted to stop the scheme without telling me first. I felt that I was deemed too weak to care for you. Elizabeth pointed out that I was acting petulantly." He smiled. "She did so in a very kind way, but behaving as a child, I certainly was." Seeing that she was still crying, he pulled her to him in a slight embrace. That unusual act stopped her tears instantly, and she held him tightly. Darcy increased his hold.

"I will not have to marry. . ."

"No dear, you will marry when you wish, and whomever you wish."

"You mean whoever will have me." She sobbed. "Nobody will ever want me now!"

Darcy's eyes filled with pain, hearing her hopeless voice. "You do not know that. Besides, you are too young to worry about such things. Give this time. You are a very good girl, and with Elizabeth's help you will have a wonderful life. All that matters is you finding happiness." He pulled back and lifted her chin. "I promise."

"I wish that I could believe that." She sat up and wiped her eyes. "I do feel a little better, but I am so afraid of behaving wrong."

"Yes, Elizabeth said that your shyness has been remarked upon. She would like to spend this month helping you to overcome it in company." He squeezed her hand. "Perhaps you might even be brave enough to play a duet with her at Longbourn or here at Netherfield one evening." Her eyes grew wide at the prospect, and he spoke hurriedly. "Or not, it is not necessary." He smiled a little, and was relieved to see her relax.

"William, you explained why the letter upset you, but why were you unhappy last night? You looked at me so sadly."

Darcy sighed and stood up. "Last night a man approached me, making accusations that I have heard many times before . . . the story that I cheated George Wickham of the bequest by our father." Georgiana gasped at the name. Darcy pressed on. "I spoke to Mr. Bennet this morning about it, so that he would know the rumours were false in case they found their way to his ears, and in the process . . ." He turned and knelt in front of her. "I learned that Wickham may be here in Meryton, serving with the militia."

"Oh, no!!" Georgiana began sobbing in earnest. Darcy was at a loss, he reached for her, but was not sure if he should embrace her or take her hands. The sound of knocking and the door handle rattling drew his attention and he heard Richard's voice calling. He helplessly looked at his sister and jumped up to open the door. Richard entered and looked to Georgiana, then Darcy. "I told her that I believe Wickham is here with the militia." Darcy closed the door and glanced at her then at Richard.

His eyes were wide with the news, but he hurried over to Georgiana's side. "There, there, sweetest. He will not get to you here. You are quite safe from him." He patted her hand, and Darcy sat on her other side, vaguely rubbing her back. The men looked at each other with the same lost expression. Finally Darcy drew a breath and wrapped her up in an embrace. Georgiana quieted, and Darcy closed his eyes in relief.

"Are you better?" He asked tentatively. She nodded. "You will not have to see him. Mr. Bennet assures me that Wickham will not be welcome in his home."

Richard chimed in. "Yes, and I met the militia's colonel today. He tells me that the men spend their days training, so it will be quite safe to visit town during the day, and I sincerely doubt that he would ever appear in church, so there is nothing to worry over." He raised his brows and smiled.

"I do not wish to be the cause of any problems for you and Elizabeth." Georgiana sniffed and drew back.

Darcy was relieved and attempted a smile. "How could that be? We are publicly engaged, Mr. Bennet has signed the settlement and I have already sent Danny to London with the papers to be kept with our attorney. All that is left to do is take our vows. There is nothing to stand in our way. You, my dear, can not possibly cause us any worry, not that you ever would." He kissed her head.

Georgiana looked at Richard then her brother. "I do not know what I would do if I had to hear those people saying things about me again." She looked down at the handkerchief clutched in her hands.

Worriedly Darcy glanced at Richard then at her bowed head. "Well, I can not imagine a single reason for Wickham to want to tell the tale of how he attempted to elope with an innocent young girl. It would only bring him shame here and likely lose him his position in the militia. He is obviously in dire straits if he joined with them." He saw Richard's confirming nod. "So as we have lived here for a month with no hint of the scandal, I daresay we will be fine for the next four weeks. You have nothing to fear."

———～～～———

Mrs. Bennet dragged Elizabeth in triumph around her Aunt Philip's sitting room four times before she finally made her escape and found a chair in a corner to rest. Despite her apparent recovery from the fever, the frenzy of crowing by her mother had left her feeling dizzy and longing to lie down. A voice with a familiar accent caught her ear and she looked up to see an officer standing nearby, smiling and laughing with Lydia. She watched them interact. Lydia was entirely too friendly, and Elizabeth was about to rise and advise her on proper behaviour when the couple turned to her. "Lizzy, you must meet my new friend, Mr. Wickham!" She beamed at him, and then looked up at Kitty calling to her. "Oh bother. Well, I will leave him with you, Lizzy; you are engaged so I do not have to worry about you stealing him away!!" She giggled and smiled at him before dashing off across the room.

Wickham watched her go, thinking of when he would make his move, and then looked down at her sister. *So this is Darcy's choice.* "Miss Elizabeth? It seems that your sister did not finish introducing us." He smiled and took a seat next to her. "I understand that you are to be married soon? Congratulations."

Elizabeth smiled and nodded, but looked at him warily. "Did I hear her correctly, sir? Your name is Wickham?"

Wickham was instantly on alert. Darcy had spoken of him. He affected an easy attitude. "Yes, it is. A common name, I have found."

Her brow wrinkled. "I can only agree with you, as I have not travelled often beyond Hertfordshire." She tilted her head. "Where is your family, sir?"

Smiling he relaxed. "My family is from the northern counties."

"Derbyshire?" She asked, watching carefully.

He did not flinch. "I believe I have some relations there. Why do you ask?" He smiled again, charmingly, he thought.

Elizabeth's eyes wandered over his face and she affected an equally charming smile. "Why your voice, sir. The accent reminds me of the man I will soon marry. Mr. Darcy is from Derbyshire, and coincidentally knows a family by the name of Wickham." She raised her brow.

Wickham was suddenly unsure how to respond. He could not decide if she was baiting him or not. "Well, that is a coincidence, indeed!" He leaned forward. "How does he know the family, perhaps I may be related to them?"

"Perhaps, the gentleman he knows was a favourite of his father, and was left a living in his will, which he rejected in favour of a great sum of money." Her eyes danced, but she was watching him closely. "It seems the man felt that he was not suited for the church."

He was entranced, even with her challenging his own tale; her impertinent delivery was intriguing him. "Well, how good it was that the man recognized his own abilities in time to allow a more worthy candidate to take the position."

"Ah yes, what a good man he is, indeed!" Elizabeth laughed. "So tell me Mr. Wickham, what brings you to the militia? Men seem to prefer missing this particular duty."

Laughing he sat back again, regarding her with delight. "I needed an income, and frankly, joining the regulars and risking Napoleon was simply not in my plans. This will do for a while, until something better comes along."

Her eyes sparkled at him with challenge. "Such as?"

"Ah, I hope to marry a girl with a great fortune!" He tilted his head and took in her smile, her lips, and her enticing form, yes; he could understand what attracted Darcy to this girl. She was so much more than her sisters.

"Well sir, I am afraid that you will have to look beyond this village for such a catch. There are few ladies who will serve your desires here." Elizabeth was not sure if this man was Georgiana's seducer or not. She had no description of him, and it was possible that George Wickham did have relatives in other parts of the country. That he was undoubtedly charming was clear.

"I am sorry to hear that news, and to hear that you have been captured already." He met her eyes and saw her brow rise slightly. That move was very provocative and he wet his lips. "Alas, I will have to perhaps settle for someone less amiable."

"You flatter me sir, but I have no doubt of your eventual success." Elizabeth began to feel uncomfortable, and stood. Wickham was immediately on his feet. "I believe that I should join my sisters, sir. I wish you great success in your chosen profession." She began to move away when she felt Wickham's arm brush against hers. She looked up immediately, and saw for just a moment a disturbing glint in his eye, and then it was gone.

He smiled. "I hope that I have not offended you in any way, Miss Elizabeth. I only wish to compliment you, both for your beauty and your great fortune in securing Mr. Darcy. He is a lucky man, indeed."

Elizabeth searched his face, still unsure of his intent, or who he was. "I can not be offended by a sincere compliment sir; however, I did not set out to secure Mr. Darcy. It was, as you say, a matter of fortune for both of us." Wickham bowed in acknowledgement and watched her move to the other side of the room. He took up a station by the window and watched her reflection in the glass.

Chapter 23

*D*arcy arrived early at their stile, determined to never again risk the chance of Lucas finding Elizabeth alone. He checked his watch and impatient, he directed his horse onto the path for Longbourn, and spotted her walking towards him. Riding forward, he stopped near a closely planted stand of trees and dismounted, tying up his horse.

"Good Morning!" Elizabeth called when she came closer.

Darcy strode forward and wrapped her up in his arms. "Good morning, my love." He smiled and squeezed her, delighting in her warm laugh. "I missed you last night." He said heatedly and captured her lips before she had a chance to speak, and they were soon engaged in an ardent exchange. Elizabeth's arms wound around his neck and her fingers trailed up the back of his head. Darcy pressed himself upon her and he attempted to recreate the sensation of her soft nude body rubbing against his. "Oh my Lizzy . . ." He whispered, and his mouth moved to her throat, where he groaned at the impediment of her bonnet ribbons.

"Will . . ." Elizabeth turned his face back to hers and she tenderly licked his upper lip. "Ohhh." He moaned and traced his tongue over her parted mouth. She stroked his softly caressing tongue with her own and Darcy embraced her so tightly she could feel all of him, even through the heavy coat. Their tongues began to duel and their mouths fought to see which would dominate the other. Elizabeth moaned softly and that was the only sound that could stop Darcy from trying to tear her bodice open and claim her right there against a tree. He started to softly chuckle. His frenzied kisses slowed and Elizabeth relaxed with him, feeling his growing smile. "Will?" She murmured, still seeking his mouth with gentle caresses.

Moving away slightly, he met her passionate eyes. *She is so beautiful!* He nibbled her lip. "I can not begin to tell you how I love your moan, Lizzy." His fingers traced her cheek.

Elizabeth's eyes flashed. "I do not moan!"

"Oh darling, yes you do, and I dearly cherish the sound." He hugged her to him.

"No, I do not." She said stubbornly, and buried her blushing cheeks against his coat. She felt his chest move and heard his deep rumble of a laugh, and they stood quietly embraced until their bodies calmed.

"How do you feel, Lizzy? Did you rest after I left you?"

"I wish I had rested, but Mama had other ideas."

"Ah, she wished to talk with you?" He laughed. "I imagine she was curious of your visit to Netherfield."

Elizabeth sighed heavily. "I wish it had been just that. We went to my Aunt Philip's so that she could parade me before the neighbours, crowing over her daughter's, and by association, her fine capture of a husband."

Darcy drew back and searched her face. "You went out? Lizzy, I was sure you were to stay at home, resting. That is why I did not remain with you longer." He watched her head shake. "Why then was I not asked to accompany you on this presentation?"

"You mean you would want to be the object of attention?" She laughed, seeing his brow still furrowed, and stroking it she explained. "Mama planned to visit the dressmaker to begin choosing fabrics for my wedding clothes. I imagine she thought that you would not wish to be there."

He was incredulous. "You had to go shopping as well?!"

"No, I convinced her to delay until tomorrow. I only had to go to my aunt's." She continued to stroke his brow soothingly, and he only appeared slightly mollified. She bit her lip and looked down, then back up to his penetrating gaze. "William, I met a man there. A soldier . . . his name was Wickham. I asked if he was from Derbyshire, his voice reminded me of yours." Darcy's eyes narrowed. "He said his name was common, but he may have relatives there . . . William, what is wrong?"

Darcy's face grew red and his eyes burned with anger. "HE was there?!" Darcy let go of her and strode away, his hands were opening and closing into fists. He tore off his hat and ran his hand through his hair. He looked back at Elizabeth's worried face and returned to her side. He took her hands and asked urgently, "What did he say? Was he uncivil?"

"He . . . he spoke of wishing to marry well . . . he . . . oh William, it will sound silly, but he brushed against me and I thought he looked . . . he made me suddenly feel uncomfortable, like Mr. Lucas sometimes does."

His voice shaking he squeezed her hands. "He *touched* you??" He closed his eyes and bit his lip. "Did he . . . no, he would not be direct." He pulled her to him and held her tightly.

"William, was that . . . him?"

"Yes, I am sure of it, and he knows that we are engaged. I spoke to your father of him yesterday, he said that he would speak to you, and ban him from Longbourn." Darcy searched her face, silently asking for an explanation.

"I did not speak to him before we left for Meryton, and I was so tired when we returned, I went straight upstairs . . . I have not seen him yet today."

He moved back and held her chin in his hand, and stared into her eyes. "Promise me Lizzy, swear, you will go nowhere alone. Never. I do not trust him."

Elizabeth's eyes grew wide. "You think he would try to harm me? Why?"

"Revenge, sweetheart. He lost Georgiana's dowry." Darcy held her to him and thought of what Wickham might do. "Promise me, Lizzy. I know you think you are capable of caring for yourself, and I am sure that you probably think me far too overprotective, but . . ."

"Will." He stopped his pleading and looked down at her upturned face. Elizabeth saw the concern in his eyes. "I promise. I will not walk alone. I only hope that you are wrong."

"I fear what he will do." He said frankly. "Your father said he will keep him from Longbourn, but I can not stop him in the village. How can I expose him without telling of Georgiana's ruin? People would not accept a vague reference to some unknown girl as proof." He kissed her forehead. "I talked to her, Lizzy. I told her of Aunt Catherine's plans, and that Wickham is here. I will not withhold the truth from her, but she is so vulnerable, so sure that she has ruined everything, so sure that she will make another mistake. I did my best . . . but oh, how I needed you there."

"Bring her to Longbourn tomorrow; she can come with us to the dressmaker. That should be a pleasant afternoon for her." Darcy nodded. "You will come here for dinner today as well, Mama invited all of Netherfield. We will work together to care for her. There is no reason for anyone to learn what happened with Wickham, and we can just pass the time before our wedding in peace."

"I hope so Lizzy. I wish your father would just let us marry so we could go home." His embrace tightened to the point of being almost painful, but she did not stop him. "Come back with me for breakfast." She whispered.

"I want breakfast in our chambers, in our home, alone." He whispered back, and then sighed. "I will take you home, and then I must return to Netherfield to dress for church." He drew back, and attempted a weak smile. "Come, let us walk."

After untying his horse, he held the reins in one hand and Elizabeth's hand in the other, and began to walk. They arrived at Longbourn, stopping at the garden gate. Kissing and resting their foreheads together for a moment, Elizabeth squeezed his hand and turned, leaving him to watch her progress to the house. Only when she was safely inside did he leave.

From a distance John and Wickham sat on their mounts. "You know their habits well. Do they meet at the stile every day?"

John finally tore his eyes from Longbourn after the door shut behind her. "On fine mornings, they do. He gives her riding lessons at Netherfield as well."

Wickham cocked a brow at him. "They certainly seemed to enjoy each other's company, although, I would say he had a burst of temper at one point, I quite feared for her."

John nodded. "You seem to be correct; he does have a violent streak about him. But she did not slap his face."

"Does she make a habit of that?" Wickham asked, and watched him flush and look away, realizing that she had indeed slapped his companion.

"She has done it before when angry."

Wickham laughed. "I would like to see that at close range, quite a lady to be tamed, eh Lucas?" John's glare made him laugh some more. "Have you been telling the truth of him to the town?"

John glanced at him. "I have told of his offences against you, and spoken of his personal habits."

The smile vanished and was replaced by a glare. "That is all?! You have not spoken of his sister's ruin? You have not told of his violent behaviour? This will not work if you do not perform your part! His sister's story and his behaviour with her is what will convince the parents to end the engagement!"

"I approached the men outside of the tavern, and I was about to tell them all, and then I saw a young girl, and thought of my sisters. I could not speak of Miss Darcy. Him, yes, I can tell of his proclivity, he is an adult, a man, but I can not hurt a child, she has borne so much already." He looked down, then back at Longbourn.

Wickham snarled at him. "She deserves to be hurt!" John's head snapped up in surprise. Wickham regained control. *It seems I will have to do the work myself, the coward!* He looked at John with disgust. "You must not want this enough, Lucas."

"Perhaps not. Perhaps I should walk away; Miss Elizabeth has made her choice. If what I have said is not enough to end it, nothing else will work. I should have just gone directly to her father; I regret what I have said in town already."

"And you will have her be his victim as well. You should rethink your priorities." John said nothing. "Well, I should take my leave. You have to attend church, I believe." He nodded and spurred his horse, and was soon gone, leaving John alone again with his thoughts.

———〰———

"Well Lizzy, how was your walk?" Mr. Bennet asked as he watched a servant take her bonnet and spencer.

"Too short." She smiled up at him and pulled off her gloves.

He crossed his arms and leaned against the doorframe to his bookroom. "Ah, you mean Mr. Darcy left too soon?" He smiled at her surprise. "Come now daughter, I am old but no fool."

She laughed then sobered. "May I speak to you, Papa?"

He stepped back and she entered the bookroom, taking a seat as he closed the door. "What is it Lizzy? Is something wrong?" He asked with concern.

"William agreed with me. The man I met yesterday at Aunt Philip's home was Mr. Wickham, the man who hurt Miss Darcy."

Mr. Bennet nodded. "I will tell your mother and sisters that he is not welcome here, and to avoid him in Meryton. There is not much else I can do. Mr. Darcy asked that I speak to him if I hear any rumours."

Elizabeth looked at her hands. "He is so worried, Papa. He wishes to leave Meryton . . . he wishes we could marry sooner." She looked up at him and saw his head shaking.

"I will not have rumours spread over your rapid marriage, Lizzy."

"But why would there be any? Everyone knows we are engaged. You said yourself that it was expected!" She stood and began to pace in agitation. "Why should Georgiana have to live in fear of seeing her seducer, and why should William have to choose between taking her away and remaining here to be close to me? Why can we not simply marry? You have agreed to the settlement, and I know he has the license!" She turned to face her father, tears were starting to form.

He tried to soothe her. "Lizzy . . . I have seen the effect of scandal on a family. I have no wish to see it again. Surely Mr. Darcy understands this, despite his impatience."

She shook her head, he did not understand. "I do not believe it is merely a case of impatience, Papa." She remembered William's worried expression, and could feel the crushing strength of his embrace.

Mr. Bennet smiled knowingly. "Ah well, not only am I not a fool, but I was also once a young man in love." His eyes grew wistful and he seemingly forgot Elizabeth's agitation. "Now, go my dear, soon your mother will appear with demands for attention. Let us enjoy our peace while we can." Elizabeth wished to question his dismissal, as well as the statement of his love for a woman, but obeyed. She sensed that the love he spoke of was not for her mother.

The Bennets arrived at church and the Netherfield coaches appeared almost at the same time. Darcy handed out Georgiana, and Richard followed, claiming her arm. Elizabeth smiled and stepped forward to accept Darcy's offer, while Jane blushed shyly at Bingley before moving to sit with their family. Bingley sighed in resignation watching her go, and then turned to escort Caroline inside. Hurst raised a brow and laughed, drawing Louisa's attention. "Well, if he would just ask to court her, he could take her inside, could he not?"

As the parties entered, Darcy's attention was focussed solely on his Elizabeth, and he missed the sudden flurry of whispers that began as they passed. Richard was more observant, and noticed heads tilting and fingers pointing. He could not make out the conversations, but simply assumed it was gossip over the betrothed couple and passed it off as typical wedding noise. As the service progressed, Richard would cast amused glances at his cousin, watching as he would stroke Elizabeth's hand as they shared the prayer book, or how he would bend his head a bit closer than necessary as they sang. Of course, he noted that she was hardly innocent either, and caught her shifting slightly so her legs touched his. Richard looked up once and noticed the amused smile on Hurst's face and rolled his eyes at him. Hurst sat back, and ignoring the sermon, listened to the fevered whispers behind him. The smile left his face and he tried his best to make out the words.

By the time they left the church, people were staring openly at Darcy, and shaking their heads sadly at Elizabeth. Mrs. Bennet thought all of the whispering was in awe of the excellent match her daughter had made, and she beamed and preened as Mr. Bennet guided her along. He had no desire to listen to the gossip of the town and wishing to get his family home quickly, led them out to his and Darcy's waiting carriages. John stood and listened to the rumours spread, and realized with some discomfort that they were already growing and worsening beyond the few truths he had told, but the news was only of Darcy, and not of Miss Darcy. He watched as Darcy handed Elizabeth into his carriage, then his sister. He hoped that exposing the truth of the man would be enough to save her in time. Elizabeth looked out of the window of the coach and their eyes met for a moment. John took it as a sign that all would be well. Elizabeth felt uncomfortable.

"Are you well?" Georgiana asked, seeing her shudder.

"Oh, of course," she smiled. "It is a little chilly today."

Darcy leaned over to Richard. "That is Lucas."

Richard observed him as they pulled away to go to Longbourn. "Ah, I see why you were able to beat him, Cousin. A very scrawny specimen." He laughed. Darcy shook his head. He would speak to Mr. Bennet about Wickham meeting Elizabeth and warn him to remain alert. After Hurst informed them of the snippets of conversation he heard in church, they were certain that the story of Wickham's lost inheritance was making the rounds of the town, but at least Mr. Bennet knew the truth of that. They could think of no good reason for Wickham to speak of Georgiana, not when Darcy and Richard could just as easily identify him as the seducer. They expected him to take revenge in some way, but thought it would come in a physical confrontation. Richard would go and speak to Colonel Forster about him in the morning, and hopefully have him agree that he did not belong in the militia, until Wickham made a move; there was little else that could be done.

———～～～———

That evening, back at Netherfield after enjoying a late supper, the men gathered in the billiards room. "You really should watch yourself, Richard." Darcy said to his cousin.

He laughed. "Am I in danger?" He looked around the room, and bent under the table, his eyes wide with feigned fright. "Are the French coming?"

Darcy rolled his eyes and Hurst and Bingley laughed. "No, Cousin, but Miss Bingley is giving you the eye."

Richard laughed louder. "Darcy, I am most assuredly not in danger of being trapped by Miss Bingley. She wants nothing of my soldier's portion. I am merely a conduit to your still-unmarried person, despite the fairly spectacular refusal you imparted upon her." He looked apologetically at Bingley. "And I assure you, she is in no danger from me."

Bingley smiled and shrugged. "I was not concerned."

"Then why do you pay her such attentions?" Darcy prodded him as he bent to take his shot.

"I did not realize I had." He missed his shot and his amusement calmed. "Come now Darcy, I did nothing beyond the bounds of propriety. I was just enjoying . . . well after all, she is the only available young woman in this house." He grinned, "Unless you hold with our dear aunt's desire that cousins marry?"

The glare Darcy delivered wiped the smile from his face. "Forgive me, Darcy. I went too far." He sighed. "I could have remained at Longbourn; there is a houseful of distracting unmarried ladies there."

Hurst poured himself some more port and walked slowly around the table, watching Darcy sink three balls with a sharp strike. He waved his glass between Bingley and Darcy. "Watch out gentlemen, he is after your ladies now."

"I believe that my Elizabeth is quite safe." Darcy's smug smile travelled the room and ended with a glare upon Richard's face.

"You did not hear how well they got along the other night." Hurst smirked. Darcy's brow rose as he remained staring at Richard. "Really?"

"Oh come now, you know Father sent me here with a purpose. You do not expect me to observe and not speak to the girl do you?" He slapped Darcy on the back. "You have absolutely nothing to fear, that woman is as loyal as my uniform is red. She may tease and have a twinkle in her eye, but her heart is yours exclusively."

Satisfied, Darcy relaxed. "Then I presume that you will report these findings to your parents?"

"I will. Her family . . . well, let us say the two youngest girls require refinement, but as for Miss Elizabeth . . . I believe that you have made an excellent choice." He grinned. "Which leaves four young ladies at Longbourn to enjoy!" He clapped his hands and rubbed them together.

It was Bingley's turn to glare. "Sir, may I remind you that Miss Jane Bennet is spoken for."

Richard cocked a brow. "Are you courting her?"

Bingley flushed. "Well, not officially."

"Have you spoken to her father?"

"Um, no, but I intend to soon." Richard grinned. "Well sir, until you do, the lady is fair game, is she not?"

Hurst and Darcy watched with interest. "How serious are you about Miss Bennet? I admit this is the longest I have seen you without a new lady on your arm for some time, but I thought that was merely because the neighbourhood had so little to offer."

Bingley spoke through clenched teeth. "You know of my intentions, Darcy!"

He bowed his head and leaned on his cue stick. "I do, and yet you make no move. Miss Bennet is probably wondering what is wrong." Bingley's eyes were full of worry. "Do you think so?"

"Expectations are high for a match, so I have heard." Hurst said. "But it seems that many mamas in the area think they still have a chance at you. You are entirely too friendly to all the ladies you meet."

"You really must curb your enthusiasm, Bingley if you are serious. I will not have my future sister hurt." Darcy's face grew serious.

"I have!" He protested.

Richard took pity on him. "I have a feeling that you and I are more alike than not, Bingley. We both enjoy the attention and company of a lady on our arm, and can not help ourselves chatting to each new one that comes along. IF you are not ready to settle down, do not let anyone push you."

"But I AM ready. I want to marry Jane!"

Darcy's brows rose, a little smile appeared on his lips. "Jane is it?" Bingley looked down.

Richard raised his glass. "To Bingley and Miss Bennet. May she say yes . . . and may he find the courage to ask the question!"

"Hear, hear!" Cried Hurst.

Bingley was still red-faced. "Come now Bingley, I will call at Longbourn for breakfast tomorrow to deliver Georgiana for her day of shopping. Ride along with us and you can speak to Mr. Bennet then." He nodded and stared at his toes.

Richard clapped his back. "Good for you, man, I envy you; she is a lovely woman."

Bingley finally looked up. "Thank you, I could not agree with you more."

Hurst made his way up the stairs to the room where slept alone each night. His relationship with Louisa had started out quite happily at first, the only son of a gentleman with an estate similar in size to Netherfield, he had expectations that were attractive to the well-to-do tradesman's daughter with aspirations of higher society. At the time of their courtship, he was far more svelte and sober; those changes came with the nearly constant presence of Louisa's sister Caroline. It stifled their intimacy, and Caroline's vindictive behaviour and overblown sense of her own worth rubbed off on her sister. Hurst missed the woman he married, but until Caroline was gone, he doubted he would have a chance to change her. So he spent his time drinking, or pretending to drink, overindulging in food, and dealing with his father's estate issues from afar, as his parents made it clear they did not want Caroline at their home either.

Hurst dismissed his valet, and hearing Louisa moving around in the next room, decided to break with precedent and visit her. He knocked on the adjoining door and heard her startled voice. "Come in?"

He stepped into the room. "Good evening, Louisa. I was surprised to hear you still awake."

"Oh, I . . . had a long talk with Caroline. I am quite tired now." She pulled the covers up to her neck and stared at him.

He shook his head and took a seat on the bed. "Do not worry, my dear. I am not here to demand my husbandly rights, although it has been quite some time." He sighed at her unwelcoming gaze. "I wished to ask you if you overheard anything odd in church this morning."

Louisa was caught off guard, and lowered the counterpane. "Odd? Do you mean, about Mr. Darcy?"

"So, you heard it too? I only caught a few words here and there, but it seemed that the tales of the summer have reached Meryton. Do you agree?"

She nodded and met his eyes. "I believe you may be correct. I heard only his name, and some reference to a living. I considered asking Caroline if she had heard it as well, but . . ."

Hurst raised his brow. "But?"

"I did not wish to hear a diatribe about Mr. Darcy's engagement. I am so sorry that I ever supported Caroline's desire to win him, especially after Miss Darcy's ruin. It was cruel to try and take advantage of him at such a terrible time, and now, he appears so happy with Miss Elizabeth."

Hurst smiled. "Louisa, what has come over you?"

She looked down at her hands. "I am tired of being angry all of the time. What do I have to be angry about? It is my own fault that I have driven you away."

Hurst reached out and took her hand. "I did nothing to help you. I chose to hide in the bottle rather than assert myself to win you back. I think that we are agreed, however, that Caroline has come between us."

Louisa looked up at him and nodded. "You are correct, but what can we do? Charles will probably marry soon, and he will not want her in his house."

Hurst laughed and Louisa looked at him with surprise. "Forgive me, my dear, it seems everyone is agreed that Bingley will marry Miss Bennet, yet he has not had the courage to ask for a courtship yet. We were just discussing that with him in the billiards room." He smiled and squeezed her hand. "Your brother is obligated to care for Caroline until she reaches the age where she will receive her inheritance or marry. He will not want her in his house, I am sure of that, but perhaps he will allow her to live in London while he is here."

"Do you wish to try and repair the damage to our marriage?" She looked back down at her hands.

Hurst nodded. "If you do." She looked back up and nodded. Hurst stood and pulled back the counterpane and slipped into the bed. He put an arm around her shoulder and drew her down beside him. Louisa lay stiffly in his embrace. "One step at a time, my dear. Tonight, we will just sleep." He heard her sigh of relief and smiled. "Tomorrow, however . . ." She gasped, and he kissed her cheek. "Good night, Louisa."

Longbourn was in an uproar. Mr. Bennet had just announced to Mrs. Bennet that Mr. Collins, the heir, would be arriving that afternoon for a fortnight visit, to extend an olive branch between the families so long separated by animosity. Mrs. Bennet was furious that the man had the audacity to come into her home, no doubt to count the silver or take inventory of the furnishings. It was only when Mr. Bennet mentioned his surmise that Mr. Collins was also interested in a bride that Mrs. Bennet's angry mutterings ceased.

"A bride, Mr. Bennet? From one of our girls?"

He contained his smirk. "Indeed, Mr. Collins counts out several times in his letter the number of daughters we have. I should think that one mention was quite enough, however, he chose to speak of it three times. I look forward to meeting such a verbose and enthusiastic gentleman." He smiled at Elizabeth. "Unfortunately I will have to inform him that his choices are only four daughters, as one is decidedly taken, is that not correct, Lizzy?"

"Quite decidedly." She said with determination. Jane looked down and twisted her hands sadly. Elizabeth patted her back and whispered softly. "Jane, it is clear that Mr. Bingley favours you, he has called regularly over the past month, and has been here so much that he could not possibly have time to call on other ladies. I am sure that he does not want to rush into things, and wants to be sure that you both know your feelings before approaching you, after all a courtship is a very serious step."

She looked up hopefully then back down. "I suppose you are correct, I guess that seeing you so happy with Mr. Darcy makes me wish for my own time. I do not want him to rush to pay his addresses."

Elizabeth leaned in close. "Oh yes you do!" She grinned at Jane's small smile and squeezed her hand.

A sudden flurry of activity at the door announced the arrival of the Darcys and to Jane's delight, Mr. Bingley. He bowed and stammered and then turned to Mr. Bennet. "Sir, may I have a moment of Miss Bennet's time before breakfast?" Mr.

Bennet raised a brow and his lips twitched. "I was not aware that you were invited, sir."

Bingley grew pale. "Forgive me, I will leave immediately after we speak, but I can not wait any longer."

Elizabeth stared at her father expressively and he relented. "Very well, Mr. Bingley, Jane would you come this way?" The three disappeared down the hallway and Elizabeth walked over to greet Georgiana and William.

"You were successful, I see." She whispered as he lovingly kissed her hand. He laughed. "It took all three of us, and some threats by Richard to come courting your sister, but he finally made a decision."

"I am not so sure that I want such an indecisive man marrying my sister." She shook her head in exasperation.

Darcy pressed her hand between both of his and smiled into her dancing eyes. "Oh, he is much improved, I assure you. He will make a fine husband for Jane."

"I choose to trust you then, sir."

Georgiana was watching their interaction. "My brother is always trustworthy, Elizabeth. He abhors deceit. You must always believe what he says."

Elizabeth tilted her head. "Must I?"

His brows rose. "Of course, my dear. Everything I ever say is the absolute truth, and of course, always correct." Elizabeth began to laugh heartily at the idea. "I will have to remember that declaration for future use!" Darcy glanced around the room and bent to quickly kiss her lips.

"William!" She admonished.

He grinned. "Your father is engaged."

"Hmm. Well, it seems one of my sisters is due to be engaged to our houseguest." She led them to some chairs and explained about Mr. Collins.

"Elizabeth, do you realize that this man is my aunt's pastor?"

"Lady Catherine?" Darcy nodded and looked at Georgiana, who grew white. Darcy turned to Elizabeth with panicked eyes. Elizabeth immediately moved to the sofa where she sat and put her arm around her. "Certainly you can not fear my foolish cousin, Georgiana."

"Oh, but he will tell her of your engagement."

Elizabeth looked at Darcy. "Is that a problem?"

"I do not see how it is; she certainly can do nothing to stop us. She will simply be learning the news sooner than I had anticipated." He smiled and patted Georgiana. "All is well."

Inside of the bookroom, Jane stood blushing before Bingley. Mr. Bennet stood outside of the closed door, watch in hand. He decided to give Bingley five minutes.

Bingley ran his hand nervously through his hair, then cast his eyes around the room, looking everywhere but at Jane. "Um . . . Miss Bennet, I . . ." He stopped and sighed. "I . . . oh why is this so hard?!" He finally looked at her and saw that her eyes were cast down, and her hands were twisting in agitation. The realization that she was just as nervous occurred to him. "Miss Bennet . . . please look at me."

Jane's eyes slowly travelled up from the floor, she saw his finely polished boots, his green breeches, the matching topcoat, a cream silk waistcoat, then the stickpin in his cravat and finally rested on his wide green eyes. She swallowed hard and saw his expression. He was nervous and hopeful, just as she was. It gave her some strength. "Yes, Mr. Bingley?" She whispered.

"Oh Miss Bennet, I am such a fool." Bingley ran his hand through his hair, and then rubbed it on his coat. "I have come here, tagging along with Darcy for weeks, thinking that I was lending my shy friend moral support as he tried to court your sister. What a fool I was! He was engaged to her the moment he came here! He needed my help as much as . . . as much as your mother needs prodding to speak of finding husbands for her daughters!"

Jane giggled and hid her smile by looking down. "But you see, Miss Bennet, in the course of coming with my friend, I . . . I have also come to . . . like you." He bit his lip and tried to see her eyes. "I have known so many ladies, and enjoy meeting new people and talking to them . . . my . . . my friends have questioned that. Why Darcy has told me many times that I . . . well, that is neither here nor there . . . the point is since coming to Hertfordshire, you are the only lady who has . . . attracted my attention." Jane looked up at him, confused but still listening. "I have known for weeks that I felt an attraction to you that I have never experienced with any woman before. I suppose I was simply enjoying it so much that I . . . I did not realize that I should speak to you. I . . . I have never really considered attempting a courtship, and I . . . I never thought that my friendly behaviour would be seen as anything other than that . . . especially as we have only known each other such a short time and in all of my previous friendships nobody expressed any expectations . . . but I believe that you are the woman I once declared to Darcy I was searching for. I am a fool because I did not readily recognize this, and it took a roomful of men and the threat from one of them to take you away to force me to come here today." He drew a breath. "Miss Bennet, will you do me the honour of allowing me to court you?"

Jane swallowed and thought over his rambling speech. This is what she had been waiting to hear, and what she dreamed of every time she saw Darcy and Elizabeth together, but she had to ask one question. "You were coerced to speak to me?" She said softly.

Bingley shook his head. "Did I say that?" He laughed. "That is a sentence more worthy of Darcy's tripping tongue. I can see him complimenting and disparaging his object all at once and thinking it was all perfectly fine because he was honest." Sighing he met her eye. "I am avoiding your question, forgive me. No, I did not need to be coerced; I was just too stupid to see what was in front of me. My friends simply chose a particularly pointed way of forcing me to acknowledge what I already knew. I think that you are the loveliest, sweetest young woman I have ever met, and I hope you might care for me a little, and I hope with all of my heart that you will accept my offer of courtship and we may see where it leads us. Will you accept me?"

Jane blushed. "Yes, Mr. Bingley, I will. Thank you so much." Bingley raised her hand to his lips and kissed it fervently. Before anything else could be said, Mr. Bennet opened the door.

"Breakfast is ready." The beaming smile on Bingley's face and Jane's blush answered his conjecture; the boy had finally made his move. Mr. Bennet's lips twitched. *It is about time, sir.*

Chapter 24

"*M*ama, have you heard the rumours about Mr. Darcy and Miss Darcy?" Charlotte asked Lady Lucas.

She put down the menus she was studying and looked up at her daughter, then at the open door to the hallway. Charlotte caught the glance and quickly closing it, took a chair near her mother. "What exactly have you heard?"

Charlotte looked at her hands. "Maria and I walked into Meryton this morning; that is where I heard . . . I understand that Miss Darcy is ruined. She tried to elope with a man, and that Mr. Darcy caught them and killed him. I believe that Miss Darcy was left with child and that Mr. Darcy employed . . . methods learned from his mistress to rid her of the child." She looked up. "Oh Mama, do you think that he physically harmed the poor girl? I have heard of women throwing themselves down stairs or being . . . beaten." She swallowed. "I can not imagine Mr. Darcy being so violent towards his sister."

Lady Lucas took her hand. "I would hope that these are merely the imaginations of gossips, my dear. As much as I wanted Eliza to marry John, I can see how deeply attached she is to Mr. Darcy. I would hope that she has not been charmed into accepting a man who would prove to be so violent."

"But even if he did not . . . hurt his sister, she is so quiet."

"Well, she is likely being shunned by society. There is always some truth at the bottom of gossip. I imagine that Miss Darcy did try to elope with some man." Lady Lucas sat back. "She is but fifteen, and likely has an impressive dowry, I wonder what could have driven her to do such a thing?"

"But that is it, Mama! Mr. Darcy must be a horror to live with! What might he do to Eliza if he lost his temper? Oh, I fear for her, Mama!" Charlotte sat back and wrapped her arms around herself.

"Charlotte, do you know why John had a bruised jaw?" Charlotte shook her head. "John was trying to force his attentions on Eliza. Mr. Darcy came upon them after witnessing him grabbing at her. Mr. Darcy was fully justified in his response, which is why you have heard nothing from your father, or even John about it."

Charlotte was shocked at her brother's behaviour, but could not let go the things she had heard. "He has mistresses."

Lady Lucas smiled slightly. "While distasteful, it is not uncommon, my dear." She patted Charlotte's hand. "You certainly are gaining an education today."

"I feel that I should go and visit Eliza. Perhaps she has not heard these things."

"Are you going to be of aid or to crow that Mr. Darcy is unworthy? I know how much you wished her to marry John, just as I did. And I even had hopes that Mr. Darcy and Mr. Bingley would choose you or Maria, but it is clear that their attention was drawn to Longbourn." She shook her head. "No, Charlotte. You would be most unwelcome. Besides that, Mr. Darcy has done our own family a great service, and I can not forget that."

"What has he done?" Charlotte asked with confusion.

"In truth, it is what he has not done. He easily could have spoken against John's behaviour towards Eliza, and even made a greater issue over the hunting incident. He could have told the neighbourhood and hurt our family with scandal, but he chose to speak to your father quietly, and walk away. No, I will not fuel these rumours that we are hearing, if anything, Mr. Darcy's behaviour makes me wonder of the truth of these rumours against him and who suddenly started them. I have been guilty of spreading stories in the past; it was not until now that I realized the impact a small tale expanded by many tongues can have on a family." She shook her head. "I will not disparage him, or his sister, and I hope that you will hold your tongue as well. I will tell the same to Maria."

Charlotte sat quietly and thought over her mother's words. "But if Eliza is in danger . . ."

"I believe that her father is the best judge of that, not we." Lady Lucas paused. "I wished for John to marry Eliza because it was the match he wanted, and she is such a wonderful girl. Her dowry is not too significant, but enough for John if he was to be happy. I pushed too hard when it was clear that Eliza was not interested, I admit, but that is a mother's prerogative. You pushed the match quite hard yourself, and I have wondered, why do you believe that John would throw you from our home if your father died? He certainly would not dare to send me away, and I would not stand for him doing that to you."

"It is just little things that he has said through the years, how he looked forward to running the estate his way, without so many family members about. He said he would be sure to marry off Maria and me to have plenty of room for his children . . ." She looked up at her mother. "It frightened me."

Lady Lucas sat up. "I will speak to your father about this. I will make sure that he stipulates in his will that John must take care of his unmarried sisters. Will that reassure you? I have a feeling though that your brother was not thinking clearly of the impact of his words when he spoke."

"Thank you, Mama. Should I go and speak to Eliza?"

Her mother shook her head. "No, I think that on this subject, Lucas Lodge should remain silent."

"Thank you so much for asking me to come with you today, Elizabeth." Georgiana said softly when they all sat down for breakfast. "I was not looking forward to another day with Miss Bingley."

"Is she rude to you?" Elizabeth asked with concern. Darcy, sitting on Elizabeth's right leaned closer to listen.

Georgiana glanced at Bingley then said in a low voice. "No, not exactly, but she seems to be less friendly now. I hope that I have done nothing to offend her, but I can not imagine what it would be."

Elizabeth glanced at William whose eyes had narrowed. "I am sure it is nothing that you have done, but rather something that your brother has done." She smiled and felt William's hand creep onto her lap and take hers.

"What do you mean?" Georgiana looked at him and saw his smile.

"I chose Elizabeth, Georgiana. Miss Bingley need not fall all over you anymore. This is a good thing, is it not? I believe that she has been keeping much to herself of late."

Bingley smiled at Georgiana then at Darcy. "Indeed she has. If I knew that the way to silence her was to take away her funds and her object of prey, I would have done it years ago!"

"Object of prey!" Elizabeth smiled up at William and he squeezed her hand. "How did it feel to be hunted?"

"I hated it. I am delighted to only belong to you now." He raised her hand to his lips and bestowed a kiss.

"AHEM!" Mr. Bennet cleared his throat. "Not at my dining table, please Mr. Darcy. I suspect the purpose of your frequent assignations with my daughter, but I have no wish to observe them."

Elizabeth and Darcy blushed. "Forgive me, sir." She caught his eye and winked, and he bit his lip.

Mr. Bennet watched them and shook his head, then turned to Bingley. "Well sir, I was surprised to have you join our little family party this morning. Tell me is there a purpose to this or can you not bear to be separated from your friend?"

Bingley's eyes grew wide and he looked to Darcy, who was suppressing a smile. He glanced over at Jane then swallowed. "Yes sir, I hoped to speak to you privately this morning on a matter of great importance."

Mr. Bennet's brows rose. "Indeed?" He saw Jane blushing bright red. "Well, sir, I look forward to hearing you, and might I add, it is about time."

This time Darcy laughed, which drew the attention of the rest of the table. "Mr. Darcy, what brings on your levity?" Mrs. Bennet asked indulgently.

He looked at the pleading eyes of his friend and relented. "I am merely delighted with your daughter's good humour, Mrs. Bennet, and I look forward to spending my life listening to her."

Elizabeth tilted her head and grinned. "Is that so, sir? Well, I will have to be sure to entertain you daily."

"Ah Mr. Darcy, you are a good man to wish to take on my Lizzy." Mr. Bennet smirked.

He smiled. "Yes, I am." Elizabeth pinched his leg and he jumped.

Leaning down he whispered, "Miss Elizabeth, I will exact my retribution for your behaviour."

She stroked his leg where she had inflicted the pinch, and he closed his eyes. "Oh, yes sir, I am certain you will." Darcy's hand lay atop hers and their eyes met.

"Ahem." Mr. Bennet coughed.

When the meal was finished, Bingley followed Mr. Bennet into his bookroom and the rest of the family had only just taken their seats in the sitting room when the pair returned. "I am pleased to announce that Mr. Bingley has asked my permission to openly court Jane, and I have granted it. I assume daughter that this pleases you?" Jane blushed and nodded her head and Bingley immediately claimed a seat next to her.

Mrs. Bennet crowed. "Yes, yes, it is all going as I planned. Did I not say this summer that Mr. Bingley would wish for Jane?" She looked around the room, and noticed that nobody was paying her any attention.

"Congratulations, Bingley!" Darcy shook his hand. "Jane, I am happy for you. I assure you that my friend is a good man."

She smiled. "I have no doubt of that at all, sir." Bingley puffed up like a peacock, and the four friends laughed.

"I am sorry that we will be leaving soon Mr. Bingley, so your time with Jane will be short today."

"No, Miss Elizabeth, I will gladly relinquish her for such a good purpose. I understand that you are to purchase your wedding clothes today?"

"Yes, and I think that I am very fortunate to have Georgiana here to help me. She knows what a lady needs far better than I." She squeezed her hand. "I am counting on you."

Georgiana's face broke out in a wide smile and she looked at Darcy who was nodding his head. "Really? Oh, why thank you, Elizabeth!"

Darcy caught Elizabeth's eye and mouthed, "Thank you."

Elizabeth was pleased to realize that with William and Bingley also riding in the carriage, there would be no room to include Lydia and Kitty on the trip to the dressmaker. Her sisters' complaints fell on deaf ears, as Mrs. Bennet was so delighted with the chance to ride in such a magnificent carriage, she chose not to listen to them. Instead she granted permission for them to visit Maria Lucas and they immediately left the house. The rest of the party was just readying to depart when Mrs. Philips arrived in a breathless flurry, and visibly balking at the sight of Darcy and narrowing her eyes at Georgiana, grabbed Mrs. Bennet and whispered urgently in her ear.

Darcy looked at Elizabeth who shrugged and continued putting on her gloves. Mrs. Bennet turned to her with a red face. "Lizzy, you just go on to the dressmaker without me. I am sure that you will be fine." Elizabeth stared at her mother then at Jane.

"Are you sure, Mama? I know how you were looking forward to this."

"No, no, you go on. I have more important matters that require my attention. Really Lizzy, you are always thinking of yourself!" She pushed them along and closed the door behind them.

The group stood in confusion on the porch. "What was that about?" Elizabeth asked Jane. "I am always thinking of myself?"

Jane shrugged. "Perhaps Aunt Philips has some news."

"Gossip you mean. It must be something very exciting to keep Mama from shopping."

"I do not know, but Lizzy, are you not grateful?"

The girls smiled at each other and Elizabeth slipped her arm onto William's. "It seems we have been given a reprieve from lace and ribbons, let us escape while we can!" Darcy laughed and handed her up into the carriage, followed by Georgiana. Bingley reserved the honour of taking Jane's hand for himself. The group was on their way for the short ride to Meryton. The coach received a great deal of attention as it rolled into town, and Elizabeth thought that it was due to the fine quality of the equipage, rather than who was inside. They arrived at the shop and Darcy jumped out to hand the ladies down. He whispered to Elizabeth and rejoined Bingley. The coach would take them to Netherfield and return to await the ladies.

Inside of the shop, all went as expected, fabrics were chosen, and not one argument over lace was heard. Georgiana made quiet suggestions, and Jane helped Elizabeth choose patterns. The dressmaker seemed to hover more than usual, and seemed very interested in Georgiana, but once she realized how many gowns were being ordered, she was all business. After hours of endless choosing they finally emerged to enter the coach. None of the ladies noticed that upon their exit from the shop, fingers were pointing and heads were coming together in consultation.

"Colonel! Welcome, it is an honour to see you again, sir!" Colonel Forster smiled and shook Richard's hand with enthusiasm. "Have you grown tired of the gentleman's life and crave the company of soldiers?"

Richard looked about the large tent that served as the militia's office and grinned. "Ah, the smell of camp, it stirs one to battle." The two colonels laughed.

"Well, let us hope that neither one of us sees it very soon, me in particular, if my militia is truly called to defend England then we are in trouble."

"I can not but agree, sir." Richard lifted the glass of brandy that a lieutenant set in front of him before disappearing. "May your skirmishes be limited to feuds between farmers!" Colonel Forster laughed and lifted his own glass, "And may yours be eliminated by Napoleon's permanent defeat!"

Downing the drink, Richard set down the empty glass and leaned back comfortably. "Tell me sir, how do you like your group of volunteers?"

Forster rolled his eyes. "We make due with what we are given, a few are here as a career, the rest are simply here for an obligation. There is not a great deal to do. We require a bit of training everyday, just to keep the order and remind the men why they are here, but well, as I told you before, I try to keep the men busy during the day."

Richard nodded. "I understand; there is not really a great deal for the regulars at this time either." He sat up and decided to come to his point. "Sir, I have become aware that you have a lieutenant in your militia who is of very questionable character."

"I daresay I have a great many of that description, sir. Is there one in particular to whom you refer?"

He sighed. "Indeed, Wickham, George Wickham." Richard watched as the colonel thought.

"Ah, yes, Wickham, joined up about a month or so ago, when we were still in Brighton." He frowned. "What is his offence?"

"He makes a habit of running up large debts of honour, as well as leaving behind debts with local merchants."

"Ah, one of those." He ran his hand through his hair. "And my superiors wonder why the coming of a militia into town is not met with open arms." He returned his gaze to Richard. "I have a feeling though that there is more to it than debts?"

Richard laughed harshly and stood. "Yes sir, there is." He stepped to the entrance of the tent and looked out, then returned. He bent near Forster. "You met my cousin Darcy; Wickham enjoys claiming that my cousin cheated him of an inheritance from his father, a living. He does not tell the additional facts that he actually refused the living and accepted a generous compensation for it. He prefers to play on the sympathies of the populace." Richard tilted his head. "Have you heard this story told? My cousin had it repeated to him recently, so Wickham is certainly at work spreading it about."

Forster shook his head. "No, I have heard nothing of it . . . let me call in some of the men, they are more likely to hear such things than I." The colonel called for several men to be found and brought in. While they waited he watched Richard. "Sir, what else?" He asked quietly.

"This is between officers." Forster rose and shook his hand.

"Wickham attempted an elopement with an innocent this summer, and was stopped before reaching Scotland."

Forster's eyes narrowed, and he became angry. "Scum! I will not have him in my militia! Do you have sure knowledge of this?"

Richard nodded grimly. "Yes, I was witness to his dissuasion." He flexed his fist in the memory and Forster watched him with understanding.

Three men arrived in the tent. "Denny, Marks, Jones, you are friends of Wickham are you not?" Forster demanded.

"Yes sir!" The three replied, and then shot glances at each other. "Has he been telling tales of how he was cheated of an inheritance?" They all nodded. "Has he been successful at the gaming tables?"

Marks snorted than straightened. "Sorry sir, he was caught cheating once so we all watch him now. Since then he's been losing badly. He has quite a fair number of accounts to settle when the pay comes around."

Forster looked to the other men. "And what of in town? How is he with the merchants?"

Denny's brows furrowed. "Well we have not been here all that long, sir, I could not say. I think he owed some in Brighton, but I'm sure he cleared that up before we left."

Richard spoke for the first time. "And the ladies, how does he treat them?"

Denny again spoke. "He likes them, enjoys the maids in the taverns, and he's kind of sweet on the Bennet girl, Miss Lydia. I went with him to pay a call on her other sister, Miss Kitty a few days ago."

Forster saw the fire brewing in Richard's eyes. "Very well then, you are dismissed." They glanced at each other and quickly departed. Forster sighed and sat down. "It seems that your claims are correct. I will have to speak to him personally, of course, and check with the merchants in Meryton and Brighton, but I would say that it seems that Mr. Wickham does not belong in my militia."

"Good, I am glad that you see that, he would only become a black mark on your record."

Fixing him with a penetrating stare, Forster asked, "Was it your family that he hurt?" Richard returned the stare and nodded. "Too many times." He bowed and left the tent. Forster called his lieutenant in to give orders that Wickham be sent to him as soon as he returned to camp. In the meantime, he would write to officers still stationed in Brighton.

"Oh Mr. Bennet!!" Mrs. Bennet had no sooner seen her sister out the door than she was inside of the bookroom and had slammed the door shut.

"What on earth is the matter?" He had been attempting to ignore the caterwauling from his wife's sitting room, located just above his head and rejoiced when it stopped, only to be startled from his book.

"Mr. Bennet! My sister has just brought me the most horrible news! Mr. Darcy, the very man who has plans to marry our Lizzy, Mr. Darcy is a cad, a rake, a man of disrepute, and oh, Mr. Bennet, a horrible violent man!! I will not have my daughter go to a man who will beat her! No! I can overlook many vices to have my daughters settled, but violence, no! You must end this engagement immediately!!"

"WOMAN!" Mr. Bennet roared, and instantly Mrs. Bennet's tirade stopped and she stood before his desk, twisting her handkerchief in agitation. "What foolishness has your sister told you?"

Mrs. Bennet proceeded to expound on the litany of accusations against Darcy and Georgiana, from the cheated inheritance, to the elopement, to his amorous encounters, and finally, dramatically, to the regular beatings he delivered upon his sister in anger for ruining their name. Mr. Bennet closed his eyes, and listened; when Mrs. Bennet finally quieted he looked to his agitated wife, who was now fanning herself energetically. "Mrs. Bennet. It is fortunate for us that I am in possession of the facts of this case. I assure you that Mr. Darcy is none of those things that you describe. He is a good man, and Lizzy is fortunate to have found him."

"Do not be ridiculous Mr. Bennet! His sister is ruined, absolutely!"

Mr. Bennet nodded. "I do not dispute that fact. Miss Darcy did attempt an elopement this summer; she is ruined in the eyes of society. There is no hiding from that. However the details that you describe are grossly incorrect. Mr. Darcy did not shoot the man; in fact he was in this very house, only days ago."

"Here?" She stared at him in shock.

"Yes, Mrs. Bennet. Mr. Wickham, the soldier you so favoured for our Lydia is the man who was supposedly cheated of his bequest, and also attempted to elope with Miss Darcy. As you see he is very much alive. Also, for this reason he will never be allowed in this house again, and I will forbid any daughters of mine to ever speak to him."

"But . . . but what of the child?" She whispered, clutching her breast. "Mr. Darcy beat his sister!"

Mr. Bennet stood. "No, there was no child. Mr. Darcy found them before she could be harmed by Mr. Wickham. Where did your sister hear this news?"

"In town yesterday afternoon, all of Meryton must know by now! Why did I not hear any of this at church?"

Mr. Bennet studied her. "I imagine it was because you were entirely occupied in telling Lady Lucas of Lizzy's fortune in securing Mr. Darcy. I believe that you held her attention exclusively the entire time, and then we left the church before you could expound to any others." He looked out the window, and saw a curricle pulling in and sighed. "It seems our cousin has arrived, Mrs. Bennet." He turned to her. "Not a word of this is to be spoken. I will not tolerate it. Mr. Darcy is a good man, no matter what the gossips may say. I can only wonder what started the talk." He bent down and put his arms on the chair where she sat. "You are aware Mrs. Bennet, of the effect of scandal on a family; it is in your best interest to keep this to yourself. I will not have my daughters suffer as my sister did. Do I make myself clear?"

Mrs. Bennet nodded and sniffed. "Yes, Mr. Bennet. If you are satisfied, then I am sure that Mr. Darcy is a fine man. But will his sister's ruin hurt our girls?"

He straightened up and sighed. "I do not believe so. Mr. Bingley certainly knows of it, and he wants our Jane, so I am not in fear of the other girls losing opportunities." He took her hand and helped her to her feet. "Now, wipe your eyes, and let us greet our guest. Perhaps he may be interested in one, and we will only have two left to worry over." Mrs Bennet's eyes brightened at the prospect and they exited the room to meet the effusions of Mr. Collins.

John sat in the tap room at the Meryton inn, listening to the buzz of conversation around him. Various friends came up to talk, and the only subject of interest seemed to be Eliza and how terrible it was that she would be tied to Mr. Darcy. Others talked of the sister, seen only at church and during the one dinner at Lucas Lodge. The talk of her was terrible, and the people seemed to relish it. John felt ill. He wanted to get Elizabeth safely away from Darcy, not to further disparage a young girl. He thought of his young sister Maria, and knew that she would never recover from hearing the words that were being thrown around about Miss Darcy. He was horrified to realize that Wickham had obviously taken matters into his own hands. John had not spoken a word about Darcy since meeting Wickham on Sunday morning. He waived off some more acquaintances and stared down into his empty tankard, things were spiralling out of control.

A man slipping into the booth made him look up and see Wickham. He had just returned from a thorough interrogation by Colonel Forster, and it was clear that his days of welcome in the militia were numbered. He could not think of why, unless some of the men he owed money had complained to his commander. He never meant to stay in long, and now he just wanted to finish this situation with Darcy, then he would be ready to go. "Well, it seems the news has spread quite rapidly."

John studied him, Wickham's teeth were slightly bared, and a look of satisfaction was on his face. "It seems that you have been busy, it has taken on a life of its own. Why did you speak of Miss Darcy?"

"You did not have the courage to speak the truth, so I did." Wickham laughed. "I thought that you wished to save the fair Miss Elizabeth from Darcy. You have changed your mind?"

John looked at him, not at all liking being the subject of his humour. "I do not wish to see her or Miss Darcy hurt. I wished to limit the exposure to telling the truth about his offences against you."

He met Wickham's amused brow. "I believe it will undoubtedly hurt both of them, but you will certainly be there to comfort Miss Elizabeth, will you not? Or are you afraid of Darcy?"

"He is no longer alone, his cousin is here."

Wickham sat up straight. "Cousin? A colonel?"

John nodded, and watched with great interest the changing expression on Wickham's face. "I saw him in church yesterday."

Wickham sat back again. Now he knew the source of his trouble in the militia. Fitzwilliam had been there. The window of opportunity was closing rapidly. He needed to learn more of Elizabeth, and it seemed his stooge would not be of use for much longer. "Tell me, what is it that drives you towards this girl? I met her, I rather enjoyed the experience, in fact, I would welcome a great deal of experiences with her. . ." He saw John's eyes narrow. "As I am sure Darcy already has. You have seen them together enough times, Lucas; you see how compliant she is with him. Do you not imagine what she would be like in your embrace?" He nodded, grinning. "Ah, so you do, I can see it in your eyes. You often imagine the feel of her skin against yours, her muff opening to your stick; I daresay you think on it constantly."

John glared. "I will not have you speak about her in such a vulgar manner!"

Wickham bent his head in contrition. "Then what is it? Why not approach one of the other ladies of the neighbourhood? Surely you must be of interest to them?"

"I am." John shook his head and opened his soul to the devil. "I have known Eliza for all of my life. She and I spent countless hours wandering the fields and lanes, climbing trees, imagining adventures of all sorts. She had no brothers, and her sisters were not at all interested in such things. And she read so many wonderful stories that her imagination was just . . ." He looked down. "I was a lad who had a wonderful playmate. Of course, I had to leave for school when I was twelve, and when I came home on holiday, she was deemed too old to be playing with a boy my age, it was no longer proper, so I only saw her from afar. I watched her grow up into the beauty she is today. We always danced together at the assemblies, and it was all in good fun, but when I returned from graduation . . . I . . . . well, she was not only beautiful but so different from every other girl. She knew who I was, and what I had, and treated me with friendship and laughter, and teased me. No other woman does that, they all worry about my fortune or what I can do for them, Eliza just cared about the person I was." His eyes grew bright. "And arrogant fool that I was, I did not recognize that. I came home from school thinking I could have any woman, my inflated self-worth . . . I had a treasure in my grasp and I let her slip away by acting a boy. Eliza needs a man. A man she can respect and love. She did not want a boy." He spoke bitterly.

Wickham regarded him speculatively. He could not appreciate the sentiment behind the confession, but he did recognize the power of emotion and behaviour. "She seems quite worth the effort then." John nodded his head. "And Darcy was the man, as you say, who came along and took her away, and now you know what he is truly like. But you are the man who will save her from the life Miss Darcy suffers. Miss Elizabeth may not appreciate it now, but you are doing her and her family a great service. These rumours have undoubtedly spread to her home by now. Do you really think that her family will allow this engagement to continue?" Wickham met his eye. "You are doing the right thing by her."

"Not if it will hurt them. I should have gone to Mr. Bennet directly with this information. This idea of yours to spread gossip, I should not have listened to you . . . I should have let her go, let her find her own way. I should have listened to her. Maybe my pushing drove her to the first man who paid her attention. I do not deserve her any more than Darcy. I should just go to Mr. Bennet now."

"The work is finished, friend. He surely knows. Now you may reap the benefits."

"I do not want them. I do not deserve her." John looked up to see the sardonic smile on Wickham's face and made his decision. *Tomorrow I will go and speak to Mr. Bennet.*

The coach containing the three ladies stopped at Netherfield first to drop off Georgiana. Elizabeth insisted that be done so that the young girl did not have to travel alone back from Longbourn. As much as she hoped that William would be there, she knew that he and Mr. Bingley were to visit a neighbouring estate for a hunt that afternoon, and would not be home for many hours. It was disappointing, but with the news of Mr. Collins arriving, it was likely for the best. They should greet their cousin without being surrounded by other guests.

Elizabeth and Jane passed back through the village and once again the coach was the subject of great interest. "Why do they stare so?" Jane wondered. "Surely this coach is familiar to everyone by now; after all, Mr. Darcy has been here for over a month."

"It is strange, but I can not imagine the reason either." Elizabeth watched the groups of people pointing and talking. "I suppose some sort of gossip about my engagement, perhaps? Remember all of the neighbours who came to the house to speak to Mama after the assembly?"

Jane smiled. "I am sure that is it."

"Perhaps they will do the same now that you are being courted, Jane." Elizabeth squeezed her hand. "What did Mr. Bingley say to you?" Jane blushed and shook her head. "Oh no, Jane Bennet; I have shared my letters from William with you. It is only fair that I hear of Mr. Bingley's words." She crossed her arms and stared at her. "We will be home soon, so be quick about it!"

'Oh Lizzy, you are such a bother sometimes!" Jane complained. "All right, Mr. Bingley closed the door, and . . . said that he was a fool and begged me to allow him to court me."

She tilted her head. "That is all?"

Biting her lip, Jane nodded. "He tried to explain his delay in asking, he was very sweet, tripping over his words and chastising himself, he was afraid of offending me while telling me his feelings . . . Why are you laughing?"

Elizabeth was trying hard to keep a straight face. "Oh Jane, forgive me, but I do think that you two will get on very well together."

"Do you think me a fool?" She looked offended.

Elizabeth wiped her eyes and hugged her. "No, dear Jane, I think that you and Mr. Bingley are both very sweet and neither one of you would ever want to cause any person offence."

She looked confused. "Well of course not, why would we?" Elizabeth was saved from her answer by their arrival at Longbourn. They entered the house where they were greeted by their mother.

Mrs. Bennet took Elizabeth's hands. "Oh my dear, come and tell me of your day."

"Mama, I would be happy to . . . but has our cousin arrived?" She could hear an unfamiliar male voice coming from the sitting room.

Mrs. Bennet closed her eyes. "Miserable little man."

Elizabeth exchanged a surprised glance with Jane. "You do not like Mr. Collins?"

"Oh, I suppose someone will have to . . . perhaps Mary would like him, she is so fond of her sermons, after all." Mrs. Bennet bit her lip and looked back at the room. "He was most disappointed to hear that you and Jane were quite attached. I suppose he expected to have the pick of the litter!"

Elizabeth and Jane stifled their laughter and Elizabeth touched her arm. "Mama, I do not recognize you!"

Mrs. Bennet looked at her soberly. "Come Lizzy, we must talk. Your father will wish to speak to you as well, but I want to see you first. Jane, you go in and meet your cousin."

Elizabeth followed her mother upstairs and into her bedchamber. "Lizzy, your aunt Philips came this morning." She nodded. "She brought me news from town, about Miss Darcy and your Mr. Darcy . . ." She proceeded to tell her the conversation. Elizabeth's anger flared, and she began to pace about the room in agitation.

Mrs. Bennet watched in fascination and startled when an expression of sudden enlightenment came over her daughter's face. "That explains the odd behaviour in town."

"What do you mean?" Mrs. Bennet asked with confusion.

"People were pointing at the carriage." She resumed her pacing. William needed to know about this, but she would not see him until he and Mr. Bingley came for dinner tomorrow.

"Oh my." Mrs. Bennet began wringing her handkerchief. "Lizzy, do you believe any of the tales about Mr. Darcy? I will demand that the engagement be broken if you fear him."

Elizabeth could not say that she was completely surprised; she knew that she was hardly her mother's favourite child, but she also knew that despite her desperate desire to see her children settled, she did love them. She felt more touched than anything, and stopped her movement to take her mother's hand. "Mama, I assure you, Mr. Darcy is the best of men. Do not believe a word of this gossip about him, please."

"Your father said the same, but I wished to hear it from you." Mrs. Bennet raised her chin. "Well then, we will just see what those gossips say when you are married and living in his grand estate, and their girls are lucky to win a clerk from a counting house"

Smiling at her sudden change in support for William, Elizabeth said gently, "There are many good men who are clerks, Mama, and you may win one as a son someday."

"That may be, but none of them will have jewels like that necklace Mr. Darcy gave you!"

Elizabeth left her mother after hearing her raptures once again about her pin money and carriages to go to her bedchamber, and wrote William a long note, telling him of the gossip in town. Georgiana was to come visit in the morning, and they had planned to walk into Meryton as a rare adventure for the girl, but she asked him if they should now forgo that plan. She sealed up the note and gave it to a servant to take over to Netherfield. She knew he was not there, so she did not ask that a reply be given. Caroline was passing the front door when the note arrived, and told the butler that she would take charge of it. She saw that it was from Longbourn, and knew it was from Elizabeth. She had no desire to read her love letters to Darcy, but she also felt he could do without them as well. She walked past the burning fire and casually dropped the letter in with a satisfied smile.

Chapter 25

*G*eorgiana arrived at Longbourn in time for breakfast. Darcy was miserable watching her go, wanting to climb into the coach with her instead of Mrs. Annesley who would ride along then return with the coach to Netherfield, but he had promised a morning for Bingley to help him understand matters of the estate. Richard and Hurst would occupy themselves with billiards during that time, then they were all going to go shooting in the afternoon before Bingley, Darcy, and Richard travelled to Longbourn for dinner. Hurst said that he and Louisa had plans to eat dinner with Caroline and retire early. Georgiana delivered a note for Elizabeth, which she fully expected. It was sweet and loving, and he missed her, but made no mention at all of the gossip, or of any objections to them walking into Meryton.

"I thought he would be incensed." She tucked the note inside of her gown and followed the rest of the family back into the sitting room after they ate, thinking all the way. *Should we go? William certainly would have made it clear that we should not go if he was worried somebody would approach us. I am sure that nobody would say anything to Georgiana, why, she is practically a stranger here, and so young, but . . . what of me? Would they say anything to me?* She thought and thought, and could not remember any instances where a person was publicly accosted over any rumour. *Perhaps there were people whispering behind their back, but they were safe . . .* She nodded and looked at the smiling girl, anticipating her adventure. *No, everything will be just fine, nobody bothered us yesterday after all, and the gossip was certainly known then. William is correct not to worry, and tonight we can talk about all of this and decide what should be done. We certainly should not hide away as if we are guilty of something.*

The evening before, when Mr. Bennet invited Mr. Collins into his bookroom for a glass of port, the obsequious little man tried to impress upon him that his fair cousin Miss Elizabeth could not possibly be engaged to Mr. Darcy, the nephew of his esteemed and noble patroness, as he knew that he was in fact long engaged to his cousin, Miss Anne de Bourgh. Mr. Bennet listened to the man's fevered assurances, wondering if his motive was to protect Miss de Bourgh's interests, or to further his by making Elizabeth available for his own marriage prospects. Mr. Bennet called for Elizabeth to join them and gravely informed her of Mr. Collins' news. Elizabeth patiently explained to Mr. Collins that she was well aware of Lady Catherine's desires, but was also certain of Mr. Darcy's, and that she was, in fact, his choice for wife. Mr. Bennet watched the man's face fall, whether for himself or his patroness, he would speculate over with great amusement later that evening, alone.

Mr. Collins was cautious meeting Georgiana. He had heard so many complaints of her from Lady Catherine that he was quite unsure how to receive her. Mr. Bennet was amused to see his effusions die away whenever he looked in her direction, which was quite delightful for the rest of the family. During one particularly long soliloquy, uncomfortably directed towards Mary, she leaned over to Georgiana. "I wish you had been here last night, and then we would have heard less of him."

"Mary!" Georgiana gasped. "Elizabeth told me that your mother hopes he will be attached to you." Mary gasped this time. "No! Oh I will not accept such a . . . oh Georgiana, why would you wish him on me?"

"I do not, it was your mother." She said in her defence.

Mary sighed. "I am invisible to mother until she wants a convenient daughter to marry off to a toad."

Georgiana giggled. "You will not kiss him and see if he is a prince?"

Mary made a face. "I would likely get warts."

Elizabeth tilted her head and smiled at the two. "What are you giggling about?"

Mary looked down. "Mama wishes me to marry Mr. Collins."

"Yes, but Papa will not make you marry anyone you do not wish. So the decision is yours. With Jane and me settled, the fear over the loss of Longbourn after Papa passes is not as urgent. We will simply bear Mr. Collin's attentions while he is here, and with luck, he will find some other lady in the neighbourhood to be the partner of his future life."

All three girls giggled and Jane leaned in. "I can hear what you are saying . . . and I agree!"

Elizabeth looked up at the clock. "Well, if we are to walk into town and back before dinner, we should begin. We must not waste this beautiful day. Do you still wish to go Georgiana?"

"Oh yes, Elizabeth. I know that I am not a great walker as you are, but I have never done anything like this before. It is quite exciting!"

Elizabeth laughed. "Well, if this is what passes for excitement at Pemberley, I may have to rethink your brother's offer!"

Georgiana turned white. "You are teasing me are you not, Elizabeth? You would not reconsider William? He would just die if he lost you!"

"You, my dear, must learn to laugh. Yes of course I am teasing; your brother is stuck with me. Nothing will stop me from meeting him at the altar, I won him, and I will keep him!" She smiled warmly and stood, and announced their intentions to leave. Within a quarter hour they were out the door and on their way to Meryton. Mr. Collins was panting and trying to keep up. Elizabeth and Jane led the way, and to Mary's dismay, Mr. Collins attached himself to her arm. Georgiana took her other arm to lend support, and Lydia and Kitty drew up the rear. Mr. Bennet watched them go, and thought briefly that perhaps they should have skipped this trip, but then, with a group so large, and in the company of a vicar, surely nobody would dare say a thing to them. He returned to his book and sipped his port.

"Lizzy what happened?" Mrs. Bennet watched as Elizabeth and Jane practically carried Georgiana in the door. "Not now Mama, we need to take her upstairs." With surprising speed and silence, Mrs. Bennet led the way upstairs to the guest bedroom and opened the door. Elizabeth dragged the hysterically sobbing girl into the room and gratefully pushed her onto the bed. Jane removed her shoes and lifted her legs, and Mrs. Bennet covered her with a blanket. Mrs. Hill appeared and called for a maid to start a fire.

Elizabeth wrapped Georgiana up in her arms, rocking her, whispering reassurances. She looked to Jane. "Laudanum?" She nodded and left the room.

"Lizzy, what happened?" Mrs. Bennet asked again, and sat beside Georgiana and rubbed her back.

She took a moment and caught her breath, then sat shaking her head. "Oh Mama, it was horrible. We walked into Meryton, and it was as if we were fools on display. People were hurling insults at Georgiana, I saw women shielding their daughters from looking at her, they acted as if she was diseased . . . and then the things they said about William . . . oh Mama, if I had not Georgiana to care for, I would have taken them all on! The lies that spew from the lips of people I considered friends!" Elizabeth was crying. Hot tears of anger fell down her face. "How could they accuse him of hurting Georgiana? Or speculate on my future? And defending that . . . man! Mr. Wickham! How did these stories spread? Who would wish to harm Georgiana or William?" She stared at her mother and clutched Georgiana to her fiercely. "They have been suffering so long with this!"

Mrs. Bennet's face grew pale. "Lizzy, did they speak of the stories that my sister told me yesterday?"

She nodded while stroking Georgiana's hair, her wails had finally ceased, and she was now shaking and staring at a corner of the room. Mrs. Bennet looked at the girl. "I do not think that the laudanum will be needed now."

"Georgiana, how do you feel?" Elizabeth whispered. Jane appeared with a glass, some wine, and a small bottle.

Georgiana looked at her and whispered. "No, not laudanum, I . . . I wish to just lie down here alone, please."

"Are you sure? I will be glad to stay and hold you." Elizabeth stroked her hair.

Georgiana spoke softly. "You are a wonderful sister. You will take good care of William. He needs you so much."

"And I need him just as much, Georgiana. I will take good care of you as well." She nodded and lay down on the bed, closing her eyes. "Just let me rest here for awhile."

The three ladies exchanged glances. "Very well, just call if you need anything." Georgiana did not answer. One by one they left and Elizabeth was the last. She turned to watch her with concern as she closed the door.

Mr. Bennet was waiting in the hallway. "Lizzy, I heard from Mr. Collins and your sisters what happened. I have sent a message to Netherfield for Mr. Darcy to come."

"Thank you Papa." Elizabeth rubbed her face and felt the tears begin to flow again. Mr. Bennet embraced her as she cried. Jane and Mrs. Bennet left them standing in the hallway and went downstairs.

"Come Lizzy, you know that what was said is false. Mr. Darcy is no villain, and Miss Darcy did not . . . well, she was not with child."

"I can not imagine what she feels, and this is not the first time she has suffered a public humiliation. In London she was told she was cut from society, and here . . . oh Papa, the people seemed to take delight in her downfall. Why? What did she do to them?"

"She is very wealthy my dear. Those who have little often rejoice in the fall of those who have everything."

She sighed. "This will hurt William terribly. Oh I wish we were married . . . Papa, I am sure that William will want to take Georgiana home to Pemberley . . . may we marry now and just go?" She looked at him pleadingly.

"No. Not in the midst of a scandal. I think that if you marry, it will have to be delayed."

Elizabeth tore herself from his arms and searched his face. "What do you mean IF we marry? Are you taking back your consent? You just said that William is blameless!"

Mr. Bennet drew her back. "Shh, shh . . . I only meant that Mr. Darcy may wish to rescind his offer now that the scandal has grown . . . to protect you."

Elizabeth's eyes flashed and she pulled again from his embrace. "That is the most ridiculous thing I have ever heard! I will not permit it!"

He closed his eyes at her anger. "Calm down, Lizzy, we will have plenty of time to discuss this later. Come downstairs and have some wine. We will let Miss Darcy rest."

Georgiana drew away from the doorway, and sat down at the writing desk to compose a note, sealed it, and left it on the bed. She glanced around the room, and finding nothing of use, looked out the window and saw a stream off in the distance. She slipped her shoes on, and listening for people, stepped into the empty hallway, hurried down the stairs, and out of the house.

The gentlemen were just returning to Netherfield when the messenger from Longbourn arrived. Darcy opened the note and cried out, "My God!" He spun around to the groom and ordered, "Leave that saddle on!"

"What is it?" Richard took the note as Darcy remounted. "Georgiana! Elizabeth!" He leapt back onto his horse.

Bingley and Hurst exchanged glances and remounted as well, unsure of the problem, but it was clearly dire. They quickly raced through town, and were moving too fast to hear the jeers or see the people pointing. John saw them speed by. He had arrived in town and listened in paralysed horror to the accounts of the verbal flogging received by Elizabeth and Georgiana. It was precisely what he feared happening as a result of telling Wickham's gossip. This was why he decided not to spread it himself. His decision to speak to Mr. Bennet that afternoon was too late. He thought of Darcy flying past with the other men following, and knew without a doubt that Darcy's devotion was indeed very real. Spotting some red coats, it hit him like a thunderbolt. "Wickham!" His whispering, his manipulation,

John saw it now. "Why did I listen?" He jumped on his horse and raced to Longbourn. He had to go. He had to know that they were well.

From his perch on a hillside, just behind the trees, Wickham watched. He saw the reaction in town and quickly circled around the walking party through the fields, and arrived at Longbourn well in time to witness their arrival. He sat and waited, soon he saw a servant racing off, undoubtedly to summon Darcy. He grinned. Soon Darcy would have to take Georgiana back to Pemberley and Miss Elizabeth's parents would announce the engagement ended. Darcy's heart would be broken. Wickham took great delight in that thought. He saw the couple's interaction. It was obvious Darcy loved her. He would never recover from this. Wickham's only regret would be not having his chance at her. That truly would have made his revenge complete.

He noticed a woman leaving the house; her blonde hair caught the sunlight. Seeing her hair at all drew his attention, as no woman would go outdoors without her bonnet. He watched her steadily hurry in his direction and he recognized her. "Georgiana!" He grinned. "Well, the game is not over yet!"

After his impotent display in Meryton, Elizabeth could no longer abide Mr. Collin's sermonizing. He already wrote Lady Catherine about her nephew's engagement, and was furiously scribbling another letter about today's events. Mr. Bennet watched her as she paced the room, then left to go upstairs and check on Georgiana. She knocked lightly then opened the door quietly. The bed was empty. She looked around the room and seeing the note, quickly broke it open and read. She clasped her hand to her mouth and her eyes lifted to the window, and there, far in the distance, she saw Georgiana disappearing into the trees. Elizabeth raced down the servant's stairs, and into the kitchen.

"Susie, give this note to Mr. Darcy when he comes. Tell him that I am going to the stream we once visited."

"Yes, Miss Elizabeth!" Susie held the crumpled paper in her hand and watched as she flew out the door, as fast as her feet would carry her.

Georgiana made her steady way into the woods, her mind on one purpose, to follow the stream to a pond she remembered from a walk with Elizabeth. She had put William through enough; all would be well if she was simply out of his life. He could marry Elizabeth and be happy. He should have sent her to Scotland when she was ruined, he was just too kind to remove her from Pemberley, so she would do the work he refused. She did not belong there; after all, she was no Darcy. If she had been banished, he would have come to Netherfield with Mr. Bingley, met Elizabeth, and fallen in love. *No, everything would be better if I am gone.*

Wickham watched her coming his way and as she passed his location, followed her far into the woods. Georgiana paused, staring at the small pond that had formed in the stream's path. He slipped off of his horse and stood watching her carefully. He was unsure of what exactly was unfolding. When she was brought back to Longbourn he could tell, even with the great distance from his observation point, that she was hysterical. Now, barely an hour later, she was standing with calm serenity, alone in the woods. The thought that he had driven her to an act of desperation suddenly occurred to him. Just as he came to that conclusion, he heard a woman's voice calling, and moved behind a tree to see what was going to happen.

"Georgiana!" Elizabeth called repeatedly, searching the familiar woods, looking off of the path and wondering where she was headed. "Georgiana!" She ran, even with the setback of her recent illness, Elizabeth was very strong and was barely out of breath when she crested a small rise and came upon the girl. She stopped, and watched her transfixed gaze upon the still water of the pond. Elizabeth moved forward very slowly and quietly, hoping not to startle her to run, or worse, jump in. Georgiana was seemingly oblivious to all around her. Elizabeth touched her arm and then took a firm hold of her. The girl jumped, then looked over to see Elizabeth's concerned gaze and dissolved into tears. She fell into Elizabeth's arms and began to sob, and rested her head on her shoulder. "Shhh. Georgiana, shhhh. It is well, you are safe." Elizabeth held her and rocked her gently, stroking her hair and inwardly breathing a sigh of relief. The sobs continued, her body wracked with the pain and sorrow she had been carrying since the horrible day when she ruined her life.

Eventually she began to calm, and she accepted the handkerchief Elizabeth offered her. She tried to catch her breath, and dabbed at her face. Elizabeth held her hand. "What has happened Georgiana? Why would you leave such a note and run off like that? If I had not seen you entering the woods, I would have had no idea where to find you. Can you imagine how devastated William would have been to find you gone, let alone to find that you had harmed yourself? Please tell me what was wrong?"

"I . . . I . . . I thought that everyone would be happier without me. I have brought so much pain to William and my family . . . and now to you. Oh Elizabeth, it was bad enough to hear them saying things about me, but to hear what they said to you. . . And William, how could they accuse him of such horrible things? I . . . I wish he had sent me to Scotland."

"What good would that have done you or him? He has done the best he can to support you. Surely you know how hard it is for him to express it, but he loves you so much, as do I. Has he not proven that already by the way that he followed when Wickham took you?" Georgiana looked up from where she was staring at her feet to nod, but then her eyes grew wide with fear.

Elizabeth spun around to see Wickham standing behind her. "I hardly would call what I did as taking you, Georgiana. I seem to remember you climbing into the carriage with great excitement for our future together."

Stepping so that she was standing between Georgiana and Wickham, Elizabeth demanded, "What are you doing here?"

Wickham looked down on the woman who was glaring at him, her head barely came to his shoulder, and she had no weapon beyond her sharp tongue. He began to laugh. "My, my, and what exactly do you intend to do, Miss Elizabeth? You are not a foolish woman; that is perfectly clear. I can easily take my betrothed with me and sweep you away with a push of my hand."

"Georgiana is not betrothed to you. Her brother's consent is required for that, and neither Georgiana nor William have given that to you."

"Ah, but you are mistaken, Georgiana did indeed agree to marry me . . . did you not my love?" He smiled and stepped closer. "Do you not remember our kisses when you said yes?" Georgiana cowered behind Elizabeth and he laughed louder. "You fear *me* now? When moments ago you stood here, contemplating your death? Surely marriage to me would not be half so bad!"

"Marriage to you would be worse than death!" Elizabeth exclaimed.

Wickham returned his gaze to her. "You should watch your tongue."

"I am not afraid of you!" He stepped ever closer. Elizabeth glanced behind her, and realized that she had nowhere to retreat; the pond was only a few feet away.

Wickham stood and smiled as she saw her trap. "Perhaps you might like to rephrase your last statement?"

"What do you want from us?" Elizabeth demanded. Georgiana whimpered behind her.

In a flash Wickham reached around her and grabbed Georgiana's wrist, pulling her forward and away. "Why, I want my wife, we have an appointment at Gretna Green, do we not, my dear?" Georgiana screamed and tried to wrestle away from his grip. As she fought him, Elizabeth searched the ground and spotting a fallen branch, picked it up and struck him hard across his head. Wickham grunted and stumbled, releasing his captive as he fell to the ground.

"Quick, Georgiana, run!" Elizabeth pushed her, but she stood paralysed. "MOVE!" She screamed at her.

Elizabeth took her hand and they started to run away when Wickham grabbed her ankle, wrenching it painfully, and she fell to the ground. Georgiana screamed again. "Go, run, Georgiana!!" Elizabeth cried.

"No, I can not leave you!" She looked around desperately, searching for the branch Elizabeth had used.

Wickham rose to his feet and drew his sword. "You run and your would-be sister dies." Georgiana stopped dead and stared, her gaze travelled between the sword, Wickham's face and Elizabeth's eyes. Wickham dragged her up to her feet and slipped the sword back into his scabbard.

"Let go of me!" Elizabeth screamed. He pulled her head roughly to him and kissed her, biting her lips and leaving them swollen. She tried to kick him and he quickly drew out a knife and held it to her throat.

"Now, I suggest that you cooperate, my dear." Elizabeth saw the blade and felt it prick her skin. Wickham pulled it away and she saw a drop of blood on the tip, and raised his brows. "The more compliant you are, the easier it will be."

Elizabeth stared at him and he raked the knife across her face. "You will not kill me."

He raised his brows in amusement at her defiance. "You think not?"

"You would have done so already. What do you want?" He laughed and watched as she thought rapidly. "You could not have planned this . . . go . . . get away while you can."

His voice lowered. "Oh, I have time." He stroked his hand over her breasts and smiled.

She attempted to ignore his touch. "Help will be coming very soon. Everyone at Longbourn will be looking for us when we do not return at our appointed time."

He laughed again. "Ah, very good Miss Elizabeth, but you forget, I watched Georgiana running from the house and you obviously discovered her gone and came after her. She was bent on suicide, and as you are wearing neither a bonnet nor coat, I believe I am quite safe in assuming that you told nobody of your departure or your destination; else there would have been a houseful of people accompanying you. No my dear, I believe that we have plenty of time for our conversation."

Elizabeth grasped at what to say. "A note was sent to Netherfield."

Wickham smiled. "I realize that, but even if Darcy was found quickly, he still has no idea where you are, does he?"

Yes he does. She turned her head to Georgiana. "Go, run back to Longbourn, find help."

Wickham looked back at Georgiana and smirked. "You will remain right where you are, will you not?" He took the knife and again drew it across Elizabeth's throat.

Georgiana's eyes grew wide. "I am sorry, I am so sorry Elizabeth." He laughed and turned back to Elizabeth.

"Why do you want to hurt me?"

His gaze returned to her breasts, his voice was calm. "I am angry with you."

"What did I do to you?"

He looked back to her confused eyes. "You love Darcy."

"Is that so offensive?"

"Oh yes, I want him unhappy forever."

She shook her head, not understanding. "What has he done to you?"

Wickham bared his teeth and snarled. "He lives."

Trying to understand his tortured reasoning she asked, "Do you think you would have Pemberley if he did not?"

"He STOLE IT from me!"

"It is his birthright, not yours! You are the steward's son!"

"I am a GENTLEMAN!!" He shouted in her face.

Elizabeth saw the anger and madness in his eyes and became deeply afraid. She decided the only course she had was to keep him talking, she could not possibly get away, even if her ankle was not injured, and Georgiana was clearly too petrified to be of any use, her flash of courage left with the appearance of Wickham's knife. Assuming a calm voice she said as steadily as she could, "A true gentleman does not hold a knife to a woman's throat." That statement seemed to give him pause. She jumped at the opportunity. "Why do you not tell me of your grievances, perhaps you can convince me that you have the right of it?" She held her breath and maintained her air of calm, while inside every bit of her was screaming to run. Wickham studied her in silence and tilted his head. "Tell me about growing up at Pemberley. It must have been wonderful to receive Mr. Darcy's favour."

He breathed heavily and reached to entwine his fingers with the curls resting on her shoulder. "You are very pretty."

She attempted to still her trembling body as he stroked her cheek, and tried not to recoil. "Do you know that Mr. Darcy gave me everything I wanted?" His eyes met hers. "Everything." He whispered. She felt a chill move through her, but she kept her eyes locked with his. He ran his hand down her shoulder. "You are cold."

"I . . . I did not think to bring a coat." He nodded and drew his finger over her lips, then examined the effect of his bite. "I was cold once. I accompanied my father to Pemberley on a winter day. He went to take care of something and I was left to my own devices. Mr. Darcy found me in the kitchens. He was there looking for Darcy. He was hiding as usual."

Feeling her heart ache for William, she could not stop her question. "Why did he hide?"

His eyes flashed at her concern. "Why not? He was invisible to his mother; that is until Mr. Darcy saw me." He smiled at the memory. "I once heard him tell his wife that if she would not bear him another child then he would make another son out of the first boy he saw . . . and that was me. I became the son he never had." Georgiana covered her mouth and tried to cover her sob, her eyes were fixed on the knife.

"But he had a son." Elizabeth said softly.

Wickham shrugged. "All I know is that suddenly I had fine clothes and a new pony."

"How old were you?" He again cocked his head at her, reading her face. Nobody ever asked him about his childhood.

"Eleven. We are almost the same age you know. I am older." Again his fingers stroked over her breasts. "He called me Son." Elizabeth closed her eyes, trying to ignore his touch and suddenly her chin was raised by his hand. Wickham's eyes burned into hers. "His ELDEST son."

Beginning to understand Wickham's delusion of a birthright, she tried to distract him from his obvious anger. "What happened when Mrs. Darcy died?"

"We went to school and always roomed together. Darcy was the perfect student, always winning the prizes, trying to make his Papa proud." He laughed derisively and stepped slightly away from her, but took her hand and held it tightly.

Looking down at his grip she swallowed. "You did not like to study?"

"Why study when I could just take his work as my own? He would never complain. He knew I was his father's favourite." A smile of intense satisfaction came over his face, and he let go of her hand to begin stroking over her hips. "I enjoy taking things that are his. I enjoy seeing his face in misery." She could see that he was losing interest in the conversation. She desperately sought to make him talk again, but at the same time she felt her strength fading, it was so painful to stand. "He did not wish to lose his father's favour?"

Ignoring the question he continued running his hands over her. "Did you know that his father told me to harass him? He told me to force him to fight back, to keep pushing him. He paid me to do what I would have done on my own!" He laughed.

"Why?" Her anguish for William inspired a deep dislike for his father.

"To make a man of him."

"But you were boys!" She cried and Wickham glared at her.

"He told me that if Darcy did not improve he would prefer to leave Pemberley to me since I WAS a man." He smiled again. "I have great plans for Pemberley."

Elizabeth watched him, knowing instinctively that this was not the truth, but his delusion of it. She knew only that she must keep him talking. "But what of your family?"

"My father died when I was seventeen, just as I finished at Eton with Darcy. My mother remarried. Mr. Darcy kept me as his ward."

"What about your time at Cambridge?"

Wickham scowled. "I no longer frightened him. He was stronger and learned too many ways to avoid conflict. He had many influential friends. He still paid my debts and covered my . . . adventures, likely out of loyalty to his father, but no matter what I did, he never folded. Nothing I did ever got under his skin again. He never lost control. His father's attitude was changing too." Elizabeth did not hear the bitterness intensifying in Wickham's voice, she was envisioning the man she loved being formed, no longer a boy to be abused; and far better than the creature before her could even dream of being. Her pride for William and his strength grew.

Wickham was watching her face. She was thinking of Darcy, he could see it in her expression. The love was undeniable, she glowed with it, and the sight infuriated him. He could not stand to see Darcy happy. His eyes grew dark with anger. "He told me for years . . . YEARS, that I was his son. He gave me everything, clothes, money, women, everything I wanted. I acted the fool for him, praising him, stroking his pride . . . And what did he leave me? A pittance and a living as a parson!!! After what he promised me!!! He promised me Pemberley!! I want it!! I EARNED it! Darcy TOOK it from me!!!" Reaching forward and taking her hips, he pulled her against him, and kissed her roughly. "Now it seems that I will take something of HIS."

Wrenching away, her fear provided the courage to fight him again. "YOU squandered what was given you!"

His eyes narrowed; he had delayed long enough. "You are playing with fire. Your life is in my hands. You had best learn obedience." He pressed his body to hers and stroked his hands down her hips, the knife still firmly in his grasp.

Elizabeth looked desperately over his shoulder, saw Georgiana standing helplessly watching, clutching a branch but clearly terrified to use it; and searched for any sign of William's approach. *Where are you?* She began to lose hope. "Go, just go." She begged.

Wickham saw her gaze, and how she was weakening. He moved one hand up through her hair. "I see why Darcy wants you. You are everything he is not."

Her head snapped back up. "He IS a gentleman. You are dirt under his feet!"

Furious Wickham held the knife back to her throat. Georgiana screamed. "He would never fight for you like this!" Elizabeth flinched then spotted movement in the trees.

Defiant, she declared. "You do not know him!"

His eyes were wild. "He is a coward!"

"You are speaking of yourself!" Elizabeth looked up and feeling a surge of hope, she tried to grab the knife from his hand. He slapped her hard across the face and threw her down on the ground.

The men rode into Longbourn's yard and came to a halt. Darcy jumped off of his horse and opening the door, strode in, following the voices to find the family gathered in the sitting room. Mr. Bennet came forward. "Mr. Darcy, you came very quickly. Your sister and Lizzy are upstairs." Mr. Bennet led the way and they arrived at the guest room to find the door ajar. Confused, Mr. Bennet stepped in and saw that it was empty.

Darcy turned to him and demanded, "What is the meaning of this, sir? Where are they?"

"I do not know." He looked about for any signs, seeing only the mussed bed.

Richard had followed them up and scanned the empty room. "Are they nowhere in the house?" Darcy shook his head then spotted a maid coming down the hall. Susie appeared in the doorway.

"Pardon me, Mr. Darcy, but Miss Elizabeth asked me to give you this when you arrived, and said that you can find her by the stream you visited."

His brow wrinkled in confusion, then he read Georgiana's note and swore. Richard snatched it from him. "Good Lord! She could not be serious!" He looked at Darcy's face. Shock, worry, and anger warred for dominance of his expression.

"Thank God Elizabeth has gone to her." He turned to Susie. "How long has Miss Elizabeth been gone?"

"No more than half an hour, sir." She stared at the men with wide eyes.

"Come on Richard, I think that I know where to go." He glanced at Mr. Bennet and began to leave the room.

"Do you think that she would . . . ?"

Darcy stopped. "Georgiana has a habit of running away and hiding when she is distressed. Do you remember her doing that at Pemberley when you were visiting? I am counting on the hope that she is overwrought by what she experienced in Meryton and wrote that note without thought. Of course Elizabeth would see it as a serious declaration and go after her."

"Perhaps it is a serious declaration, Darcy." Richard turned to the window and scanned for any sign of the women. He looked at Susie. "Did you see Miss Darcy leave?"

Susie nodded. "Yes sir, she was walking quickly."

"Was Miss Darcy carrying anything?"

She shook her head. "No sir, but come to think of it, she wasn't wearing a coat or bonnet either."

Darcy and Richard's eyes met. Mr. Bennet spoke. "Lizzy told me that Miss Darcy seemed to calm and asked to be left alone."

Darcy was desperately trying to reassure himself that his sister had just wished to be alone with her thoughts, but increasingly he wondered about the stream where Elizabeth had directed him to go. A memory intruded. "Georgiana had a kitten once that fell into a pond and drowned. She asked me if I thought the animal suffered and I told her that it was an easy death. Not that I knew, I was trying to comfort her." They looked out the window at the distant stream. "Does that stream lead to a pond of some sort?"

Mr. Bennet nodded. "Yes, it is not large . . . but it would be sufficiently deep, and I do believe that Miss Darcy walked with Lizzy in that direction one day." Richard glanced at Darcy and together they flew down the stairs, and were immediately joined by Bingley and Hurst. They went out the door just as John Lucas arrived.

Darcy met his eye for a moment then jumped on his horse and rode out towards the stream. The other men were right behind him. Their progress was slowed in the woods; they had to traverse paths not normally used by horses. They followed the stream, calling their names and looked everywhere for them. Darcy prayed that his first thoughts were correct, Georgiana simply wished to walk. He derived comfort in knowing that Elizabeth was likely with her and would be able to speak to her calmly. She probably followed the girl so quickly that Georgiana would have had little chance to go forward with her claimed plans. He fought back the combination of anger and guilt he felt over her actions. *She will be safe.* He kept telling himself. *She is with Elizabeth.*

Almost a half mile into the bare trees of the woods; he began to hear the sound of a man and a woman arguing. He could not make out the words but looked back at Richard, he had heard it too. He put his finger to his lips and Darcy nodded, approaching cautiously. He saw the flash of red that could be nothing else but a soldier's uniform, then with relief saw Georgiana's golden hair. Suddenly he realized that Elizabeth was being held by the soldier, and then, as the words of the argument became clear, he realized who her captor was. Darcy dismounted, and the other men instantly copied him. Darcy pointed and Richard drew his blade, then nodding, they carefully advanced. Wickham held Elizabeth against a tree. Darcy began to lunge forward but Richard held him back, pointing to the knife that was in his hand. With growing rage he watched Wickham's hands travel over her, and saw the expression of fear in her face as she looked over his shoulder, searching for help. Georgiana stood nearby, sobbing and begging Wickham to let her go. Richard's hand was firmly gripping Darcy, holding him back, but his strength was nothing to the fury that was intensifying in his cousin's mind. Over the pounding of his heart in his ears, Darcy could hear the words of their argument carrying across the void. Staring, he saw the moment when she noticed them. He watched as Elizabeth's courage rose and she declared Wickham a coward. Her eyes met his a second before he saw her grab at the knife and witnessed the strike. Darcy heard her cry and he tore from Richard's grip. With a roar, he ran up to Wickham, jumping on his back and tumbling them over so they were tangled beside Elizabeth.

"YOU DO NOT TOUCH HER!!"

"DARCY!" Wickham cried in surprise.

The men struggled with each other, Richard held up his hand, silently telling the others to let them continue the fight for now. Grunting as they twisted and fought Darcy growled, his face practically touching Wickham's. "I heard you. I heard your lies. You were given a charmed life, but you threw it away."

Wickham pushed his palm over Darcy's face, trying to lift his head up and away from him. "You know what was promised me!!"

Darcy slammed his shoulders hard on the ground and his rage-filled eyes burned into Wickham. "You fool, there was no promise made to you. Do you truly believe that a man as proud as my father would give HIS birthright to YOU?! Ignore his BLOOD??" Wickham finally managed to push off Darcy's chest, and used the heel of his boots to kick him away. He scrambled to his feet and stood before Darcy, watching him jump back up to face him. Both men were aware of no other person; they were caught up in their long-awaited showdown.

"He called me SON!"

"HE called you MY BOY!"

"It is the same!"

"He called ME Son, and his favourite stable hand "my boy", what does that make you? You were nothing but his pet!"

"He TOLD me to hurt you!"

"Do not try your lies on me, Wickham; I know what my father was."

The men stood glaring at each other, their chests heaving. Darcy's hands were balled into fists, and Wickham bared his teeth and snarled.

"You owe me Darcy . . ."

Darcy nodded his head emphatically. "Yes, at last you are correct. I owe you for the years of torment. I owe you for taking my father away. I owe you for the money and the women, and the countless merchants you cheated. I owe you for my sister and now I owe you for touching my wife. She was correct, you ARE a coward! Only a coward would try to feel power by manipulating and striking a woman. Only a coward would spread lies and rumours to seek revenge!"

Wickham suddenly bent to retrieve the knife at his feet and crouched down, ready to spring upon him. Darcy ran forward and gripped his wrists, twisting them until the weapon dropped, and in the struggle they fell back to the forest floor. Darcy wrapped his hands around Wickham's throat.

Wickham struggled, his hands tearing wildly at Darcy's grip. He finally managed to break the hold as Darcy's leather gloves slipped on his sweat-covered neck. He gasped for air and landed a blow to Darcy's jaw, knocking him back. Instantly Darcy returned the favour, sending a crushing strike to Wickham's temple. He fell back against a tree, momentarily stunned, and Darcy turned away from him, feeling satisfied at last. His attention returned to Elizabeth. She looked up at him and he knelt by her side, removed his gloves and caressed her cheek. He tried to catch his breath, swallowing repeatedly, and stared into her eyes. Neither one could find words, but their tears said all that was necessary.

Bingley and John were standing back in paralysed silence, watching the couple. Richard held Georgiana's shaking body in his embrace, but his eyes were fixed upon Wickham. He saw Wickham shake his head and regain his faculties, then suddenly dart to the side and away, running up to the horse that had followed him to the scene. He jumped on and began urging it quickly through the trees. Hurst cried out to alert them. "DAMN!" Richard cursed, shoved Georgiana into Bingley's arms and ran back to his horse.

Darcy stood at his cry. "Where are you going? Let the militia take care of him."

Richard paused and looked down at him then fixed his gaze on Elizabeth. "No Darcy, I started this, I will finish it." He turned his horse's head forward and soon disappeared into the trees.

"Damn!" Darcy cursed and looked after him. Elizabeth touched his leg. "What did he mean, he started this?"

He dropped down to kneel by her side. "When Wickham tried to elope with Georgiana . . . when we found them at the inn . . . Richard beat him. I told him then that it was a mistake. I knew Wickham would seek some sort of revenge, especially if society had already learned of Georgiana's ruin before he had a chance to take advantage and blackmail me for his silence. Once the gossip began, his opportunity for profit was gone. I have dealt with him almost my entire life. I know how he reacts. He might have just slunk away . . . but the beating, that would make him seek his revenge. He must have realized the opportunity when he knew I was here . . . and happily engaged to you." He stroked the back of his fingers against her cheek.

John listened with increasing mortification. "Wickham was the one? He took your sister?" His eyes turned to the girl sobbing against Bingley's coat.

Darcy nodded then returned his attention to Elizabeth. She took his hand and kissed it, and he pulled her to his chest. Their eyes closed and his cheek rested on her head. "I saw him with the knife and thought I would lose you." Elizabeth burrowed into his neck and breathed in his reassuring scent. "That is impossible, I knew you would come in time."

The three other men stood back and consulted amongst themselves, wondering if they should stay or go after the colonel, none of them were armed, they had left their guns back at Netherfield. John's attention was caught by the expression on Darcy's face, and watched as his eyes scanned down Elizabeth's body and how he ran his hand down her side, smoothing the fabric of her skirts with a firm touch. The others stopped talking and watched. His stroking told everyone there; particularly Elizabeth, that she belonged to no other, and she felt safe again.

Bingley signalled Hurst to come and take charge of Georgiana, and knelt by Elizabeth's feet. "Miss Elizabeth, your ankle is swollen. Have you tried to stand?"

She took a great breath. "Yes . . . I did, but I could not run away . . . I hit him with a branch and he fell, but he tripped me. I think that was when it twisted." She attempted a smile. "I should have left my boots on when we returned home, these slippers were not meant for walking."

"May I see if it is broken?" Bingley asked, and then turned to meet Darcy's eyes. They both nodded and gently Bingley moved her foot. Elizabeth gasped with pain. "Forgive me, but I believe it is sound." He removed his cravat and used the long strip of fabric to quickly bind up the ankle.

Elizabeth gripped Darcy's arms tightly while he worked and when finished, gasped again, and then managed a weak smile. "You have unheralded skills, sir."

Bingley returned the smile. "No, I was uncommonly clumsy as a lad. I have much practice in this particular manoeuvre."

Darcy kissed her cheek and turned her face back to his. "Now, what is this about you hitting Wickham?"

Her smile warmed a little. "I wished to gain his attention."

He shook his head and his mouth curled slightly. "You undoubtedly did, and I imagine it was not of a sort you craved." The glance between them communicated more of the frightening experience than a recounting of the facts ever could. He encircled her with his arms and nuzzled his face against hers. "I must go to Georgiana, but I will return to you in a moment, then we will take you back to Longbourn."

She nodded and caressed his face. "I love you."

He kissed her palm and whispered. "My Elizabeth."

Standing, he walked to Georgiana, and held out his arms for her. She fell into his embrace and began sobbing anew. "I am so sorry, William. I tried to fight him, but . . ."

Darcy kissed her head and murmured in her ear. "We will return you to the house, and then we will talk. We need to care for Elizabeth; I think that she needs us." He looked down at her and raised her chin. Georgiana flinched, seeing the swelling of his jaw. "Will you help me? I can not do it all alone; she is far too obstinate for me."

Georgiana gave him a tremulous smile. "Yes, Brother."

He kissed her cheek then turned to Hurst. "Will you ride back with Georgiana? I will take Elizabeth." Hurst smiled and offered Georgiana his arm, and Darcy returned to Elizabeth where he bent and scooped her up in his arms.

"What did you say to her?"

He smiled slightly. "I told her we would talk but that in the meantime I needed her to help me keep you still." Elizabeth laughed softly and rested her head on his shoulder as he walked back to the horses. He lifted her onto the saddle and swung up behind her. The others had mounted and begun to thread their way back through the trees.

Darcy watched his sister clinging to Hurst, tears silently running down her face. "Why Lizzy? Why would she wish to . . . end her life? That is what she claimed in the note."

"That is what she wrote, and I ran after her so quickly because I believed her. When I found her, she spoke of having brought so much misery to you and her family, and thinking we would be better off without her. She thought you should have sent her away . . . but I think that if she truly did wish to die, she would not have spoken to me so easily. She seemed immediately relieved when she saw that it was me standing by her side."

Darcy closed his eyes in frustration over hearing of his sister's foolish reasoning. "We both have spoken to her about working together to find her a promising future."

Elizabeth stroked his face. "You can not imagine how horrible it was to be attacked as we were. Her recovery was so tenuous; it would not take much to send her back over the abyss of self-loathing."

He nodded with resignation. "She has always run off when she is distressed, and if I did not find her, eventually she would return on her own. But this time . . ."

"Wickham's presence was the last thing any of us could have expected. I believe that we would have met you on the way back to the house if he had not been there. You know her well, William. She is in a great deal of pain, but she did not truly wish to harm herself. She did try to fight him until she saw the knife, I was happy to see that."

"I am grateful that you were there, and able to hold on until we arrived. God knows what would have happened otherwise." He gently kissed her head.

"I am not sure how much longer . . ." She shook her head. "We will need to talk to her, and I imagine, watch her carefully. After what she witnessed today, she will undoubtedly feel even more guilt."

Darcy saw her determination to remain strong and ran his hand lovingly through her hair. "How can I ever thank you for what you have done today?"

She relaxed against him, feeling so safe with his touch. "I do not want your gratitude, William. It is you and the others who should be thanked for rescuing us." They rode in silence for some time then Elizabeth's head popped up. "Should you go after the colonel? I am well; I can wait for your return." Darcy kissed her forehead, and smiled at her belated concern for Richard. "Do you truly wish me to leave you, my love?"

"No." She admitted and clung tightly to his waist.

"Good because I would not go. Richard is a seasoned soldier. Whatever his intentions, I am sure they will be successful. He will turn up in his own time." Darcy drew back and gently kissed her bruised lips. "I feel strangely liberated; I no longer care about Wickham. He has perpetrated more harm upon my family . . ."

Elizabeth touched his cheek. "I know, he told me some of what you experienced at his hands. I found it incredible."

Darcy searched her eyes. "You kept him talking to buy time." She nodded and looked down. He gently caressed her jaw and lifted her face to his. "You are so brave, Lizzy. I am so proud of you. I heard you defend me."

She held his gaze. "I was merely stating the truth."

"I love you." Darcy's lips tenderly touched hers. "Does that hurt?"

She shook her head. "Only if you stop."

Chapter 26

"**D**amn you, Fitzwilliam!" Wickham cried Richard raised his brow and turned from where he was tethering his horse. He regarded the bleeding man. "Would you have preferred to have been run through? I considered lopping off your arm, but then I did not wish to hear of you pretending to be a war hero, as you have pretended to be a gentleman all these years. It seems a quick stab to the shoulder was all that was required. You obviously have not learned how to handle a blade during your time in the army. I imagine that you have disgraced your uniform just as freely as you disgraced the fine clothes my uncle purchased you." Richard settled against a tree and folded his arms.

"Will you not give me any aid? I can barely see let alone tend this wound." Wickham pressed his hand to the tear in his uniform.

Richard stepped forward and offered his handkerchief. "Will this suffice?" The cloth fluttered down to the ground and Richard smirked and stepped back. "No? Well, I am sure that the militia has a surgeon available, he will see you soon. I am certain that Darcy will notify them of our location."

"What, do you want me hanged as well? What is your game, Fitzwilliam, why did you spare me?"

Richard smiled. "You think that I would spare you?" Wickham's vision was becoming murky, and his voice was taking on a decided sluggish tone. The loss of blood was slowly beginning to take its toll. Richard crouched down to his eye level. "I want to know why. You failed with Georgiana; you lost the dowry, why did you spread the stories about Darcy around the town?"

"Have you no concept of revenge?" Wickham spat. "I like seeing Darcy miserable. I have enjoyed causing it for years." He coughed and shook his head. "I had been waiting for my chance, then I heard that he was engaged to marry . . . and not to that miserable cousin of yours, and it made me angry . . . I would have left him alone if he were to marry that sickly example of a woman." He groaned and his head rolled.

Richard slapped him. "Soldiers never express pain!"

Wickham's eyes opened. "I watched him; I would ride out to see his daily appointment with her. He was in love." Wickham sneered. "I could not allow that. I decided that would be my revenge, to drive them apart, make her parents end . . . the . . ." His voice trailed off. Richard slapped him again and he blinked.

"Why did you follow Georgiana? Why did you try to take Elizabeth?"

Laughing, Wickham met his stare. "Surely Fitzwilliam, you would not pass on such an opportunity?"

Richard glared at him in disgust. "Your quarrel was with Darcy, not with two defenceless women."

"Georgiana is defenceless, but Elizabeth . . . that woman has a fire any man would enjoy taming."

Richard stepped forward and struck him hard on his jaw. "You do not speak of her like that!"

Wickham swore and spat out some teeth. "What is it Fitzwilliam, do you love her, too?" Wickham spat out some more blood and sneered at him. "My, my, Darcy has quite the competition, does he not? First a foolish local gentleman and now his own cousin."

"Do not try to taunt me with your ill-conceived theories, Wickham." Richard resumed his position leaning against the tree.

"Then why would you come after me? Should this not be Darcy's fight? Oh yes, he is too much of a coward to take me on."

Richard's brow rose. "I seem to recall the man leapt upon you while you were accosting Elizabeth and beating you soundly."

Wickham spat again and groaned as he held his shoulder. "He did not finish the job."

Richard smiled. "You did not oblige him by staying put." He shook his head. "No, Darcy does not need to be a murderer. He does not need to carry that on his shoulders . . . I have killed a great number of men, what is one more?"

The bleeding man's eyes took on a look of fear. "You do mean to kill me."

Richard laughed quietly. "You always were a fool Wickham. Do you not realize that I already have? It is just a matter of waiting now." He glanced over to the shoulder wound and Wickham followed his gaze, then looked back at him with wide eyes.

"Why?"

"Do you really have to ask? You are vermin Wickham. You spent your youth and your adult life torturing a boy, now a man, who would have rewarded you far more than you ever dreamed to have had your friendship. You took away his father, and threw away the favour my uncle bestowed upon you. You could have had a very comfortable and pain-free life if you had accepted his generosity as the gift it was, but instead you coveted Darcy's home, his fortune, and now the woman who has at last given him a life. You disgust me. You have had everything handed to you and you still want more. I may have been born a second son, but I never held my brother's fortune in contempt. I accepted my lot and chose my destiny. I have seen death and suffering and misery. I know hunger and deprivation. I know what it is to live in filth and freeze, and see my comrades lose their limbs and die in agony. I have done this willingly to defend my country and because I am proud of my heritage. You have never done anything in consideration for anyone but yourself. You are the worst of vermin, because you dress in your gentleman's costume and draw in your marks. You convinced a lonely little girl that you loved her, and now drove her to nearly take her life. I will give you no more mercy than will the maggots that will soon be infesting your gaping, lifeless mouth."

Wickham's face fully reflected the terror that he now finally realized. This was no longer a game. The cold eyes of the man before him confirmed it. "Please, Fitzwilliam, help me. . ." He closed his eyes and moaned.

Richard stood still and watched him. "It is time to make your confessions, Wickham, what have you to say before you go to hell?"

"I . . . had help."

He gasped for breath and Richard reached forward and shook him. "WHO??" Wickham made no answer and passed out, never to open his eyes again. Richard watched as the last of his life's blood flowed down from his wound and soaked into his uniform. A last gasping breath and he was gone.

Richard stepped away and retrieved his fallen handkerchief, wiped off the blood that stained his hands and threw it back onto Wickham's body. He studied the position of the wound, and made note of how long Wickham breathed after receiving it, information to be used for another day. He felt not one trace of remorse. His only regret was not learning who Wickham's accomplice was.

The four horses moved at a steady pace. Hurst led the party, and Georgiana was silent, holding onto his coat draped around her shoulders, and listening to the man's soft reassuring voice while tears ceaselessly ran down her face. Darcy had opened up his greatcoat, and Elizabeth was nestled inside, her eyes closed, enveloped in his warmth. Darcy was focused completely on her, whispering, and rubbing his cheek on her head. She whispered back and clung tightly to him. Bingley, riding beside them, reached over and unnoticed, took the reins from his grasp. He moved up ahead and took charge of leading Darcy's mount. John spurred his horse forward to match Bingley's pace, leaving Darcy alone and behind them, allowing them a little privacy. Bingley looked over to John and saw him glancing back. "What brought you to Longbourn, Lucas?"

Startled from his thoughts, John's head swung around. "I . . . I was in Meryton and heard what happened to Miss Darcy and Miss Elizabeth. When I saw you all riding through . . . I thought I could help."

Bingley stared at him in disbelief. "You thought you could help? Where were you when they were under attack? Why did you not step in then? I thought that you professed a fondness for Miss Elizabeth, surely you would have wished to leap to her defence?"

John startled. "I was not present at the time, I arrived after the fact." He looked pained then glanced back at Darcy in time to see him tenderly kiss, then caress Elizabeth's face. "I . . . I suppose that I was foolish enough to believe the rumours I had heard. I had intended to come speak with Mr. Bennet about them this afternoon. I thought that he would end the engagement to Darcy." He ended softly and looked down.

"So after hearing that the woman you hoped to win lived through a hell of torment your thoughts were centred on the hope that she would reject the man who *had* won her?" Disgust was clearly expressed. "I wonder how long you have known of these rumours and how much you helped with their dissemination." Bingley watched him without understanding.

John looked at him quickly then away again. "No, not at all, after seeing Darcy and the rest of you riding through town, I . . . I realized too late that the rumours were fabrications, clearly Mr. Darcy is not the man that he was painted to be." He could not bring himself to confess to his gullibility.

Darcy leaned and kissed Elizabeth's bruised lips, and he felt her warm response. "Lizzy?" He said softly and kissed her again.

She opened her eyes to his. Her hand released its grip on his waist and lifted to cup his bruised jaw. "Are you in pain, my Will?"

Darcy smiled slightly at her worry. "It is nothing." His lips turned to caress her palm. "How are you?"

She searched his face. "I am only now beginning to realize what happened. It all unfolded so quickly . . . I know what we almost lost." Tears filled her eyes and Darcy cupped her face in his hands.

"Do not think on that, it will do you no good, if I think of all I almost lost today, I . . ." He bent and kissed her deeply, their eyes met again and they nestled together, her head tucked under his chin.

Elizabeth, in an effort to stop reliving the events in the woods, began thinking over how the whole situation could have been prevented. "I should have kept Georgiana at Longbourn today. After yesterday, I should have been more prepared. I was surprised when you did not react at all to the news."

A look of confusion passed over Darcy's face and his brow pulled together. He bent to see her. "What news? What happened yesterday?"

"It was all in the note I sent . . ." She examined his expression. "You did not receive it!" Her eyes closed. Once again an error of understanding came between them due to a lost letter.

Darcy touched her and she looked at him. "Lizzy?"

"I sent you a note, delivered by one of our servants. When we were in Meryton yesterday, we noticed people whispering and pointing at us and the carriage, Jane and I decided that it was just gossips talking of our engagement." Darcy nodded, but knew there was more. "When we returned home, my mother took me to her chambers and told me why my aunt was so upset . . . you remember her coming in as we were leaving?"

"Yes, your mother stayed at home which you seemed to think was unusual."

Elizabeth nodded then moaned, putting her hand to her head, she had a mind-numbing headache. Darcy kissed her forehead and cradled her to him. "My mother told me that there were rumours in town about Georgiana's ruin . . . and of how you mistreat her." Darcy's eyes changed from their steel blue to black in a second. "They spoke of how she was with child from her lover who you killed and that you beat her to . . ." She could not say it, and he had a fair idea of what she meant.

"Good Lord." He breathed.

"I wrote all of this to you and asked if we should forgo the walk into town, when your note this morning made no mention of it, I thought that you were not concerned . . . what a fool I was! Of course you would have said something. Do I not know you well enough by now?" She chastised herself, shaking her head and ignoring the pain from her intense headache. "This is entirely my fault! I should never have gone into Meryton, but Georgiana was so excited, I was so happy to see her smiling and . . . well, acting like a young girl instead of a . . . oh William, I am so sorry!" She began to cry again and he held her tightly, wondering what could have happened.

"Lizzy, this is not your fault. You asked for my opinion and when my note said nothing of the subject you thought that all was well. You had a male companion, an obviously useless one, and all of your sisters. You were as safe as could be, and truly, you were walking into a town full of people you have known all of your life. You could not have expected such a vicious turn from those you always considered to be friends. This is *not* your fault." He kissed her forehead, and looked up. "Bingley!"

Bingley stopped his horse and waited for Darcy's mount to amble up. "Elizabeth tells me that a very important note was sent to Netherfield yesterday, warning me of this gossip spreading. I did not receive it. Do you know of anything coming in?"

He shook his head, thinking. "No, the post was on my desk as usual, and anything that comes for you would go directly to Roberts if you are not at home." He could see the fury in Darcy's eyes. "Would this note have prevented what occurred today?"

"Today, yes, eventually, I could not say. I wish I knew . . . well, it is obvious that Wickham was behind it all." He turned to John, who had stopped when Bingley did. "Wickham told you the lie about my father's bequest, did he not?"

John's stomach dropped. *So that too was a lie.* Darcy had told him to be sure of his facts before spreading rumours. "Yes, he told me at the officer's dinner."

Darcy's eyes were searching his face. "So, he was there. I did not see him."

John drew a breath. "He departed suddenly when we were talking; he said he had duties to perform . . . courtesy of you. He seemed surprised by your attendance." He hung his head. "And I was a willing listener for his lies."

Darcy said nothing, only clutching Elizabeth closer to him. He could only imagine just how eagerly Lucus would have listened to Wickham, and wondered if he was guilty of their spread through town. He looked back down at Elizabeth who had closed her eyes again, but the tears were still shining on her cheeks. He noticed that the reins were not in his grasp and tugging them, Bingley let go. Darcy kicked his horse and they continued to the edge of the woods and entered the meadow. Nearly a half-mile away, Longbourn could be seen. Hurst and Georgiana had not stopped and were already ahead of them.

A group of soldiers were just leaving the house and approached rapidly. Hurst stopped his mount and looked back at the others, then remained still as they caught up. Colonel Forster was leading the group and reined in. "Mr. Darcy, I see that you have recovered Miss Darcy. I had heard of the difficulties in the village. I was told that some of my men participated, and I wished to tender my apologies. Mr. Bennet told us of your sister's flight and we were just on our way to be of aid. I can not express the relief we felt when you all emerged from the trees." He saw the bruises to Elizabeth's face and Darcy's. "It seems that more has occurred here, however."

Nodding, Darcy looked down at Elizabeth. "Miss Elizabeth followed my sister and when she found her, they were accosted by Wickham. Our search party came upon them in time." Elizabeth met his steady gaze. Colonel Forster listened with growing anger. "Where is Wickham now?"

Darcy lifted his jaw towards the woods. "He ran off and my cousin Colonel Fitzwilliam gave chase. Lucas can show you the path they took; hopefully you will find them quickly." John nodded and turning his horse, waited for the colonel to finish his conversation.

"It seems he did some damage before he fled."

They each touched the other's face. "He did but Elizabeth and I left our own marks upon him, and I can well imagine that if my cousin catches up to him, he will no longer be in a pristine condition."

Colonel Forster's brows rose. "Indeed? Miss Elizabeth, you defended yourself against the scourge?"

Before she could answer, Darcy smiled at her and said proudly, "She kept him talking and distracted him until help arrived. She struck him with a tree branch and resisted his advances, she duelled him with her wit as sharply as you could do with your blade." His eyes were shining with his admiration and love.

Not to be outdone Elizabeth turned to the colonel. "I did those things, I admit, but Mr. Darcy leapt upon him when his cousin was clearly holding him back. He easily could have killed him, but acted as a gentleman, struck his opponent and when he was down, turned to care for me. I am exceedingly proud of him."

Colonel Forster smiled at the two. "Well, I imagine he received his due from you both. You will make quite a fearsome couple."

Darcy breathed deeply and nodded. "That we will."

The colonel's brow rose and he was glad to see such a good result come for the family. He turned to John. "Lead on Lucas." They departed and were soon in the woods.

"I wish I could take you to Netherfield. I wish for us to be alone." Darcy kissed her cheek and watched for her reaction.

"William, I would like nothing better than to be alone with you, not just now, but forever . . . but we have family anxiously waiting for our return . . . I fear we have no choice but to go to Longbourn." Elizabeth stroked his cheek when he closed his eyes in denial.

"All I want to do is take you home to Pemberley, and never let you go again."

Elizabeth smiled at his obvious unhappiness. "I think that should be something we speak to my father about. I want to go, too. I have had enough of waiting." Darcy nodded and resigned, kicked the horse back into motion.

Mr. Bennet stood watching the slow progress of the two riders with an increasing agitation that was only exacerbated by the endless cries and questions from his wife and daughters, and exclamations by Mr. Collins. "Why do they move so slowly?" Jane asked her father worriedly.

Mr. Bennet patted her hand. "I fear it indicates that Lizzy is injured. Do you see how Mr. Darcy holds her? Miss Darcy seems unwell, too."

Darcy felt his chest tightening the closer they came to the house. It just brought him closer to the moment when Elizabeth would be whisked away from him. She could feel his tension. "Will, I . . . please do not leave me."

"How did you know what I was thinking?" He leaned and stroked her lips gently. "I will do everything I can to remain with you."

She embraced him and buried her face against his waistcoat. "I am being selfish. Georgiana will need you." His only response was to increase his grip. He could feel that he was soon to be pulled in many directions, and regretted more fiercely than ever not taking her to Netherfield.

Hurst arrived first, and dismounted awkwardly. Between him and Mr. Bennet, they helped Georgiana down, and Mary came forward to take charge of her with Mrs. Bennet. Kitty and Lydia stood back, their questions silenced by first seeing her swollen eyes, then upon spotting Elizabeth and Darcy's bruised faces.

"Lizzy!" Jane ran up to the horses and gasped at her sister's appearance. Bingley quickly jumped down and hovered by her side. Darcy carefully dismounted and Elizabeth slipped into his waiting arms. He used his last seconds of privacy to tell her his feelings with one intense look. She nodded, returning his silent declaration. He slowly turned to face the family. Silence reigned until Mr. Bennet spoke. "Lizzy, Mr. Darcy, what happened?"

"Sir, perhaps it would be best to take Elizabeth inside, she requires care."

"Of course, of course, it appears you do as well, sir." He stepped aside and Darcy walked past him and followed Jane upstairs. Behind him he could hear Mrs. Bennet calling for bath water to be prepared. Entering Elizabeth's bedchamber Darcy paused; and his mouth turned up slightly, seeing all of the feminine touches in his beloved's room. Amongst the ribbons and combs and bottles of scented water belonging to a woman, were scattered the treasures of her childhood. Well-loved dolls and oddly shaped rocks, a sea shell, and bottles made of coloured glass. Elizabeth felt him relax the moment he entered her little sanctuary. The essence of lavender gently permeated the air and Darcy drank it in. "William?" Elizabeth was watching him. He gazed at her and his smile grew. He shook his head, it was something he could not explain, seeing her room made him realize how well-matched they were, and he could not wait to have the barren rooms of Pemberley filled with the evidence of her life.

Gently, he set her down on the bed. He knew he could no longer kiss her lips, no matter how much he wished for it. To distract himself he turned to Jane. "Miss Bennet; where is my sister?"

"She is with Mary in the guest room. I will see to her as soon as we have Lizzy settled." Darcy nodded.

Elizabeth noticed Jane's desire to care for her, and William's unwillingness to leave. "William, perhaps my father's valet can help you to clean up while I change. When I am finished, you can come and keep me company, we have much to discuss." She squeezed the hand that had remained tightly gripping hers.

"Yes . . . I . . . forgive me. I am in your way . . ." He still would not let go. Elizabeth brought her free hand up to stroke the one that held hers. "You know that is not true. I do not wish to be parted from you either." He smiled gratefully at her.

Mr. Bennet appeared. "Sir, Mr. Hurst has left for Netherfield. He anticipates you staying here tonight and will return with a change of clothes for you and Miss Darcy. You are welcome to use my chambers."

Darcy received another squeeze from Elizabeth and bent to kiss her cheek. "I will return soon." He walked back out of the door and Jane closed it behind him. Mr. Bennet stopped him when he entered the hall. "When you are comfortable, I would like to hear just what happened today." Darcy met his eyes and bowed his head. "Yes sir."

Colonel Forster and Colonel Fitzwilliam sat in the tent that served as headquarters and sipped the whiskey that was poured out for them. "I suppose that the churchyard will take his body . . . unless you know of some relatives?"

"He was an only child, and his parents are gone. As far as I know, nobody would want him. Perhaps the local surgeon would like him for some practice." Colonel Forster smiled then shook his head.

"Unbelievable. You know, I heard some of the gossip that was going around about Darcy, but I gave it no credence. I met the man, admittedly, he is not the most open person to know, but he is polite and when I saw his sister, why she seemed shy, and perhaps nervous in company, but beaten? No. I have seen what an abused child looks like. This girl seemed as if she would have gratefully hid in her brother's tailcoat if he would let her."

Richard laughed without a sound. "She has suffered a great deal."

"So Wickham was the man who compromised her." Richard nodded. "Ran away with her . . . we found them in time."

"Well, I see nothing to require any charges against you, sir. You were clearly pursuing the man who assaulted two of your cousins and his betrothed; you have witnesses in three prominent residents of the district, not to mention Mr. Darcy himself and Miss Elizabeth. I do not believe that any details concerning the attack upon Miss Elizabeth or Miss Darcy need to be given, nor of your cousin's retribution upon Wickham. I will speak to the magistrate with my report, and that should be the end of it." He met Richard's eye. "It *will* be the end of it. I should have locked him up after you last visited."

"You had to conduct your investigation; I can not fault you for following protocol." He drained his glass and lifted the bottle to refill it, filling Colonel Forster's in the process. He sat back and sighed. "My concern now lies with the destruction left behind. You say that you heard the rumours. May I ask how and when?"

Colonel Forster put his feet up on his desk and crossed his arms over his stomach. "I believe it was my wife who told me." He nodded. "Yes, she had been invited to some tea or other in one of the local's houses. Apparently it was all over Meryton on Sunday . . . Philips! Yes, Mrs. Philips was the woman." He looked back at Richard who was frowning.

"Well, I suppose Mrs. Philips heard it all in town and was just repeating and likely embellishing what she learned. That does not help. I am sure that it all leads back to Wickham. He mentioned that he had help though. I wish that I knew who, and even what that meant."

He watched Richard thinking. "Did he say why he acted as he did? Was it purely for revenge? Somehow I do not see Wickham as being a man to exert himself without a clear profit in mind."

"Ah, I disagree with you there, sir. Revenge is very profitable if the goal is to see as much pain as possible inflicted." Richard remembered months ago, Darcy's agitated reaction to his beating Wickham, and how he was sure that he would find a way to hurt them terribly. Darcy was absolutely correct, Wickham found his way, and even admitted to it. The question was how long he would reach from beyond the grave to continue his plans. "Sir, if you could speak with your wife, and see if she knows where the rumours began . . . I just want to be sure this ends with Wickham's death." He stood and finished his drink. The colonel joined him and they shook hands.

"I will be happy to do what I can."

———~~~———

Louisa and Caroline watched as Mrs. Annesley boarded the carriage to Longbourn. She was going to spend the night sitting with Georgiana. "Do you see Louisa? This is what comes of Mr. Darcy mixing with such people! He should have stayed with his own circle!"

"Caroline, when are you going to let this drop? Mr. Darcy is engaged to Miss Elizabeth and that is not going to change, and even if it did, he certainly would never offer for you."

Caroline glared at her. "Who says that I want him?"

"Oh come off it, you can not fool me. His rejection of your advances has done nothing to cool your determination. I have watched you watching him. You only seem to have retreated, but I can tell you have an unending stream of ideas running through your mind. Leave the poor man be. Return to London and find some man to marry."

"In the middle of winter? Nobody is there! And what is for me in London? I have no money until this spring! What would I do; sit in the parlor and drink tea?"

"I imagine that is what you will do wherever you are." Their argument was interrupted by Bingley's return. They watched as he mounted the steps, and heard him in the foyer, speaking to Hurst and removing his coat. Bingley's voice rose in anger as he questioned the butler; and the sound of apologies was heard. He then appeared in the doorway and looked straight at Caroline. Her eyes darted around, searching his face.

"Charles, where is Mr. Darcy, and Miss Darcy, will they not be coming back?" Her distraction did not work. He was obviously angry, and it was directed at her.

"No, Caroline, they will remain at Longbourn, at least overnight. Miss Darcy is sleeping after taking a draught, and Darcy wishes to remain near Miss Elizabeth."

Louisa glanced at her brother's unusually angry eyes that were boring into Caroline's. "How is Miss Elizabeth, Charles?"

His gaze did not change. "She is injured, but thankfully the physical damage should heal in time. But what she experienced will likely scar her forever. I know that what I saw will never leave me."

Caroline could stand no more. "Charles, why do you stare at me so?"

He walked further into the room and stood directly in front of her with his arms crossed. "A letter for Mr. Darcy from Miss Elizabeth was delivered here yesterday. It was given to our butler. He tells me that you took it and promised to give it to Darcy. It was very important. Where is it, Caroline?"

She looked from his eyes to Hurst's who was standing behind him, looking just as angry. "I . . . I gave it to his valet, he must have lost it."

"Hurst spoke to Roberts, who said that he did not receive any letters for Darcy yesterday. Try again." Bingley's hands were balled into fists. She glanced at Louisa who was looking at her incredulously.

"I . . . I might have dropped it." She looked down at her hands and twisted them together.

"Where, Caroline?"

"In the fire in the drawing room." She whispered.

"Pardon me? You dropped a personal letter into the fire? Did you read it first?" Bingley was bellowing.

"No, I . . . I thought it was a love letter from that Miss Eliza, and . . . he did not need to read that sort of . . . I . . . how could it be that important?" She looked at him defiantly.

"I will tell you how it is important. Miss Elizabeth was asking Darcy if he felt it was safe for her to take Miss Darcy into town this morning. When he did not express an opinion not to go, she decided that he felt all would be well. This entire episode, the loss of a man's life, the behavior of Miss Darcy, the abuse I did witness of Miss Elizabeth, could all have been avoided if you had simply given Mr. Darcy his letter." Bingley's face was red, it was the angriest anyone had ever seen him. "I have had enough of you Caroline. You are no longer welcome in my home. You will go to London. You may stay at the townhouse until I can meet with the attorneys. You will receive your dowry, and then I will wash my hands of you."

Caroline's eyes opened in panic. "Charles, what are you saying?"

"I am saying that you will have to establish your own house. Perhaps one of our relatives will want you. I can no longer stand the sight of you." He bowed to Louisa. "I am sorry that you had to witness this. If you and Hurst choose to take her in, that is your prerogative. I will not be visiting when she is in residence." He turned on his heel and left the room to begin writing letters to the attorneys. Caroline watched him go in stunned silence, then spun to face her sister.

"Louisa, he can not do that! He is obligated to care for me!"

Hurst answered from the doorway. "He is, but it does not have to be under his roof. I imagine that his attorney will tell him that an establishment must be formed for you, and that your own apartments must be found, but once that is addressed, I am afraid you are on your own. You should settle in London, perhaps you will find a husband there, but at least you will be in walking distance to whatever you may need, since I doubt you will have a carriage at your disposal anymore." Hurst nodded to Louisa. "And no dear, we will not be hosting your sister." He turned and walked down the hall to join Bingley in his study.

"Louisa!" Caroline took her hands, but Louisa pulled away in disgust.

"Why, Caroline, why did you need to interfere in Mr. Darcy's business?"

She sank onto a sofa and held her face in her hands. "I was humiliated after his rejection. I hated knowing that he was in love. As long as he did not feel love, I thought I had a chance, that is why I tried to convince Mr. Lucas to compromise Miss Eliza, but that failed as well."

Louisa sat down. "What do you mean about Mr. Lucas?"

"I approached him at the dinner at Lucas Lodge. I said that I was hoping to win Mr. Darcy, and it was fine until Miss Eliza stole him away. I knew that he wanted

Miss Eliza, and suggested that if he compromised her . . ." She shook her head. "He must not have tried. I heard nothing of it, but I did notice he had a bruised jaw . . . but Mr. Darcy would never strike anyone."

"Until today, it seems."

"Because of me." Caroline said morosely. She stood. "I should probably start packing for London." Louisa made no move to go and help her, but sat and wondered about Mr. Lucas and his bruised jaw.

———~~~———

Darcy quietly closed the door to the bedroom where Georgiana lay in peaceful slumber. He sat with her in Mary's silent company until his thoughts of guilt and helplessness overcame him and he was driven to rise and seek out Elizabeth. He walked down the hallway and knocked lightly on the door. It opened to reveal Jane. "Miss Bennet, I . . ." He looked over her to see Elizabeth sitting by the fire drying her hair. He let out a small sigh and swallowed.

"Mr. Darcy, her bath took some time to accomplish, with her ankle, but as soon as her hair is dried, I will send someone to fetch you." She smiled and patted his arm. "Do not fear sir, she is just as impatient to see you." Darcy nodded and looking once more into the room turned away.

Jane shut the door and sighed. "Lizzy, your Mr. Darcy has the most soulful eyes of any man I have ever seen."

Elizabeth smiled. "Everything is in his eyes, I learned that very quickly." She looked at the door. "Was that him?" Jane nodded. "Well why did you send him away? Call him back!"

"Lizzy! You are not dressed!" Jane admonished.

"Well it is not as if he has never . . ." Elizabeth saw Jane's eyes widen and dart to Susie who was picking up the discarded clothes from the floor. Elizabeth blushed and beckoned her over. "Jane, Mr. Darcy will be staying tonight." She met her eyes and stared at her meaningfully.

"Lizzy! You can not wish to sleep . . ." She looked at Susie and whispered, "with him?"

"I do and I will. I made him come here instead of to Netherfield as he wished, and I need him just as much as he needs me. Now, how can we work this out?"

———~~~———

Darcy wandered down the stairs and back into the public rooms of the house. He could hear Kitty and Lydia arguing and turned in the opposite direction. He walked into the sitting room and leaned against the fireplace and stared into the flames, reliving the events of the last hours. "Mr. Darcy, I do not believe that we have been formally introduced. I am William Collins and I am the recipient of the living at Hunsford Parsonage, courtesy of my esteemed and noble patroness, Lady Catherine de Bourgh."

Turning, Darcy looked down at the self-important man. "Mr. Collins." His eyes returned to the fire, having no use for the man who had failed utterly in protecting his sister and cousin.

"It is my understanding sir, that you are the great lady's favorite nephew and I should congratulate you on your upcoming nuptials to Miss Anne de Bourgh. You are bringing much happiness to your aunt with this marriage."

Darcy turned back to him and stared. "Sir, perhaps you are unaware, but I assure you, I am not engaged to my cousin as I am, in fact, engaged to yours. Miss Elizabeth will be my wife, and no other. My aunt's perception has been corrected time and again; however, clearly her delusion continues. I advise you sir, to take anything that she says with great care, and enjoy the situation you have for as long as it lasts. She can be quite temperamental about such things."

Collins swallowed. "Sir, but I was given to believe that since Miss Elizabeth has clearly been ruined by the actions of today, you would surely end this engagement, which of course would allow you to reestablish the fondest dreams of my patroness to join your two great estates!"

"You were told that I would reject Elizabeth because she was attacked? Who spouted off this nonsense?" Darcy's eyes pierced the little man.

Mr. Collins' eyes grew wide. "Why, Mr. Bennet . . ." Darcy looked up and strode straight from the room, leaving the sputtering parson behind. He walked to the bookroom door and pounded on it. Mr. Bennet opened it immediately and seeing who it was and the expression on his face closed his eyes and stepped back.

"I see you have been speaking to Mr. Collins."

Darcy swept into the room and stood facing Mr. Bennet, there was murder in his eyes. "I see that his words were not the work of his imagination." He glared as he watched Mr. Bennet close the door and walk back to his desk where he sat down. "Please be seated, Mr. Darcy."

"I would rather stand, sir. Now, what is this . . . idiocy that I would wish to end my engagement to Elizabeth?"

"That is not what I said . . . I thought that she might end her engagement to you." Mr. Bennet said quietly.

"ON WHAT GROUNDS, SIR?" Darcy bellowed.

"On the grounds that the rumors of your and your sister's behavior would gravely affect the rest of my daughters were my Elizabeth to continue her association with you." He said softly, looking down at his hands. "They have undoubtedly been affected already."

Darcy stared in shock. "You know the rumors to be false! You would allow the man who tried to RAPE your daughter to achieve his goal of tearing us apart? That was the goal, sir. He told my cousin that as he lay dying. His desire was to see me miserable for all of my days. I love Elizabeth, sir. I will not have her taken away from me now. It is my intention to take my sister and MY WIFE home to Pemberley as soon as possible." His hands were resting on Mr. Bennet's desk and he was bent staring directly at him. "What is your response, sir?"

"You will not marry. Not now." He still would not look up at him.

"Mr. Bennet. You have told me of the pain your family suffered after your sister's ruin. You seemed to admire the fact that I did not follow your father's example and send Georgiana off to a remote estate, never to be mentioned again.

You even told me of your own loveless marriage and regret over a lost relationship and admired how Elizabeth loved me despite all of the pain that my family has faced. And here you sit, condemning me, both of us, to the same hell that you professed to live day after day? I will not have it, sir! The marriage contracts have been accepted and signed by you. I have the license. There is nothing to prevent me from sprinting up those steps this minute, claiming my bride, and taking her to the nearest church to be my wife. I will not relinquish her now or ever! What say you to that, Mr. Bennet?"

Mr. Bennet still would not look at him. "You will not do those things because you are a gentleman."

"What good is being a gentleman if I am not sufficiently worthy of marrying the woman I love and who loves me?" Darcy turned around and strode to the window, his eyes were burning and he reached into his pocket to find the ribbon and wound it tightly around his fingers. Up the drive came a carriage; and he saw Mrs. Philips getting out with several other women. Mr. Bennet heard them arriving and sighed. "Do you not see what has happened, Mr. Darcy? We will be inundated by the gossip mongers, trapped in our own home, and surrounded in the village. I thought that I could ignore the gossip that was spread around the town, but after the attack this morning in Meryton, and this incident with Wickham, I can no longer hope that it will die away. Everywhere we step we will be subjected to the whispers and rumours. I have lived this once already, I can not see my daughters live through it."

Darcy turned from the window. "But your daughters have done nothing wrong!"

Mr. Bennet shook his head. "When has that ever mattered? As long as you are part of Elizabeth's life, your taint will be on my family. If the engagement is ended, all will gradually go back to what it once was." He stood and walked over to Darcy and put a hand on his shoulder. "I am sorry."

Darcy could not look at him, his entire life was crumbling around him and he could not see a way to repair the damage. "I thought . . . I thought that you had accepted me as your son." He blinked and looked down at the ribbon in his hand. "You said that you supported me, I thought that if anyone could appreciate what happened to my sister and how hard I have tried . . . how much I dearly need Elizabeth." He swallowed and grew silent. His face became as stone and he stared off into the distance.

Mr. Bennet sat down heavily on the edge of his desk. "Darcy, I would be proud to call you Son."

Darcy remained at his post. "Sir, I WILL NOT accept this. I WILL NOT allow Wickham to continue to haunt me every moment for the rest of my life. We will find a way to deal with this. I have spent too much of my life alone. Elizabeth is the air I breathe; I refuse to give her up." He finally turned and looked at her father. "Excuse me; I will be with my Elizabeth."

Darcy left, oblivious to the sound of women's voices in the sitting room, or anything else in the house. His feet began moving faster and he ran up the stairs, pounded on Elizabeth's door, pulled it open, and the look on his face alone sent everyone in the room running out. He slammed the door shut and locked it, and strode straight over to the chair where Elizabeth sat by the fire, gathered her in his arms and fixed his burning gaze upon her. "I will not leave you."

Chapter 27

"Leave me, William, of what are you speaking?" Elizabeth tried to pry his face from where it rested against her neck but he refused to move. She kissed the top of his head and wrapped her arms around the man nearly twice her size who was crushing her, rubbed his back and waited. It had been such a horribly emotional and exhausting day, perhaps it had just finally taken its toll on him. Darcy sank into her embrace and absorbed the love she gave to him. He had fought for her that day, finally breaking free of the constraints he had lived under all of his life, and in a burst of emotion took out the pain of Wickham's abuse by paying him back with a response that was years in the making. Only now did he realize that if it had not been for his gloves slipping, he would have throttled Wickham there in front of everyone. He would have been a murderer, and somehow, that thought did not bother him because Wickham was harming the most important part of his life and for once, he fought back. He listened to Elizabeth's comforting voice confessing her love and decided that if he allowed Mr. Bennet to take her away, he may as well have joined Georgiana in her pursuit of that deep pool. He lifted his head and cupped Elizabeth's cheeks in his hands and searched her worried, bruised face. No, he would not allow anything to come between them ever again.

"Lizzy, I just left your father. He wishes to end our engagement."

Elizabeth's eyes grew wide with shock. "WHY?" Of all the consequences of the day's events, the last she expected was this.

"He feels the gossip that caused all of this will continue to grow, especially now that there is a death, and it will only serve to hurt you and your sisters." He watched her struggling to understand his words, and looking away from her expression of pain he said softly, "Your father feels that all will return to what it once was when I am removed from your life."

"Do not tell me that you accepted this!" Elizabeth's eyes flashed. "That is the most ill-reasoned, ridiculous . . . William, do you know that when we returned from town this morning with Georgiana, my father took me aside in the hallway and told me that you would likely wish to end our engagement? He said that you would wish to protect me from the scandal. I refused to give that any credence. I believe that when he saw that you would have no intention of abandoning me, he took it upon himself to appeal to your goodness and use his arguments to influence you. Obviously he was thinking of this even before Wickham attacked." Elizabeth searched his eyes. "Is that what happened? Were you fighting for me and he used this upon you?"

Darcy sat back on his heels with a look of understanding spreading over his face. "Yes, that is precisely what happened. I threatened to come up here and carry you out the door that instant and marry you at the first church that would take us tomorrow morning." He took her hands in his. "I told him that I will not give you up, that we will find a way to deal with this. Lizzy, I think that I know what is behind his demand. He is remembering his family's ruin and is thinking that it will happen to his daughters by association. Hearing what happened to you in Meryton today must have been similar to what he experienced and he thinks it is the same situation. He could not be further from the truth! The situation is as different as night and day!"

Elizabeth squeezed his hands urgently. "What scandal? There is no scandal in our family." She watched him, it was clear that he was thinking hard. "William, what do you know of my family that I do not?"

Darcy startled from his conjectures. He would hold no secrets from her and told her of her aunt, her banishment, her father's lost love, and his forced marriage. Elizabeth's expression changed from shock to understanding, to anger. "So, because of my father's experiences, I am to suffer . . . WE are to suffer the same fate? We are to exist in a life without love or the companionship of the person we need and want because of what? He worries of the opinions of the residents of Meryton? Does he forget that these same residents this morning delighted in disparaging one of their own, believing the lies of a would-be rapist and murderer? Does he think that I have any care for those people's opinions any more than you care for the society you so easily rejected? I refuse to let public opinion determine my life!"

Elizabeth's eyes bore into his. "I have grown up in a household with a loveless marriage and lacking in any respect between the parents or the children. It is painful and sad, and I can imagine it was nothing compared to the hellish childhood you experienced. I refuse to allow the actions of a man so evil destroy my hope of happiness, or yours. I understand now why my father was so supportive of my decision not to accept the attentions of men I did not respect. But I do not understand why now, after a lifetime of indifferent parenting, he suddenly feels that he can dictate to me that I must not marry the man who I *have* chosen. I have determined my path. I will marry the best man I have ever known or will spend the rest of my life in a sad and lonely existence because I will accept no other. Well, Mr. Darcy, tell me, what is my life to be?"

Darcy stared at the beautiful woman who had endured so much, and still had the strength to fight for their marriage. The fire in her eyes filled his heart with pride. "Miss Elizabeth Bennet, will you do me the very great honour of saving my life, of giving me a life, and accepting this fool as your husband? Will you be my wife?"

Elizabeth's glare lessened and she nodded. "That was good, but I think that it can be improved."

Darcy smiled slightly then became very serious. He took her hand in his. "Miss Elizabeth Bennet, I am telling you here and now that you *will* be my wife. I will not accept another woman, and I will not tolerate any person who ever attempts to separate us again. *You* will be my wife."

At last Elizabeth smiled and they stood, wrapped up in a tight embrace. "Now that is the man I love! Yes, Mr. Darcy, I will marry you." Darcy held her to him and kissed her. "I would not have left you my love; I already told your father that.

I do not believe that he wishes for it either. I can not begin to tell you what I was feeling when I walked into this room."

"I guarantee that you would not have left me, because I would have run after your carriage to chase you down!" She smiled and hugged him fiercely to her.

Darcy laughed and looked down at her bandaged foot. "That would have been a sight to behold." She blinked back some tears that were threatening to fall. Darcy brushed her hair with his lips. "I can not tell you how happy I am that you would fight for me."

Elizabeth lifted her head and he saw her brimming eyes. "It seems that we are taking turns defending each other today." She took a tremulous breath. "William, I can not possibly live without you."

Darcy blinked back the emotion he felt overwhelming him. "I am nothing without you." He kissed her forehead, and tried to regain control. He cast about for a neutral subject. "How do you feel?"

She understood his need, and responded with a return of her humour. "My headache was gone until you entered this room." She looked at him pointedly.

He cast his eyes down. "Forgive me." He looked back up and smiled at her warm gaze. The break in the tense mood helped them both to relax. He brushed the curls from her face that had fallen from her pins. "What do we do now? I told your father that we would find a way to address his fears."

Elizabeth rested her head against his chest and closed her eyes to think. Suddenly she looked up. "William, was it my imagination, or did I hear a group of women downstairs?"

"Yes, your aunt and several ladies of the neighbourhood arrived just as your father was telling me that I may not marry you . . . I believe that is what convinced me that he truly did care for both of us, and how pained he was with his ill-conceived decision. They are undoubtedly here to learn what has happened today. I am sure that Wickham's body coming through town in the cart inspired a fresh round of speculation about my violent tendencies." He said the last with bitterness.

Her eyes lit up. "That is it, William! Not one of these ladies has ever heard your side of the story!"

"What are you suggesting?"

She spoke quickly, looking up at him and pressing her hands to his chest. "I am suggesting that you and I go down there and visit with the ladies of the neighbourhood and give them the truth, let them see the good man that you are, and address their speculation. I am sure that when presented with the evidence of our love and commitment, they will have a great deal more to wag their tongues over."

"I am not sure Lizzy . . . you know how difficult it is for me to speak." He looked at her nervously. "I may make things worse."

She took his hand and squeezed. "William, I believe that if all you do is display your affection for me, they will be sufficiently impressed with you. I will do the talking."

He looked doubtful. "Do you mean that simply seeing me pay you attentions will change their opinion? That can not be, after all of the vile rumours that these same women have said of me and Georgiana, how could they possibly be so easily swayed?"

"Trust me William." Her determined smile convinced him that it would not hurt to try. He bit his lip. "If this does not work . . ."

Elizabeth interrupted. "It will, watch and see." He drew a deep breath and nodded. She began to move away towards the door and he stopped her progress by drawing her back into his arms. "Lizzy, I told your father that I will marry you and take you and Georgiana to Pemberley as soon as possible . . . but that was when I thought that . . . well, we no longer need to leave immediately, but I realize that removing her soon from Hertfordshire probably is wise. Will you come with us to Pemberley? Even if we have not yet married? I need you there; I do not know that I can care for her alone. I do not know what to expect when she awakens."

"Of course I will come!" She smiled and hugged him.

He sighed with relief then looked at her with concern. "Do you think that your father will allow you? Besides convincing him that we will marry, and the impropriety that I suspect you have no care about, but your injuries . . . can you walk?"

"I can limp with extraordinary grace, sir, especially if I am on the arm of a handsome gentleman from Derbyshire."

Darcy smiled. "Thank you. Have you much practice in the art of limping?"

"I have climbed, and therefore fallen from many trees." Her eyes danced, and she tilted her head. "And you sir, your injuries? How are they?"

"Ah, and I have fallen from many a tall horse." He kissed her nose, and basked in the optimism that flowed from her.

"You? But you are such an excellent horseman!" He lovingly kissed her lips then gently stroked his thumb over the bite mark, suddenly becoming teary-eyed. Elizabeth touched his face and brought him back.

"I . . . it takes practice, as anything does." He clutched her to him and they held each other for several long moments. "I wish that I could sleep with you tonight." He whispered in her ear.

"Keep wishing." She whispered back.

Darcy drew away and gazed at her. "What do you have planned?"

She smiled. "You will see."

He pulled her back in his arms and kissed her forehead. "My God, I love you."

Elizabeth drew his face down and smiled into his eyes. "As I love you." Their lips met tenderly, until Darcy drew away to rest his forehead against hers.

"I am surprised that we are left alone like this so long." He whispered in her hair.

"You have no idea the expression on your face when you came in here."

He closed his eyes as the emotion rushed over him again and he swallowed down the pain. "If we are to meet the ladies we should go."

"Will you help me down the stairs?" Darcy swept her up into his arms. "I will carry you as the treasure you are."

Elizabeth shook her head and smiled. "I am not a helpless damsel, sir."

"You most certainly are not, and I am grateful for it." Darcy stepped to the door, and Elizabeth turned the key. He kissed her again, then opened the door to go and repair the damage.

―――ᨀᨀ―――

Richard wearily climbed the steps to his chambers in Netherfield. He was told that Bingley and Hurst were in the study and he informed the butler he would join them as soon as he washed and changed. His batman was ready for him, and skipping the bath he deeply desired, he washed as thoroughly as he could with a basin of hot water and donned a fresh uniform. Glancing at his reflection, he saw nothing different about his face besides an obvious need for sleep. He had killed before and would likely kill again someday; there was nothing new to see there.

He knocked and entered the study and was greeted warmly by the other men. "What news have you Fitzwilliam?" Bingley asked eagerly while pouring him a drink.

"Nothing significant, Wickham will be buried in a far corner of the churchyard. He was not convicted of a crime so they will accept his body, but the grave will be unmarked, and no service will be said over him. They already looked through his belongings . . . it is fortunate that he has no known relatives else they would be liable for over five hundred pounds in debts of honour that he leaves behind. Colonel Forster is going to total up what he owes the merchants . . . I will not be surprised if Darcy pays those debts himself."

"Why? They are not his." Hurst asked.

Richard smiled slightly. "Darcy has spent nearly his entire adult life cleaning up after the man. I can bet that he will see this as an obligation. His father created the monster by giving Wickham a good taste of a life he could never support, and by indulging him almost as a pet to anger his estranged wife. Why he continued the practice after her death, I will never understand. Perhaps he saw something in Wickham that he had crushed in Darcy. If he had stopped then and given his attention to his own son . . . well, it is useless to speculate on what might have been. I suppose too much had happened by then." He sat in thoughtful silence and considered the letter he must write that night to his father. He had only just received a letter confirming the Earl's happiness in Darcy's engagement to a worthy woman, now Richard would have to tell him that he had no idea when the wedding would occur.

"Hurst and I have been speculating over the gossip . . . you said that Wickham claimed he had help?"

Withdrawing from his musings, Richard returned his attention to the men. "Yes, it was his dying statement. I have been thinking it over myself, chewing on the clues, as it were. I wonder; do you have any ideas?"

Bingley glanced at Hurst who encouraged him. "Well, when we were riding from the woods, I asked Lucas how he came to be there, he thought he would be of use after learning of the attack on Miss Darcy and Miss Elizabeth. He admitted that he had hopes that the rumours in town would encourage Mr. Bennet to end her engagement."

Richard's brows rose. "Is that so? Surely he would not expect the rumours to go so far to lead to such violence."

"I imagine not, but later as we were approaching Longbourn, Darcy asked him about Wickham, and he admitted that he had eagerly listened to his stories."

"My wife told me this afternoon that Caroline admitted to approaching Lucas to propose a compromise of Miss Elizabeth, but that it obviously did not happen."

Hurst leaned back in his chair. "We know that Darcy hit him for touching Miss Elizabeth. Perhaps that was the compromise that Caroline proposed? Darcy never disparaged him in town or really even to us. He hit him and dropped it."

Richard nodded and said thoughtfully, "The fact that Darcy acted in a violent manner at all is remarkable, what he did today was extraordinary, which goes to prove his intense feelings for both Miss Elizabeth and Wickham. I would have stepped in if he had continued throttling him . . ." Richard's voice trailed off. He never wanted Darcy to know what he did of delivering death. He roused himself from his thoughts. "Today was an important day for him."

"One likely never to be repeated I would wager." Hurst nodded.

"I would hope not!" Bingley said with wide eyes.

Hurst smiled. "No, not *that* Bingley, I mean, such an expression of emotion on his part, it seems quite unusual."

Bingley nodded in understanding. "It seems to be a great day for unusual expressions of emotion." Hurst looked at him and smiled. Richard tilted his head and raised his brow. Bingley sighed. "I essentially threw my sister out of the house. She burned the letter from Miss Elizabeth that told Darcy of the new rumours of his violence and Miss Darcy's ruin. If he had received it . . ."

Richard shook his head. "So many what-ifs are in this tale. I am sure that your sister is only receiving a recompense that has been long in coming." He watched Bingley look down and nod, then sipped his drink. He would allow the young man to clean up his own house. His sights were focussed elsewhere. "Well, I can not help but speculate that Lucas is somehow involved in this. I should like to interview him. Colonel Forster is making inquires from his wife about where she heard the rumours, but the very nature of gossip is that it is insidious, like smoke, getting into cracks and crevices and growing with each new breath of air. I suppose that each new tidbit was gobbled up and embellished as it passed from one person to another. I have a feeling that when I speak to him, he may admit to spreading the rumours, but will equally claim that he had no idea of Wickham's ultimate plans or the damage it would all cause." He looked at his audience and raised his glass to his lips. "Of course, ignorance of the result is not an excuse from punishment."

"What will you do if he is guilty?" Bingley asked, and watched in fascination as the cold eyes he had seen on the soldier as he rode off to follow Wickham reappeared. He suddenly realized how fortunate Caroline was that the punishment he had determined for her was all she would be receiving.

"He hurt my family, I will have to consider if I should extend mercy." Bingley swallowed and looked to Hurst who puffed his cheeks and blew out his breath. They realized that they were in the presence of a very dangerous man. Bingley hoped that he would speak to Darcy before acting, since he was likely the only person Richard would heed.

"Oh Mr. Bennet! You will be so proud of me!" Mrs. Bennet came into the bookroom with a triumphant gleam in her eye. She stopped dead and stared at her husband. "Mr. Bennet are you . . . weeping?"

Mr. Bennet was seated at his desk, and nothing could stop the tears that were pouring down his face. He rested his head in his hands, no matter how hard he tried; he could not blot out the stricken expression of utter agony in Darcy's eyes. His willingness to fight for Elizabeth, and find a way to protect her and her sisters only confirmed the goodness of the man, something he had acknowledged long ago. "She will never forgive me."

"Who? Mr. Bennet?"

He lifted his head and said mournfully, "I have told Mr. Darcy that I wish to end his engagement to Lizzy. I do not want his . . . family's ruin . . . to touch our girls." He sighed. "Mr. Darcy refuses to comply. He went to speak to Lizzy about it."

Mrs. Bennet blinked in disbelief. "Mr. Bennet! Have you lost your senses? Mr. Darcy fought for our Lizzy! He saved her life! He saved her from . . . his cousin fought that . . . Mr. Bennett, I just told my sister, Mrs. Goulding, and Mrs. King that Mr. Darcy is the finest example of a gentleman that ever entered Hertfordshire and if they choose to believe the lies spread by a . . . criminal bent to . . . KILL . . . and . . . harm our children, then they are FOOLS!" Mrs. Bennet's face was red and she wrung her hands. "How can you possibly tell Mr. Darcy he may not marry Lizzy? He cares for her . . . I can not imagine what it would be to enjoy the . . . affection Mr. Darcy so freely displays for our daughter . . . NO SIR, I never question your judgement but on this I will not let up. YOU GET OFF THAT CHAIR AND YOU GO TELL MR. DARCY . . . GO! NOW!" Mrs. Bennet was hysterical in her declarations.

Mr. Bennet could not recognize the woman before him. "Mrs. Bennet, you defended Mr. Darcy to the neighbourhood?"

"I most certainly did! I told all of them that they would be grateful to have half such a good man marry their daughters! And THEN, Mr. Darcy brought Lizzy downstairs to visit with the ladies. He and Lizzy had not eaten since breakfast and she wished to have some tea. He carried her into the room, insisting that he serve her, and there they sat side by side, holding hands in front of everyone . . . oh and he kissed and caressed her hands, too . . . and the way he looked at her! Everyone could see how tender he is with her! They did not stay long, as they are both so tired . . . well it was clear that Lizzy should not be out of bed, the injuries to her face were horrid enough, but you should have heard them talking about Mr. Darcy's jaw and blackened eye! And nobody missed Lizzy stroking his poor swollen hands. I can imagine that the dear man is simply COVERED in bruises! He did not say very much, but he was exceedingly polite, and so obviously a gentleman. AND THEN Lizzy told them all about that horrible Mr. Wickham! How he imposed himself upon Miss Darcy, luring her away from the cottage, and trying to marry her to get her dowry. WELL Mr. Bennet, they were shocked! Nobody knew how wicked Mr. Wickham was! Lizzy told us that Mr. Wickham made a habit of taking in innocent girls and has many natural children left in his wake!! Poor Miss Darcy was betrayed by the woman who was supposed to protect her, and well, Mr. Bennet, she is but fifteen; imagine if our Lydia was faced with such a wolf in sheep's clothes? What would have become of her? After that Mr. Darcy swept her back up in his arms and took her upstairs. They all remarked upon how mistaken they must be about him, and I told them that they simply must agree with me that he is a very good man and that he and his sister were the ones wronged in all of this. They are all going to tell the truth of the matter to the entire town!" She shook her handkerchief at him. "Now you go speak to him before he listens to you and ruins everything for Lizzy!"

Mrs. Bennet actually began pushing him up and out of his chair. "I will not see our daughter miss this opportunity to . . . have a fine husband." Her frantic energy finally dissipated and she stared at the floor.

Mr. Bennet stood and turned to face her. "You mean that you will not have her miss the chance to be loved."

She looked up at him and the silly vacant woman was gone. "Mr. Bennet, I know full well that you have never loved me, and that I was forced upon you. It was not the match I wished for either, but I made the prudent choice and have done the best I can. Who would you have her marry now, surely not Mr. Collins or John Lucas?"

He examined this serious woman before him with wonder. "No, no, she would not accept either of them."

"Mr. Bennet, I think that it is doubtful that Elizabeth would accept anyone other than Mr. Darcy."

A knock at the door interrupted them. "Come in." Mr. Bennet called.

Mrs. Hill entered the room with a note and left. Mr. Bennet opened the folded piece of paper and shook his head, then read it aloud to his wife. *Papa, Mr. Darcy told me of your ridiculous dictate, and I hereby inform you that it will be ignored.* Mrs. Bennet smiled in triumph and nodded. "You are not my most beautiful child, Lizzy, but you are by far the cleverest!" She looked up to her husband. "Well, Mr. Bennet, what have you to say about that?"

After being called back down to Mr. Bennet's bookroom, and receiving the man's sincere apologies and pleas for forgiveness, Darcy informed him of his desire to quickly remove his sister to Pemberley, in the company of Elizabeth, who he stated would prefer to go as his wife. Mr. Bennet asked to have the night to think over the plan, but Darcy knew that regardless of Mr. Bennet's decision, Elizabeth would be in his carriage the day they departed, wedded or not. His patience was at an end.

Upon returning upstairs, he learned that Georgiana had awakened, and he cautiously entered her room to visit. "Georgiana, how do you feel?" She turned from where she lay facing the wall and saw his injuries. She cried out and her hand went to her mouth. "Oh William! Your jaw . . . does it hurt? Oh, this is all my fault!" She burst into tears and Darcy looked at Mrs. Annesley, then reached over and pulled her to him. He was relieved to feel her calm.

"Georgiana." He paused, thinking, and decided he had always been truthful with her. "Yes, it does hurt. I imagine I will feel quite stiff in the morning, but . . . I am glad for these marks." Her muffled voice could just be heard from where her head was pressed to his shoulder. "How can you be glad?"

"I was able to defend the woman I love, and pay him back for harming the sister I love. I did not allow him to continue taking from me as he has for as long as I can remember. I was able to end it on my terms, before our cousin ended it on his, Wickham is dead." She gasped, and he hugged her. "I do not want you to blame yourself for this anymore Georgiana, but I do want to know why you felt that your only recourse was to do yourself harm."

He pulled away and held her away from him. "If you are not ready to speak of it yet, I understand, and if you would prefer to speak to Elizabeth instead, I will accept that, but I do want you to think carefully about your answer and when you are ready, tell us why. I would have blamed myself forever if you had succeeded, and I could not have stood to follow the law in the manner dictated to bury one who takes their life. When you understand why you acted as you did, then Elizabeth and I will be able to help you. You must know that we both love you very much and want only your happiness. Now that I have found mine, and I will no longer be the morose brother you have grown up knowing, I believe that we can find yours. Elizabeth will help us both to be better people." He watched her carefully, and held her hand. "I was very proud to hear Elizabeth tell me that you fought back. I think that was very important, and shows how you truly do want to live."

Georgiana remained silent. Darcy looked back to Mrs. Annesley who smiled and nodded her head. He sighed. "It has been a very long day dear, and I am going to retire. Tomorrow we will talk. I plan for us to return to Pemberley soon, and hopefully Elizabeth will join us. Will that please you?" She nodded and he kissed her forehead. "Very well then, good night." He stood and nodded to Mrs. Annesley and left the room. Looking down the hallway, he saw that the door to Elizabeth's room was open, but he could hear the sound of women's voices inside. He hung his head and instead walked to the door to the chamber that would be his for the night. Just as he raised his hand to knock, Mr. Bennet's man approached and offered his assistance to prepare. Darcy accepted and the valet opened the door for him and he entered, glancing around at the simply appointed, but obviously feminine room. He paused as the man swept by him and he took in the scent of rosewater. He smiled slightly, wondering if Bingley would be as affected by Jane's scent as he was when entering the lavender filled room belonging to Elizabeth. The unfamiliar servant worked quietly and efficiently, and seemed to take great pleasure in handling the very fine clothes that were methodically removed from Darcy. With Roberts at Netherfield, he did not expect any special attention, and in truth he did not want it this night.

Finally alone, he stood in his robe and nightshirt and leaned on the window frame, resting his head on the cold glass. It was a very dark night, heavy clouds blocked the moonlight but occasional breaks allowed him brief glimpses of the garden and of the trees creaking in the brisk autumn wind. He waited, Elizabeth told him to wait. In the distance the noise of a house full of women created an uncomfortable din. He was not at all accustomed to so much activity, except perhaps when staying at an inn while travelling. He searched around the room for something familiar and just felt lost. Darcy turned his eyes back to the garden when a soft knock on his door was heard. "Enter."

Jane slipped into the room. "Good evening, sir." She closed the door and would not look at him. He supposed it was his dress that was making her blush violently, so he stood out of her way and watched her as she quickly opened the closet door then stood aside, staring down at her hands. She gestured to the door. "Please go ahead Mr. Darcy."

He stepped forward and tried to see her eyes. "In the closet?" She nodded and kept her gaze averted. Cautiously, Darcy stepped into the dark space, and was suddenly surrounded by a stronger scent of rosewater, obviously captured in all of her gowns. Ahead he saw a sliver of light around a doorframe and walked further. Gradually the roses dissipated and he was enveloped instead by lavender. *Elizabeth.* He pushed open the door and blinked upon entering the softly lit room. He scanned the familiar space and upon seeing her smile he relaxed. He was home.

Chapter 28

*D*arcy gradually woke and felt a sensation that was entirely new and pleasant. His eyes opened to behold Elizabeth's hair fanned out over his chest like a blanket, her face pressed against his shoulder, her arm draped around his waist and her leg entwined over his. It was so very warm and comfortable. The steady beat of a cold November rain brought his glance to the window, and he regretted that they were not at Pemberley where a day such as this could be spent quite happily in their bed or at the least, curled together in the library under a warm blanket, pretending to read. He sighed as his imagination ran with the thoughts of his future domestic life, far away from the society he so hated, and making a home with this beautiful woman.

He brushed back her hair and saw the edge of her bruise, and could just make out the deepening discoloration of her skin. It would look far worse as it began to heal, he knew that well enough. He attempted to suppress the rising tide of his anger for the man who had caused so much destruction, he was dead, and they must focus on their next steps. Lifting his hand to stroke his jaw, he could feel that the swelling seemed to be down, but it was still sore, and he could feel the stiffness in his hands and arms from the struggle. He closed his eyes and began thinking through the events of the day before. Above everything that had happened, the one constant through it all had been Elizabeth and her strength. Once she was away from Wickham, she had, through every turn, been optimistic, encouraging, unyielding . . . everything that he felt he was not. He never could have taken on Wickham if he had not been attacking Elizabeth. He likely would not have confronted Mr. Bennet if it was not to save his engagement, and he wondered if he could have comforted and spoken to Georgiana had Elizabeth not taught him how. His love for her seemed to grow with every moment, and he wondered if there was a limit to her strength, or if she was a master at hiding her feelings just as he was.

Elizabeth murmured in her sleep and he bent to listen. "Willllll." His smile grew and he brought his arms around to hold her close. His meandering gaze took in the shadowed details of her bedchamber, seeing the little touches that he had not noticed before, and realized that she had filled the room with her memories, just as he kept little reminders of happy moments. His eyes rested on the door to her closet, where Jane had blushingly directed him to enter when she appeared in her own chambers the evening before. He had walked cautiously through the small forest of gowns and ladies' clothing hanging on pegs to appear with delighted surprise in front of Elizabeth's bed, where she sat smiling warmly. He heard the firm click of the door behind him on Jane's side and he copied the motion by turning to close Elizabeth's door. It was the work of a moment to tear off his robe and slippers and climb into the bed beside her. It was also the work of only a few more moments for them to realize that despite the desire they both had to share their love in a physical way, they were exhausted. After a few sweet kisses and caresses, Darcy spooned his body to hers and they were soon asleep.

It was just as well. He gently wrapped a long curl around his finger. *If we had given in to loving each other, there may have been the consequence of that action to address, and until we have a wedding date in mind, it would be best to try to rein in our desire.* He closed his eyes again and rested his cheek on her head, and was just drifting back to sleep when he became aware of Elizabeth's shoulders shaking. Darcy lifted his head and bent to study her face. She was crying, her eyes were squeezed tight and she clearly was trying to muffle her sobs by pressing her face down into his chest. "Lizzy!" Darcy turned to lie on his side, and pulled her against him. "Please, sweetheart, tell me what is wrong?" He petted her hair, rubbed her back, rocked her, and still she wept. Wracking sobs shook her body, and his nightshirt was soon soaked with her tears. Darcy was desperate to comfort her, but not knowing how, he held her and whispered how much he loved her. He was not sure if she was simply spent or if he said the correct words, but eventually her sobs became gasps, and then she quieted, burrowing against him. Darcy breathed a sigh of relief as she regained control and kissed her cheek. "Lizzy, please talk to me, what troubles you?" She sniffed but said nothing, only clutching him tighter.

He searched for something to say. "Is it your father? I know that he asked for a day to think about when we would wed, but between your mother and my talk with him yesterday, he has agreed that our engagement will continue. I personally would prefer that we marry before we leave for Pemberley, but if he is obstinate, we have a beautiful chapel on the estate, and I am sure my aunt and uncle will gladly come from Matlock to attend."

She sniffed. "No William, I am not so worried about the wedding, we will marry very soon, like you, I too am tired of the delays. If Papa had simply allowed us to marry a month ago, none of this would have happened."

Darcy kissed her gently, feeling the bite mark on her perfect lips and internally cursing Wickham anew. He wiped away the tears on her cheeks with his thumb. "What bothers you, my love? It seems I have too many choices of terrible topics, so you will have to help me along if I am to help you." His lips curled with his little smile and his eyes warmed.

"I believe that I am overwhelmed with everything. All day yesterday as each new event occurred, I kept saying to myself, *I want to go home.*" She smiled at the confused look that spread over his face and caressed his furrowed brow. "I realize that sounds ridiculous coming from a girl lying in her own bed, but . . . I think that it just means that I want to go home, to our home, wherever that is, and be with you. It seems that even if we have managed to repair the damage created by the gossips in Meryton, I will never look upon that village as a friendly place again. I will never see the people there as my friends, and will always see the sneers on their faces, and wonder what they are thinking under their smiles. I can never walk into the woods of Longbourn again without remembering Georgiana's flight or feeling Wickham's hands on me. And even here in this room, how can I sit in here without remembering you bursting through the door with a look of deepest despair when you thought you had lost me forever?" Elizabeth caressed his face and looked up into his eyes. "I want to go home with you."

"Lizzy." Darcy whispered and kissed her. "Then perhaps we should simply make our own plans, and not wait for the influence of others. Georgiana will be well enough to return to Netherfield today, she only had some bruises on her arms, although she is very troubled still, but Mrs. Annesley can keep a watch over her. I will need to speak with Richard . . . he seemed determined to understand the meaning of Wickham's claim of having help, and I have a feeling that I will need to check his lust to seek retribution. I see no reason why we could not arrange a small wedding in two day's time, and then we can depart for Pemberley. My relatives may be disappointed in missing it, but their attendance was mostly desired to show society their approval. If we go to London in the spring, they can just as easily hold a dinner for us, and that will hopefully be enough. Does that sound reasonable to you?"

She sniffed and nodded. "That sounds perfect. My only regret is that you will not be here tonight. I am afraid that I have grown rather fond of sleeping by your side."

Darcy smiled. "I believe my love, that fond does not begin to describe my feelings. Although I have done the best I can with your nightdress, it is not the same as holding the woman who owns it."

Elizabeth laughed. "You have been holding my nightdress when you sleep?" He smiled shyly and looked down. "Why do you think that I demanded it?"

She wrapped her arms around his waist and laid her head back on his chest. "I thought that you kept it in your treasure box." He chuckled. "It is not that large, my love." He began brushing his hands up and down her back. "What have you done with my nightshirt?"

Her face lifted and she caressed his jaw. "I sleep in it."

His eyes grew wide and he smiled. "You do?" He turned to kiss her palm. "Thank you."

Elizabeth gently touched the dark skin around his jaw, and her tears reappeared. Darcy touched her mouth. "Are you sure that it does not hurt when I kiss you?"

She looked down and the tears fell faster. "No, it does not. Please do not stop."

He pulled her to him and kissed her, gently, then began kissing her tears away. "Dearest, tell me what hurts." He kissed her forehead. "Is the headache gone?" She nodded. He kissed her cheek. "Does this hurt?"

She nodded again. "Only a little." He moved and instead kissed her unbruised cheek and she smiled at his care. She gently touched his face and met his eye, and he smiled. "Yes, it is sore, but I will gladly accept your touch."

Elizabeth's tears ended. She nestled against him and he wrapped her up in his embrace. His hands gently travelled up and down her arms and he kissed her forehead. One hand moved down to caress her hip and he felt her stiffen and shrink away. He immediately moved his hand back up to her waist and she relaxed. Darcy closed his eyes and squeezed her. Wickham had done his damage, he would be delighted. "Lizzy, I just had an idea."

Nestled safe in his arms, Elizabeth did not realize that she had retreated from his touch. She looked up into his serious gaze and smiled. "What is it, Will?"

"I thought that perhaps you might like to wait until our injuries have healed to marry, then we can go home to Pemberley and enjoy our honeymoon . . ." His voice trailed away.

She sat up to look at him with concern. "But you just said that we could marry in two days, you said that Georgiana should return to Pemberley . . . our bruises will require weeks to disappear."

"I think that bruises are not the only injuries to heal." Darcy brushed her cheek with the back of his hand and saw her confusion. His eyes remained locked with hers, but his hand ran down her side and again rested on her hip. She jumped and her eyes widened. "Oh, Will!"

"What did he do to you Lizzy? You have not spoken of it. Please tell me, I need to know." The expression on his face was a mixture of worry and pain.

She dropped her head onto his chest and began to cry again. Darcy held her close, and fiercely kissed her head. "I saw his hands on you. Did he . . . touch you the way I did at Netherfield?" He held his breath and prayed.

"No, but, he did run his hands over me." Darcy closed his eyes, and attempted to blot out the vision that his mind created. "But mostly it was just . . . oh, I guess trying to unnerve me, he had that knife and he would . . . it was the way he spoke, it was quiet then shouting, he touched me, and the things he said that he did to you and your father's wishes . . . He was just so angry with you and wanted you to be unhappy. I could not believe what he said was true. I was just concentrating so hard on keeping him occupied, and hoping that someone would come. Georgiana was afraid to run away, he threatened to kill me if she did." She sobbed then said softly. "It was not a physical torture . . . but one of anticipation."

Darcy held her head to his chest and her body to his, gripping her tightly around her waist. "Damn him!" His clutch was possessive and he felt her shaking. He squeezed his eyes shut and attempted to calm. "Forgive me, love." He blew out his breath and kissed her, then slowly relaxed his grip, and her trembling stopped.

"Do you truly wish to delay our wedding, William?"

"No . . . of course I do not . . . I . . . oh Lizzy, I wanted to give you a beautiful wedding. I wanted our family around us; I wanted to have a simple ceremony where we pledged ourselves to each other forever. I wanted to take you home and love you . . . I dream of making love for the first time and giving you everything of me. I have been imagining you coming to me at the altar . . . since the moment that Danny brought me your letter and saved me from my despair. Please tell me how to reassure you. Please . . . I can not bear to have you fear my touch."

She sat up again and held his face in her hands. "I do NOT fear you." She sighed seeing his anguished expression. "Perhaps we do need time to heal a little. At least, so that I can walk down the aisle instead of leaning on my grandmother's cane." She smiled, but saw that it had no effect on him. He was still looking at her with great worry. "Just love me, Will. How did you manage to survive the pain that your parents inflicted upon you? That was not of a physical nature." Darcy's expression changed, and a light of understanding seemed to fill his eyes.

"Yes, I can see the comparison." He bit his lip and studied her face. "I retreated into a private world of my imagination, where everything was bright and happy."

"And created your treasure box." He nodded. Elizabeth smiled. "Is that why you chose Benedick as your horse's name?"

He smiled a little and looked down. "Yes. As an adult I read the comedies to bring me a smile that my real life could not." He looked back up at her shyly. "Until I met you."

"I think that you have found a way to reassure me." Darcy's head tilted and he brushed her curls while drawing his brows together. "How?"

"If I was the key to reassuring you, then you must be the key to reassuring me. Just love me. That is what you needed for all those lonely years, and I know that is what I need from you. I think that you are correct. A rush to the altar is unnecessary. My only concern is Georgiana. If she must return to Pemberley, I doubt that my father will allow me to come with you. It is quite an accomplishment to have changed his mind on the engagement; I do not think we should push his tolerance any further. I will; however, be having a very candid conversation about his reasoning and the family secrets that he saw fit to tell you and not his own daughters."

As much as delaying the wedding pained him, the thought of a separation was worse. It was only the return of his obstinate Lizzy, with the flash in her eyes at her father's behaviour that gave him any sense of hope that all would be well. "Let us see how Georgiana is this morning, and perhaps Richard could accompany her back to Pemberley. I will write to my aunt and uncle, and they could stay with her. We could remain here and marry when we originally planned, then go to Pemberley. I have a feeling that removing Richard from the area will be a good idea."

"I like that idea very much, I would still have you, and Georgiana would be safe at home . . . but why do you worry about your cousin?"

Darcy pulled her back down to cuddle against him and kissed her gently. "Oh, I just know how he likes to find trouble when he is unoccupied." He sighed and closed his eyes. Elizabeth knew there was more to it than that, but hearing the clock chime five times, she decided her time would be better spent healing in the arms of her William than in worrying about his cousin.

———∽∾∿———

As usual, Mr. Bennet did not sleep well, but he was particularly troubled after the long and terrible day past. He paused on his way down the stairs in the early hours of the morning. He thought he could hear the sound of a woman sobbing, and following the cries determined it came from Elizabeth's chambers. He knew that Jane was with her, and would provide the comfort she needed. Lowering his head, he continued down the stairs. He thought over his sudden decision to try and stop her wedding because of the gossip, and realized if he had just allowed them to marry when they wished, the gossip over a seemingly hurried wedding would have been a pittance to what grew instead.

Mr. Bennet lit a lamp and sat back in his chair, considering the conversation he had with Darcy after he had received the terse and unrepentant note from Elizabeth. He looked over to the empty chair and could see the exhausted, beaten man, staring at him defiantly, his energy revived by Elizabeth's obvious devotion.

Darcy was correct, he did think of him as a son. He liked the solemn young man who had wooed his daughter in their clandestine letters. He could sense how much Darcy had come to like him as well, and even, he thought, Darcy would regret losing a father figure, even one as flawed as he. That realization struck him to his core. He knew that he was not a good father, but to have such a man as Darcy regret him . . .

"I received Lizzy's note, I believe that I owe you an explanation for my behaviour today."

Darcy's jaw was clenched. Mr. Bennet saw the muscle working, and noticed how his hands were balled into fists. There was no expression on his face, only the demanding, relentless glare. "What can possibly explain it? Notice sir, that I do not use the word excuse."

Closing his eyes to break the contact, Mr. Bennet sighed. "When Mrs. Bennet told me of the gossip in town, my reaction was . . . typical, I suppose. I told her to ignore it, to not speak of it, and foolishly thought that inaction would make it disappear." He glanced back at Darcy who had seemingly not blinked. "Obviously that was incorrect. I had a niggling thought that perhaps the girls should not walk into Meryton today, given my knowledge, but did I stop them? No, because I would not be bothered with it, not wishing to hear the complaints I was sure would come." He bowed his head again. "Then Lizzy returned with your sister, and I heard what happened in town. I . . . I was brought back, years back, to my sister's ruin. I could hear the accusations, the gleeful vindictive jeers by the townsfolk for one of their own. The way it stopped then was to send my sister away, by removing the source of their gossip . . . well, you see that my parents were equally ineffectual in dealing with such matters and I learned from them. I foolishly thought that you would wish to end the engagement to protect Elizabeth, being the gentleman that you are. But then you came and they were gone, and you gave no indication of anything other than, well of course your focus was on finding your sister." He sighed again and rubbed his face with his hand. Darcy had not moved. "When you left, Mr. Collins settled in my bookroom and proceeded to expound continuously about your aunt, Lady Catherine, and her desires for you to marry her daughter. He told of the great disappointment the family suffered over your sister's behaviour, he explained in explicit detail what happened to your sister in London and how your aunt attempted to secure her future by marrying her off, and that you refused . . . he filled my already overwrought mind with rubbish. I should have known better than to listen to such a man." He looked over to the port sitting nearby and resisted the urge to take a drink. "And then you returned here, with my Lizzy in your arms, beaten. I could not bear any more. I had to act, for once in my life I felt that I had to take control. I made a foolish, ill-conceived demand of you both. I did what I thought a good father would do; I thought that I was protecting Elizabeth and my other daughters by removing you from her life, but in truth I was acting as I always have, ignoring the problem rather than facing it. My parents sent my sister away to save their reputations, and instead they died of heartbreak. I was forced to accept an unwanted marriage because of that same notion on their parts, and because of that, I have failed to acknowledge my sister *since their deaths. I stupidly thought that I was doing the right thing for my family by demanding that you leave Elizabeth."*

"Your poor attempt to assert yourself was cruel, in so many ways." Darcy said quietly.

"I realized that the moment you left this room." Mr. Bennet finally met his eye.

After that, Mr. Bennet could not possibly deny him further, and apologized for his foolish attempt to protect his family's reputation. Clearly his wife and daughter's approach to deal with the gossip head on was far more effective than his family's method of hiding and ignoring it. He asked for a day, but he knew what his answer would be. Yes, they may marry before going to Pemberley, if not; he would not be present to give Lizzy away. He wanted that privilege. Standing, he looked outside at the dark garden, and could hear the servants moving about the kitchen to begin the work of the day. Sitting down, he wrote a note, telling his decision, and asking that they talk, then went upstairs to slip the note under her door and paused to listen. The tears had stopped and the room was silent but for the creak of the bed. He touched the wood and walked away.

The sound of the paper sliding across the floor was just loud enough to wake Elizabeth from her light doze. She was again curled on her side, her cheek resting on William's chest. Her head rose and fell with each steady breath, and she cuddled into his warmth and thought over her reaction to his touch. Why should she draw away from him? Would not the feel of his hand giving love be different from Wickham, who was taking from her? She looked up at his peaceful face, the soft glow from the fire lit up his features, and she could see his dark lashes fluttering slightly as he dreamed. Elizabeth smoothed his hair and his mouth lifted in a small smile. She determined at that moment that she would not allow Wickham to frighten her away from receiving William's touch.

"Will?" He did not wake. She raised herself up so that she was lying over his shoulder and tenderly began kissing his lips. Darcy stirred and mumbled incoherently. Elizabeth smiled and studied him, then began pressing kisses over his cheek, and down his neck to the point where his open nightshirt ended and his shoulder began. Her soft lips wandered over his throat, tickled by the new whiskers, and she found his beating pulse and settled there, nibbling gently, and rousing him. "Ohhhhhhh." He moaned, and his eyes blinked open.

Darcy bent his head and met Elizabeth's warm gaze. He scanned her face, and saw her welcoming smile. His breath hitched and he swallowed, feeling the rising tension between them. "Lizzy . . ." He rolled over so that he laid on his side, embracing her, then closed his eyes as he captured her lips, tenderly caressing and stroking her as she returned his kiss by suckling his soft tongue. They lay entwined that way, only kissing and caressing for seemingly hours. Darcy's lips slowly travelled down her throat, and finding her pulse, indulged his desire to taste her, allowing his mouth to caress that sensitive spot relentlessly to draw out her low moan. At the same time, he lifted from her just enough to untie the ribbons of her gown and drew it from her shoulders. His kisses travelled lower to her soft mounds, and languorously, he tasted the nirvana of her breasts. Around and around his tongue passed over her tightening nipple, and his teeth nipped gently at the bud, each time making her back arch in response. She moaned and he rose again to reclaim her mouth, and kissed her love-swollen lips. Elizabeth ran her hands over his back, drawing him closer and clinging to the hard muscle and comforting weight of his body. Darcy's kisses returned to her throat, and he searched until he found the secret spot he knew would be there, her shudder told him he had reached his goal and he suckled, licked, nibbled and kissed over and over while running his hands around her breasts until he was rewarded by her lips on his ear, crying the soft moan he craved to hear, while her body writhed and arched below him and her hands entwined in his hair as she reached the pinnacle of her pleasure. As she calmed he withdrew enough to kiss her lips and look again into her eyes. "I love you." He whispered, then moved from her to lie back on the pillows and drew her to his chest. She closed her eyes and regained control of her breathing while his hand slowly stroked her waist. Elizabeth reached and placed it on her hip, where he paused, waiting to see what would happen. When she did not flinch or move away, he began stroking lazy circles over her curves.

Elizabeth's hand stole down Darcy's chest to lie over his arousal. He thought of protesting, but it was clear that she had made a decision. He would gladly follow her wherever she felt comfortable going, and he could not deny that it felt so very good. Darcy closed his eyes and melted into the enjoyment of her hand on his body, and remembered her sweet touch from when she caressed him before. Elizabeth watched her fingers drifting up and down. Somehow she had pulled up his nightshirt, and was lovingly stroking his ever-hardening flesh. Darcy became lost in the pleasure of her agonizingly slow caress. He moaned and Elizabeth moved to cover his mouth with her own to silence him. Darcy responded by wrapping his arms around her and they kissed, while she stroked and fondled and soon, much too soon, his body twisted and arched, his cry swallowed in a deep kiss. He fell back against the pillows and Elizabeth hovered above and kissed him. "I love you, too." Darcy smiled and tenderly ran a finger down her cheek. She reached for a handkerchief from the table by the bed and wiped her hand and his stomach. He sat up and took it from her, looking at it for any embroidery, and seeing that it was plain, wadded it into a ball and tossed it into the fire. She laughed and hugged him. "No evidence?"

He smiled and pulled her back down to lie on his chest. "Precisely." They both closed their eyes and listened as the clock chimed six times. "Thank you."

Elizabeth looked back and smiled. "You enjoyed yourself?"

Darcy squeezed her. "Immensely . . . but that is not why I am grateful Lizzy, you came to me . . ." He sighed and struggled to put his thoughts into words. "I will not pretend to understand what you experienced yesterday, but I do know what it is to feel vulnerable and frightened at the actions of another. For you to come to me . . . it tells me that you are willing to face your fears where I respond by withdrawing. Your willingness to approach me . . . you told me how much you need . . . ME . . . Lizzy I can not express how deeply I cherish your trust. I wish so much that I could find a way to make you feel what I do."

"Will, do you not realize that you have succeeded? I know how difficult it is for you to express yourself. I treasure each time that you tell me your feelings. I recognize the gift that it is. You tell me in so many ways that you need and trust me." His embrace tightened, and she whispered. "Everything is going to be well."

"Yes, it is."

She smiled to hear him express optimism and raised her brow. "Colonel Forster was correct when he said that we would be a formidable couple." Darcy laughed out loud and Elizabeth hurriedly covered his mouth, and looked to the door.

He shrugged and smiled. "Well dearest, if we are caught, we will just have to marry today!" Laughing, he kissed her. "Do you not realize that I have been trying to be caught and forced to marry you sooner every time that I kiss you in the open?"

"No!" Elizabeth looked at him with wide eyes.

Nodding, he smiled. "It was a lost cause, it seems. Your father was equally determined to ignore that behaviour as well; he knew full well what we were doing."

"You chose the wrong parent to work on, Will. When it comes to marriage, you should have opted for Mama to offend." Elizabeth laughed and squealed as he happily pulled her over to lie on his chest and looked up at her smiling face.

He brushed back the curtain of hair that fell over him and murmured against her lips before capturing them again, "I propose that we offend your mother as soon as possible."

Bingley left for Longbourn at the earliest decent time. He needed to see Jane, after all of the misery from the day and night before; he found that he was craving the comfort of the woman he now knew he loved. While riding through the village, he viewed the residents going about their daily tasks in blissful serenity, as if their behaviour had not in the least changed irrevocably so many lives. Netherfield was a fine property, precisely what he could afford and handle at this time, but he was seriously considering giving up the lease and looking elsewhere . . . but only after he had secured Jane's hand. Somehow living amongst these people had lost its appeal.

One good thing had come of all of this mess. Seeing Darcy and Elizabeth's reunion made him desire such a love. His commitment to his courtship was strong and he was determined to care for Jane as Darcy did his Elizabeth, he only hoped he was worthy of her. He was welcomed into the house and shown into the dining room. Darcy and Elizabeth sat side by side, not even attempting to hide how their hands were clasped under the table. The bruises of yesterday were now dark purple and ugly. Georgiana sat by Mrs. Annesley, and gave him a weak smile. He noticed that she would not look at her brother at all and would speak to her plate when addressed by Elizabeth, and only in one word answers. The other sisters were much subdued, almost silent. The evidence of the previous day's events was too clearly displayed before them to be able to make light of the matter.

Only Mrs. Bennet seemed able to maintain her cheer. "Mr. Bingley, so good of you to call! How are things at Netherfield?"

"Oh, well, my sister Caroline is preparing to remove to London, and I thought that Darcy would need the carriage this morning to bring Miss Darcy and Mrs. Annesley back." He glanced up at his friend.

"Miss Bingley is leaving? I was not aware of her plans to return." Darcy could see that Bingley's expression was very troubled.

"Ah, yes, she . . . decided that she would prefer to remain in town." He met his eyes and it was clear that he did not wish to discuss the issue before the Bennets.

Darcy nodded. "I see. I am surprised that Richard did not come with you."

"The colonel had plans for the morning, but I suggested that he speak with you before going forward. I must say that it took a great deal of convincing. He must be a spectacular leader on the battlefield, and I imagine it would take a strong man to dissuade him from his set course." Bingley again stared at Darcy meaningfully. Elizabeth watched the exchange between the men, as did Mr. Bennet.

"William, perhaps we can go to my father's bookroom after we finish eating, we have much to discuss." She looked at her father, who nodded. "Mr. Bingley would you care to join us?" His relief was evident. "Indeed, yes." He finally was able to relax and turned to Jane to see her concerned gaze.

"Is Miss Bingley well, Mr. Bingley?"

He grimaced and whispered. "I am afraid that my sister has raised my ire for the last time.

Her eyes grew wide. "What happened?" Bingley noticed the other girls were trying to listen and shook his head while indicating her sisters with his eyes. "Later." She looked around and nodded.

When breakfast ended, Darcy insisted that he carry Elizabeth to the bookroom. "I have a cane, William." He smiled. "As long as I am here, you will be carried. Besides, what better excuse do I have to hold you close?" She laughed and settled against his neck. Georgiana looked up at their retreating backs with tears in her eyes, and got up to rush back to her room. Mrs. Annesley sighed and followed her, along with Mary and Jane. Bingley and Mr. Bennet joined Darcy and Elizabeth.

"Well, what is it, Bingley?" Darcy asked when they were assembled and the door was closed. "What happened with Miss Bingley?"

He paced and ran his hand through his already unruly hair and told them the story of Elizabeth's burned note. Darcy held her hand tightly and she covered her mouth with a gasp. "Of course, who else would try to prevent me from receiving Elizabeth's note?" He looked at her. "It can not be undone."

She nodded and turned to Bingley. "And you have decided to sever your ties with her?"

"It has been a long time in coming, Miss Elizabeth, I assure you. I will have to consult with the attorneys; they will tell me what I may do." He glanced at Mr. Bennet who was listening quietly. "My greater concern right now is your cousin, Darcy. We spent some time puzzling out what Wickham meant with his last words."

"As have I." Darcy lifted Elizabeth's hand to his lips and kissed it then unconsciously pulled her closer to him. "I have a suspicion . . . what did you conclude?"

"We believe that John Lucas may have been Wickham's dupe. He admits being in his company; and he clearly had a goal." All three men looked at Elizabeth, who flushed and looked down.

"I had reached the same conclusion . . . you say that my cousin is . . ."

"Darcy, if he could call for torches and pitchforks I would say that he would have descended upon Lucas Lodge last night. As it is, it was all Hurst and I could do to convince him to stay his action before meeting with you. I will not say that Lucas' involvement is innocent, but neither do I think he should be drawn and quartered. Lucas expressed his remorse for believing Wickham, and he did try to offer help here. He could not have possibly imagined such an outcome. I am not trying to excuse him. Clearly he wished to separate you." He glanced between Darcy and Elizabeth, and saw that Darcy wore a fierce expression of possession on his face and Elizabeth's eyes were closed, her head was resting on his shoulder.

"Wickham preyed on the weak. He used them to his advantage. Look at my sister, my father, the countless young ladies he defiled, and the debts he undoubtedly left behind." He attempted to control his anger. "I am not surprised that Wickham would use Lucas to spread his vile lies. Lucas wanted to hear the worst of me. And the gossips of the town likely embellished it with great amusement." Darcy turned to see that Elizabeth was crying and wrapped his arms around her. He could care less who saw. "How many times was he warned away from you, my love? Even before we were together, you told him that you were not interested. His obsession has hurt so many."

"So must he die for it? That is what Mr. Bingley is implying. Your cousin seems bent on revenge just as strongly as Mr. Wickham was." Elizabeth opened her eyes and looked up at his angry face.

"What would you have me do, Lizzy?"

"Send Georgiana to Pemberley with Colonel Fitzwilliam so that will get him away from here. Then you can speak to Mr. Lucas. He has committed no criminal act. Spreading lies is not punishable by the law, but if he truly is repentant, and if he did come to Longbourn yesterday to help and not to see his wishes fulfilled, perhaps . . ."

"You wish me to forgive him?" Darcy shook his head in disbelief. "Lizzy, I almost lost you, I almost lost Georgiana, and the town thinks of us all as . . . well I do not even know. He accosted you, he shot me . . . my forgiveness has limits, my love. I am no longer a man who will silently accept what the world gives me. I will fight for what is mine."

Elizabeth nodded and stroked his cheek. "But what do you do when the fight is clearly won? Do not change your cause into a mission of revenge. Then you are no better than Wickham."

"It seems Darcy, that the idea of sending your volatile relative to Pemberley with your sister is sound. She seems desirous of being out of your company in any case." Mr. Bennet raised his brow and Darcy's gaze dropped to his lap.

"She is having difficulty seeing our wounds. She blames herself."

Mr. Bennet nodded. "You have my permission to marry whenever you wish, today, or next year. It is on your timetable. If you have decided to delay until you have healed a bit, I suggest that you and I, and perhaps Mr. Bingley and Mr. Hurst, pay a call on Lucas Lodge. A final call."

"You will break your ties with them?" Darcy asked.

"Should I?"

"They are your neighbours, sir. Once we are married, I do not expect to spend time in their company again."

"Well then, perhaps we might leave that decision to be made after we visit. I would suggest you call him out, and you would undoubtedly win, but . . . perhaps it is time to frighten him thoroughly and move on to your future." He smiled.

A small smile appeared on Darcy's face. "Frighten him?" He looked at Bingley then Elizabeth. "Now that is an interesting idea."

<center>~~~~</center>

"There you go." Darcy set Elizabeth down before Georgiana's door and looking up and down the hallway, bent and kissed her, then licked his lips. "Why are there never any witnesses?"

"What am I going to do when you leave me tonight?" She smiled up at him with a twinkle in her eye. "I suppose I will have to enlist Mr. Collins to carry me about."

"If I hear of any other man daring to touch you, I will employ my newly-learned throttling skills most effectively." He growled. She laughed and caressed his jaw. "No, no, my love, I do not care to have your face completely blackened."

"You are implying that I would lose? I am hurt!" He looked affronted.

"Forgive me, I meant no such implication, I only point out that your opponent may not quietly find his way to dusty death, so to speak." Her bubbling laugh made his lips twitch and he traced his finger over her cheek.

"You make a sound point. Forgive me. However, I am serious." She looked around them and seeing they were still alone stood on her toes and kissed him.

"I know, William. Now, let me see if I can coax your sister to talk." He nodded and knocked on the door.

Jane opened it and looking behind her slipped out and closed it quickly. "Lizzy, I am so glad that you are here. She is berating herself for what she has done."

"Well at least she is speaking. Do you think she will see me?" She looked at William, who nodded. "See us?"

"I really do not know. She is very disturbed by seeing your injuries, and feels that it is her fault that you have them at all."

Elizabeth folded her arms. "Well, if you think about it, it is her fault." Jane's eyes grew wide and Elizabeth reached for the handle and opened the door. She strode in to see Mary sitting by the bed and Mrs. Annesley holding her hand. "Mary, Mama needs you downstairs. Jane, Mr. Bingley would like to visit with you. Mrs. Annesley, if you would like to enjoy a cup of tea, I am sure that cook will be able to accommodate you." Darcy stood back and watched as the women exchanged glances and filed out of the room. He closed the door behind him and waited to see how Elizabeth handled the situation. She sat down in the chair Mary had occupied and looked at Georgiana, who was now hiding her face in her hands.

"Enough of this Georgiana. Stop hiding whenever William and I are in the room. These bruises will not disappear overnight, so you may as well grow used to them." She sniffed and peeked up at her then to Darcy, who was standing behind the chair with his hand on Elizabeth's shoulder. "I understand that you are blaming yourself for what happened?"

"Yes." She whispered.

"Well, I am glad of it. I am glad too that you did not run for help. Not because I believed Wickham's declaration that he would kill me if you did, he had other plans for me, but because I feel that it was good for you to witness the consequences of your rash decision to run away and claim to attempt suicide. I do not for one moment believe that you would have gone through with it. You were understandably upset by what occurred in town, as was I, as was everyone else who was there, and I accept the blame for taking you there at all." She placed a hand on Darcy's arm, staying his protest. "But instead of remaining in this house and talking about it when we returned, you left that note and ran off. Wickham's appearance and the subsequent events have nothing to do with your initial behaviour which put us in that situation. Your flight was not an act of desperation, but one of selfishness."

"I thought everyone would be happier if I was no longer here. William should have sent me to Scotland to live at his estate there!" She looked at him with anger.

His brows furrowed and he bent his head to look at her. "What good would that have done? I would have been left alone, carrying the guilt of banishing my sister, wondering constantly if you were well or happy, and feeling an absolute failure in caring for you. With you home, I had the opportunity to try and make your life the best it could be, I thought that you had improved quite significantly over the past months, especially with Elizabeth's letters and then with her here in person, you did not think of the pain you would bring to those people who love you."

"But nobody loves me." She said mournfully. Elizabeth's eyes flashed. "Pardon me, Miss Darcy, but there are two people in this room who love you dearly. Three others were just sitting with you. You have your cousin who twice risked his own well-being to take on the man who attacked you, not to mention your other relatives. You are old enough to know better."

Darcy sat down on the bed. "When you arrived at the pond, before Elizabeth found you, what were you thinking?"

"I was thinking . . . that I wanted to go home." She looked up at him with tears in her eyes. "I wanted to go back to Pemberley and just . . . be away from anyone who would talk of me."

Elizabeth took her hand. "So you did not really wish to drown yourself?"

Georgiana shook her head. "I was so relieved when you found me, Elizabeth. I guess that I would have eventually turned back to Longbourn, but . . ."

"Wickham came." She sighed. "I will tell you what I told William yesterday. The whole day as each event occurred, I thought to myself that I wanted to go home, and not here, but to Pemberley."

Georgiana's face came up. "You did?"

Elizabeth nodded. "Yes. And I was very proud that whatever your reasons for not going for help, at least you did fight him. That was very important." Georgiana's eyes grew wide with her declaration. "What is equally important is for you to think about how your decisions affect others before you act, not just yesterday, but back to when you first ran away with Wickham." She relaxed. "Now, William and I will marry soon. We have decided to allow our wounds to heal a little more first. I am asking you for an answer, do you wish to return to

Pemberley tomorrow with your cousin, or stay here and return when we marry? The decision is yours."

"I would not like to miss your wedding." She bit her lip and looked between them.

Elizabeth smiled. "Georgiana, it is merely a ceremony, something for the law and the church, and a memory for William and me, but truly, I feel that I have been married to William since the moment he asked me, the service is a formality. If you wish to return to Pemberley, do not let witnessing our wedding stop you."

Darcy took Elizabeth's hand and kissed it. "I feel the same way, my love. You have been my wife for quite some time, perhaps from the moment I first saw you. But I suppose that I am a sentimental fool for wanting to see you come down the aisle." She smiled at him "And I am an incurable romantic who wants to see you waiting for me."

"I think that I will go home if Richard will take me." Georgiana said softly. "I promise to think about all that you have said, and when you come home, I hope to be ready to learn to be like you, Elizabeth."

"I do not want you to be like me, Georgiana, but I will be honoured to help you become yourself." She moved to the bed and embraced her. Darcy wrapped his arms around them both, and rested his head on Elizabeth's shoulder. Sniffs were heard then Darcy sat back and took Elizabeth's handkerchief from his breast pocket and discretely wiped his eyes. She took the cloth from his hand and dabbed at her own face, then Georgiana's. "Well, it seems that you need to speak to the colonel now." She handed him back the cloth which was carefully returned to its home.

"Maybe you should come with me?" He suggested with a smile.

Elizabeth laughed. "Ah, you finally found a way to bring me to Netherfield!"

Chapter 29

Sir William stood from behind his desk. "Gentlemen, please be seated." His eyes darted nervously from one man to the other, taking in the expressionless faces, and finally settled his gaze in horrified fascination upon Darcy's battered features. He swallowed. "What . . . what may I do for you?"

"Is Lucas home?" Darcy asked quietly. "We would like to speak with him."

"Oh, yes . . . yes, of course, so much to say . . . quite the day you had . . ." He leapt back to his feet and walked hurriedly to the door. "I will just fetch him, shall I? Yes?" He seemed afraid to turn his back on them. He blindly reached behind for the door, opened it, and disappeared.

Richard glanced at Darcy. "Twitchy fool, is he not?"

Darcy's lips lifted slightly. "He grows worse with excitement."

"I am glad that we left the others at Longbourn. A front of all five of us may have been effective, but this particular battle is a family matter, *our* family."

Nodding, Darcy watched the door. "This is my conversation to direct, Richard."

"I promise I will not say a word until you are through, but give me that, Cousin."

The door opened and Sir William reappeared with John. "Mr. Darcy, Colonel, how may I help you?" He smiled slightly.

Darcy did not hesitate. He stood and glowered over John. "Wickham's last gasp of breath proclaimed he had help in his destruction. After careful consideration, we have concluded that you were his most likely partner in this." His eyes speared him. "You have this one opportunity to explain yourself. I have, to this point, held my tongue regarding your countless offences against me and my family, which includes my future wife. You should know that I could ruin you without batting an eye. This is your chance, Lucas. I suggest that you take it."

John broke the penetrating stare only to encounter Richard's deadly gaze. He turned back to Darcy. "I . . . I believe you already know that I admit to listening to his tale." Darcy made no sign. "I . . . Wickham told me . . . well, you know the rumours, you know what he said."

"I know what he said Lucas, the question remains, what you did with it? Obviously you did not confirm the information with me or at the least, Mr. Bennet."

"I was going to speak to Mr. Bennet yesterday, but events prevented . . ."

"You were going to speak to him AFTER disparaging me and my sister?" Darcy bellowed.

John shrunk back. "I *never* spoke against Miss Darcy! I never said one word of Wickham's claims about her or your reported behaviour against her. I swear! I only spoke of your denial of the bequest and your . . . proclivities."

Richard snorted in disgust. Darcy shot him a look. "Both of those claims you now know are false." He snarled. "Why should I believe you? I know how you wanted Elizabeth. You disregarded her repeated and vehement resistance of your unwanted, ungentlemanly, and uncivil advances! Clearly you cared not for her feelings, but only for your own. Why would you hesitate to spare my sister in your quest to conquer Elizabeth's opposition?"

He swallowed repeatedly. Darcy was so close he could see every variation in the bruises on his perfectly smooth skin. John glanced down and watched Darcy's fists clenching and unclenching, and the memory of Wickham's purple face as those same hands choked the life out of him flashed in his mind. "Mr. Darcy . . . I thought of my sisters and could not hurt yours."

Darcy stepped back and relaxed his stance. John breathed and licked his lips. "Sir, I was wrong, completely wrong in every action, word, thought, everything. I deluded myself into thinking that I was protecting Miss Elizabeth from you. I wish I could take it all back . . . I apologize sincerely for listening to Wickham, for spreading the false tale of your father's bequest, but I swear on all that I hold dear that I spoke nothing of your sister. Wickham knew that I refused to do so and spread those lies himself."

"You did nothing to stop him." Darcy said quietly.

"I did not . . . I . . ."

"You still hoped they were true." Darcy spoke with the same emotionless voice.

"I am not proud of what I have done, sir." John's eyes cast down to his feet.

"What made you think that Elizabeth would have ever turned to you? I am fully cognizant of her opinions of us both."

"I understand the treasure you have won." John said softly.

"I *have* won, do not *ever* forget it again." Darcy did not move until John met his gaze.

"I will not, sir."

Darcy's eyes swept over him and caught Richard's. He nodded, satisfied with the ghostly white face of the petrified man before him. John took a shaking breath, his heart was pounding. Darcy leaned forward. "If I believed that you were complicit in beginning the rumours of my sister, or participated in the attack in Meryton, we would be outside, and you would be lifeless on the ground by now. No magistrate would convict me."

"Yes, sir." John whispered.

Darcy then strode towards the door. Sir William ran ahead and opened it quickly for him. They stepped into the hall but were arrested by Richard's voice. "Oh, Cousin, I will be with you in a moment. I would like a brief word with Lucas." Darcy's lips lifted and he inclined his head, then closed the door behind him.

———∿∿∿———

Darcy was in his bedchamber at Netherfield less than two minutes before Richard appeared at his door. "Now *that* was an afternoon well spent."

"And no blood was shed." Darcy scanned over him, assessing his mood, "I am pleased that you agreed to our plan to scare the living daylights out of Lucas."

"In a gentlemanly way." Richard laughed. "I thought he was going to soil himself when I asked for a moment alone with him at the end."

Darcy smiled at the memory. "What did you say? I could not hear you in the hallway. I had an urge to tie down Sir William; he was bouncing around so much."

"Well with Bingley and Hurst lying in wait for us in the lanes, I could not very well tell you then. This is our secret." Richard grinned widely. "I, shall we say, offered to demonstrate some of my skill with the sabre. I showed him precisely where my blade entered Wickham, and described in detail his demise. The man turned red, then green, then white. Quite entertaining!"

"I do not believe he will ever be anything but an outstanding citizen from this moment on." Darcy smiled with satisfaction.

"Did you believe his confession?" Richard asked while closing the door.

"I did. I know how strongly he wanted Elizabeth, and how deeply he wished to prove me inferior and prove himself right, so I comprehend his susceptibility to Wickham. However, what is more significant is that I can also appreciate his desire to protect Georgiana from further shame by not exposing my supposed sins, as well as her behaviour. That is truly the sole factor that has kept me from becoming violent with him. Well that, and Elizabeth's good sense." Darcy turned and walked to his writing desk. "I appreciate your willingness to allow humiliation and fear to be his punishment."

"I admit to not feeling terribly pleased with the decision when we arrived, and not understanding your desire to approach him in such a manner. I would have expected you to relish the justifiable opportunity to make an example of him. It seems that your head won out over your emotion." Richard watched him opening a deep drawer. "Is it my imagination; or do you actually look . . . happy?" Darcy smiled slightly and said nothing, only glancing up while he unlocked a large ebony case and removed something wrapped in a bit of red silk that was secreted in his pocket. He carefully placed it within, locked it, and returned the box to the desk, locking that as well. Richard's brow rose. "What was that, some crown jewels?"

Darcy turned and still wearing his slight smile; leaned against the mantle and folded his arms. "I truly appreciate you agreeing to take Georgiana home tomorrow."

"Do not try to distract me, Darcy. What was that and why are you so blasted happy?"

"It is none of your business. Now, do you wish to discuss Georgiana or not?" The stare down commenced, and Richard knew from years of experience that Darcy was far more stubborn than he.

"All right, you win . . . for now." He took a seat in the chair before the fire. "Yes, I do agree with you, she needs to go home. I wrote Father to join us at Pemberley. Perhaps we should just go to Matlock with her, you will not want a sister underfoot when you are honeymooning." He gave him a wicked grin.

"I will not discuss my honeymoon with you, Richard. Pemberley is quite a large house . . ."

"Ah yes, but with her home you can not indulge in some rather intriguing past times of the newly wed."

"And what do you know of those?" Darcy raised his brow.

Richard laughed loudly. "More than you do, I would wager!" He stood and walked over to him. "I am intensely jealous of you, Darcy. You have found yourself a lovely girl. I would love her for what she has done for you and Georgiana alone, but watching her take on Wickham, well, she has my unending respect as well. Please forgive my ever doubting you. I look forward with great anticipation seeing her introduction to the rest of the Fitzwilliams."

"You are certainly forgiven Richard, and thank you." He paused and met his eye. "I rather suspected that you admired her."

"I do. She is damned beautiful; and just listening to her talk and laugh . . . but she is yours Darcy. You had the great fortune of noticing her that day, not me. I would not have seen her in any case, when I am in my soldiering mood, well, I am not fit for courting the ladies." He said the last morosely and sat down again, staring at his hands. "I have only killed in battle before . . . it is rather difficult to transition between my civilian and soldiering personas." He looked up at him. "I do not regret killing Wickham, he was in uniform, and he disgraced it. He was touching Elizabeth and God knows what he did to terrify Georgiana . . . I simply fear losing control. I feel my anger flaring up and if there is no one to check me . . . well; you heard how I wished to kill Lucas. If you had not returned here when you did, I likely would have set off after him on my own. Bingley and Hurst could not have stopped me."

"Perhaps it is time to retire."

"And do what? I am nearly thirty years old. What else am I fit to do but be a soldier?" His eyes closed as Darcy sat down.

"You could marry Anne." He smiled and was glad to see his cousin's eyes open and glare at him.

"You are in a good humour to suggest something so ridiculous!"

"Forgive me . . . have you spoken of this to your father?"

"No, what could he do for me?" He sighed and regarded his cousin. "I am the second son, I chose the army. I suppose I could have joined the church . . . could you see me delivering a sermon?" He laughed.

"I know that he has set aside funds for your sisters' dowries."

Richard looked at him as if he was mad. "I have no sisters." Darcy raised his brows and stared at him pointedly. "Do you mean that Father has held those funds in trust . . . for me? How do you know this?"

"We were speaking of Georgiana's prospects for marriage someday, perhaps increasing her dowry, the conversation somehow turned to the preparation of marriage settlements and what is involved . . . it just slipped out in the conversation." He watched Richard's mind thinking rapidly.

"And when was I to learn of this, did that news happen to just slip out as well?"

Darcy grinned. "Indeed, I am not a fool, I had to ask. He said that upon your showing interest in marriage, even before finding the girl, just expressing the desire; or if you were to be sent to the continent. Your parents can not bear to see you sent to war again."

"Well, I will be damned." He sat back in stunned silence. "Is there enough to . . . I do not know, buy a home, live from the interest, anything?"

Darcy nodded. "I believe you could afford a small estate, like Longbourn, if you wished. He may have some place in mind."

A huge smile lit up Richard's face, and he stood to come wring Darcy's hand. "Thank you, thank you for telling me this." He laughed. "I may just have to find myself a bride!"

"Miss Bingley is available, and she does have twenty thousand pounds . . ." Darcy smiled and laughed at the horrified expression on his face.

"Watch it Darcy, this new-found levity is dangerous in your hands. You have not learned when it is safe to apply it. I may just have to steal your bride away from you."

The smile instantly left Darcy's face and he fixed a burning glare upon his cousin. "Do not even think of it Richard, nobody touches my Elizabeth again."

Richard clapped his shoulder. "Well done, Darcy. I would not think of it."

———

"Henry, when should we leave for Hertfordshire?" Lady Matlock asked her husband as she finished dressing for the day. She nodded to her maid who curtsied and departed.

Lord Matlock wandered into her dressing room while fiddling with his pocket watch and drew his brows together as he concentrated. "I am not sure. Richard's letter gave no timeframe for the wedding, well, he said by the end of the month, but no actual date has been set as far as he knew."

Lady Matlock stood and looked out the window at the falling snow, then back at her husband. "I am afraid winter is setting in early this year. I do hope we have some definite news soon, or we may be unable to attend at all."

He glanced out at the weather. "It is not that bad, this early snow is always light." He settled onto a chair before a large mirror and watched her examine her appearance. "You know, Miss Elizabeth will not have time to prepare a proper trousseau."

"And when have you ever concerned yourself with ladies' clothing?" She asked in surprise. He cleared his throat. "I will have you know, my dear, that I am always concerned with the clothing of one lady in particular."

"Henry!" She admonished then smiled. "Thank you, dear." He smiled back. "You do make a good point. She will need many things that the local dressmakers can not possibly provide. I wonder if they plan to go to London after the wedding, and what they will do with Georgiana. Richard said that she is quite taken with her future sister."

"I believe that Richard is quite taken with her as well." Lord Matlock muttered.

She spun around to face her husband. "What do you mean?"

He regretted it instantly. "Oh, it is nothing, I just have never heard him heap praise upon a woman before . . . especially one that he was seemingly determined to reject."

"Perhaps that is why he is praising her so passionately now Henry, to make up for his lack of faith in Darcy's choice."

Lord Matlock looked down at the fingers templed over his stomach. "Yes, perhaps." The parents exchanged looks and sighed. "Well, I suppose we can do nothing but wait for the next letter to determine when we will depart."

"I am pleased that you have come around Henry, and that you have accepted Miss Elizabeth."

He glanced up at her. "I am not accepting her so much as I am supporting Darcy. I want him happy, and Richard says that this woman is genuine, and exactly as Darcy proclaimed. I accept her for his sake."

"But you still must meet her before you will truly believe she is what you have heard." She raised her brow and smiled, knowing her husband's thinking.

Nodding, he smiled, seeing her amusement. "Do not tell me that you feel differently."

"I trust Richard's judgement, and I will help her all that I can. She will need our support. The *ton* will not be kind."

"He has not chosen an easy path back to society." Lord Matlock sighed.

"He is his own man, Henry." Lady Matlock finished her hair and looked at him expectantly. He stood and held his arm out to escort her down to the breakfast room.

They arrived to see James already eating and looking through the post. "Father, I see that you have a letter from Richard and one from Aunt Catherine." He smirked. "Well which will you choose to open first, the bad news or the worse news?"

Lord Matlock sat and watched as a servant hurried to pour his tea. "And which exactly is Richard's?"

"I would say his is the bad news, more details on this foolish match of Darcy's." His father shook his head. "You remain unconvinced, James? Surely you trust your brother's judgement?"

He laughed. "I trust him to be capable of having his head turned by a pretty girl."

"It is well that your brother's troops have more faith in his judgement than you do, James, else how many of them would no longer be living?" Lord Matlock's eyes bore into his eldest son's and he was satisfied when he looked away. Sighing he took up his sister's letter and read. His eyes rolled.

"What is it, Henry?"

"Catherine insists that the dower's house is insufficient, and that we must go to the lawyers to change the will so that she can remain at Rosings." He looked up at his wife over the letter. "That; will not happen." He looked back down and read. "Oh no, she is back on her tear over Darcy marrying Anne. I swear, she must have some sort of ailment in her mind, how many times must she be told that he will not marry her? That boy had better take his bride soon so that we can be spared of this nonsense permanently."

"I am confident that Darcy would agree with that proposition. Perhaps Richard's letter brings us news of the date." Lady Matlock glanced at the other letter and looked at her husband pointedly.

He laughed. "Yes, dear, I will open it." He took a sip of tea then broke the seal of Richard's letter. He read silently, but it was clear to his family that the news was not just bad, but horrific. His face grew red and his fist pounded down on the table. "Good Lord! Has Satan himself come to live in Hertfordshire?" He read it over again and sat back in his chair, shaking his head. "Can not anything go well for this poor man?"

"Henry, what is it?" Lady Matlock demanded. He looked up and passed her the letter. "It will be easier this way."

She read it and her mouth dropped open. "Oh, poor Darcy, and Georgiana, and Miss Elizabeth . . . and Richard killed him, well good for him!"

James had waited long enough and snatched the letter from his mother and took in the news. "My God, Wickham!" He turned to his father. "I never understood why Uncle George fawned over him, and look what it all came to!"

"Should we go there?" Lady Matlock asked.

"No, no, what good could we do? Besides, this was two days ago . . . who knows where things stand now? Hopefully he will be writing us daily, so we can expect another letter tomorrow." He stood up and stared out at the swirling snow. "If the roads are good." He picked up a muffin and strode out of the room.

James looked at his mother. "Where is he going?"

"I imagine that he is writing to Darcy and Richard." James hastily finished his meal and was out the door after his father. Lady Matlock sat back and considered her son's letter. She decided that Darcy would likely want to take Georgiana home to Pemberley as soon as possible, and that was where they should go to meet them. She stood up and went to write a note to Mrs. Reynolds, then would begin their packing.

On the third day, Elizabeth slowly walked into breakfast with the use of her grandmother's cane. The bruise on her face had faded slightly, and the edges had taken on a yellow tinge. The bruises on her neck from Darcy's lovemaking were also fading, but those she looked upon with great affection. When she spied them that first morning; she remembered spinning around to glare at him. He laughed and wrapped his arms around her from behind and regarded their reflection in the glass.

"I have wanted to mark you as mine for so long, Lizzy, and I thought that nobody would notice . . ."

"William!" She whispered furiously.

He cast his eyes down apologetically. "I was simply doing something worthwhile in an adverse situation." His eyes met hers again and she smiled as he continued. "You seemed to enjoy it."

Her mouth opened with a retort, and closed, then she caressed the bruises she had left on his neck. "I did, and I hope very much to have it repeated often." Darcy growled and turned her around to hold her possessively. "That, I can guarantee."

Elizabeth startled from her recollection with her father's voice. "It is good to see you smiling, Lizzy. Are you feeling better?"

She looked at him and saw his worry. "Yes Papa, a little better every day. Perhaps we can have our talk this morning. William will be occupied seeing his sister and cousin off, and will not be able to visit until this afternoon."

"Of course, come to my bookroom after you have eaten." He stood and folded his paper, then patted her shoulder. "It is good to see your improvement." He left the room and she watched him go.

She closed her eyes and her thoughts turned to her visit to Netherfield the day before when she accompanied Georgiana, William, and Mrs. Annesley back. Bingley returned on Darcy's horse, but only after he had a little more time to visit with Jane. She remembered entering the sitting room on William's arm and Caroline coming to a dead stop as she rushed forward to greet him. Her hand came to her mouth as she surveyed their faces, then stifling a cry, she flew from the room. Louisa watched her go and nodded with satisfaction, and later told Elizabeth privately that she was pleased that her sister could see in person the result of her foolish, jealous action.

"My dear cousin, I hope that your health has improved." She opened her eyes to see Mr. Collins had taken a seat by her side.

"Oh, Mr. Collins, I did not hear your entrance. Forgive me. Yes, I am feeling better." She noticed that they were alone and wondered where the rest of her sisters were.

"That is good news indeed." He eyed her bruises speculatively. "I understand that Mr. Bennet has agreed that the wedding plans will continue with Mr. Darcy." Elizabeth knew of Mr. Collins' influence on her father from William, and had not forgiven his interference, and even wondered at his motivation.

She mustered up her ability to remain civil. "Yes, they will. We will wed in ten days. Will you still be here sir, or will you have returned to Hunsford by then? Forgive me for not remembering your schedule."

"Ah, it is so good of you to ask me to your nuptials, however, no, I must return to my duties and will be leaving for my humble abode in only five days." He stopped and eyed her. "Miss Elizabeth, are you quite certain that you wish to marry Mr. Darcy?"

She fixed him with a glare. "And why would I not be?"

"Well, it is certainly a fine, prudent match for you, but now that you have been ruined. . ."

"Mr. Collins!"

"I am only concerned over the effect of such a bride upon his reputation, after all, his own sister . . ."

"Mr. Collins!"

"I am also quite worried of the reaction of my noble patroness to this news. She was gravely disappointed when her nephew rejected her lovely daughter, and I informed her in my letter that he was engaged to marry my own cousin, why I can only imagine her surprise."

"Sir, what is the point of this?"

"Oh, I received an express from Lady Catherine yesterday; you can expect a visit from her."

"A visit? For what purpose?" She had heard enough of this woman to know that a visit from her would not be an invitation for tea.

"Why, to dissuade you, of course!" He looked at her as if that was the most natural act in the world. "Now, when you are free of this engagement, you will be in need of a suitor to repair your reputation, so I do believe that a man of the cloth would be ideal in such an endeavour! And no doubt Lady Catherine would approve of such a sacrifice on my part." His eyes passed over her form with appreciation; he could excuse her fall to gain such a comely wife.

"I beg your pardon?"

She stared at him as he bobbed his head and smiled knowingly. "Even Mary Magdalene was redeemed, Cousin Elizabeth."

Elizabeth stood and stared at him. "Mr. Collins! I take great offence to your implication, and I assure you, Mr. Darcy and my father will as well! Excuse me, sir!" She could not leave him fast enough and was soon knocking on the bookroom door. She heard her father's call and entered, closing the door with a loud snap. Mr. Bennet removed his reading glasses and regarded her flushed face. "Lizzy, what on earth has happened?"

"That obsequious toad has proposed to me!" She wrapped her arms around herself and began pacing the room the best she could with her limp. "He had the gall to imply that I am RUINED and compared me to a . . . I can not even say it!" She fumed and turned to her father. "Why, why must we put up with him a moment longer? Mary does not want him, and clearly Kitty and Lydia are not suited to him, can we not send him on his way?"

Mr. Bennet smiled, seeing his daughter's spirit. "I am afraid that we must continue to host him a few more days, unless he finds another suitable candidate for his hand in the village. Have you no friends in search of a mate?"

"I would not wish him on my worst enemy!" She stopped pacing and stared out the window, seeing Lady Lucas and Charlotte approaching the house. "Well, then again . . ."

"What is it?" Mr. Bennet joined her at the window. "Miss Lucas?" He smiled down at her. "I noticed a falling out between you, Lizzy, but I did not realize it had gone quite that far." Elizabeth glanced up at him and smiled. "I suppose not. Well, I will leave them to meet and see what comes of it." She sighed and looked at him. "I know that I should go speak with them, but . . ."

"You are waiting for an explanation of our family's scandal." He nodded and took his seat behind the desk. She sat down and watched him close his eyes. "Sarah, your aunt's name is Sarah Bennet, although she does not go by that name. She calls herself Douglass now."

"To protect the family name?" She saw his face become pained. "No, she is married, although it has been so long now . . . a lifetime, just over Jane's lifetime." He opened his eyes. "She is much like you, Lizzy. I suppose that is one of the reasons you are my favourite child."

He proceeded to tell her the story of his childhood, and growing up in a very happy home. He was just graduated from Cambridge when the news that Sarah was with child by the stable hand came out. "I thought the gossip was horrible until I witnessed what happened with you. I tried to shield you from it by, well, you know what I did, and I am sure that Darcy told you of our conversation. I am very sorry. I like Darcy very much; I have come to regard him as a son. I could not have wished you to find a finer man. If I had fathered a son, I could only wish that he would be so admirable."

"Then why would you wish to end our engagement, especially after the day we had just experienced?"

"I thought I was protecting you . . ." He sighed at her expression of disbelief. "I know my faults Lizzy, I am a terrible father, your sisters are unchecked, your mother is acutely aware of my lost love, and has dealt with it her own way. It was not a desired marriage."

"Have you ever even tried to appreciate her? Even if you were forced to marry, it is for your lifetime. Was there ever a time when you made an attempt at some felicity?" Mr. Bennet shook his head, allowing her interrogation of his behaviour. "No child. The first years I was too upset over losing . . . and then with you girls coming, life settled into a routine. She had her life, and I had mine." He smiled sadly. "But I am happy for you, Lizzy. You should know that Darcy has some darkness in his past. I think that a bright girl like you will be able to coax him out."

"I believe that I already have." She just did not have the strength to discuss this further, it was a fruitless pursuit, her respect for her father had been deeply damaged. "Papa, I would like to write my aunt. Do you think that she would like to hear from me?"

His eyes grew bright. "She would, she would be delighted. She knows all about you." He quickly wrote her address and handed it to Elizabeth.

"Thank you." She stood and took the paper and read the direction. "What became of the child?"

He sighed. "The girl died at birth, if the facts of the ruin were not so well known, perhaps Sarah could have been brought back home. . ." His voice trailed off.

"Does she have other children?"

"Yes, two boys and a girl. Her eldest son is just joining his father in their business. He is a brewer, quite successful from what she tells me."

Elizabeth's brows rose. "Well it seems that she found happiness in the end. I hope that Georgiana might find the same one day." She studied the paper in her hand then looked back at her father. "I believe my sisters would like to know of her as well." She looked at him pointedly.

He nodded and looked down. "I will speak to Jane and Mary first."

Elizabeth turned and left the room, and walked down the hall to see the Lucas'. They were the first callers since the ladies on the first day. She drew breath and entered the room, not knowing what to expect. Charlotte stood immediately and took her hands. "Oh Eliza, I am so sorry, are you well?" She led her to a sofa and looked at her anxiously. Lady Lucas sat next to her. "John has refused to speak any details of what happened. He said that a gentleman does not discuss such things. He only assured us that you were well and that Mr. Darcy was taking exceptional care of you. He praised him without hesitation, and called your future cousin an extraordinary leader of men. I understand that they called on him yesterday and he was quite impressed with what they had to say."

"Mr. Lucas said these things? Of Mr. Darcy?" She looked at them both then met Jane's surprised gaze.

"Yes Eliza, he went throughout Meryton last night, telling all he met how extraordinary Mr. Darcy is."

"Forgive me Charlotte, but that is quite a change." She did not answer as Mrs. Bennet appeared with Mr. Collins, who stared unhappily at Elizabeth. Introductions were made, and Mrs. Bennet lamented in a rather transparently false way that Mr. Collins had hoped to make a match with one of her daughters but apparently none of them suited. Elizabeth held her tongue and watched in fascination as Charlotte obviously recognized the opportunity and latched onto it with a fervour previously unseen. Taking a seat next to the parson, she expressed great interest in his conversation. Lady Lucas was happy to help them along, and invited him to dinner that very night.

"If you are certain Mrs. Bennet, I do not wish to deprive your family of my company and counsel at this difficult time." Again he stared at Elizabeth who met his gaze with indifference clear in her expression. He turned his eyes to Charlotte's eager face and he looked her up and down, nodding.

"Oh, Mr. Collins, we have enjoyed your counsel for several nights, certainly we can spare you!!" Mrs Bennet happily pushed him to accept and gladly waved him out the door to spend the rest of the day at Lucas Lodge.

When he had gone Lydia giggled. "Well Mama, I pity poor Charlotte, it seems she may have caught a husband, but who would want to kiss that every night!"

"At least he would want her, my dear. There is a great deal to be said for that as well." Mrs. Bennet caught Elizabeth looking at her with understanding and startled, resumed her frenetic activity. "You should be resting Miss Lizzy, Mr. Darcy will be here soon enough and he will want to see you improved. You are not married to him yet!"

"Yes Mama." Elizabeth said quietly and left to go write her aunt a letter.

Sarah Douglass took the stack of post on her writing desk and sat down to answer her letters. Amongst the correspondence there was an envelope from Longbourn, but the handwriting was definitely not her brother's. Opening it she began to read and gasped, putting her hand to her mouth.

20 November 1811
Longbourn
Hertfordshire

Dear Aunt Douglass,
Please forgive this long delay in writing to you, but you see; I only just learned of you in the past few days. Recent events have brought to light your history and how it relates to circumstances which affect a dear friend of mine. I can only say that I regret not knowing you and my cousins, but am so delighted to finally have the opportunity. My father told me that you were once living in Scotland, and by your surname, I suppose that is where you married, but now you live in

Derbyshire. That is quite extraordinary news as I will be marrying and moving to Derbyshire within the next fortnight. I will marry Mr. Fitzwilliam Darcy, and join him and his sister at his estate, Pemberley. Perhaps you have heard of it? I understand it is within five miles of the village of Lambton. I do hope that someday we may take advantage of our proximity and meet. Papa tells me that we resemble each other; so naturally, I am all curiosity to see you now!

I shall write to you again when we are settled at home.

Sincerely,

Elizabeth Bennet

Sarah wiped the tears that flowed down her cheeks and read the letter again. Finally, after nearly five and twenty years, she was again acknowledged as a Bennet. She did not know what to think, but there in her hand was the connection to her past that she felt was missing for so long. Her letters from her brother were always welcome, but she felt his shame when each one arrived bearing news of people she was not permitted to meet. It was a cruel punishment, but she accepted it for what she had willingly done.

"Sarah, there you are! I wanted to ask you . . . Sarah dear, whatever is wrong?" Angus Douglass touched his wife's shoulder and pulled out his handkerchief to wipe her tears. He saw the letter still clutched in her hand. "Did you receive bad news?"

"No, Angus, I have received the most extraordinary news . . . my brother has spoken of me, this is from my niece Elizabeth. She wishes to know me." Her teary eyes met her husband's and he knelt as she threw her arms around him. Angus was inclined to be angry with her brother and wished to never see him darken his door for the way he had continued to refuse to publicly acknowledge his sister, especially after his parent's deaths, but at the same time he knew his wife's feelings. He drew away and held her hands.

"What does your niece have to say?" Sarah handed him the letter and he took a chair nearby and holding her hand, held the letter in the other and began to read. His eyes grew wide. "Sarah, do you realize what this says?"

"I believe so . . . what do you see?" She was very confused.

"Darcy! Your niece Elizabeth is marrying Darcy!" He laughed. "Remarkable!"

Sarah continued to stare at him in confusion. "You know Mr. Darcy?"

"Know him? You have met him! Why he is my greatest supplier of wheat and barley. I visited Pemberley in August with Marshall." He thought and grinned. "As I recall, our son was quite taken with a brief glimpse of Miss Darcy."

Sarah's mouth hung open. "Oh, forgive me Angus; I do not know where my mind was, of course, Fitzwilliam Darcy, how could I forget . . . such a very sombre young man."

Angus grinned. "And he is to marry, well that is excellent news!" He stood and walked around the room. "Your niece says that she reminds your brother of you. If that is the case, I would say that Mr. Darcy will not be sombre for long!"

Her eyes grew wide. "ANGUS!"

He laughed and kissed her hand. "Forgive me, my dear, but I am very fond of that young man, if he has found happiness in a young woman who even approaches your charm, he is very fortunate indeed."

"Thank you, dear."

He smiled and began thinking. "I will have to make a wedding gift for him, perhaps a few kegs of our finest ale, made with his corn! You know, I was planning on stopping there next month when I toured the alehouses in that area, perhaps you would like to come along, meet your niece?"

"I will wait for an invitation."

"Nonsense! You have waited long enough to be part of that blasted family again!"

"Angus it is not Elizabeth's fault. I do not wish to impose."

He sighed and smiled at her. "I was going to impose myself in any case. So what does it hurt for you to be with me . . . and take Marshall along as well?"

"Angus, I will not be party to your matchmaking. I will write Elizabeth back and mention our connection. If we are invited, it will be by the Mistress of Pemberley, and not for business reasons." She fixed a determined eye on him.

"You are a stubborn mule sometimes, Sarah." She smiled and caressed his cheek. "And you like me that way." Angus kissed her lips. "Aye, Lassie; that I do!"

——◦◦◦——

"I thought that we were going to London, Mother." Anne de Bourgh looked out the carriage window as the horses took a road to the right, going north instead of on the familiar turnpike to the left, leading to London.

"So we are, daughter, but we must pay a call first." Lady Catherine fixed her determined gaze on the horizon.

"Where?"

"We are going to see Miss Elizabeth Bennet."

Chapter 30

"**M**other!" Richard walked into Pemberley and saw his parents and brother waiting just inside the front door. Before she could respond, Georgiana rushed past him and into her arms. "Aunt Ellen!"

Lady Matlock hugged her tightly and looked questioningly at her son. Richard shook his head and closed his eyes. "I am so happy to see you arrived safely dear. How was the journey?"

Georgiana kept her head on her aunt's shoulder and sniffed. "It was fine, but I am so happy to be home. I never wish to leave Pemberley again."

The adults all exchanged glances and Lady Matlock pushed her away and looked at her face carefully. "I think that I will join you in your rooms. We can talk a bit while you change clothes. How does that sound?" Georgiana nodded and the two women departed upstairs.

"Well?" Lord Matlock looked at his son.

"Let me change; and I will join you and James . . ." He looked at him questioningly, this was not their home.

"Ah, yes, shall we meet in the library?"

Richard smiled. "I imagine Darcy will not mind if we pilfer some of that fine port he keeps in there?"

James grinned. "Oh, have no fear; we have been making good use of our host's assets!"

Some twenty minutes later Richard was comfortably ensconced in Darcy's favourite leather chair before the fire, glass in hand. "I was surprised to see you here. Darcy only wrote to you three days ago."

"That is your mother's doing, as soon as I read your letter, she was packing for Pemberley. She was certain Georgiana would be coming home soon. I imagine that he should be receiving our letter today. I am rather surprised that he chose not to return with his sister." Lord Matlock's brows went up and he subtly demanded an explanation.

"Father, Georgiana had me and her companion, and . . . Darcy will never leave Miss Elizabeth's side." James snorted and Richard frowned at him. "Watch yourself, James. I will not tolerate any disparaging remarks from you concerning Miss Elizabeth. If Darcy is not here to defend her, I will."

"So, you have been suckered in by the notion of love."

Before he could reply to the jab, Lord Matlock interjected. "Or do you have feelings for the lady yourself?"

Richard stared at him. "Pardon me? Where on earth did you devise that ridiculous idea? I greatly admire my future cousin, that I freely declare, to you and to Darcy, but if you are implying that I have lost my heart to the woman . . . you are very much mistaken." He stood up and poured another drink. "Why would you make such an accusation?"

"Your letters from Netherfield were very complimentary, effusively so, I have never heard such praise from you about any other woman. Unless you include that mare you once rode."

"I would hardly compare Miss Elizabeth to a horse Father, and I can assure you that the lady would take great exception to it as well. I admit that had I met her on my own, without Darcy being involved, yes, I believe I would easily have fallen in love with her." Lord Matlock's head tilted, watching as he returned to his seat and sipped his drink. "I walked into Netherfield expecting to see a fortune hunter, but I met a lovely, genuine, happy and sincere woman, who was absolutely besotted with Darcy, and the most extraordinary thing of all was to see HIM displaying his undeniable devotion to her. He is moon-eyed over her. It would be amusing if it was not so wonderful. You will see; they are a joy to see together, especially after this hell that they just experienced."

"Very well then, Son, I am mistaken and your mother is once again correct."

Richard grinned. "Ah, she predicted that my enthusiasm was happiness for Darcy, and you chose to see only torment?"

Lord Matlock cleared his throat. "Hmm. Something along those lines. In any case, your letter was disturbing enough, but I would like to hear everything."

Richard settled back and methodically described everything that had occurred in Hertfordshire. When finished, he poured a new drink and went to stand by the mantle, affecting a pose that mirrored the estate's absent owner. James and Lord Matlock sat in silence, digesting the information.

"Georgiana resembles what she was in London this summer."

"Indeed, I attempted to elicit conversation with her, but she steadfastly refused my attempts. Her companion took me aside at one point and quietly suggested that I leave off for now. Perhaps Mother will have better luck."

James seemed finally impressed with the woman Darcy had chosen. "She took on Wickham when he held a knife to her throat? I can not imagine such bravery from a man, let alone a girl."

"I am pleased to hear that she has at last managed to garner your praise, James. They will come to Pemberley directly after the wedding, which will take place a week from now. I suggested to Darcy that we might bring Georgiana to Matlock to give them a bit of a honeymoon, perhaps return her for Christmas?" He looked at his father who nodded.

"Absolutely. I wish to meet this woman, but I do believe that Darcy deserves a honeymoon without having to worry about anything but his wife. I will speak to your mother."

"What will your behaviour be towards her?" Richard asked his father.

Lord Matlock saw Richard's protective stance and looked at him with interest. He had never seen this side of him before. "I recall saying that we would trust your opinion."

"You did, but that does not tell me how you will receive her. Elizabeth's status is not of our circles, but I assure you that Darcy will not tolerate incivility."

Lord Matlock did not flinch away from the colonel's glare, but he sensed the strength of the leader before him. "I will tell you this. We will welcome Mrs.

Darcy because of, as you say, all that she has accomplished. Make no mistake; I am already impressed with her. However, I must see her for myself; I must see them together before I can truly accept her."

Richard nodded. "Be prepared to be humbled quickly, Father."

Still caught up with the story of Wickham's death, James shook his head in wonder. "A woman taking on an armed man with nothing but her wit! Extraordinary!"

"Goodbye, Caroline." Bingley stood stiffly in front of the Hurst's carriage. Louisa was already inside, and Hurst was standing beside him, waiting for Caroline to enter. The Hursts agreed to accompany her to London, and see her settled in Bingley's townhouse. They would return in a few days, to attend the wedding. Hurst would also deliver the letters Bingley had prepared to his attorney, so that the disposition of Caroline's dowry and her future could be determined.

"Goodbye Charles." Caroline hesitated. She had convinced herself that her always pliable brother would relent and let her stay, but he had remained firm in his resolve. "I hope to see you again soon, perhaps for Christmas?"

"I am afraid that I will be unable to join you, it is my hope that I will be spending my time with the Bennet family." Bingley kept his eyes focussed on the feathers of her turban. He knew that if he met her gaze he might not follow through with his decision. Caroline opened her mouth, and then closed it again. Lifting her chin, she climbed into the carriage and took her seat.

Bingley blew out the breath he was holding when he felt Hurst's hand on his back. He turned to his brother, and away from the carriage. "Hang on, Bingley we will be gone in a moment. Do not give in now."

"I thought for a few moments that she was repentant when she saw Darcy and Miss Elizabeth, but she seemed to have returned to her fawning over him almost the moment that Miss Elizabeth departed. There was a glimmer of compassion, why would she not accept the truth of her involvement? I might have been inclined to show some mercy if she had."

"I do not know, Bingley. Louisa and I talked about it last night. Caroline's desire for Darcy was very strong and long-lived. I imagine that it will take time for her to let go of the delusion that she would ever marry him. I hate to say this, but I wonder if upon looking at Miss Elizabeth, she was sorry that her injuries were not more grievous."

Bingley was horrified. "She can not be that cold!"

Hurst shrugged. "Well, I have a long carriage ride with her ahead, so I am certain to hear quite a lot, perhaps I will conveniently fall asleep." He smiled and winked at Bingley. "You are doing the correct thing. Do not forget that. Perhaps someday there will be reconciliation, but I do not see that coming until some poor fool decides to marry her."

"Fool indeed." Bingley shook his hand. "Thank you for doing this, Hurst; I do not know how I can repay you."

He laughed as he climbed into the coach. "Oh, I will remember you said that!"

The door was shut and latched and Bingley took one last look at Caroline, and then signalled the driver to walk on. He turned to the house and slowly climbed the steps. Inside the entrance, Darcy waited for him.

"Come on Bingley, I think that I know precisely what you need at this moment."

"What would that be?" He said quietly.

Darcy smiled. "Have you forgotten Jane?"

His head snapped up. "Of course! I will be but a moment, let me change into my riding clothes!" Darcy laughed. "I will see you at the stables." He watched Bingley bounding up the stairs and smiled as he pulled on his gloves. It seemed that Bingley would now understand what it was to need the comfort of the woman he loves.

Darcy took his time walking out to the stables. It was a welcome sunny and warm day, and reflected his mood. He would not admit it to anyone, but he was glad to have Georgiana returned to Pemberley. This was the first time that he would truly be able to concentrate on nothing but Elizabeth. No sister, no John Lucas, no Wickham, not even family would intrude. It would only be his dearest friend and himself, and he intended to make good use of the time.

He swung up into the saddle and took the opportunity while waiting for Bingley to work on some equestrian skills. Although this horse was not his own, he could not resist the urge to train it to do his bidding. As a boy, he was taught to ride early, since it was a very important skill to possess as master of the estate, but very quickly he realized that his mount was the only part of his life where he was able to exert control. When riding he was his own master, and that time alone was invaluable for helping him survive returning to the house. He took out his ribbon and held it tightly in his hand, seeing the contrast between his black leather glove and the yellow satin. The next time he entered Pemberley, he would not be alone, and with Elizabeth on his arm, or better yet, in his arms, their entrance would forever banish away his memories of dread when walking inside.

Bingley's hurried approach startled him from his reverie and he returned his token to its place. "You took long enough, Bingley!"

"I could not locate Bates! He had gone below stairs and I had a deuce of a time getting him back!"

"You are incapable of dressing yourself? How old are you?" Darcy's lips twitched as he watched his friend leap upon his horse and they began their ride. "I seem to recall that Jane said that she liked you in green, Bingley." Darcy laughed as he saw his face fall while staring down at his blue coat. "Forgive me; I am making sport with you. She will find you handsome in whatever you wear."

"Do not do this to me, Darcy! Did I harass you when you were courting Miss Elizabeth?" His glare fixed on Darcy's amused face. "And how can you stand being so happy and amiable? It is just not you, Darcy, you should rethink it."

"You find my mood to be irritating?"

"No . . . no disconcerting." He sighed and looked down at the ground. "Did I do the correct thing with Caroline? Have I made an enormous mistake?"

"Charles." Darcy met his surprised expression. "Your sister's behaviour over the years that I have known her has always been directed only to serve herself. I have not once observed her extending a hand or even a kind word to anyone else.

Not even towards Mrs. Hurst or yourself. This is not your fault, but rather a result of the lax upbringing she received. Your father was too busy making his fortune and you mother was too busy trying to climb society's ladders. They did these things to benefit their children, but I fear that all three of you lost out in the process. As for Miss Bingley, she attended the finishing school that you father could afford, and it was probably a very good institution. It taught her social skills that are necessary for her to move about the *ton*, however, all of the education in the world does not make up for a lack of compassion or goodness. Something seems to be innately missing in Miss Bingley. I can only hope that her new situation will help her to appreciate what she once had. Perhaps someday you will both wish for reconciliation." Bingley acknowledged his thoughts but sank into his own.

They entered Meryton, and could not help but notice the people stopping to watch them go by. Neither acknowledged the stares, but rode by in silence until exiting the village to continue to Longbourn. "I have decided not to keep the lease at Netherfield."

"The area no longer suits?"

"No, it has lost its charm." Bingley looked up. "If you hear of any place, perhaps something in Derbyshire . . ." He smiled. "Do you not think that the sisters will enjoy living closer together?"

"Indeed they would, but I do believe that you must propose first, Bingley." Darcy smiled back at him.

"Ah yes, a small detail that slipped my mind!" He laughed and took a deep breath. It was so soon after asking for the courtship, but he had made his decision. The enormous trees situated in front of Longbourn house came into view. "You are correct about my parents, they were proud to have their children, enormously proud to have an heir to establish an estate, but they did not understand what it was to have a fortune. Possessing money is only a part of it. And I am afraid that my sisters, Caroline in particular, felt my parent's great fear that it could all be taken away in an instant. They were climbing out of being categorized as people in trade, and Caroline felt their fear of being dragged back down. She grew to hate all that our past represented, and thought that nothing but the first circle was acceptable."

"She has no respect for your forefathers whose hard work raised you to the level you are today, or the time it will take to bring the next generation higher."

"Exactly, she sees it as a birthright now, instead of what it is, enormous luck and hard work." He looked at Darcy carefully. "I never have seen you look at your fortune as a given, you take pride in Pemberley, but you are also aware of its history and are grateful for it, despite your childhood."

"My childhood does not change the history of my name. I would be a fool to disparage hundreds of years of work because of one bad marriage. I do wonder what my father would have been without my mother . . . but then I would not have been born, would I?" He smiled at Bingley.

"I suppose that is the silver lining in your tale, where would your Miss Elizabeth be without that happenstance?" Bingley raised his brow at him as they turned into the drive up to Longbourn.

"I do not even care to think about it." Darcy said softly as his eyes were drawn to the sight of Elizabeth on Jane's arm, strolling slowly around the garden paths.

The men dismounted and strode quickly to their ladies. "I will take charge of your sister now, Jane." Darcy held out his arm and Elizabeth grinned while slipping her hand over it. "Do I seem unable to walk without someone holding me up?"

Seeing that Bingley had already steered Jane away to a convenient copse, Darcy glanced about then brushed her mouth lingeringly. "Mmmm. No, I simply have the unfathomable pleasure of being the one man in the world who has that honour, and I mean to take advantage of it as often as possible."

Elizabeth regarded him carefully. The twinkle was back in his eyes. "You sir, are happy."

"That is the second time today I have been accused of being happy." He pursed his lips and tried to suppress his grin, and failed. "Do you dislike it, my love?"

"No, not at all, I find it rather . . ."

"What?" Darcy's mouth hovered over hers. "Intoxicating." She whispered wickedly.

Darcy moaned and he took her hand and moved as quickly as her still tender ankle would allow. They found a bench behind a tree, well hidden from the house, and sat down. "Now, where were we?" She sighed as his lips began wandering down her cheeks and found their way to her throat. "I truly dislike bonnets."

A warm laugh filled his ear and he drew back to see her smile. "And what do you suggest I wear?"

His lips returned to her cheek and he whispered. "Do you have any idea how much I wish to see you wearing nothing at all?" His warm breath sent shivers down her spine, and Elizabeth shuddered. "I have seen bits of you, but not the whole. I have held your nude body to mine, and felt the promise of our union, but Lizzy, I dream of the day when I may lay with you in my arms and love you completely. I can not begin to describe how I need to feel your skin upon mine. You have allowed me a taste, and like an opium addict, I will never have enough of you."

"Oh Will."

"Do I frighten you?"

"No darling, I . . . I imagine seeing you as well." She felt his cheek move with his smile. "Truly?" He could not hide the delight in his voice.

"I am afraid that I am rather taken with you, too." She whispered into his ear.

"Lizzy?" Darcy's lips softly caressed hers.

"Mmmm."

"What do you say we marry tomorrow?"

She could feel his arms clutch her tighter. "I would say yes, but . . ."

Triumphant he leaned away from her. "No, no, you said yes. It is settled."

"Will, it is not. My aunt and uncle are coming from London, Mama has planned a breakfast for us; we can not change our plans now." She heard his frustrated sigh. "Besides, my love, I promised to walk down the aisle to you, and that will require a few more days of healing."

"I was being foolish; of course I want you to walk to me . . . I just want you to know how very much I want to marry you."

Elizabeth caressed his cheek and then snuggled against his chest, safe in his embrace. "I know Will. I am ready as well." They sighed and closed their eyes, not daring to do more for fear of becoming carried away. So lost were they in their communion, neither heard Bingley and Jane approach.

"Charles, stop, you must not disturb them!" Jane pulled him back and away from their bench.

Bingley took a close look and flushed. "I nearly walked into them!" He grinned. "It is so good to see . . . and I hate to disturb them . . . oh Jane, I must!" Bingley pulled her hand and bounded up to the embraced pair. "Darcy!"

They jumped. "Bingley have you lost your mind!" Darcy glared at him as Elizabeth adjusted her bonnet.

"Forgive us, William, but Charles wishes to tell you our news." Jane was smiling and clutching his arm.

"Charles?" Elizabeth asked and looked from one to the other, then to William. Darcy had a slow smile crossing his face. "You did it, Bingley? Well done!" He stood and Elizabeth joined him in their congratulations.

"Oh Jane! I am so happy for you!" The sisters hugged.

Jane was bursting with joy. "I was so surprised that he asked me today! Oh Lizzy, if only you could delay your wedding, then we could marry together!"

Darcy heard that and looked at Elizabeth in a panic. She saw it and shook her head. "No Jane, I am afraid that can not be. Besides, Mama decreed that Mr. Bingley would marry you, so she should have the pleasure of preparing your wedding clothes. I will have practically nothing new." Darcy's brow knit hearing her words, but he was soon distracted by his friend.

"We shall be brothers Darcy!" Bingley wrung his hand vigorously.

"Indeed, my friend, we shall." Darcy turned to Jane and kissed her cheek. "Congratulations, Jane, I am sure that you will find my friend to be quite tolerable."

"I would hope she would find me better than that!" Bingley laughed and accepted a hug from Elizabeth.

"Welcome to our family . . . Charles?" He laughed again. "Indeed, thank you Elizabeth."

The couples began to walk towards the house, Jane was anxious to bring Bingley inside to speak to Mr. Bennet. They were laughing and talking, enjoying the moment, when they came around the side and were confronted by the sight of an enormous coach and four parked directly in front of the door.

Darcy's smile was wiped from his face as he noted the crest emblazoned on the coach's door. "Aunt Catherine." The other three stopped and stared. Elizabeth's hand went to her mouth.

"Oh William, Mr. Collins said that he wrote to her!" She turned to him, "I never believed she would come!"

He drew a deep breath. "I am not at all surprised." He held her hands. "Please do not take anything she says to heart. She will be rude, cruel and angry. Remember, not only is she losing the opportunity for me to marry her daughter, but she is also losing her home in the process." Elizabeth nodded and taking his arm, he led the way into the house.

Mrs. Hill was hovering outside the drawing room door, listening in to what could best be described as the screeching of cats in heat. Quickly Darcy moved past her and pushed open the door. What they found was jaw-dropping. Standing toe-to-toe were Mrs. Bennet and Lady Catherine. Anne was sitting on a sofa, a handkerchief to her mouth, Mary, Kitty and Lydia were standing and staring at the two women in awe, and Mr. Bennet was following the volley of words like canon at battle.

"This will NOT be borne!! HE is engaged to MY DAUGHTER!!"

"THAT will come as a GREAT surprise to HIM!!!"

"IT WILL NOT! He has known of this engagement since he was a child. He is shirking his duties by entertaining the wanton behaviour of your daughter. He is merely acting as any man toying with the allurements of the feminine sex. HE will REGRET his choice. I am here to make sure that HE DOES NOT FORGET HIS DUTY!!

"ARE you calling MY DAUGHTER a . . . woman of the night??"

"I have heard of her luring in the neighbour's son, and I have heard of her compromise by another man in the woods!!!"

"MY DAUGHTER was protecting YOUR NIECE!! MY LIZZY is a good and kind girl. She would fight tooth and nail for Mr. Darcy. SHE LOVES HIM. I will not let some fortune hunting . . . SOW take away her happiness!"

"WHAT did you call me?"

"YOU HEARD ME!" Mrs. Bennet's face was red and her hair was falling from her pins. She spotted Darcy and Elizabeth standing and watching her. She ran over to them. "LOOK!" She pointed to Elizabeth's face then Darcy's jaw. Lady Catherine blanched at seeing the nearly faded marks. "THEY fought for each other. THEY belong together. I WILL NOT permit YOU or anyone driving them apart!" She huffed and caught her breath. "MY DAUGHTER WILL MARRY the MAN who LOVES her, and who she LOVES! SHE will have a marriage that HONOURS her vows. YOU are intruding where you are NOT WELCOME!"

"Do you KNOW who I AM?"

"You are nobody to me." Mrs. Bennet regained some control over her breathing and Darcy stepped over to her. He took her hand and led her to a chair, saw her seated and kissed her cheek. "Thank you, Mother." Mrs. Bennet blushed and patted his face. "You are welcome . . . Son." Elizabeth gave her a handkerchief and stood by her side, holding her hand.

Darcy turned to his aunt. "I believe that Uncle Henry will be most displeased to hear of this Aunt Catherine."

"What have these people done to you Darcy? You have been brawling! Did they catch you fighting the girl? Is she compromised by you? Pay them off; you can be released from this!"

"Aunt Catherine, Elizabeth is my choice. I will not describe to you what happened here, I am sure that Mr. Collins will be more than happy to give you the details."

"I will demand that he relinquish all ties to this family!"

Darcy rolled his eyes. "Aunt, this will someday be his estate. He would be a fool to relinquish his inheritance.

"I will end my patronage!"

"You know that you can not revoke a living once given. Although I have no desire to defend the man who has done nothing to serve his family, and has insulted my betrothed with his assumptions and impositions, I can not see you taking out your ire over your failed plans on him. I will speak to Uncle Henry, but I am sure he will agree that if Mr. Collins suddenly finds himself driven to abandon his pulpit, you will suddenly find yourself in new accommodations as well."

She spoke quickly. "I do not have to go to the dower's house until Anne is thirty."

"I was not speaking of the dower's house, Aunt. I believe that a place at Bedlam is waiting for you." Silence so deep filled the room that the only sound was the rasping breath of the old dowager. "You heard of Henry's threat?"

"I have, and it is not a threat." Darcy's face was unreadable. He had retreated behind his protective mask.

"Mother, I believe we should depart now." Anne's voice broke the tension. She stood and walked to Elizabeth; she took her hand and stared at her face, taking in her every feature. Elizabeth felt as if the woman was measuring herself to her. Finally an expression of regret and resignation came over her. "I hope that you give Darcy what he needs, Miss Elizabeth. I never could."

"I will." Elizabeth looked to William who knit his brows and exchanged a glance with her. He then looked at his cousin who approached him.

"Allow me to see you to your carriage, Anne." He held out his arm and she placed her thin hand upon it. "Aunt Catherine?" He held out his other arm and she rose but did not take it. In silence they left the room.

"Mama, thank you." Elizabeth bent and held her tight.

Mrs. Bennet whispered in her ear. "I do not want you to be unhappy in your marriage, Lizzy. I know that Mr. Darcy is a fine man."

Elizabeth kissed her cheek. "I think that he would wish you to call him William now." She smiled and wiped the tears from her mother's flushed face.

Mr. Bennet appeared by her side and bent to her. "Fanny, that was the most remarkable speech I have ever heard, and I wish to apologize to you. If it were not for the marriage we have had, you would never have been able to deliver it so well." He held out his hands and confused, she took them. "Come." He nodded to his daughters and led Mrs. Bennet out of the room and upstairs.

Outside, Darcy watched Lady Catherine enter the coach and then turned to Anne. "When I asked you if you wished to marry me, you said no."

She smiled slightly. "I said no because I knew that you did not want me. If I had said yes, you would have felt obligated to proceed, would you not?"

Darcy looked down. "I do not know. I never considered marriage until I met Elizabeth."

Anne patted his arm. "I saw the relief in your eyes, Darcy." He looked pained. "I am not in love with you; I was seeking escape from Mama." She looked at the silenced woman in the coach. "It seems I will find it in any case."

"I doubt that Uncle Henry will send her to Bedlam, Anne."

She laughed. "No, perhaps I will one day, but I will consider removing her from Rosings. I will write to him of it." Anne kissed his cheek, and touched the faded bruise on his jaw. "You truly did fight for each other?" He nodded and she smiled. "Good for you Darcy, I will not regret you, but will you allow me a bit of jealousy?" She patted his cheek and climbed up the steps and took her seat. "Go and be happy, it is about time."

"I will." He closed the door and signalled the driver to leave.

Elizabeth appeared and slipped her arms around his waist and he rested his head on her hair. "Are you well?" She felt his head nod. "Do you regret not marrying her?" She asked in a small soft voice.

"No, she wanted me only as a means to her own desires, not as her friend or to love." He looked down, and saw her worry. "I do not regret a match that I never desired, and even if she had answered me in the affirmative, I . . . I admit I would have been torn with my decision . . . but I believe in the end my desire not to fulfil my mother's wishes would have given me the ability to continue to resist. I feel that I was always waiting for you." He fixed her with the same intense stare that he gave her the very first time they met. It seared her soul then and it did again now. Both times she was branded as his. Elizabeth held his face in her hands and kissed him, gently suckling his upper lip. Darcy moaned softly and closed his eyes, pulling her tightly to him, and turned his head to deeply kiss her in return. He heard the soft sound of her moan and drew away, waiting to see his dearest friend's eyes open. Elizabeth gazed at him and smiled, feathering her fingers through his mussed hair.

"Tomorrow, Lizzy. No more waiting."

She caressed him, following the curves of his face, and knowing that in this man she had found love, friendship, and a future that very few could imagine, let alone own. "Yes, Will. No more waiting."

Darcy drew a deep breath and blinked rapidly, then rested his forehead on hers. "Thank you."

Upstairs in the window of Fanny Bennet's room, the married couple watched their children. "I suppose that such a display should be stopped." Mr. Bennet observed, looking down at his wife.

"No, leave them be Mr. Bennet. Perhaps they can teach us a lesson or two."

Mr. Bennet turned to her. "I had no idea the woman I had married. I never knew the force you are. Why have you hidden behind the silly façade all these years?"

"Have you never wondered why Lizzy was so strong or why I looked upon her as my least favourite?" He shook his head. "She is as I once was. I saw you loving and appreciating her, when I knew that she was like me . . . she has your intelligence and humour without a doubt, but the rest is me. You never gave me a chance. You dwelled on . . . the one you lost. I simply did the best I could with what you offered me."

"I like this woman Fanny, do you think she could stay and grow old with me? Will you give me a chance?" He took her hand and stared into her eyes.

She looked down at the hand that had only rarely held hers. "Are you lonely, Thomas?"

"Yes."

She looked up to see him still staring at her. "So am I."

Mr. Bennet tugged her hand and pulled her against him, hugging her for the first time in years. "Well my dear, let us do something about it."

After they had returned to the house, Darcy found Mr. Bennet walking down the stairs and requested that they speak in privacy. Mr. Bennet was not pleased with the change in plans, but as he had promised that he would allow them to marry whenever they were ready, he could not object. He wrote a note to Reverend Mosby asking if the church would be available in the morning. Mrs. Bennet heard the news and sent a servant and Mary into town to retrieve all of Elizabeth's finished gowns from the dressmaker, with orders to also bring matching ribbons and lace for use in trimming bonnets. Jane and Elizabeth set to work packing her clothes with Susie's help. The girl's sister was summoned to the house to observe since she would be taking her place as the Bennet's maid on the morrow. Darcy apologized to Bingley for this disruption of his plans to speak with Mr. Bennet, but Bingley only smiled and assured him that he would have plenty of time to talk to the man once Darcy had finally quit his home. Mary returned with nine of the dresses, and one made of a light yellow silk was chosen as the bridal gown. Lydia immediately set to work preparing a bonnet, and Kitty began retrimming some others. Darcy stayed in the bookroom, writing letters. It was a whirlwind of activity and by the end of the day, everyone was exhausted.

The two couples walked outside to say goodnight before it became too dangerous to ride back to Netherfield. The family called their farewells and Darcy shook Mr. Bennet's hand, and leaned to kiss Mrs. Bennet's cheek, his newly established parting ritual. Elizabeth took his hand and led him out the door behind Bingley and Jane. "She loves that, you know."

He chuckled. "Yes, she turns beet red every time. I hope you are not jealous."

"No, I believe that I can spare a few of your kisses for my mother." He laughed at her smile, and raised her hand to his lips, brushing it. "I always have loved your generous heart."

They reached the porch and saw that Bingley had spirited Jane away to steal a few moments alone. Elizabeth drew him to a darkened corner and pulled his head down to hers, kissing his lips and pressing her body to his. "Oh Lizzy . . ."

"After tomorrow, we will no longer have to say goodbye."

Chapter 31

"**F**arewell Lizzy." Mr. Bennet leaned against the window frame and watched Elizabeth set off in the early morning light. He took note of her stride, unfaltering, and returned to the quick, assured steps of his confident daughter. No longer did she need to lean on her sister or her Darcy, although, he suspected, Darcy would not mind her leaning on him for the rest of his life. She disappeared from view and returning to his desk, sank heavily down. Today his daughter would leave him forever. He blinked several times and picked up the letter from his sister.

23 November 1811
Onich Hall
Buxton
Derbyshire

Dear Thomas,
I am at a loss. What has, after all of these years, driven you to finally welcome me back into the family? I received a letter from Elizabeth, and I was overwhelmed. She wishes to know me, and the most extraordinary circumstance is that her husband is known to mine. Mr. Darcy is a very well-respected man by not only my husband; but all of Derbyshire. How ever did Elizabeth meet him? He has quite clearly not been in search of a wife. I know the disparity in their stations and I pray that this was not a case of a compromise, please reassure me.
Whatever the reason, I look forward to meeting her when she is settled at Pemberley. Perhaps Brother, our family will at last be healed.
Your sister,
Sarah

"No sister, it was decidedly not a compromise." Mr. Bennet sharpened a pen and settled down to tell her the story of Elizabeth's courtship, if ever there was a woman who would understand and sympathize with all of the parties, it was she.

———

Elizabeth wandered over Longbourn's park, visiting her favourite haunts, walking up to and touching special trees and making memories of the views. Her ankle was sore, but she was determined to take this final walk to say goodbye to her childhood. She would be a married woman in only four hours.

She wished to visit Oakham Mount one last time, but she realized that such a journey was just too far, and she listened to William's voice in her mind. She smiled thinking about his serious gaze, holding her hands and begging her to behave, somehow knowing that she would walk this morning. He would forever worry over her, it seemed. She returned to her favourite place at Longbourn, and climbed up on the stile to look out over the meadow towards Netherfield, and wondered what William was doing then, and if she was on his mind.

"I hoped I might find you here." John sat upon his horse, twenty feet from where Elizabeth sat. "Oh, Mr. Lucas." She stood up and suddenly found that she did not know where to look or where to place her hands.

"Please, Miss Elizabeth, do not fear me." He sighed. "May I dismount? I only wish to talk. I will not come any closer."

Elizabeth bit her lip and closed her eyes, then nodded. She knew that this was the true reason why William did not want her to walk, and here it had happened. He quickly slid out of the saddle and stood by the horse's head, reins in hand. "You seem to be completely recovered; your face . . ."

"Yes. I was hoping to look myself by the wedding. Mr. Darcy's appearance is nearly restored as well." She paused and added, "We have decided to marry this morning."

"Oh." Silence fell over them. He drew a deep breath. "Miss Elizabeth, I was hoping for an opportunity to apologize to you. I had no idea that Wickham was leading me down a path . . ." He stopped. "Well, regardless of what Wickham did, it is my fault for not letting you go when it was clear that you had no interest in me. I was at fault for hearing only what I wished to hear, and spread stories that grew far out of proportion from what I first stated. I believed a man whose acquaintance I barely had made instead of listening to the assurances of a friend I have known all of my life. If something worse had happened to you at Wickham's hand . . . or to Miss Darcy or her brother or cousin . . . I could not have lived with myself. I have a very difficult time living with myself after witnessing . . ." He hung his head.

"At least you did come to help when you realized your mistake, and it is likely that Wickham would have found someone else to do his bidding, were it not you." She felt uncomfortable, but realized she would likely never speak to him again, so allowed him to purge his conscience.

"Yes . . . but it does nothing to excuse my arrogance in assuming you would wish for me in the first place. May I ask . . . when did you first meet Mr. Darcy? I remember your mother speaking of some gentlemen coming to Netherfield . . ."

"We met early in June."

"So, you were already disinterested when I first returned from Ireland, before I had even begun my poorly executed attentions." He sighed and stared down at the reins in his hands.

"Mr. Lucas . . . John . . ." He looked up in surprise. "I considered you a friend. Neither of us can say what may have happened if I had never met Mr. Darcy, but I did, and I will marry him today. I . . . I never perceived love from you . . . friendship once, perhaps even some admiration, but . . ."

John could not help himself; he had to express his feelings just once, despite Darcy's warning, and despite already knowing her response. "I think that if given the chance, it would have grown to love . . . perhaps for us both."

Elizabeth closed her eyes, hating this conversation. "You must not dwell on that. My father spent four and twenty years doing just that. It brings nothing good. Please, let whatever you imagined with me go. Find your future and be happy. You know how rare love is in marriage, and if you find friendship with another woman, I think that you will be satisfied."

"You are irreplaceable, Elizabeth. I did not deserve you." He said in a soft regretful voice.

"No, I am hopefully irreplaceable to Mr. Darcy. You can not feel such possession for something that you never had, and if you are honest with yourself, never loved. I do not know what I represented to you, but you never respected me. If you did, you would have listened to my pleas to let me go. I believe that at first you were simply overly confident that I would accept you, and when I did not, you were hurt and wanted to force me to accept your will. That is not love, it is not friendship, and anything less is unacceptable to me."

"You are not Charlotte. She has accepted Mr. Collins. Did you know?"

"Yes, she told me after he departed. She wishes for security, and one day she will have Longbourn."

"She does not feel that she needs more."

"No, but as you said, we are different. You must decide what you want, and you will have to find the woman who suits you. I never was that woman. You must let me go." Elizabeth met his eye and smiled, relieved to have told him the truth. "You have changed John, as terrible as this experience was; I think all of us have grown from it. I believe that you will take from this the knowledge that will make you a fine master and hopefully someday a good husband for some fortunate woman."

John smiled in return, relieved for her forgiveness. "Thank you for that, I hope that someday I will prove you correct."

Across the field Darcy rode up to the crest of the hill and looked to the stile where he suspected Elizabeth had walked, despite his plea. He thought he would just take a look there before returning to Netherfield to prepare for the day. He spotted her and began to shake his head with a smile when he noticed the man. His chest grew tight; it was as he feared, Lucas. He kicked the animal and began galloping across the field. John saw him and his eyes grew wide. Elizabeth turned to follow his gaze and saw William flying to her. She knew what he was thinking, so she turned completely around and waved, and smiled. Darcy was watching her closely and breathed a sigh of relief, slowing the horse from its breakneck speed. He arrived and with an unspoken command, they leapt the fence.

"Good morning William!" Elizabeth smiled warmly at him. Darcy glanced at John then dismounted, tying his reins to the fence, and then walked to her side. He placed his hand on her back, curving his fingers around her waist, and bent to kiss her lightly.

"Good morning, Lizzy." He looked back up and fixed his eyes on John.

"Lucas."

"Darcy."

"Mr. Lucas was just wishing me joy on our wedding, were you not, sir?" She smiled at him.

John startled and broke away from Darcy's stare, glanced at the placement of his hand and nodded. "Indeed. I was most happy to come across Miss Elizabeth this morning. I understand that you will only have family at the service?"

Elizabeth paused, waiting for William to speak, and proceeded. "Yes, we wished for a private ceremony."

"Have you honeymoon plans?" John asked awkwardly.

"Yes, we do." Darcy finally spoke, and then turned to Elizabeth. "I have been thinking, my love, that you should at least see our home in London before we venture north for the winter. What do you say to going to town for a few days?"

"Really?" Elizabeth smiled. "I would love to see your home!"

Darcy smiled back. "Our home, Lizzy."

John cleared his throat; Darcy was obviously asserting his territory. "Well, I shall take my leave then. Mr. Darcy, Miss Elizabeth, may you have every happiness." He bowed and mounted. Darcy met his eyes with a protective glare. "Congratulations to you both." Before they could reply he kicked his horse and was gone.

Darcy wrapped both arms around her and brushed his lips over hers. "Now, my dear Elizabeth, what was that really about

She raised her brow. "You did not believe me?" He chuckled and kissed her forehead.

"No, my love, I know a ruse when I see one, and that was pathetically transparent."

"Hmm. I see that I will have to work on my machination skills." She pursed her lips and her eyes danced.

Darcy smiled and drew her against his chest, then began trailing kisses down her cheek. "Oh, I do not think that you will have difficulty with that. Now, what did he want?"

"Mmmm. He wanted to apologize."

"And did he?" Darcy untied her bonnet and pulled it from her head, then nuzzled his lips below her ear

Elizabeth's knees were growing weak. "Did he what?"

"Apologize."

"Mmmmmmm." Darcy found her pulse and nibbled gently while his hands made a slow circuit of her body. Elizabeth's hands found their way into his hair and she pressed against him as tightly as she could. His lips finally found hers and they lovingly embraced. He shuddered and forced himself away, breathing raggedly, and returned his mouth to her ear.

"Do you know why I really want to take you to London?"

"Tell me."

"I want to make you moan. I want to hear you call out your pleasure. I want to express my love for you and hold nothing back. We can not do that at an inn, and I do not want to wait for Pemberley to make you mine. We will be in our home, in our bed, and I will finally love you the way I have imagined since the first moment I saw you." He moved away to read her expression, and was thrilled to see the passion in her eyes and a smile on her lips.

"Oh, Will."

"You bewitch me."

"You fascinate me."

His arms encircled her and they remained clasped until their breathing and his body calmed. When they both relaxed again she withdrew and caressed his face. "I suppose I should return to Longbourn."

Darcy wound a curl around his finger and watched the play of sunlight on her hair. "Have you finished your farewells?"

Elizabeth laughed. "How did you know what I was doing?"

"We are very much alike; we are both very sentimental about things." He touched the chain to her locket and met her smile. "Tell me, is there anywhere else you would like to visit? May I take you there?" Elizabeth's brow rose and she shook her finger at him.

"I think, Mr. Darcy; that you are simply looking for an excuse to stay with me. We both need to prepare." He kissed her finger, and with a sudden grin, scooped her up and placed her in the saddle. "William!"

He jumped on behind her, drew her body to his, took up the reins and kissed her upturned face. "Ah dearest, I have missed your lessons!"

―――⁓⁓⁓―――

"I hope that I will always see you wearing such a smile Lizzy." Jane sat by her side, watching as she brushed her hair.

"I suspect that with such a silly man as my husband, I am bound to be smiling."

"What did he do?"

Elizabeth sat on the bed and shook her head. "Before we returned, his eyes lit up with what I can only call a look of inspiration. He jumped off of the horse, and took out his knife. I watched him working by the stile, and when I said that we really must return, he stepped aside and showed me where he had carved our initials into the wood." Jane covered her mouth and laughed. "He was so proud of himself!"

"How can you not but laugh at such antics?" Jane closed the last of the trunks and looked around the empty room. "I think that is everything, Lizzy. I am sure that you will be purchasing a great deal more, you have not had much opportunity as yet."

"No, and in some ways I am pleased about that. I hope to ask Lady Matlock to help me, and perhaps I can coax Georgiana to visit the dress shops as well in the spring." She stood and looked over the last of the bonnets and decided to leave them for her sisters. "You will have Aunt Gardiner's help. When do you plan to go to London for your wedding clothes?"

"Charles needs to go to town for some business this coming week, so I will ask if I might travel with him, along with Mary, and we will do our shopping with Aunt Gardiner then."

"Oh, then perhaps we will see you . . ."

"Lizzy, I do not think that William will be in any mood to entertain, do you?" She tilted her head and smiled.

She blushed then grinned. "No, perhaps not." The girls laughed and Jane helped her to slip the gown over her head, and began arranging her hair, while

Elizabeth adjusted the diamond choker's position. "Have you set a date for your wedding yet?"

Jane's smile disappeared. "It all depends on what happens with the attorneys. He is meeting them to work out Miss Bingley's future. I do not think that he wishes her to be residing in his townhouse after our marriage . . . so . . ." Her voice faltered.

Elizabeth turned and hugged her. "I am sure it will be soon."

"He does not wish things to be this way, Lizzy. He hopes so much for her to see the effect her actions have had on others and change her ways. He would prefer reconciliation; it is just that she finally pushed him too far."

"And he is standing up to her. You should be glad of it and support him, Jane."

"Oh I do!" She peeked up at her. "Lizzy, could you tell me of . . ." Elizabeth watched her. "You seem to have given William much comfort . . ."

She began to understand and smiled. "Do you wish for advice on kissing Charles?"

Jane blushed but sighed in relief. "I wish to know everything, Lizzy."

Elizabeth laughed and watched her sister's embarrassed but eager face in the mirror. "Well, I do not know everything yet!"

The sister's conversation was interrupted by Mrs. Bennet bursting in the door. "Lizzy! Are you not ready? You must be at the church within the hour! Why you chose this morning to go gallivanting in the fields, I will never know. YOU decided to marry today, if you had simply waited a week . . . OH, my poor nerves!"

Elizabeth stood and put a calming hand on her mother's arm. "Mama, please relax. All I need are my bonnet and spencer."

Mrs. Bennet looked to Jane. "Please leave us Jane; this is not for your ears." The girls exchanged glances and Jane hurriedly left the room. Mrs. Bennet took Elizabeth's hand. "Lizzy, I know that I have not been the best of mothers or even wives, but I have tried my best with what I was given."

"Mama, I know about Aunt Sarah, and how you came to be married to Papa."

She stared at her in shock. "You do? But how? He said never to speak of it!"

"He told William, and I confronted him. I have written to my aunt. I now understand so much of your marriage, Mama. I want you to know that I am very happy, and . . . I do not fear what will come tonight."

"Are you sure, child? I can offer few words of comfort, only to say that . . . no, Mr. Darcy cares very much for you. Anything I could say would be useless." She patted her hand and smiled slightly. "Your husband will be gentle and kind, I am sure. Follow his lead and you will be well."

Elizabeth smiled and kissed her cheek. "I know that I will." Mrs. Bennet embraced her.

"I expect many letters, daughter. I want to know how you get on." She sniffed and turned quickly to the door and opened it. Elizabeth watched her go, her heart ached for her, seeing the devastation that a loveless, friendless marriage could wreak, and realizing again how extraordinarily rare her relationship with William was.

She gathered her spencer and looked about for the bonnet, and remembered it was downstairs. Lydia and Kitty walked up to her with giggles and handed it to her. "It looks lovely Lydia, thank you. You have a great talent for this."

Lydia's eyes widened. "Thank you, Lizzy!"

Kitty bit her lip and drew out a confection of yellow ribbons and lace. "There are no flowers in the garden anymore, so I thought you might carry this."

Elizabeth laughed. "It is beautiful!" She looked at the roses she had formed with the ribbons and lifted it to her nose. "Did you sprinkle this with rosewater?"

Kitty giggled. "You noticed! That was Mary's idea!" Mary appeared from around the corner and smiled slightly. Elizabeth took her hand.

"Thank you, it was a wonderful idea."

Mary suddenly flung her arms around her and whispered. "I shall miss you so much."

"Then you will have to come and visit, Georgiana will like that, and so will I." Elizabeth hugged her tightly. "Until then I want you to write." Mary nodded and sniffed.

"All right ladies, to the carriage!" Mr. Bennet appeared and shooed them all away, then looked sadly at her. "Well, you have chosen to fly the nest."

Elizabeth laughed. "Yes, Papa, you should be glad, one less mouth to feed."

He shook his head. "No my dear, I would have gladly kept you here forever, but it seems that Darcy had other plans."

———〰———

"Are you not nervous?" Bingley stood by Darcy's side, watching the unreadable face. Darcy's eyes were bright and alive.

"No."

"I would be nervous."

"How fortunate that I am not you, then."

"Come now man, this is forever! Every day, the same woman, the same voice, the same . . ."

Darcy raised his brow and looked at him speculatively. "I believe that you became engaged yesterday Bingley, are you certain that you are not speaking of your own misgivings?"

"NO! No, no . . . I am . . . This is not right Darcy. You are so damned stoic!" Bingley glared at his friend's perpetually calm demeanour.

Darcy's lips twitched. "Would you prefer me to be pacing, twisting my gloves, shaking in my boots . . . perhaps resembling you?" Bingley's hat was in his hands and he was ruining the brim with his twisting. "I am the one marrying this morning, and I am calm because I will at last be happy, and my home truly will be a place that I can not wait to enter, and be with my love. Why on earth are you so nervous?"

"I . . . I am just seeing my future is all." Darcy tilted his head. Bingley sighed. "I am hoping that I am seeing my future. Do you realize that Jane is the only woman I have not disappointed by running away to find another? Our courtship was so short, I proposed yesterday on an impulse, I am afraid that my old habits might return and I might never be standing in this position, at an altar, again."

"Do you love her Bingley?"

"With all of my heart, with a fervour that I have never known, that I did not even realize I was capable of possessing." Bingley stopped his nervous twisting and leaned against the pulpit, looking at his serene friend. "I am . . . Darcy, you know my habits. In honesty they are not that different from yours."

Darcy's cough made him smile. "Well, you know; my habits in bedding ladies. I daresay I visited the courtesans no more often than you . . . well, perhaps a little more often."

Darcy grew uncomfortable and looked down. "I am not proud of that Bingley, and I told Elizabeth of it. She accepted my honesty, but I know it hurt her." He looked up. "It will never happen again."

"I doubt that I will ever speak of it to Jane, she is all that is sweet and pure . . . not that Elizabeth is not." He added hurriedly. Darcy shook his head and indicated that he continue. "I have never bedded any woman of society. I was tempted, it was offered, but I did not. I also never felt an inclination to marry any of them either, Jane is the first . . ." His voice trailed off.

"Do you doubt your ability to remain constant to her, despite the obviously elevated feelings you have for her, beyond everything you have ever experienced before? Truly Bingley, you should have held this debate before proposing. Your honour is engaged now." Darcy's gaze pierced him, and Bingley knew what was being left unsaid. His friend had told him many times not to trifle with Jane.

He looked up and drew a deep breath. "I suppose . . . I suppose that I . . ." He smiled. "I suppose that I am finally growing up. I no longer want to flit from lady to lady. I want to have a wife, a home, and children." He nodded as he looked at his friend who was forced to instantly become an adult at an age when Bingley was only concerned of the next dance partner and if she was pretty. The realization finally sunk in. Darcy knew long ago what responsibility was, and he was only just feeling it, first with his sister, and now with this new commitment to Jane. "I guess Darcy, it is that being in this place right now, and preparing to witness the awesome pledge that you are about to take with Elizabeth . . . I am leaving my boyhood behind. I may not be taking the vows today, but when I look at Jane, I will be repeating them to her."

Darcy smiled widely; his friend had finally taken the great step to being his own man. "Then you will be here soon. I have every faith in you." Darcy clapped his back and turned to greet Reverend Mosby and his clerk. Bingley; still lost in his epiphany, jumped at their sudden appearance.

"Mr. Darcy, are you prepared? Do you have the ring?"

Darcy smiled. "Well, my friend does."

"The ring! My God . . . Oh, forgive me Reverend . . . Oh where is it?" Bingley began patting his coat, searching desperately. Darcy tilted his head and calmly reached forward, grabbing his flying right hand.

"Bingley." He stopped and stared. Darcy pointed to his little finger, where the wedding band rested on the tip.

"Oh, thank heaven." He smiled ruefully at his friend. "I suppose that I am nervous now about failing you at your time of need."

The church doors opened and Mrs. Bennet and the girls entered. Jane took her place at the altar, smiling at Bingley, and then looking concerned at his somewhat flustered appearance. He smiled at her and she relaxed. She glanced at Darcy, but his eyes were riveted to the back of the church, where the vision of his dreams stepped into reality. Elizabeth stood with Mr. Bennet and saw nothing but William's gaze fixed upon her. Mr. Bennet looked between them.

"He is worthy of you."

"Then take me to him, Papa."

Mr. Bennet swallowed down the lump in his throat and began walking. Elizabeth's eyes remained locked on William's, noticing the slight smile that played on his lips, but concentrating on his expressive eyes, bright and glowing with love and unshed tears. She could barely make out his face by the time they arrived at his side, her own vision was so blurred.

Mr. Bennet placed her hand in his warm clasp. Elizabeth felt the tremble that showed nowhere else, and knew that it was not fear. The Reverend began the service, and the words encircled them, bound them, just as tightly as the invisible spirit of the love and commitment they already shared had done long ago. When asked for the ring, Bingley's gaze was fixed upon Jane, and he did not hear the request. Darcy bent and removed it from his unmoving finger, and found the payment for the service inside of his coat, serving as his own best man. Elizabeth's eyes danced and Jane furrowed her brow at him. Bingley suddenly realized that he had been asked to perform his duty and closed his eyes in mortification to see the ring already resting on the bible. He caught his friend's eye and shook his head. Darcy's lips twitched; then he turned to face Elizabeth and his eyes twinkled in barely repressed glee as he promised her everything that he was or ever would be. She promised him forever her love and devotion, and when Darcy finally slipped his great grandmother's ring on her finger, the smile that lit his face matched perfectly the joy on hers.

They knelt, holding hands, half-listening to the final blessings, and taking turns wiping the tears pouring down the other's face. When finally the prayers ended, Darcy stood and beaming, aided Elizabeth to her feet. Bingley met Jane's smile and looked down, shaking his head and smiling to his shoes. "Darcy will never let me forget this."

A deep warm chuckle began in Darcy's chest, followed by Elizabeth's bubbling laugh. Soon the church was filled with the sound of laughter. Elizabeth held out her arms and Darcy, towering above her, fell into her embrace for the homecoming he had wished for his entire life. They walked to the register, and he sat, signed his name, then handed the pen to his wife, who leaned over his shoulder to write her maiden name one last time. He took the pen from her, and then captured her hand, holding it to his chest.

"I do not have the words, Lizzy . . . Thank you."

"Take me home, Will."

Chapter 32

"Two hours, Mr. Hendricks! Two hours!" Mrs. Hendricks glared at her husband as she tore around the master suite, watching the chambermaids fluffing the bedding and dusting furiously. "What was the master thinking? He was not to marry until next week and then they were to go to Pemberley!"

"It seems that he made the decision to come here just this morning."

She ran through the door into the adjoining sitting room, checked to see that supplies for the fire were in place and then entered the Mistress' chambers. She paused, watching the activity of the maids. "Well at least this room was completely redecorated this summer." She turned to him. "He must have known he would marry her then."

"I do not know. Roberts and Danny are very tight-lipped about Mr. Darcy; they only seem to talk to each other."

"I heard that, Hendricks. Mr. Darcy only entrusted the secret to us, and specifically said not to speak of it to the staff. They were engaged for almost two months." Roberts came into the room and looked around. "Well, this is quite a change."

"Mr. Darcy wanted nothing to be left untouched. The wall coverings, the furniture, the rugs, even the mattress was replaced. He wanted no memories of . . ." Mrs. Hendricks grew silent, and the three old staff members looked at each other, remembering Mrs. Darcy and her turbulent marriage. He had done something very similar to the master's suite when his father passed on.

"It will be good to have a mistress again." Mr. Hendricks said softly.

"What is she like, Roberts?"

He smiled slightly. "Well, I saw her but rarely, but I can say that she has had a remarkable affect upon the master. Perhaps you should ask her abigail."

"Susie!" The young girl appeared from the dressing room and stood in frightened anticipation before her new superiors.

"Yes ma'am!"

"How long have you served Mrs. Darcy?"

Susie startled, not used to the new appellation. "Oh, three years, I cared for all of the Bennet girls."

"Well then, you know her best. Will this room please her?"

Susie looked around the room and smiled. "Yes, it looks like it is set in a garden. Miss Eliz . . . Mrs. Darcy is very fond of the outdoors."

"She does not seem to have a great deal of luggage." Mrs. Hendricks looked at the few worn trunks, now being carted away by two footmen.

"No, there was little time for preparing her wedding clothes, especially after . . ." Her eyes widened and she looked at Roberts, unsure if she could speak of what had happened in Hertfordshire. The housekeeper and butler turned to regard the valet.

Roberts cleared his throat. "Later."

Mrs. Hendricks turned back to the girl. "Is your mistress particular about anything? Any likes or dislikes that we need to address before she arrives? Anything urgent?"

"I can not think of a thing. She is a very happy, warm lady. Very kind and . . . I like her very much." Susie blushed and looked at her toes.

"Very well then, return to your duties." Mrs. Hendricks swept out of the room to speak with the cook. Mr. Darcy had sent specific requirements for a supper to be left in the sitting room. He wanted no large meal waiting for them, which was fortunate as there was no time to prepare it in the first place. She cast a critical eye over the house, everything was spotless, as usual, despite the fact that the master had not been in residence in nearly five months. As the time flew by, a footman was stationed by the front door, and at almost the exact predicated moment, he raised a cry. "They are here!"

The staff hurried to assemble in the foyer; Mr. Hendricks inspecting each of them for their uniform and deportment, then joined his wife at the front door. Two footmen raced out to open the coach's door and begin collecting whatever luggage remained. The older couple leaned and watched as Mr. Darcy's finely polished boot appeared on the step and he descended, immediately offering his palm to someone inside. A small, slender gloved hand appeared and rested in his, and then a bent, bonneted head. The small woman looked up and smiled into the eyes of her husband. Darcy took her arm and turned towards the house, a warm, glowing smile on his face. Mrs. Hendricks's breath caught and she lifted a hand to her mouth, and glanced at her husband, who was fighting back the tears in his eyes. He cleared his throat and straightened, awaiting their approach.

Elizabeth looked up at the house and faltered a moment. Darcy immediately looked down. "What is it, Lizzy?"

"I . . . Oh William, it is so . . .." She looked at him in distress. "How am I ever to be mistress of this?"

Darcy smiled and kissed her hand. "My love, it is merely a house. If I could run it with the help of my staff, you can as well. Come, come into our home." Elizabeth nodded her head and drew a breath, then took a determined step forward. Darcy chuckled softly, thinking that she could hardly fear a household after taking on Wickham.

They climbed the steps and Mr. and Mrs. Hendricks greeted them. "Sir, congratulations."

Darcy smiled widely, and they stared at the novelty. "Please forgive my impulsive decision. I only made it this morning. I will understand if there was not enough time to prepare for our arrival."

"Not at all sir, all is in readiness, as you requested." Mrs. Hendricks smiled, and then looked to Elizabeth, who was watching him.

"Ah excellent." He paused, then noticing the assembled staff, he moved forward. He stood before them and stepped slightly away from her. "I would like to introduce you to Mrs. Fitzwilliam Darcy, my dear wife. Please welcome her into our home, and give her the courtesy and respect that you have given me. I have no doubt that you will soon count yourselves as fortunate to have such a mistress."

Elizabeth blushed deeply with his praise and the staff broke into a round of applause. "Thank you all for your kind welcome, I very much wish to continue the traditions of Darcy House, and I hope that you will all bear with me as I learn." Her warm smile and the master's apparent happiness with his wife settled any questions they had over her.

"Sir, your baths will be ready in a quarter hour, the meal you requested is in the sitting room. Is there anything else?" Mrs. Hendricks asked.

"No, not at all. We will require nothing until the morning, and . . ." He looked down at Elizabeth then back to his housekeeper. "We will ring when it is wanted." Elizabeth blushed again and Mrs. Hendricks nodded and held back her smile. "Yes, sir."

Darcy breathed out a long sigh. That was finished, now, to get his wife upstairs! "Come my love; let me show you your chambers." Instead of offering his arm, he took her hand, and entwined his fingers with hers. Elizabeth squeezed and they made their way up the steps. He watched her taking in the home with some anxiety. "Do you like it, Lizzy?"

"It is beautiful. Perhaps we might have a tour tomorrow?" She smiled and felt his squeeze.

"Perhaps . . . If you wish to leave our rooms."

"William!" She glanced around to make sure that no servants were near, and he laughed in delight. "It seems you have great plans for me."

Darcy raised her hand to his lips. "For us, my love."

They arrived on the second floor, and he showed her the door to his chambers, and then took her farther down the hallway to her door. "This was completely redecorated this summer. I . . . I did it with your memory in mind, you see . . . I knew, even before we came to Hertfordshire that I would ask you to be my wife." Elizabeth lifted her hand to caress his face. He covered the hand with his own, and then kissed her palm. "Thinking of you in this room is what kept me sane while waiting for . . ." His eyes grew bright.

"My letter." She whispered, and he nodded. Reaching out, he turned the handle and they stepped into the room. "Ohhhh."

They stood together, taking in the décor. "It is . . . oh William; it is like a walk in a garden on a spring day." She turned and embraced him. "It is perfect, thank you!"

Darcy beamed. "I am so glad that you like it."

Susie appeared and immediately blushed. "Mrs. Darcy, your bath is ready." They broke apart and Elizabeth nodded. "Thank you." She looked back at William. "How long . . ."

He leaned and kissed her softly. "I shall meet you in the sitting room in an hour." He indicated the door and raised his brows to her. "Agreed?"

Elizabeth laughed. "Agreed." He squeezed her hand and she watched him disappear through the door.

Turning around to look again at the room, she saw all of the little touches that he had chosen for her, the colours, the carving in the furniture, even the fabrics themselves seemed to be symbolic of the bits of information he had discerned in her letters. A great deal of thought and dreaming went into the decoration of this room. Susie cautiously reappeared. "Are you ready, Mrs. Darcy?" She nodded and smiled, walking into the dressing room, and noting the full-length mirror and dressing table, already holding an assortment of perfumes for her use. The closets were yawning with their emptiness. Her small supply of clothes barely made a dent in the capacity that was available. She could not imagine filling the room, but knew someday she would. Susie helped her out of the wedding gown, and took down her hair. The necklace was placed in its box and she watched with a smile as Susie carefully placed it in the safe hidden in the back of one closet. They entered the room that contained the bathtub and Elizabeth stood still in astonishment. Susie glanced at her. "It took me by surprise, too!"

"You could fit three people in that!" Elizabeth whispered, admiring the enormous copper tub. It was a far cry from the family tub she grew up using, one she could barely fit inside.

The bath was accomplished quickly, and Susie dried and brushed out her hair. "I did not know what you would like as your nightdress, Mrs. Darcy, there is nothing new . . ."

Elizabeth looked sadly at the three muslin gowns that were displayed. "No, this is not what I had in mind for tonight either." She sighed and then looked down at the yellow robe she was wearing. "I think that this will have to do." Susie's eyes widened. "But . . ." Elizabeth smiled. "That will be all, Susie. I will ring for you in the morning."

Susie bobbed and looked her over one more time. "You look very beautiful, Mrs. Darcy."

Elizabeth stood before the mirror, adjusting her curls, and smoothed the silk robe that her mother had slipped into her trunk. She took a deep breath and noting the time, walked into her bedchamber and paused at the open door to the sitting room.

William stood by the fire, leaning and looking into the flames. He was turned sideways, and she could clearly see the evidence of his prominent arousal pushing the silk of his deep blue robe away from his body. Her breath caught, and she must have made a sound as he instantly looked up and towards the doorway. She would never forget the expression on his face when he saw her. He stood frozen, drinking her in, and commanded himself, *Remember this!*

After seemingly hours of staring, Darcy advanced towards her, and Elizabeth met him in the middle of the room. "You are lovely." He breathed, and entwined his fingers in her long, loose hair, combing them through. Elizabeth's hands rested on his hips and Darcy cupped her face in his hands, "I love you." He lowered his mouth to kiss her once, then hovered above to watch her tongue appear to wet her lips, and covered them again, stroking the warm, trembling flesh. Elizabeth moaned softly and pressed her body to his, encircling him with her arms, and stroking his back. His arms lowered to surround her shoulders and draw her against his chest.

She moaned again when he began moving his lips slowly down her face to her throat, and lingered there, tasting her earlobe, and finding her pulse. Elizabeth closed her eyes and relaxed into the sensations that were flowing through her, the gentle brush of his hair against her cheek, the warm softness of his tongue, his hands, travelling possessively over and up and down her back, and his heady scent that seemed to encompass her senses with everything that was him. "I love you, Will." She whispered in the ear that was so close to her mouth, and she tenderly drew in his lobe, inspiring his low moan.

Darcy's lips returned to hers, and his hands moved to the front of her robe. While they kissed with increasing passion, his fingers untied the belt and he spread the fabric open. His hands reached inside to touch, then suddenly stopped and drew away. "Lizzy . . . you are. . ." He stood back, holding her hands and looked with pleasure and delight at the nude body of his blushing wife appearing within the open robe. Darcy's smile grew and he pushed the silk back and off of her shoulders to puddle on the floor. "Oh, my love . . . you are beautiful!" He laughed and reached out to touch her firm and intoxicatingly soft breasts, then down her waist, over her enticingly curved hips then around to pull her to him, while running his hands over her back. "What a gift you are!" Elizabeth recovered a little from her embarrassment and slipped her hands between them, tugging at his belt.

"I believe that it is time to open my gift, Will." Darcy's delighted laugh rumbled in her ear, and he moved away a little, fixing his twinkling warm eyes on her face while she looked down to untie his robe. To her great surprise, she found that he too wore nothing beneath the silk. There before her was the tight, muscled body she had imagined and felt, but never fully seen. She caressed her hands upwards through the soft black curls blooming on his chest, then down to touch and fondle the velvety skin of his potent manhood. Darcy growled and shuddered with her touch. "Lizzzy." Elizabeth bit her lip and looked up at him, lowering her hands to weigh his stones in one palm, and then stroked him slowly with the confident precision that her knowledge allowed. He drew her hands from him then clasped her body to his, and bestowed deep, wet, lingering kisses. He nibbled the tender swollen lips then soothed them with his tongue, and drew hers into his mouth to caress. Darcy released her and bent, scooping her up in his arms. He stared at her with intense, dark eyes. "Come wife, to our bed." Elizabeth smiled and touched his reddened lips, then brushed his cheek with her fingertips. Lifting her chin she breathed in his ear, "Take me, husband."

They entered the softly lit room, a fire blazed, a few candles glowed, and an open and forgotten bottle of wine sat on a table near a sofa. A tray piled with specially selected fruits and sweets, meant to inspire a seduction, waited for another time. Darcy lowered his precious burden onto the bed, disappeared for a moment to retrieve their discarded robes, and then climbed in beside her. He rested on his side touching her face, and ran his hand down her body. "Are you nervous?"

"Are you?"

Darcy smiled and laughed, nuzzling her face with his. "Yes." He admitted then looked back up to her, seeing the warmth and sparkle in her beautiful eyes.

"So am I."

He closed his eyes, trying to think of ways to reassure her, and felt her finger delicately tracing over his lips. Looking at her he saw the love shining from her face, and ardour in her expression. *She wants ME!* He thought in joyous disbelief. Elizabeth turned on her side and pressed against him, kissing him lovingly.

"I have dreamed of you in this bed." His lips wandered down her throat to taste the silk of her shoulders. Elizabeth breathed deeply. His hair brushing against her face made her skin tingle and his skilful fingers circling and tenderly kneading her breasts encouraged the moan he craved. He continued exploring down and rubbed his face in the valley between. His mouth replaced his hands, caressing and savouring the tight peaks. "Will." She moaned, desperately combing her fingers through his hair, and writhed against him. He looked longingly down to the dark triangle of curls between her legs, then back up to her parted lips. There were so many places he needed to love. "Do you want more, my wife?"

"I do, I love you. I want you." Darcy kissed her, and groaning, turned her onto her back, settling between her parted legs, and murmured against her lips, "I beg you to trust me, Lizzy." He could feel the heat of her loins inviting his entry and breathed in her scent. He dragged his mouth away from hers and looked again into her eyes, seeing the same passion and desire that he was feeling. He kissed her again, stroking his hands possessively over her breasts. Positioning his body, he very gently touched her, spreading the wetness over his fingers, and carefully pushed inside. Her gasp matched his moan and he sank into the warm abyss as he slowly entered. The anticipation of this moment began the first day he had seen her, and now the reality of feeling his heavy rigid member pushing into her narrow walls nearly caused his instant release. Breathing raggedly he fought for control, and felt the caress of her hands on his bottom, urging him forward. Gratefully he settled onto her, wrapping her in his embrace, and steadily continued to open her until she possessed all of him. Darcy was overwhelmed by the feeling of finally loving her, and could not read the expression that came over her face when their bodies were completely joined.

"Does it hurt?" He whispered anxiously.

Elizabeth drew his face back to hers. "No, it . . . it feels like . . ." She closed her eyes and moaned. "Oh Will, it is indescribable."

His voice caught with emotion as he watched tears begin to appear in her eyes. "Please let those be tears of joy." She nodded and wiped his eyes. Relieved, he bit his lip then kissed her deeply, and confidently began to move, thrusting steadily and slowly, building into a rhythm that she gradually learned and matched. Before long her arms were around his neck, her hands in his hair, and his body was gliding over hers. Their mouths joined, their tongues moving in time with his thrusts, and muffling the sounds that would have filled the room. Neither one heard the rhythmic rocking of the bed, it simply added to the other sensations of the moment; the smell of their lovemaking, the warmth of their skin, the bunching of the counterpane, and the strong constant sound of their bodies coming together, again and again and again. Elizabeth felt the building tension within her, and knew what would follow. She allowed the powerful feeling of rapture to spread up and over her, thrilling him with her cry. Darcy felt her squeezing him and immediately covered her mouth with his own, and suddenly, joyously, lost himself in his own coming of ecstasy. For the first time, he had made love. He opened his eyes again to see his Elizabeth looking to him with devotion. "You are mine." He whispered hoarsely. She smiled, "And you are mine."

He kissed her and hugged her to him. "Forever, my love, forever yours."

———

Elizabeth woke and felt the wonderful warmth of William's nude body curled around her. One hand was resting possessively on a breast, the other; she could feel beneath her pillow. His face shared the pillow as well, and his breath tickled her neck. On the three occasions when they had slept together, there had been a slight nagging fear of discovery, but now, all she felt was the comfort and safety that she had craved her whole life. Knowing her William's history, she could only imagine that he felt even more fulfilled. The clock chimed and she realized that it was only ten. They had skipped supper to instead consummate their marriage, and now she began to feel the hunger that both the long day and wonderful exercise inspired.

Spotting the dance of the fire reflected in the wine bottle, she cast a longing glance at the tray full of fruit. Elizabeth bit her lip, and slowly began to extricate herself from her husband's embrace, pausing and listening, and eventually managed to slip free. She knew that her robe was somewhere in the room, but could not remember where William had placed it. Glancing at him she picked up a small blanket thrown over the sofa and held it to her breasts, then stole across the room to the table where she found oranges and lemon biscuits, little cakes, apples, and several fruits she did not recognize.

It took only moments for Darcy to sense that Elizabeth had left the bed and he awakened, sitting up and searching the room for her. The soft glow of the fire revealed her bending near the table, her nude back turned to him, her only covering the curtain of hair. The sight stole his breath. Before she could notice him he was out of the bed and by her side. He stood behind her and encircling his hands around her waist, he whispered. "You are beautiful Elizabeth." One hand cupped her breasts while the other lowered to fondle her curls. She rested her head against his chest and looked up to him, and before she could utter a word, his mouth encompassed hers in a demanding kiss. The orange on her tongue made him hungry, but not for food.

Elizabeth turned, forcing his probing fingers to change position to instead cup her bottom. Her hands travelled up and down his back, mirroring his touch, and pulled his hips forward to press his swollen groin against her belly. His kisses crushed her lips, and he devoured her with the fervency he had held in check for so long. She felt the intensity of his desire, so different from anything he had displayed before, and encouraged him, drawing her lips away to whisper in his ear while he raked his teeth and tongue over her throat. Her whispered words of passion drove him wild. "More Lizzy, tell me more."

"Show me what you have imagined, Will."

He groaned and pulled her down to the thick rug before the fire, and lingered over her, searching her eyes. Elizabeth reached between them to stroke his straining pride. They both moaned with the contact, and he abandoned all control. His hands possessed her breasts, stimulating the nipples relentlessly while his mouth fell upon her vulnerable and exposed throat. He kissed and suckled, leaving his mark, and glorying in her moans. His mouth and hands travelled further down her soft, warm body to find the glistening pink flesh peeking from her dark tangle of curls. He stroked her lovingly with his tongue, and tasted the sweet flavour that only he would ever know.

Elizabeth felt his lips kissing her, his rough cheek brushing her thighs, and was unable to make a coherent sound, only concentrating on not flinching or drawing away from the unfamiliar, overwhelming, and disconcertingly wonderful feel of his tongue lapping over her most sensitive place. She wanted him to continue, to love her, to . . . "Ohhhhhhhhhhh. Oh Will!" His lips sucked and he nibbled something that made her hips buck and writhe. "Ohhhhh!" Her cries moved from whimpers to moans, as the new sensations travelled throughout her body. Panting, she grasped his head to drive his ravenous mouth closer. Darcy's hands spread her legs farther apart, and he drank in the intoxicating aroma of his lover. Her ecstasy arrived and his attention never wavered, never gave her a chance to relax. He revelled in her harsh cries of release. When the flood of her sweet essence touched his tongue, he immediately rose up and in one thrust, plunged deep inside of her. They both gasped at the feeling, but even in this, he did not cease his motion. It was the pounding vigour of his strokes, possessing, demanding, inextricably joining them that finally freed Darcy's expression of passion. His deep hoarse voice told her with every powerful thrust of his hips how he loved her, how he wanted her, how he craved her. Wicked, private words that he had kept bottled inside poured from his lips and thrilled her to the bone. Elizabeth clung to his driving body, wrapped her legs around his waist and instinctively matched her hips to his pace, trying to draw him in deeper with each fevered motion. His arms straddled her, and his head hung down, watching as he moved within her. Elizabeth reached up to drag his face to hers and silenced his words with a desperate kiss. That kiss was his undoing, and he let go to find euphoria, filling her with his seed and collapsing onto her soft, slick, yielding, delicious body.

Elizabeth wrapped her arms around his heaving back, not wanting to relinquish the feeling of their union. "I am crushing you." He finally managed to say after catching his breath. He rolled onto his side, bringing her clinging form with him, and kissed her.

"That was . . ."

"I do not know what came over me."

"Whatever it was, please let it happen again."

Darcy had been preparing to apologize. He hardly knew what he had said to her, but surely his lovemaking was too . . . much for his sweet wife. He stared at her in astonishment. "You . . . you are not . . . angry?"

"Angry?!" She started to laugh. "Oh Will, how could I be angry with such passion? I would not wish for such . . . every time, but oh yes, I want this again."

He beamed and laughed, hugging her tightly to his chest. "Oh Lizzy, what a wanton wench I have married!"

A bubbling laugh rose near his throat, and she lifted her head to kiss his chin. "And what does that make you?" Her eyes danced and she caressed his cheek.

Darcy nuzzled his nose against her face and growled. "A rake."

"I like the sound of that."

"I think, dearest Lizzy, we will enjoy our marriage bed very much." He kissed her tenderly. "Slowly, and . . ."

"Exhuberently?"

He chuckled again. "Indeed."

They rested before the warm fire a little longer before they decided to rise. Elizabeth, walking with a slight wobble, donned her robe and left for her dressing room to tidy herself, and when she reappeared, she was surprised to see William pouring glasses of wine at a table set before the fire in her bedchamber.

"What is this?"

"You were hungry." He smiled and led her to a chair, bent and kissed her, caressing her cheek, then took his own seat.

"Why did we move into here?"

Darcy took her hand and kissed it. "Do you remember when I said that I dreamed of seeing you in my bed?" She tilted her head and nodded. "That was the truth. I thought of that . . . well, not long after we met." Elizabeth blushed and he tenderly kissed her hand again. "I have spent years alone in that room . . . this room is for you, for us . . . this is where I wish to live the rest of my life."

Elizabeth leaned forward and kissed him. "A fresh beginning?" He nodded. "And at Pemberley? Shall we exorcise the ghosts in one room before moving to another?" Her smile relaxed the seriousness of the conversation.

Darcy laughed. "That is precisely my plan. Do you approve?"

"I do, very much." It took fortitude, but Darcy resisted the sudden urge to take her to their new bed that moment. They had the rest of their lives ahead of them.

The Darcys remained in London for five days. And much to Elizabeth's surprise, they managed to leave their room to tour the house and take care of some business. Their first stop was at the modiste who Georgiana favoured. Darcy informed the woman that Elizabeth would purchase her entire wardrobe for the coming Season there if she produced a wardrobe suitable for winter within a fortnight. He indicated that no expense would be spared. Elizabeth was measured, fabrics were chosen, patterns were picked over, preferences noted, and within three hours, under the watchful gaze of her husband, and the efficient work of the modiste, a vast array of clothing suitable for the Mistress of Pemberley was ordered. It would all be delivered the week before Christmas, to ensure a sizable bonus. The next stop was the furrier, to purchase a warm coat and gloves, then on to the cobbler, for fur-lined boots. Those would be ready before they departed. They spent one evening at dinner in Gracechurch Street, and Darcy was delighted to meet the pleasant Gardiner family. Learning that they were to come to Lambton in the summer, he invited them to stay at Pemberley. The day before they were to leave for Derbyshire, Mrs. Hendricks requested a few hours of Elizabeth's time, to acquaint her with the household, and establish her preferences for meals and servant's behaviour before they returned in the spring. Darcy took the opportunity to pay an important call.

He exited the carriage, and looked up at the façade of his club. He had not set foot inside since his last visit with Bingley. Most members would be at their country homes, but there were always some men inside, so he prepared himself for whatever words they would offer. He entered, and walking up the staircase, passed through the doors to the main room, and went directly to the case where the betting books were kept.

His presence did not go unnoticed. The small group of men in the room stopped their activity and observed as Darcy found the record he desired and paged through. A slight smile appeared, then taking up the pen that lay nearby, dipped it in the ink pot, wrote quickly, replaced the volume, flicked his eyes over the interested crowd, and exited without a word.

Several men rushed up, found the book and turned to the newest entry.

Married 26 November 1811 to Miss Elizabeth Bennet.
Betting closed.
Fitzwilliam Darcy

"Well, I will be damned." Pendergast murmured. "Who is she?" The others shook their heads.

"Who won?" Forrest asked.

"Gilbert Hurst."

Chapter 33

"**W**ell it seems that the joyous Master of Pemberley is on his way home with his beloved wife. If the weather cooperates, they will likely arrive in two days." Lord Matlock put down the letter and glanced around the table. His eyes fell upon the empty chair at its head, and then moved to take in his niece's downcast eyes. "You will be pleased to see your brother and sister, will you not, Georgiana?"

"Oh yes, of course, I have missed them both." Tears suddenly sprang to her eyes and she stood, murmured her excuses and ran from the room.

The men's gazes turned to Lady Matlock. "No, I am not chasing after her again." She resumed her meal. "What does Darcy have to say, Henry?"

He stared at his wife for a moment then looked again at the letter. A small smile played on his lips. "If I was not familiar with his handwriting, I would say some unknown man had written this letter and forged his signature. He is effusive in his happiness, praising his wife, his servants, the air of London . . . well he must be besotted to do that!" They all laughed. "Well Richard, it seems we shall at last meet this wonder that is Elizabeth Darcy. Your own pronouncement of her worth will finally be put to the test."

Richard took a sip of wine and grinned. "I have no worry over my triumph, Father. You will be enchanted."

"Hmmph. I wonder though, will her new sister be equally enchanted. Ellen, what is wrong with the girl?"

She sighed. "I believe that she fears Darcy's anger. She thinks that he will never forgive her impulsive escape from Longbourn which led to Elizabeth running after her and being placed in harm's way. Mrs. Annesley told me that it is clear how dearly he loves his wife, and how devastated he was with her injury."

"I think . . ." All eyes turned to James. He cleared his throat. "I think that she is jealous that her brother is giving all of his attention to Elizabeth instead of her."

"Now that is an interesting theory. What a wonder to hear it coming from you!"

James glared at Richard and continued. "Well, think about it. If all of these tales of Darcy being besotted with Elizabeth are to be believed . . ." Richard sighed with frustration. ". . . then it seems that he has easily given his attention to her in a way that he has never really displayed to his sister. I imagine she was rather hurt that her brother did not escort her to Pemberley himself."

Richard laughed without mirth. "At the time she could not stomach looking at his face. It was the best decision to have me take her home. She needed to leave the area, well, hang it, I needed to leave the area, and frankly, Darcy needed to be alone with Elizabeth. Her father would not have allowed her to come here unmarried, and she was not able to walk without aid. She needed to remain at Longbourn."

Lady Matlock agreed. "I have spoken many times to Mrs. Annesley. Georgiana admits freely that the loss of her father's affection and the absence of its display from Darcy is what drove her to accept Wickham's attentions and keep the secret."

Thoughtfully, Richard nodded his head. "Darcy was hardly able to pat her shoulder when we found her at the inn, but when we left for Pemberley; he was wrapping her in a tight embrace."

Lord Matlock met his son's eyes. "Something learned from Elizabeth, no doubt."

"Aye, and something that she missed and likely regrets losing again now that he is married."

James looked around the table in confusion. "Just a moment, if what you say is true, then my theory is incorrect. It makes no sense for her to think that she will suddenly lose all of her brother's affection now that he has it from Elizabeth. I can not put the blame for her impulsive behaviour with Wickham, or even after what happened in Meryton, on Darcy's shoulders. He may not have held her, but what feelings he was capable of displaying were solely for her and done far more easily than for any other person, including us. Growing up with him, she should have been fully aware of his limitations and accepted them. If anything, she should rejoice in his newfound happiness."

"I daresay he will display it more freely now that he is happily married." Lord Matlock said as he stared again at the empty Master's chair.

Richard watched his father's gaze. "She does not understand that."

"I will speak to her." Lady Matlock wiped her mouth and stood. "I hope you boys are taking note of all of this . . . that is IF either one of you ever marries. I want to see grandchildren before too long." She glared at both of her blushing sons and looked at her chuckling husband before leaving the room.

"You heard her, boys. You have your marching orders. Go forth and procreate! But do marry first!"

They all laughed with the change in mood and Richard raised his glass. "To the lovely lady who can bear my love!"

"Hear, hear!" James called, grinning. "Do not worry, Father, I intend to make a selection this coming Season. I suppose whatever wild oats I had are most efficiently sown. I am quite ready to settle down. I suppose that I just want to take a gander at this so-called love match that Darcy has found, who knows, maybe that is what I have been anticipating."

Richard nearly choked on the piece of ham he was swallowing. "LOVE? YOU?" He shook his head and looked out the window. "No, I see no donkeys flying about the garden, so it must be a true statement. What has come over you?" James shrugged and said nothing.

Lord Matlock watched his heir then turned to his second son. "And what of you, have you given serious thought to this? You did mention once that had Elizabeth been free . . ."

"I did, and I was serious, but have I found my true love? No, but then I have not looked as yet." He paused and met his father's gaze. "I hope to find her soon.

I am desirous of a home and a family. However, I am afraid that I will be unable to find a lady who will wish to be married to a man who might disappear for years of war and no guarantee of return. It will take either a very special or very desperate woman to accept such a fate."

"I believe Son, that it is time we had a talk." Lord Matlock said carefully.

"About my sister's dowry?" Richard asked.

James looked up in confusion. "What??"

Lord Matlock's eyes widened. "You know?" Richard nodded. His father sighed. "Darcy told you. Well, what do you think?"

"I wish I had known years ago, but Father . . . I am grateful if it is true."

"It is. I will show you the papers when we return to Matlock, but . . . please, go ahead, and find your bride."

Richard smiled and reached across the table to shake his father's hand. "Thank you, sir."

James looked from one to the other. "Will someone tell me what the deuce is happening?"

"I have just promised a significant portion of your inheritance to your brother, James. He shall be given fifty thousand pounds and a small estate worth three thousand a year located near Matlock. He will receive this as soon as he resigns his commission. He, of course, must find himself a bride as well."

"Do you object?" Richard fixed a challenging stare upon his spluttering brother.

"Object!" He calmed and relaxed. "No, of course not. What funds are these, what is this of sisters?"

Lord Matlock smiled. "I was merely preparing for my younger son. Something that I hope both of you remember someday."

———— ∿∿∿ ————

"Well?" Bingley shoved his friend into the bookroom at Longbourn and closed the door. The Darcys were stopping there to rest the horses and collect the last of Elizabeth's purchases from the Meryton dressmaker before continuing on with the first day of their journey to Pemberley.

"Well what?" Darcy turned and folded his arms across his chest, and raised a brow at his beaming friend.

He sighed. "The wedding . . . the marriage . . ." He lifted his brows and whispered while leaning forward. "Is it all that you imagined?"

Darcy fixed a burning glare upon him. "A gentleman does not speak of such things, Bingley, and I AM a gentleman."

"Do not pull rank on me, Darcy. Come now, tell me all." Bingley plopped down on a corner of Mr. Bennet's desk, folded his arms, and smiled at him angelically.

A slight smile appeared on Darcy's lips and a distinct twinkle appeared in his eye. Bingley jumped up from the desk and clapped him on the back. "Well done, Darcy!!" He laughed and wrung his hand. "Excellent! I can be nothing but pleased and insanely jealous of you!"

Darcy relaxed and smiled fully. "I have said nothing, and mind you, Bingley, I never will discuss such things with any man, but I will confess to being . . . for the first time in my life . . . truly happy. It is . . ." He shook his head and just smiled at his shoes. Bingley laughed again. Darcy looked back up. "So when will you join me in this state of euphoria?"

"Ah, seemingly ages, I am afraid. We will marry at the end of February."

Darcy's brow knit and he took a seat. "Why so long?"

Bingley resumed his perch on the desk. "Darcy, you courted Elizabeth for three months and were engaged for nearly two. When you add it all up; our wait for the altar will be nearly identical."

"So it will, I suppose that I just remember how terribly long that wait was." He met his friend's knowing smirk and smiled.

"Well hopefully my time of engagement will not be quite as tormented as yours."

"Speaking of torment . . ."

The amusement left his face and he sighed. "Yes, Caroline, well she is in my townhouse. I will go to London tomorrow to meet with my board of directors for our quarterly review, and will also meet with my lawyers about Caroline. From what I have heard so far, I should leave her dowry alone, at least to the end of the year, to get the last quarter of interest paid in from the funds, then search out some apartments to have her established by my wedding date."

"Have you heard from her?" Darcy sat back and resting his elbows on the chair arms, templed his hands.

"Not a peep. Louisa took her around in their carriage, dropping off her cards to every member of the *ton* with whom she could claim acquaintance. It was a kind gesture that I do not know I would have permitted . . . she and Hurst have decided to remain in town, but they are not telling Caroline that." He grinned.

Darcy shook his head and his lips twitched. "Hurst won the betting on my marriage date.

"Yes, I know, he wrote crowing about it. The day they arrived in town, he high tailed it to the club and laid down his cash. He was wrong on the exact date, but was certainly the closest. That man is fond of cards, but this was a sure thing. I only regret not winning a piece of it myself!"

Darcy chuckled and shook his head. "What will he do with the winnings?"

"He spoke of a second honeymoon with Louisa for the winter. They are really working to overcome the years of Caroline's interference in their marriage, and, well, obviously it will take them far away from her."

His brows rose, realizing how high the stakes were in this particular betting pool. "I am delighted to have been of assistance in such a noble endeavour." Charles rolled his eyes. "What are your honeymoon plans?"

"I think that we will remain in town. Jane should be presented, and she has never experienced a Season. It really will be good for us both to be introduced as a couple, I think."

Darcy gave a resigned nod. "Well, with your wedding, we will come here and then continue to town. But at this point I am undecided about society. I truly dread the scrutiny we will doubtless have to endure. I know that Elizabeth must eventually be presented, and we must do our duty. Even if it is too late for

Georgiana, we must think ahead to our children. I am battling with this decision, as you can see. I have no desire to associate with the majority of them ever again."

Bingley looked at him sympathetically. "You do not wish to put on a show for those who openly disparaged your family."

He sighed heavily and nodded. "It would not be done with enthusiasm, but at least it will be far more bearable having Elizabeth there by my side. I can not imagine what the next Season would have been were I still unmarried."

"The matrons would be licking their chops, smelling blood and desperation." Bingley grinned again and Darcy grimaced with agreement. "They are all such hypocrites, you know."

"Yes, I do, I am fully aware of the hidden behaviour of society. However, if I had been there for the next Season alone, I know that my aunt and uncle would have had to drag me to the dinners to re-establish my place. My greatest fear now is what they will do to Elizabeth. You know as well as I do that they do not like outsiders, they will attack her roots, suggest mercenary motives . . . I hope that my aunt will sponsor and guide her. That is if she accepts her as my wife in the first place, but I suppose I will have that answer in a few days when we arrive at Pemberley." He shook his head. "Our time in London was short, and we had no contact with society. Elizabeth only let it show briefly, but I know that Darcy House intimidated her. I can not imagine what her reaction to Pemberley will be when she sees it; I have hardly prepared her for this role." He ended softly, looking at the floor.

"Darcy . . . she will be fine. She is an extraordinarily strong and intelligent woman. And I have no doubt that you will be by her side in everything. Your staff will be so overjoyed to see you happy that they will likely fall all over themselves to help her learn."

"I do not wish her to regret accepting me. She deserves only the best, not more troubles." He continued to stare down at his shoes.

"I believe that she would say that she has the best already." Bingley smiled, tilting his head.

Darcy eyes lifted to his friend and lit up. "She has mentioned that."

"She will be fine Darcy. Your staff will not allow their mistress to fail. They have waited too long to see Pemberley a happy home."

"As have I." The two friends smiled at each other and started when the door opened.

Mr. Bennet entered the room. "Gentlemen, I am sorry to interrupt this reunion, but I would like a word with my son."

Bingley jumped to his feet and grinned. "Certainly, Mr. Bennet. I will go join the ladies." He winked at Darcy and exited, closing the door behind him. Mr. Bennet took his seat behind the desk and regarded the countenance of his son-in-law.

"My Lizzy appears very happy, Darcy."

Darcy smiled. "I believe sir; that Elizabeth is predisposed to such an emotion, but I can only be pleased that she continues to possess it under my care."

"Indeed. I have no doubt that shall be the case for both of you." Darcy inclined his head and watched Mr. Bennet with concern. Something of weight was on his mind. "I wonder sir, are you acquainted with a man named Angus Douglass?"

"Mr. Douglass? Yes, he is a very successful brewer in the North. He purchases a great deal of his corn from Pemberley. Why do you ask?"

Mr. Bennet ignored his furrowed brow and ploughed on. "Have you met his wife?"

Confused, Darcy spoke slowly. "Yes, she occasionally accompanies him on his trips, especially now that the children are older, their youngest is in Eton now, and their eldest, Marshall, just began to work in the family business this summer after graduating from Oxford."

"Does Mrs. Douglass remind you of anyone?"

Darcy's brow creased again, wondering his point, and he attempted to recall a woman he had met only briefly and over a year earlier. "I am sorry sir, but I only remember dark hair, and . . ." He stopped, tilting his head in question, and staring at Mr. Bennet.

"Yes?" He sat forward and nodded urgently.

"Eyes, she had very expressive eyes." Mr. Bennet nodded again and leaned back. "Sir, what are you trying to tell me?"

"Mrs. Douglass is my sister, Sarah. She married Angus Douglass when he was just leaving his apprenticeship to a brewer in Scotland. The brewer died suddenly, and as he had no heir, Angus took over his small operation and it has grown to the thriving business it is today. They moved south to Derbyshire ten years ago. Elizabeth has written her, and she has written me, asking for an explanation of how you came to marry. She had nothing but praise for you. I took the liberty of explaining your sister's situation to her . . . I thought if anyone could understand . . . I hope that you are not angry with me."

Astonished, Darcy absorbed the news. "No, no, the news is hardly a secret; in fact, I prefer to have the truth spread rather than these horrendous rumours. Does Elizabeth know the connection?"

"No, I leave that to you to explain. You have a long trip to accomplish, and it will certainly fill some of the time." He smiled slightly at Darcy's knowing look. "I do know that Elizabeth wants to meet her."

"Of course she will. Mr. Douglass is a fine man, I can only hope for such a man to accept my sister someday."

"Well sir, let us rejoin the ladies. I am sure that you will wish to continue your journey soon." They stood and walked out into the hallway just as Elizabeth and Jane were coming down the stairs. Darcy smiled at them and looked at Elizabeth in confusion when Jane instantly turned bright red with embarrassment. Elizabeth looked at her sister and sighed.

"What is wrong with Jane?" Darcy looked behind him when Elizabeth came forward to take his arm and steer him into the drawing room.

She sighed again then said softly, "I was giving her a sisterly talk." He stared at her expectantly. "About marriage." Her pointed gaze met his, and Darcy suddenly felt a flush coming over his face.

"You . . . you did not tell her . . . Lizzy, you did not tell her what we . . ." He glanced around the room and bit his lip, then dragged her as inconspicuously as possible back into the hallway. "Lizzy, please tell me that you did not speak of our lovemaking!" His mouth was pressed close to her ear and his hands were grasping her to him.

Elizabeth attempted to clamp down the stirrings that his deep voice in her ear always inspired. "I only told her of the mechanics, not tales of your prowess." Her warm breath against his neck and the soft feel of her body against him was inspiring enough, but to hear her speak of his . . . ability was just too much.

"My prowess, Mrs. Darcy?" He growled. A shiver went straight down her spine, and he felt her reaction. His instant arousal pressed urgently against her. "I think that we need to discuss this further."

"But we are to leave very soon." She said weakly in protest.

"I have a feeling that it will not require much time." Darcy licked his lips and met her gaze. Glancing around the empty hallway, he took her arm and led her quickly up the stairs to her old bedroom, and soundly closed the door.

Mr. Bennet watched them depart from the open drawing room door, smiling in amusement at the enthusiasm of the newly married, then his gaze met his wife's and he was surprised to see her raised brows and expectant smile. He shook his head and she nodded, and then returned to her work.

Twenty minutes later, Darcy and Elizabeth entered the room, flushed, bright-eyed, and smiling. Bingley barely held in his laughter, but vowed to tease his friend about it in the future. Soon the couple took their leave of the family. Darcy again invited the Bennets to Pemberley for Christmas, only four weeks hence, and Mr. Bennet said that it would ultimately depend on the weather, as he did not relish such a difficult journey in the snow.

"Take care, my daughter, and if you should meet your aunt, well, tell her that I hope we might see each other at Pemberley someday." He allowed her to peck his cheek and he patted her shoulder.

"I will, Papa, perhaps at Christmas?" He smiled and nodded. "We shall see."

Elizabeth turned to see Mary's sad face. "It is not the same here without you, Lizzy."

"Oh Mary, I am sorry, but perhaps this is your chance to become the impertinent one in the household. Papa will need someone to warm the chair in his bookroom. Why not you? And I promise, we shall ask him for permission to bring you to town in the spring. You and Georgiana can keep each other company while William and I face the approbation of the *ton*."

"They will love you, Lizzy." She said with conviction. "But, I would like to come, thank you."

"Good! And you know that Aunt Gardiner told me she would ask you to come with them on their trip this summer, so you will be at Pemberley as well. We will see a great deal of each other." The sisters hugged and Elizabeth turned to see her mother.

"You seem to be keeping your husband well-occupied, Lizzy. You will have his heir before too long, I suspect."

"Mama!" She whispered and glanced at Lydia and Kitty.

Mrs. Bennet smiled and patted her cheek. "It is your greatest duty as a wife, my dear. But it seems you are enjoying the experience. I am happy for you."

Elizabeth blushed, realizing that their little escape had been noted and murmured her thanks before saying her farewells to the other girls. Jane was last and she hugged her fiercely. "Now, I want you to enjoy this long wait for your wedding, Jane."

"You did not tell me everything, did you, Lizzy?" She whispered.

She squeezed her sister's hand. "No, I did not. There are some things that you will have to wait and discover on your wedding night. I just did not want you to be fearful." A warm smile appeared. "Now, in the meantime, do not restrain your affection for Charles too much, you must keep him interested!"

"Oh Lizzy, you sound like Mama!"

"Well I am an old married woman now!" She laughed and felt William's hand upon the small of her back.

"Come my love, we have many miles to cover before we rest for the night." He smiled and she took his hand, entwining her fingers with his. "I can not wait to bring you home."

Lady Matlock determinedly strode down the hallway in search of her niece. It was time to put a stop to the never-ending tears, and the habit of running off to hide. She asked a passing footman of her location and he indicated the music room. The sound of laughter coming from the doorway stopped her in astonishment, and she looked in to see Georgiana seated at the instrument, searching through a large pile of sheet music, a bright smile lighting her face. "Georgiana! What is this?" Lady Matlock demanded.

"Aunt Ellen?" She blushed and looked with confusion at Mrs. Annesley.

Closing the door and walking up to the two women she moved her eyes between them. "Georgiana, you just ran from the dining room in tears upon hearing that your brother and Elizabeth were happy and on their way here. You have done nothing but cry and remain silent when questioned since you arrived. Your cousins are warring with theories that you are angry with William for not bringing you home himself, to guilt over causing their injuries, to jealousy that he loves his wife and that you feel that he is abandoning you. Now either you have been putting on quite a show for the benefit of your relatives, or we have been entirely wrong in reading your mood. Which is it?"

Georgiana's mouth gaped. "I am not at all angry with William, or Elizabeth, or jealous or . . . anything! I am so very happy for them! William is the dearest of brothers, and Elizabeth is just so wonderful!"

"Then why did you run from the room?"

"I am just so happy that he is finally loved, and to hear that it appears in his letters . . . oh you can not know what joy it brings me to know that he smiles! I just become so emotional when I think of him being loved and I . . . I thought that I should leave the room so that you would not have to look at me." She said softly then added. "If I feel jealous, it is only with the desire that someday I will feel such affection from a man who might accept me, despite my transgressions."

Lady Matlock took a seat and stared at her niece. Mrs. Annesley broke the silence. "My Lady, I understand how Miss Darcy's behaviour could be misunderstood. She has endured, and in some ways caused, a great deal of distress in the past months. But we have spoken of this very often. She understands where her actions caused some events to be far worse than they might have been, and she also understands how others have affected them by their own behaviour. Each person contributed to the whole in a significant way. I assure you though; she feels nothing but the greatest admiration for Mrs. Darcy, and only hopes that she can be a good sister to her. She can not wait to . . . share her with her brother." Mrs. Annesley smiled and patted her hand.

"Aunt Ellen, since my return home, I have taken time to reread all of the letters that Elizabeth sent me after Ramsgate, and I have spent a great deal of time meditating on the conversations we had in Hertfordshire, as well as when William talked to me. I know that it is in my hands to determine my future. I can sit and cry over what I can no longer change, or move on. That is what everyone has told me. I regret every one of my actions, but I know that I can not be bitter about them; otherwise I will be no better than my mother. I have no desire to live as she did. I think that my brother's marriage will be a great example to me of what my future could be."

"Well, I must say, this is a great relief. I was ready to give you a thorough tongue-lashing and threaten you to paste a smile on your face for your brother's return. I do not want this joyous time for him and Elizabeth to be spoiled by your behaviour." Georgiana's eyes widened. "However, as it seems that your entire family has mistaken your motivation, I will instead apologize and ask; how do you wish to welcome them home?"

"Really?" Georgiana looked to Mrs. Annesley who nodded her encouragement. "I . . . I had thought of a special dinner for them, with all of William's favourites and I think that I know some of Elizabeth's, too, and I was just looking through the sheets here to put together a little concert for them . . . and oh, I wanted to ask if there were any flowers in the hot house that we could use to decorate their rooms . . ."

"That all sounds just wonderful, Georgiana. We shall give them a grand welcome! I imagine though that when they arrive, the first thing they will wish for is a warm bath!" The three ladies laughed and moved to some chairs around a table. Georgiana brought some paper and a pen, and they began working out the details of the homecoming.

———~~~———

Caroline Bingley sat alone in front of the window that looked out upon Hanover Square. Muffled sounds of servants going about their work could be heard. The clock chimed, carriages made their way down the street, people walked by, but nobody approached her door. She had dropped off calling cards at thirty addresses with Louisa her first day back. Nearly all of them went to people who she could hardly call friends, but the barest acquaintances, ones she had been introduced to at various balls and parties. The only thing she had in common with those people was the shared connection to Mr. Darcy. They were all far above her in status, and in fact, the majority of them were not at home, but in the country at their estates. The other cards had been delivered to friends she had made in finishing school, girls, nearly all married now, who were from her true circle, tradesman's daughters who were taking the first steps into the gentry, or lower-status gentlewomen, below the rank of Hurst's family. These were the only people who had responded to her calls and allowed her visits. The others either were not at home or had decidedly shut her out.

She tried to reason it out, thinking that it was Mr. Darcy's fall and her association with him that made the members of the *ton* less welcoming to her. However that made no sense, she knew full well *he* would be welcomed back the next Season. But slowly, very slowly, the thought that perhaps it was *she* that was the problem began to enter her mind. She looked down at the society page, reading the wedding announcement again. It was done. He was gone, and had never been there for her in the first place. She set her sights far too high, and now she was paying the price. She looked forward to the next day's paper, and the gossip about what a mistake Darcy had made. She looked forward to being invited into the homes of the ladies who mattered and telling them what a country nobody Eliza Bennet was. She thought of entering a tea room and being the centre of attention when she spoke of her knowledge, then the growing vindictive smile fell from her face. She had no carriage, and no funds to hire a cab. She would have to walk to the fashionable places. She could not hang about shops making purchases while gossiping. All she could do is sit in that window, and wait, and watch the world go by. Charles' punishment was going to be most effective.

The carriage lurched again as a gust of wind hit it hard, and Elizabeth braced her body by holding tightly to the strap with one hand, and clutching William's arm with the other. His chuckle made her glare at him. "What is so amusing?"

"Forgive me, I was only thinking that it is a fine thing that my coat is so heavy, else my arms would be quite bruised from the abuse they are suffering at your hand." She had been comfortably reclined against him until she sat up to take in the view.

The rocking seemed to have stopped and Elizabeth cautiously relaxed her grip. "Is it always like this?"

Darcy closed his book and tossed it across the carriage to land on the opposite seat, glanced out the window as they made a turn, then wrapped his arms around her waist to draw her back to his side. "No, but it is still autumn; and the weather is always changing. Although I think that the period of warmth we just experienced is already a fond memory. Winter in Derbyshire is cold."

She snuggled into his embrace. "I am not so concerned about the weather once we arrive. I am simply very unfamiliar with travel. The only place I have ever been is London, and I had never slept at an inn before. It seems that every moment with you is a new experience." She looked up at the lips that were curved in his familiar little smile. "I should think that you would be quite pleased with my fortitude."

His smile grew. "I am delighted with you, my love." He kissed her nose. "How may I distract you from the rigours of travel?"

"Tell me of Pemberley." He laughed. "Not the house, but tell me of your day. I have no idea what to expect. Will you leave me every morning only to return at dark? Will you shut yourself away in your study and not wish to be disturbed? Will you go on long trips?"

"It seems that you are anticipating my abandoning you almost as soon as we arrive. I did not marry only to separate from you, Elizabeth." He kissed her forehead. "I think that you are worried over your role, but dearest, remember, Pemberley has had no mistress for sixteen years. You will be establishing what your duties will be. Whatever you wish to take over from Mrs. Reynolds is entirely your decision." He peeked down at the face resting on his chest. "Surely you are familiar with running a household from observing your mother?"

"Yes, of course, she is many things, but she did train us very thoroughly in that."

"Well, think of Pemberley House as a slightly larger version of Longbourn." He smiled at her raised brows.

"How much larger?"

"Oh, well, I would hazard a guess of about . . . five times?" Elizabeth spun around to face him.

"FIVE!" She cried.

"Six?" He bit his lip and attempted to hold back his laughter and failed. Instead he pulled her struggling body tight to his and began showering kisses over her. "I do not mean to frighten you, but it is a very large estate. We will do this together. And to answer your questions, I do like to ride over the estate every day in good weather, and I wished you to improve your skills so that you could join me. I do like to know my tenants and their concerns, and I hope that you will visit them with me as you did your father's. I do work in my study and meet with my steward, but I would be overjoyed if you were to spend your time with me when you are not busy with your own activities. I very occasionally need to make overnight trips to other estates to discuss concerns with other landowners, but I notice that they always brought their wives with them. I intend to bring you with me whenever I can. I will no longer bury myself in work to find a way to make the day pass. I wish to share all of my life with you, Elizabeth."

Their faces were nose to nose, his legs were stretched out across the seat, and she was lying on top of him with her arms around his neck. "You are an unusual man."

Darcy's lips twitched, then he resumed his favourite occupation of nibbling on her throat. "Do you mind so terribly?"

"Oh no, not at all . . . in fact, I feel very smug about it." He returned to his previous position and regarded her sparkling eyes and waited. "All of these women who cover themselves in lace and feathers to attract their husbands, and it seems that all I need to do is appear dishevelled and work by your side."

"I prefer you dishevelled." Darcy growled in her ear. "And I take great pleasure in destroying the careful work of your abigail."

"I noticed." Elizabeth moaned as she felt his hand begin to travel up her legs and cup her bare bottom. "Oh, Willlllll."

"Mmmmm?" He captured her lips and began stroking his tongue with hers. Elizabeth moved to sit up, and quickly unbuttoned his coat and the fall of his breeches, reaching inside to release his very potent arousal. She stroked up and down and saw him watching her closely.

"What are your intentions, Mrs. Darcy?"

She straddled him, and slowly sank down onto his hardened shaft. Darcy's head fell back and he groaned while biting his lip. "I think Mr. Darcy, if I am to travel the estate with you, I must be thoroughly acquainted with my mount." She whispered seductively.

He sat up and turned so that her knees rested on the seat, and he drove his hips upwards, burying himself deeper inside. She gasped with his move. "Prepare for a hard ride then, my love. Your mount is quite restive." He pulled her tight against his chest and attacked her lips. The carriage struck a rut and they flew up off of the seat for a moment, and she landed, impaled deeper than ever. They both groaned. She began to move upon him, and he rested his hands on her hips, helping her rise and fall. The wind blew and the carriage buffeted them from side to side, and still they rode, hanging on to each other as the springs creaked and groaned, and masked the unrepentant cries of pleasure they both exclaimed. With one last thrust upwards, Elizabeth fell over the brink and clutched him, nearly strangling him with her hold, and nearly suffocating with his kiss. Darcy soon followed and revelled in the heart-stopping release. Breathing heavily they finally drew far enough apart to rest their foreheads together. Darcy opened his eyes and glanced out of the window. He kissed her cheek. "Lizzy, look."

Elizabeth opened her eyes and looked out of the window. The carriage had paused, and there below her, seemingly rising from the landscape as naturally as the surrounding hills was a great stone house. "Pemberley." She whispered.

"Welcome home."

Chapter 34

"*H*ow much time do we have?" Elizabeth demanded.

"I would say about twenty minutes." Darcy had fixed his attire, and was sitting back against the cushion, watching with amused fascination as Elizabeth desperately worked to repair the mass of curls that their lovemaking had released over her shoulders.

"I will never forgive you for this Fitzwilliam Darcy! You knew that we had entered Pemberley!" She glared at him as he held out another pin from the collection in his hand, and failed completely in stopping the smile he wore from spreading over his face.

"I rather thought that you enjoyed your welcome." He laughed outright. She grabbed the bonnet to place over her hair, and prayed it would not all come tumbling back down when it was removed. "Come my love, you can not be so upset with me, can you? You started it after all." He looked at her with contrition and took her hand as she gave her skirt a final tug, buttoned her coat, and finally settled back against the seat, ending her fevered movements.

Elizabeth looked down at the large warm hand that encompassed hers and was suddenly filled with the memory of the first time he removed her gloves and touched her skin, when he proposed. His loving gaze melted her ire. "No, I am not . . . I . . . I just want to make a good impression." She looked out of the window and saw a new view of the house, which included spotting a stream of people pouring out of the door and lining the steps. She took a shaking breath and Darcy felt her tremble.

He drew her against him. "It is only the staff assembling to welcome you home."

"There are so many." She whispered.

"Yes, but they are very loyal and will do their best to help you."

"Oh William, I do not want to fail you. I was worried enough over Darcy House, but now when I look at this beautiful place . . ." Her voice trailed away.

Darcy turned her around so he could see her face. "It is a house Elizabeth, only a house. And I am just a farmer." She looked at him and slowly shook her head, knowing how very simplistic that statement was. He brought his other hand to encase hers. "You, my love; are my dearest friend, and lover, and wife. This is the place where we will live, and God willing, raise our children. I never allowed myself to dream of this moment ever happening, but here I am with you, and I can not wait to embrace our future and see what each day will bring. Please do not be afraid. You will only fail me if you do not trust me."

"I do trust you." She reached up to caress his cheek, then smoothed a lock of hair from his forehead.

"Then believe me when I say that you will be magnificent." He leaned forward and gently kissed her, then moved away.

Elizabeth swallowed and nodded, then drawing her shoulders back, smiled. "I will." Darcy smiled, she was always so positive, but it felt good to be the one reassuring her for a change. "But I do wish that I was not appearing before everyone in a state of dishevelment."

He sat back and laughed. "I LIKE you that way!" Elizabeth sighed with exasperation and returned her gaze out the window. They soon rolled up before the house, and footmen jumped to open the door. Darcy stepped down first and turned to hold out his hand. Elizabeth took one last moment alone inside of the carriage to steel herself. She closed her eyes and said a prayer to give her strength and to be all that her husband needed, then placed her hand in William's palm, smiled, met his glowing face, and stepped down. Darcy kissed her hand and turned to face the shivering staff; who stared at him in wonder.

"The Mistress of Pemberley, Mrs. Fitzwilliam Darcy." The crowd broke into loud applause and Elizabeth smiled.

"I am sure that I will soon meet you all, but I believe that you will agree; that would be best performed indoors!" The servants laughed and Darcy entwined his fingers with hers. He started to bend and she shot him a warning look and whispered. "Do not even think of carrying me inside!"

He chuckled and squeezed her hand. "I just wanted to see what you would do." He laughed at her raised brow, and giving her hand a tug, they quickly mounted the steps and entered the foyer. The servants followed, and returned to their duties, but not without sending surreptitious looks to their new mistress as they passed.

Their outerwear was quickly removed, and Elizabeth was relieved that her hair stayed up. An older woman approached and curtseyed. "Mrs. Darcy, this is Pemberley's housekeeper, Mrs. Reynolds."

Elizabeth bowed her head in acknowledgment. "I have heard many wonderful things of you, Mrs. Reynolds, from both Mr. and Miss Darcy. I do look forward to your guidance as I learn my role."

"It will be my pleasure Mrs. Darcy." She studied the small, obviously nervous, glowing young woman, then looked to Darcy and was struck by how young he appeared. His face was lit with a warm smile and his eyes were sparkling with happiness. In all of her years of knowing him, she had never seen such an expression on her master's face, and she nearly gave over to tears with the sight of it. "Mrs. Darcy, bath water has been ordered, and your clothes have been unpacked. Your family is waiting for you in the yellow drawing room. Miss Darcy has planned a special dinner in honour of your wedding tonight."

Elizabeth was a little startled to realize that as mistress, this information would be told to her, not William, but she recovered quickly. "Thank you, Mrs. Reynolds, we will go and greet our family and would appreciate the baths in a half-hour." Mrs. Reynolds nodded, and looked back to Darcy who was standing and watching with pride as his wife took charge of their home. The extraordinary change in him warmed the woman who had witnessed so much sadness in this home.

"Come my love, it is time that you met the Earl." He took her arm and placed it on his, then led the way up the grand marble staircase. Elizabeth began to take note of her surroundings. "It is just beautiful, William. I look forward to my tour." She gave him a brave smile.

"I look forward to taking you, and I am sure that Georgiana will as well." He tilted his head and saw her obvious attempt to remain calm, but her trepidation was clearly reflected in her expressive eyes.

"I have no doubt of needing many. I have confidence that I shall frequently be lost for quite some time." She turned her head around, and began to focus on the overwhelming splendour.

This time Darcy felt her body tremble as she clutched his arm. He needed to find a way to relax her. He kissed her forehead, bringing her eyes back to him. "Shall we put up signs indicating the proper direction?" He suggested with a smile.

Elizabeth laughed, and Darcy placed his free hand over hers, giving it a squeeze. She relaxed a little. "That is an admirable idea, but it would take away from the décor. I believe that I will have to rely on a good memory, and perhaps a scattering of breadcrumbs."

His smile grew. "The mice will thank you for that, but not Mrs. Reynolds, I fear."

She gratefully fell into his warm eyes and leaned against him as they walked. "Well, then I will rely on my wit. I have no desire to raise her ire so soon in our acquaintance."

Darcy kissed her hand and stopped outside of a door, and looked down at her. "Do not be nervous. You know that they questioned my choice, but that was because they care for me, not because they do not like you." Elizabeth nodded and bit her lip. "You are beautiful, your hair is perfect so stop fretting over it, and they will love you as I do." He brushed his lips over hers. "Ready?"

She let out a deep breath and smiled. "Into the examination, Mr. Darcy!"

He shook his head and turned the handle, opening the door. They stepped in and immediately the occupants stood. "William! Elizabeth!" All possibilities of a dignified and elegant entrance were destroyed when Georgiana ran to them. She eagerly embraced Elizabeth then turned to her brother who gave her a hug. "Oh, I am so glad that you are home! We were watching the sky, it looks like snow, and then we received word that you were seen entering at the lodge, and oh, how the servants flew about! It was fascinating! I never knew such activity! Bells rang, and they were calling out directions, it was so exciting! How was your trip? Was it terrible? I want to hear all about the wedding! What did you wear? What did you do in London?"

"Georgiana!" Elizabeth exclaimed. "My goodness, what has become of you?" She laughed and took her sister's hands.

Calming, she blushed and peeked at her astonished brother's expression. "I . . . I decided to think only of the past as it gives me pleasure." Darcy's eyes met Elizabeth's. He knew where that phrase had been learned.

She blushed this time. "You have decided to move on?" Georgiana nodded. "Good for you!"

A clearing throat caught their attention and Darcy held his hand out for Elizabeth. They stepped forward. "Uncle Henry, Aunt Ellen, James, oh and you too, Richard. . . May I present my dear wife, Elizabeth. Dearest, this is the Earl and Lady Matlock, the Viscount . . . and you know Richard." A little smile was playing around his lips, his eyes were twinkling, and he was entirely incapable of being formal. His family stared at him in awe.

Elizabeth saw his mirth and delighted in the sight, however, she did manage to curtsey. "I am very pleased to meet you all . . . including you, Richard." A warm smile appeared and Richard began to laugh.

"It seems that I am the ugly stepchild here." He stepped forward and kissed her rosy cheek. "I am delighted to see you looking so well, Elizabeth. And what exactly have you done to my cousin?" He held out his hand and they shook. Richard looked back to her then raising his brow, took in his cousin's similarly imperfect appearance. "If ever there was a man who looked satisfied with his situation . . ."

"Careful, Cousin." Darcy glared. Richard stepped back, laughing louder.

"Mrs. Darcy, it is good to meet you at last." Lord Matlock had been watching everything and kept sending knowing looks to his wife, who was smiling at Darcy's obvious happiness.

"I am very happy to meet you as well, sir." Elizabeth said and smiled warmly at him.

Lady Matlock stepped closer. "Our family had its share of turmoil over these past few months, my dear, and I can not begin to imagine what state my nephew and niece would presently be living in were it not for you coming into their lives. I first wish to thank you for your care, and I wish to welcome you. My son and niece have spoken very highly of you, and even after seeing you for only a few moments, I am already sure that William has made precisely the match that he needed. I will be glad to help you any way that I can, in your household or in society."

Elizabeth could not believe how quickly she had earned such a blessing and looked to William. He leaned and kissed his aunt's cheek. "Aunt Ellen, I can not thank you enough for your support."

She patted his hand. "No my dear, to see your face lit up with joy is reward enough. I never imagined seeing such an expression on you. If this is the woman who coaxed it out, I will be eternally grateful to her."

Elizabeth blushed while looking from her then up at William. "Thank you Lady Matlock. I can only tell you that William is most capable of inspiring the most heartfelt joy in me, and I am honoured that he would wish me for his wife."

"Aunt Ellen." She smiled. Elizabeth nodded and Darcy squeezed her hand.

James had stood, taking in the scene, looking first with amazement to Darcy then settled his gaze upon Elizabeth. When her eyes turned to meet his, he suddenly felt his brother's fascination, and approached. "I admit that I have been the one who doubted this match from the moment I first heard of it, more so than my father or brother, but Darcy," he looked over to him, "I understand your convictions now." He bowed to Elizabeth, and took her hand, kissing it. "Please accept my apologies for ever doubting you."

"Of course." Elizabeth was overwhelmed, then the Earl took her hand from his son.

"Thank you, my dear. My sister was the last mistress of this great house. She neither wanted nor appreciated the role. I am convinced that at last Pemberley has the mistress it deserves." He kissed her hand then gave it a squeeze. "Please call me Uncle Henry."

"I will." She looked up at William.

Darcy regarded her with pride and turned to his uncle. "I believe that we would like to change and rest after our journey. I understand that Georgiana has something special planned for dinner, so we will meet with you all again in two hours?" They all nodded, and Darcy held out his hand to Elizabeth. She started to reach for it and he leaned down and scooped her up in his arms.

"William!" She cried and blushed furiously.

Darcy laughed and kissed her lips. "You know that I have been thinking about this, my love!" He nodded to his family and strode out the door.

They stood staring at each other, listening to the receding sound of Darcy's boots, and the mixture of his deep chuckle and Elizabeth's bubbling laugh. "Incredible." Lord Matlock said.

"Lucky dog!" Richard exclaimed.

"I will be damned." James whispered.

"Finally." Lady Matlock nodded with satisfaction.

Georgiana smiled and held back her tears. "I have a home."

Darcy lay back in the enormous bed and looked down at his Elizabeth's sleeping face nestled on his chest. Tenderly he traced the curve of her jaw, and then wound a curl around his finger. His other hand held her nude form to his, and he rested his cheek against the top of her head, closing his eyes. At last. Years and years of lonely nights, some spent in this magnificent room, and many more spent in first the nursery, then his boyhood bedchamber, were at last a memory. Elizabeth's soft steady breathing gave him so much comfort. The sound effectively drove away the screech of the howling wind outside of the window. He was safe, he was warm, and he was loved. At last.

He thought over the conversation he had with his uncle and cousins after Georgiana's wedding feast. To say that he was surprised with their easy acceptance of Elizabeth was an understatement. He knew that Richard had written them with his recommendation, and certainly he and Georgiana had told of their experiences in Hertfordshire, but somehow, that deeply ingrained streak of pessimism did not allow him to hope for such an extraordinary outcome. He suspected that they were accepting her for his and Georgiana's sake. The family saw the change in both of them, and were, in truth, giving Elizabeth a chance. He had no doubt in his mind that she would win them over on her own merits soon enough, but in the meantime was grateful for their kindness towards her, whatever the motivation. They were to depart in the morning and Georgiana would remain. So, he wondered, what should they do next? He thought over his conversation with Bingley.

It was tempting, he supposed, to simply hole up in this house and never leave again. Truly it was what he desired. But . . . he was married now, and at any time Elizabeth could come to him and announce that their first, hopefully of many, child was on his way and now he must think of him. He could not limit his children's opportunities simply because he felt anger and disdain for society. The souls of the past, and the image of the future inhabitants of this room were all seemingly gathered outside of the drawn bed curtains, and he felt the responsibility he carried for them all. It was up to him, and Elizabeth, to correct the mistakes of his parents, and his sister, and to assure that the Darcy name was as great and respected as it ever was. They would have to return to London in the spring.

Aunt Ellen would be key in this plan's success. She would act as Elizabeth's sponsor. She would educate her in the proper and expected behaviour in the drawing rooms of society. She would teach Elizabeth how to walk, speak, dress, perform, entertain . . . his head spun with the details, and he knew that his occupation in all of this would be to give her a comforting shoulder and willing ear to abuse when her fear of failure or indignation over the absurdity of it all became too much. Georgiana, he decided, would remain at Pemberley. Perhaps Mary Bennet could come and keep her company. He and Elizabeth would go to town alone.

Darcy felt Elizabeth stir and he opened his eyes to see her watching him. A sliver of light from the fire fell through a crack in the curtains upon her. "You are lost in thought, my love."

He smiled and caressed her cheek. "I have been caught."

"Putting away the ghosts of this room before we move into the beautiful haven you created for me?"

"Hmm. In a way, putting them aside and preparing for the future."

"You wish to return to London."

"No, I do not wish it, but I know that we must." He pulled her up so that she lay on top of him, covered her with the counterpane and kissed her nose. "How did you know?"

"I imagine that you heard a similar speech from your uncle as I did from your aunt tonight."

"Ah, so it was a two-pronged attack. They did not waste time, did they?" He smiled and kissed her softly. "Well, what is your opinion my good wife?"

"I believe that they likely are seeing this with much more objectivity than you can, and as I am truly inexperienced in the whole realm of the first circles, I believe that I should bow to their superior knowledge. As much as I do not relish this, and would prefer a simple life here . . ." She sighed. "We must go." Gently she stroked the unruly strands of hair that fell across his forehead. "I know that it will not be easy, and I realize that I must still prove myself. My greatest hope is that I will not embarrass you, but I am willing to subject myself to your aunt's moulding if it is of benefit to our and our children's future."

"On one condition." Darcy pressed his finger to her nose and then shook it at her.

Elizabeth laughed. "What is that my dear husband?"

"You must promise NOT to become one of those ladies of society that I have avoided all of my adult life. I want the girl I married to retain her smile and laugh, to be intelligent and witty, to be kind and lovely."

"Is that not the opposite of everything that I am supposed to be?"

"I want the cats of London to see WHY I rejected them."

"May I dance with you too much?" She raised her brow and pursed her lips.

He chuckled. "I will demand it."

"May I occasionally hold your hand in public?"

"Only if I may steal a kiss."

"Oh the scandal, sir!!" She pretended horror.

"Will." He corrected.

"My Will." She declared.

"My Lizzy." He lifted her chin and gently traced his tongue over her parted lips, then captured them for a slow deep kiss while caressing his other hand over her bottom, drawing her hips to his.

"ohhhhhhhh." She moaned softly.

"Let me love you, darling."

A footman on duty in the hallway startled with an unfamiliar sound. Catching up his branch of candles, he walked cautiously towards the master's chambers and paused. His eyes widened as he realized what the sound of the steadily creaking bed meant, and hurried away, but not without a smile.

"I am not sure of this Angus." Sarah Douglass worriedly looked at her husband and he smiled as he guided her into the carriage.

He took his seat and seeing Marshall just leaving the inn, he turned to her. "Come, my dear, you are as anxious to meet your niece as I am, and after reading your brother's extraordinary letter about Miss Darcy, well, I would think that you would like to meet the girl as well. I have always felt a great respect for Mr. Darcy, but seeing how he handled his sister's fall, I admire him even more. It seems that Mrs. Darcy was indispensable in her recovery, and obviously won the heart of a good man in the process."

"I just do not like coming unannounced like this." She fretted and looked at him anxiously.

Mr. Douglass looked into the wide expressive eyes that had captured his heart and imagination so many years ago. "My dear, I have sent a note to Pemberley asking to see Mr. Darcy. It is not entirely unreasonable, the threshing should have just been completed, so he will know exactly the yield of his crops now, and since I happen to be in the area . . ."

"You are in the area by design, Angus."

He laughed. "Indeed, but he does not know that." Marshall climbed up into the coach, and Mr. Douglass patted her hand. "It will be fine." She looked at him doubtfully.

"What will be fine?" Marshall asked.

"Visiting Pemberley today."

"I heard that the Darcys have been home a fortnight. I suppose that they have likely been disturbed by many neighbours since the wedding. Isn't it customary to give the couple a week to settle in before coming to call?"

Mr. Douglass smiled in triumph. "There, you see Sarah? Even our son knows that this is not improper."

"Hmmm." Sarah looked out the carriage window and worked to calm her nerves. This would be the first time in nearly a quarter century that she had seen any blood relative besides her own children. She would be lying if she professed that she was unaffected by the prospect. Her brother's remarkable letter made her think that perhaps she could be of use to the Darcys. His regret in not welcoming her back into the family after their parent's deaths was great, and she admitted that forgiveness for the continued banishment was not easily found. But that was a quarrel with her brother, not with her innocent niece. She resolved to be open and friendly, and she hoped to reconnect with the rest of the Bennets through her.

The Douglass' travelled the thirty miles from their home to Lambton the day before. It had been a difficult journey, winter was closing in and the roads were snowy, causing both the horses and carriage wheels to slip on occasion, but they had arrived, tired and relieved, to sleep and present themselves to the owners of Pemberley.

"It is just as magnificent in winter as in summer, don't you think?" They peered out the carriage windows at the view of the frosted mansion just before they began to descend into the valley below.

"I think that it is in some ways lovelier." Sarah said. "It blends in even more perfectly now." Slowly the carriage made its way down the drive, and finally came to rest before the steps. Alert footmen appeared and opened the doors to let them out, and guided them inside.

Mrs. Reynolds was waiting for them, and watched the staff efficiently take their things. "Mr. and Mrs. Douglass, we have been expecting you. Mr. and Mrs. Darcy are waiting for you upstairs, if you will please follow me?" Mr. Douglass raised his brows at his wife. This was the first time he had been invited up to the public rooms of the house; all other visits had been conducted in the study or dining room. He held out his arm and they followed the housekeeper up the steps. Marshall made a studied attempt to keep his jaw from falling open at the grand interior. His father was wealthy, but it was nothing to this. He could feel the gravitas of the family permeating through every portrait, wall sconce, and carpet.

Arriving outside of the selected sitting room, Mrs. Reynolds knocked and hearing Darcy's call, entered. "Mr. and Mrs. Angus Douglass and Mr. Marshall Douglass, sir." She stepped back, then exited, closing the door behind her.

Darcy stepped forward. "Mr. Douglass, it was a most pleasant surprise to hear that you and your family were in the area. May I present my dear wife, Elizabeth Darcy, and my sister, Miss Georgiana Darcy." He smiled down at Elizabeth who was holding his hand tightly and looking with fascination at the older woman whose features vaguely resembled her own. "Elizabeth, Georgiana, this is Mr. Angus Douglass, his wife, and their eldest son, Mr. Marshall Douglass."

Elizabeth felt his fingers squeeze her hand and she startled from her occupation and laughed. "Forgive me; I believe that I was lost in a mirror." She smiled and letting go of William's hand she stepped forward. "Aunt Sarah?"

Sarah Douglass was similarly mesmerized with Elizabeth, and startled herself. "Oh, I . . . well, yes; I suppose that in fact I am . . . niece." She smiled and was surprised to be on the receiving end of a warm embrace. Suddenly the years of shame and guilt over her foolish behaviour were wiped away with that simple act of acceptance, and she began to cry. Elizabeth held her and cried as well, for the lost years, and for the harsh punishment that the woman had suffered. Holding her made her appreciation of William's decisions for Georgiana's future so much greater, and she felt her pride in him grow.

The men stood by looking at each other and unsure of what to do. Marshall was entirely confused, he had not been told of the relationship, but his eyes drifted to Georgiana, who was blushing while alternating her glances between him and her sister. Finally Darcy stepped up and touched Elizabeth's shoulder. "Perhaps we should be seated my dear, or would you like to be alone with your aunt?"

Elizabeth drew away from Sarah and still holding her hand looked at her with a smile. "What would you like Aunt Sarah? Shall we ladies have a little talk? I daresay the men would prefer not to see any more tears."

Sarah laughed, a warm bubbling laugh, which startled Darcy just as much as Elizabeth's expressive eyes startled Mr. Douglass and Marshall.

"Yes, let us leave them to their own devices. I hear that my husband claims that they were to discuss crop yields today."

"Ah yes, well, I admit that we were suspicious of his intent when the note arrived." Elizabeth gave the fascinated man an oddly familiar smile. "Forgive me sir, but your ruse was seen through immediately."

He laughed. "Well, Mrs. Darcy, it gained us entry didn't it?"

Darcy took her hand and spoke. "It would not have been refused in the first place. Nonetheless, shall we go down to my study and leave the ladies to their discussion?" Darcy kissed Elizabeth's hand and smiled warmly at her and Georgiana; bowed to Sarah and led the way out the door. Marshall looked at the three women in wonder and then hurried to catch up, a million questions in his mind. They proceeded to the stairs, and Marshall found his voice.

"Is . . . is Miss Darcy recovered from her sadness of the summer, Mr. Darcy? She looked very well." Marshall asked cautiously.

They arrived in the study and Darcy closed the door after them, indicating chairs by his desk. He did not answer until he took his seat. He looked at the young man carefully. He had not missed the behaviour of either of them and decided to follow through with the decision he and Elizabeth had made. "My sister is returning to herself. I wonder if you have heard the story of why she was so distressed?"

Marshall looked at his father who was nodding his head in affirmation. "No sir, I have not, but it seems my father has."

"I have Son, and if Mr. Darcy decides to share the information with you, I want him to know that I understand the suffering that his sister has endured, and I support with great pride his decisions regarding the matter."

"Thank you, sir. I imagine that you are a man who would understand much better than most, and I respect what you have done as well."

Mr. Douglass nodded. "Go ahead, sir. I would rather he hear it from you than from the gossips."

Darcy grimaced. "Ah do not even mention the gossips, they have done enough." He then proceeded to lay out the basics of Georgiana's ruin. He did not mention what happened in Hertfordshire, it was not pertinent to the story. He only said that the man at fault was no longer alive. Marshall listened, absorbing the information. He had not been able to forget Georgiana in all of the months since he last saw her. He was struck by her almost ethereal beauty, but also by the despair that he sensed about her.

"I share this information with you Douglass because, as you have probably realized by now, my wife is your mother's niece. As a member of our extended family, I prefer that the truth be known to you. We have suffered quite grievously with those who took my sister's story and chose to make it fodder for the gossip mills. I understand that your mother suffered a similar situation, and it gladdens my heart to see proof that my sister has the chance of a happy life." He looked over to Mr. Douglass and nodded. "My sister has only very recently been removed from a painful situation, and she is still recovering from the incident. As you are now likely to be invited to Pemberley for more than business, I feel that you should be aware of the reasons behind her behaviour. I do not wish you to think poorly of her when you are in company if she . . . falters or withdraws."

"It seems that she is in need of a friend."

"She is, and that was how I met my wife. She was offering friendship to my sister at her moment of greatest need."

Marshall thought over the overwhelming information and looked between the men. "Perhaps, when I am visiting, I might . . . talk with her?"

Darcy smiled. "Certainly, that would be welcome. I expect that you will occasionally call on Pemberley in accordance with the contracts that we have between ourselves, beyond any family event that we may be hosting." He looked to Mr. Douglass who was nodding. "Sir, in that light, I would also like to take this opportunity to invite your family to Pemberley for a family dinner on New Year's Eve and to stay the night. The entire Bennet family will be coming for Christmas, and I hope that your wife will wish to reunite with her brother and meet her other nieces. You will, of course, be welcome to stay longer if you all feel comfortable after the introductions."

"Really sir? Well, I will need to consult my wife, but I would be very happy to accept your offer of hospitality." He smiled at his son. "What do you think, Marshall?"

"I would like that, sir. Thank you." Darcy nodded then pulling out some papers smiled. "Well, until our wives finish their talk, shall we speak of wheat, sir?" Laughing, Mr. Douglass pulled up his chair and leaned over the desk, and the talk turned to business.

Georgiana sat quietly watching the two women fall into animated and easy conversation. To look at them they would appear to be acquaintances of a lifetime, not minutes. Sarah was aware of her family's doings from her brother's letters, and was most interested in learning about changes in Longbourn and Meryton. Elizabeth wished to hear of her other cousins, and where her aunt lived. When their combined curiosity had been sufficiently sated, Elizabeth took Georgiana's hand and turned to her aunt.

"Aunt Sarah, my husband told me that you have been informed of what happened with my sister this summer. You should know that I have told her of you. She has come a long way from where she once was in her recovery, but recent incidents have set her back, despite her current appearance of cheer. I have tried the best that I can, but I admit that I hope you might lend her some advice, or be able to answer questions that I have no experience to aid me in replies. Would you be willing to counsel both of us?"

Sarah looked at Georgiana's downcast eyes. "Of course I would be glad of it. You are not so very alone, there are many of us." She patted her hand and met her surprised expression. "My dear, when a girl is ruined, the family has four options. Each carries its own burden. They can marry her off to the man who compromised her, they can marry her off to another man who is willing to accept her, they can send her away either permanently or until the confinement is over and the child abandoned, or they can keep her home and face the scorn of their society. I believe that your brother's insistence that you remain at home was very brave, and proves his love for you is far greater than his concern over his status. You are very fortunate. I hope that you recognize the sacrifice he made for you."

"I had not thought of it that way." She whispered and looked to Elizabeth with wide eyes. "He has never spoken of it."

Elizabeth smiled. "I think that your brother is actually grateful for it because his temporary fall gave him the ability to see me as worthy, instead of an impossible choice."

"He is a very good man." Sarah smiled. "Now, I am sure that you wonder what your future may hold?" Georgiana nodded. "You are young, you are very wealthy. I know that you have been the subject of scorn and derision, but I am sure that you are well aware that a family may inherit a title, but entailments prevent them from selling property to provide funds for the estate and lifestyle they must maintain. They must marry a woman with a dowry. You will not be scorned by such families as a possible bride."

"But I want what William and Elizabeth have."

"Ah then, I hope that you will find a man like my husband. He courted me when he was still an apprentice, and when it was over and he was free to marry, I told him of my past. He accepted it for what it was; a foolish mistake of youth; that I admitted was partly my fault. He still wanted me, and we have been married happily for three and twenty years."

"Everyone in London knows what I did." She said softly and looked down at her hands.

Elizabeth squeezed her hand. "No, I would say that everyone in London *thinks* they know, but have embellished it with their own version. Unfortunately, it will be very difficult to change that opinion, even with those families who would accept you for the dowry."

"Well then, I suggest that you widen your prospects. Not every eligible man lives in London, and not all of them are peers." Sarah smiled. "But you will not need to worry about such things for a few years yet."

"No." Georgiana bit her lip and looked between the ladies. "I thought that Mr. Douglass was quite handsome." She blushed furiously and looked back down.

Elizabeth and Sarah smiled at each other, each lifting identical brows to matching dancing eyes. "I think he is quite handsome as well, Georgiana." She looked at her aunt. "Would you like a tour of the house while we wait for the gentleman to finish their business?"

"I would indeed, Elizabeth."

Chapter 35

"Let us see then . . . ." Elizabeth sat in Mrs. Reynolds' office, looking over the menu for Christmas dinner. Mrs. Reynolds had not failed to appreciate the mistress coming into her domain, and the rest of the staff had noted it as well. Elizabeth wished to demonstrate that she was approachable. "Roast beef, venison, capon, goose . . ."

"Cook has some nice fat peacocks as well, Mrs. Darcy."

"Oh, I hate to kill such a beautiful bird!"

"Noisy bird, if you ask me madam, no great sin to silence one or two."

Elizabeth laughed. "Well, since I have not had much exposure to them, I will have to take your word for it." She sighed. "What we are planning is quite beyond anything that I have ever experienced, and I thought that my mother always set an excellent table." She smiled at her housekeeper, and then her eyes grew wide. "Oh, did I remember to give you the recipe for the Bennet family Christmas pie? Papa would be devastated if it was not on the table!"

"Yes madam; and I have located the Darcy family recipe for Christmas pudding."

"Was it not made every year?"

"No, madam. Christmas was never really celebrated at all, other than attending services and a family meal. This recipe is from your husband's grandmother. It was tucked away in an old cookery book."

"This truly was a sad house." Elizabeth watched the woman's downcast eyes and pursed lips. "Mrs. Reynolds, how long have you been at Pemberley?"

"I have been here just over four and twenty years. My husband, bless his soul, was here when your husband's parent's married."

"I have heard it was . . . difficult."

"Mr. Darcy was a good man when he was younger. I understand that it was his wife who turned him into a very bitter and angry one." Mrs. Reynolds' eyes flashed. "Pardon me madam, I should not speak ill of the dead."

"Did you know George Wickham?"

"A clever schemer that boy was!" She shook her head. "He worked his way around Mr. Darcy and used him, and hurt the young master!" Her eyes closed. "Pardon me again madam; I should not be speaking so plainly to you."

"Mrs. Reynolds, please do not apologize. I appreciate how protective you feel about my husband and sister. He thinks very fondly of you." The older woman practically glowed with the praise. "I have been trying to piece together the information I have received from so many different sources . . . Mr. Wickham was favoured by Mr. Darcy? He once told me that Mr. Darcy wished that he was his son and would leave him Pemberley because he hated my husband. Did you ever see any evidence of that?"

Her eyes grew wide and indignant. "I remember that boy, strutting about as if HE was the heir, belting out orders to the servants, giving himself airs. WE knew what he was, and paid him no heed. He shut up quick enough when his patron was about. He was always polite when the young master was with his father too, but when they were alone . . ." She shook her head. "Sometimes I thought Master Fitzwilliam was just too much a gentleman. I would not have minded seeing him knock that wastrel down!"

"Well, I am happy to tell you that he did, but that is between us." Elizabeth smiled.

Mrs. Reynolds' eyes grew wide and she grinned. "Really?" She smiled with pride.

Watching her carefully, Elizabeth asked. "How did Mr. Darcy's parents treat him?"

The woman's eyes filled with tears. "Please do not ask me of those times, madam. I am grateful they are in the past." Elizabeth nodded and wondered what had happened, but seeing how the mere mention of it distressed Mrs. Reynolds, she more than ever understood her husband's lapses into silence and his need for her embrace.

Wiping her eyes, Mrs. Reynolds resumed her formal address. "Is there anything else, Mrs. Darcy? Will you need a seamstress to make any alterations to your new gowns?"

She smiled ruefully. "Mrs. Reynolds, I am at last appreciating the skill of an excellent modiste. I can honestly say that not a stitch must be added to any of the beautiful things Mr. Darcy insisted we order when we were in London. I have no idea how those women even completed so many items, it must have taken up every moment of their time."

"I am pleased to hear it, Mrs. Darcy. Is there anything else that we need to discuss?"

"Oh, the tenants, does Mr. Darcy give them anything for Christmas?"

"Yes, madam, he wrote me of the baskets in October. We have been putting them together. They are all laid out in the ballroom. Each household will receive some fruit and biscuits, socks for the children, some good wool yarn for the women and a purse for the men. Mr. Darcy likes to deliver them on Christmas Eve."

"He goes himself?" Elizabeth was pleased to hear of his participation.

"Oh yes, ever since his father died, he makes a point of doing this. The tenants were always appreciated."

"He shall have company this year." The women smiled at each other. "And has he thought of gifts for the Pemberley and Darcy House staff?"

"Yes, that has been addressed."

"That leaves the decorations. I suppose that we must start some new traditions there as well. Please ask the men to cut greenery for the doorways, and to find a Yule log. My father is bringing the end of our log from last year. Is there any hope of making a kissing bough?" She raised her brow.

Mrs. Reynolds laughed. "Ah, yes indeed, I am sure that we will be successful in that!"

"Good, Mr. Darcy and I will have to inspect it thoroughly." She winked and stood.

"Mrs. Darcy?" Elizabeth paused as she was about to leave the room. "Thank you. The servants here at Pemberley are delighted to help you in any way."

"Thank you Mrs. Reynolds, I am entirely lost without all of you." She smiled and walked out the door and up the stairs to the first floor. After three weeks in residence, she had a fairly good feel for her way about the house. *I suppose all of those years wandering the forests have honed my wayfinding skills!* She looked towards William's closed study door. He had been sequestered there with Mr. Barkley, his steward, for hours, as he had been nearly every day that past week. His long absence from the estate left many issues to review and resolve, and being the man he was; William could no longer neglect his duty. She used the time to learn her own duties, and Mrs. Reynolds was gradually introducing her to each one. Knowing that William would be hoping for her to come and keep him company after his steward was dismissed, she glanced at a clock and decided that she had time to complete one more task before joining him.

She continued up to the deserted guest wing, and began opening doors, looking over the bedchambers. The Matlocks all had assigned places and would simply stay where they always did. Richard's presence would disrupt Bingley's preferred place, and Elizabeth was toying with the idea of choosing a room for him that was conveniently close to Jane's. She bit her lip and giggled as she stood just inside the doorway of a lovely room, calculating how long it would take her future brother to sneak across the hallway, when she felt two hands steal around her waist and heard a deep voice in her ear.

"What are you plotting, Mrs. Darcy?" Warm lips began nibbling her lobe.

"You finished early!" She smiled and tilted her head upwards. "Mmmm, that is so nice."

His chuckle rumbled and his embrace tightened, drawing her back against him. "I am happy to bring you pleasure; my love. Now, you have not answered my question." He nibbled down her neck to her shoulders, and began lightly caressing circles around her rapidly hardening nipples. Elizabeth wiggled back against him and felt an insistent pressure against her back.

"I . . . I was just wondering . . . .ohhhhh . . . how convenient it would be . . . oh, Will, please . . ."

Darcy's hand continued its slow torture of her breasts, while the other drifted down to stroke over her centre. "Convenient?" He whispered huskily.

"For Jane and Charles . . ."

"You are encouraging them paying calls during the night?" His tongue found its way back up to her ear.

Elizabeth's back arched and her writhing was exciting him in dramatic ways. "It . . . ohhh . . . it did us no harm . . . did it?" Her voice died away and he turned her around to bestow a slow, loving kiss. She clung to him and he cupped her bottom, pressing her tightly against his groin.

"No my love, the only harm it did was to make me mad with wanting you." He spoke against her lips. "Lizzy, is it over, may I love you again?"

She smiled; it had been a difficult week for her passionate husband. "Yes, Will. You no longer have to wait."

"I have no patience for waiting." He kicked the door shut and scooped her up to drop her, bouncing slightly, on the bed. Elizabeth laughed and met the intense eyes that were staring at her with unhidden desire. Darcy tore off his coat and cravat, and dropped his hands to unbutton his breeches.

Watching his fevered movements, Elizabeth asked innocently, "Should we not undress, Will?"

Shaking his head vehemently, he advanced to stand at the edge of the bed. "I want you now, Lizzy."

"In the middle of the day?" She teased, rising up on her knees to wrap her arms around him, and began kissing his wonderfully exposed neck.

Darcy's eyes closed and he groaned, running his hands over her back. "Soon this house will be full of people, and with the weather, who knows how long they may remain. I have been denied my wife for the past week, I want you now." His lips found hers and they met in a voracious kiss.

"I think that you missed me." She whispered in his ear, then reaching down, firmly caressed his exposed arousal, and bent to tenderly suckle the tip. Darcy gasped. Elizabeth straightened and looked at him with worry. "Did I do something wrong?"

"NO!" He began tearing off his waistcoat and shirt, and paused long enough to look at her. "What are you waiting for?" He demanded. Elizabeth laughed and unbuttoned her gown, deliberately removing her clothes, while she watched him struggle out of his.

"If you would slow down . . ." She began and watched as a boot sailed across the room. He hopped on one foot and tore off the other, then quickly stripped off his breeches and drawers. Elizabeth bit her lip and neatly folded her gown, then slipped off her shoes and stockings. All that remained was her chemise and stays. Suddenly she found that two shaking hands were untying the ribbons and she watched as the remaining items fell to her feet. His fingers travelled through her hair, and a cascade of pins hit the floor, followed by the curtain of her hair dropping down to a swaying halt around her shoulders. She looked up at her husband's burning gaze and ran her hands over his expansive chest. "Now, what was it that you wished for, Will?"

With a squeal she found herself in the air and dropped back onto the bed. Darcy dove on top of her and pinned her down. "You are teasing me cruelly, my love." His nose was touching hers.

"Forgive me; you are simply irresistible when you are amorous." She pulled his face down and kissed him, drawing the upper lip into her mouth, and delighting in his low moans. "How may I win back your favour?"

"Turn over," he whispered. He lifted up from her and she rolled onto her belly. Darcy gathered her long hair up and pushed it aside, then beginning with her ear, slowly kissed his way down over her shoulders, tracing his tongue down her back, caressing her silky skin and gently nibbling her delightfully soft rump. "You could not possibly lose my favour." He murmured as his hands spread her legs apart and he looked hungrily at her treasure, wet and ripe for his embrace. "Oh, Lizzy. . ." He lay down on her back, and reached below, touching her, spreading her essence over himself, and slowly entered. "Ohhhhhhhhhh." They both moaned. "Does it feel good, dearest?"

"Oh, yes." She moaned.

He nuzzled his face against her neck and bit her shoulder. One hand caressed over her back, down to her hips, and returned as the other arm wrapped around her waist, holding her against his steadily moving body. His hips travelled in an endless circle as he ground into her. It was a quiet, impassioned coupling. They were both soon lost in the bliss, the only sound was their erratic breathing, and then Elizabeth's soft, "Will." He felt her arching back, and gasping, he allowed his release to rush over him, "Oh, Lizzybeth." He groaned.

Luxuriating in the wonderful lassitude, Darcy could not even consider moving from her, and instead drew her closer to his chest, curling around her, and caressed the place where he felt their bodies still joined. He closed his eyes and nestled his face on her shoulder. "I missed loving you so much, Elizabeth."

Elizabeth's hand lowered to touch where his lay, and feeling his softening flesh, entwined her fingers with his. "I missed you as well."

"Now that I know what it is to be one with you, it seems that I can not bear to separate for too long." He gently kissed her neck.

"You were dreaming of this?" She felt his head nod. "Did I neglect you this week? I . . ."

"Stop that." He kissed her. "Of course not, I . . . oh Lizzy, I am simply a man who deeply appreciates his wife. This week I buried myself in work, hoping to distract my mind from you, and failed terribly."

"Do you mean that you really did not have to meet with your steward?" She looked at him with surprise.

"No, I did, I just . . ." He sighed. "I no longer want to spend all of my time engaged in work. I have used work as an excuse to . . . avoid living, avoid people. I have you now, and I want to experience so much that I have neglected before."

"This can not all be about lovemaking." She rolled over and caressed his face.

He chuckled. "No dearest, it is not, but I can not deny the attraction." Elizabeth laughed as well. Darcy pulled the edge of the counterpane up to drape over them. It was suddenly very cold in the unheated room. He wrapped her up in his arms, and kissed her hair, tucking her head under his chin. "Most of the gentlemen I know leave the management of their estates to their stewards, and only concern themselves with being sure that the rents are collected."

"As my father does." She said softly.

"Yes, but at least he is aware of what crops are planted." He looked down at her closed eyes and gave her a squeeze. "I can not consciously remain idle, not when I am aware of how intrinsically the land is tied to my heritage. Not to pay attention to it; or its improvement, is entirely against everything that I believe . . . but now . . ."

"You must find a balance that was unnecessary before." She looked back up into his intense blue eyes. "As much as I love you Will, I know that we can not be together all of the time. I understand that, and certainly do not question your need to work, if anything I admire it." Smiling she kissed his lips, then touched them. "Besides, if you were always by my side, you would grow tired of me and wish me away."

"Impossible."

Laughing she kissed his nose. "You must also make time for the activities that you enjoy, your fencing and riding, for example. After all, I enjoy looking over my handsome husband and wish him to remain that way." She ran her hands over his tightly muscled body and he sighed with her touch.

He then looked at her with concern. "I want you to be happy, and not waiting for me."

"I think that an enormous house full of servants will keep me occupied, and I can walk to remain healthy for you, I do have quite the spectacular park to explore, and of course there is Georgiana to look after as well."

"That all sounds well and good, but I need my time with you, and not just keeping company while I work. I need to be alone with you. I need to finally live." He met her with his earnest gaze. "I have no desire to be parted from you for endless hours. I want you to share this with me. This is why I married, I need you."

"This is the result of loving your wife, you know. Those who marry for convenience do not face these problems." She smiled and his gaze did not relent.

"I am serious, Elizabeth." He held her face in his hands. "Help me. This week you were unable to . . . be with me as we had been, and without that temptation I thought that I would try to return to my work and see what sort of a life it would be, and I . . . I did not like it. What I told you the day we arrived here was the truth. I did not marry to be separate from you."

Elizabeth stared into his searching eyes and stroked his hair while she thought. "Perhaps if we establish working hours, you could attend to business in the morning, and depending on the season and your activity we could meet for breakfast, perhaps leave your paperwork for the afternoon when I could keep you company after addressing my duties for the house in the morning? Then from dinner time on we will be a family?"

He nodded slowly. "I think that might work." He looked at her sharply. "It will not be set in stone. We must leave room for spontaneity."

"Oh yes, by all means!" She smiled and kissed him, and a sparkle came to her eyes, wondering if he had ever allowed himself to behave with such freedom before. "I think that we will be spontaneous more often than not."

Darcy relaxed. "Forgive me, Lizzy. This has occupied so much of my thought this week. I want to make you happy, and I want to be happy, and . . . I suppose that until we arrived here and, well I was forced to see all that needed to be addressed, that I . . ."

"The honeymoon has ended." She said sadly.

"No, I do not ever want it to end, it will NOT end." He said with determination, and saw her expression. "Dearest, oh what have I done? I should never have spoken of this!" He hugged her fiercely. "I am so sorry!"

"Will, I . . . please stop." She squeezed him. "This is new for both of us. Now that we are . . . not over our honeymoon, but perhaps . . . ready to . . . begin our true marriage, we will just have to talk to each other and . . . make our plans accordingly for each day." She saw his worried expression, and decided it was time to lighten the mood. "Have you noticed that we seem to have our most serious conversations when we are lying together in bed or holding each other?"

Darcy's little smile appeared. "I have, and I truly love this." Squeezing her he whispered. "I think that all of our conversations should take place in such a manner." She laughed and his smile grew. "I love you, Elizabeth."

"I love you, William." They kissed slowly and entwined their limbs in a tight embrace. Elizabeth bit her lip and decided to broach a new subject. "Will, you have never wished to lay behind me before; is this something that you have thought about? We sleep that way, is that what inspired you? I was just curious. . ."

Darcy lifted his head, "Sweetheart, were you uncomfortable? There are many ways to make love."

She looked away from him. "No, I was not uncomfortable, far from it . . . I am not completely unfamiliar, at least I think that I am not quite as unfamiliar as I thought I was before we married, but we have only been married a few weeks, I mean, I think that . . ."

Turning her head towards him, Darcy caressed her face and gave her a confused smile. "Lizzy, what are you trying not to say?"

"I . . . Do you remember when I said that I looked into my father's locked drawer and saw his books?" She blushed and looked down again.

"Yes." He continued his caress, and delighted in the feel of her increasingly warm cheek under his fingers. He suddenly had an idea of what his once innocent bride saw but did not understand until their wedding night. "Dearest, did your father have engravings showing couples engaged in acts of love?" He felt her face grow warmer and she nodded, still not looking at him. He bit his lip but could not restrain his laugh.

Elizabeth looked up sharply. "I amuse you?"

"Yes, you do. I can just see you now, engaged in your clandestine peeking, and wondering just what you were seeing." He hugged her, and wondered if Mr. Bennet had a copy of the scandalous book by Fanny Hill as his father did. "Did you see a picture that resembled what we just experienced?"

"I did, I . . . I did not realize at the time that . . . Will you said that there are many ways to love each other?"

He smiled and nodded, and saw a shadow cross her face. "And before you wonder, I truly have not experienced many, Lizzy. I truly have not, but my father collected a great number of books and engravings that I suspect are similar in nature to your father's, and as I did know what I was viewing, and I have a very fertile imagination, well, I have often envisioned us in such positions." Elizabeth's gaze was fixed on his warm eyes. "Perhaps you would like to look at the drawings with me, and we might find something that you would enjoy?" He smiled at her wide eyes and traced his finger over her mouth. "I wonder if your desire to taste me was inspired by such a drawing." He raised his brow and watched her guilty smile appear. He whispered, "I enjoyed that very much." The smile on her face grew and he laughed, then kissed her. "That settles it. Tonight after we bid Georgiana goodnight, we shall enjoy an evening of education."

Laughing, Elizabeth stroked back the hair from his brow. "And shall we require many lessons, my Will?"

"Oh, undoubtedly!" He smiled at her with twinkling eyes. Their foreheads rested together, and their noses touched. "So, my love, what was that you were saying about Jane and Bingley?"

"Jane." Bingley grabbed her hand and pulled her into the empty parlour. The coaches were packed and they would be leaving for Pemberley in only a few minutes.

"Charles, be careful, if Papa catches us again . . ." Bingley smiled and embraced her.

"I know, but it will be two days before I can be sure of a private moment with you again! I am certain that we will have no opportunity at the inns, but I am aware of many secluded places in Pemberley . . ." He kissed her soundly and wiggled his eyebrows.

Jane blushed. "You are a little boy, Charles Bingley!"

Charles laughed. "I am a very big boy, I assure you, Miss Bennet." He tilted his head and brushed her cheek with his fingers. Jane regarded him for a moment and looked down. He kissed her softly. "I may behave as a little boy sometimes, dear Jane, and I admit that I do not always do the right things and my inexperience shows, but I do believe that I am the man you need and want as your husband." She looked up at him in surprise. "I am not a fool, Jane, just young and learning, and I want to do this all with you."

Jane nodded and smiled. "Thank you, Charles." She peeked out the door and kissed him. He laughed with delight and let her go when they heard Mrs. Bennet's call. "Come on, we must go!" She took his hand and pulled him down the hallway. Bingley smiled and wondered how Darcy ever survived his engagement.

The family boarded the two coaches, Mr. and Mrs. Bennet, Lydia, and Kitty in theirs; and Jane, Mary, and Bingley in the other. It was just after dawn and they were on their way. "I can not wait to see Lizzy and Georgiana!" Mary said with a smile.

"Have you no excitement over your brother, Mary?" Jane asked.

"Oh, of course I want to see William, too!" She blushed. "He is becoming livelier according to Lizzy's letters. She said they had a snow battle last week and she knocked his hat off five times before he finally just threw it away!"

Bingley laughed. "I can not imagine this wonder that my friend has become, but I am delighted to hear of these tales. His last letter to me was so joyous; I admit that I wondered if he was truly the author. Your sister has worked a miracle on the man."

"My sister could make a statue smile." Jane grinned. "Oh, I can not wait to see her. Do you truly hope to find an estate near Pemberley?"

"Yes, I do. I have no desire to remain in Hertfordshire. The area has been irrevocably ruined for me. I can not look at the people without remembering the disdain they showed for my future family. Would you not like to live near your sister?"

"Oh yes, although, I will miss the rest of my family." She smiled at Mary. "Have you decided to accept Lizzy's invitation to spend the spring at Pemberley?"

"I have. I want to take this opportunity to see what is beyond Hertfordshire, and I do not know that I would have been comfortable in London for the Season. I think that Georgiana is relieved that William does not want her to accompany them there. She is afraid to return. I think that we will have a wonderful time by ourselves."

"I doubt that Elizabeth and Darcy will remain long in town. They will visit the theatre and bookshops mostly, I think. After the presentation, I understand that they only plan a few dinners with his loyal friends, and Lord and Lady Matlock will hold a ball in their honour to expose them to greater society. Of course, we must hold some sort of affair." Bingley smiled across the coach at Jane. "Beyond that . . . well, it depends on their reception. If I know Darcy, he will be back home by May."

"Do you think that is long enough to repair any damage?" Jane asked with interest.

Bingley shrugged. "Who knows? It will be enough to let the *ton* get a good look at both of them, and hopefully there will be some other poor souls who will attract their interest. Truly, Darcy's wealth and name alone would have done the trick; it is the addition of Elizabeth which will provide the challenge. I wonder if they will go to Rosings for Easter, Darcy does every other year."

"Have you heard from Miss Bingley? You have not mentioned her."

He shook his head. "That is because she only raises my ire. She requested funds for transportation to Bath for Christmas. I refused. She will remain in London. I believe that Louisa and Hurst will have her over for Christmas dinner, and then they will leave for their trip, and return for our wedding. Caroline is still unrepentant, and until I hear something sincere from her, I will continue with my plans. I think that she is still counting on me giving in. She is quite incorrect."

Mary studied her hands, thinking of scripture verses. "Are you sure that you should not be the first to offer forgiveness?"

Bingley smiled. "I have thought of that, Mary, I truly have, but some people, my sister being one of them, would look at an offer of forgiveness as an opportunity to take advantage and not a chance to reform. I believe that she has not ever felt the sting of rebuke before, and . . . I do believe that she needs to feel it for some time. In this, she must find her way."

"Through reflection and prayer." Mary nodded.

"Hmmm. Mary, I admire your optimism, but you can not project your faith onto my sister." He smiled kindly and she tilted her head, thinking that there was a great deal of truth in his statement.

Jane broke the silence. "I look forward to meeting my Aunt Sarah."

"How does your father feel about this?"

"He is excited and apprehensive, I think."

In the smaller carriage that travelled behind Bingley's Mr. Bennet sat and studied his book, ignoring the noisy conversation of the ladies. "Well, I am looking forward to it! Imagine; a whole new set of relations! And they are quite wealthy are they not?" Lydia asked with excitement.

"I know that they are quite comfortable, my dear, but it is not your place to point that out." Mrs. Bennet calmly addressed her daughter and Mr. Bennet looked at her with admiration. Since her confrontation with Lady Catherine and the subsequent improvement in their relationship, she had allowed her flutterings to lessen and her sense to appear. Of course, the marriage and engagement of two of her daughters to wealthy men did not hurt either.

"Thank you, Mrs. Bennet." He smiled at her and turned to his daughters. "I am looking forward to seeing my sister as well. I hope that upon meeting us, she will not regret the reunion. I expect both of you to conduct yourselves with proper decorum." He raised his brow.

"And does that include Lizzy, Papa? What if she decides to race William again on those donkeys he bought her as a wedding gift?" Kitty giggled.

They all laughed. "Whatever possessed him to do such a thing?" Mrs. Bennet wondered.

"Oh Mama, do you not know? He fell in love with her when he saw a donkey tear her bonnet off in the street! He tried to find the exact same one, but he had to settle for the pair he bought." Lydia giggled. "Lizzy said he stuck an old bonnet on one and a beaver on the other and had them waiting for her in the stable when he took her for a riding lesson!"

"Your sister has certainly found a man full of boyish spirit." Mr. Bennet smiled and shook his head, remembering the sombre man who stiffly told him that he was taught to never express any emotion. He missed his daughter's presence in his life every day, but he did not for a moment regret giving her away to a man who treasured her so dearly. He looked upon his other girls and hoped they would find the same joy someday.

He felt Mrs. Bennet lightly touch his hand. "It will be wonderful to see the children at play, will it not Mr. Bennet?"

He laughed. "Indeed. I look forward to seeing them with their own."

"Back again!" Lord Matlock shook the dusting of snow from his hat and shrugged out of his coat. "The house looks beautiful, Elizabeth!"

She smiled and accepted the kiss he bestowed on her hand. "Thank you, Uncle Henry. Georgiana and I have had a grand time thinking of ways to decorate."

Lady Matlock gave her a hug. "It is lovely, my dear. Perhaps next year you might consider opening the house to tours?"

"Oh my, that would take a great deal of planning!" Her eyes grew wide. "I would not know where to begin!"

"Hmm. Well, we have done it for years, in honesty; I am rather pleased to be missing it this year!" She laughed.

"And you expect me to be excited now?" Elizabeth smiled and turned to greet James, who was standing quietly by her side. "It is good to see you!"

"And you, Elizabeth. You are still glowing with happiness. I assume that my cousin has not reverted to his dour self as yet." He smiled warmly.

"No sir, he has not, and it is my wifely duty to ensure that he never will." She received his kiss on the hand and laughed at his gallant bow. James' smile grew with the sound of her amusement.

Richard walked straight up and kissed her cheek, then grinned at her. "You do glow Elizabeth! Where are my missing cousins?"

She smiled at the two men. "Georgiana is occupied with Mrs. Annesley, and will join us for tea after you have refreshed yourselves. William is dealing with an emergency on the estate, but expects to be with us very soon."

"An emergency?" Lord Matlock turned a concerned eye to her.

Nodding, her expression became serious. "One of the tenant families lost their home to a fire last night. Thankfully, nobody was injured, other than a few burns. William went to the scene as soon as he was informed, and is very relieved at the providential outcome. The loss of the home is sad, but the tragedy that was avoided has made everyone grateful. Fortunately, a tenant home on another part of the estate is empty, so William has directed the boys in the stable to help bring over supplies and move the family in. Many other tenants are donating belongings and William has given them some funds to buy whatever else they may have lost, to give them a start. They will rebuild in the spring."

Richard listened in admiration. "No wonder he has such success at Pemberley, he always cares for his people."

Elizabeth raised her brows. "Without those people's efforts, Pemberley would not be the great estate it is."

"Something for you to remember, Son." Lord Matlock reminded him.

Elizabeth directed the family to their rooms and returned to the drawing room to make sure that all was ready for their guests. A maid was just stoking the fire and another brought in the tea service when Darcy arrived. "Mrs. Darcy, did I miss anything?" The two servants bobbed and quickly departed.

"No, they are upstairs changing. How are the Hoyts?" She regarded his tired face with concern.

He sighed and ran his hand through his hair then stared at the soot that coated his fingers. "They are devastated, but grateful to still be intact. They should be fine though, they already seem to have more than they owned before with the generosity of the neighbours." He paused, and closed his eyes. "It could have been so much worse . . . my relief for such a fortunate outcome . . . I have not seen a fire at Pemberley since the one that claimed Danny's family. He was there today, helping out. I think he looked worse than they did." He shook his head and attempted to move away from the memory. "I am thinking of bringing him into the house."

She saw his effort and encouraged his thinking. "Would he like that?"

"I do not see him being a messenger forever, especially if he wishes to marry Susie . . ."

Elizabeth smiled. "You are matchmaking, Mr. Darcy?"

He smiled at the sparkle that appeared in her eyes. "No, that is your position, my love. I am simply preparing for the inevitable."

"Perhaps you should ask him his preferences, maybe he would be happier in the stables, or perhaps he could become an aid to your steward." She raised her brow.

Growing thoughtful, he considered the suggestion. "Groom him for a greater position, you mean?"

"Well, what could he be inside of the house? Do you see him as the butler?" Darcy tilted his head and smiled. She laughed. "I did not think so. And if Susie does marry him, I suppose I would need to find a new maid, she surely could not take on all of the duties for me and care for her husband as well."

Darcy sighed. "You, dearest, are very sensible. I will talk to him. I just feel that he should be rewarded for all that he has done for us." He kissed her and laughed at the dirt he left on her nose. "I believe I should bathe." He nudged her to face the mirror over the mantle to see her reflection, and she rolled her eyes and lightly hit his arm, then moaned at the fine cloud of soot that rose from him.

"You! Out! Immediately!" She pushed him to the door.

Darcy made to wrap his arms around her. "Come, my love, do you not wish for my embrace?" Elizabeth squealed and ran away. Darcy laughed and left the room, still chuckling as he climbed the stairs. He met Richard on the landing and his wide grin only inspired a wider one from his cousin. They shook hands and Darcy laughed to see the black paw that his cousin now possessed and continued on to his chambers. Richard stared at the dirt and sighing, returned to his own.

That evening at dinner, the halls of Pemberley rang with laughter. Unrepentantly, Darcy sat next to his wife and held her hand, kissing it frequently and smiling warmly. Georgiana entertained her relatives with a recital. Elizabeth watched it all and hoped the easy atmosphere would continue when her family arrived. As if he was reading her mind, Darcy leaned over and whispered in her ear. "I have not a doubt in my mind that all will be well, my love. How could it not be? You are here."

"Thank you." Elizabeth whispered with shining eyes. Darcy lifted her hand to his lips, his eyes just as bright, and whispered. "No, my love. Thank you."

Chapter 36

"*O*h my!" Jane craned her neck to catch another glimpse of Pemberley as their carriage left the top of the rise and descended back into the forest. Bingley grinned. "I have seen it so many times, I suppose that I am in some ways immune to the affect it has upon the first viewing. It is rather awe-inspiring." He leaned across the carriage. "I am afraid, Jane; that whatever we purchase will not be nearly as impressive."

Jane touched his hand. "When have I ever proclaimed a desire to live in a palace, Mr. Bingley?"

He laughed and sat back. "Never, thankfully."

Mary's eyes were wide with anticipation. "To be the mistress of all this would be something." She smiled at Jane. "And to think our sister won the position!"

"Won it is a good description, I think!"

"Oh Mr. Bennet!" Mrs. Bennet stared at him. "I never really understood just how rich Mr. Darcy was until this moment!"

"Neither did I. He told me his income, but numbers on a page do not translate to the reality that is before us." He met her eyes. "Our Lizzy is a grand lady indeed."

"She must be frightened to death!" Kitty whispered.

"Lizzy? Scared?" Lydia snorted. "After she took on Wickless?"

"Lydia! Where did you hear such talk?!" Mrs. Bennet scolded.

She shrugged. "That is what I heard the grooms call him."

"No more gossip, young woman. You saw how hurtful it is. I will not tolerate it. Do you understand me?" Mr. Bennet glowered at her.

"Yes, Papa." Lydia sighed and looked around at the endless trees. "There is nothing here. I think that when I marry, I must live in a town. I do not think that I would be happy with nothing but trees to look upon."

"Well my dear, I hope that your wish will be fulfilled someday." Mrs. Bennet nodded her head, and wondered if she could persuade Jane to take her to town in the spring, since Elizabeth had already said that she would not.

The carriages arrived and soon the passengers were inside and receiving the overwhelming attention of the servants. Elizabeth and Darcy waited to greet them, as the cacophony of exclamations by the ladies filled the air. Mrs. Bennet was blushing profusely with Darcy's kiss on her cheek. She patted his face. "You just grow more handsome every time I see you, William."

He smiled and offered her his arm. "Thank you, Mother." He shot a look and a wink at Elizabeth who suppressed a laugh and kissed her father.

"How was the journey?"

"Long, cold, noisy, and thankfully over." He kissed her cheek and held out his arm. "This is quite the little cottage you live in, my dear."

"Yes, William's family has done well with what little they have." Her eyes twinkled. "I shall take you to your rooms, and then you can join us all before dinner." She smiled at Bingley. "Charles, since you know your way around, I am counting on you to help direct everyone to the yellow drawing room."

"It will be my pleasure. I assume that I am in my usual chambers?"

Darcy was at the first landing and was about to continue to the living quarters when he turned to his friend. "Ah, no Bingley, my cousin beat you to them, but Elizabeth has selected a place especially suited to you."

Bingley looked at him in confusion and followed the family upstairs. Darcy paused at the first door in the guest wing. "This is yours, Bingley."

He opened the door and looked in; it was a finely appointed room, decorated in masculine colours. He looked back at Darcy with a question in his eyes, and then heard Elizabeth's voice.

"You are in the family wing, Jane. I will show you your room after we have everyone else settled."

Bingley looked back at Darcy. "Well?"

Darcy smiled. "Would you be able to stay away from her if she was convenient to your chambers?"

He turned red and started to protest, then smiling slightly he looked down. "No, and I would have no willpower to stop once I arrived. So you are doing this as a favour to me?" He met his friend's nodding head and laughed at how well Darcy knew him. "How ever did you survive your engagement, Darcy?"

Laughing, he clasped Bingley's shoulder. "Perseverance, my friend, and a great deal of wishful thinking."

———※———

The Bennet ladies were thoroughly intimidated with their introduction to the Fitzwilliams. Richard and Elizabeth managed to start and encourage the conversation. Bingley had no trouble joining in. Darcy, for all of his happiness, remained a quiet man, happier to contribute as needed, but happier still to sit back and watch his wife effortlessly put the disparate group at ease. He sipped his wine and observed her laughing with Jane far away at the opposite end of the table, taking her place for the first time in the mistress' seat. His thoughts drifted to the coming Season.

Lord Matlock, sitting to his right, leaned over to him. "Where are your thoughts, Darcy? You appear concerned."

He smiled slightly. "I am worried for Elizabeth. What will society do to her?" He looked at his uncle, and his brow creased. "I could not bear to see her changed to be like them, and I can not bear to see her hurt because she is not. I dread returning to London, but yet I know that we must." His gaze returned to her and their eyes met. "She is so precious to me."

Lord Matlock watched as Elizabeth's brow wrinkled, reading Darcy's expression. "Smile man, before she starts to worry."

Darcy managed a little lift to his lips. Elizabeth studied him then nodded, and returned to her conversation. He knew that he would be interrogated later and his smile widened at the thought. He looked at his plate and heard his uncle's voice again. "Son, your aunt has no intention of making Elizabeth into something neither of you will recognize. She will instruct her on the rules of engagement. I think that it is quite clear to us that neither of you wish to fully participate in the Season, nor is it necessary. With such a marriage as you have made, even without the scandal, Elizabeth would only have been accepted by your best friends, and those who would benefit by association with the Darcy name. Those above you who do not need your connection would have rejected or accepted you on their terms, no matter how you present yourselves. If you had chosen the daughter of a peer, as was always expected, things would be different. No Son, you have disappointed a great many people with your wedding. You will have the curious and the indifferent, the friends and the toadies. I would go to town, complete her presentation, reconnect with those you feel you must, then when you have fulfilled your duty, return home."

"I would like to take her to the theatre."

"Well, there is certainly no reason not to go."

"I would like to dance with her as well, and take her to Gunter's, and . . ." He looked down at his plate again. "I want to give her the world."

Mr. Bennet had been listening in silence on his left side. "Son, from the letters I have received, I can honestly say that I believe you are her world." He chuckled at Darcy's puffing chest.

Lord Matlock laughed. "Well, if you can not believe the girl's father, who can you trust?" He nodded at Mr. Bennet. "Who knows sir, perhaps you will have news of a grandchild on its way by then, and this conversation will be moot!"

"Ah, yes, I look forward to that!"

Darcy, despite the embarrassment he felt over the implications of the conversation, was now sitting with a wide smile on his face, staring down the table at her. Elizabeth stopped in mid-sentence and cocked her head at him, her own smile growing. "What is he up to, I wonder?"

"What?" Jane asked and leaned to look down the table.

"William, he is . . . he is being so silly."

Jane laughed. "From what I understand he is quite accomplished in the art."

Mrs. Bennet was watching her husband. "When does Sarah arrive?"

"We originally invited them for New Year's, but we decided to ask them for Christmas instead. I did not wish to disrupt their plans with the Douglass family, but Aunt Sarah said that they are all in Scotland, and her family never makes the journey there in winter. So they will arrive tomorrow afternoon. William and I will deliver baskets to our tenants all day, and hopefully we will be returned in time to change before they come."

"Are there a great many baskets to distribute, Lizzy?" Kitty asked.

"Yes, but our steward and his staff take them around as well; it will not be just the two of us. We will take the tenants closest to the house so that we will return as soon as possible. Unfortunately it means that you will all have to entertain yourselves for most of the day." She smiled.

"I think we will manage." Jane looked at Georgiana. "Perhaps you might lead a tour for us?"

"Oh, yes, I could do that, Aunt Ellen, will you help me?"

"Of course, my dear." She returned her gaze to Richard who was oddly silent and sending little glances down the table towards Mary.

Mary was blushing and looking everywhere but at him. Lydia poked her. "Are you ill? Your face is red."

"It is not. Eat your dinner."

Lydia began glancing around the room, and caught Richard's eyes resting upon Mary then flick away again. She grinned and whispered loudly. "He is looking at you!"

"Nobody is looking at me. Now mind your business." She hissed.

"Colonel Fitzwilliam!" Lydia sang. "Will you be returning to your regiment soon?"

Startled he looked at her. "Well, yes, in a way. I will return in January to resign my commission."

"Oh, how terrible!"

Richard laughed. "And why is that, Miss Lydia?"

"Why then you will not be in a red coat. I simply adore a man in a red coat!"

"Lydia!" Elizabeth admonished.

"Oh as if that was a secret, Lizzy!" Kitty giggled. "A red coat does make the man, sir. You should really reconsider your decision."

Elizabeth rolled her eyes. "Forgive them Richard, they are being silly. I am afraid that the travel has made them overtired."

"No, I understand the attraction. However, I have the opportunity to be a gentleman with an estate, and I am preparing to settle down to be a dull old man like my cousin Darcy."

James lifted his brow. "And here I was thinking you wished to emulate your wiser elder brother."

Darcy coughed, and Richard laughed. "Why on earth would I want to resemble you?" James rolled his eyes. "Besides Brother, I have yet to see you settle down."

"Oh, I am preparing for it."

"But it seems that I shall be master of the estate first!" Richard declared triumphantly.

"Ahem, Son, I find that preferable, otherwise I would be dead." Lord Matlock reminded him. Richard flushed as the rest of the table laughed.

"So you must marry." Lydia bobbed her head at Richard and glanced at Mary.

"I suppose I should." Richard grinned and then met his mother's raised brow. He closed his eyes and when he opened them, he saw that he was being speared by the entire table. "I have no announcement to make, if that is what you are asking. Now Darcy, I saw a fine bottle of port in the library, when shall we sample it?"

Laughing, Darcy stood. "Gentlemen, if you will join me? I believe the ladies have some plotting to accomplish."

"William, will you please teach me to drive?" Elizabeth had curled as close to him as possible, her arms wrapped around his left, as he drove the open sleigh through the snow. They had just finished delivering the last of the baskets to their tenants, and ate, yet again, a piece of gingerbread and sampled their cider.

Darcy looked down at his wife, her eyes were bright, her cheeks red with the cold, and leaned down to kiss her pink nose. "No."

"Why not?" She demanded. "I see many women driving. And here at Pemberley, I would be able to perfect my technique before arriving in London."

Darcy pulled up the horse and looked at her incredulously. "You do not seriously think that I would allow you to drive in London?"

"No?"

"NO!"

"Then may I drive here?" She bit her lip and looked up at him through her long lashes. Darcy groaned and took her face in his gloved hands and kissed her lips.

"You are quite cruel, Mrs. Darcy."

"Is that a yes?" She laughed.

"No, it is not." He smiled at her disappointment. "Darling, you have yet to manage controlling a horse well. You have made wonderful progress with your riding, but until I am satisfied that you have mastered the reins of your mount, I will not risk you losing control of a horse pulling a gig. To see you injured . . . please do not ask this of me."

"I was simply thinking that I should be able to pay calls on the tenants when they need medicine or just an opportunity to tell their needs to me. I thought it would be less intimidating for the women to speak with me than you."

"Do you think they are afraid of me?" Darcy's brow wrinkled in concern.

Elizabeth stroked the crease. "You are rather imposing, my love. And you are the master of the estate."

"I never meant to . . ." He sighed. "I am so glad that you wish to take on this role. It has been needed for so long. I am afraid that I have left a great deal of the communication between the tenants and myself to my steward."

"I do believe that you have done quite well with the myriad of duties you have assumed. I am simply relieving you of one." She smiled. "But it would be easier if I could drive."

"No."

Elizabeth sighed. "Well, I tried." She looked ahead and folded her hands in her lap.

Darcy sat staring at her, and did not set the sleigh back in motion. "Are you angry?"

"No."

"Yes you are."

"Let us go home, it is cold, and my aunt should arrive soon."

"Lizzy."

"Please William, you have made your wishes clear, and I promised to obey." Darcy closed his eyes and groaned to himself. She was obstinate, he knew it. But he was, too. And he would NOT give in to this request. In silence he flicked the reins, and they began to move. Elizabeth sat quietly, no longer holding his arm. There was not one sign of anger or upset, but the absence of her voice and touch was unsettling him. He kept his eyes on the path, but shot glances at her. It was at times like this that he cursed his terrible powers of speech. About a mile from the stable, they came upon an open field. Darcy stopped the sleigh.

"Come here." He held the reins out for her.

Elizabeth looked up at him. "I thought that you said no."

"I want you to feel what it is like, then you can decide for yourself if you are ready for this demand you have placed upon me."

She studied his face, it was unreadable. She could see the deep worry in his eyes and decided to accept his offer without petulance, but address it with the seriousness that he obviously felt it deserved. She sat up straight and watched how he wrapped the straps in her grip. He put his arms around her, poised to take hold at the instant it was required, and told her to slap the reins to urge the horse forward. The sleigh lurched and she cried out. Very quickly Elizabeth felt overwhelmed, and just as quickly, Darcy took charge and stopped the sleigh before it tipped over. He did not say a word, but unwrapped the reins from her grip and resumed his place. Soon they were back underway and moving smoothly along.

"You were correct."

"I know."

"You do not need to be smug about it!"

Darcy gave her his little smile. "Do you understand my reasoning now? Will you accept being driven until I am sure that you can handle this safely?"

"Yes William, but first I must master my horse."

"Perhaps we should master the donkeys first?" He grinned and she slapped his arm, and snuggled back up to him.

"Mr. Bennet, please stop pacing." Mrs. Bennet watched her husband walking in circles in the sitting room with windows that directly overlooked the courtyard in front of the house.

"What am I going to say to her?" He sighed and stopped to look at his wife. "I have apologized in my letters, but that does not make up for the continued separation after our parents died. I should have welcomed her back then, or at least soon after. I should have told the girls about her long ago, they should have known their cousins . . ." He shook his head. "Darcy truly has my great admiration and respect for keeping his sister at home."

"She seems to have accepted your parent's decision to send her away. I imagine that she had no choice but to go, did she?"

"No." He looked at her. "None at all. I remember helplessly watching her leave, her face . . ."

A movement caught his eye and he watched Elizabeth and Darcy walking up to the front door, arm in arm and laughing. He was grateful for the distraction. "They are happy."

A footman met Darcy at the door. "Sir, a carriage has just turned in at the lodge."

"Thank you. Please inform Mr. Bennet that the Douglass' will likely arrive within the hour." Darcy took Elizabeth's hand. "Well, we have no time for a warm bath, I am afraid."

She smiled at him and they began walking up the stairs. "Hmm. Well, we will have to find another way to warm."

His eyes grew wide. "Lizzy, what are you suggesting?"

"Hot tea, of course, what did you have in mind?" She arched her brow and twinkled at him.

Darcy leaned down. "NOT tea!" Elizabeth laughed and started running up the steps with Darcy chasing after her. They flew down the hallway and into her chambers, closing the door firmly behind them. Mary stared in awe and smiled at their playful antics. A warm chuckle from behind caught her attention and she turned.

"Colonel, I did not see you there."

"I came to see the commotion, Miss Mary. I would guess by the smile on your face that you do not disapprove of their behaviour?"

"I wonder at their hurry, I suppose that they wish to prepare for the Douglass' arrival. But no, I do not disapprove, they seem very happy." She blushed. "I have always wished to be more like my sister."

"Well, that is a very admirable goal. There is nothing about her wanting. She is a fine example of a happy woman. There are things about you she would probably like to copy as well." He smiled and left to join the men in the billiard's room, leaving Mary staring after him and wondering what about her he could possibly like.

"Come on, Mary, I heard that the Douglass' carriage is on its way!" Lydia and Kitty grabbed her arms and dragged her to the sitting room where their parents and Jane stood staring out into the distance.

A short time later, Georgiana and Lady Matlock walked past the room and observed the gathered family. "I think that we should retire to the music room. This is a reunion that should be amongst the Bennets and the Douglass'." She hooked her hand in her niece's arm and they walked off down the hall, meeting Darcy and Elizabeth about to descend the stairs.

"How were the deliveries? It must have been terribly cold, you are both still flushed!" Georgiana observed. Lady Matlock regarded her nephew and niece with amusement and watched him try to explain their appearance, and was rescued by his wife.

"It was wonderful to meet so many of the tenants, Georgiana. I hope that you help us in the future." Elizabeth took his arm and guided him down the stairs to the foyer. "I suppose that we did not fool your aunt."

"No, and I am certain that it will not be long before we do not fool my sister either." He smiled and stood with her by the door and watched the carriage stop. Trunks were unloaded and Mr. Douglass handed down his wife and daughter, then Marshall and a young boy climbed out.

"Welcome to Pemberley! Happy Christmas!" Elizabeth declared as their coats were removed. She smiled warmly at the new visitors and enjoyed the expressions of wonder at the house. She embraced her aunt. "Everyone is waiting for you upstairs. Would you like to relax first or complete the introduction?"

"I believe that for the sake of all of our nerves, we should meet first." Sarah said.

Darcy was busy greeting Mr. Douglass and Marshall. "And may I know the names of our other guests?"

Mr. Douglass smiled with pride. "Mr. and Mrs. Darcy, this is my daughter Bonnie, and my son Errol."

Elizabeth smiled and immediately hugged them both. "I am so happy to meet you at last!" Darcy bowed and solemnly shook the young boy's hand. "Come upstairs and meet your other cousins!" Elizabeth took Bonnie's hand. "I understand that you are my age?"

"I am just twenty." She smiled nervously.

"Good, then you will fit right in with the rest of your cousins. I am afraid that Errol will be the odd man out, though. Perhaps the more boyish of our male guests will find ways to entertain him." She looked back and winked at William, who flushed a little. He had behaved as a little boy more since he married than he had during his entire childhood.

They arrived at the sitting room and for a few moments the family stood staring at each other in silence. Finally, Elizabeth saw that her father was overcome with emotion and made the first move. "Aunt Sarah, Uncle Angus, Marshall, Bonnie and Errol, may I present my family, Fanny Bennet, Jane, Mary, Catherine, Lydia, and my father, Thomas Bennet." Mrs. Bennet gave her husband a little push on his back and swallowing hard, he stepped forward.

"Sarah . . . you have barely changed . . . you have a beautiful family." He looked down at his nervously twisting hands.

Sarah took a deep breath and Angus whispered in her ear. She nodded and moved to take his hands in hers. "We can not change what has happened between us, but I hope that we can now . . . begin again." Mr. Bennet nodded.

"Please forgive me."

"It was not your doing. It was mine and our parents, and . . . another."

"I did not end it when I should."

"I did not ask you to."

"But you hoped for it."

"I did."

"It is over now." He turned and picked up a wooden box. "This was Mother's, it should be yours."

She opened the box with a shaking hand. Inside were her mother's rings, her grandmother's combs, all of the little symbols of the Bennet women for generations. Mr. Bennet looked at her with tears rolling down his face. "This should go to your daughter, and hers, it is your history. I hope that someday you will be proud of it again."

"You do not wish this for your daughters?" She asked in a tremulous voice.

He choked back his tears. "They will receive things from their mother. These have always belonged to you and yours."

Sarah handed the box to Bonnie and held out her arms. Mr. Bennet pulled her to him and they burst into tears. There was not a dry eye in the room. Soon the invisible line separating the families was broken and the sound of questions and greetings and laughter filled the air. Eventually Elizabeth offered to show them to their rooms and Mr. and Mrs. Bennet were left alone again. He wrapped his arms around her and held her tightly to him, and they looked out at the beautiful peaceful landscape together.

———～～～———

The Christmas celebration began that evening with a visit by the families and some of the servants to the Pemberley chapel. Mr. Higgs, the young man who Darcy had given the living at Kympton, arrived early to conduct the service at the estate before returning to his church to repeat the same for his parishioners. It was a favour performed every year by that pastor. Christmas had never really been celebrated by the family in years past. The servants decorated their domain and were permitted to enjoy the day, but the unhappy marriage, and generally quiet nature of the orphaned Darcys inspired only a day for exchanging a few gifts and sharing a large meal. This year was to be a revelation.

The addition of the noisy Bennets, the jovial Douglass', the unendingly happy Bingley, and the bemused but pleased Fitzwilliams, not to mention the deeply in love Darcy and Elizabeth, created a scene that had not been witnessed in the halls of Pemberley in ages.

Marshall, under the watchful gaze of his father and nearly every other male in the room, approached Georgiana to compliment her on the beautiful decorations that he had seen throughout the house, and asked her easy questions about the furnishings and people in the various paintings he had noticed. He had asked his mother for guidance, and Sarah, knowing very well the shame and caution that Georgiana would be feeling, advised him to simply appear friendly, and expect nothing in return.

Darcy watched apprehensively, and Elizabeth saw the worry in his eyes. "She is fine, William. She needs to learn how to talk to a gentleman, well actually talk to anyone who is not in the immediate family. This is a good experience, and you started it by encouraging him to be friendly."

"I do not want her to be hurt."

"He is asking her about your great-uncle Horace's painting, how could that possibly hurt her?" Elizabeth's raised brow and pursed lips met his frown. He glanced at the portrait and a small smile appeared.

"I suppose that Uncle Horace is enough of a frightening incentive to quell any feeling of romance in a young lady."

"He is rather frightening, and I doubt very much that Georgiana is in any way ready to think of romance." Elizabeth squeezed his hand, and she felt him relax. "Now the answer I desire is what are your cousin's designs on my sister? What is that all about?"

Darcy glanced over to a corner where Mary sat at the pianoforte looking through the music, and Richard stood attentively by her side. "I honestly do not know." He knit his brow. "I am afraid that my attention at Longbourn was not on my cousin, so if something was brewing there, I certainly missed it. He spoke of his attraction to you and Jane . . ."

"Really?" Elizabeth smiled and saw Darcy look at her sharply, scanning her face with worry. She pinched him. "Stop that!"

He smiled a little. "I will always be jealous, Lizzy." He raised her hand to his lips.

"What will you do when we arrive in London?" She tilted her head, and grinned.

"I am hoping that nobody will wish for our company and I can keep you all to myself." Darcy smiled and drew her to him for a soft kiss on her cheek.

"Mmm. I like that plan!" They moved, hand in hand, across the room to speak with Lady Matlock.

Jane and Bingley were standing beneath the kissing bough and he nudged her. "It seems a shame to waste this perfectly good ornament." He raised his eyebrows and puckered his lips.

"Charles, you could not possibly think of kissing me here!" She whispered furiously and glanced around the room.

"Why not? Is that not the purpose of this lovely bit of decoration?"

"Yes . . ."

"I need your kisses to give me life. You are the only woman who can save me." He held his hand to his forehead dramatically.

She rolled her eyes. "Oh that is the silliest bit of nonsense I have ever heard!"

Charles laughed and squeezed her hand. "Your sister said that I was a charmer, you do not agree?"

"Well of course I agree . . . but that does not excuse you from silliness." Jane shook her head.

"You are avoiding my kisses." He whined.

"Charles! Shhh! You ARE a little boy who wants his own way!" She looked around to see if anyone was watching, then moving very quickly she rose up on her toes and kissed him.

Charles grinned widely. "Was that so hard?"

Mr. and Mrs. Bennet observed them from across the room. Sarah and Angus watched as well. "When is their wedding?"

"At the end of February; I hope that you will be able to make the journey, and of course stay at Longbourn." Mr. Bennet looked at her hopefully.

Sarah stared at her hands. "Would there be room for us? I imagine that Elizabeth and William will be with you, and other family."

Mrs. Bennet patted her arm, bringing Sarah's eyes back up. "The Gardiners will come, but all other guests will stay at Netherfield."

"I would like to see Longbourn again." She looked at Angus.

He read her expression and nodded. "Then we will certainly be there. We will go on to London afterwards. Marshall can look after things at home and I will have some business to attend in town by that time."

"I understand that you are a brewer, sir?" Lord Matlock approached the couples.

"Yes, My Lord, I am." He drew himself up.

Lord Matlock waved his hand. "Matlock will do, sir." Angus relaxed and nodded. "Darcy tells me you are doing well?"

"Yes, quite so, it is certainly an appreciated product." The men laughed and Mrs. Bennet moved away with Sarah. Richard and James wandered over, and Elizabeth, wanting to interview Mary, nudged William to go join them. Jane sent

Charles on his way as well, and gradually the sexes separated to their own conversations.

Lady Matlock stood near Jane and observed her for some time. "You seem quite interested in my nephew, my dear." She said quietly.

Jane jumped and turned, blushing, to look at her. "I . . . I am happy for my sister's choice."

"Are you perhaps regretting yours?"

She looked down at her hands. "Of course not, I . . . I am quite content with Mr. Bingley."

"What do you see in my nephew? I notice that you have similar dispositions. You are both quiet and very dedicated to your loved ones."

"Yes." She turned back to look at Darcy.

Lady Matlock followed her gaze. "I think that he is much better suited to Elizabeth, she has the liveliness that he lacks. She draws him out like no other person I have ever seen. She gives him the confidence to express the joy of life he has always forced himself to suppress. He is behaving as a rambunctious boy for the first time, but only with her. He is laughing out loud, he is smiling and free. I think that a woman who resembled him in nature never would have drawn him out in this way. Besides your sister's matching him in intelligence, she is teaching him how to live. He will teach her of the world, but her gift of happiness will far exceed his offerings. Certainly you would not begrudge your sister or Darcy such love?"

"Oh no, I . . . I suppose that I admire that he is . . . a man." She glanced at Bingley and back at Lady Matlock.

"Ah, I see. Well, yes, your Mr. Bingley does have some growing to do, but he is handling his sister, and he is taking the steps to secure an estate. I understand that he oversees the operation of several factories in Scarborough, although he does not really have a hands-on approach as Darcy does with Pemberley. And most important, he has decided to give up his old life in society and marry you. It seems he already possesses the boyish joy to live that Darcy is only beginning to discover."

"But will I hold his attention?" Jane said softly.

Lady Matlock's eyes widened and she nodded her understanding. "Is that what worries you? Is that what you admire most in Darcy, his unwavering constancy to Elizabeth?"

"I suppose it is."

"I can not guarantee that your Mr. Bingley will not wish to return to his old habits, but have you ever spoken to him of his past life? Have you questioned his ability to be true to you alone? You must address these fears now, before you marry, or they will gnaw at you every time that he leaves you. And he *will* need to leave you alone from time to time." She patted her arm. "Talk to him. I have a feeling that he will appreciate it." She smiled at Jane's furrowed brow. "And do stop coveting your brother-in-law. Your sister will strangle you if she finds out."

"I do not covet him, but I do admire his devotion. Thank you Lady Matlock." She thought over the older woman's advice. She hated confrontation and knew that Charles did as well, and Lady Matlock was correct, he was changing and growing, had he not said as much to her at Longbourn before they left? Jane chose to suppress her worries and settled back into happy complacency, there was no need to broach the subject.

Bingley approached Darcy who was standing by the fireplace, staring down at the flames, but was surreptitiously sending little glances into the mirror and smiling, watching Elizabeth talking animatedly and encouraging sensible conversation between her younger sisters and newfound cousin. "So are you still blissfully happy?"

Darcy turned to regard his friend. "It has barely been a month, Bingley, but I suspect that I will be this happy fifty years from now."

"Fifty!" Bingley laughed at his friend's confidence in both his felicity and long life.

Darcy lifted his brow. "I look forward to every moment of my marriage, the good and the bad. Tell me, has your confidence improved over the past month?"

Bingley looked over to Jane and smiled. "As a matter of fact, it has."

"How so?"

He returned to meet Darcy's gaze. "I had to go to London after I saw you at Longbourn. There were papers that I needed to review and sign concerning Caroline . . . I made a point of visiting, well, my haunts of bachelorhood." Darcy nodded, remembering Bingley's tales of the boxing parlours, taverns, and the gentleman's clubs. "Do you know what I found? I found that I did not belong there anymore. I knew that I had a beautiful, sweet, loving woman who trusts me and was waiting for me in Hertfordshire, and my only thought was how can I finish my business and return to her as quickly as possible." He smiled. "I actually felt pity for all those lonely fools I saw in the clubs."

Darcy grinned and clapped him on the back. "Excellent Bingley! You have come far!"

"You gave me a great deal to ponder, my friend, I am indebted to you." Bingley clasped his hand and looked at him seriously.

Darcy looked down, unable to accept the praise. "Have you told Jane these revelations?"

"No, should I?"

Lifting his head again, Darcy placed his hand on Bingley's shoulder and met his eye. "Yes, Bingley. Do not hold back your thoughts, whatever they are. Talk to her. I started with letters, and now, I share everything with Elizabeth, although I admit sometimes she must cajole it out of me, and there are some things still . . ." He paused and looked down again. "But I could not imagine living with her and holding back something as important as this. I can not understand a marriage of convenience where the couple lives essentially separate lives and shares only an occasional evening in the marriage bed." He looked back up. "Does that make sense to you?"

Bingley smiled. "Yes, it does, but . . . I am not you, Darcy, and the thought of having such a conversation with Jane is not one that I would relish. And she is so happy, why should we speak of unpleasant things, especially if they are in the past?"

Darcy knew of no easy way to explain his convictions, and also knew that his friend likely would not ever feel the intense devotion that he experienced for Elizabeth, despite his declarations of love. Bingley was correct, they were not alike, and Jane was not Elizabeth. "Bingley, you know your mind and heart, and hopefully Jane's as well. I will not attempt to impose my ways upon you."

"You are not imposing Darcy; you are simply being my friend." Their private conversation was interrupted by Richard joining them. Bingley took the opportunity to walk away and mull over Darcy's words.

Darcy glanced at Elizabeth with Mary and elbowed him. "All right Cousin, explain yourself."

"What?" Richard followed Darcy's eyes and flushed. "I am merely curious about her."

"Why?"

"What kind of a question is that?"

"She is hardly your type, Richard." Darcy said quietly. "I know the sort of ladies who attract you."

Richard spoke softly so no one could hear. "I am not attracted, I just . . . Darcy my life is about to change . . . we have talked about my need to get away from soldiering and start over, it just occurred to me that perhaps I need to reevaluate my choices in women as well." Darcy's gaze was unwavering, demanding more. Richard shook his head. "I like her, Darcy. She is not the least attracted to my uniform, or to my status. Even as a second son, I have attracted women simply because I am the son of an Earl, but she is unimpressed. If she blushes, I think it is from receiving the attention of any man. I could just as easily pay attentions to Miss Douglass." He glanced around the room and said quietly, "I know that I am very fortunate to be receiving this estate and money from my father, but it is nonetheless a small estate. No woman of the *ton* will want to come to me there."

"So you are looking elsewhere." Darcy said and nodded his head in understanding. "But why Mary? She is a quiet young woman, I know her fondness for sermons and . . . well frankly Richard; she is not your type."

"And Elizabeth is yours?" He laughed. "You two are complete opposites."

He smiled slightly. "Yes and no. Where Elizabeth is joyful and happy, I am quiet and withdrawn, but we are both passionate and well . . . we are well-matched."

"You present an impossible example, Cousin. You are the rare love match."

"Then do not look to us as your example, your parents would serve you better. But as for Mary, perhaps her time here at Pemberley this spring will allow you the opportunity to . . . know each other."

"That is what I am hoping. I will have my hands full, learning all that I need to know for my new home and life, but I do hope to come and visit Georgiana while you are away. If Miss Mary is here I could . . . see how she is getting on while she is in the area. So do I have your permission?" He looked at him with a mixture of command and pleading.

Darcy smiled and clapped his back. "Of course, Richard. Just please do not suggest anything more to her or anyone else. Elizabeth was suspicious of your motives and sent me to speak to you."

Richard laughed. "Women are adept at spotting possibilities, even if they are only fantasies."

"I will make no comment." He glanced back at his wife and sister. "If nothing else, perhaps you may find a friend."

"That I would like, and you are correct, although you have not said the words. I know that I am not ready to marry."

"Did I say that?" Darcy smiled. "Well, yes, I implied it. One thing at a time; let us see you in a cravat for a while."

"That will not produce the grandchildren my mother is demanding!" The men laughed and James wandered over to them. Richard nodded at him. "Speak to my brother if you want to speak of marriage."

"Why me?" James stared at him and sighed. "All right, yes, I have agreed that this is my year. Let the Season begin!"

Bingley returned to the group and laughed. "I am thrilled to not have to participate in the manhunt this year, or ever again."

Richard grinned at him. "I rather thought you enjoyed the experience. How many . . ."

"It no longer matters. I have found my angel." He looked lovingly over at Jane.

Darcy smiled, realizing that his ideal of marriage could not be applied to either his friend or his cousin. That did not stop him from poking fun at him, though. His lips twitched. "I think that Richard may have spotted one."

"Enough Darcy." Richard glared at him. "This new frivolity of yours is most unbecoming."

Darcy laughed. "Blame my wife for that!"

Eventually the sexes mixed together again, and Darcy happily sat beside Elizabeth at the pianoforte, turning pages for her and trying stoically to pay attention to the music instead of becoming lost in the bewitching sound of her voice. Bingley sat next to Jane, smiling and talking with Bonnie. Jane watched him and shifted uncomfortably. He noticed and turned to her, lifting her hand and kissing it. "Jane, you are so quiet."

"I am always quiet next to you, Charles." She said softly.

"I suppose that is true, but I do love to hear your voice, and I think, my dear, that something is on your mind?" He kissed her hand again and fixed his gaze on her wide blue eyes.

She looked at him, then away to Darcy and Elizabeth. "They are so perfect together."

Bingley turned to regard his friend. "I hope to someday be the man he is." He smiled and looked back at Jane, seeing her startled expression. "Jane?"

"I . . . I thought the same." She bit her lip and looked away.

"My behaviour concerns you." He said softly, thinking over his conversation with Darcy. "I am doing my best Jane, and I do love only you."

"You love me?"

"Have I not said so?" He closed his eyes. "Not often enough, it seems." His gaze wandered over towards Bonnie and he suddenly realized the problem. "Dear Jane, do you fear for my constancy?"

She would not look at him. "I . . . oh, Charles of course not."

"Jane, I did not tell you this, but when I was in London last, I made a point of visiting my old haunts of bachelorhood; and do you know what I found? I discovered that I could not wait to run home to my angel. Sweetheart, I am a friendly person, you know that . . . I am like Elizabeth in a way, but you know that she may smile and talk to others, but she would never stray from Darcy. Can you not see that same behaviour in me?" He gazed at her with all sincerity.

Jane lifted her eyes back to him. "Forgive me for doubting you. I see the comparison between you and Lizzy. I just love you so much, Charles, I suppose I am frightened of you someday forgetting me."

"You have no reason to ask for forgiveness because I am not offended. I . . . I will do my best for you, my dearest Jane. I will stay true to you." Again he lifted her hand to his lips, and they moved a little closer to each other. Her hand remained tightly clasped in his and he turned his eyes back to Darcy and Elizabeth, now risen from the instrument and standing under the kissing bough. Darcy looked down at her, his eyes twinkling, and cocked his head, raising his brows in question. It was an expression that Charles only saw given to Elizabeth. She pursed her lips and rose up on her toes to softly kiss him and caress his cheek. *You give me quite an example to follow, my friend.*

Christmas morning brought with it new snow and a leisurely breakfast. Gifts were exchanged, mostly within the separate families, although Elizabeth gave all of the women assortments of scented soaps and perfumes and Darcy presented the men with fine bottles of port and cigars. Elizabeth handed him a small box and bit her lip when he looked at her with surprise.

"I was not expecting anything from you, Lizzy. We certainly had no opportunity to shop in London."

"Open it." She smiled as he carefully untied the ribbon, and slipped it into his pocket. Inside he found four new handkerchiefs; embroidered with their flowers and his initials, and a journal. He looked up to her and smiled. "Thank you, they are beautiful, and I will treasure them." Elizabeth opened the journal so that he could read the inscription.

25 December 1811

To my husband,
Our lives have just begun together, and this empty book is yours to record the memories of our future days. I hope that this is only the first of many volumes. Whatever those times bring, joy, laughter, children, or sorrow, know that I am with you in all things. Your days of loneliness are over, and I pray that the days of happiness far outweigh the times of sadness. I love you, and ask only that you hold my hand while we face our future together.
Your loving wife,
Elizabeth

"Lizzy." He whispered, and setting down his gift drew her into his arms to kiss her, entirely forgetting the other occupants of the room. Soon all of the conversation ceased and the rest of the family stared at them. Elizabeth's head was nestled to his chest, and Darcy's face was buried in her hair, their eyes were closed and they were lost in their embrace. Gradually the conversation resumed and they drew apart, each wiping the other's tears. Darcy swallowed and pulled a small box from his pocket. "This is for you."

Elizabeth opened it with shaking fingers. Inside was a key, and an oval cut piece of parchment. She looked up at him. "The key is to a special place where only you and I will ever go." He picked up the parchment and biting his lip, took the locket from around her neck and opening it, placed the note inside along with his lock of hair. He handed it back to her. She read the note and began to cry again.

This is a piece of me, but in truth, you carry my heart in your hands. It did not begin to beat until the day I first saw you. Your arms are my shelter, your smile is my light, your laughter is my joy, and your kiss is my salvation. I love you.
Always,
William

"Oh Will." Darcy carefully placed the locket back around her neck and taking her hand rose to his feet.

"Will you excuse us?" He did not wait for a reply. He smiled and led her out of the drawing room and down the hallway.

"Where are we going?" She sniffed and dabbed at her wet face. Darcy smiled and leaned down to kiss her softly.

"To show you our little sanctuary."

Elizabeth looked around as they travelled the halls. "Is it far?"

He laughed as her tears gave way to her curiosity. "As far as your imagination will allow us to go."

Chapter 37

"*T*his house truly is an island in the midst of a great white wilderness." Elizabeth murmured as she stood looking out of the window. A blizzard had raged for nearly a week, depositing several feet of snow and completely isolating Pemberley from the rest of the world. She was grateful that all of their Christmas guests had departed and were either home or well on their way and travelling south before the storm appeared. She rubbed her arms, feeling the cold radiating from the glass, and turned to find her shawl. William was speaking with Mr. Barkley, making plans to put men to work, cutting ice to store away in the several ice houses scattered over the estate. It was backbreaking work, but the gift of allowing the preservation of food in warm weather would make it all worthwhile. Georgiana was grateful to have all of the guests return home, even the Fitzwilliams. She finally felt free to just be herself and continue to heal.

Elizabeth looked down at her sewing, tossed carelessly on the chair before the warm fire, but could not bring herself to take it up. Instead she decided that if it was too cold to walk outside, she should take some exercise by briskly roaming the halls. William had led her on countless tours, but even now she noticed that there were certain rooms that he avoided, or earned only passing comments. There were also certain alcoves and pieces of furniture that inspired silence. Slowly he would allow bits of information to be revealed, but each item was so heartrendingly painful to hear, and seemed more so to tell, that they would soon change the subject to happier topics.

Her steps led her towards the music room where Georgiana sat alone working determinedly through a difficult passage. Elizabeth stood watching her quietly for some time, and when she stopped, applauded her efforts. "Well done, Georgiana!"

"Elizabeth, how long have you been there?" She blushed and looked down. "It was awful."

"It was very good, and I would not even attempt it. I hope that you might give me some instruction sometime. I do not practice as I should; and it shows when I play." Elizabeth touched her shoulder and smiled.

"You have a household and a husband to run." Georgiana provided an excuse with sincerity.

"I am not sure if your brother would agree with you that I run him . . . well, maybe a little." Elizabeth's eyes sparkled.

"He is very happy, and so am I." Struck by a thought, her brow creased and she looked earnestly at her sister. "Did I perform well for our guests? I was trying to be part of the conversations."

"I think that my sisters drew you out. They were determined to bring you good cheer. Kitty and Lydia seemed to have formed a sort of conspiracy for you."

"They did?" She smiled with surprise. "That was very kind!"

Elizabeth nodded and sighed. "They are good girls, silly and without direction, but perhaps Papa will listen to William and send them to school, or at least find them some instruction to improve themselves before they grow much older. He offered to help, but Papa said he would take care of it himself."

"But what of Mary?" Georgiana asked worriedly. "Would she not want the same benefit?"

"She is eighteen, and feels that she is too old for school. But when she is with you this spring, perhaps you can take her in hand."

Her eyes grew wide. "Me? Oh I am not so accomplished as that!"

"Of course you are! You had the benefit of school and the masters. Surely you remember their techniques. She would appreciate your knowledge, I know she would." Elizabeth smiled and patted her hand. "Now, I will stop interrupting your work, and continue my walk. Thank you for giving me some lovely music to accompany me. You are a gifted musician." Georgiana sat up a little straighter and began to play again, and Elizabeth set off.

Her wandering feet next took her to the portrait gallery, and she stopped before the likeness of Lady Anne Darcy. She was beautiful, but did not really resemble Georgiana, other than their colouring. The girl naturally did not resemble Mr. Darcy at all, he was dark and imposing just as his son was. There certainly could be no doubt that William's blood was definitely that of a Darcy. Elizabeth studied the woman who had caused so much pain, then turned to the father whose response was to be so brusque with his son. She thought over her husband's quiet confessions, and how she knew it was only the barest hint of his experience, and felt an intense desire to confront them.

"How could you do this to your son?!" She demanded of the two faces staring blankly at her. "All he wished for was to be loved; you were both fools to reject such a dear child, and exceptional man!" She paced back and forth before the portraits, then turned to look at them. "What a foolish woman you were!" She gestured to Mr. Darcy. "You were given every chance at happiness, and he DID care for you! You drove him away for the lack of a title!" Then she turned and glared at Mr. Darcy. "And YOU! What were you thinking treating your son and heir like so much a prized stallion! When did brutality succeed in producing quality? You nearly broke him, is what you did!" She stormed down the gallery then returned to them. "Oh how I wish you two were before me and I could really give you a piece of my mind! Fitzwilliam Darcy is the finest example of a gentleman that was ever born, and he became that way DESPITE your horrible parenting. On second thought, I am grateful you can not see him; you do not deserve to claim such goodness as the product of your upbringing! I love him, and our children will adore him. HE will be the parent that neither one of you could ever hope to become!"

Darcy stood at the end of the long gallery, watching Elizabeth pace before the paintings. He heard every word, and it did more to help melt the stone that still seemed to reside in his heart from his troubled past than anything. He slowly walked down to where she stood with angry tears running down her face. "Lizzy, are you fighting for me again?"

Startled she turned and saw him. "Oh Will, I am so sorry, I . . . I went for a walk to warm, and it seems that I chose to pick a fight with two ghosts instead. Did you hear me?" She looked down and asked softly.

He tenderly lifted her chin and smiled. "I did, my love, and I thank you for your fierce defence." He took her handkerchief from his pocket and wiped the tears.

She grasped his hand. "Forgive me, but I just can not understand your parents."

"My father . . ." Darcy glanced at the portrait. "I know what Wickham said to you, but . . . you must realize that he saw what he wished." He took her hand and kissed it.

Elizabeth stroked back the hair that fell across his eyes. "You can not deny the harshness of your father's behaviour towards you."

"No, that is true." He tugged her hand and she settled her head against his chest. They stood embraced as he rested his cheek on her head and studied his parents' portraits. "When my mother was alive he was so angry, and I was so small that he had no real use for me. It was not as if he could speak to me as a man, and often I felt that seeing me made him angrier for some reason, perhaps it was the reminder that I would likely be his only child, I do not know." He felt Elizabeth's arms squeeze him and he kissed her head. "After she died, I was at school, so we had contact only during the summer and on holidays. I would come home and it would be very . . . stiff between us, but gradually as the holiday continued, we would relax more and by the end of the visit he was . . . more like the man he *could* be, if that makes sense. He was teaching, not ignoring, instilling pride in our heritage and the land. As I approached majority, he spent a great deal of time educating me, challenging me to thoroughly know the workings of Pemberley and all of our holdings. But always, even in my youngest, loneliest days, I knew his pride for our family, even if he did not express it in a kinder way. Perhaps that is why I tried so hard to win his attention and was so devastated when he pushed me aside."

Elizabeth heard him seemingly making excuses for his father and was confused. "But what of Wickham?"

"I believe that my father abused that relationship, at first out of a desire to anger my mother, and then later after she was gone, he gave Wickham more than he ever earned or deserved. By then Father was charmed by him. It formed the man Wickham became. I do not believe that Father ever told him to be deliberately cruel to me. I think that was entirely Wickham's jealousy at work." He sighed and began a delayed and painful confession. "You told my parents that I was good man, but you did not know me before . . . before Wickham convinced Georgiana to leave with him."

Elizabeth lifted her head. "What was different about you? I find it hard to believe that you simply manufactured this persona that I love in a day, and surely your family and the servants would not care for you as they do if you were anything but good and kind."

Darcy let go of her and stood before his parents' portraits. "I . . . learned to protect myself by . . . being arrogant. I . . . treated those below me in society with disdain, and held myself above others. I know that in part it was to convince myself that I was better than Wickham, and also an attempt to earn my father's praise, even beyond his death." He stared into his father's eyes. "I tried to emulate him. It became ingrained, so much so that I was not even aware of what he had created in me." An expression of disgust appeared, and Elizabeth hugged herself, watching him finally confront his father's influence. "Knowing you as I do now, I wonder if you would have tolerated the man I was then, or even wished to have known me. Would I have even allowed the attraction I felt when I first spied you to grow, or would I have simply assumed that you would want me because of my status? I was accustomed to being pursued in society. And worse still, would I have then rejected you because I was too proud to . . ." He stopped. "Bingley heard me questioning if I was worthy of you after Georgiana's fall, and pointed out that I never would have considered you before, no matter what my heart said. I know that I mentioned some of this to you before, but I never really explained why." He turned to her. "You, and only you, allowed my true self to emerge from behind the shadows of my past. I will forever be grateful that you found me."

"You give me far more credit than I deserve. I was struck by you the first moment that we met, before I knew anything of your status, and before this transformation of yours took place. What you were in essentials was plainly before me. I saw the man Fitzwilliam Darcy when you first captured my eyes." She observed the emotions playing across his face. "I believe that you have brought out the best in me. I know that all we have experienced over these past months has matured me, and I would no longer wish to be the girl I was eight months ago. Perhaps I am the one who would have been found intolerable."

Darcy shook his head, and his intense gaze bore into her. "Elizabeth, do not disparage yourself in an attempt to placate me. I know . . . I am deeply aware of the man I was then." He spoke urgently. "Think of Caroline Bingley. Do you not think that she saw something similar in me to herself? Do you not think that her brand of insufferable selfish arrogance lived in me? Why else would she latch onto me so vehemently?"

Elizabeth's anger began to rise again. "You were the wealthy, connected, and conveniently available friend of her brother!"

He clenched his jaw and closed his eyes. "You are not listening to me!"

Her eyes flashed. "I have heard every word, and yes, perhaps it is true . . ."

"Perhaps?!" He demanded.

Elizabeth stood straight in front of him and clenched her fists. "Yes, PERHAPS! But whatever caused your behaviour, whatever continued it, whatever it was . . . you have conquered it. Obviously it was not your true nature otherwise I would not be here with you now. If I wished to marry an arrogant, selfish man, I would have accepted John Lucas or Mr. Collins for that matter. I chose YOU." She continued to glare at him. "I am not afraid to question you, William, especially when it concerns your fundamental goodness."

Darcy's eyes searched her face, taking in her expression, and he relaxed, holding out his hand. "I appreciate that more than you can ever know. Nobody questions me, and I need that." Sighing, he pulled her hand and drew her back against his chest. "Whatever you and I were before; I thank God that we have each other now." Resting his cheek on her head, he felt her arms wrap around his waist.

"You desperately needed someone to take care of you." She said softly.

"I think that you did, too." He kissed her nodding head. "I have never truly spoken of these things before. I have only thought about them."

"Do you feel better?"

He soaked in the comfort of her embrace. "Yes, I do, but enough for today Lizzy, please?"

Elizabeth looked up and saw his sad eyes. She knew how difficult it was for him to be so open, and could feel how he still wished to respect his father. His confessions of his failings were hard to hear, and impossible for her to imagine. Drawing a breath, she smiled and kissed him, it was time to move forward. "Of course, shall we go to the library? It is always warm there." He smiled and released his embrace, then taking her hand; they strolled to one of their favourite rooms.

Settling in a large chair before the fire, Elizabeth sat on his lap and drew a blanket over them. They nestled together in silence with their eyes closed, listening to the crackle of the flames, and the howl of the wind outside the window.

"You will be a wonderful father."

Darcy's eyes opened and he tilted his head, seeking her face, his future role worried him and he sought her reassurance. "How can you be so confident? My example was poor."

She looked at him with surprise. "But it is just that example that will make you successful. You know how *not* to be."

He laughed softly at her reasoning. "I will be the opposite of my father and you will be the opposite of your mother?" Comforted, he gave her a hug.

"Oh, I hope so!" She laughed. "At least the mother I grew up knowing. Now she is changing, but then . . . well, both of my parents had their own demons, as you know." She kissed his chin. "Do you hope for children soon?"

"Yes and no." He smiled at her eyebrows climbing her forehead, and the eyes that demanded an explanation. "Oh, I look forward to it; anticipate it eagerly actually, although I do fear for your well-being very deeply." Elizabeth gave him a gentle kiss and he caressed her cheek. "I know that most men wish for their heir to arrive right away, but I would enjoy at least one summer with you, free to just be together."

"And what do you wish to do with me over this beautiful summer?" She smiled and then laughed at the passion that suddenly flared in his eyes. "Besides the obvious, my love."

He chuckled and squeezed her. "I would like to show you the entire estate, and continue your riding lessons. Perhaps we could go to Scotland and visit our estate there, spend some time in the Lake District, or maybe go to the shore . . . or, would you enjoy going to the continent, Lizzy? We could go to Italy? Where has your imagination taken you when you were sitting in your tree?"

"So many places, but always the trip was wonderful because of my companion, so it did not matter where I roamed, as long as he was there."

He smiled widely. "You were dreaming of your husband? I did not think you a devotee of romantic novels!"

She giggled. "I admit nothing, my love, only that I have a fairly healthy imagination without the help of novelists." He laughed loudly and kissed her cheek. "I would enjoy any of the ideas you mentioned. I know that travel to the continent would probably be best before we have children, but I believe I would be just as delighted to see the beauty of England, or even this wonderful estate. I would love to see your boyhood haunts. I wish I had been with you then. I dream about it sometimes, the two of us playing as children. What fun we would have had!" She laughed and furrowed her brow at the appearance of tears in his eyes.

"I have often thought the same, dearest, how different things would have been." He blinked and smiled, leaning to kiss her, "I think that we are making up for that loss with our current childish antics."

"Will you take me skating?"

He chuckled with her distracting request. "I believe we would have trouble locating the ice beneath the snow. It is just too deep for now, but I have no doubt that the wind will do its work soon enough and we will have a patch to try. Have you skated before?"

"Once, and I was an utter failure. I will rely on your strong arm to support me." She smiled up at him and squeezed his waist.

"I do believe that I will enjoy that immensely." He kissed her warm lips and then took her hand, studying the band of gold he had placed there. "Mrs. Darcy, I recall you saying that you began this excursion today in search of warmth. Ice skating hardly qualifies."

"I did, and I know that skating is not warm, but I just wanted to do something with you. I would like to bring a healthy glow to my cheeks." Her eyes danced and his grew dark. "Do you have any suggestions for warming me further?"

"Well obviously you feel that this blanket and a shared chair before the fire is insufficient, but I think that I have determined a far more productive occupation."

"Oh, and what is that?" She asked innocently.

"You have declared that I would be an outstanding parent, I think, my love, that some work on both of our parts is required to fulfil that declaration. It is something that most definitely we must accomplish together." He smiled his little smile, but his lips were threatening to allow it to grow.

She nodded solemnly in understanding. "Ah, and you believe that you know the best way to accomplish this desired outcome?"

"Yes my love, and as with all things, you know that practice makes perfect." He growled softly in her ear.

"And you feel that I am lacking?"

His lips caressed her lobe as he felt her melting into his arms, and heard the soft moan he coveted. "Oh no, my dear wife, but I desire that you stay in top form. Come let me warm you from the inside out."

———

The weeks passed, and soon they would be leaving for Hertfordshire. Elizabeth strolled through the house, and taking out her Christmas key, approached the door to their little sanctuary. As always when the door was opened she was greeted with a rush of humid air and the intoxicating smell of warm earth and fragrant flowers. This was a special room, separate from the much larger orangery next door. This room had three keys, one for Darcy, one for Elizabeth, and one for the head groundskeeper of Pemberley. He was allowed in to do his work at a very specific time; otherwise it was to be left locked. Within the beautiful room were tropical blooms, outrageous in their bright colours and intoxicating scents, trees with huge, heavy leaves, and the aura of fantasy and escape permeated every nook. There were two comfortable chairs and a table, and a new addition, a long, wide, fainting couch, just large enough to accommodate two people seeking solitude in each other's arms. The heavy greenery blocked any view whether inside or out, and a solid wooden door inside of the house gave no hint as to the place that lay behind. Darcy built this escape after his father died. In his imagination and loneliness, he dreamed of someone spending time with him there. The couple often disappeared within for hours. Today Elizabeth entered to read a letter from Jane while William met with his steward. She settled back on the couch and almost immediately began smiling and shaking her head.

Dear Lizzy,

I do hope that you and William are well, and enjoying your peace, I believe that I am quite envious of you! If our mother had never married, I think that she would have been of great use in helping people plan affairs. Does such a position exist? Well, in any case, she has taken over the staffs of Longbourn and Netherfield with her ideas for decoration and food. Oh Lizzy, at the time that you were married I admit that I felt sorry for your simple wedding, but now, I think that you and William had the correct idea. I will say no more, you will be here soon enough to experience the madness in person! At least Papa is laughing about her frenzy, and she even laughs at herself, as well.

Papa has absolutely forbidden Kitty and Lydia from speaking to any of the officers beyond common courtesies. After what happened with Georgiana, he trusts none of them. It is not truly fair to group them all together in such a state of dislike, but he says that they are too young to be so flirty and he has no intention of hosting another wedding anytime soon, unless it is for Mary. Poor Mary just blushes. She is ever so anxious to come to Pemberley. It is so kind of William to send another coach with you to take her there after the wedding. Papa was relieved to know that he was sending Mrs. Annesley and several men along as well.

John Lucas inquired after you when we saw him in church yesterday. He said that he had heard from Charlotte and that she was settling into Hunsford Parsonage, and hoped to see you when you come to visit Lady Catherine. I was not sure of your plans on that subject so said nothing. He seemed pleased to hear how well you and William were getting on. He has been very quiet, keeping to Lucas Lodge, and not really participating in the various dinners of the neighbourhood. I understand from his mother that he has thrown himself into preparations for the coming growing season, and is quite serious about learning his responsibilities.

Now, to my Charles. Oh Lizzy, I know that I had expressed some worries that he might regret choosing me, but I must tell you that he is becoming quite more admirable every day. We have been in so much company of late, with engagement dinners and teas. There are always many pretty girls there, and he does talk and is friendly to them, but I see now how his friendliness is tempered. It is not flirting, but enthusiasm, a joy of life. I suppose it is what attracted him to me, we both want everyone around us to be happy, but he is able to express it more openly. Why would I wish to change that? I am assured of his constancy at every turn, and he always returns to my side. I am truly content. He and the Hursts travel to London tomorrow to move Miss Bingley from his home and settle her in the new apartments he found for her. He has stuck to his decisions, and not wavered at all. I feel sorry for her, but I do not blame him.

I look forward to seeing you, dear sister.

Jane

Elizabeth closed the letter and sat wondering over all of the news. It seemed that everyone in Hertfordshire had experienced some form of improvement in the past months. She did not look forward to seeing John again, but at least it appeared, from Jane's always rosy point-of-view, that he had moved on.

———～∽～———

Jane and Bingley were wed on the 27th of February, a bright morning, and the wedding breakfast was everything that Mrs. Bennet had dreamed of producing. She outshone every woman in the area with the vast array of foods and drink. The gowns on her daughters were exquisite, the guests, curious to spot the Darcys and the rumoured return of Sarah Bennet were satisfied. John cautiously approached Elizabeth and Darcy, and gave them a friendly greeting, which was returned in kind before they quickly separated, both sides feeling relief with the accomplishment. The Darcys were polite to the neighbours but for the most part kept company with the family party. The wedded couple were oblivious to all and were anxious to be on their way to London. Darcy was delighted to see his friend appear at the altar without a single nervous twitch.

Sarah's reunion with Longbourn was both painful and revealing. She was struck with how small the house seemed, and how tall the trees had grown. Very little had changed; other than some of the furnishing and fabrics for the drapes. It was as if she had left only a week earlier instead of nearly a quarter century. She and Angus were given her old bedroom, which was also Lizzy's old room. She looked about the walls, remembering oddities in the plasterwork, finding old creaking floorboards, saw small nicks in the closet door showing her growth, and for a little while was once again a Bennet. Her brother and sister had done everything they could to make her stay comfortable. None of the current servants knew Sarah, which in many ways was a relief to her. They only stayed the one night, leaving immediately after the wedding breakfast. She visited her parent's graves, standing before them in the snow, and made her peace. Angus stood behind her, ready to give her whatever she needed, and was pleased to see her turn away from the headstones with a look of serenity.

One guest was missing, and that was Caroline Bingley. The Hursts offered to transport her from London to stay at the Meryton Inn, but she declined. She instead moved quietly into her new apartments with her companion, her lady's maid, a housekeeper, and cook. Charles turned over her dowry to her solicitor to manage and wished her well. He had received no indication of a desire to reconcile, so he proceeded with his life without her. Caroline sat alone in the window of her new sitting room, looking over the noisy street in the less-fashionable part of town and wondered what she could do now. It was a feeling of extreme disbelief that dominated her that day. Somehow, she just could not grasp that Charles would follow through with his plans. But he did, and now she was truly alone. The Season would begin soon; perhaps this was her last opportunity to find a husband before the silent apartment would be forever her home. She was six and twenty, but she had an attractive dowry, perhaps it was not too late.

On the day before the wedding, Elizabeth and Darcy took a walk through the light snow that covered the ground. The cold there was nothing to what they had experienced at Pemberley, so their walk felt like a warm spring day in comparison. They held hands and naturally headed towards their stile. Darcy brushed the snow off of the step and Elizabeth sat while she watched him draw out his pocket knife.

"What are you doing?"

"Well, we were in such a rush on our wedding day; I was not able to complete my project." He grinned mischievously at her while he knelt on the ground and worked at the wood.

"May I see?" She leaned and tried to look past his imposing shoulder. He moved to block her view.

"No."

"Will!" He chuckled and after a few more minutes of work he brushed a few stray bits of wood from his carving and sat back, admiring his masterpiece. Elizabeth jumped down and leaned over his back. "You added our wedding date, and, oh Will . . ."

"Does it please you?" He looked back at her and she kissed his hair. "I will ask your father to save this post when the wood must be replaced, but for now, anyone who passes will know . . ."

"Our love was born here." Elizabeth quoted then hugging his broad back, whispered in his ear. "You are a sentimental fool, Fitzwilliam Darcy."

He stood and swept her up into his arms, and laughed at her furious protests. "You do not yet know the extent of it, Lizzy."

It had been a long day, and Elizabeth was grateful to finally arrive in London after the wedding. They ate, then wearily climbed the stairs to bathe and change into their nightclothes. She walked into her bedchamber and stood before the fire, warming her hands. Darcy entered carrying a large ebony box.

She looked up and smiled. "What is this?"

He bit his lip and taking her hand, they settled on top of a thick rug in front of the hearth. "This is my treasure box. I left it here after we married by mistake. I wanted to show it to you at Pemberley, especially after seeing your father's gift to your aunt Sarah. I thought that you might like to see . . ." He looked down, embarrassed and shy.

"Of course I want to see inside!" She kissed his cheek and he leaned against the side of a chair as she cuddled next to him. He placed the box on their laps. Elizabeth caressed his face and he kissed her hand.

"This is . . . full of little happy memories. They are the things that . . . brought me comfort when I was . . . so alone." He looked away and concentrated on unlocking the box. He slid back a panel on the side. Elizabeth's eyes grew wide.

"I bought this box in Germany while on my tour. There was a cabinet maker, and I was admiring his skill, and I wanted something I could bring home with me. He was very fond of secret compartments. I am not entirely sure that I have found them all." He looked up at her and delighted in her wide eyes. "This replaced a plain box I had since childhood."

"This is fascinating!" Elizabeth watched him withdrawing his first treasure. He handed her a faded and threadbare square of wool. She examined it, feeling the worn fabric. "This was your blanket." He nodded. "You have always needed to hold something at night." She teased.

"Holding you is my greatest comfort." They leaned and kissed softly.

Darcy returned the blanket to its place and withdrew a ribbon. "From cigars?" She asked.

"My father." Elizabeth now understood how he could hold some fondness for the man, which more than anything exposed the goodness of his heart.

One by one each treasure was revealed; special rocks for skipping on the lake, a button, a thimble, drawings, poems, letters, small toys, many, many things, each with a story, or attached to a person who showed him kindness.

He withdrew a hairpin and Elizabeth took it and looked up at him. "This looks like mine."

He smiled. "From our carriage ride to Pemberley." Elizabeth blushed with the memory.

Next he showed her the worn yellow ribbon and dried lavender, and a pair of small gloves. She wiped the single tear that ran down his cheek. "What is this?" She picked up a folded piece of red silk. Darcy carefully unwrapped it, and inside was long curl of chestnut coloured hair, tied with a bow of yellow ribbon. Their eyes met. "I cut this while you slept at Longbourn, and carried it with me when we went to see Lucas."

"Oh Will." She took his hand and kissed it while he swallowed hard. "I wondered why you never asked for a lock of my hair." He softly kissed her cheek and carefully replaced her hair in the silk.

Slowly they continued opening compartments and examining each item, talking about their significance before replacing the bits in their proper places. Every letter and note that she had given him was carefully folded and secreted in a special location. Elizabeth noticed a last folded square of white silk that he had not shown her. She touched it and looked up at him. "Why is this special?"

He did not answer, and locked the box back up and set it aside, then drew her tightly into his embrace. "Will?" Darcy nestled his face in her neck. He whispered in her ear and she blushed deep red.

"You kept . . . that?" She said softly.

"You gave yourself to me that night, Lizzy. Of course I treasure that gift above all others."

Elizabeth's hand rested on his cheek and he pulled her onto his lap. They began kissing slowly, softly, taking their time. Their tongues caressed and tasted, and their lips grew increasingly swollen and sensitive, and still they did not stop. Darcy fondled her breasts and then returned his hands to tenderly cup her face. He simply could not relinquish her mouth. Elizabeth drew away, sliding from his embrace, and his searching lips followed her. "Will . . . come to bed."

His eyes, dark and drunk with passion opened to see hers. He slowly stood and held out his hands, lifting her up to her feet, then walked with her to their bed. She undressed him, untying his nightshirt and lifting it up over his head, and then urged him to sit on the silk sheets. She stood before him, removing her robe and her gown, never looking away from his intense gaze. Darcy drew her between his legs and suckled her breasts, so perfectly placed before his mouth. His hands ran over her bottom and she embraced his neck. Elizabeth withdrew and he moaned in protest. She smiled and pressed him down against the pillows. "I want this night to be for you, my love."

Beginning with his toes, she kissed and caressed her way slowly up his legs, pausing to tenderly touch and love the prominent features that made him a man, then traced her lips upwards to suckle his tight nipples, his enticing neck, his sweet handsome face, and finally to love his wet, open, eager mouth. As she climbed his body, she rubbed him with her own, and stroked his soft skin, leaving a trail of sensation that made him moan and beg for more. He was not passive during her gentle assault. As soon as he could reach her, his hands stroked over her warm luscious body, her hair, her arms, her back, her gorgeous swaying breasts, touching more as she advanced ever higher up his form. He was dying to be inside of her, but held back, wanting to let her incredible, tender loving last.

Eventually her delicately exploring lips drove him to consummate. He rolled her over and slipped inside as easily as breathing. Their bodies joined for a slow, rhythmic dance. So slow. So warm. Long, deep, trusts, accentuated with equally deep, sensuous kisses. His hands embraced her with loving caresses. His erection drew out almost completely, only to plunge back in. Their eyes locked and they drank again another kiss, until he paused, pulling her shoulders up. "Look darling, watch us move together."

Elizabeth rested back on her elbows and her gaze travelled down to where she saw his slick thick shaft, shining in the firelight, and watched as he slid into her, disappearing and filling her, then back out. She moaned with each smooth movement. His eyes followed the motion then closed in the pure ecstasy of their joining. "Will." He panted and looked back to her, and she held his face and urged him back down to kiss again. Their moaning grew louder, their whispers became heated, and the pace increased, causing the gently creaking bed to now thump, the headboard of the massive piece of furniture steadily striking the wall. Thrust after powerful thrust sent their bodies slamming together; faster, harder, deeper; straining to feel the exquisite torture grow until her climax arrived and she embraced him with her entire body, inside with her clasp, and with her legs and arms rocking and loving him outside until his own explosion sent him reeling. "I love you!" He gasped, collapsing and shaking, and held her to his chest.

They fell apart, and held hands as they gradually calmed. Darcy looked over to her and smiled, kissing her hand and then pulled her back against his damp body. "I have no words, Lizzy."

She laughed and brushed back the hair that clung to his forehead. "I do not think they are needed." She kissed him and smiled. "I love you." He expelled a long breath and shook his head. "Amazing." Sitting up, he retrieved their night clothes. As much as he wished to hold her naked body to his, it was February, and it was cold. They dressed and he tended the fire as she closed the bed curtains.

They climbed in under the blankets and snuggled together in their embrace.

"Well, my love, are you ready to face the *ton*?" He kissed her neck and she giggled, kissing the hand that rested on her breast.

"Oh yes, when each one of those sour women tries to disparage me, I will only need to smile sweetly and think of you loving me, and I will have already triumphed over them all."

Darcy laughed and nuzzled his face into her shoulder and sighed. "Sweet revenge."

"What is that?" She whispered.

"A happy life with you."

———

The next month was spent preparing for the Season. Lady Matlock took Elizabeth in hand, drilling her on the lessons she had practiced at Pemberley during the time after Christmas. She was very pleased with her student. Elizabeth was well-versed on every aspect of the home, from menus to place settings, preparing invitations, to addressing peers. Even her playing and singing had improved under Georgiana's guidance. Helping Elizabeth prepare for the Season served as an exercise in improving the girl's confidence, and she dove into the work with enthusiasm. Now Elizabeth was in London, and had to work on those intangibles that could not be learned without an experienced member of society at her side. She was taught how to take her curtsey, and the presentation gown was prepared. She visited the modiste and ordered a dizzying supply of clothes.

One afternoon her task was to study the gossip pages, learning the names, the scandals, the conversation needed in the drawing rooms, no matter how annoying she found it all to be.

"Must I really care about gossip?" Elizabeth complained to Lady Matlock.

"I am afraid that you must my dear, if for no other reason then to learn who may be seated together at your dinner parties."

"But we only intend to invite friends, why would there be animosity amongst them?"

"Oh dear, there is always some undercurrent of social upheaval underway." Lady Matlock laughed as Elizabeth's eyes rolled. "Come, there is much to accomplish." Elizabeth was grateful that Jane was permitted to attend some of these lessons, so at least she had someone with whom to suffer the education she received. Louisa Hurst was proving invaluable to Jane as well, instructing her on the ways of the circles located below the Darcys'. The day continued on, until Lady Matlock realized that it was time for her return to her own home. Elizabeth thanked her again for her assistance, and watched the carriage departing with relief.

In need of some conversation of a sensible nature, she entered William's study. "What has wrinkled your handsome brow?" She smiled and took a seat across from him.

He laughed. "Hmm. A letter from Anne."

"Is she well?" Elizabeth asked with concern.

"Yes, seemingly," he paused. "Lizzy, she asks that we come to Rosings for

Easter."

"Oh." She bit her lip. "I know that you always visited there at that time before."

"Yes, but every other year I had not been suffering my aunt's attentions so . . . dramatically." He looked up from the letter. "I hesitate to go. I can not imagine her disposition has improved."

"But she is no longer mistress, Anne is." She pointed out.

"That does not prevent her from exercising her tongue. I have no desire to travel somewhere only to see her disparage us."

"Does Anne truly need your help?"

He sighed and looked back down at the letter. "She should not, she has an excellent steward. She says that she wants my assurance that all is well." He met Elizabeth's eyes. "I feel that I should honour her request, despite my misgivings."

Softly Elizabeth spoke while looking down at her hands. "Perhaps she misses you."

Confused, Darcy tried to catch her eye. "We saw each other very rarely before."

"Yes, but you were not married then, and she could still imagine . . ."

He understood now. "She said that she did not love me, Lizzy."

Elizabeth looked up at him and spoke shortly. "Love has nothing to do with it. She based her dreams of escape on your offer."

"I hope that your suggestions are merely the product of your fertile imagination." He raised his brow and smiled slightly.

Elizabeth relaxed then shrugged and smiled at him. "I am not worried for your safety or felicity, Will. If you feel that we should visit, we will go."

"Easter is at the end of March, the 29th. I believe. We will go, but only for a short stay, long enough to reassure Anne, and hopefully escape Aunt Catherine unscathed." His smile grew.

"And we shall come back to the welcoming embrace of London society!" She smiled fully at him.

"Hmmmm." He smiled and Elizabeth walked around to kiss him before returning to her neglected duties as mistress. He watched her depart with regret. She had been so busy with his aunt they had spent not nearly enough time alone together. The Season's commencement might actually bring them some relief.

Of course he had his own assignment during this period. Their knocker was not on the door, so they were not forced to endure calls, but he was strongly encouraged by his uncle to visit his club, and re-establish relationships with the men there. Bingley accompanied him after honeymooning for a week, and Lord Matlock came as well. Darcy enjoyed none of it, not the speculation, the direct questions about his choice of wife, nor of her willingness in their bed. It took a great deal of work for Bingley to keep him in his seat, whether to prevent him from thrashing the men or simply leaving. The questions about Elizabeth were difficult enough, but the references to Georgiana made him fume. There was nothing he could do, and eventually he found that by not responding to the barbs, the men left him for more reactionary victims. Gradually, they left him alone. His sister remained unquestionably ruined, she was not old enough to allow her dowry to buy her way back into society yet, but as predicted, he seemed to have been allowed back into the fold. It was a relief, but he knew it would only begin again once the Season started and Elizabeth was by his side. He was being given a temporary pass, and he knew it.

———

"Darcy." The tall older man with greying, but still blonde hair stood nearby; fidgeted with his sword, and looked expectantly towards the open doorway.

"Lord Rutherford." Darcy glanced at the man, then turned his gaze in the same direction.

"My daughter." He nodded to the doorway, and looked back at Darcy. "Surely your sister is not . . ."

"She is too young." Darcy said without emotion. "My wife is being presented."

"Of course, yes, I read of your marriage. Congratulations. It has been a long time since Pemberley has had a mistress. I remember visiting frequently when your mother was alive."

Darcy turned and looked at him with greater attention. "Yes, I believe that I remember you." The men's eyes locked, and Lord Rutherford flushed. Movement in the doorway caught their attention and a young woman with golden blonde hair and wide blue eyes came into the room, escorted by a striking older woman.

"Ah, there is Julianne and my wife. Excuse me, I wish you felicity with your marriage." He quickly made his way across the room to greet the ladies.

Darcy stared at the girl. She could have been Georgiana's twin. The memory of laughter and voices, knowing winks and quiet footsteps filled his mind. He watched the man before him as he turned and caught his eye, holding it for a moment before leaving the room. Darcy stared down at his shoes and clenched his fists, a combination of pain and fury filling up his heart.

"Will?" He looked up to see Elizabeth, beautiful even in the ridiculous attire of the newly presented. "Are you well?"

He cleared his throat and took her hand, kissing it. "Yes, of course." He smiled slightly. "How did it go?"

She was silent for a moment, taking in his red-rimmed eyes, and how he bit his lip in agitation. "It was the most overblown bit of nonsense I have ever experienced and I am delighted that it is over." She squeezed his trembling hand. "What is wrong?"

He looked down and shook his head, knowing he could never hide anything from her and whispered. "I think that I have identified Georgiana's father."

"Lord Rutherford?"

Darcy's head snapped up and he stared at her in surprise. "How do you know?"

"I thought I was standing behind Georgiana. I was surprised that your aunt did not notice." She smiled softly, and squeezed his hand as she saw the agreement in his eyes. "What will you do?"

He lifted his shoulders and spoke in a terse whisper. "Nothing is to be done, other than avoiding his sons as suitors. I very well can not chase after him, demanding that we meet at dawn for a duel." He then closed his eyes; confirmation of the truth was difficult. He expelled a held breath and returned his gaze to her. "I should instead be grateful for my sister's life."

Elizabeth knew that he was feeling much more than he could speak about at that moment, she could feel the anger radiating from him. Their conversation would have to wait for home and privacy. Her goal at that moment was to remove them from the situation. Lady Matlock, who had been speaking with some friends, joined them. "Well, shall we return to Darcy House so that we can rid ourselves of these horrible clothes? I often wonder how many of these presentation gowns find their way to the ragman the next morning."

Elizabeth laughed and hooked her hand onto Darcy's arm. "Oh yes Aunt Ellen, please! And we must rid my husband of this sword before he begins to feel the need to use it on someone." She smiled up at him and he relaxed a little.

"I am not a man of violence." He said softly.

"Violent affections, perhaps?" She squeezed his arm and felt the tension that remained.

"Well . . . yes." He attempted a smile and hugged her arm to him, and then offered his other to his aunt. They returned to Darcy House for the little family celebration they had planned. Bingley and Jane would join them later; they were far back in the queue. His status was not nearly as high as Darcy's, and Jane, with Louisa as her sponsor, would have some time to wait before her turn arrived. As of the next morning, the knocker would be on the door, and they would finally face the *ton*, together.

"Well my dear cousin, what trouble have you found in the absence of your brother and sister?" Richard settled onto the sofa, took a bite of a biscuit and grinned at Georgiana.

"Oh Richard, do not tease me. You know that I do not look for trouble."

He smiled and thought, *No cousin, it finds you.* "Hmmm. I do not know if I should take your word . . . Miss Mary, oh excuse me, Miss Bennet, what have you to say about this?"

"I am still not used to being called that!" She smiled shyly. "But sir, I suppose that we are cousins by marriage, are we not? I would not object to you calling me Mary." She blushed with her boldness and looked down at her hands. Richard grinned.

"I would be delighted! But only if you call me Richard, I am still trying to grasp the moniker Mr. Fitzwilliam, and it has been two months since I resigned my commission." Mary looked up and smiled at the comparison. "Now, please tell me your doings. You have enjoyed a month without proper supervision."

Georgiana sighed loudly. "Mrs. Annesley has been quite attentive, and Mrs. Reynolds, I swear has spies or at least eyes on the back of her head. There is no opportunity to misbehave, even if we wished. We have spent the time playing music and taking advantage of the library, and I thought that now with the weather improving, perhaps I could try to teach Mary to ride."

He sat up and looked at her with interest. "Really? Well that is certainly a worthwhile occupation! I would be glad to lend my expertise to the endeavour."

"Oh, but then she would only learn to ride into battle!" Georgiana teased.

Mary laughed. "I do believe I can safely say that I will never be going to war, sir."

Richard chuckled and tilted his head. "No, as fetching as you might be in red, I would prefer the ladies to remain safe at home." She blushed furiously and he smiled. "But I nonetheless would like to at least accompany you on your attempts. I will be visiting for a fortnight before I must return to my new home, and would certainly appreciate the occupation."

"Why are you staying so long?" Georgiana asked.

"You do not want me? I am offended!" Richard laughed.

"No, oh that came out all wrong!" Georgiana bit her lip and glanced at Mary then back at him. "I . . . just thought that Shee Onnoroil required your attention, such an odd name, why did you choose it?"

"Well, I suppose I will eventually come to call it Onnoroil, but well, you know our Fitzwilliam ancestry is Gaelic, correct?" She nodded, this was her blood family and she was very curious about it. "The phrase shee onnoroil means *peace with honour*. I thought it rather appropriate for a retired man of war. Do you agree?"

"What a beautiful sentiment!" Mary exclaimed. He smiled warmly at her.

Georgiana laughed. "That is perfectly lovely, Richard. What did Uncle Henry have to say about it?"

"He told me he would never have guessed me to be a sentimental fool, but I do believe he was very pleased with my attention to our roots."

"Perhaps Richard, if you could while you are here, perhaps you might teach me about the Fitzwilliam family? I know now that I am not a Darcy, and as wonderful as it is to be accepted as one . . . I would like to know my true history. I could never speak to William about the Fitzwilliam side of our family; it was just too painful for him to think of Mother, but for you . . ."

"Of course, I would be glad to tell you the bloody tale of our clan!" He cocked a brow at Mary. "I am afraid that you will be bored to tears, Mary."

"I have a feeling that you are capable of making any tale exciting, sir."

"Ah, I am cursed with a golden tongue!" He laughed, and saw the little sparkle in Mary's eyes, reminiscent of her sister, but unique to her. Darcy was correct. Take this time to become friends, show her his true self, and see what came of it. "Well if I am to deliver a dissertation, I am afraid that I will require something more than tea. Ladies, excuse me while I request some port."

Clutching Mary's arm in mock terror Georgiana exclaimed. "Oh no, you are winding up for a long talk, Mary, do you think that we can bear him for such a period?"

Mary smiled gently and met Richard's warm and friendly smile. Elizabeth told her to simply enjoy his visit, to let down her guard and be the girl she always imagined and wished herself to be. She determinedly forgot all of Fordyce's advice about a modest woman's behaviour and laughed. "Well, Georgiana, I believe that if you can bear his effusions, I will as well."

Chapter 38

"**M**iss Bingley, may I have the next set?" Caroline looked into the gentleman's eyes. They were not particularly warm, certainly not the soulful blue of Darcy's or the bright green of her brother's. They were brown, sharp, and most importantly, directed at her alone. "Yes, of course, Mr. Thatcher." She took his offered hand and glanced at Louisa, who gave her an encouraging smile. The gentleman led her away to the dance, and they stood opposite each other, assessing their partner and wondering if this would be their view for life.

Louisa turned to her husband. "What do you know of him, Gilbert? He approached you at the club?"

"Yes, he heard of Caroline's removal from Bingley's home upon his marriage and that she has a significant dowry. He has an estate, I would say about the size of my father's, in Yorkshire, but the entailment upon it prevents him from selling any property as he hoped to eliminate some debts."

"Why does he need the funds, is he a gambler?" She watched the couple move through the pattern, making some conversation in the process. Caroline seemed to be attempting to smile, and Mr. Thatcher's eyes were roaming over her.

"Not that I am aware, but his father was, and left debts of honour behind when he died. Mr. Thatcher is obligated to pay them."

"So his recourse is to marry a woman with a dowry." She said grimly.

Hurst turned to watch them. "Yes, and quickly . . . he is not a bad man, Louisa."

Louisa caught his eye. "But is he a good one?"

"He is not me or Bingley, and certainly not Darcy, but he is a gentleman. A marriage of convenience is all he ever wanted or expected. Do not be surprised to hear of his mistress, or of him preferring his club to his home. He wants a wife to produce his heir and run his household, and of course for social occasions such as this. He told me that he has observed Caroline in company, and that she has a sharp wit that would complement his own. He finds her handsome enough." Louisa looked at the couple dancing sadly and he saw her expression. "They would marry because he needs the money and she needs the security. It is cold, but in all honesty, that is all that Caroline expected with Darcy, is it not?"

"She wanted the first circles and his riches. Instead she will endure a loveless marriage, without even companionship as a benefit, I suspect. She has alienated so many women with her cruel remarks . . . few of them would recommend her to their brothers. It is the lot that she cast for herself."

"Well, she will be the same as you and I, which given your family's very recent roots in trade, is not a bad accomplishment, if I may toot my own horn." He smiled, then took her hand and bestowed a kiss. "I believe that you and I had a bit more of a romantic inclination when we first met, and I think that we have restored that now."

"Well, you certainly are returning to the dashing figure you had when you courted me!" She smiled and he laughed, patting his stomach.

"My tailor is pleased for all the new business!" He smiled again and then looked soberly back at Caroline. "This may be her only chance, Louisa. The gossips are all discussing her removal from Bingley's house. If he had not married, they would be crowing over it even more, at least they seem to have latched onto that as a reason. Her window of opportunity is closing quickly. Surely you would prefer her in her own home rather than living alone forever?"

"Of course, it is not what she desired, but her hopes were too high, and her methods despicable. I regret ever encouraging her. Will Mr. Thatcher speak to Charles?"

"Yes, it is not necessary, she is independent, but he wishes to follow the formalities. If Caroline is agreeable, I can see them marrying within the next two months."

"I admit that it will be a relief." She sighed then laughed at her husband's nod. "Well, let us leave them to their courting. I feel no compelling desire to chaperone what is a business transaction." She tilted her head. "So, Mr. Hurst, will you ask me to dance?"

He offered his arm and grinned. "By all means! May I demonstrate my newly acquired lightness of foot to match my new lightness of figure?" Hurst led her out to line up for the second set and smiled, his gaze resting on the small bump on his wife's belly.

Darcy walked slowly around his nervous wife, his arms folded, studying the way the fine fabric draped so sensuously over every curve. He stood behind her, admiring her bare shoulders, the soft skin like a siren, beckoning for his touch, the caress of his lips. Three long curls draped down her back, and moved with each quiet breath. Those curls would be enticing him all night. He slipped his hands around her waist and unable to resist, pulled her back against his body. He wanted her to feel what she had done to him merely by entering the room.

He tenderly kissed her throat. "No, you may not wear this gown tonight."

"Will . . ."

"I will not share your beauty with any other man. Do you not have a gown of sackcloth you might wear instead?" He gently nibbled below her ear and gloried in the soft moan.

"Will . . ."

"Let us stay home." He breathed. Slowly he turned her towards him and saw her beautiful, sparkling, but worried eyes. Her fear was all that kept him from carrying her off to their bed that moment.

Elizabeth smiled softly at his warm and intoxicated gaze, and wound her fingers gently through his hair. Darcy's eyes closed and he leaned into her touch. They reopened with the brush of her lips against his, and he knew she was seeking his reassurance. "Lizzy . . ." Her tongue tasted his mouth and he groaned, pulling her hard against his chest, and firmly held her hips to his, rubbing slowly. Both of them moaned with the growing sensation. "You can not wish to go . . ."

"I . . . I wished to dance with you.

"We will dance here."

"There is no music." She sighed, feeling his tongue on her ear.

His deep voice sent a thrill through her. "Our cries will be our music, my love." His lips wandered down to her shoulder and lovingly nibbled the silky skin.

"I know what you are doing." She whispered.

"What am I doing?"

"You are behaving badly to make me demand that we go."

"And why on earth would I wish us to go?" His muffled voice asked.

"Because we must, and you know it." Elizabeth looked down.

Darcy tilted his head and placed his hands on her shoulders. "Yes, my love, we must go. But know this, I am not at all reluctant to attend this ball out of fear for some misstep by you, and I hope with all of my heart that you do not fear that you will somehow embarrass me. Dearest Wife, do you not know me?"

"You obviously know me."

"I do, and I wish to know where my courageous Lizzy has disappeared. You have been unusually quiet all day."

She drew a shaking breath. "I know how important this night is, Will. I have not been blind to the response of your peers as we travel about town. I realize that your return to London was not supposed to be as a married man. Especially as a man married to . . . someone who was required to spend endless hours being formed by your aunt into an acceptable . . . I know that my education was poor. I am very much aware of . . ."

"What, Lizzy?" He said softly.

"How unworthy I am of you." She whispered and looked down.

"Oh Elizabeth, please, do not say that!" He cried, and dropped his hands to enfold hers in their warm clasp. "There is no other woman in the world for me." Darcy then lifted one hand to hold her face up, so that she had no choice but to look into his eyes. "Remember what you said to me at Pemberley. You refused to believe my confession of arrogance, and said that if you had wanted that sort of man you would have married Lucas, or Collins, do you remember that?" She nodded. "I spoke the truth then and I speak it now. Believe me when I say that you outshine every woman I have ever known. If I had wanted what society had to offer, I would have married into the cold formality and existence that was expected of me years ago. I waited, and although I declared that I would never marry, deep in my heart, I hoped I would be blessed with someone to love. Is it not obvious that I found all of the ladies of London lacking?" He stroked her jaw with his thumb. "You hosted a brilliant dinner for our friends last week."

"Yes, our friends, the ones who stood by you through this trouble, and willingly accepted me as your wife on your recommendation. They all wanted me to succeed. Your aunt's guests will not be so generous. I have seen the reactions to me everywhere we have gone." Elizabeth tore her eyes away from his.

"Why would you allow a ballroom full of Caroline Bingleys and Lady Catherines bother you?" She looked back up in surprise. "My aunt has not invited my greatest enemies. They are powerful members of society, yes, but they are not . . ." Her sigh stopped him. "Lizzy, I hate going to this ball. I hate knowing that every move we make, our expressions, the tone of our voices, everything will be examined and discussed. I hate performing for others, but I am also very proud of the woman who married me, and I can not help but want to . . . show her off." Darcy's little smile appeared and he stepped away, still holding her hands. "Come my love, I can not do this without you. Please help me."

He watched as her shoulders lifted and the fear left her expression. That was it; she needed to hear him say that he needed her. "I believe Mr. Darcy, that you and I shall have a very good time tonight." A small smile appeared on her lips and she tilted her head. "I look forward to my waltz."

Immediately Darcy grabbed her waist and spun her around the room, eliciting a delighted squeal. "And I, my dear, look forward to all of your dances." Their twirling came to a breathless end and they stood staring at each other. "Lizzy . . ."

Elizabeth gasped, seeing the unmistakable desire in his eyes. "Darling, we must go."

"Not yet." His hands embraced her face and he leaned down to tenderly kiss her. Elizabeth's arms wound around his waist and she clung to him. His lips slowly wandered down her jaw to her throat and then he spoke softly in her ear. "Are you ready for this? Are you still frightened?"

Elizabeth looked down and he gently lifted her chin so she looked into his eyes. "I am nervous . . . but you will be with me, and your aunt and uncle, I will be fine, we will be fine."

"Yes, we will." They kissed again. "And when we return home . . . I will love you properly." His lips found their way back to her throat and he felt her giggle. Lifting his face he encountered her dancing eyes.

"It is a wonder that I am not yet with child." She pressed her lips together to suppress her smile, and Darcy began to chuckle, the dark passion in his eyes gave way to a twinkle. Resting his forehead to hers he kissed her nose and smiled. "Indeed."

Merely thirty minutes later they stood before the silent ballroom, hearing their names announced. Elizabeth felt William's tension increase as they entered the house, and knew that it was not for fear of failure, but for distaste over the charade they must put on. He avoided being the object of attention in any location, and this night he and Elizabeth were unquestionably the objects of all eyes. It was indeed time for Elizabeth to show her strength. Lord and Lady Matlock came forward and greeted them, exchanging kisses and embraces. With that show of acceptance the volume of conversation rose again, and the couple was left alone for a moment.

"You are lovely tonight, my dear." Lady Matlock smiled. "You look very well in green; it brings out the depths in your eyes."

"I would think that the emeralds were sparkling enough for that, another heirloom?" Lord Matlock examined the spectacular necklace and earrings with interest.

"No, I purchased them specifically for this evening." Darcy raised Elizabeth's hand and kissed it. "I wanted to create a memory with them."

Lady Matlock laughed. "You and your little treasures, Darcy. Do you know Elizabeth, that he kept a robin's egg in his pocket for months until it was smashed when he fell off of his horse?"

Elizabeth laughed and squeezed his hand, seeing his blush. "And why did you do that, William?

"Because he thought it was a pretty blue." James strolled up and kissed her cheek. "You said it looked like the sky on a summer day, and you wanted to be like the bird and fly away." He grinned and Darcy continued to blush.

Elizabeth realized that what the shell represented to him was escape. "You must have been very sad when it broke." He nodded and said no more. She entwined her fingers with his and they stood clasping their hands tightly. She turned to James and grinned. "So Viscount, have you found your bride?"

He groaned and his parents laughed, Darcy's little smile appeared and he relaxed. "Excellent Elizabeth, he can hear it from you for a while!" Lord Matlock cheered.

"That is enough. I am moving on, it seems I have work to do." James bowed and left for friendlier companions.

"Come dear, we must make some introductions before the dancing begins." Lady Matlock led the couple around the room. Darcy knew them all, and as they approached each presentation, he would lean over and quietly give a warning as to them being friend or foe. Always his pronouncement was quickly proven correct. Through it all they maintained some form of physical contact, which reassured her, as he had retreated so far into his masked persona that she otherwise might have feared that he was displeased. By the time the dancing began they had managed to meet at least a third of the guests.

The relief of being alone, standing opposite each other and waiting for the music to begin, was felt by both. Darcy paid great attention to Elizabeth's expression and when they at last advanced to join hands he bent to her ear. "What are you thinking? Your mind is at work."

They moved apart and came together again. "It occurs to me that we were not being introduced so much as we were humbling ourselves."

His brow creased, and then he smiled. "I had not considered that, but you are correct."

"It is as if we are behaving as repentant sinners, and you are holding me up, saying, *Look, she is witty and lovely enough, I did not ruin my life by accepting her, please forgive me for being a besotted fool.*" Her eyes were dancing.

Darcy hooked his arm with hers and they spun. "I am shocked that I did not see the parallel so easily, which proves your superior social skills. I do, however, have a proposition."

"Ah, to prove your superior analytical skills?" Elizabeth grinned.

"I will not touch that statement." She laughed and his eyes twinkled at her. "From this moment on, we will enjoy this ball. We will dance and speak with friends and family, and no longer allow our aunt to parade us about the room. If someone wishes to know us, they may approach, but we will not beg for their sanction."

"I like this plan Will, very much!"

Darcy's face lit up with his first real smile since leaving their home. "They will have plenty of opportunity to observe us and draw their conclusions."

"And I have no doubt that tongues will be wagging at our impertinence." She raised her brow and he took her hand to bestow a kiss as they danced side-by-side. "William!"

"I told you I would steal kisses . . . and my love, you dance with nobody but me tonight." His gaze burned into hers.

"Not even Charles or James?" She tilted her head and delighted in his possessive expression.

"I will allow family, no others."

"You are a determined man!" Darcy swung her around one last time and they ended the set standing opposite each other. He bowed and lifted his head.

"I have played by their rules, now it is time to live by ours." He held out his hand and they walked off together to join Bingley and Jane.

Elizabeth hugged her sister. "I am sorry that we have not been able to greet you sooner."

"I have been watching you Lizzy, you were certainly well-occupied. How are you holding up?" Jane looked at her worriedly.

She smiled and accepted a kiss from Charles on her cheek. "As well as can be expected." They laughed and moved to a relatively quiet corner. "Tell me about Miss Bingley's romance. How is that coming along?"

Charles laughed. "Romance!" Jane shot a look at him and he lifted her hand to his lips. "Come my dear, call it what it is. It is the epitome of a marriage of convenience. She will be married to a gentleman, although not the grand one she wanted." He grinned at Darcy who coughed. "Thatcher is not the warmest individual I have ever known, but then neither is Caroline. In that they are well-matched. She will have an estate to lord over, he will have her dowry to spend, perhaps they will produce an heir, and they will always have a dance partner. She will essentially be no better than Louisa or me." He smiled, "Well, perhaps I will surpass her a bit."

"Knowing Thatcher I would say so." Darcy said quietly

"What does that mean?" Elizabeth asked curiously.

"Thatcher just recently inherited his estate, but from what I know of him, he will be like his father, and will not invest in its improvement. A wise man looks to the future, and should be aware of the changes that are occurring in the world. A man's income must not be all tied to the land, even though the status from such ownership is undoubtedly vastly important in society."

"And are you looking to the future in such a way?" Elizabeth tilted her head and he smiled down at her.

"You can be assured that I am." He took her hand and held it tightly. "Our children will be well-provided for."

"Well then man; do not keep these secrets to yourself! Share the wealth!" Bingley laughed and Darcy smiled. "In any case, they are engaged and will marry at the end of April. It will be small, as her dowry has other purposes besides frills and bows." He grimaced. "And then it will be done."

"Is she happy?" Elizabeth asked Jane.

She blushed and glanced at Darcy. "Louisa tells me that she remains bitter over your winning William. She feels that you do not deserve him and that she earned the right to be his wife by waiting so long for him."

"I never indicated any desire to marry her." He said with frustration.

Charles held up his hand. "It was her choice. Perhaps she could have won someone who actually cared for her, if she had given in sooner. But she did not, and she will instead have a cold marriage of convenience. It is her bed, she shall lie in it. I will not allow it to bother me again." He smiled and looked around at the crowd. "Now, enough of this. This is a ball, and I intend to dance. Elizabeth, will your husband tolerate letting go of your hand for one set with your brother?"

Elizabeth looked down at her tightly gripped hand and smiled. "I think he may be persuaded, but only if he dances with his sister."

Darcy looked at Jane who was smiling at him widely. "I will dance only with my sister. No other woman."

"I am honoured, sir!" Jane laughed as he took her hand and bowed.

He smiled and they followed Elizabeth and Bingley to the floor. "If I can not have my wife, I will have the next best thing, and that is you, Jane."

"William." She smiled and he looked at her enquiringly. "Have you been learning how to speak charmingly from my husband?"

Darcy laughed and grinned. "I suppose it had to rub off sometime!"

The rest of the evening went as Darcy and Elizabeth planned. He steadfastly refused any further attempts by his aunt to introduce the couple. When Elizabeth was occupied dancing with James, Lord and Lady Matlock pulled him aside. "Darcy what has happened? Why are you hiding Elizabeth from the guests?"

"I am hardly hiding her, Uncle. There she is in plain sight." He gestured to the dance floor, caught her eye and smiled.

Lady Matlock followed his gaze. "You have stopped the introductions. Was someone rude to you? Surely you know that not everyone here will accept you with open arms, but they can not make a decision without first meeting her."

"Aunt Elaine, Elizabeth and I realized that the people here will observe us no matter what we do. If they want to know us, here we are, they are welcome to approach, but I will not go to them. I have found since Elizabeth's presentation that I have friends, people whose loyalty I have earned through supporting them when they were in need of my help, and now that I am in need of theirs, they are with me. I will not spend my precious time with Elizabeth asking some haughty peer to lower his nose enough to look me in the eye. I may not be titled, but my ancestry is ancient and great. I am proud of it, and my children will have nothing to feel shame over. I do not need them." He smiled warmly and kissed his aunt's cheek. "I appreciate very much what you have done for us tonight. This event will indeed give the important members of the *ton* the opportunity to see my Elizabeth, but after tonight, we will participate no more."

"What are you saying?" Lord Matlock demanded.

"I am happy, and I do not need anything more than what I have right now. Those who continue to disparage me are ones who have done so since I was in school. Those who are above me do not need my friendship and I refuse to toady to them. I have never really participated in society, although admittedly that was due to my own feelings of distaste for the proceedings, and likely limited my appeal to many. However, there is no denying that seeing us now putting ourselves out for the pleasure of society's inspection is behaving in a different manner than I ever have. Seeing me dance happily with my wife should prove novel enough to entertain or enrage whoever is here. On Friday we will go to Rosings for Easter, returning on Monday. For the remainder of our time in town, I intend to enjoy the theatre, take my wife through the parks, indulge in buying her gifts and see only those who share our pleasures. Then we will go home to Pemberley." He smiled as James approached with Elizabeth. "Did you survive my cousin's poor dancing?"

Elizabeth laughed and patted James' arm. "I have no bruised toes."

"You know, Richard should be here to take some of these barbs!" He looked affronted, then relaxed. "I say Darcy, how am I ever going to find a wife like yours?"

Darcy took her arm to lead her back to the dance and said over his shoulder, "By dancing with someone else!"

"I am not sure if his decision is wise, Henry." Lady Matlock looked after them worriedly.

"It is his to make, my dear." Lord Matlock scanned the room. "In all honesty do you truly like most of the people you invited tonight?"

She first looked at him in shock then smiled slowly. "No, in all honesty I do not. But you are in parliament, and we are saddled with them. Darcy does have that freedom to choose his friends."

They watched as Darcy, smiling warmly to Elizabeth's glowing face, glided and turned her gracefully around the room. There was no question what their expressions said, the devotion was there for all to see.

———

The Darcy carriage arrived at Rosings late Friday afternoon. They were greeted by Anne, who had replaced her mother as mistress after her horrendous display at Longbourn. Lord Matlock did not back down from his promise to go to the attorneys. They were surprised that Anne allowed her to stay, but not at all surprised that Lady Catherine did not join them for dinner.

"Do you think that your aunt truly was ill?" Elizabeth asked as they retired.

Darcy climbed into the bed and drew her to his body. "There is no doubt in my mind that she is quite well. She will appear when she has formed whatever vitriol she wishes to deliver."

"I am proud of you." Elizabeth gently kissed him and smiled.

"What have I done to deserve that?" He smiled and lifted her up so that she lay on his chest. Elizabeth lovingly kissed him again, and he licked his lips. "Mmmm."

She laughed and caressed his hair. "Despite your justifiable anger with her, you were still willing to come here."

"If Anne was not mistress, we would not have come. We are here solely for her. Perhaps Aunt Catherine will do us all a favour and remain in her rooms until we depart." Elizabeth laughed and he hugged her to him. "I have come to this wretched mansion every Easter for as long as I can remember. For the last, oh, nearly twenty years I was told repeatedly that I would marry my cousin Anne, my fate being pronounced more vehemently every year. I often thought of what it would be to come to this place with a wife of my choosing, and love her."

"An act of defiance? From you?" She laughed. "I do hope that you would want me for better reasons than that." She arched her brow and pursed her lips.

"Well of course I do, but I can not deny the glee I will feel knowing that I am here with the woman I wanted to marry; and not one that was forced upon me." He shrugged and regarded her with a twinkle in his eye. "Call me an adolescent boy, but there it is."

"I think that there is a great deal of little boy in you, and that I have only begun to meet him." She grinned and caressed his jaw.

"Just wait until we return to Pemberley my love, then we shall truly get down to the serious business of play." He smiled brilliantly and kissed her palm as she laughed.

Elizabeth rested her head on his shoulder. "Anne has invited Charlotte Collins to visit tomorrow while you are working. They have become friends and I understand that Charlotte has spoken of her family's interference in our lives."

"Are you ready to mend your friendship?" His hand ran through her hair, and stroked her back with the other.

"I suppose that I will find out." She said softly. Darcy watched her conflicted expression, and attempted to bring her relief.

"Shall I anticipate hearing your sobs of regret after seeing her, realizing your mistake of refusing Mr. Collins' proposal after he so graciously offered to rescue you from ruin?" His lips twitched. "I believe that I did detect a gasp of disappointment when we drove past the parsonage and you viewed all that could have been yours." Darcy tilted his head and saw her fighting a smile. He laughed loudly and Elizabeth joined him.

"No, Mr. Darcy, although living in such proximity to your aunt may have been rewarding, I do not feel that I would have suited to be a parson's wife."

He drew her face to his and began nibbling on her jaw. "Mmmmm. No, my wanton wife is most definitely not formed for such a life." Pulling away he smiled at her. "I am being silly." His expression changed. "Do I demand too much of you? I imagine that at times you must think me insatiable, but it is only because I love you so much. If you wish me to leave you alone . . ."

She placed her fingers over his lips. "No dearest, you are everything wonderful, and you have never asked anything of me that I was unwilling to give." Elizabeth kissed him and moved back down onto the bed where they fulfilled his dream.

In the morning, Darcy rode out with the steward early and Elizabeth joined Anne for breakfast, again without Lady Catherine. The two ladies were beginning to know each other. Anne told her that she felt it would be easier for Elizabeth to meet Charlotte away from Mr. Collins, who apparently expressed frequently his thoughts on her marriage to Darcy, no doubt parroting Lady Catherine's opinion. Charlotte arrived and Anne stayed for a short while, then murmured an excuse to allow the two friends time alone, leaving to speak to Darcy who had returned to work in the library.

Elizabeth sat next to Charlotte on a sofa and poured some more tea. "How do you find marriage, Charlotte? Are you happy?"

"I am content Eliza. I never wanted or expected a passionate marriage. I only wished for protection. Mr. Collins keeps to his duties and I have mine. We seem well-matched. It is as much as I ever wanted. I look forward to soon becoming with child and fulfilling my duty to him." Elizabeth accepted the statement, but noticed the flat tone of her voice and her rigid posture. Clearly she was looking forward to ending her duties. Charlotte looked down then smiled slightly. "I suspect that you and Mr. Darcy are content as well, if his smile upon seeing you when he returned is any indication. Is marriage everything that you dreamed it would be?"

Elizabeth thought of their delay in finding sleep the night before, his tender love and concern, their unending mutual support, and their desire to share their lives, and smiled. "Yes, we are very happy."

Charlotte watched her expression and wondered what it meant, clearly Elizabeth's marriage was precisely what her own was not. "You truly are happy. I am so sorry on behalf of my family. We all tried to force something upon you that was never wanted."

"It is over. Please let us move on, Charlotte. There is no need to dwell upon a past that can not be changed. How is your brother?" Elizabeth looked at her with determination.

"Very quiet, but working quite hard on the estate. He has taken over all of Papa's duties."

She looked at her with surprise. "Really?" *Perhaps he was growing up. Perhaps he had become a man.* "He is quiet?"

"Yes, he regrets his behaviour very much. He said that he will not marry for many years, not until he can earn a good woman's respect." Charlotte looked at her meaningfully.

Elizabeth smiled, understanding the compliment. "That is quite a change."

"I believe that you and Mr. Darcy have given him a great deal to think about." Charlotte said very seriously.

Elizabeth looked at her hands. "I am happy for the woman he will someday marry. She will have a good husband."

"He is so sorry . . ." She began, wanting to explain John's feelings.

She looked at Charlotte sharply. "He does not regret me, does he?"

She met Elizabeth's gaze and spoke with sincerity. "He regrets hurting you and not listening to you, as do I."

"Please tell him that Mr. Darcy and I are happy and I think that what he is doing is admirable. Now, tell me about life as a parson's wife." She smiled warmly and squeezed her friend's hand. The subject was forever closed. They spent the next hour in conversation before Charlotte took her leave to return to the parsonage. She had a letter to write.

In the library, Anne knocked on the open door. "May I come in, Darcy?"

He stood. "Of course, it is your home." Darcy smiled then resumed his seat. "What can I do for you?"

She looked at the papers strewn over the desk. "Is everything in order? Do I have anything to worry over?"

"Your steward is a good man. He did not say directly, but he is very pleased that you are now mistress."

A small smile crossed her lips. "I am less tight-fisted than my mother, I think." She studied him.

"I can only agree." He met her eyes and his brow creased. "What is wrong,

Anne?"

She said nothing for a few moments. "I watched you and Elizabeth last evening, the way that you sat together at the pianoforte, and how you simply seemed to fit, completing each other. You and I would not have had such a marriage."

"No." He was very uncomfortable. "Anne . . ."

"I am sorry Cousin. I can see your wariness. I am afraid that I am unable to speak subtly, too much exposure to my mother, I suppose. I no longer regret you, truly."

"But you did." He sighed.

"Yes."

"I suspected it . . . Anne, why did you ask us here? Clearly your steward is performing his duties well and has everything in hand. You really did not need me to come and look over his work."

"It was selfish, I know, but I needed to see you." Darcy closed his eyes, and she quickly continued. "I needed to see that you were truly happy." He pressed his lips together, and she could see his face reddening in anger. "I did not wish this as a means to interfere with your life, I am not Mama." His eyes opened and he stared at her. "I could not help but observe you with Elizabeth. Darcy, I am very happy for you." His gaze softened, seeing her warm smile appear. "She has changed you."

He relaxed. "For the better, I hope."

"Very much so." Darcy smiled and she saw the pleasure that gave him. "Although I never witnessed it in London, I certainly knew of your opinion for society, and obviously understood your taciturn and unsociable behaviour. I was aware of the general unhappiness of the ladies of who threw themselves at you. Mama crowed over each one you rejected as a sign that you would eventually offer for me."

Darcy looked down. "I remain rather unsociable, but Elizabeth refuses to believe I could ever be so . . . dismissive of others."

"Why would you wish to convince her of your faults? Whether past or present?"

"I suppose that I fear her being taken by surprise someday." He smiled. "But it seems that I am so amiable that she would find that to be impossible."

"I know your wife only briefly, Darcy, but I have an inkling that she would find that statement laughable." Anne smiled and laughed and Darcy's rueful expression.

He tilted his head and regarded her carefully. "Do you wish to marry?"

"And give my husband the income of Rosings?" She laughed and shook her head.

Darcy seemed confused. "He would not own the estate; he could not sell or mortgage it."

"Oh Darcy, you are such a man!" He looked at her quizzically. "If I do not have control of the income, it may as well be sold. No, I have waited so long to be independent of Mama. I will not give it up now. I said that I no longer regret you, and this is the reason."

Darcy nodded in understanding; it never was love, but escape for her. *That* he could appreciate. "It is interesting. She wished to keep Rosings for herself by marrying you to me, but she did not wish the same independence for you by forcing such a union."

"Of course you would have had control of the income then." She pointed out.

"But she would have lived here alone, still queen of the manor." The two cousins smiled at each other, both feeling the success of thwarting Lady Catherine's plans.

"I plan to leave Rosings to you." She said matter-of-factly.

His brow creased. "Why? Leave it to Richard. He has an estate, but it is very small."

"But he has not suffered mother's machinations as we have. And you suffered even more so with your own parents. No, I wish it to go to you and your children. I will not marry; I doubt I could safely bear a child if I did. I think that both of us have found happiness, though. I like the idea of you receiving Rosings without either of us being forced to accept an arranged marriage." She watched him thinking. "This is why I wished to be assured of your happiness. I needed to see it for myself."

Darcy smiled in understanding. "It is your decision, Anne, but if you proceed down this path, I thank you on behalf of my family."

"May it be a brood; Darcy." He gave her a brilliant smile. She shook her head at the sight of it and stood. "I will see if the meal is ready, you must be famished."

"Thank you Anne. Please tell Elizabeth I will join you soon."

Darcy bent back to his task. The sound of the door opening made him look up quickly, anticipating Elizabeth coming to keep him company. Instead of the welcome arrival of his wife, he was faced with the intensely unwanted appearance of Lady Catherine. He stood. "Aunt Catherine. I hope you are well, we missed seeing you last night." She took a seat and he returned to his.

The old woman regarded him imperiously. "I am surprised that you are concerned at all, Darcy. You are obviously devoid of all familial feeling. Why would that change now?"

"I fail to understand your implication." He said steadily.

"You have forsaken your duty to your estate by taking this . . . person as your wife." The venom was clear in the tone of her voice.

His jaw set and he spoke in a low voice. "I believe that you have already expressed your opinion, madam. It is not necessary to repeat yourself, particularly so far past the date of our wedding."

"I once wished you for my son. Now I am grateful for your betrayal. I would not wish such a fool as my daughter's husband. You deserve the misery you will suffer married to that person." She sniffed and looked down her nose.

"I asked you not to disparage my wife." He gritted his teeth and clenched his fists

"I am not. I disparage you. You brought nothing but misery to my sister. You and your sister; and SHE killed Anne."

The words spewing from his aunt's mouth grew more vicious and cruel, never had she spoken to him in such a way. She had fawned over him, complimented him, it was demanding but was always done with her single-minded goal of gaining him as her son in mind. Now that her dream was destroyed, she let him feel the full force of her anger. Darcy barely heard the words; instead he focussed on her eyes, and the tone of her voice. He was transported back, years back. Those familiar eyes, that voice, that sneer on her lips . . . it was no longer the wrinkled old face of his aunt, he saw, he heard, he felt . . . his mother. The young boy alternately ignored or berated by the angry woman who bore him stood paralysed before his aunt as a man.

The feel of a hand in his startled him back to the present. He looked down to see Elizabeth gripping him. At some point he must have stood. The buzzing sound of his aunt's unending diatribe became recognizable speech again, and he understood that her fury was now venting upon Elizabeth. He fell into the eyes that had changed his life and he saw that she was dying to respond, but was waiting for him, this was his fight. He felt her grip tighten and saw her lips form the silent words, "I love you, Will."

He turned to his aunt and roared. "ENOUGH!!"

Lady Catherine's mouth snapped shut. "My mother is dead, and I will not allow you to drag her back to the world of the living to haunt my life again. Your demands are as selfish and arrogant as hers were, and your delivery is no different, you have only lived long enough to see them crushed, as they should have been at their inception." He watched her narrowed eyes and again felt the reassurance of Elizabeth's hand in his. His eyes dropped to hers. "Fortunately I am old enough now to protect myself where others failed me before. Nobody can hurt me again. I am loved." His mouth turned up slightly and his chest swelled, seeing the unmistakable pride for him that Elizabeth's intense gaze communicated. "I am free." He turned to his aunt. "You are as significant to me as the mud on my boots. Go ahead and make your noise, I will dismiss it as the braying of the donkeys I purchased my dearest wife."

Elizabeth relaxed and smiled at him. "Shall we rename the female donkey Catherine, my love?"

Nodding, he met her gaze. "Indeed, what an excellent idea. I will enjoy watching her work pulling the wagon that hauls manure from the stables each day." He looked again to his aunt. "It will remind me of your words, and what they mean to me."

"Darcy!" She snarled.

Darcy turned back to Elizabeth and wrinkled his brow. "Do you hear something, Lizzy?"

"I think that it is the sound of birds singing, Will." Elizabeth's eyes sparkled and her smile grew.

"Ah yes, well then, shall we go take a stroll in the park and enjoy them? I would like to show you the groves, they should not be missed." They walked from the room, past Lady Catherine, ignoring the revival of her speech completely.

"Do you wish to remain at Rosings?" Elizabeth said quietly as they made their way outside into the sunshine.

He took a deep breath of the fresh air and lifted her hand for a kiss. "I wish to finish the work that I began, although I know that all is well. Tomorrow is Easter, a day of hope and renewal. Perhaps the sermon will do Lady de Bourgh some good. In any case, we can not travel tomorrow, and it is too late to leave today."

"But if she begins berating us again . . ."

"We will retire to far more productive conversation in our rooms." He saw Elizabeth's eyes demanding a serious response and said softly, "I have no desire to spend my time arguing with a woman who is clearly implacable. My tolerance for poor behaviour is gone, Elizabeth. I have borne it for all of my life, and have no intention of doing so ever again. I would prefer to spend time loving my wife who has rescued me more times than I can count. When did you enter the room?"

"Not long before you noticed me, you awakened from your stunned state as soon as I touched your hand; I could hear her speech begin when I was coming to keep you company." They walked in silence down through the precisely manicured hedges and entered the natural beauty of the groves.

Darcy stopped and leaning against a tree, drew her into his arms to kiss her. "I would likely still be there if you had not arrived."

"No dear, I am sure you would have strangled her eventually." Elizabeth laughed. He chuckled and began nibbling her neck. "What are your plans, Mr. Darcy?" He just smiled and continued his kisses up to her ear. She sighed and melted into him. Darcy rested his cheek on top of her head, and ran his hands lovingly over her body.

"Mine."

Elizabeth gave him a squeeze. "Perhaps we should spend the rest of our visit out here."

"What an excellent idea." He smiled. "Thank you, Lizzy. You helped me to confront my father at Pemberley, and my mother here. I hope so much that it is truly in the past now. My future is in my arms."

Back in the study, Anne stood before Lady Catherine. "I should have had you removed to the dower house months ago, Mama." Anne said softly.

The old woman looked at her daughter with alarm. "You said that I did not have to go there!"

"That was before you insulted my cousins." Anne felt the power of her position, and finally decided to apply it.

"Very well, I will keep my thoughts to myself." She said with some pleading in her tone.

Anne shook her head slowly. "No Mama, you made this decision for me. I will have the house opened for you, and then bid you farewell."

Lady Catherine did not join the family for any other meals, and did not sit with them at Easter services. Anne gladly spent time alone with Elizabeth while Darcy finished looking over the estate papers. The two new cousins came away from their brief visit with a new appreciation for each other. Elizabeth no longer feared Anne's feelings for William, and Anne was able to feel happiness for herself and him. Although William was now full of positive thoughts for a future free of memories, speaking to Anne gave Elizabeth greater insight into her husband's past lapses into brooding silence. It had been a trip worth taking.

———∿∿∿———

"Do you miss the army yet, Richard?" Mary asked. They were strolling around the flower beds, admiring the early daffodils while Georgiana was busy with Mrs. Annesley.

Richard smiled and picking a bloom, handed it to her. She blushed and looked down.

"I miss certain friends, and perhaps the power of command, and I suppose the soldier's routine will always remain with me, but in truth I am glad to leave it behind. I needed to leave it behind." He hesitated and decided to chance opening to her. "It was not all glory and honour."

Mary lifted her eyes back to his. "I am certain it was not." She searched for something to say. "You did see the world, though."

Richard was relieved that she was not scared away, but realized she was still very young. "Hmm. Yes, and not always the pretty parts." He closed his eyes for a moment and felt a gentle pressure on his arm. He looked down in surprise and met her gaze.

"But you are safe now." She removed her hand. "Tell me of your brother."

"James?" He smiled. "Are you attracted to him?"

She stared. "Certainly not! I . . . you are teasing me!"

He laughed. "I am, but truly I can not think of any other reason for anyone to express interest in him."

"He is not so terrible! He seemed very pleasant when we met at Christmas." She admonished.

"Oh, I suppose not, but he is rather full of self-importance, the curse of his status, why do you ask of him?" Richard's head tilted and he studied her.

"Lizzy told me he was to find a bride this Season. I wondered if he . . . well how can you approach such an important decision unemotionally?" Her expression of confusion made him smile.

"Most people do, Mary." He said gently.

"I suppose that I have been spoiled watching Lizzy and Jane." She sighed then laughed. "Your aunt sent my cousin to Longbourn to find his bride and gave him an entire fortnight to do so."

"How generous of her! It only proves how foolish your cousin is, and how domineering is my aunt. Do you admire your sisters' methods?"

"Well Jane and Charles followed a traditional courtship, and Lizzy and William . . ."

He laughed. "Were an enormous exception to every rule." She remained quiet and he watched her. "What I admire most of Darcy and Elizabeth is that they were friends, good friends before it became love."

"Yes, I admit I was very confused at the assembly when they danced the first time, they seemed so close, and it was only after they were married that Lizzy told me about their letters . . ." She blushed.

"What do you think of their letters?"

She shot him a quick glance and looked down. "I would have been shocked if I had known at the time, but now . . . they are the happiest people despite everything."

"Indeed, of course they are both very unusual, but it only makes me admire them more." They walked along in silence for several minutes. He finally made a decision. "I return to my estate in a few days."

"Yes, Georgiana will miss her cousin, I think." She spoke softly and kept her gaze on the ground.

"And I will miss her . . ." He hesitated then plunged forward. "I will miss our conversations as well." Their eyes met. "Would you consider writing to me? I would like to continue our friendship, if you can bear the impropriety."

"I . . . I do not . . ." She saw his resigned acceptance of her refusal. "Why?"

His face brightened. "A fair question. I like you, and I would enjoy hearing from you, instead of waiting until our paths crossed again."

"I . . . I like you too, Richard." She bit her lip. "Well, I will be here at Pemberley all summer, so my parents would not know."

"And certainly your sister and Georgiana would not mind." He smiled and tilted his head at her.

"No." Mary thought of Elizabeth and the closeness she had always observed between her and Darcy. She looked up to him, and saw the hopeful expression that was directed solely at her, and decided to take the risk. "Yes Richard, I would welcome your letters."

Richard grinned. "Excellent! I will look forward to my post for a change, so much better than receiving the demands of my aunt!"

Mary smiled. "What does she ask of you?'

"Nothing of sense, I assure you!"

———∿∿∿———

Two weeks after their return from Rosings, Elizabeth stood in her study with her hands on her hips, staring at her husband in barely contained exasperation. "Are these men at least *friends* of yours?"

Darcy regarded her and said carefully, "Of course, I would not ask them to dinner otherwise. We need to discuss a very sensitive subject and could not do so at the club."

"What is so sensitive?"

"I am not at liberty to say."

She stared at him and he met her with a steady eye. "Will their wives be coming?"

"No." He bit his lip and spoke quickly. "I am used to inviting friends for dinner without thought." This time he could not meet her eye.

"Without thought is precisely how you have acted." He was behaving oddly and it was upsetting her. It was very unlike him to be deceitful with her; in fact, she had no memory of it happening before.

He closed his eyes then lifted his chin, twisting his neck, a sure sign of agitation and she saw it. "We are attempting to re-establish our place, these men are very influential, and seeing you . . ."

"Behaving charmingly?" His continued evasion raised her ire. They had decided weeks ago that they would not perform for the benefit of the *ton*. She waved her hand over the enormous pile of invitations and calling cards on her desk. "And am I to accommodate the rest of these people as well? I have spent hours answering letters to strangers today William, while you were away for an unexpectedly extended period. I was left alone to attempt to evaluate who is a friend and who is curious, I . . . Go. Just go, William. Go to your friends. I will

⌐ of dinner." She closed her eyes and bent her head, holding back the ⌐ughts that were bursting to spill out.

He did not move; his eyes showed his distress. "Lizzy . . ."

"Please go, William. We both have work to do."

Darcy took her stiff hand and kissed it, then pressed a kiss on her unwelcoming mouth. He did not like that feeling at all. "I am sorry, Lizzy." She nodded without looking at him, and he slowly turned to leave. He felt horrible; he had never lied to her before.

Elizabeth was already overwhelmed with the invitations which were pouring in, particularly since they had stopped attending events that put them on display, but now he was asking her to suddenly entertain strangers, charm them, and do it with no idea as to why. It was so unlike William to keep anything from her. She realized that made her angrier than the sudden guests. She felt as if he did not trust her, and it hurt, and she could not help but wonder if he was becoming like every other man, now that they had been married for almost five months.

Calling for Mrs. Hendricks, together they worked out a suitable menu, using the fare they had planned and expanding upon it as best as they could on short notice. Elizabeth apologized to her and asked her to speak the same to the cook. With time passing, she was able to put aside her ire and think about the situation. William had not really made an unreasonable demand of her, just unexpected and unusual, and she thought with a resigned sigh, poorly delivered. She decided that she needed to take a look at these so-called friends, and now fearing that something was very wrong, became worried for him. Determinedly she walked to his study door, and could hear the low rumble of men's voices within. She knocked and suddenly there was silence, followed by William's voice calling to enter.

She walked in and was taken aback by the scene. An older man sat with his head in his hands, two young men by his side, a fourth at the window. William stood near his desk, an expression of deep disgust and sorrow warring on his face, and his ribbon was twisted through the fingers of his left hand. Elizabeth's anger dissolved instantly seeing his obvious distress, this was not a meeting of a boy's club; it was a support group.

"Excuse me for interrupting, gentlemen." Elizabeth met her husband's intense gaze, and smiled at him. The relief her smile gave him was instantly expressed, and he strode to her side, claimed her hand and gratefully felt her squeeze.

"May I introduce you all to my wife, Elizabeth? Dearest, this is Edward, Howard, and Philip Fletcher, and their cousin Gregory Rhodes." The men all stood and bowed, murmuring their greetings.

"Please forgive our intrusion, Mrs. Darcy." Rhodes, the man at the window, said.

"Only if you forgive my interruption, I came to offer you refreshments before dinner, I am afraid it will be delayed a short while this evening." She smiled and tilted her head, reading the pained and anguished expressions on their faces, and felt William's hand still squeezing hers hard.

"No thank you, madam, I believe we will simply wait for what will certainly be a delicious repast." Said Rhodes; obviously acting as the spokesman for the family.

"Very well then, I will leave you all to your work." She looked up to William who had not stopped watching her.

"I will return in a moment, gentlemen." He led her out into the hallway and closed the door behind him. They stepped into the empty dining room and he immediately wrapped his arms around her. "Lizzy, I apologize, I do not know why you seem to have forgiven me, but I am grateful for it."

"I was angry because you would not tell me what was wrong. I could see you were not being truthful and darling, it does not sit well with you. It hurt me to be so treated, but then I realized that you would never behave that way without reason. And now seeing those men . . . William, what has happened, are they demanding something of you?"

"I did not mean to hurt you, believe me; I have no desire to be a man who orders around his wife. They wished to keep this as quiet as possible and when I asked to bring you into the room, they were incapable of understanding our marriage." He watched her eyes soften and they both relaxed. "Their sister ran away with a man, a militia soldier, and they have only just located her. Howard Fletcher is her father."

She gasped. "Oh dear heaven! What can be done?"

Darcy's cheek pressed against hers and he spoke softly in her ear. "They had wished to make them marry as they have not already."

"Has the soldier refused?"

"He has disappeared, much like Wickham did with every woman he defiled." He sighed and was silent for a moment. "They are asking me for advice, what I did for Georgiana. They would prefer to bring her home instead of finding someone to accept her. But she has three unmarried sisters at home, and their reputations would be destroyed if this all comes out. Honestly Lizzy, they should be talking to you. You had a greater hand in restoring Georgiana than me."

"No, my love, it was your decision to bring her home that gave her any chance at all, everything else we did together." She caressed his cheek and he kissed her palm. "I would be glad to speak with them if they are willing. I understand now why you could not tell me what was really wrong. Please forgive me for doubting you."

"They asked for silence, but I knew I would have to tell you. You read me too well." He kissed her hair, and held her tight. "I feel so much better telling you the truth. How do men keep secrets from their wives?" He looked down at her.

Elizabeth smiled and brushed the hair from his eyes. "The difference is that we both love and respect each other, Will."

His lips curved up. "Come, let us return to the room and offer your advice. It can not hurt."

Hand in hand they walked down the hall. "I can not imagine what our family would have done had this happened with one of my sisters."

Before opening the door, Darcy gently caressed her cheek. "Thank heaven we will never have to find out. Your father is keeping a close eye on all of his girls." She smiled and he let them in. Once again conversation stopped.

"Darcy, we do have much to discuss . . ." Rhodes looked at Elizabeth.

"Indeed, and my wife was instrumental in my sister's recovery. I believe that you will find her opinion to be invaluable, as I do." He smiled and still holding hands, they sat down together.

Howard Fletcher raised his head and regarded Elizabeth through his bleary gaze. "Mrs. Darcy, no woman should have to hear of such depravity, Darcy tried to convince us earlier to allow you entry. I assume that your husband has told you of our misfortune?"

Elizabeth decided that these men needed decisiveness, not coddling, and immediately set to work. "He has, sir, and I am sorry for your pain. I understand that your daughter is recovered?"

"Yes, she is in our London home. The rest of the family has remained in the country."

Her brow creased as she thought. "Is that normal? Would it cause more conjecture if the family strayed from their usual routine?"

Darcy immediately understood her. "My wife makes a good point, sir. It is fortunate that no neighbours are aware of your daughter's flight. You quickly explained her absence as a trip to town with her brothers."

"Yes, her come out is this summer, we were to buy her some more gowns." Mr. Fletcher's gaze sharpened watching the couple working together, then was overcome with a wave of anger. "Why would she do this now?" He pounded his fists on the table. He sighed. "Forgive me, Mrs. Darcy."

Elizabeth waved it off. "She was undoubtedly charmed by the man and poorly supervised by whoever had her charge, whether it was her parents or her governess. Also, you can not forget that she exercised her own free will." The men stared at her in surprise of her bluntness. Elizabeth continued, "Could she be with child?" Their eyes grew wider and they looked at Darcy, who flushed, but was nodding with her reasoning. She looked around the room. "Come now gentlemen, that is the crux of the matter and you know it. She can easily be returned home if she is not, but if the possibility exists, that limits your options, at least for now."

"She claims not." Mr. Fletcher said quietly, "But she may not be truthful in this. They were gone three days before we found her at an inn."

"I think that we must prepare for the worst, Father." Edward said softly.

"Do you have any other relatives she could visit for the summer? Far from your estate?" Darcy asked.

Rhodes nodded. "My parents live several counties away."

"Send her there, then. You will know within a few months the truth, and she could still have some of her Season if it is well for appearance's sake. If it is not, then she could remain there for her confinement. Then bring her home, if you wish, or find a man willing to marry her." Darcy continued in his quiet voice, "I considered these possibilities when I was searching for my sister."

"What of the child?"

"You would be responsible for finding a suitable home and supporting him until adulthood; that is if you are a gentleman." Darcy met his eye and held it.

"This is difficult to hear. This would be my grandchild." Mr. Fletcher said softly.

"Surely you did not come to my husband and expect an easy answer, sir?" Elizabeth scanned the room. "You should be prepared for a long recovery for your daughter. I do not know her temperament, but if she was shy before she could become more withdrawn, if she was bold, this may temper her. In either case, will she realize her error? That I believe is the key to her improvement, and accepting that is the key to yours." She looked up at Darcy who smiled.

"Yes, it took me a great while to accept that I was not entirely to blame." He kissed her hand. "I think that we will leave you now to discuss this in privacy." Darcy stood along with Elizabeth and they left the room.

"What do you think? Will they listen?" She said as they made their way to the library.

He shook his head. "It depends. Her brothers are full of blood lust and speak only of killing the man. Her cousin though, he is not as directly involved and has a clearer head. Hopefully he will be able to cut through her father's guilt." They took a seat on a sofa and he drew her to his side. "Why do I have a feeling that this will not be the last time that a family comes to us in search of such advice?"

"I hate to think that it would be needed by anyone again, but if Georgiana is a success, and we are seen as a successful couple, I believe you are correct, it may happen again." Elizabeth reached up and gently kissed him and he warmly responded.

"That is better." He sighed against her cheek. "I did not like that angry kiss at all."

"Then you are wise to avoid inspiring my ire." She whispered.

"Forgive me."

"I already have. Trust me."

"I do, my love. I would have told you, you know I would."

A servant knocked and they were summoned back to the study. Mr. Fletcher stood. "Mr. and Mrs. Darcy, thank you for your time and forbearance. We have decided to take your advice and remove my daughter to her aunt's home until we can be certain of the outcome. In the meantime, our family will join us here." He sighed and looked at his hands. "We will wait and see what our next course is. In the meantime, we feel that we have trespassed on your hospitality for far too long and will remove ourselves from your home."

"Sir, please, you are welcome to stay for dinner!" Elizabeth assured him.

"No, Mrs. Darcy, we will leave you in peace." He looked at the couple and smiled. "I am very happy for you. The rumours of your marriage were claiming a country upstart had captured Darcy for his fortune. I beg to disagree. I have never seen such a relationship in a marriage, and can not pretend to understand it."

Rhodes looked them over with speculation. "Perhaps poetry is not drivel. Perhaps it is true that a lady can capture a man's heart." Darcy smiled and Elizabeth blushed. He shook Darcy's hand and bowed to Elizabeth, as the other men did the same. Soon they were gone, and Elizabeth noticed Mrs. Hendricks watching their departure.

"Please tell cook it will just be the two of us tonight; and please apologize again." Mrs. Hendricks pressed her lips together and disappeared downstairs. Elizabeth took William's hand and they walked back to her study where he regarded the piles of invitations.

"Lizzy, what do you say to just declining all of the invitations?"

"All of them? Even from friends?"

"We have visited with everyone who are truly our friends, and today's experience confirms that if there is somebody else who wishes our friendship, they will seek us out. I think that it is very safe to say that these invitations and calling cards are from those who wish to get a look at us, or desire a connection. Let this time be for our benefit, which means not wasting yours by writing letters. We will be here another fortnight, we will spend time with our families and enjoy what else London has to offer."

"Oh Will, I love that idea!" Elizabeth threw her arms around him and hugged him fiercely. Darcy chuckled and picked up the stack of calling cards and gleefully dropped them in the fire. He began to do the same with the invitations and she stopped him. "Wait, I will answer those properly." He was disappointed but set them down. "It is wise not to burn bridges, my love. A simple note of refusal is no trouble."

"As you wish, my love."

Chapter 39

*J*ohn rode beside the fence that separated Netherfield and Longbourn, unconsciously moving towards the stile. It took him by surprise to see the man sitting on the steps, staring off towards the hills that hid Netherfield. "Mr. Bennet, good morning." John said and brought his horse to a halt.

"Lucas." Mr. Bennet blinked and smiled. "Not watching the planting this morning? I am surprised."

"I could say the same to you, sir." John smiled and dismounted, and holding the reins he moved forward, glancing at the initials carved into the wood as he walked.

Mr. Bennet noticed. "I leave it to my steward; I have never really been a very hands-on landowner, which has been to my and my family's detriment. Do not follow my example." John met his eye. "But I believe that you have made enormous strides in that direction. You are already a much more accomplished gentleman than I or your father have been."

"My father was not born to this, I was." He said softly, glancing again at the stile.

"You do not regret her still, do you?" Mr. Bennet asked, tilting his head. John's surprised expression made him smile. "Let me tell you a story. I was very much in love with a young lady. She said that she loved me, but when my sister was ruined . . . you know that story now, I suppose?" John nodded and looked down. "Well, I lost her." He grew silent for a moment. "Maria, her name was Maria, just like your sister. My Mary was named for her, not that my wife knows." He sighed. "I spent all of my marriage, until these last few months, comparing my wife to her. It was a waste of a potential felicity. I have fortunately recognized my error and we have begun to repair the damage that years of neglect have wrought upon us. It is not easy." Looking back at John he met his gaze. "Do not make my mistake, Lucas. When you find the woman you will marry, put all others from your mind. Do not compare your wife to another." He glanced at the initials then back at his companion.

"That is an important lesson, and one that I am grateful to hear second hand and not have to experience myself. I do not know that I regret Mrs. Darcy now so much as I regret my behaviour that ruined what might have been. I know that I can not spend my life dwelling on what will never be." He drew a breath. "She made a man of me."

Mr. Bennet laughed, and John's brow creased. "Forgive me, but it seems that she made a boy of Darcy." He glanced again at the carving and John smiled, both knowing that Darcy was more of a man than either one of them ever would be.

"And what has he done for her?"

"Ah, he gave her the respect and love that she deserves." Mr. Bennet smiled. John nodded and looked down. "My son Bingley is giving up the lease on Netherfield. He will search for a home near Pemberley."

John shook his head. "I once told Mrs. Darcy that she would be better with me because she would remain near to her sister. It seems that argument is proving wrong as well." He smiled and met Mr. Bennet's amused eyes. "Well, perhaps the next lease holder will have a lovely daughter for me to court."

Nodding, Mr. Bennet stood up. "Perhaps that will be so. I am glad to see your willingness to move on; you have made great strides in the neighbourhood. I think that you will be a fixture in the area, just as your father has been."

Rolling his eyes, he laughed. "Well, thank you for the vote of confidence, sir." He turned and mounted his horse and looked again at the stile, then to Mr. Bennet. "I have to get back to my fields; I have an estate to run. I enjoyed our conversation, thank you."

Mr. Bennet watched him gallop off and looked at the stile once again. "Well done, Darcy and Lizzy."

"There you are." Darcy rose from his crouched position in front of the lake. He had been wiping his sweaty face with a dampened handkerchief and upon hearing the familiar voice, turned and saw Richard galloping towards him. "You have been working hard at your duties, I see." Dismounting, he strode forward and clasped Darcy's hand.

"I believe that you should be doing the same, what brings you here? Have you forgotten your new position?" Darcy grinned and clapped his back.

"My estate takes a fraction of the time to prepare that yours does, being a fraction of the size." Richard's face was glowing with good humour and he looked around him. "I am overwhelmed Darcy, how do you do it?"

"I have a great deal of help, and have hired excellent people to aid me. I am not afraid to delegate duties, either."

"Delegate? You?" Richard looked at him askance. "I know you, Darcy; you have an iron grip on every aspect of this operation. I doubt that even your enticing bride can pull you away from your duties."

Darcy's brow rose at his description of Elizabeth, but let it pass. "I am firmly in charge, I assure you. However, yes, my Elizabeth is most capable of making me change my ways. I . . . I no longer *want* to be lost in the work, it is time to live." He smiled and tilted his head. "I have help from my wife as well."

"What does she do, rub your temples and bring you libations?" He laughed, then saw Darcy shake his head.

"You truly do not understand our love, do you? Well, I will attempt to explain a bit of it. A fortnight after we returned from London, I came into the house after spending a morning out with my steward, and anticipating a long afternoon with my paperwork. I walked into the study to find Elizabeth sitting behind my desk, opening the business letters and sorting them into categories of importance. She was organizing the correspondence for me, saving me the time it would take to read and do so myself, and even pointing out the ones that seemed especially urgent."

"She was acting as your secretary?" Richard stared at him in amazement. "But what of your personal letters?"

"Those were unopened. She knows well-enough who my friends are, and she has spent enough time watching me answer correspondence, and well, listening to me tell her all of my business that she knew who everyone was. Any return that she did not recognize she left unopened. It was truly gratifying." He smiled at his cousin's confused expression. "I had always hoped, even back to last summer when I was just dreaming of marrying her, that she would wish to be my partner, and here it has come true. I admit that I thought she was simply humouring me at first, listening with seeming interest to my ramblings and rages, but once again she has proven me wrong in my assumptions. She does care, and she has a great talent for it. She told me that she hoped to help me in this way, only she needed to learn her duties as mistress first."

"You heap praise upon her, but do you recognize the unusual behaviour in yourself? I know of no man who would include his wife in such things, regardless of whether she were interested or capable of understanding. My mother certainly knows nothing of Matlock, it would be unthinkable of my father to speak of such to her, just as she would not share the household accounts with him."

"I did it all alone. It does not intimidate me in the least to share the burden with Elizabeth, and frankly, it is what I wished for all along. By helping me, we have more time for each other." Darcy laughed and taking the reins of his horse the cousins began walking to the stables. "Do not follow our example Richard, we have rejected so many conventions of our peers, I imagine we will continue to amaze and intrigue, and doubtless inspire wagging tongues forever, but we are happy, and that is what matters. You must find your own path to happiness."

"That is what brings me here today." Darcy raised his brows, and Richard cleared his throat. "I understand that Mr. Bennet has given you leave to look after Mary's interests while she remains in your care."

"He has."

"Ahem, well, I . . . I have decided that . . . I have decided that I wish to ask for a courtship." He glanced at Darcy who was smiling slightly and staring at him. "Well SAY something!"

"What would you like to hear?"

"Your blessing would be a welcome beginning." Richard said in frustration.

"Have you spoken to her? You have only been corresponding for three months, after all . . ." Darcy was fighting his smile.

"Yes, I spoke to her when I arrived, and she said yes, and I seem to recall that you PROPOSED to Elizabeth MOMENTS after seeing her in person after only THREE MONTHS of clandestine correspondence, and furthermore, I have at least KNOWN Mary since last fall; and . . ."

Darcy held up his hand and stopped walking. "You do have it bad, Cousin! I am simply toying with you. Of course you have my blessing. I will be proud to someday call you brother." He laughed seeing Richard's fighting stance relax.

"That was bad form, Darcy."

"I said very little, you jumped to the defence rather quickly." Darcy tilted his head and they began walking again. "How is that temper coming along? It will not do to frighten your tenants too often, nor may I add, your wife. If you do anything to upset my sister . . ."

Richard blew out a long breath and smiled at his cousin's willingness to fight him. "I find that reading one of Mary's letters instantly restores my good humour. I imagine that actually living with her will do wonders for my temperament."

"Well, she does know a great many sermons. . ." Darcy relaxed with a grin and Richard laughed. They gave over the horses to the stable hands and walked to the house. Elizabeth met them at the door and gave William an enquiring look. He kissed her hand and smiled. "It seems we must begin chaperoning duties, my love."

Elizabeth looked over to Richard whose face fell. "I think that you and I benefited from our lax chaperones William, perhaps we can extend the favour to Mary and Richard."

"Hmmmm." Darcy considered him.

"Darcy . . ." Richard growled.

"I will think it over." He gave Elizabeth a wink and walked up the stairs to change clothes, with Richard hard on his heels and arguing steadily his case. She laughed and returned to the sitting room where her two sisters sat together.

"Well?" Mary asked nervously.

"Of course William said yes Mary, he is just torturing Richard now." Mary sighed in relief and Georgiana gripped her hand, bouncing excitedly.

"When will you marry?"

"For heaven's sake, Georgiana, they have only begun the courtship!" Elizabeth admonished.

"Oh, you and William skipped all of that, why not Mary? Besides, she is to return to Longbourn in two months, would it not make sense to have the wedding before then and she could simply move to Onnoroil from here?"

"Mama would not be pleased to miss hosting a wedding." Mary said, blushing and looking down at her hands. "Listen to me, he has not even proposed and we are making these plans!" She looked up at Elizabeth, "I must go and lie down; I am so flustered!" She quickly left the room and Elizabeth and Georgiana sat looking after her in amusement.

"I am happy for her; she would be so excited when a letter would come. I am glad to be able to see them together now; she stopped telling me what he said. Now I can watch!" Georgiana said with a sparkle of mischief in her eye.

"I did show Jane all of mine, well, until your brother's thoughts became much more . . . personal." Georgiana giggled. "He is a very romantic man." Elizabeth added with a soft smile.

"You do not have to convince me of that! I can not help but see you two!" Georgiana laughed at her blush. "Do you hope for children soon?" She saw her sister's look of surprise and laughed again. "I am not so naïve; I was taught what would bring a child." Elizabeth wondered how much she really understood, and thought she would have to explore the subject sometime.

"We hope to be blessed with many children, but they will come in their own time."

"I think that William will be happy to be a father, he is so changed from how he was only a year ago." Georgiana's excited expression clouded over.

Elizabeth gripped her hand, seeing a memory intruding, the anniversary of her flight with Wickham was approaching. "He will be happy; I am sure of it, and frightened, too." Georgiana was distracted from her memory with Elizabeth's statement.

"He fears being like Papa." She said perceptively.

Elizabeth nodded. "That, and many other things, I will simply have to reassure him!" She smiled and laughed at Georgiana's rolling eyes. "What does that mean, young lady?"

"I know what your reassuring him will entail; I might as well go and plan another afternoon alone with Mrs. Annesley, because we will certainly not be seeing you two!"

"Georgiana!"

"Oh, I was blind to you disappearing all of the time before, but not any more!" She giggled and stood, then spun around. "Lizzy loves Will!" She sang and ran out of the room, leaving her sister behind to ponder the education Georgiana was gaining.

—⁓—

"Ahem." Darcy cleared his throat and watched Mary's blush and Richard's posture straighten. He looked over to Elizabeth who reached under the table and pinched him. "Ow!"

"Leave them be!" She whispered.

"What did I say?" He smiled at her pursed lips. "I am acting in place of your father, dearest. How many times were we admonished at the table?"

Elizabeth relaxed and laughed. "Well, if that is your purpose, I suppose that I can tolerate some correction." She looked over to Mary and Richard and shook her head. "But it seems that any words from you will have a very short effect."

He took her hand and kissed it. "I believe that your father's had none on us, either." Raising his voice he startled the couple. "What news have you of your brother, Richard? The last I heard he may have made a selection from the debutantes?"

"Oh, yes, James." Richard tore his eyes from Mary and blushed with his inattention to the company. "Indeed he has, I believe, chosen a lady from the crowd. I have not met her, but of course, Mother and Father have, and they like her. She is two and twenty, not a child, and I think that is a good decision on his part. He is only a year older than me, but he needs a mature woman, not a girl."

"Then what does that make me, Richard?" Mary asked softly, smiling at him.

"You, my dear, have more maturity in your little finger than most debutantes have in their entire bodies. Their intelligence is lost in their hair. You have spent your time far more productively with your books, and were not distracted by frivolities; it is one of the qualities that I admire greatly in you." He raised her hand to his lips and bestowed a kiss, as Mary blushed furiously.

"So tell us of this girl, what is her name?"

Richard returned his hand to begin eating again and looked up at Georgiana. "Her name is Rebecca Farnesworth, yes one of *those* Farnesworths." He saw Darcy's eyes close and then looked to Elizabeth. "They include several sisters who chased Darcy quite determinedly last spring. Fortunately Rebecca was not one of them. I suppose you will have to meet the others, still unmarried by the way, at the wedding. She has turned down many a good offer, and was quite worrying her mother, but it seems she and James met at St. James' and, well, they were instantly attracted, or enough to decide to begin paying calls; and it has proceeded from there. I expect the wedding will take place in August, just at the end of the Season, at her parent's estate in Devonshire. Of course you will be invited." He glanced up at Darcy, whose brows were knit, then at Elizabeth who was biting her lip. "Is something wrong?"

"That is the height of the harvest, Richard, I should not be away. James was not at our wedding, well hardly anyone was, but I am not sure that we can be travelling then." He looked to Elizabeth whose countenance had been restored. "What do you think, dearest?"

"You know what your responsibilities entail William, this is my first harvest here." He smiled and nodded.

"I look forward to having you by my side." He squeezed her hand and she smiled.

"There they go again. Between them and now Richard and Mary, I believe that I will be invisible soon!" Georgiana observed.

"Not at all cousin! I propose that you impress us all with your playing, and we," Richard again kissed Mary's hand, "may dance!"

"Are you willing, Georgiana?" Elizabeth asked.

"If I might have a dance with my brother and my cousin in trade." She bargained.

"Well done, Georgiana!" Richard applauded. "I agree, and I am sure that your amorous brother will be delighted to acquiesce."

"I am, and I thank you." Darcy stood. "Shall we retire to the music room?" The remainder of the evening was spent in happy company. Surprisingly it was Elizabeth who ended the frivolity, begging for sleep after a tiring day. Darcy saw that Richard desired a private farewell for Mary, and giving him a stern look, which was promptly ignored, he escorted his wife and sister upstairs to retire.

Richard turned to Mary, who had blushed crimson and sat back down at the pianoforte. He walked over and took a seat by her side, and watched her fingers touching the keys. He placed his right hand over hers, silencing the instrument, then drawing her to him with his left, he looked down into her lifted face, and smiled softly into her warm, gently sparkling eyes. "You are trembling."

"I . . . I do not know what I am supposed to do." She said nervously.

"Close your eyes." He whispered. "Let me teach you."

Gathering up the papers scattered over his desk, Darcy neatly arranged them in a pile and handed it to Mr. Barkley, thanked him, and watched as he left the study, closing the door behind him. He settled back in his chair and a small smile appeared. "Well Douglass, I am glad to have had the opportunity to speak with you today, but surely this business could just as easily have been addressed through a letter. Was this a special trip? I know that you are taking over the brewery and your father has kept the duties of visiting the taverns."

Marshall shook his head and met Darcy's eye. "Why do I feel like a schoolboy waiting to be rapped on the knuckles?"

Darcy's brows rose in amusement. "Your troubles are that difficult?"

"Mr. Darcy, you were once my age . . ."

"I am eight and twenty; please to not paint me as a man with one foot in the grave, and please, we are family, you may address me as Darcy."

Flushing with embarrassment he nodded. "Thank you, sir. I meant to say that you probably faced the attentions of eager mamas and daughters at one time, and you would understand how overwhelming it is."

"Ah, you do not enjoy the attention you receive?" Darcy smiled.

"I know it is not of the same circle as yours, but I expect there is a similarity in the experience." Darcy nodded his understanding. "My father never experienced this so where he offers excellent advice in other arenas, in this I am on my own, perhaps even more alone due to his enthusiasm for me." He paused and sighed. "Sir, could you offer some advice?"

Smiling wider, Darcy laughed. "Why me?"

"You obviously resisted the fray for years, and I observed your happiness with my cousin. I have the example of a happy marriage in my parents, I want that for myself. You could tell me what to do."

"Well, that is quite a gratifying compliment." Darcy considered the young man. "Are you in a hurry to marry?"

"No, I wish to work and concentrate solely on the brewery for another year or so, but I do not wish to live in seclusion either."

Darcy considered his words. "I was, and in many ways remain, a recluse. Obviously I am vastly different from you in that aspect. You can attend the balls and parties and enjoy yourself. You are a social being, how can you not be with such a gregarious father and pleasant mother? My advice would be to simply be sure not to give attention to any lady in particular. Dance only once with each, and for other needs, keep it to a reputable establishment. Surely you are aware of any behaviour that would be deemed as a compromise and you will avoid such. Keep yourself under good regulation. I might note though that a day may arrive when you do find the woman you love, and you will have to consider your past behaviour and if you will regret it, and further, if you will confess it to her."

Marshall's eyes grew wide. "Did you?"

"That is a subject between me and my wife." Darcy was not smiling.

"Forgive me, sir." Marshall said hurriedly.

Darcy relaxed. "Is there anything else?"

Biting his lip he asked, "How is Miss Darcy getting on? Mother has shown me her letters from Elizabeth. Is she recovered?"

He regarded the young man appraisingly. "You know the whole story now?" Marshall nodded. "She is improved. Mary has been here since February and was a good companion and friend during that time, however, when we returned at the end of April, she clung to Elizabeth, and it seemed what progress she had made was erased. Elizabeth said it reminded her of her nieces and nephews when their parents would return from a trip. She refused to tolerate the reversal, and made it clear over the past month that she expected growth, not stagnation from Georgiana." He laughed quietly. "Elizabeth has a strength about her . . . well; in any case, I would say that Georgiana is well on her way to recovery. Elizabeth will accept nothing less, and Georgiana has risen to the challenge. The transformation has been breathtaking. As you can probably tell, I admire my wife's ability a great deal, after all, I can testify to her improvements to myself." He smiled, thinking of his wife's love. He remembered his guest and met his fascinated gaze. "We will not be leaving Pemberley again until next spring, so Georgiana will have a great deal of uninterrupted time in the company of her sister. She will likely be a far more confident person in a year's time."

"She will be seventeen then?"

"Yes, she recently celebrated her sixteenth birthday, but we will probably delay her come out until the following year. We are hoping for the *ton* to have moved on to greener pastures by then. Now, why are you interested, this is more than a polite inquiry, I assume?"

Marshall twisted his hands and looked down. "I like her. I enjoyed our time at Christmas. She seems so fragile, like a delicate flower . . ."

"A delicate flower is pleasant to observe, but do you truly wish to live with one?" Marshall's brows knit. "I do not wish to discourage you, but she needs time to come into her own, and knowing her as I do, I realize that she will never be the strong woman my Elizabeth is, but she will undoubtedly be far more than she ever would have been without her. I suspect she will likely end like your cousin Jane. If you are going out to experience society, do not hold back in anticipation of Georgiana's entrance. You do not know her well enough to limit your social life. Perhaps in a year, with this misery behind her somewhat, that will be the time to come courting. And do not use the idea of perhaps winning Georgiana as a way to avoid the demands of society. You must face that regardless, it is an important learning experience, and one that will give you a sound basis for deciding if, in fact, your interest does belong with my sister. For now, be a friend. If you have not found someone by then and remain interested, I will not discourage you."

"I suppose I was a bit premature in my hopes." He could not hide his disappointment.

"Perhaps, but as neither of you are in a hurry . . . well, it is not necessary to discuss this further. I hope that you are free to visit with us for awhile. You are very welcome to stay." Darcy raised his brows and smiled.

Marshall relaxed. "I would like that, thank you."

"I believe that Mary, Richard, and Georgiana are at the stables. I am sure that they would welcome your company." The men stood and Darcy led the way out of the study. Mrs. Reynolds had already prepared a room for Marshall at Elizabeth's direction and the surprised young man was led away to change his clothes.

Darcy laughed softly watching him go, thinking that Elizabeth had no doubt of this alliance someday taking place, and was not about to discourage it. He walked the short distance down the hallway to her boudoir. She was bent over the desk, a quill trapped in her teeth as she read over a letter. The windows were wide open and a warm breeze drifted in, gently blowing the curtains. Darcy stood behind her and rested one hand on her shoulder, and entwined the other in the curls at her nape. Elizabeth looked up and saw his eyes focussed on the view, watching the gardeners tending the newly planted lavender border. A serene expression was on his face, and she smiled, continuing her letter, and leaned into his gently caressing fingers. Darcy did not speak, he simply enjoyed touching her and waited for her to finish. When the letter was at last folded and sealed, he leaned down and kissed her. "May I steal you away now, dearest?"

"Where will you take me?" She asked, rising to her feet and holding both of his hands. She smiled seeing the glee in his eyes.

"Why, on an adventure, of course!" Grinning, he squeezed her hand and escorted her out of the house towards the stables. "Douglass asked me for advice on love."

Elizabeth laughed. "So that is to be our lot is it? We shall advise on all spectrums of love. Well, at least it was not another family with a ruined daughter. Did he enquire after Georgiana?"

Darcy tilted his head and his eyes twinkled. "How do you know his feelings?"

"Well, I saw how he looked at her; it reminded me of someone I know."

Darcy stopped their walk and bent to kiss her. "You are very perceptive, my love." Elizabeth caressed his cheek and they continued on. "Do you know her feelings?"

"She thinks him very handsome, but she is not ready . . ."

"That is what I told him, and I said not to wait." He sighed. "He is precisely the type of man I would hope for her." Elizabeth's hand squeezed his and they exchanged resigned smiles. It would have to wait a little longer.

They arrived at the stables to see Mary and Georgiana laughing while Marshall regaled them with some story of his travels. Richard stood with his arms folded, looking at the young man speculatively. Again Elizabeth squeezed William's hand. "Friends first, correct?"

"It certainly worked for us." He smiled and kissed her hand.

Approaching the group, Darcy laughed. "Richard is acting as a guard dog."

"He suspects Marshall's feelings?" Elizabeth asked.

"Well they are obvious to us, why not Richard? He has a heightened sense of how romance appears, now that he is embroiled in it himself."

They arrived and Elizabeth said to Mary, "I thought that you were hoping to show Richard the new foals in the pasture. Why not take a walk over?"

"Oh, I was not sure if Georgiana and Marshall would wish to come . . ." She looked at Richard who was beaming at Elizabeth's suggestion.

"No, I am sure that they are not at all interested." He said instantly, and stepped up to Mary's side. Darcy smirked.

Georgiana saw the hopeful expression on the couple's faces and spoke up. "Mr. Douglass and I will just have to get on without you." She then looked quickly at Darcy. "Is that all right, Brother?"

"You will keep to the stables or the house?" He said sternly, directing his gaze to Marshall.

"Yes, sir." Marshall answered. "We will not stray. I am enjoying talking with Miss Darcy. We have discovered a similar sense of humour, have we not?"

Giggling a little nervously she blushed and glanced at him then at Elizabeth. "Yes, it is far more entertaining than Richard, he teases too much."

"Well, he knows you better, Georgiana. If you and Marshall become good friends, you may have to refine your assessment of his worthiness as a companion." Elizabeth smiled.

"Oh I think that I will continue to like him." Her eyes grew wide and she blushed. "Forgive me, I did not mean to imply . . ."

"It is quite all right, Miss Darcy, I will own to liking you, too." Marshall smiled warmly and she looked back up at him, her confidence restored. Darcy felt Elizabeth's hand squeezing his again and with a tug, she told him it was safe to go.

"Very well then, enjoy your visit." He smiled and decided to get in a dig. "Perhaps my sister would enjoy your tales of pursuit by the matchmaking mamas?" Marshall shook his head and Elizabeth laughed while Georgiana looked at him expectantly.

"Remind me not to tell your brother any secrets again."

The couple continued to the stables and were met by Danny. "Sir! I will have Benedick and Beatrice brought out right away!" He went inside and ordered the grooms to fetch the two animals. Darcy leaned against the paddock fence and pulled Elizabeth to rest her back against his chest, and loosely wrapped his arms around her waist.

"He seems to have made the transition to his new position quite readily." He observed. "I was afraid that he would feel constrained after so many years of essentially being his own man, and not answering to anyone but me."

"I think that he sees the opportunity and appreciates the chance to perhaps establish a home and have a family. Besides, Mr. Greeley is getting old, and will wish to turn over the responsibilities to a younger man in a few years. By then Danny will surely be well trained to take over. And Susie will be wishing to start her own family."

Darcy laughed and kissed her cheek. "Greeley will always be hanging about the yard, dispensing advice whether wanted or not, but that is not a bad thing. I am happy to do this for Danny."

The horses arrived and Darcy gave Elizabeth a leg up to her mount and seeing her seated, leapt up onto his favourite stallion. The grooms had attached the saddlebags filled with their picnicking supplies and with a nod, they set off. He grinned over to her. "Where shall we go?"

"This is your adventure, Will. You tell me." She smiled and kicking her horse picked up the pace and rode in front of him. Darcy watched with appreciation as her bottom bounced slightly on the saddle and began to consider where they would have the most privacy. Nodding his head he caught up with her and took a slight lead. They rode for over an hour, still well within the boundaries of Pemberley's park, steadily climbing through pasture and meadows, up steep paths and through the walnut groves, until finally they arrived at a seeming dead end. "Where do we go now?" Elizabeth asked, knitting her brow. Darcy jumped down, and following his lead, she did as well.

"Tie off your reins here." He pointed to a tree on the edge of a grassy area. Taking the saddle bags, he offered his hand, and led her around a boulder on a very faint trail, and suddenly they appeared on a grassy outcrop high above the valley, and below them spread a perfect view of Pemberley House, the lake, the gardens, and some of the outbuildings that were not hidden by the tall trees.

"Oh, William!" Elizabeth turned and beamed. "What a beautiful place!"

Darcy scanned the beauty before them. "I spied this spot from the valley below when I was a lad. It took many attempts before I finally discovered my way. I spent countless hours here with my books and thoughts."

She looked back at the prospect. "If you could convince an artist to sit here, would this not make a magnificent landscape to hang in your study, or better yet, in mine?"

Laughing, he took her hand and pulled her against his chest, untied her bonnet and tossed it on the ground. He rested his cheek on her hair. "Why would it be better in your study?"

"Why because I could sit and look upon it and remember what happened here while taking in the view." She gazed up at him and then turned in his arms.

"What exactly happened here, my love?" Darcy whispered. Elizabeth stood on her toes and held his face in her hands, kissing him softly and slowly. His eyes closed and he moaned. "Ohhhh." Darcy's hand rose to entwine in her long curls, and the other pulled her waist firmly against him. Gently his tongue met hers and caressed it, drawing her into his mouth, heightening their pleasure, while his arms wrapped around her body and held her so firmly to his. It was heaven and they had just begun. Darcy's hand drifted down to cup her bottom and tenderly ran over the tempting, rounded curves. Elizabeth's hands at last moved to deftly untie his cravat, pulling it loose and without breaking the motion of their stroking mouths, tossed it to the ground. Her hands managed to slide between them and worked open the buttons of his coat; as her searching lips finally broke free of his mouth and brushed down to taste his deliciously exposed neck. "Ohhhhh yes, Lizzy!" He moaned, loving her suckling him there. The buttons free, she pushed his coat and waistcoat off of his shoulders and they dropped to the grass below, and immediately she began pulling his shirt free from his breeches, slipping her hands under the loose fabric and touching his warm skin, then up to caress the thatch of hair on his chest and tease the hard flat nipples. Darcy shivered with the touch, and let go of her long enough to rip off his shirt and pull her back against his skin. Immediately Elizabeth began suckling and nipping the small puckered circles and he moaned, whispering in her ear. The hands continued their work, drifting between them again, to now open the breeches, and slid them over his hips. He stopped her advances by clasping her tightly and tilting her head back, taking possession of her throat, suckling and kissing her aggressively, feeling her tremble and hearing the moan he adored. His fingers set to work now, and quickly he opened the buttons on her gown and pushed it down her shoulders to form a billowing pink cloud as it descended to the grass below. The palm of his hand rested over one of her breasts, and the fingers had barely touched her nipple when she moaned. Tweaking the tight bud, he drew away from her reddened neck and looked, admiring the way her breast spilled over the palm of his hand. "You wore no stays. Thank you, my love." He bent to kiss the beautiful mounds, while rubbing her body up and down.

Breathing heavily they paused, and Darcy quickly reached for a saddle bag, removed a blanket, unfurled it and taking her hand pulled her down onto the ground. Immediately he drew her nearly nude body to his and began to renew his attentions to her breasts. Elizabeth's fingers were entwined in his hair, and she was quaking with the feel of his tongue tasting her, drinking from her deeply, while one hand drifted between her legs and into her folds, rubbing, stroking, fondling relentlessly to bring her to the brink of ecstasy. "Do not stop, oh please do not stop!" She cried. Darcy's fingers lowered and he plunged them inside her wet ring, and withdrew. The eyes that had bewitched him from the first moment of their lives together begged him to continue. Smiling, he rose and kissed her lips, then moved to quickly pull off his boots and the rest of his clothes, removing her boots and stockings just as quickly.

Darcy hovered over her. "What would you like, my love?"

"You." She reached up to his face, and stroked his cheek, then lowered her hand to caress the arousal that rested on her belly. "I want this, inside of me, please William; do not make me wait."

"Kiss me first." He looked at her with intense desire. "Please Lizzy, please kiss me."

"Come." Motioning him forward, he moved so that his erection rested on her lips. He groaned as her tongue appeared to taste him. Slowly he entered, watching as he moved in and out of her warm welcoming mouth, the reddened swollen lips swallowing him. "Oh Lizzy, oh I love watching you take me." Her eyes opened and her hands drew his bottom closer. She could not take all of him, but she tried, and her tongue swirled over him as she brought him such pleasure. Trembling, he withdrew and moved back, regaining his control. Darcy bent and rewarded her with his passionate kiss to her heated lips. "Thank you, dearest, now it is your turn."

He kissed his way down to her thighs and began suckling her pearl the same way she had just loved him. It took but a moment and her back was arched, her body rippling and the sound of her gasping moan filled him with pride. He lifted his wet face from her curls and smiled to see the expression of ecstasy. Now he was ready to love her and spreading her legs wide, joyously penetrated her nest. Elizabeth's eyes flew open and she gasped. "More darling?" He asked, pausing for the moment.

"Yes, please, more." Panting he wrapped her legs around his waist and began thrusting vigorously, pounding her slick tunnel, her wetness becoming a froth with the power and speed of his delivery. His arms straddled her and his eyes drank in the vision below, as her breasts rolled and swayed with his frenzied movement. Their moans echoed off of the surrounding rocks, filling the valley below with the sound of their lovemaking. Darcy rode her, giving her everything he had, and she met his hips, stroke for stroke, holding on to his muscular arms and staring up into his eyes. The words he spoke told her everything of his love. This was the moment when he was completely free, when he could tell her his deepest feelings. Elizabeth knew this and waited for it, lived for his declarations and never closed her eyes. She wanted him to know that he was heard. Watching his face she saw his jaw shaking, his body trembled and he was hanging on, waiting for her. When at last her eyes closed and he felt her clasp and milk him, he let go with a shout and released his seed deep inside, finally collapsing onto her and then moving to his side to hold her tightly, their bodies still joined, as they slowly recovered.

Darcy kissed her hair and took a long breath. "Lizzybeth, I can not possibly explain how much I love you." He swallowed with emotion and nuzzled his face against hers. "How does it get better every time?"

Elizabeth calmed and kissed his ear, "I love you Will, and I think it gets better because we want it to, my desire is to bring you pleasure, and yours is to love me just the same. How could we fail with such goals?"

"Promise me we will endeavour to always be this way." He finally withdrew his softened root from her and lay by her side. "I hope so much that forty . . . fifty years from now we will be just as caring for each other."

"You will not be tired of me by then? The same woman for so long?" Her eyes danced and she stroked the damp hair back from his brow. "Perhaps we will not be quite so vigorous then."

"I think that we are quite accomplished at loving in slow methods as well, dearest. And no, I will not be tired of you. I believe that you and I have very active imaginations, and we will undoubtedly think of unending adventures to make our encounters fresh . . . but right now, everything is new. I never had any expectation of ever making love outdoors. What would society say of such a thing?" He grinned.

"Well, I believe that we have quite firmly established what our opinion of society is. Let them have their separate bedrooms and joining only in the dark and with their nightwear in place. Let them lie still and derive no pleasure. We know better." Elizabeth smiled up to his twinkling eyes. "You know, I especially enjoy loving you after we have had an argument. It is so much better than my mother's method of hiding in her room in a snit."

Darcy laughed. "Perhaps we should argue more often, then!"

"No, we will argue only on special occasions. It is hard to disagree with you too often, I am afraid that I am rather susceptible to your charms, even when angry." She hugged him tightly.

"I will use that to my advantage, you know." He murmured into her ear. She giggled and he sighed happily. His head rested on the pillow of her breast. Elizabeth shifted and she moaned quietly. Lifting his face his brow furrowed. "Is something wrong?"

"I am just a little tender there, sweetheart."

"Was I too rough with you? I am sorry." He looked at her with concern then gently caressed her, again seeing how her breast spilled over his palm. Stopping he looked to her. "Lizzy . . ." He watched her face, she was biting her lip. Slowly his eyes drifted down her body and rested on her belly. His caressing hand moved to rest over the swelling that had not been noticed before. He heard a sigh. Trembling, his hands cupped her face. "Lizzy?"

Meeting his searching eyes Elizabeth rose to hold his face as well. "Yes, my love. I am carrying our child." She heard a quick intake of breath, and rejoiced, seeing the spreading incredulous smile.

"Really?" He whispered, then looked back to her belly and to her face. "Are you sure?"

"Yes." She nodded and laughed to see him looking like a giddy fool. "Yes my love, I felt the quickening only yesterday. I will give birth in six months."

Darcy laughed and pulled her up in his arms and squeezed her. "I am going to be a father!" The sound of his declaration filled the hills around them. He grinned and kissed her. "How long have you suspected? Why did you not tell me?"

"I have suspected for several weeks, but I know that it is wise to wait before . . . being as excited as you are. Forgive me for keeping this from . . ." She gasped with the tight embrace she received. "Have you not noticed that a monthly event has not come, and that I seem to take many naps of late?"

"I have, but . . . I thought, well, I thought that I was wearing you out." He looked at her sheepishly.

"Well there is that." Elizabeth grinned at him and caressed his cheek. "You are rather enthusiastic."

"Forgive me. Should we curtail our affections?" He asked somewhat worriedly.

"No, perhaps at the end when it is uncomfortable, but I have spoken with Mrs. Reynolds, there is no reason to stop." She laughed again seeing the expression of relief.

"You have suffered no ill effects? I would have noticed them."

"No, only a brief aversion to meat, but that seems to have gone by the wayside. I am fortunate." His face lit up again and she smiled at his joy. "Come, we can not lay out here unclothed, no matter how remote this location." They dressed enough to achieve some semblance of modesty, and Darcy opened the saddle bags, pulling out bread and cheese and wine. They settled in to eat, toasting their good fortune and continually exchanging smiles of celebration and anticipation.

Darcy studied her bright eyes. "You are more emotional."

Elizabeth blinked and took a deep breath, then caressed his cheek. "I am." His eyes filled as well and he kissed her gently.

When the meal was finished, Elizabeth could not hold back a yawn. Darcy settled against the warm boulder, and invited her to lay by his side where she settled for a nap, her hands creeping beneath his shirt to hold on to her anchor. He closed his eyes and drifted into his own short slumber then awoke to see her still sleeping comfortably, her head on his chest. He drew her close, wrapping his arm around her shoulder and rested his other hand over the slightly swelled belly. A feeling of contentment filled him as he looked out over his land. A slight movement brought his eyes down first to his hand, then up to Elizabeth's peaceful face. He kissed her forehead gently, and he blinked back the emotion in his eyes.

Darcy rubbed his child, and spoke softly. "I promise. I will love you and care for you. I will teach you about your heritage. I will give you a home where you will long to return. I will never give you reason to fear or not respect me, and if you are my heir, I will teach you everything that you need to know to be a good steward of our people and our land, and if you are . . . my little girl," his tears began to fall, "I will protect you from harm until the day I must give you away to a good man."

He wiped his face then returned his hand to his baby. "You have a beautiful, kind, wonderful mama. She taught me how to love, and she will fill our lives with such joy. I can not wait to see her holding you." Elizabeth's eyes remained closed, but she was listening to William's quiet voice. She could hear the emotion.

Feeling her embrace he looked down, and spotted her warm eyes upon him. "You heard me." He said shyly.

"I did." Her hand brushed his wet cheek, then she sat up to embrace his face with her hands, and kissed his lips. "Thank you, Will. You will not be a father who looks at his child at his birth and ignores him for years, leaving him to the care of his governess. You will be a magnificent father because you know what you have missed from your own."

"If I am good, it will be because you are my wife." He kissed her gently and laid his palm on her cheek.

"This is an argument that I fear we will hold perpetually." She smiled as he enfolded her in his arms.

"And one that I will assuredly win!" He kissed her and recovering from the moment, allowed a smile to appear. "Did you sleep long enough, dearest?"

Elizabeth laughed and drew away, shaking her head. "Oh no, the fussing has begun!"

Laughing, he took her hand and kissed it. "Yes, and my love, I will not relent, so you may as well grow used to it." Darcy drew her up to rest on his lap. "Bear with me, mama, I am going to be a very protective papa." He smiled down at her and kissed her nose, then caressed her lips, and began to tenderly love her again.

She sighed and whispered as she melted into his arms. "Of that I have no doubt."

Epilogue

April 1813

Elizabeth bent and gently brushed the fringe of hair away from his forehead, and listened to his soft steady breathing. His long lashes fluttered slightly and she held her breath, hoping that she had not awakened him. After a small sigh and wiggle, her son settled back down to sleep. She closed her eyes and was startled when two hands crept around her waist.

A gentle mouth began wandering down her throat, a nose nudging away the curls that were in the way of its meandering path. She leaned back against William's chest and relaxed. "Stop worrying." He whispered.

"I just hope that the noise will not wake him."

"Lizzy, canon fire could not wake this child."

She laughed and turned around to see her husband's twinkling eyes. "You do make an excellent point." She held his face in her hands and they kissed slowly. Darcy lowered his hands to her bottom and drew her against him.

"Do you think anyone would miss us if we do not go to the ball?" He whispered huskily.

"As it is being held for your sister one floor below us . . . yes, darling, I do believe it would be noticed."

He sighed. "At least it is small."

Elizabeth stroked the fringe of hair from his forehead, just as she had done for their son moments before. "I believe that both you and Georgiana would have preferred a small ball regardless of the circumstances."

Smiling, he nodded. "That is true. I will be so relieved when this is over. She survived the presentation. Without Aunt Ellen's pull, I wonder if she would have been allowed at St. James', perhaps we should have waited three years . . . but now that is done. Douglass had his levee, and now . . . ."

"Now it is up to them." Elizabeth kissed his nose and carefully resting her head on his chest attempted not to disturb the intricate creation of jewels and sweeps that was her hair. "I am so proud of Marshall for waiting; another year might have been too much to ask. I realize that Georgiana likely does not really know what her feelings are, and I know not to press her towards him, but I do feel for Marshall, who does. It had to have been very difficult; there must have been quite a number of young ladies throwing themselves in his path."

"There were, he lamented it all to me frequently, but also like me, none of them caught his eye." Darcy held her and drank in her scent. "I listened with sympathy, having lived through it myself."

"Your ladies were of a different circle."

"That does not make his any less determined."

"They are still angry with me for stealing you away." She glanced up to see his satisfied smile.

Darcy tilted his head down and kissed her. "I think that some have quite come to admire you, my love."

Elizabeth sought his warm blue eyes. "Really? How? I certainly have not pushed myself to be accepted by them. I do not treat others with disdain, or cater to the whims of the *ton*."

"I believe dearest, that there are those who wish they had your courage to be so dismissive." He laughed to see her grin. "I have certainly received enough quiet pats on the back from gentlemen who admire my attitude." He stroked his finger along her cheek, then raised her chin to kiss her lips again.

"Your long-held contention that walking away from a fight was the wisest course has been proven correct. It seems that those who wished to hate you are now seeking you out." Elizabeth smiled and raised her brow.

Darcy nodded and kissed her forehead. "You are certainly aware of how many people wished to be invited tonight."

She rolled her eyes and sighed. "Not to support Georgiana."

"No, I realize that it was to curry favour with me. The Darcy name has been restored to its prominence, and I imagine, once Georgiana is married, her past indiscretion will be a memory."

"Well then, let us go downstairs and greet our guests. The sooner the ball is over, the sooner Georgiana can begin her Season . . ."

"And the sooner we can take our baby home." He whispered and gently stroked her belly. "I want a girl next time."

"Will you tolerate a boy?" Elizabeth smiled at his misty expression.

"Of course, but I want a girl just like her Mama." His eyes bore into hers.

"Only she will learn how to ride at a younger age." She teased.

He chuckled and kissed her lips. "A *much* younger age; and properly."

"You will never let me drive, will you?"

He hugged her tightly. "NO." Elizabeth shook her head and smiled, thinking she would test that objection when they returned to Pemberley, he could not use pregnancy or winter as an excuse now. "I think that we should begin to work on this new family member." He whispered in her ear.

She smiled up to his passionate eyes. "I believe that we have been addressing that desire quite frequently, my love."

"You know how I feel about constant practice, Lizzy." He growled. Shaking her head she pulled away and led him to the door, but was instantly drawn back into his arms. "Not so fast, Mrs. Darcy." She giggled and gladly accepted his fervent kisses.

Finally sated, Darcy resigned himself to hosting the ball. They wandered slowly down the stairs, watching the servants still rushing about, putting the last touches in place. Richard met them at the bottom. "Have you seen my wife? She disappeared after I supposedly destroyed her careful coiffure." He laughed. "For a woman who never worried about her appearance before, she is fretting inordinately over this evening."

"Mary wants to look her best for you, Richard. You should feel the compliment." Elizabeth saw Mary hurrying down the steps. "See, there she is!"

"Does it look right, Lizzy?" Mary patted the curls, and blushed at Richard's appreciative smile.

She laughed. "Perfect, now stop touching it before it all comes down." Mary stopped her fussing, and startled when a knock was heard. "I am certain that will be Marshall." He entered, accompanied by his hosts in town, the Bingleys, and the Hursts. Greetings were made all around and Marshall's eyes travelled the entrance. Elizabeth smiled. "Are you looking for anyone in particular?"

"Oh, um, yes, I . . ." He sighed. "I was hoping that I could speak to Miss Darcy before everything began, I wanted to secure my dances with her." He bit his lip and glanced at Darcy, who was not smiling.

"How many dances?" He glowered.

"Stand down, Darcy. The man has waited long enough for this." Richard laughed and turned to Marshall. "I am sure that you wished for no more than two, am I correct, sir?"

"Yes, of course, only two." He looked a little disappointed.

"I seem to recall that we had three dances when we attended the Meryton Assembly, William." Elizabeth raised her brow.

"That is correct, Darcy, I remember my sisters speaking of it incessantly afterwards!" Bingley jumped in.

Hurst laughed. "Caroline did not have anything charitable to say after that dance, and neither did you, my dear." He smiled at Louisa.

She shook her head. "You promised not to remind me of that, Gilbert!"

"Forgive me, dear. You may extract retribution by the method of your choosing."

"Do not tempt me, Mr. Hurst." His laughter wiped the scowl from her face.

Jane turned to Elizabeth. "Do you remember the ladies of the neighbourhood all came by to remark upon your dances to Mama?" She grinned and smiled at Darcy's closing eyes.

"It seems that you all are usurping my role as my sister's guardian. Perhaps I should simply go upstairs and spend the night with my son. He will not object to my protection." He opened his eyes only to see the amused smiles of his family.

Elizabeth took his arm. "No dear, but I think that you should go upstairs and collect Georgiana. I believe that she is nervous to make her appearance, and needs your courage." They walked to the foot of the stairs and she reached up to touch his cheek. "This is something that only you can do for her."

"Thank you, Lizzy." He kissed her palm and set off up the stairs. Elizabeth stood watching him for a moment then returned to her guests.

"So, your husband is feeling powerless to stop the inevitable?" Richard noted, watching his retreating form.

"He feels his obligation to care for those he loves, no matter how seemingly inconsequential the situation." She smiled and laughed. "When I was with child, he was far worse." Elizabeth looked at Mary who widened her eyes and glanced at Richard, then shook her head. Apparently she had not shared her suspicions with her husband yet.

Darcy reached Georgiana's door and knocked lightly. It was opened by her abigail who bobbed a curtsey and departed with his nod. "Georgiana, our guests have begun to arrive, shall I escort you down? Douglass is waiting to speak with you." She turned from where she stood at the window and he smiled. "You look lovely tonight, dear."

"Thank you." She said softly. "I . . . I want to thank you for giving me Mother's jewels."

"I see that you have chosen not to wear any of them." He walked in further and closed the door.

"No, I wished to wear the necklace that you gave me for my presentation, I did not know Mother, this means so much more to me, and I thought on this night . . ." Her voice trailed away.

Darcy took her hands in his and looked down into her worried eyes. "Two years ago, well nearly two years ago, when I was riding through the countryside, thinking the worst, and wondering what your future could possibly be if I did find you in time, I barely allowed myself to imagine that this night would ever occur. I feared so many possibilities . . . but here we are. You were presented at court, you have gained so much confidence, and downstairs there is a fine young man who is very anxious to finally be allowed to call on you. I could not have dreamed of such an outcome after that desperate ride, but it has happened. I can not begin to tell you how proud I am of you."

"Oh William, thank you!"

He drew a breath, and continued his speech. "You are out now. This is your opportunity to meet other young men. I do not want you to feel obligated to accept Douglass' attentions despite his unwavering friendship. I do not want you to regret not taking this time . . ."

Georgiana interrupted him. "Brother, stop. Mr. Douglass has never looked at me as anyone but a friend. He has liked me for myself, and not for the dowry that every other young man would value, at least those who would be willing to look at me at all. I know that the rumours of my ruin still exist. He understands everything of me. Why should I look elsewhere?"

"It would be a different life than what you have known, dear." He said gently. "And before I will allow you to consider it, you must meet other young men. You must be sure. I want you to have no regrets, Georgiana."

"I have enough of those already. But I look forward to my future now, and I understand your wish for me to meet others, as much as I fear doing so." They embraced, both teary eyed. He kissed her forehead and stepped back, dabbing his eyes with his handkerchief. Georgiana noticed. "Is that the same one that Elizabeth gave you?"

Smiling he placed it back in his coat. "I am never without one of them, but yes, this is that particular one." He took her hand and placed it on his arm. "Now, my dear sister, my wife sent me up here to fulfil my brotherly duty and to bring you downstairs. Douglass indicates that he wishes to ask for many dances with you."

"How many?" She asked, suddenly excited.

He sighed, and shook his head, his day was done. "Well, I suggested two and the assembled crowd laughed at me, but I will not relent. However, the first is mine."

"But what of Elizabeth?" Georgiana asked worriedly.

"I am sure that she will make do with Douglass, do you not agree?" He laughed at her thinking it over. "Surely you do not fear Elizabeth stealing him away? I assure you, that until I have my own daughter, this will be the last time that I do not open a ball with my wife."

She laughed and blushed. "I am just being silly."

Opening the door, they stepped out into the hallway. The increased volume of noise indicated that the remaining guests had begun arriving. Elizabeth stood near the entrance, greeting them as they entered. She caught sight of the couple at the top of the stairs and paused, smiling up at them. People turned and Darcy sedately descended with Georgiana. Murmurs of appreciation for the striking girl were heard, and she took her place at Elizabeth's side.

"You are glowing, Georgiana." Elizabeth whispered.

"I am so worried of making an error." She whispered back.

"If you do, I promise to do something worse, so all of the gossip will be about me instead." She grinned and squeezed her hand and felt her relax. Darcy's hand rested on the small of her back and she looked up. "Are you well?" He could not so easily hide the evidence of his conversation with Georgiana from his observant wife.

"Stay with me tonight, Lizzy." He said softly.

"Of course, my love." She leaned against him and he closed his eyes. "Oh, what will you do at her wedding?" He heard her gentle laugh and looked back down at her dancing eyes.

"I will be deeply in need of your love." His little smile appeared.

"Hmm. That does not sound at all bad!" They laughed and were startled back to awareness with Lord Matlock's booming voice.

"Well, it seems that everyone is here, shall we get this night underway?" He clapped Darcy's back and then kissed Georgiana. "We are delighted for you, my dear!"

"Thank you, Uncle Henry." Georgiana laughed. "Where is Aunt Ellen?"

"Oh she is about here somewhere, always politicking that woman is." He grinned and offered his arm to Elizabeth. "Come Mrs. Darcy. Your husband has a duty to perform!"

Elizabeth glanced back at him and smiled. "Yes he does, and where do you take me?"

"I have decided that we need to dance together." He lifted his chin. "Now I know that young Douglass had tried for your hand, but I told him no, your husband will have to give you up some other time to him."

"But what of your wife?"

"She does not like to dance with me for some reason." Elizabeth's eyes grew wide and she looked at Lady Matlock who had spotted her husband's determined advance to the floor.

"No Henry, I will not have you tread on Elizabeth's toes." She pulled him away and spotting Marshall lifted her finger. "Sir, I understand that this dance is yours? Well then, please take your place." Lord Matlock protested but Marshall quickly stepped up.

"I am sorry, Elizabeth, I could not very well say no to an Earl." He whispered softly.

"Fortunately for my feet his wife could!" She smiled and they lined up, the men opposite the ladies. Darcy looked at her sadly. She looked pointedly at Georgiana and he laughed, focussing again on his sister. The dance began and Elizabeth caught Marshall staring at Georgiana, and sighed at the two besotted men. "You will dance with her soon enough. Now, how are your parents? I am sorry that they could not come today."

"They are well, but with me in London, father felt that he could not leave the brewery unsupervised. Your parents could not come either, I see."

"No, they were here for Easter, but Papa hates town, and Kitty is being courted back home . . . and of course a suitor in hand is more important to Mama than searching for a new one for Lydia, so they returned just last week." She smiled. "Papa seems to be receiving regular inquires from Mr. Collins on the status of his health. I gather that our cousin is most anxious for Papa's demise and his inheritance. I wonder Marshall, should you not be the rightful heir of Longbourn? You are father's nephew."

"But Mother was disowned, I suppose that I could speak to your father now that the family has been reunited. I do not know if any legal proceedings took place or if she was simply disavowed but . . . I do not know that I would want it, not after she was sent away from there. I would rather carry on my father's work." He looked at Georgiana. "I will be forever grateful that Darcy brought Miss Darcy home."

They continued through the first dance and when it ended, they waited for the music for the second in the set to begin. Darcy leaned over and whispered to Marshall who looked at him with surprise. The two men switched positions, and now Darcy was standing opposite of Elizabeth, and Marshall was smiling warmly into Georgiana's wide eyes. The dance began and Darcy held out his hand for his wife.

"That was very kind of you, Will, but what happened to allowing only two dances?" Elizabeth said as they turned together.

He raised her hand to his lips, then smiled. "Ah, but everyone saw that it was me who made the request to change partners, so they will give him a pass and be amused at my besotted behaviour." He laughed at her sceptical expression. "I put myself in his place, and remembered how much I wanted to dance the first with you." Elizabeth's eyes softened and she shook her head.

"This is entirely different; you are no threat to him."

"No, but I hate seeing anyone else touching you." His eyes darkened and they moved apart, their fingertips barely touching. "Since I have been told that my days of protecting my sister are numbered, I will instead protect my wife."

"From a young man enamoured with your sister!" She laughed and he grinned. "Such worries you have!" Moving around him and she whispered, "Perhaps I need to protect you from your cousin James' sisters?"

"Why did you invite them?" Darcy whispered back, and looked across the ballroom to see James dancing with his wife.

"Your aunt asked me to. She hoped that someone would catch their eyes and they might be married off and gone from visiting Matlock." She laughed at his rolling eyes. "I promise Will, they will not bother you."

"And how do you plan to keep this promise?" He watched as she passed by his shoulder.

"I will spirit you away so nobody can find you." Elizabeth said mischievously. Darcy's eyes lit up and he began looking around the room. "What are you seeking?"

"The Farnesworth girls, perhaps they can annoy you now and you can initiate the rescue!" His eyes twinkled and the dance ended. Soon the music began again for the second set, and Elizabeth took his arm. Slowly they made their way through the crowd, speaking to their guests. Elizabeth checked to see how Georgiana fared, noting that Lady Matlock was beside her, and eventually their meandering path brought them to the doorway and they exited the ballroom. "You are kidnapping me!" Darcy suddenly realized, unable to hide the delight in his voice. Elizabeth glanced up at him with a wicked grin and kept leading him forward to slip into his study for a few moments of pleasure.

Bingley watched them disappear down the hallway and Richard leaned over to him while they waited their turn to begin dancing. "Are they incapable of keeping their hands off of each other for even a few hours?"

"Apparently so." Bingley laughed. "It seems that we mere mortals will never keep up with them."

"I admire his stamina." Richard said with awe.

Bingley grinned and stepped forward to take Jane's hand. "What are you two boys whispering about?"

"Oh, we just were remarking on our hosts." She looked around the room for her missing sister and brother. Bingley watched, knowing how she tried to emulate her sister's marriage. "Jane dear." She returned her attention to him. "They amuse us, but what we have is everything that I ever wanted. I love you."

"Oh, Charles Bingley, now you will make me cry!" She wiped the happy tears with her glove. He laughed and took her arm for a spin, and noticed Elizabeth and Darcy had already returned.

Across the room, Georgiana was surrounded by a group of young men when Marshall approached. "Miss Darcy, may I have a moment?"

She turned and gave him a bright smile. "Oh, I wish that you would!"

Surprised he smiled back, and taking her arm, led her to a relatively unoccupied corner of the ballroom. "Why would you make such a wish?"

"You are the friendly face in this crowd." She said honestly.

"Has anyone treated you badly?" Concern crossed his brow and he looked back at the abandoned suitors.

"No, but I feel as if everyone is staring at me." She whispered and looked down.

He relaxed and laughed. "You are the guest of honour; of course you are the one who they came to see."

"Oh I wish that this was over!" Georgiana cried in frustration.

Marshall's expression changed, and his voice lowered. "And then you would like what to happen?" She blushed as he moved closer.

"William wishes me to experience my Season. He wishes me to . . . be sure that I am . . . aware of . . . he wishes for me not to regret any impulsive decisions I might make, I think. I believe that he is not quite convinced that I am mature." She said the last softly and looked down.

"Miss Darcy." Georgiana looked up at her friend and found comfort in his smile. "Your brother loves you dearly, and I believe that you should not take his . . . request for you to meet gentlemen as a sign that he thinks you are immature or might make the wrong choice, but rather that he wishes you to be sure that the choice you make is correct. He said much the same thing to me last year. He told me to participate in society, to experience meeting different people and to learn from each encounter, and not to sequester myself away in the hopes that . . . well, not to limit my choices by fixating on what may never be. As difficult as that advice was to hear, I listened, and I have indeed benefited from it. He is a wise man, even if he is your brother." Marshall smiled. "He knows that you have not really known many young men, and he wants you to learn. I have no doubt that he and Elizabeth, and all of your family, will be by your side to help you through this time. Perhaps you will meet someone who is . . . the one you need."

She looked up to him and watched the expression on his face. "Will you stay in London for the entire Season?" *Please stay with me.*

He met her searching eyes. "I will not leave." *I will not leave you.*

Georgiana nodded. "Very well then, I will do as my brother requests for this Season." Marshall smiled and saw her relief. They startled as a young man approached and bowed.

"Miss Darcy, I believe I am your partner for the next set?" He offered his arm. Georgiana smiled and took his elbow, then glancing at Marshall's face walked off to the dance. He drew a breath and went to stand on the side, his eyes never left her.

Darcy and Elizabeth stood together, their hands clasped and hidden by her skirt, and watched the tender scene unfold before them. "Shall we send the guests home, Will? It seems that these suitors are unnecessary." He laughed at her pursed lips.

"Dearest, I want this match as much as you do, and if we had waited until next year, perhaps I would not be so adamant about her meeting others . . ."

"I know your motivation and I agree with it, I just feel so terrible for Marshall, being forced to watch her with others. You know that you would not have endured it with grace were it me." Elizabeth squeezed his hand.

"No, I doubt very much that I would, but both of us had much more experience, and knew what we wanted in our partner. All of the young men who were invited here are worthy. Some are certainly more interested in her dowry than she, well likely most of them are, but they are also all good men, they would not be here otherwise. Douglass is of a different sphere. She needs to be sure . . ."

"We do not need to justify our actions, William. I agree with you. I just know that despite your best intentions, the match is already made." She smiled at him and he laughed softly, lifting her hand to his lips.

"Well then if we are forced to endure guests, then be prepared to dance your slippers off!" He caught the musicians' attention in the balcony above the ballroom and nodded. Instantly a waltz began. Cries of excitement and dismay filled the room as married couples assembled to take part in the scandalous dance, and the single guests were relegated to the sides. Darcy grinned and held out his arms. "Come, my love."

Elizabeth took his hand and smiled up to his twinkling eyes. "You had this planned!"

"I did." He laughed and stood still, waiting for the cue to move. "If I must host a ball, then I will do it on my terms."

—⁓—

May 1821

Sealing her letter to Jane, Elizabeth could hear the sound of her children racing down the hallway, and the stern voice of her husband telling them to walk. She shook her head and smiled with the thought of the expression on his face. William was delighted with fatherhood from the first moment he learned that he had won the title. Her eyes lifted to examine the painting hanging across from her desk. It was a landscape that he had commissioned. The view was of Pemberley, and the painter had sat at the same grassy outcrop where they had made love the day she shared the news that she was with child, nine years earlier.

Nine years. It was nearly ten years since she met William, and the time had passed in the blink of an eye. So much had happened, births, deaths, weddings, tragedies, and many, many joys. Even the world around them was changing. The seemingly endless war did end, and the increasing importance of industry affected everyone and everything. She smiled and thought of how once she and William hoped to retire to Pemberley and never have to participate in the world again, but they realized, thankfully, how important it was to be willing to grow. Those who did not would be left behind. Her husband was determined that his family would prosper.

Elizabeth awoke from her musings to a silent house. Walking through her home, she smiled at the footman who rushed to open the front door. She could hear her family in the distance, and above the din of the children, William's warm deep chuckle reigned. Laughing softly, she followed the sounds.

"Help me, Papa!" Emily Darcy held out her arms to her father and he lifted her tiny form onto the donkey's back. He kissed her little nose, and tugged playfully her long chestnut curls. At four she was the apple of his eye, and only her mother surpassed her as the woman he loved the most.

"Me too, Papa!" Thomas Darcy, a black-haired six-year-old stood nearby, tugging on his coat. Darcy laughed.

"You are old enough to be mounting yourself, Son." He lifted the tall boy onto the donkey behind his sister.

"He can mount by himself, Father, but he still likes you to pick him up." The eldest son, eight-year-old Matthew, called out from his seat on his pony. He bore a striking resemblance to his father, particularly around his soulful blue eyes, which were always either crinkled in a smile or lost in deep thought.

Darcy regarded his second son. "So young man, you have been hiding an accomplishment from me? I suppose that you have acquired some new riding skills as well? Show me what you can do."

Thomas kicked the donkey. "Come on Catherine, let us show Papa!" The donkey brayed and began a slow stroll. Emily giggled. "Papa, why are all of the donkeys named Catherine?" Darcy laughed as he walked alongside them.

"Oh, have you not heard the story of how your mother and I met? I am sure that she has told it many, many times."

"She has, but we have not heard it from your side, yet." Matthew said. "She always makes it into a great tale, where the knight was riding to save a kidnapped maiden, and it was the work of an enchanted donkey that brought the attention of the good knight to a princess, and together they saved the maiden from the evil dark lord."

Darcy was laughing so hard that he had to wipe the tears from his eyes. "And what is the explanation for the donkey's name?"

Elizabeth strolled over from where she had been watching her children play, "Why she is the wicked witch, of course!"

Slipping his arms around her, he smiled down into her dancing eyes. "You have a fascinating imagination, my love." She smiled warmly and caressed his cheek.

"Is it true?" Emily demanded.

He kissed Elizabeth and looked over to her mirror image. "Yes dear, every word." Returning his gaze to Elizabeth he kissed her again, "We discovered the maiden and saved each other in the end." Lowering his voice he whispered. "I dare not think what my life would have been without you."

"It was fate." Elizabeth hugged him.

"No, Lizzy, it was love."

The End